READER'S DIGEST
SELECT EDITIONS

READER'S DIGEST
SELECT EDITIONS

www.readersdigest.co.uk

The Reader's Digest Association Limited
11 Westferry Circus Canary Wharf London E14 4HE

For information as to ownership of
copyright in the material of this book,
and acknowledgments, see last page.

Printed in Germany
ISBN 978 0 276 44286 5

CONTENTS

Widely reviewed as one of the best new novels of the year, this gripping story is narrated by a professional ghostwriter, hired to help former British prime minister Adam Lang compile his memoirs. The 'ghost' thinks he's landed a real coup, as the fee is generous and his subject fascinating, but as the interviewing commences, in an isolated house on windswept Martha's Vineyard, the writer finds that he is in far deeper water than he ever imagined possible.

A debut novel by a lively and thoroughly engaging writer, *Sacrifice* brings a new twist to the popular forensic crime genre. The heroine of the story, consultant surgeon Tora Hamilton, has found moving to Shetland unsettling enough, even before she makes a gruesome discovery in a field beside her house one rain-drenched Sunday morning. It is a woman's corpse, bearing strange, rune-like markings, and it leads Tora to delve into a fascinating legend from the island's distant past.

SELECTED AND CONDENSED
BY READER'S DIGEST

THE READER'S DIGEST ASSOCIATION LIMITED, LONDON

THE MAN IN THE PICTURE

SUSAN HILL

341

The author of *The Woman in Black*, one of the longest-running stage plays in London's West End, has returned to a supernatural theme in this, her latest book. The story begins in the college rooms of a retired professor, as he recounts the bizarre history of one of his oil paintings. Depicting a Venetian carnival scene, it shows costumed revellers by a canal, their faces and expressions concealed behind exotic masks. In their midst, one unmasked man gazes beseechingly at the onlooker . . .

A group of high-powered executives from Hammond Aerospace is on a retreat, ensconced in a remote hunting lodge in the middle of a wilderness. No computers, no BlackBerries, no phones; it's the perfect place to sort out the company's financial problems. The trouble is, it's also the perfect spot for a kidnapping, and within a few short hours the executive team find themselves held at gun-point, unable to call for help and stuck in a nail-biting, high-stakes battle for survival.

POWER PLAY

JOSEPH FINDER

407

JOSEPH FINDER
POWER PLAY
Five hunters. Thirteen hostages. One reluctant hero.

ROBERT HARRIS

the
ghost

For a celebrity ghostwriter
the rules are simple: tell a
convincing story and make the
subject look good. Getting
caught up in the story yourself
shouldn't be on the agenda.
Especially when you're writing
about a former British prime
minister, whose past is about to
catch up with him . . .

ONE

The moment I heard how McAra died, I should have walked away. I can see that now. I should have said, 'Rick, I'm sorry, this isn't for me, I don't like the sound of it,' finished my drink and left. But he was such a good storyteller, Rick—I often thought *he* should have been the writer and I the literary agent—that once he'd started talking there was never any question I wouldn't listen, and by the time he'd finished, I was hooked.

The story, as Rick told it to me over lunch that day, went like this:

McAra had caught the last ferry from Woods Hole, Massachusetts, to Martha's Vineyard two Sundays earlier. I worked out afterwards that it was January 12. It was touch-and-go whether the ferry would sail. A gale had been blowing since midafternoon and the last few crossings had been cancelled. But towards nine o'clock the wind eased, and at 9.45 the master decided it was safe to cast off. The boat was crowded; McAra was lucky to get a space for his car. He parked below decks, then went upstairs to get some air.

No one saw him alive again.

The crossing to the island usually takes forty-five minutes, but the weather this night slowed the voyage considerably: docking a 200-foot vessel in a fifty-knot wind, said Rick, is nobody's idea of fun. It was nearly eleven when the ferry made land at Vineyard Haven and the cars started up—all except one: a new tan-coloured Ford Escape SUV. The purser made a loud-speaker appeal for the owner to return to his vehicle, as he was blocking the drivers behind him. When he still didn't show, the crew tried the doors, which turned out to be unlocked, and freewheeled the big Ford down to the quayside. Afterwards they searched the ship—nothing. They called the terminal at Woods Hole to check if anyone had been left behind—again: nothing. Finally, an official of the Massachusetts Steamship Authority contacted the Coast Guard station in Falmouth to report a possible man overboard.

A police check on the Ford's licence plate revealed it to be registered to one Martin S. Rhinehart of New York City, although Mr Rhinehart was eventually tracked down to his ranch in California. By now it was about midnight on the East Coast, 9 p.m. on the West.

'This is *the* Marty Rhinehart?' I interrupted.

'This is he.'

Rhinehart confirmed over the phone to the police that the Ford was his. He kept it at his house on Martha's Vineyard for him and his guests to use in the summer. He also confirmed that, despite the time of year, some people were currently staying there. He said he'd get his assistant to call the house and find out if anyone had borrowed the car. Half an hour later she rang to say that someone was indeed missing, a person by the name of McAra.

Nothing more could be done until first light. But everyone knew that if a passenger had gone overboard there would be a search for a corpse. Rick is one of those irritatingly fit Americans in their early forties who look about nineteen and do terrible things to their bodies with bicycles and canoes. He knows that sea: he once spent two days paddling a kayak round the island. The Woods Hole ferry plies the strait where Vineyard Sound meets Nantucket Sound, and that is dangerous water. At high tide you can see the currents sucking the huge channel buoys onto their sides. Rick shook his head. In January, in a gale, in *snow*? No one could survive more than five minutes.

A local woman found the body early the next morning, on the beach four miles down the island's coast at Lambert's Cove. The driver's licence in the wallet confirmed him to be Michael James McAra, aged fifty, from Balham in south London. I felt a shot of sympathy at the mention of that dreary, unexotic suburb: he was a long way from home, poor devil. His passport named his mother as his next of kin. The police took his corpse to the little morgue in Vineyard Haven, then drove over to the Rhinehart residence to break the news and to fetch one of the other guests to identify him.

'It must have been quite a scene,' said Rick, when the volunteer guest showed up to view the body: 'I bet the morgue attendant is still talking about it.' There was a patrol car from Edgartown, a second car with four armed guards and a third vehicle, bombproof, carrying the instantly recognisable man who, until eighteen months earlier, had been the prime minister of Great Britain and Northern Ireland.

THE LUNCH had been Rick's idea. I hadn't even known he was in town until he rang the night before. He insisted we meet at his club. It was not *his* club, exactly—that was a similar mausoleum in Manhattan, whose members had reciprocal dining rights in London—but he loved it all the same. At lunchtime only men were admitted. Each wore a dark blue suit and was over sixty. Yellow electric light from three immense candelabra glinted on dark polished tables and rubied decanters of claret.

'I'm amazed this hasn't been in the papers,' I said.

'Oh, but it has. Nobody's made a secret of it. There've been obituaries.'

Now I came to think of it, I *did* vaguely remember seeing something. But I had been working fifteen hours a day for a month to finish my new book, a footballer's autobiography, and the world beyond my study had been a blur.

'What on earth was an ex-prime minister doing identifying the body of a man from Balham who fell off the Martha's Vineyard ferry?'

'Michael McAra,' announced Rick, with the emphatic delivery of a man who has flown 3,000 miles to deliver this punch line, '*was helping him write his memoirs*.'

And this is where, in that parallel life, I express sympathy for the elderly Mrs McAra, fold my napkin, finish my drink, say goodbye and step out into the chilly London street with the whole of my undistinguished career stretching safely ahead of me. Instead I excused myself and went to the lavatory.

'You realise I don't know anything about politics?' I said when I got back.

'You voted for him, didn't you?'

'Lang? Of course. Everybody did. He wasn't a politician; he was a craze.'

'Well, that's the point. Who's interested in politics? In any case, it's a professional ghostwriter he needs, not another goddamn politico.' He glanced around. It was an iron rule of the club that no business could be discussed on the premises—a problem for Rick, who never discussed anything else. 'Rhinehart paid ten million dollars for these memoirs on two conditions: it'd be in the stores within two years, and Lang wouldn't pull any punches about the war on terror. He's nowhere near meeting either requirement. Things got so bad around Christmas, Rhinehart gave him the use of his vacation house on the Vineyard so Lang and McAra could work without any distractions. I guess the pressure must have gotten to McAra. The medical examiner found enough booze in his blood to put him four times over the driving limit.'

'So it was an accident?'

'Accident? Suicide?' He casually flicked his hand. 'Who'll ever know? What does it matter? It was the book that killed him.'

'That's encouraging,' I said.

While Rick went on with his pitch, I stared at my plate and imagined the former prime minister looking down at his assistant's cold white face in the mortuary—staring down at his ghost, one could say. How did it feel? I am always putting this question to my clients. I must ask it a hundred times a day during the interview phase: How did it feel? *How did it feel?* Mostly they can't answer, which is why they have to hire me to supply their memories. I rather enjoy this process, to be honest: the brief freedom of being someone else. If that sounds creepy, let me add that real craftsmanship is required. I not only extract from people their life stories, I impart a shape to those lives; sometimes I give them lives they never even realised they had.

I said, 'Should I have heard of McAra?'

'Yes, so let's not admit you haven't. He was some kind of aide when Lang was prime minister. Speechwriting, policy research, political strategy. When Lang resigned, McAra stayed with him, to run his office.'

I grimaced. 'I don't know, Rick.'

The people whose memoirs I ghosted had usually fallen a few rungs down the celebrity ladder, or had a few rungs left to climb, or were clinging to the top, desperate to cash in while there was still time. It was ridiculous to think that I might collaborate on the memoirs of a prime minister.

'I don't know—' I began again, but Rick interrupted me.

'Rhinehart Inc. are getting frantic. They're holding a beauty parade at their London office tomorrow morning. Maddox himself is flying over from New York. Lang's sending the lawyer who negotiated the original deal for him—the hottest fixer in Washington. I've other clients I could put in for this, so if you're not up for it, tell me now. But I think you're the best fit.'

'Me? You're kidding.'

'No. I promise you. They need to do something radical. It's a great opportunity for you. And the money will be good. The kids won't starve.'

'I don't have any kids.'

'No,' said Rick with a wink, 'but I do.'

WE PARTED on the steps of the club. Rick had a car waiting outside. He didn't offer to drop me anywhere, which made me suspect he was off to make the same pitch to another client. Rick had plenty of ghosts on his books. Take a look at the best-seller lists: you would be amazed how much of it is the work of ghostwriters. We are the phantom operatives who keep publishing going.

'See you tomorrow,' he said, and in a puff of exhaust fumes, he was gone: Mephistopheles on a fifteen per cent commission.

I stood for a minute, undecided. I was in that narrow zone where Soho washes up against Covent Garden: a trash-strewn strip of empty theatres, dark alleys, snack bars and bookshops—so many bookshops you can feel ill just looking at them. I often drop into one of the cut-price behemoths of Charing Cross Road to see how my titles are displayed, and that was what I did that afternoon. Once inside, it was a short step across the scuffed red carpet of the biography department from 'Celebrity' to 'Politics'.

I was surprised by how much they had on the former prime minister—an entire shelf, from the early hagiography, *Adam Lang: Statesman for Our Time*, to a recent hatchet job titled *Would You Adam and Eve It? The Collected Lies of Adam Lang*, by the same author. I took down the thickest biography and opened it at the photographs: Lang as a toddler, feeding milk to a lamb, Lang as Lady Macbeth in a school play, Lang dressed as a chicken in a Cambridge Footlights Revue, Lang as a merchant banker in the 1970s, Lang with his wife and young children on the doorstep of a new house, Lang waving from an open-topped bus on the day he was elected to parliament, Lang with his colleagues, with world leaders, with pop stars, with soldiers.

I looked up McAra, Michael, in the index. There were only five innocuous references—no reason, in other words, for anyone outside the party to have heard of him. I flicked back to the photograph of the prime minister seated, smiling, at the cabinet table, his Downing Street staff arrayed behind him. The caption identified McAra as the pale, burly, dark-haired figure in the back row. He looked exactly the sort of unappealing inadequate who is congenitally drawn to politics. You'll find a McAra in any country, standing behind any leader with a political machine to operate: a greasy engineer in the boiler room of power. And this was the man who had been trusted to ghost a ten-million-dollar memoir? I felt professionally affronted. I bought myself a small pile of research material and headed out of the bookshop with a growing conviction that perhaps I *was* the man for the job.

It was obvious the moment I got outside that another bomb had gone off. At Tottenham Court Road people were surging up from all four exits of the tube station. A loudspeaker said something about 'an incident at Oxford Circus'. I carried on up the road, unsure of how I would get home—taxis, like false friends, tending to vanish at the first sign of trouble. In the window of an electrical shop, the crowd watched a news bulletin relayed on a dozen televisions: aerial shots of Oxford Circus, smoke gushing up out of the station. An electronic ticker at the bottom of the screen announced a suspected suicide bomb, and gave an emergency number to call. Above the rooftops a helicopter circled. I could smell the smoke—an acrid, eye-reddening blend of diesel and burning plastic.

It took me two hours to walk home, lugging my bag of books. The entire tube system had been shut down; so had the main railway stations. The traffic on either side of the street was stalled. Occasionally a police car or an ambulance would mount the kerb, roar along the pavement and attempt to make progress up a side street. I trudged on towards the setting sun.

It must have been six when I reached my flat. I had the top two floors of a high, stuccoed house in what the residents called Notting Hill and the Post Office stubbornly insisted was North Kensington. It was grim—used syringes glittered in the gutter. But from the attic extension that served as my office I had a view across west London that would not have disgraced a skyscraper: rooftops, railway yards, motorway and sky—a vast urban prairie sky.

Kate had let herself in and was watching the news. Kate: I had forgotten she was coming over for the evening. She was my—? I never knew what to call her. No one the wrong side of thirty has a girlfriend. Partner wasn't right, as we didn't live under the same roof. Lover? How could one keep a straight face? Mistress? Do me a favour. I suppose it was ominous that 40,000 years of human language had failed to produce a word for our relationship. (Kate wasn't her real name, by the way, but it suits her better than the name she has: she looks like a Kate—sensible but sassy, girlish but willing to be one of the boys. She worked in television, but let's not hold that against her.)

'Thanks for the concerned phone call,' I said. 'I'm dead, actually, but don't worry about it.' I kissed the top of her head, dropped the books onto the sofa and went into the kitchen to pour myself a whisky. 'The entire tube is down. I've had to walk all the way from Covent Garden.'

'Poor darling,' I heard her say. 'And you've been shopping.'

I topped up my glass with tap water, drank half, then topped it up again with whisky. I remembered I was supposed to have reserved a restaurant.

When I went back into the living room, Kate was removing books from the carrier bag. 'What's all this?' she said. 'You're not interested in *politics*.' But then she realised what was going on, because she was smart—smarter than I was. She knew I was meeting an agent and she knew all about McAra. 'Don't tell me they want *you* to ghost his book?' She laughed. 'You cannot be serious.' She tried to make a joke of it—'You *cannot* be serious' in an American accent, like that tennis player—but I could see her dismay. She hated Lang, felt betrayed by him. She used to be a party member.

'It'll probably come to nothing,' I said, and drank some more whisky.

She turned back to the news, her arms tightly folded—always a warning sign. The ticker announced that the death toll was seven and likely to rise.

'But if you're offered it you'll do it?' she asked, without looking at me.

I was spared having to reply by the newsreader announcing that they were cutting live to New York to get the reaction of the former prime minister. Suddenly there was Adam Lang, on a podium marked 'Waldorf-Astoria', where he had been addressing a lunch. 'You will all by now have heard the tragic news from London,' he said, 'where once again the forces of fanaticism and intolerance . . .'

Nothing he uttered that night warrants reprinting. It was almost a parody of what a politician might say after a terrorist attack. Yet, watching him, you would have thought his own wife and children had been eviscerated in the blast. This was his genius: to refresh and elevate the clichés of politics by the sheer force of his performance. Even Kate was briefly silenced. Only when he had finished and his audience was rising to applaud did she mutter, 'What's he doing in New York, anyway?'

'Lecturing?'

'Why can't he lecture here?'

'I suppose no one here would pay him a hundred thousand dollars a throw.'

She pressed MUTE. 'There was a time,' she said slowly, 'when princes taking their countries to war would risk their lives in battle—lead by example. Now they travel in bombproof cars with bodyguards and make fortunes three thousand miles away, while the rest of us are stuck with the consequences of their actions.' She turned to look at me. 'I don't understand you. All the things I've said about him over the past few years—"war criminal" and the rest of it—and you've sat there nodding. And now you're going to write his propaganda for him. Did none of it mean anything to you at all?'

'You're a fine one to talk,' I said. 'You've been trying to get an interview with him for months. What's the difference?'

'*What's the difference?*' She clenched her slim white hands and raised them in frustration, half claw, half fist. 'We want to hold him to account—that's the difference! To ask him proper questions! About torturing and bombing and lying! Not "How does it feel?" *Christ!* This is a complete waste of time.'

She got up and went into the bedroom. I heard her filling her bag noisily with lipstick, toothbrush, perfume. I knew if I went in I could retrieve the situation. We'd had worse rows. I'd have been obliged to concede that she was right, affirm her moral and intellectual superiority in this as in all things. A meaningful hug would probably have got me a suspended sentence. But the truth was, at that moment, given a choice between an evening of her smug left-wing moralising and the prospect of working with a so-called war criminal, I preferred the war criminal. So I carried on staring at the television.

She didn't slam the door as she left but closed it carefully. Stylish, I thought. On the television screen the death toll had just increased to eight.

RHINEHART PUBLISHING UK consisted of five ancient firms acquired during a vigorous bout of corporate kleptomania in the 1990s. Wrenched out of their Dickensian garrets in Bloomsbury, upsized, downsized, rebranded, renamed, reorganised, modernised and merged, they had finally been dumped in Hounslow, in a steel-and-smoked-glass office block with all its pipes on the outside. It nestled among the pebble-dash housing estates like an abandoned spacecraft after a fruitless mission to find intelligent life.

I arrived, with professional punctuality, five minutes before noon, only to discover the main door locked. I had to buzz for entry. Through the darkened glass I could see the security men checking me on a monitor. When I finally got inside I had to turn out my pockets and pass through a metal detector.

Quigley was waiting for me by the lifts.

'Who're you expecting to bomb you?' I asked. 'Random House?'

'We're publishing Lang's memoirs,' replied Quigley in a stiff voice. 'That alone makes us a target, apparently. Rick's already upstairs.'

'How many've you seen?'

'Five. You're the last.'

Roy Quigley was about fifty, tall and tweedy, and in a happier era would have smoked a pipe and offered tiny advances to minor academics over large lunches in Soho. Now he took a plastic tray of salad at his desk overlooking the M4, and received his orders from the head of sales and marketing, a girl of about sixteen. He had three children in private schools he couldn't afford. As the price of survival he'd been obliged to take an interest in popular culture, to wit, the lives of various footballers, models and foul-mouthed comedians, whose customs he studied in the tabloids with scholarly detachment, as if they were Micronesian tribespeople. I'd pitched him an idea the year before, the memoirs of a TV magician who had been abused in childhood but had used his skills to conjure up a new life, etc., etc. He'd turned it down. The book had gone straight to number one, and he still bore a grudge.

'I have to tell you,' he said, as we rose to the penthouse, 'that I don't think you're the right man for this assignment.'

'Then it's a good job it's not your decision, Roy.'

Quigley's title was UK Group Editor-in-Chief, which meant he had all the authority of a dead cat. The man who really ran the global show was waiting for us in the boardroom: John Maddox, chief executive of Rhinehart Inc., a big, bull-shouldered New Yorker whose bald head glistened like a massive, varnished egg. Next to him was Lang's Washington attorney, Sidney Kroll, a bespectacled forty-something with floppy raven hair and a damp handshake.

'And Nick Riccardelli I think you know,' said Quigley, completing the introductions. My agent winked up at me.

'Hi, Rick,' I said, and took my seat beside him, feeling nervous.

Maddox sat with his back to the window. He laid his massive hands on the glass-topped table and said, 'I gather from Rick that you're aware of the situation and that you know what we're looking for. So perhaps you could tell us exactly what you think you'd bring to this project.'

'Ignorance,' I said brightly, which at least had the benefit of shock value, and before anyone could interrupt I launched into the little speech I'd rehearsed in the taxi coming over. 'You know my track record. There's no point my trying to pretend I'm something I'm not. I'll be honest. I don't read political memoirs. So what?' I shrugged. 'Nobody does. But actually that's not my problem.' I pointed at Maddox. 'That's your problem.'

'Oh, please,' said Quigley quietly.

'And rumour has it,' I went on, 'you paid ten million dollars for this book. As things stand, how much of that d'you think you'll see back? Two million? Three? That's bad news'—I turned to Kroll—'especially for your client. Because this is Adam Lang's opportunity to speak directly to history. The last thing he needs is to produce a book that nobody reads, a life story that ends up on the remainder tables. But it doesn't have to be this way.'

I know what a huckster I sounded. But this was pitch talk, remember—which, like declarations of love in a stranger's bedroom at midnight, shouldn't necessarily be held against you the next morning. Kroll was smiling to himself, doodling on his yellow pad. Maddox was staring at me. I took a breath.

'A big name alone doesn't sell a book,' I continued. 'What sells a book is *heart.*' I believe I even thumped my chest at this point. 'That's why political memoir is the black hole of publishing. The name outside the tent may be big, but everyone knows that once they're inside they're going to get the same old tired show, and who'd pay twenty-five dollars for that? You've got to put in some heart, and that's what I do. And whose story has more heart than the guy who starts from nowhere and ends up running a country?'

I leaned forward. 'Here's the joke: a leader's autobiography ought to be *more* interesting than most memoirs, not *less*. So my ignorance about politics is an advantage. I *cherish* my ignorance, frankly. Adam Lang needs no help from me with the politics of this book. What he does need is the same thing a movie star needs, or a baseball player, or a rock star: an experienced collaborator who knows how to ask him questions that will draw out his heart.'

There was a silence. I was trembling. Rick gave my knee a reassuring pat under the table. 'Nicely done.'

'What utter balls,' said Quigley.

'Think so?' asked Maddox, still looking at me. He said it in a neutral voice, but if I had been Quigley I would have detected danger.

'Oh, John, *of course*,' said Quigley. 'Adam Lang's autobiography is going to be a world publishing event. A piece of history, in fact. It shouldn't be approached like a . . . a feature for a celebrity magazine.'

Beyond the tinted windows the traffic was backing up along the motorway. London still hadn't returned to normal after the bomb.

'It seems to me,' said Maddox, in the same slow, quiet voice, 'that I have warehouses full of "world publishing events" that I can't get off my hands. And a lot of people read celebrity magazines. What do *you* think, Sid?'

For a few seconds Kroll carried on smiling to himself and doodling. I wondered what he found so funny. 'Adam's position on this is straightforward,' he said eventually. 'He takes this book very seriously—it's his testament, if you will. He wants to meet his contractual obligations. And he wants it to be a commercial success. He's therefore more than happy to be guided by you, John, and by Marty also, within reason. Obviously, he's still very upset by what happened to Mike, who was irreplaceable.'

Obviously. We all made the appropriate noises.

'Irreplaceable,' he repeated. 'And yet—*he has to be replaced*.' He looked up, pleased with his drollery. 'Adam can certainly appreciate the benefits of trying someone different. In the end, it all comes down to a personal bond.'

'How do you see this working practically?' asked Rick.

'First off, we need it wrapped up in a month,' said Maddox.

'A month?' I repeated. 'You want the book in a month?'

'A completed manuscript does exist,' said Kroll. 'It just needs some work.'

'A lot of work,' said Maddox grimly. 'OK. Taking it backwards: we publish in June, so we ship in May and edit and print in March and April, which means we have to have the manuscript in-house at the end of February. The newspapers need to see it for the serial deals. There's a TV tie-in. Publicity tour's got to be fixed well in advance. So the end of February—that's it, period. What I like about your résumé,' he said, consulting a sheet of paper, 'is that you're obviously experienced and above all you're fast. You deliver.'

'Never missed once,' said Rick, squeezing my shoulder. 'That's my boy.'

'And you're a Brit. The ghost has to be a Brit, to get the jolly old tone right.'

'We agree,' said Kroll. 'But everything will have to be done in the States.

Adam's locked in to a lecture tour there right now, and a fund-raising programme for his foundation. He's not coming back to the UK before March.'

'A month in America, that's fine—yes?' Rick glanced at me eagerly.

I could feel him willing me to say yes, but all I was thinking was: A month, they want me to write a book in a *month* . . . I nodded slowly. 'I suppose I can always bring the manuscript back here to work on.'

'The manuscript stays in America,' said Kroll flatly. 'That's one of the reasons Marty made the house on the Vineyard available. It's a secure environment. Only a few people are allowed to handle it.'

'Sounds more like a bomb than a book!' joked Quigley. Nobody laughed. He rubbed his hands unhappily. 'You know, I will need to see it myself at some point. I am supposed to be editing it.'

'Actually,' said Maddox, 'we need to talk about that later.' He turned to Kroll. 'There's no room in this schedule for revisions. We'll revise as we go.'

As they carried on discussing the timetable, I studied Quigley. He was upright but motionless, like one of those victims in the movies who get stuck with a stiletto while standing in a crowd and die with no one noticing. Yet he'd asked a reasonable question. If he was the editor, why shouldn't he see the manuscript? And why did it have to be held in a 'secure environment'? I felt Rick's elbow in my ribs and realised Maddox was talking to me.

'How soon can you get over there? Assuming we go with you rather than one of the others—how fast can you move?'

'It's Friday today,' I said. 'Give me a day to get ready. I could fly Sunday.'

'And start Monday? That would be great.'

Rick said, 'You won't find anyone who can move quicker than that.'

Maddox and Kroll looked at one another.

'We'll go with you,' said Maddox. He stood up, reached over and shook my hand. 'Subject to reaching a satisfactory agreement with Rick, of course.'

Kroll added, 'You'll also have to sign a nondisclosure agreement.'

'No problem,' I said, also getting to my feet. Confidentiality clauses are standard procedure in the ghosting world. 'I couldn't be happier.'

And I couldn't have been. Everyone except Quigley was smiling, and there was a kind of all-boys, locker-room-after-the-match feeling in the air. We chatted for a minute or so, and that was when Kroll took me to one side and said casually, 'I've something here you might care to take a look at.'

He reached under the table and pulled out a yellow plastic bag. My first thought was that it must be the manuscript of Lang's memoirs, but when he saw my expression Kroll laughed and said, 'No, no, it's not that. It's a book by another client of mine. I'd appreciate your opinion if you get a chance to look at it. Here's my number.' I took his card and slipped it into my pocket.

'I'll give you a call when we've settled the deal,' said Rick.

'Make them howl,' I told him, squeezing his shoulder.

Maddox laughed. 'Hey! Remember!' he called as Quigley showed me out of the door. He struck his big fist against his blue-suited chest. 'Heart!'

As we went down in the lift, Quigley stared at the ceiling. 'Was it my imagination, or did I just get fired in there?'

'They wouldn't let you go, Roy,' I said, with all the sincerity I could muster. 'You're the only one left who can remember what publishing used to be like.'

'"Let you go,"' he said bitterly. 'Yes, that's the modern euphemism, isn't it? As if it's a favour.'

A couple on their lunch break got in at the fourth floor and Quigley was silent until they got off to go to the restaurant on the second. When the doors closed, he said, 'There's something not right about this project. The way no one's allowed to see anything. And poor old Mike McAra, of course. I met him when we signed the deal two years ago. He didn't strike me as the suicidal type. He was more the sort who makes other people want to kill themselves, if you know what I mean.'

'Hard?'

'Hard, yes. Lang would be smiling away, and there would be this thug next to him with eyes like a snake's. I suppose you've got to have someone like that beside you when you're in Lang's position.'

We reached the ground floor and stepped out into the lobby.

'You can pick up a taxi round the corner,' said Quigley, and for that one small, mean gesture—leaving me to walk in the rain rather than calling me a cab on the company's account—I hoped he'd rot.

IT MUST HAVE taken me half an hour to find a ride back into town. I had only a hazy idea of where I was. There was a steady, freezing drizzle. My arm was aching from carrying Kroll's manuscript. Eventually I stopped at a bus shelter. Wedged into its metal frame was the card of a minicab firm.

The journey home took almost an hour and I had plenty of time to take the manuscript out of the yellow plastic bag and study it. The book was called *One Out of Many*. It was the memoir of some ancient US senator, and by any normal measure of tedium it was off the scale. I put the manuscript back into the bag and paid the driver. The fare was forty pounds.

I was crossing the pavement towards my flat, head down, searching for my keys, when I felt someone touch me lightly on the shoulder. I turned and walked into a wall, or was hit by a truck—that was the feeling—as some great iron force slammed into me, and I crumpled, felt the wet stone of the gutter against my cheek, and gasped and sucked and cried like a baby. Then I was conscious, through this much greater pain, of a smaller and sharper one as a foot trod on my hand, and something was torn away.

One of the most inadequate words in the English language is 'winded', suggestive as it is of something light and fleeting—a graze, a touch of breathlessness. I hadn't been winded: I had been semiasphyxiated. My solar plexus felt as though it had been stabbed with a knife. I was aware of people taking my arms and propping me up against a tree. When at last I managed to gulp some air into my lungs, I started blindly patting my stomach, feeling for the gaping wound I knew must be there. I inspected my moist fingers for blood, but there was only dirty London rainwater.

When I realised I wasn't going to die, all I wanted was to get away from these good-hearted folk who had gathered round me and were asking me about calling the police and an ambulance. The thought of having to wait ten hours in casualty, followed by half a day hanging around the police station, was enough to propel me out of the gutter, up the stairs and into my flat. I locked the door, peeled off my outer clothes and lay on the sofa, trembling, for an hour. Then I went into the kitchen and was sick in the sink.

I poured myself a large whisky, and felt myself moving out of shock and into euphoria. I still had my wallet and my watch. The only thing missing was the yellow plastic bag containing Senator Alzheimer's memoirs. I laughed as I pictured the thieves stopping in some alleyway to check their haul: *My advice to any young person seeking to enter public life today . . .* Then I realised this could be awkward. The memoirs might not mean anything to me, but Sidney Kroll might view matters differently.

I took out his card. Sidney L. Kroll of Brinkerhof Lombardi Kroll,

Attorneys, M Street, Washington, DC. After thinking about it for ten minutes or so, I went back and sat on the sofa and called his cellphone.

He answered on the second ring: 'Sid Kroll.' I could tell he was smiling.

'Sidney,' I said, 'you'll never guess what's happened.'

'Some guys just stole my manuscript?'

I gulped. 'My God,' I said, 'is there nothing you don't know?'

'What?' His tone changed abruptly. 'Jesus, I was kidding. Is that *really* what happened? Are you OK?'

I explained what had happened. He said not to worry. The manuscript was *totally* unimportant. He'd given it to me because he thought it might interest me in a professional capacity. He'd get another sent over. What was I going to do? Was I going to call the police? I said I would if he wanted, but I preferred to view the episode as just another round on the gaudy carousel of urban life: 'You know, *che sarà, sarà*, bombed one day, mugged the next.'

He agreed. 'It was a pleasure to meet with you today. It's great you're on board. Cheerio,' he said, and there was that smile in his voice again. *Cheerio*.

After I hung up, I went into the bathroom, stood in front of the mirror and opened my shirt. A livid red horizontal mark, three inches long, was branded into my flesh, just below my rib cage. It was curiously sharp edged. That was caused by a knuckle-duster, I thought. That looked *professional*. I started to feel strange again and went back to the sofa.

When the phone rang, it was Rick, to tell me the deal was done. 'What's up?' he said, interrupting himself. 'You don't sound right.'

'I just got mugged.'

'No!'

Once more I described what had happened. Rick made sympathetic noises, but when he learned I was well enough to work the anxiety left his voice. He soon brought the conversation round to what really interested him.

'So you're still fine to fly to the States on Sunday?'

'Of course. I'm just a bit shocked, that's all.'

'OK, well, here's another shock for you. For one month's work, on a manuscript that's supposedly already written, Rhinehart Inc. are willing to pay you two hundred and fifty thousand dollars, plus expenses.'

'*What?*' They say every man has his price. A quarter of a million dollars for four weeks' work was roughly ten times mine.

'That's fifty thousand dollars paid weekly for the next four weeks,' said Rick, 'plus a bonus of fifty if you get the job done on time. They'll take care of air fares and accommodation. And you'll get a collaborator credit.'

'On the title page?'

'Do me a favour! In the acknowledgments. But it'll still be noticed in the trade press. I'll see to that. Although for now your involvement is strictly confidential. They were very firm about that.' I could hear him chuckling. 'Oh, yes, a whole new wide world is opening up for you, my boy!'

He was right there.

TWO

American Airlines flight 109 was due to leave Heathrow for Boston at 10.30 a.m. on Sunday. Rhinehart biked round a one-way business-class ticket on Saturday afternoon, along with a contract and the privacy agreement. I had to sign both while the messenger waited. I trusted Rick to have got the contract straight, scanned the nondisclosure undertaking in the hall and signed without a qualm.

It took me about five minutes to put my London life into cold storage. All bills were paid by direct debit. There were no deliveries to cancel—no milk, no papers. My cleaner would retrieve the mail from downstairs twice a week. I'd cleared my desk of work. I had no appointments. Kate had likely gone for good. Most of my friends had long since entered the kingdom of family life, from whose distant shores no traveller e'er returned. My parents were dead. I had no siblings. I could have died myself and, as far as the world was concerned, my life would have gone on as normal. I packed one suitcase with a week's change of clothes, a sweater and a spare pair of shoes. I put my laptop and minirecorder into my shoulder bag. I would use the hotel laundry. Anything else I needed I would buy on arrival.

I spent the rest of the day and all that evening up in my study, reading through my books on Adam Lang and making a list of questions. As the day faded, I could feel myself beginning to get into Lang's skin. He was a few years older, but our backgrounds were similar: an only child, born in the Midlands, educated at the local grammar school, a degree from Cambridge, a passion for student drama, a complete lack of interest in student politics.

I went back to look at the photographs. *Lang's hysterical performance as a chicken in charge of a battery farm for humans at the 1972 Cambridge Footlights Revue earned him plaudits*. I could imagine us both chasing the same girls, taking a bad show to the Edinburgh Fringe in the back of a beat-up Volkswagen van, sharing digs, getting stoned. Yet somehow, metaphorically speaking, I had stayed a chicken, while he had gone on to become prime minister. This was when my normal powers of empathy deserted me, for there seemed nothing in his first twenty-five years that could explain his second. But there would be time enough, I reasoned, to find his voice.

Heathrow the next morning looked like one of those bad science-fiction movies 'set in the near future' after the security forces have taken over the state. Two armoured personnel carriers were parked outside the terminal. A dozen men with machine guns patrolled inside. Passengers queued to be frisked and X-rayed, carrying their shoes in one hand and their pathetic toiletries in a clear plastic bag in the other. This is how they'll manage the next holocaust, I thought, as I shuffled forward in my stockinged feet: they'll simply issue us with air tickets and we'll do whatever we're told.

Once I was through security, I headed towards the American Airlines lounge. A satellite news channel was burbling away in the corner. I fixed myself a double espresso and was just turning to the football reports in one of the tabloids when I heard the words 'Adam Lang'. Three days earlier I would have taken no notice, but now it was if my own name was being called out. I went and stood in front of the screen.

To begin with, the story sounded like old news. Four British citizens had been picked up in Pakistan a few years back—'kidnapped by the CIA', according to their lawyer—taken to a secret military installation in eastern Europe and tortured. One had died under interrogation, the other three had been imprisoned in Guantánamo. The new twist was that a Sunday paper had obtained a leaked Ministry of Defence document suggesting that Lang had ordered a Special Air Services unit to seize the men and hand them over to the CIA. Expressions of outrage followed, from a human rights lawyer and a representative of the Pakistani government. A spokeswoman for Lang was quoted as saying the former prime minister knew nothing of the reports and was refusing to comment. The programme moved on to the weather.

For some reason I felt as if someone had just run an ice pack down my spine. I pulled out my cellphone and called Rick. I couldn't remember if he had gone back to America or not. It turned out he was sitting about a mile away, in the British Airways lounge, waiting to board his flight to New York.

'Did you just see the news?' I asked him.

Unlike me, Rick was a news addict. 'The Lang story? Sure.'

'D'you think there's anything in it?'

'Who cares if there is? At least it's keeping his name on the front pages.' Down the line I heard a loudspeaker announcement howling in the background. 'They're calling my flight. I got to go.'

'Before you do,' I said quickly, 'can I run something past you? When I was mugged on Friday, somehow it didn't make sense, the way they left my wallet and ran off with a manuscript. But looking at this news—well, I was wondering—you don't think they thought I was carrying Lang's memoirs?'

'But how'd they know that?' said Rick in a puzzled voice. 'You'd only just met Maddox and Kroll. I was still negotiating the deal.'

'Well, maybe someone was watching the publishers' offices and followed me when I left. It *was* a bright yellow plastic bag, Rick. I might as well have been carrying a flare.' Then another alarming thought came to me. 'It's not possible, is it,' I said hesitantly, 'that Sidney Kroll gave me that manuscript because he thought—if anyone was watching—he thought it would look as though I was leaving the building carrying Adam Lang's book?'

'Why the hell would he do that?'

'I don't know. To see what would happen? It sounds mad, but why are the publishers so paranoid about this manuscript? Why won't they let it out of America? Maybe they think someone over here is desperate to get hold of it.'

'So?'

'So perhaps Kroll was using me as bait—sort of a tethered goat—to test who was after it, find out how far they'd be willing to go.' Even as the words were leaving my mouth I knew I was sounding ridiculous.

'Lang's book is a boring crock of shit!' said Rick. 'The only people they want to keep it away from are their shareholders! *That's* why it's under wraps.'

I would have let the subject go, but Rick was enjoying himself too much.

'"A tethered goat"!' I could have heard his shout of laughter from the other terminal even without the phone. 'Let me get this straight. According to your theory, someone must have known Kroll was in town, known where he was Friday morning, known what he'd come to discuss—'

'All right,' I said, feeling a fool. 'Let's leave it.'

'—*known* he might give Lang's manuscript to a new ghost, known who you were when you came out of the meeting, known where you lived. Because you said they were waiting for you, didn't you? Wow. This must've been some operation. Too big for a newspaper. This must've been a *government*—'

'Forget it,' I said, finally cutting him off. 'You'd better catch your flight.'

'Yeah, you're right. Well, you have a safe trip. Get some sleep on the plane. You're sounding weird. Let's talk next week.' He rang off.

I stood there holding my silent phone. It was true. I was sounding weird. I went into the men's room. The bruise where I'd been punched on Friday had ripened, turned black and purple fringed with yellow, like some exploding supernova beamed back by the Hubble Telescope.

A short time later they announced that the Boston flight was boarding, and once we were in the air my nerves steadied. I love that moment when a drab grey landscape flickers out of sight beneath you, and the plane tunnels up through the cloud to burst into the sunshine. Who can be depressed at 10,000 feet when the sun is shining? I had a drink. I watched a movie. I dozed for a while. But I also scoured that business-class cabin for every Sunday newspaper I could find, ignored the sports pages for once, and read all that had been written about Adam Lang and those four suspected terrorists.

WE MADE our final approach to Logan Airport at 1 p.m. local time. As we came in low over Boston Harbor, the sun struck the downtown skyscrapers one after the other: erupting columns of white and blue, gold and silver, a fireworks display in glass and steel. O my America, I thought, where the book market is five times the size of the United Kingdom's—shine thy light on me! As I queued for immigration I was practically humming 'The Star-Spangled Banner'. Even the guy from the Department of Homeland Security couldn't dent my optimism. He sat frowning behind his glass screen at the very notion of anyone flying 3,000 miles to spend a month on Martha's Vineyard in midwinter. When he discovered I was a writer he couldn't have treated me with greater suspicion if I had been wearing an orange jumpsuit.

'What kind of books you write?'

'Autobiographies.'

That obviously baffled him. 'Don't you have to be famous to do that?'

'Not any more.'

'Not any more,' he repeated, with an expression of infinite distaste. He picked up his metal stamp and punched it twice. He let me in for thirty days.

When I was through immigration, I turned on my phone. It showed a welcoming message from Lang's personal assistant, someone named Amelia Bly, apologising for not providing a driver to collect me from the airport. Instead she suggested I take a bus to the ferry terminal at Woods Hole and promised a car would meet me when I landed at Martha's Vineyard.

The bus was almost empty, and I sat up front as we pushed south out of the city and into open country. The sky was clear, but snow was still piled in banks next to the road and clung to the higher branches in the forests that stretched away on either side. I had a pleasing sense of gaining time, imagining a gloomy, wet Sunday night in London, in contrast to this sparkling afternoon winterland. But gradually it darkened here as well. It was almost six when we reached Woods Hole, and by then there were a moon and stars.

It wasn't until I saw the sign for the ferry that I spared a thought for McAra. Not surprisingly, the dead-man's-shoes aspect of the assignment wasn't one I cared to dwell on. But as I wheeled my suitcase into the ticket office to pay my fare, then stepped back out into the bitter wind, it was only too easy to imagine my predecessor going through similar motions three weeks earlier. I joined the passenger queue and turned to the wall for protection from the wind. There was a wooden board with painted lettering: CURRENT NATIONWIDE THREAT LEVEL IS ELEVATED. I could smell the sea.

Most of the cars waiting to board the ferry had their engines running so the drivers could use their heaters in the cold, and I found myself checking for a tan-coloured Ford Escape SUV. When I actually got on the boat and climbed the clanging metal stairs to the passenger deck, I wondered if McAra had come this way. Once you start thinking about a thing, you can't always make yourself stop. As the boat shuddered and cast off from the terminal, I left the fuggy passenger cabin and went out onto the top deck.

The Martha's Vineyard ferry on a summer's evening must be delightful.

There's a big stripy funnel straight out of a storybook, and rows of blue plastic seats, running the length of the deck, where families no doubt sit in their shorts and T-shirts. But on this January night the deck was deserted, and the north wind blowing down from Cape Cod sliced through my jacket and shirt and chilled my skin to gooseflesh.

As the lights of Woods Hole slipped away, I jammed my hands in my pockets and crossed unsteadily to the starboard side. The handrail was waist-high, and for the first time I appreciated how easily McAra might have gone over. I had to brace myself to keep from slipping. Rick was right. The line between accident and suicide isn't always clearly defined. You could kill yourself without really making up your mind. The mere act of leaning out too far and imagining what it might be like could tip you over. And nobody would hear you fall! The weather wasn't nearly as bad as it had been three weeks earlier, and yet, as I glanced around, I could see not a soul on deck.

My teeth chattering, I went down to the bar for a drink.

We came into the ferry terminal at Vineyard Haven just before seven. An elderly local taxi driver was holding a torn-out page from a notebook, on which my name was misspelt. As he heaved my suitcase into the back of the taxi, the wind lifted a big sheet of clear plastic and sent it twisting and flapping over the ice sheets in the car park. The sky was packed with stars.

I'd bought a guidebook to the island, so I had a vague idea of what I was in for. In summer the population is 100,000, but when the vacationers have migrated west for the winter it drops to 15,000. These are the hardy, insular natives, the folks who call the mainland 'America'. There are a couple of highways, and dozens of long sandy tracks to places with names like Squibnocket Pond and Jobs Neck Cove. My driver didn't utter a word, and all attempts at conversation failed. I didn't know where I was, or where I was going.

After a while we came to a crossroads and turned left into what I guessed must be Edgartown, a settlement of white clapboard houses with picket fences, small gardens and verandahs. Nine out of ten houses were dark. At the bottom of the hill, past the Old Whaling Church, a misty moon cast a silvery light over shingled roofs. Curls of woodsmoke rose from a couple of chimneys. The headlights picked out a sign to the Chappaquiddick ferry, and not long after that we pulled up outside the Lighthouse View Hotel.

Again, I could picture the scene in summer: buckets and spades and fishing nets piled up on the verandah, a dusting of sand trailed up from the beach. But out of season the big old wooden hotel creaked and banged in the wind like a sailing boat stuck on a reef. I watched the lights of the taxi disappear round the corner with something close to nostalgia.

Inside the lobby, a girl dressed as a Victorian maid with a white lace mob-cap handed me a message from Lang's office. I would be picked up at ten the next morning and should bring my passport to show to security. I was starting to feel like a man on a mystery tour: as soon as I reached one location, I was given a fresh set of instructions to proceed to the next.

The hotel was empty, and I was told I could have my choice of rooms, so I picked one on the second floor with a desk I could work at and photographs of Old Edgartown on the wall. After the receptionist had gone, I put my laptop, list of questions and the stories I had torn out of the Sunday newspapers on the desk, then stretched out on the bed.

I fell asleep at once and didn't wake until two in the morning, when my body clock, still on London time, went off like Big Ben. I spent ten minutes searching for a minibar before realising there wasn't one. On impulse, I called Kate's home number in London. She didn't answer. I found myself rambling to her answering machine. She must have left for work early. Or hadn't come home the night before. That was something to think about, and I duly thought about it. Then I took a shower and afterwards I got back into bed and turned off the lamp. Every few seconds the slow pulse of the lighthouse filled the room with a faint red glow. I must have lain there for hours, eyes wide open, and in this way passed my first night on Martha's Vineyard.

THE LANDSCAPE that dissolved out of the dawn the next morning was flat and alluvial. Across the road beneath my window was a creek, then reed beds, and beyond those a beach and the sea. A pretty Victorian lighthouse with a bell-shaped roof and a wrought-iron balcony looked across the straits to a long, low spit of land about a mile away. That, I realised, must be Chappaquiddick. A squadron of hundreds of tiny white seabirds, in a formation as tight as a school of fish, soared and dived above the shallow waves.

I went downstairs and ordered a huge breakfast. From the little shop next to reception I bought a copy of the *New York Times*. The story I was looking for was entombed deep in the world news section:

LONDON (Associated Press)—Former British prime minister Adam Lang authorised the illegal use of British special forces troops to seize four suspected Al-Qaeda terrorists in Pakistan and then hand them over for interrogation by the CIA, according to newspaper reports here Sunday.

The men—Nasir Ashraf, Shakeel Qazi, Salim Khan, and Faruk Ahmed—all British citizens, were seized in Peshawar five years ago. All four were allegedly transferred out of the country to a secret location and tortured. Mr Ashraf is reported to have died under interrogation. Mr Qazi, Mr Khan, and Mr Ahmed were subsequently detained at Guantánamo for three years. Only Mr Ahmed remains in US custody.

According to documents obtained by the London *Sunday Times*, Mr Lang personally endorsed 'Operation Tempest', a secret mission to kidnap the four men by the UK's elite Special Air Services. Such an operation would have been illegal under both UK and international law.

The British Ministry of Defence last night refused to comment on the authenticity of the documents or the existence of 'Operation Tempest'. A spokeswoman for Mr Lang said that he had no plans to issue a statement.

I read it through three times. It didn't seem to add up to much. Or did it? It was hard to tell any more. Methods my father's generation would have considered beyond the pale, even when fighting the Nazis—torture, for example—were now apparently acceptable civilised behaviour. I decided that the ten per cent of the population who worry about these things would be appalled by the report; the remaining ninety would probably just shrug.

I had a couple of hours to kill before the car was due to collect me, so I took a stroll into Edgartown. It seemed even emptier than it had the previous night. I had wanted to buy a windproof jacket but there was no place open. The little boutiques were stripped bare of stock, the windows filled with dust and the husks of insects. *See you in the spring!* read the cards.

It was the same in the harbour. The few yachts moored now were shrouded for winter. The only movement was a solitary fishing boat with an outboard motor heading for the lobster traps. Gulls swooped and cried. There was hammering in the distance as property was renovated for the summer. An old guy walked a dog. Apart from that, nothing occurred that could possibly have distracted an author from his work. It was a nonwriter's idea of a writer's paradise. I could see why McAra might have gone insane.

MY OLD FRIEND the taxi driver picked me up from the hotel later that morning. We drove out of town for about ten minutes, following signs to West Tisbury, into flat, thickly wooded country, and then, before I'd even noticed a gap in the trees, swung left down an unmade sandy track.

Until that moment I was unfamiliar with scrub oak. Maybe it looks good in full leaf. But in winter I doubt if nature has a more depressing vista to offer than mile after mile of those twisted, dwarfish, ash-coloured trees. We rocked and bounced down a narrow forest road for almost three miles and the only creature we saw was a run-over skunk, until at last we came to a closed gate, and there materialised from this petrified wilderness a man carrying a clipboard and wearing the unmistakable dark Crombie overcoat and polished black Oxfords of a British plain-clothes copper.

I wound down my window and handed him my passport. He scowled as he checked my name against the list on his clipboard, wiped a drop of clear moisture from the end of his nose, and walked round inspecting the taxi. I could hear surf performing its continuous, rolling somersault on a beach somewhere. He returned, gave me back my passport and said—or I thought he said: he muttered it under his breath—'Welcome to the madhouse.'

I felt a sudden twist of nerves, which I hope I concealed, because the first appearance of a ghost is important. I try never to show anxiety. I strive always to look professional. For my first-ever meeting with a former prime minister, I had decided against a suit, and selected a pale blue shirt, a conservative striped tie, a sports jacket and grey trousers. My hair was brushed, my teeth cleaned and flossed, my deodorant rolled on. I was as ready as I would ever be. *The madhouse?* Did he really say that? I looked back at the policeman, but he had moved out of sight.

The gate swung clear, the track curved and a moment later I had my first glimpse of the Rhinehart compound: four wooden, cube-shaped buildings—a garage, a storeroom and two cottages—and up ahead the house itself. It was only two storeys high but as wide as a stately home, with a long, low roof and a pair of big, square, brick chimneys of the sort you might see in a crematorium. The rest of the building was made of wood, new but already weathered to a silvery-grey, and the windows were as tall and thin as gun slits. It all somehow resembled a holiday home designed by Albert Speer.

The front door opened as we drew up, and another police guard welcomed me unsmilingly into the hall. He searched my shoulder bag while I glanced around. There were rows of African masks on the white walls and display cabinets filled with primitive carvings and pottery. From somewhere inside the house I heard a woman shouting. A door slammed and then an elegant blonde in a dark blue jacket and skirt, carrying a black-and-red hardcover notebook, came clicking down the corridor on high heels.

'Amelia Bly,' she said with a fixed smile. She was probably forty-five but could have passed for ten years younger. She had beautiful, large, clear blue eyes and exuded a sweetly opulent smell of perfume. I presumed she was the spokeswoman mentioned in that morning's *Times*. 'Adam's in New York, unfortunately, and won't be back till later this afternoon.'

'This is absolutely bloody *ridiculous*!' shouted the unseen woman.

Amelia expanded her smile a fraction, creating tiny fissures in her smooth pink cheeks. 'Oh, dear. I'm afraid poor Ruth's having "one of those days".'

Ruth. The name resonated briefly like a warning drumbeat. It had never occurred to me that Lang's wife might be here.

'If this is a bad time—' I said.

'No, no. She definitely wants to meet you. Come and have a coffee. I'll fetch her. How's the hotel?' she added over her shoulder. 'Quiet?'

'As the grave.'

I retrieved my bag from the Special Branch man and followed Amelia into the interior of the house, trailing in her cloud of scent. She had nice legs, I noticed; her thighs swished nylon as she walked. She showed me into a room full of cream leather furniture, poured me some coffee from a jug in the corner, then disappeared. I stood at the French windows with my mug, looking out over the back of the property. There were no flowerbeds, just a big lawn that expired about a hundred yards away into sickly brown undergrowth. Beyond that was a lake, as smooth as a sheet of steel. To the left, the land rose slightly to the dunes marking the edge of the beach. I couldn't hear the ocean: the glass was too thick—bulletproof, I later discovered.

A burst of Morse from the passage signalled Amelia's return. 'I'm sorry. I'm afraid Ruth's a little busy at the moment. She'll catch you later.' Her smile had hardened somewhat. It looked as natural as her nail polish. 'If you've finished your coffee, I'll show you where we work.'

She insisted that I go first up the stairs.

The house, she explained, was arranged so that all the bedrooms were on the ground floor, with the living space above, and the moment we ascended into the huge open sitting room I understood why. The wall facing the coast was made entirely of glass. There was nothing manmade within sight, just ocean, lake and sky. It was primordial: a scene unchanged for 10,000 years. The soundproofed glass and under-floor heating created the effect of a luxurious time capsule that had been propelled back to the Neolithic age.

'Quite a place,' I said. 'Don't you get lonely at night?'

'We're in here,' said Amelia, opening a door.

I followed her into a big adjoining study, with a similar view. There were two desks: a little one in the corner at which a secretary sat typing at a computer, and a larger one, clear except for a photograph of a powerboat. The sour old skeleton that was Marty Rhinehart crouched over the wheel of his boat—living disproof of the old adage that you can't be too thin or too rich.

'We're a small team,' said Amelia. 'Myself, Alice here'—the girl in the corner looked up—'and Lucy, who's with Adam in New York. Jeff the driver's also in New York—he'll be bringing the car back this afternoon. Six protection officers from the UK—three here and three with Adam at the moment. We badly need another pair of hands, if only to handle the media, but Adam can't bring himself to replace Mike. They were together so long.'

'And how long have you been with him?'

'Eight years. I'm on attachment from the Cabinet Office.'

'Poor Cabinet Office.'

She flashed her nail-polish smile. 'It's my husband I miss the most.'

'You're married? I notice you're not wearing a ring.'

'I can't, sadly. It's too large. It bleeps when I go through airport security.'

'Ah.' We understood one another perfectly.

'The Rhineharts also have a live-in Vietnamese couple, but they're so discreet you'll hardly notice them. Dep looks after the house and her husband, Duc, does the garden.'

She produced a key from her jacket pocket, unlocked a filing cabinet and withdrew a box file. 'This is not to be removed from this room, or copied,' she said, laying it on the desk. 'You can make notes, but I must remind you that you've signed a confidentiality agreement. You have six hours to read it before Adam gets in from New York. I'll have a sandwich sent up for lunch.

Alice, come on. We don't want to cause him any distractions, do we?'

After they'd gone, I sat down in the leather swivel chair and loosened my tie. For a few moments I allowed myself to swing back and forth, savouring the ocean view and the sensation of being world dictator. Then I flipped open the lid of the file, pulled out the manuscript and started to read.

ALL GOOD BOOKS are different but all bad books are the same. In my line of work I read a lot of bad books. And what they all have in common, be they novels or memoirs, is this: they don't ring true. I'm not saying that a good book *is* true necessarily, just that it *feels* true for the time you're reading it.

Adam Lang's memoir felt false, as if there was a hollow at its centre. Its sixteen chapters were arranged chronologically, starting with 'Early Years' and ending with 'A Future of Hope'. Each had been cobbled together from speeches, communiqués, memoranda, interview transcripts, office diaries and newspaper articles. Occasionally, Lang permitted himself a private emotion ('I was overjoyed when our third child was born'), a personal observation ('the American president was much taller than I had expected'), or a sharp remark ('as foreign secretary, Richard Rycart often seemed to prefer presenting the foreigners' case to Britain rather than the other way round'), but not to any great effect. And where was his wife? She was barely mentioned.

A crock of shit, Rick had called it. But actually this was worse. This was a crock of nothing. It had to be a lie, I thought. No human being could pass through life and feel so little. Especially Adam Lang, whose political stock-in-trade was emotional empathy. I skimmed the chapter called 'The War on Terror', searching for words like 'rendition', 'torture', 'CIA'. I found nothing. What about the war in the Middle East? Surely some mild criticism here of the US president, the defence secretary or the secretary of state; some hint of betrayal or letdown? No. Nowhere. I began reading again from the top.

At some point, Alice must have brought me in a tuna sandwich and a bottle of mineral water, because I noticed them at the end of the desk. But I was too busy to stop, and besides I wasn't hungry. In fact, I felt nauseous as I scanned the sheer white cliff face of featureless prose for a tiny handhold of interest to cling to. No wonder McAra had thrown himself off the Martha's Vineyard ferry. No wonder Maddox and Kroll had flown to London to try to rescue the project. No wonder they were paying me $50,000 a week. All this was rendered logical by the direness of the manuscript. And now my reputation would come spiralling down. I would be the ghost who had collaborated on the biggest flop in publishing history. In a shaft of paranoid insight, I fancied I saw my real role in the operation: designated fall guy.

I finished the last of the 621 pages ('Ruth and I look forward to the future, whatever it may hold') in midafternoon, and when I laid down the manuscript I pressed my hands to my cheeks and opened my mouth and eyes wide, in a reasonable imitation of Edvard Munch's *The Scream*.

That was when I heard a cough in the doorway and looked up to see Ruth Lang watching me. I don't know how long she'd been there.

She raised a thin black eyebrow. 'As bad as that?' she said.

SHE WAS WEARING a man's thick, shapeless white sweater, so long in the sleeves that only her chewed fingernails were visible, and once we got downstairs she pulled on top of this a pale blue hooded cagoule, disappearing for a while as she tugged it over her head, her pale face emerging at last with a frown. Her short dark hair stuck up in spikes.

It was she who had proposed a walk. She said I looked as though I needed one, which was true enough. She found me her husband's windproof jacket and a pair of waterproof boots, and together we stepped out into the blustery Atlantic air. We followed the path round the edge of the lawn and climbed up onto the dunes. To our right was the lake, with a jetty; to our left was the grey ocean. Ahead of us, bare white sand stretched for a couple of miles, and when I looked behind the picture was the same, except that a policeman in an overcoat was following about fifty yards distant.

'You must get sick of this,' I said, nodding to our escort.

'It's been going on so long I've stopped noticing.'

We pressed on. Close up, the beach didn't look so idyllic. Strange pieces of broken plastic, lumps of tar, a blue canvas shoe stiff with salt, a wooden cable drum, dead birds—it was like walking along the side of a six-lane highway. The big waves came in with a roar and receded like passing trucks.

'So,' said Ruth, 'how bad is it?'

'Well,' I said, politely, 'it needs some work.'

'How much?'

'It's fixable,' I said. 'It's the deadline that's the trouble. We absolutely have to do it in four weeks, and that's less than two days for each chapter.'

'Four weeks!' She had a deep, rather dirty laugh. 'You'll never get him to sit still for as long as that!'

'He doesn't have to write it. He just has to talk to me.'

She had pulled up her hood. Only the sharp white tip of her nose was visible. Everyone said she was smarter than her husband and that she'd loved their life at the top even more than he had. You only had to watch them on TV together to see how she bathed in his success. Adam and Ruth Lang: the Power and the Glory. Now she stopped and turned to face the ocean. Along the beach, as if playing Grandma's footsteps, the policeman also stopped.

'You were my idea,' she said.

I swayed in the wind. I almost fell over. 'I was?'

'Yes. You were the one who wrote Christy's book for him.'

It took me a moment to work out who she meant. Christy Costello. My first best seller. The intimate memoirs of a seventies' rock star. Drink, drugs, girls, a near-fatal car crash, surgery, and finally rehab and redemp in the arms of a good woman. It sold 300,000 copies in hardcover in the UK alone.

'You know *Christy*?' It seemed so unlikely.

'We stayed at his house on Mustique last winter. I read his memoirs. They were by the bed.'

'Now I'm embarrassed.'

'Why? They were brilliant, in a horrible kind of way. Listening to his scrambled stories over dinner, then seeing how you'd turned them into something resembling a life—I said to Adam then: "This is the man you need to write your book." '

I laughed. I couldn't stop myself. 'Well, I hope your husband's recollections aren't quite as hazy as Christy's.'

'Don't count on it.' She pulled back her hood and took a deep breath. She was better looking in the flesh than she was on television. The camera didn't catch her amused alertness, the animation of her face. 'God, I miss home,' she said. 'Even though the kids are away at university. I keep telling him it's like being married to Napoleon on Saint Helena.'

'Then why don't you go back to London?'

She stared at the ocean for a while, biting her lip. Then she looked at me, sizing me up. 'You did sign that confidentiality agreement?'

'Of course. Check with Sid Kroll's office.'

'Because I don't want to read about this in some gossip column next week, or in some cheap little kiss-and-tell book of your own a year from now.'

'Whoa,' I said, taken aback by her venom. 'I thought you said I was your idea. I didn't ask to come here. And I haven't kissed anyone.'

She nodded. 'All right then. Between you and me, there's something not quite right with him at the moment, and I'm a bit afraid to leave him.'

Boy, I thought. This just gets better and better. 'Yes,' I replied diplomatically. 'Amelia told me he was very upset by Mike's death.'

'Oh, did she? Quite when *Mrs Bly* became such an expert on my husband's emotional state I'm not sure.' If she had hissed and sprung claws she couldn't have made her feelings plainer. 'Losing Mike made it worse, but it isn't just that. It's losing power—that's the real trouble. And now having to sit down and relive everything, while the press go on and on about what he did and didn't do. He can't get free of the past. He can't move on.' She gestured helplessly at the sea, the sand, the dunes. 'He's stuck. We're both stuck.'

As we walked back to the house, she put her arm through mine. 'Oh, dear,' she said. 'You must be starting to wonder what you've let yourself in for.'

WHEN WE GOT BACK to the compound, a dark green Jaguar limousine with a Washington licence plate was parked at the entrance, and a black minivan was drawn up behind it. As the front door opened, I could hear several telephones ringing. A genial-looking grey-haired man in a cheap brown suit was sitting just inside, drinking a cup of tea and talking to one of the police guards.

He jumped up smartly when he saw Ruth Lang. 'Afternoon, ma'am.'

'Hello, Jeff. How was New York?'

'Bloody chaos, as usual. Like Piccadilly Circus in the rush hour.' He had a London accent. 'Thought for a while I wouldn't get back in time.'

Ruth turned to me. 'They like to have the car ready in position when Adam lands.' She started wriggling out of her cagoule.

Just then, Amelia Bly came round the corner, a cellphone wedged between her elegant shoulder and her sculpted chin. 'That's fine, that's fine. I'll tell him.' She nodded to Ruth and carried on speaking—'On Thursday he's in Chicago'—then looked at Jeff and tapped her wristwatch.

'Actually, I think *I'll* go to the airport,' said Ruth suddenly, pulling her cagoule back down. 'Amelia can stay here and polish her nails or something. Why don't you come?' she added to me. 'He's keen to meet you.'

'Then I'll travel in the back-up car,' said Amelia, snapping her cellphone shut and smiling sweetly. 'I can do my nails in there.'

Jeff opened one of the Jaguar's rear doors for Ruth, while I went round and nearly broke my arm tugging at the other. I slid into the leather seat and the door closed behind me with a gaseous thump.

'She's armoured, sir,' said Jeff into the rearview mirror. 'Weighs two and a half tons. Yet she'll still do a hundred with all four tyres shot out.'

'Oh, do shut up, Jeff,' said Ruth good-humouredly as we pulled away. 'He doesn't want to hear all that.'

'The windows are an inch thick and don't open. She's airtight against chemical and biological attack, with oxygen for an hour. At this precise moment, sir, you're probably safer than you've ever been in your life.'

Ruth laughed again and made a face. 'Boys with their toys!'

The forest track ran smooth and quiet as rubber. We ran over the dead skunk, and the big car didn't register the slightest tremor.

'Nervous?' asked Ruth.

'No. Why? Should I be?'

'Not at all. He's the most charming man you'll ever meet. My own Prince Charming!' And she gave her deep-throated, mannish laugh again.

As I glanced over my shoulder at the minivan following close behind, we came out of the forest onto the main road. We turned left and almost immediately swung right through the airport perimeter.

I stared out in surprise at the big runway. 'We're here already?'

'In summer Marty likes to leave his office in Manhattan at four,' said Ruth, 'and be on the beach by six.'

'I suppose he has a private jet,' I said in an attempt at knowingness.

'Of course he has a private jet.' She gave me a look that made me feel like a hick who'd just used his fish knife to butter his roll.

I realised then that just about everybody the Langs knew these days had a private jet. Indeed, here came Lang himself, in a corporate Gulfstream, dropping out of the darkening sky. Jeff put his foot down and a minute later we pulled up outside the little terminal. There was a cannonade of slamming doors as we piled inside—me, Ruth, Amelia, Jeff and one of the protection officers. Inside, a patrolman from the Edgartown police was already waiting.

The private jet taxied in from the runway. It was painted dark blue, with HALLINGTON in gold letters by the door, and had six windows either side. When it came to a stop and the engines were cut, the silence over the deserted airfield was unexpectedly profound.

The door opened, the steps were lowered and out came a couple of Special Branch men. One headed for the terminal. The other waited at the foot of the steps. I could make out Lang in the shadows of the interior, shaking hands with the pilot, then he came out—almost reluctantly, it seemed—and paused at the top of the steps. He was holding his own briefcase—not something he had done when he was prime minister. He smoothed down his hair, and glanced around as if he was trying to remember what he was supposed to do.

Then he caught sight of us watching him through the big window. He waved and grinned, exactly the way he had in his heyday, and the moment—whatever it was—had passed. He came striding eagerly across the concourse, trailed by a third Special Branch man and a young woman pulling a suitcase on wheels.

We left the window just in time to meet him at the arrivals gate.

'Hi, darling,' he said, and stooped to kiss his wife.

She stroked his arm. 'How was New York?'

'Great. They gave me the Gulfstream Four—you know, the transatlantic one, with the beds and the shower. Hi, Amelia. Hi, Jeff.' He noticed me. 'Hello,' he said. 'Who are you?'

'I'm your ghost,' I said.

I regretted it the instant I said it. I'd conceived it as a witty, self-deprecatory, break-the-ice kind of a line. But somehow, in that deserted airport, it hit precisely the wrong note. He flinched.

'Right,' he said doubtfully, and although he shook my hand he also drew his head back slightly, as if to inspect me from a safer distance.

Christ, I thought, he thinks I'm a lunatic.

'Don't worry,' Ruth told him. 'He isn't always such a jerk.'

THREE

'Brilliant opening line,' said Amelia as we drove back to the house. 'Did they teach you that at ghost school?'

We were sitting together in the back of the minivan. The secretary who'd just flown in from New York—her name was Lucy—and the three protection officers occupied the seats in front of us. I could see the Jaguar immediately ahead carrying the Langs. It was starting to get dark. Pinned by two sets of headlights, the scrub oaks loomed and writhed.

'Particularly tactful,' she went on, 'given that you're replacing a dead man.'

'All right,' I groaned. 'Stop.'

'But you do have one thing going for you,' she said quietly, turning her large blue eyes on me. 'Almost uniquely among all members of the human race, you seem to be trusted by Ruth Lang. Why's that, do you suppose?'

'There's no accounting for taste.'

'True. Perhaps she thinks you'll do what she tells you?'

'Perhaps. Don't ask me.' The last thing I needed was to get stuck in the middle of this catfight. 'Listen, Amelia—can I call you Amelia? I'm helping write a book. I don't want to get caught up in any palace intrigues.'

'Of course not. You just want to do your job and get out of here.'

'You're mocking me again.'

'You make it so easy.'

After that I shut up for a while. I could see why Ruth didn't like her. She was a shade too clever and several shades too blonde for comfort. In fact it struck me that she might be having an affair with Lang. He'd been noticeably cool towards her at the airport, and isn't that always the surest sign?

We were halfway down the track when Amelia said, 'You haven't told me what you thought of the manuscript.'

'I haven't had so much fun since I read the memoirs of Leonid Brezhnev.' She didn't smile. 'I don't understand,' I went on. 'You people were running the country not that long ago. Surely one of you had English as a first language?'

'Mike—' she began, then stopped. 'But I shouldn't speak ill of the dead.'

'Why make them an exception?'

'All right, then: Mike. The problem was, Adam passed it all over to Mike right at the beginning, and poor Mike was simply swamped by it. He disappeared to Cambridge to do the research and we barely saw him for a year.'

'Cambridge?'

'Cambridge—where the Lang papers are stored. Two thousand boxes of documents. Two hundred and fifty metres of shelving. One million separate papers, or thereabouts—nobody's ever bothered to count.'

'McAra went through all that?' I was incredulous.

'No,' she said irritably. 'Obviously not every box, but enough so that, when he finally did emerge, he was exhausted. I think he lost sight of what he was supposed to be doing. That seems to have triggered a clinical depression, though none of us noticed it at the time. He didn't even sit down with Adam to go over it all until just before Christmas. And by then it was far too late.'

'I'm sorry,' I said. 'You're telling me that a man who's being paid ten million dollars to write his memoirs within two years turns the project over to someone who knows nothing about producing books and who is then allowed to wander off on his own for twelve months?'

Amelia put a finger to her lips. 'You're very loud, for a ghost.'

'But surely,' I whispered, 'a former prime minister must recognise how important his memoirs are to him?'

'I don't think Adam had the slightest intention of producing this book within two years. He let Mike take it over as a kind of reward for sticking by him. But when Rhinehart made it clear he'd hold him to the original contract, and when the publishers read what Mike had produced . . .' She trailed off.

'And nobody saw this coming?'

'I raised it with Adam every so often. But history doesn't really interest him—it never has, not even his own. He was much more concerned with getting his foundation established.'

I sat back in my seat. I could see how it all must have happened: McAra, the party hack riveting together his useless sheets of facts; Lang, always a man for the bigger picture, preferring to live, not relive, his life; then the realisation that the great memoir project was in trouble, followed, I assumed, by recriminations, the sundering of old friendships, suicidal anxiety.

'It must have been rough on all of you.'

'It was. Especially after they discovered Mike's body. I offered to go and do the identification, but Adam felt it was his responsibility. It was an awful thing to go through. So please, no more jokes about ghosts.'

I was on the point of asking her about the rendition stories in the weekend papers when the Jaguar's brake lights glowed, and we came to a stop.

'Well, here we are again,' she said with a hint of weariness. 'Home.'

The temperature had dropped with the sun. I stood beside the minivan and watched as Lang ducked out of his car and was swept through the door by the swirl of bodyguards and staff. All along the façade of the big house, the windows started lighting up, and it was possible, briefly, to imagine that this was a focus of real power and not some lingering parody of it. Still twisting with embarrassment over my gaffe at the airport, I lingered outside in the cold for a while. To my surprise, the person who came out to fetch me was Lang.

'Hi, man!' he called from the doorway. 'What on earth are you doing out here? Isn't anybody looking after you? Come and have a drink.'

He touched my shoulder as I entered and steered me down the passage towards the room where I'd had coffee that morning. He'd already taken off his jacket and tie and pulled on a thick grey sweater.

'I'm sorry I didn't get a chance to say hello properly at the airport. What would you like?'

'What are you having?' Dear God, I prayed, let it be something alcoholic.

'Iced tea. I'd sooner have something stronger, but Ruth would kill me.'

'Iced tea would be fine.'

He called to one of the secretaries: 'Luce, ask Dep to bring us some tea, would you? So,' he said, plonking himself down in the centre of the sofa, 'you have to be me for a month, God help you.'

'I hope it will be a fairly painless procedure, for both of us,' I said, and hesitated, unsure how to address him.

'Adam,' he said. 'Call me Adam.'

There comes a moment, I find, in dealing with a famous person face-to-face, when you feel as if you're in a dream, and this was it for me. Here I was, conversing in an apparently relaxed manner with a world statesman. He was going out of his way to be nice to me. He *needed* me. What a lark, I thought.

'I have to tell you,' I said. 'I've never met an ex-prime minister before.'

He smiled. 'I've never met a ghost, so we're even. Sid Kroll says you're the man for the job. Ruth agrees. So how are we supposed to go about this?'

'I'll interview you. I'll turn your answers into prose. I might add linking passages, trying to imitate your voice. But anything I write you'll be able to correct. I don't want to put words into your mouth you wouldn't want to use.'

'And how long will this take?'

'I'd normally do fifty or sixty hours of interviews. That gives me about four hundred thousand words, which I'd edit down to a hundred thousand.'

'But we've already got a manuscript.'

'Yes,' I said, 'but frankly, it's not really publishable. It's research notes, it's not a book. It doesn't have any kind of voice.'

Lang pulled a face. He clearly didn't see the problem.

'The work won't be wasted,' I added quickly. 'We can ransack it for facts and quotations, and I don't mind the structure—the sixteen chapters—although I'd like to open differently, find something more intimate.'

The Vietnamese housekeeper brought in our tea. I wanted to introduce myself, but when she handed me my glass she avoided meeting my gaze.

'You heard about Mike?' asked Lang.

'Yes,' I said. 'I'm sorry.'

Lang glanced away, towards the darkened window. 'We should put something nice about him in the book. His mother would like it.'

'That should be easy enough.'

'He was with me a long time. You think you know someone pretty well and then . . .' He shrugged and stared into the night.

I didn't say anything. I've learned over the years to behave like a shrink—to sit in silence and give the client time. After about half a minute he appeared to remember I was still in the room.

'Right. How long do you need from me?'

'Full time?' I sipped my drink and tried not to wince at the sweet taste. 'If we work really hard we should be able to break the back of it in a week.'

'A week?' Lang performed a little facial mime of alarm.

I resisted the temptation to point out that $10 million for a week's work wasn't exactly minimum wage. 'I may come back to you to plug any holes, but if you give me till Friday I'll have enough to rewrite most of this draft.'

'Fine. The sooner we get it done the better.' Lang jumped up and shook my hand. 'It's good to meet you, man. We'll make a start first thing tomorrow.'

'HOW DID IT GO?' enquired Amelia as she showed me to the door.

'Pretty well, I think. It was all very friendly. He kept calling me "man".'

'Yes. He always does that when he can't remember someone's name.'

'Tomorrow,' I said, 'I'll need a private room where I can do the interviewing. I'll need a secretary to transcribe his answers as we go along. I'll need my own copy of the existing manuscript on disc. Yes, I know'—I held up my hand to cut off her objections—'I won't take it out of the house. But I'm going to have to cut and paste it into the new material, and also try to rewrite it so that it sounds vaguely like it was produced by a human being.'

She was writing all this down in her black and red book. 'Anything else?'

'How about dinner?'

'Good night,' she said firmly and closed the door.

One of the policemen gave me a ride back to the hotel. I had just opened the door to my room when my cellphone rang. It was Kate.

'Are you OK?' she said. 'I got your message. You sounded a bit . . . odd.'

'Did I? Sorry. I'm fine now.' I fought back the impulse to ask her where she'd been when I called.

'So? Have you met him?'

'I have. I've just come from him.'

'And?' Before I could answer, she said, 'Don't tell me: charming.'

I briefly held the phone away from my ear and gave it the finger.

'You do pick your moments,' she went on. 'Did you see yesterday's papers?'

'Of course I did,' I said defensively, 'and I'm going to ask him about it.'

'When?'

'When the moment arises.'

She made an explosive noise that managed to combine hilarity, fury, contempt and disbelief. 'Yes, *ask* him. Ask him why he illegally kidnaps British citizens in another country and hands them over to be tortured. Ask him if he knows about the techniques the CIA uses to simulate drowning. Ask him what he plans to say to the widow and children of the man who died of—'

'Hold on,' I interrupted. 'You lost me after drowning.'

'I'm seeing someone else,' she said.

'Good,' I said and hung up.

After that there didn't seem much else to do except go and get drunk.

The bar was decorated to look like the kind of place Captain Ahab might drop into after a hard day at the harpoon. The tables were made out of old barrels. Antique seine nets and lobster traps hung from the roughly planked walls. I ordered a beer and a bowl of clam chowder and sat where I could see the big television screen, which was showing an ice hockey game.

'You're English,' said a man at a table in the corner. He must have heard me ordering. He was the only other customer in the bar.

'And so are you,' I said.

'Indeed I am. Are you here on holiday?'

He had a clipped, hello-old-chap-fancy-a-round-of-golf sort of a voice. That, and the double-breasted blazer with the tarnished brass buttons, flashed bore, bore, bore as clearly as the Edgartown Lighthouse.

'No. Working.' I resumed watching the game.

'So what's your line?' He had a glass of something clear with ice in it.

'Just this and that. Excuse me.' I got up and went to the lavatory and washed my hands. When I returned to the table, my chowder had arrived. I ordered another drink but didn't offer to buy one for my compatriot.

'I hear Adam Lang's on the island,' he said.

I looked at him properly then. He was in his middle fifties, slim but broad-shouldered. His iron-grey hair was slicked back off his forehead. There was something vaguely military about him, but also unkempt and faded.

I answered in a neutral tone, 'Is he?'

'So I hear. You don't happen to know his whereabouts, do you?'

'No. I'm afraid not. Excuse me again.' I started to eat my chowder.

I heard him sigh noisily, then the clink of ice as his glass was set down.

'Bastard,' he said as he passed my table.

THERE WAS NO SIGN of him when I came down to breakfast the next morning. The receptionist told me there was no other guest apart from me, and was firm that she hadn't seen a British man in a blazer. I'd been awake since four, and was groggy and hungover enough to wonder if I'd hallucinated the whole encounter. I felt better after some coffee. I walked round the lighthouse to clear my head, and by the time I returned the minivan had arrived.

I'd anticipated that my biggest problem on the first day would be physically getting Adam Lang into a room and keeping him there. But when we reached the house, *he* was waiting for *me*. Amelia had decided we should use Rhinehart's office, and we found the former prime minister, wearing a dark green track suit, sprawled in the big chair opposite the desk. His trainers had sand on their soles: I guessed he must have gone for a run on the beach.

'Hi, man,' he said, looking up at me. 'Ready to start?'

'Good morning,' I said. 'I just need to sort out a few things first.'

'Sure. Go ahead. Ignore me.'

I opened my shoulder bag and unpacked the tools of the ghosting trade: a Sony Walkman digital recorder with a stack of 74-minute MiniDiscs, and a mains lead and adapter (I've learned the hard way not to rely on batteries); a silver Panasonic Toughbook laptop computer; a couple of small black notebooks and three rollerball pens. I also had my list of questions.

'I've loaded the manuscript onto this flash drive for you,' said Amelia. She handed me an object the size of a plastic cigarette lighter. 'You're welcome to copy it onto your own computer, but I'm afraid that if you do, your laptop must stay here, locked up, overnight.'

Lang said, 'So you've actually got my whole book on that?'

'We could get a hundred books on that, Adam,' said Amelia, patiently.

'Amazing.' He shook his head. 'You know the worst thing about my life? You get so out of touch. You never go in a shop. Everything's done for you. You don't carry any money—if I want some money, even now, I have to ask one of the secretaries or one of the protection boys to get it for me. I couldn't do it myself, anyway; I don't know my—what're they called?'

'PIN?'

'You see? I just don't have a clue. The other week, Ruth and I went out to dinner with some people in New York. They've always been generous to us, so I say, "Right, this is on me." I give my credit card to the manager and he comes back a few minutes later, all embarrassed. There's still a strip where the signature's supposed to be.' He grinned. 'The card hadn't been activated.'

'This,' I said excitedly, 'is exactly the sort of detail we need for your book.'

Lang looked startled. 'I can't put that in. People would think I was an idiot.'

'But it shows what it's like to be you.' I knew I had to get him to focus on what we needed. 'Why don't we try to make this book unlike any other political memoir ever written? Why don't we try to tell the truth?'

He laughed. 'Now that would be a first.'

'I mean it. Let's tell people what it *feels* like to be prime minister—the day-to-day experience of actually leading a country. What are the strains? What's it like to be so cut off from ordinary life? What's it like to be hated?'

'Thanks a lot.'

'What fascinates people isn't policy; it's the detail of another person's life. This shouldn't be a book for political hacks. It should be for everyone.'

'The people's memoir,' said Amelia dryly, but I ignored her, and so did Lang, who was looking at me quite differently now.

'Most former leaders couldn't get away with it,' I said. 'They're too stiff, too awkward, too *old*. If they take off their jacket and tie and put on'—I gestured at his outfit—'a track suit, say, they look phoney. But you're different. So you should write a different kind of political memoir, for a different age.'

Lang was staring at me. 'What do you think, Amelia?'

'I think you two were made for each other.'

'Do you mind,' I asked, 'if I start recording? Something useful might come out of this. Don't worry—the discs will all be your property.'

Lang shrugged and gestured towards the Sony Walkman. As I pressed RECORD, Amelia slipped out and closed the door quietly behind her.

'The first thing that strikes me,' I said, bringing a chair from behind the desk so that I could sit facing him, 'is that you aren't really a politician, in the conventional sense. I mean, when you were growing up, no one would have expected you to become a politician, would they?'

'Not at all,' said Lang. 'I thought people who were obsessed by politics were weird. I still do, as a matter of fact. I liked football. I liked theatre and the movies. Later on I liked going out with girls. I never dreamed I might become a politician. Most student politicians struck me as complete nerds.'

'So what changed? What turned you on to politics?'

'Turned on is about right,' said Lang with a laugh. 'I'd left Cambridge and drifted for a year, hoping that a play I'd been involved in might be taken up by a theatre in London. But it didn't happen, so I ended up working in a bank, living in this grotty basement flat in Lambeth, feeling sorry for myself, because all my friends from Cambridge were working in the BBC, or what have you. And I remember it was a Sunday afternoon—raining, I was still in bed—and someone knocks on the door . . .'

It was a story he must have told a thousand times, but you wouldn't have guessed it. He was smiling at the memory, going over the same old words, using the same rehearsed gestures—he was miming knocking on a door—and I thought what an old trouper he was: the sort of pro who'd always put on a good show, whether he had an audience of one or one million.

'. . . and this person just wouldn't go away. Knock knock knock. And, you know, I'd had a bit to drink the night before. I'm moaning and groaning and I've got the pillow over my head. But it starts up again: knock knock knock. So eventually—and by now I'm swearing quite a bit—I get out of bed, pull on a dressing gown and open the door. And there's this girl, this gorgeous girl. She's wringing wet from the rain, but she launches into this speech about the local elections. I didn't even know there *were* any local elections, but I pretend that I'm very interested, invite her in and make her a cup of tea, and she dries off. And that's it—I'm in love. And it becomes clear that the best way of getting to see her again is to take one of her leaflets and turn up the next Tuesday evening, or whenever it is, and join the local party. Which I do.'

'And this is Ruth?'

'This is Ruth.'

'And if she'd been a member of a different political party?'

'I'd have joined it just the same. I wouldn't have stayed in it,' he added quickly. 'I mean this was the start of a long political awakening for me—bringing out values and beliefs that were simply dormant at that time. I couldn't have stayed in just any party. But everything would have been different if Ruth hadn't knocked on that door that afternoon, and kept knocking.'

'And if it hadn't been raining.'

'I'd have found some other excuse to invite her in,' said Lang with a grin. 'I mean, come on, man—I wasn't *completely* hopeless.'

I grinned back, shook my head, and jotted 'opening??' in my notebook.

WE WORKED ALL MORNING without a break, except for when a disc was filled. Then I would hurry downstairs to the room that Amelia and the secretaries were using as an office and hand it over to be transcribed. On my return I'd find Lang sitting exactly as I'd left him.

I took him through his early years, focusing on the impressions and objects of his childhood: the semidetached house in Leicester; the quiet, apolitical values of the English provinces in the sixties; muddy Saturday-morning games of football at the local park and summer afternoons of cricket down by the river; his father's Austin Atlantic and his own first Raleigh bike; the comics—the *Eagle* and the *Victor*—and the radio comedies—*I'm Sorry, I'll Read That Again* and *The Navy Lark*; the 1966 World Cup Final and *Z Cars*; Millie singing 'My Boy Lollipop' played at 45 rpm on his mother's Dansette Capri record player. Sitting there in Rhinehart's study, the minutiae of English life nearly half a century earlier seemed remote and irrelevant. But there was cunning in my method, for this was not just *his* childhood we were itemising but mine and that of every boy who was born in England in the 1950s.

'What we need to do,' I told him, 'is persuade the reader to identify with Adam Lang. To see beyond the remote figure in the bombproof car. To recognise in him the same things they recognise in themselves. Because if I know nothing else about this business, I know this: once you have the readers' sympathy, they'll follow you anywhere.'

'I get it,' he said, nodding emphatically. 'I think that's brilliant.'

And so we swapped memories for hour after hour, and I will not say we *concocted* a childhood for Lang, but we certainly pooled our experiences to such an extent that a few of my memories blended into his. As it transpired, I collaborated with Lang for only a short while, but I can honestly say I never had a more responsive client. We decided that his first memory would be when he tried to run away from home at the age of three and he heard the sound of his father's footsteps coming up behind him and felt the hardness of his muscled arms as he scooped him back to the house. We remembered his mother ironing, and the book she had with a red and gold cover and pictures that young Adam would look at for hours; it was what first gave him his interest in the theatre. We remembered Christmas pantomimes he went to, and his stage debut in the school nativity play.

By the time we broke for lunch, we had reached the age of seventeen, when his performance in the title role of Christopher Marlowe's *Doctor Faustus* had confirmed him in his desire to become an actor. McAra, with typical thoroughness, had dug out the review in the *Leicester Mercury*, December 1971, describing how Lang had 'held the audience spellbound' with his final speech, as he glimpsed eternal damnation.

Lang went off to play tennis with one of his bodyguards, and I dropped by the downstairs office to check on the transcription. Both secretaries wore headphones, and the room was filled with a soothing rattle of plastic. An hour's interviewing generally yields 7,000 to 8,000 words, and Lang and I had been at it from nine till nearly one. I would have about a hundred double-spaced pages of material to show for that morning's work alone. For the first time since arriving on the island, I felt the warm breath of optimism.

'This is all new to me,' said Amelia, reading Lang's words over Lucy's shoulder. 'I've never heard him mention any of this before.'

'The human memory is a treasure house, Amelia,' I said, deadpan. 'It's merely a matter of finding the right key.'

I left her peering at the screen and went into the kitchen. It was about as large as my London flat, with enough polished granite to furnish a family mausoleum. A tray of sandwiches had been laid out. I put one on a plate and wandered round the back of the house to what I suppose you would call a solarium—with a sliding glass door leading to an outside swimming pool, covered with a grey tarpaulin. Beyond the two silvered wooden buildings at the far end was the scrub oak and the white sky. A small, dark figure was raking leaves. I presumed he was the Vietnamese gardener, Duc. I must try to see this place in summer, I thought. I sat down on a lounger, releasing a faded odour of chlorine and suntan lotion, and called Rick in New York.

He was in a rush, as usual. 'How's it going?'

'We had a good morning. The man's a pro.'

'Great. I'll call Maddox. He'll be glad to hear it. The first fifty thousand just came in, by the way. I'll wire it over. Speak to you later.' The line went dead.

I finished my sandwich and went back upstairs. I'd had an idea, and my newborn confidence gave me the courage to act on it. I went into the study and closed the door. I plugged Amelia's flash drive into my laptop, then attached a cable from my computer to my cellphone and dialled up the Internet. My life would be much easier, I reasoned, if I could work on the book in my hotel room each night. I told myself I was doing no harm.

The moment I was online, I addressed an email to myself, attached the manuscript file and pressed SEND. The upload seemed to take an age. Amelia started calling my name from downstairs. 'Your file has been transferred,' said the female voice favoured by my Internet service provider. 'You have email,' she announced a fraction later.

Immediately I yanked the cable out of the laptop and removed the flash drive, and I stepped into the living room just as Amelia came up the stairs.

'I rather lost track of you,' she said, an edge of suspicion to her voice.

'It's a big house. I'm a big boy. You can't keep an eye on me all the time.' I tried to sound relaxed, but I knew I radiated unease.

There was a squeak of rubber soles on polished wood and Lang came hurtling up the stairs, two at a time. He had a towel round his neck. His face was flushed, his hair damp, and he seemed angry about something.

'Did you win?' asked Amelia.

'Didn't play tennis in the end.' He blew out his breath, dropped into the nearby sofa and started vigorously towelling his head. 'Gym.'

Gym? I looked at him in amazement. Hadn't he already been for a run before I arrived? What was he in training for? The Olympics?

'So,' I said, in a jovial way, 'are you ready to get back to work?'

He glanced up at me furiously. 'You call what we're doing work?'

It was the first time I'd seen a flash of bad temper from him, and it struck me that all this running and pressing and lifting was simply what his metabolism demanded. He was like some rare marine specimen that could live only under extreme pressure. Exposed to the thin air of normal life, Lang was in constant danger of expiring from sheer boredom.

'Well, I certainly call it work,' I said stiffly. 'For both of us. But if you think it's not intellectually demanding enough for you, we can stop now.'

I thought I might have gone too far, but with great self-control, he hoisted a tired grin back onto his face. 'All right, man,' he said tonelessly. 'You win.' He flicked me with his towel. 'I was only kidding. Let's get back to it.'

FOUR

'Were your parents at all political?'

We were in the study once again. He was sprawled in the armchair, still wearing his track suit, exuding a faint aroma of sweat. I sat opposite with my notebook, the minirecorder on the desk beside me.

'Not at all, no. I'm not sure my father even voted. He said they were all as bad as one another.'

'Tell me about him.'

'He was a builder. Self-employed. He was in his fifties when he met my mother. His first wife had left him some while before. Mum was a teacher, twenty years younger. Very pretty, very shy. The story was he came to do some repair work on the school roof, and they got talking, and one thing led to another, and they got married. I came along the following year.'

'I get the impression, reading what's already been written, that you weren't that close to him.'

Lang took his time before answering. 'He died when I was sixteen. He'd already retired, because of bad health, and I was just getting to know him, really, when he had his heart attack.'

'How exactly did he die?'

'Trying to move a paving slab that was too heavy for him. In the garden.'

'Who found him?'

'I did.' He looked at his watch.

'Could you describe that?'

'I'd just come home from school. Mum was out doing something for one of her charities. I got a drink from the kitchen and went out into the back garden, thinking I'd kick a ball around. And there he was, in the middle of the lawn. Just a graze on his face where he'd fallen. The doctors told us he was probably dead before he hit the ground. But I suspect they always say that, to make it easier for the family. It can't be an easy thing, can it—dying?'

'And your mother?'

'She came from a strong Quaker family. She gave up teaching when I was born, and there was nothing she wouldn't do for anyone. Completely selfless. She was so proud when I got into Cambridge, even though it meant she was left alone. She never let on how ill she was—didn't want to spoil my time there. I'd no idea how bad things were until the end of my second year.'

'Tell me about that.'

Lang cleared his throat. 'I knew she hadn't been well, but . . . when you're nineteen, you don't take much notice of anything apart from yourself. I called her every Sunday night, and she always sounded fine. Then I got home and . . . I was shocked . . . she was . . . a skeleton basically—there was a tumour on her liver.' He made a helpless gesture. 'She was dead in a month.'

'What did you do?'

'I went back to Cambridge and I . . . I lost myself in life, I suppose.'

'I had a similar experience,' I said, after a silence.

'Really?' His tone was expressionless. He was looking out at the ocean.

'Yes.' I don't normally talk about myself, but a little self-revelation can sometimes help draw a client out. 'I lost my parents at about that age. Didn't you find, in a strange way, despite all the sadness, that it made you stronger?'

'Stronger?' He turned away from the window and frowned at me.

'In the sense of being self-reliant. Knowing that the worst thing that could possibly happen to you had happened, and you'd survived it.'

'You may be right. I've never really thought about it. At least, not until just lately. It's strange.' He leaned forward. 'I saw two dead bodies when I was in my teens and then—despite being prime minister, with all that entails: having to order men into battle and visit the scene of bomb blasts and what have you—I didn't see another corpse for thirty-five years.'

'And who was that?' I asked, stupidly.

'Mike McAra.'

'Couldn't you have sent one of the policemen to identify him?'

'No.' He shook his head. 'No, I couldn't. I owed him that, at least.' He paused again, then abruptly grabbed his towel and rubbed his face. 'This is a morbid conversation,' he declared. 'Let's change the subject.'

I did as he requested. 'Cambridge,' I said. 'Let's talk about that.'

I'd always expected that the Cambridge years were going to be the easiest part of the book to write. I'd been a student there myself, not long after Lang. He had gone up to read economics, briefly played football for his college's second eleven, and had won a reputation as a student actor. Yet in the manuscript, although McAra had dutifully assembled a list of every production the ex-prime minister had appeared in, there was something thin and rushed about it all. What was missing was passion. I blamed McAra, of course. But Lang himself seemed oddly evasive about the whole period.

'It's so long ago,' he said. 'I can hardly remember anything about it. I wasn't much good, to be honest. Acting was basically an opportunity to meet girls—don't put that in, by the way.'

'But I've read interviews with people who said you were *very* good,' I protested. 'And Cambridge must have been hugely important in your life, coming from your background.'

'Yes. I enjoyed my time there. I met some great people. It wasn't the real world, though. It was fantasyland.'

'I know. That was what I liked about it.'

'So did I. Just between the two of us: I *loved* it.' Lang's eyes gleamed at the memory. 'To go out onto a stage and pretend to be someone else! And to have people applaud you for doing it! What could be better?'

'Great,' I said. 'This is more like it. Let's put that in.'

'No.'

'Why not?'

'Because these are the memoirs of a *prime minister*.' Lang suddenly pounded his hand against the side of his chair. 'All my political life, whenever my opponents have been stuck for something to hit me with, they've said I was an *actor*.' He sprang up and started striding up and down. '"Oh, Adam Lang,"' he drawled, in a pitch-perfect caricature of an upper-class Englishman, '"have you noticed the way he changes his voice to suit whatever company he's in?" "Aye"'—now a gruff Scotsman—'"the man's a performer. You can't believe anything the wee bastard says."' And now he became pompous, hand-wringing: '"It is Mr Lang's tragedy that an actor can only be as good as the part he is given, and finally this prime minister has run out of lines." You'll recognise that last one no doubt.'

I shook my head. I was too astonished by his tirade to speak.

'It's from *The Times* editorial on the day I announced my resignation. The headline was "Kindly Leave the Stage".' He resumed his seat. 'So no, we won't dwell on my years as a student actor. Leave it the way Mike wrote it.'

For a while neither of us spoke. I pretended to adjust my notes, remembering Ruth Lang's words about her husband: *There's something not quite right about him at the moment, and I'm a bit afraid to leave him*. Now I saw what she meant. I heard a click and leaned across to check the recorder.

'I need to change discs,' I said, grateful for the opportunity to get away. 'I'll just take this down to Amelia. I won't be a minute.'

Lang was staring out of the window again. He made a small, slightly dismissive gesture with his hand to signal that I should go. I went downstairs to where the secretaries were typing, and gave the disc to Lucy. Amelia was standing by a filing cabinet. I suppose my face must have given me away.

'What's happened?' she said.

I felt an urge to share my unease. 'He seems a bit on edge.'

'Really? That's not like him. In what way?'

I picked up the latest transcripts. 'He just blew up at me over nothing.'

Amelia tilted her head slightly. 'You're right. There *is* something troubling him, isn't there? He took a call just after this morning's session.'

'From whom?'

'He didn't tell me. It came through on his mobile. I wonder . . . Alice, darling—do you mind?'

Alice got up and Amelia slipped in front of the computer screen. Her fingers moved rapidly across the keyboard, then slowed to a few staccato taps.

'Shit!' Amelia tilted the screen towards me, then sat back in disbelief.

I bent to read it. The web page was headed BREAKING NEWS:

January 27, 2.57 p.m. NEW YORK (AP)—Former British Foreign Secretary Richard Rycart has asked the International Criminal Court in The Hague to investigate allegations that the former British prime minister Adam Lang ordered the illegal handover of suspects for torture by the CIA.

Mr Rycart, who was dismissed from the cabinet by Mr Lang four years ago, is currently United Nations special envoy for humanitarian affairs and an outspoken critic of US foreign policy. Mr Rycart maintained at the time he left the Lang government that he was sacked for being insufficiently pro-America.

In a statement issued from his office in New York, Mr Rycart said he had passed documents to the ICC—details of which were leaked to a British newspaper at the weekend—that allegedly show that Mr Lang, as prime minister, personally authorised the seizure of four British citizens in Pakistan five years ago.

Mr Rycart went on: 'I have repeatedly asked the British government, in private, to investigate this illegal act. I have offered to give testimony to any inquiry. Yet the government has consistently refused even to acknowledge the existence of Operation Tempest. I feel I have no alternative except to present the evidence in my possession to the ICC.'

'The little shit,' whispered Amelia.

The telephone on the desk started ringing. Then another on a table beside the door chimed in. Nobody moved. As Lucy and Alice looked at Amelia for instructions, Amelia's own mobile set up its own electronic warble in a little leather pouch on her belt. For the briefest of moments I saw her panic and, in the absence of any guidance, Lucy reached for the phone on the desk.

'Don't!' shouted Amelia, then added, more calmly: 'Leave it. We need to work out a line to take.' By now a couple of other phones were trilling away in the recesses of the house. It was like noon in a clock factory. She took out her mobile and examined the incoming number. 'The pack is on the move,' she said and turned it off. For a few seconds she drummed her fingertips on the desk. 'Right. Unplug all the phones,' she instructed Alice, 'then surf the main news web sites, see if you can discover anything else Rycart is saying. Lucy, find a television and monitor the news channels.' She grabbed her black and red book and clattered off down the corridor on her high heels.

Unsure of what I was supposed to do, I decided I'd better follow her.

She called for one of the Special Branch men. 'Barry, please find Mrs Lang and get her back here as soon as you can.' She started climbing the stairs to the living room.

Lang was sitting exactly where I had left him, with his own small mobile phone in his hand. He snapped it shut as we came in. 'I take it from all the phone calls that he's issued his statement,' he said.

Amelia spread her hands wide in exasperation. 'Why didn't you tell me?'

'Tell you before I'd told Ruth? I don't think that would have been very good politics, do you? Sorry,' he said to me, 'for losing my temper.'

I was touched by his apology. 'Don't worry about it,' I said.

'And have you?' asked Amelia. 'Told her?'

'I wanted to break it to her face-to-face. Obviously, that's no longer an option, so I just called her. She should be back any minute.' Lang got to his feet and stood looking out of the window. 'He wanted to let me know there was nothing personal. He wanted *very* much to tell me that it was only because of his "well-known stand on human rights" that he felt he couldn't keep quiet any longer.' He snorted. 'Dear God.'

Amelia said, 'Do you think he was recording the call?'

'Probably. I just said, "Thank you, Richard, for letting me know," and hung up.' He turned round, frowning. 'It's gone unnervingly quiet down there.'

'I had the phones unplugged. We need to work out what we're going to say.'

'Well, at least we now know where the *Sunday Times* got its story.'

Lang returned his gaze to the window. 'Ah,' he said. 'Here comes trouble.'

A small figure in a blue cagoule was striding down the path from the dunes, the policeman behind breaking into an occasional loping run to keep up.

'Adam, we've *got* to put out a statement of our own,' said Amelia.

'All right,' said Lang. 'How about this?'

Amelia uncapped a small silver pen and opened her notebook.

'Responding to Richard Rycart's statement, Adam Lang made the following remarks: "When a policy of offering one hundred per cent support to the United States in the global war on terror was popular in the United Kingdom, Mr Rycart approved of it. When it became unpopular, he disapproved of it. And when, due to his own administrative incompetence, he was asked to leave the Foreign Office, he suddenly developed a passionate interest in upholding the so-called human rights of suspected terrorists. A child of three could see through his infantile tactics in seeking to embarrass his former colleagues." End point. End paragraph.'

Amelia had stopped writing midway through Lang's dictation. She was staring at the former prime minister, and I'd swear the Ice Queen had the beginnings of a tear in one eye. He stared back at her. There was a gentle tap on the open door and Alice came in, holding a sheet of paper.

'Excuse me, Adam,' she said. 'This just came over AP.'

Lang seemed reluctant to break eye contact with Amelia, and I knew then—as surely as I had ever known anything—that their relationship was more than merely professional. After what seemed an embarrassingly long interlude he took the paper from Alice and started to read it.

That was when Ruth came into the study. By this time I was starting to feel like a member of an audience who has left his seat in the middle of a play to find a lavatory and somehow wandered onto the stage.

Lang gave the paper to Ruth. 'According to the Associated Press,' he announced, 'sources in The Hague say the prosecutor's office of the International Criminal Court will be issuing a statement in the morning.'

'Oh, Adam!' cried Amelia. She put her hand to her mouth.

'Why weren't we given some warning of this?' demanded Ruth. 'What about Downing Street? Why haven't we heard from the embassy?'

'The phones are disconnected,' said Lang. 'They're probably trying to get through now.'

'What use is *now*?' shrieked Ruth. 'We needed to know about this a week ago! What are you people doing?' she said, turning her fury on Amelia. 'You're not telling me the Cabinet Office didn't know this was coming?'

'The ICC prosecutor is scrupulous about not notifying a suspect if he's under investigation,' said Amelia. 'Or the suspect's government, for that matter. In case they start destroying evidence.'

Ruth seemed stunned. It took her a beat to recover. 'So that's what Adam is now? A suspect?' She turned to her husband. 'You need to talk to Sid Kroll.'

'We don't know what the ICC are going to say yet,' Lang pointed out.

'Adam,' said Ruth slowly, 'you need a lawyer. Call Sid.'

Lang hesitated, then turned to Amelia. 'Get Sid on the line.'

'And what about the media?'

'I'll issue a holding statement,' said Ruth. 'Just a sentence or two.'

Amelia pulled out her mobile and started scrolling through the address book. 'D'you want me to draft something?'

'Why doesn't *he* do it?' said Ruth, pointing at me. 'He's the writer.'

'Fine,' said Amelia irritably, 'but it needs to go out immediately.'

'Hang on a minute,' I said.

'I should sound confident,' Lang said to me, 'not defensive—that would be fatal. But I shouldn't be cocky, either. No bitterness. No anger. But don't say I'm pleased at this opportunity to clear my name, or any balls like that.'

'So,' I said, 'you're not defensive but you're not cocky; you're not angry but you're not pleased. What exactly are you?'

Surprisingly, under the circumstances, everybody laughed.

Amelia abruptly held up her hand and waved at us to be quiet. 'I have Adam Lang for Sidney Kroll,' she said. 'No, I won't hold.'

I WENT DOWNSTAIRS with Alice and stood behind her while she sat at a keyboard, patiently waiting for the ex-prime minister's words to flow from my mouth. I realised suddenly that I hadn't asked him the crucial question: had he actually ordered the seizure of those four men? Then I knew he must have done, otherwise he'd have denied it outright at the weekend, when the original story broke. Not for the first time, I felt seriously out of my depth.

'I have always been a passionate—' I began. 'No. I have always been a strong—no, *committed*—supporter of the work of the International Criminal

Court.' Had he been? I assumed he had, or had pretended he had. 'I have no doubt that the ICC will quickly see through this politically motivated piece of mischief-making.' I paused. It needed one more line, something statesman-like. 'The international struggle against terror,' I said, in a burst of inspiration, 'is too important to be used for the purposes of personal revenge.'

Lucy printed it, and when I took it back up to the study I felt a curious bashful pride, like a schoolboy handing in his homework. I showed it first to Ruth. She nodded her approval and slid it across the desk to Lang, who was listening on the telephone. He glanced at it, beckoned for my pen and inserted a single word. He tossed the statement back to me and gave me a thumbs-up.

Into the telephone he said, 'That's great, Sid. And what do we know about these three judges?'

'Am I allowed to see it?' said Amelia, as we went downstairs.

Handing it over, I noticed that Lang had added 'domestic' to the final sentence: 'The international struggle against terror is too important to be used for the purposes of *domestic* personal revenge.' The brutal antithesis of 'international' and 'domestic' made Rycart appear even more petty.

'Very good,' said Amelia. 'You could be the new Mike McAra.'

I think she meant it as a compliment. It was hard to tell with her. Not that I cared. For the first time I was experiencing the adrenaline of politics.

One by one the telephones were reconnected and immediately began ringing. I heard the secretaries feeding my words to the hungry reporters: *I have always been a committed supporter of the work of the International Criminal Court.* I watched my sentences emailed to the news agencies. And within minutes, on the computer screen and on television, I started seeing and hearing them all over again. The world had become our echo chamber.

In the middle of all this, my own phone rang. I jammed the receiver to one ear and put my finger in the other. A faint voice said, 'Can you hear me?'

'Who is this?'

'It's John Maddox, from Rhinehart. Sounds like you're in a madhouse.'

'You're not the first to call it that. Hold on, John. I'll try to find somewhere quieter.' I walked out into the passage. 'Is that better?'

'I've just heard the news,' said Maddox. 'This can only be good for us. We should start with this.'

'What?' I was following the passage round to the back of the house.

'This war crimes stuff. Have you asked him about it?'

'Haven't had much chance, John, to be honest.' I tried not to sound too sarcastic. 'He's a little tied up right now.'

'OK, so what've you covered so far?'

'The early years—childhood, university—'

'No, no,' said Maddox impatiently. 'Forget all that crap. *This* is what's interesting. Get him to focus on this. And he mustn't talk to anyone else about it. We need to keep this absolutely exclusive to the memoirs.'

I'd ended up in the solarium. Even with the door closed I could hear telephones ringing. The notion that Lang could avoid saying anything about illegal kidnapping and torture until the book came out was a joke. 'I'll tell him, John,' I said. 'It might be worth your while talking to Sidney Kroll. Perhaps Adam could say that his lawyers have instructed him not to talk.'

'Good idea. I'll call Sid now. Meantime, I want the timetable accelerated.'

'Accelerated?' In the empty room my voice sounded thin and hollow.

'Sure. As in speeded up. At this moment, Lang is hot. We can't afford to let this opportunity slip.'

'Are you now saying you want the book in less than a month?'

'It'll probably mean settling for a polish on a lot of the manuscript rather than a rewrite. But the earlier we go, the more we'll sell. Think you can do it?'

No, was the answer. No, you bald-headed, psychopathic bastard—have you seriously read this junk? 'Well, John,' I said mildly, 'I can try.'

'Good man. And don't worry, we'll pay you just as much for two weeks' work as we would for four. I tell you, if this war crimes thing comes off, it could be the answer to our prayers. I'm relying on you. OK?'

By the time he rang off, two weeks had somehow become a firm deadline. I would no longer conduct forty hours of interviews with Lang, ranging over his whole life. I would get him to focus on the war on terror—if he objected, I was to remind him of his contractual obligation—and we would begin the memoir with that. The rest I would rewrite where I could.

I permitted myself a brief moment of despair, leaning against the wall, pondering the fleeting nature of human happiness. I tried to call Rick, but he was out so I left a message. Then I went in search of Amelia.

She wasn't in the office, the passage, or the kitchen. One of the policemen told me she was outside. It must have been after four by now and getting cold. She was standing in front of the house. In the January gloom, the tip of her cigarette glowed bright red as she inhaled, then faded to nothing.

'I wouldn't have guessed you were a smoker,' I said.

'I only ever allow myself one. At times of great stress or great contentment.'

'Which is this?'

'Very funny.'

I hadn't had a cigarette in more than a decade, but at that moment, if she'd offered me one, I would have taken it. She didn't.

'John Maddox just called,' I said. 'Now he wants the book in two weeks instead of four. I don't suppose there's the faintest chance of my sitting down with Adam for another interview today, is there?'

'What do you think?'

'In that case, could I have a lift to my hotel? I'll do some work there.'

'You're not planning to take that manuscript out of here, are you?'

'Of course not!' My voice always rises an octave when I tell a lie. I could never have become a politician: I'd have sounded like Donald Duck. 'I just want to write up what we did today, that's all.'

'Because you do realise how serious this is getting, don't you?'

'Of course. You can check my laptop if you want.'

She finished her cigarette. 'All right, I'll trust you.' She dropped the stub and extinguished it with the pointed toe of her shoe, then stooped to retrieve it. 'Collect your stuff. I'll get one of the boys to take you into Edgartown.'

We walked back into the house and parted in the corridor. She headed back to the ringing telephones. As I climbed the stairs to the study, I could hear Ruth Lang shouting. The only words I heard distinctly came at the tail end of her rant: '. . . spending the rest of my bloody life here!' The door was ajar. I knocked lightly. After a pause I heard Lang say wearily, 'Come.'

He was sitting at the desk. His wife was at the other end of the room. They were both breathing heavily, and I sensed that something momentous—some long-pent-up explosion—had just occurred. I could understand now why Amelia had fled outside to smoke.

'Sorry to interrupt,' I said, gesturing at my belongings. 'I wanted to—'

'Fine,' said Lang.

'I'm going to call the children,' said Ruth bitterly. 'Unless of course you've already done it?'

Lang didn't look at her; he looked at me. He invited me, in that long instant, to see what had become of him: stripped of his power, abused by his enemies, hunted, homesick, trapped between his wife and mistress. You could write a hundred pages about that one brief look.

'Excuse me,' said Ruth and pushed past me quite roughly.

At the same moment, Amelia appeared in the doorway, holding a telephone. 'Adam,' she said, 'it's the White House. They have the president of the United States on the line for you.' She smiled at me and ushered me towards the door. 'Would you mind? We need the room.'

BY THE TIME I got back to the hotel, there was just enough light in the sky to show up the big, black storm clouds rolling in from the Atlantic. I went up to my room and stood in the shadows, listening to the relentless *boom-hiss, boom-hiss* of the surf. Then I turned on the desk lamp, took my laptop out of my shoulder bag and gave the machine a comradely pat. Its once-shiny metal case was scratched and dented: the honourable wounds of a dozen campaigns. We had got through those. We would somehow get through this.

I hooked it up to the hotel telephone, dialled my Internet service provider and went into the bathroom for a glass of water. From the other room I heard the familiar announcement: 'You have email.'

I saw at once that something was wrong. There were the usual junk messages, plus an email from Rick's office confirming payment of the first part of the advance. But the email I had sent myself that afternoon wasn't listed.

For a few moments, I stared stupidly at the screen, then I opened the folder that stores sent email. To my relief, at the top was one titled 'no subject', to which I had attached the manuscript. But when I opened the blank email and clicked on the box labelled 'download', I received a message saying, 'That file is not currently available.' I tried a few more times, with the same result.

I took out my mobile and called the Internet company.

I shall spare you a full account of the sweaty half hour that followed—the queuing, the Muzak, the panicky conversation with the company's representative in Uttar Pradesh. The bottom line was that the manuscript had vanished, and the company had no record of its ever having existed.

I lay down on the bed.

One explanation was that Lang's manuscript hadn't been uploaded in the first place—but that couldn't be right, because I had received those two messages while I was still in the office: 'Your file has been transferred' and 'You have email.' Another was that the file had since been wiped from the memory of my Internet service provider's computers, by someone who was able to cover their tracks. That implied that my emails were being monitored.

Rick's voice floated into my mind—*Wow. This must've been some operation. Too big for a newspaper. This must've been a government*—followed swiftly by Amelia's—*You do realise how serious this is getting, don't you?*

'But the book is crap!' I cried despairingly at the portrait of the Victorian whaling master hanging opposite the bed. 'It's not worth all this trouble!'

The stern old sea dog stared back, unmoved. I had broken my promise, his expression seemed to say, and something out there—some nameless force—knew it.

THERE WAS NO QUESTION of my doing any more work that night. I didn't even turn on the television. Oblivion was all I craved. I switched off my mobile, went down to the bar and, when that closed, sat up in my room emptying a bottle of Scotch. For once, I slept right through the night.

I was woken by the harsh metallic tone of the bedside telephone. When I rolled over to answer it I felt my stomach keep on rolling, across the mattress and onto the floor. The revolving room was hot. I realised I'd gone to sleep fully dressed and had left all the lights on.

'You need to check out of your hotel immediately,' said Amelia. 'Things have changed. There's a car on its way.' Before I could argue, she'd gone.

I once read that the Ancient Egyptians prepared a pharaoh for mummification by drawing his brain out through his nose with a hook. During the night a similar procedure had seemingly been performed on me. I shuffled across the carpet and pulled back the curtains to unveil a sky and sea as grey as death. Nothing was stirring. A storm was coming in; even I could tell that.

As I was about to turn away, I heard the sound of an engine. I squinted down at the street and saw a car pull up. Two men got out—young, fit-looking, wearing ski jackets, jeans and boots. The driver stared up at my window and I instinctively took a step backwards. By the time I risked a second look, he was bent over the open boot of the car. He took out what at first, in my paranoid state, I took to be a machine gun. Actually it was a television camera.

I moved quickly then, or as quickly as my condition would allow. I opened the window to let in a blast of freezing air. I undressed, showered, shaved, put on clean clothes and packed. When I got down to reception it was 8.45—an hour after the first ferry from the mainland docked at Vineyard Haven—and the hotel looked as if it was staging an international media convention. There must have been thirty people hanging around, drinking coffee, swapping stories in half a dozen languages, talking on their mobiles.

I bought a copy of the *New York Times* and went into the restaurant, where I drank three glasses of orange juice straight off, before turning my attention to the paper. Lang was right up there on the front page:

WAR CRIMES COURT TO RULE ON BRITISH EX-PM

ANNOUNCEMENT DUE TODAY

Former Foreign Sec. Alleges Lang OK'd Use of Torture by CIA

Lang had issued a 'robust' statement, it said (I felt a thrill of pride). He was 'embattled', 'coping with one blow after another'—beginning with 'the accidental drowning of a close aide earlier in the year'. The affair was 'an embarrassment' for the British and American governments. 'A senior administration official' insisted, however, that the White House remained loyal to a man who had been its closest ally. 'He was there for us and we'll be there for him,' the official added, speaking only after a guarantee of anonymity.

But it was the final paragraph that really made me choke into my coffee:

> The publication of Mr Lang's memoirs has been brought forward from June to the end of April. John Maddox, chief executive of Rhinehart Publishing Inc., reported to have paid $10 million for the book, said that the finishing touches were now being put to the manuscript. 'This is going to be a world publishing event,' Mr Maddox told the *New York Times* yesterday. 'Adam Lang will be giving the first full inside scoop by a leader on the West's war on terror.'

I rose, folded the newspaper, and walked with dignity through the lobby, carefully stepping round the camera bags, the two-foot zoom lenses, and the handheld mikes in their woolly, grey, windproof prophylactics. Among the members of the Fourth Estate, a cheerful, almost a party atmosphere prevailed, as might have existed at an eighteenth-century hanging.

'The newsroom says the press conference in The Hague is now at ten o'clock Eastern,' someone shouted.

I passed unnoticed and went onto the verandah, where I put a call through to my agent. His assistant answered. I asked to speak to Mr Ricardelli.

'He's away from the office right now.'

'Where is he?'

'On a fishing trip. It was a spur-of-the-moment thing—'

'*Fishing?*'

'He'll be calling in occasionally to check his messages.'

'That's nice. Where is he?'

'The Bouma National Heritage Rainforest Park.'

'Christ. Where's that?'

Rick's assistant hesitated. 'Fiji.'

THE MINIVAN TOOK ME up the hill out of Edgartown, past the bookshop and the whaling church. At the edge of town, we followed the signs left to West Tisbury rather than right to Vineyard Haven, which at least implied that I was being taken back to the house, rather than straight to the ferry to be deported for breaching the Official Secrets Act. I sat behind the police driver, my suitcase beside me, and stared out of the window.

We were quickly into the drab forest. I was thinking of Rick in Fiji, and feeling duped, abandoned, aggrieved.

'Oh no,' said the policeman, leaning forward. 'Here we go again.'

Up ahead, the blue lights of a couple of patrol cars flashed in the gloomy morning. As we came closer I could see a dozen or more cars and vans pulled up on either side of the road. People stood around aimlessly, and I assumed they had been in a pile-up. But as the minivan slowed to turn left, the bystanders grabbed things from beside the road and ran at us. 'Lang! Lang! Lang!' a woman shouted over a bullhorn. 'Liar! Liar! Liar!' Images of Lang in an orange jumpsuit, gripping prison bars with bloodied hands, danced in front of the windscreen. WANTED! WAR CRIMINAL! ADAM LANG!

The police had blocked the track to the Rhinehart compound with traffic cones and quickly pulled them out of the way to let us through, but not before we'd come to a stop. Demonstrators surrounded us, and a fusillade of thumps and kicks raked the side of the van. I glimpsed a brilliant arc of white light illuminating a figure—a man, cowled like a monk. He turned away from his interviewer to stare at us, and I recognised him dimly from somewhere. Then he vanished behind a gauntlet of contorted faces and pounding hands.

'They're always the really violent bastards,' said my driver, 'peace protesters.' He put his foot down, and we shot forward into the silent woods.

AMELIA MET ME in the passage. She stared contemptuously at my single piece of luggage and said, 'Follow me.'

My suitcase, one of those ubiquitous pull-alongs, made an industrious hum on the stone floor as I trailed after her towards the back of the house.

'I called you several times last night,' Amelia said, 'but you didn't answer.'

'I forgot to charge my mobile.'

'Oh? What about the phone in your room? I tried that as well.'

'I went out.'

'Until midnight?'

I winced behind her back. 'What did you want to tell me?'

'This.' She opened a door, and stood aside to let me go in.

The room was in darkness, but the heavy curtains didn't quite meet in the middle, and there was just enough light for me to make out the shape of a double bed. It smelt of stale clothes and old ladies' soap.

Amelia crossed the floor and briskly pulled back the curtains, revealing glass doors that opened onto the lawn. 'You'll sleep in here from now on.'

Apart from the bed, there was a desk with a gooseneck lamp, a beige-covered armchair and a wall-length closet with mirrored doors. I could see into a white-tiled en suite bathroom. It was neat and functional, and dismal.

I tried to make a joke of it. 'So this is where you put the granny, is it?'

'No, this is where we put Mike McAra.' She slid back one of the closet doors, revealing a few jackets and shirts on hangers. 'I'm afraid we haven't had a chance to clear it yet. But it will only be for a few days.'

I've never been particularly superstitious, but I didn't like that room.

'I make it a rule not to sleep in a client's house,' I said, attempting to keep my voice light. 'At the end of a working day, it's vital to get away.'

'But now you can have constant access to the manuscript. Isn't that what you want?' For once there was genuine merriment in her smile. 'Besides, you can't keep running the media gauntlet. They'll soon discover who you are, and start pestering you with questions. This way you can work in peace.'

'Isn't there another room I could use?'

'There are six bedrooms in the main house. Adam and Ruth have one each. I have one. The girls share. The duty policemen use one for the overnight shift. And the entire guest block is taken over by Special Branch. Don't be squeamish: the sheets have been changed.' She consulted her watch. 'Look, Sidney Kroll is arriving any minute. We're due to get the ICC announcement in less than thirty minutes. Why don't you settle in, then come up and join us. Whatever's decided will affect you. You're practically one of us now.'

'I am?'

'Of course. You drafted the statement. That makes you an accomplice.'

After she'd gone, I sat gingerly on the end of the bed and stared out at the wind-blasted lawn. A small blaze of white light was travelling across the sky, swelling as it came closer. A helicopter. It passed low overhead, then reappeared a minute later, hovering just above the horizon a mile away. It was a sign of how serious things had become, I thought, if some hard-pressed news manager on a trimmed budget was willing to hire a chopper in the hope of catching a fleeting shot of the former British prime minister.

I sat there for a while, until I heard the noise of the minivan pulling up in front of the house, followed by voices in the hall, and a small army of footsteps thudding up the staircase: I reckoned that must be the sound of a thousand dollars an hour in legal fees on the hoof. I gave Kroll and his client a couple of minutes for handshakes, condolences and expressions of confidence, then wearily left my dead man's room and went up to join them.

FIVE

Kroll had flown in by private jet from Washington with two young paralegals: an exquisitely pretty Mexican woman he introduced as Encarnación and a black guy from New York called Josh. They sat on either side of him, their laptops open, on a sofa that placed their backs to the ocean view. Adam and Ruth Lang had the couch opposite, Amelia and I an armchair each. A flat-screen TV next to the fireplace was showing the aerial shot of the house, as relayed live from the helicopter we could hear buzzing outside. Occasionally the news station cut to the empty podium in the large, chandeliered room in The Hague where the ICC press conference was due to be held. Each time I saw it I felt sick with nerves. But Lang himself seemed cool. He was jacketless, wearing a white shirt and a dark blue tie. It was the sort of high-pressure occasion his metabolism was built for.

'Here's the score,' said Kroll. 'You're not being charged. You're not being arrested. None of this is going to amount to a hill of beans, I promise you. All the prosecutor is asking for right now is permission to launch a formal investigation. OK? So when we go out of here, you walk tall, you look cool, and you have peace in your heart, because it's all going to be fine.'

'The president told me he thought they might not even let her investigate,' said Lang.

'I always hesitate to contradict the leader of the free world,' said Kroll, 'but the feeling in Washington this morning is they'll have to. Our madam prosecutor is quite a savvy operator. The British government has consistently refused to hold an investigation of its own into Operation Tempest, which gives her a legal pretext to look into it. And by leaking her case just before going into the pre-trial chamber, she's put a lot of pressure on those three judges to give her permission to move to the investigation stage. If they tell her to drop it, everyone will say they're scared to go after a major power.'

'That's crude smear tactics,' said Ruth. She was wearing black leggings and another of her shapeless tops. Her shoeless feet were tucked beneath her on the sofa; her back was turned to her husband.

Lang shrugged. 'It's politics.'

'Exactly,' said Kroll. 'Treat it as a political problem, not a legal one.'

Ruth said, 'We need to get out our version of what happened. Refusing to comment isn't enough any more.'

I saw my chance. 'John Maddox—' I began.

'Yeah,' said Kroll, cutting me off, 'I talked to John, and he's right. We really have to go for this whole story now in the memoirs. It's the perfect platform for you to respond, Adam. They're very excited.'

'Fine,' said Lang.

'As soon as possible you need to sit down with our friend here'—I realised

Kroll had forgotten my name—'and go over the whole thing in detail. But make sure it's all cleared with me first. We have to imagine what every word might sound like if it's read out while you're standing in the dock.'

'Why?' said Ruth. 'You said none of this was going to amount to anything.'

'It won't,' said Kroll smoothly, 'especially if we're careful not to give them any extra ammunition.'

'This way we get to present it the way we want,' said Lang. 'And whenever I'm asked about it, I can refer people to my memoirs. Who knows? It might even help sell a few copies.' He looked around. We all smiled. 'OK,' he said, 'what am I actually likely to be investigated for?'

Kroll gestured to Encarnación.

'Either crimes against humanity,' she said carefully, 'or war crimes.'

There was a silence. We stopped smiling.

'Unbelievable,' said Ruth eventually, 'to equate what Adam did, or didn't do, with the Nazis.'

'That's precisely why the United States doesn't recognise the court,' said Kroll. He wagged his finger. 'We warned you what would happen. An international war crimes tribunal sounds noble in principle. But you go after all these genocidal maniacs in the Third World, and sooner or later the Third World is going to come right back after you. Well, they can't drag America into their phoney court, so they drag in our closest ally—you.' He turned to Encarnación again. 'Go ahead, Connie. Let's hear the rest of it.'

'The reason we can't be sure which route they'll choose is that torture is outlawed both by Article 7 of the 1998 Rome Statute, under the heading "Crimes against humanity", and under Article 8, which is "War crimes". Article 8 also categorises as a war crime'—she consulted her laptop—' "wilfully depriving a prisoner of war or other protected person of the rights of fair and regular trial" and "unlawful deportation or transfer or unlawful confinement". You could be accused under either article, sir.'

'But I haven't ordered that anyone should be tortured!' said Lang. His voice was incredulous, outraged. 'And I haven't deprived anyone of a fair trial, or illegally imprisoned them. Perhaps—perhaps—you could make that charge against the United States, but not Great Britain.'

'That's true, sir,' agreed Encarnación. 'However, Article 25, dealing with individual criminal responsibility, states that'—her cool dark eyes flickered again to the computer screen—'"a person shall be criminally responsible and liable for punishment if that person facilitates the commission of such a crime, aids, abets or otherwise assists in its commission or its attempted commission, including the means for its commission".'

Again there was a silence, filled by the distant drone of the helicopter.

'That's rather sweeping,' said Lang quietly. 'Legally—'

'It's not legal, Adam,' Kroll cut in, 'it's political.'

'It's legal as well, Sid,' said Ruth. She was frowning at the carpet. 'The two are inseparable. Richard Rycart has produced documentary evidence suggesting that Adam did in fact do all those things in the passage your young lady just read out: aided, abetted and facilitated.' She looked up. 'That is legal jeopardy—isn't it? And it leads inescapably to political jeopardy. Because it will all come down to public opinion, and we're unpopular enough back home without this.'

'Well, if it's any comfort, Adam's certainly not in jeopardy as long as he stays here, among his friends.'

The armoured glass vibrated. The helicopter was coming in again for a closer look. Its searchlight filled the room. But on the television screen, all that could be seen in the big picture window was a reflection of the sea.

'Wait a minute,' said Lang, raising his hand to his head and clutching his hair. 'Are you saying that I can't leave the United States?'

'Josh,' said Kroll, nodding to his other assistant.

'Sir,' said Josh gravely, 'if I may read you the opening of Article 58: "The Pre-Trial Chamber shall, on the application of the Prosecutor, issue a warrant of arrest of a person if, having examined the application and the evidence or other information submitted by the Prosecutor, it is satisfied that there are reasonable grounds to believe that the person has committed a crime within the jurisdiction of the Court, and the arrest of the person appears necessary to ensure the person's appearance at trial."'

'Jesus,' said Lang. 'What are "reasonable grounds"?'

'It won't happen,' said Kroll. 'Nevertheless, until this whole thing is resolved, I strongly advise you not to travel to any country that recognises the jurisdiction of the International Criminal Court. All it would take is for two of these three judges to decide to grandstand to the human rights crowd, go ahead and issue a warrant, and you could be picked up.'

'But just about every country in the world recognises the ICC,' said Lang.

'America doesn't.'

'And who else?'

'Iraq,' said Josh, 'China, North Korea, Indonesia.'

We waited for him to go on; he didn't.

'And that's it?' said Lang. 'Everywhere else does?'

'No, sir. Israel doesn't. And some of the nastier regimes in Africa.'

'Something's happening,' said Amelia, aiming the remote at the television.

And so we watched as the glamorous Spanish chief prosecutor—all massive black hair and bright red lipstick—announced that she had that morning been granted the power to investigate the former British prime minister, Adam Peter Benet Lang, under Articles 7 and 8 of the 1998 Rome Statute of the International Criminal Court.

Or rather, the others all watched her, while I watched Lang.

AL—intense concentration, I jotted in my notebook. *Reaches hand out for R: she doesn't respond. Glances at her, puzzled. Withdraws hand. Looks back at screen. Shakes head. CP says "was this just single incident or part of systematic pattern of criminal behaviour?" AL flinches. Angry.*

I had never before witnessed any of my authors at a real crisis in their lives, and scrutinising Lang I realised that my favourite question—'How did it feel?'—was a crude tool, vague to the point of uselessness. In those few minutes, a rapid succession of emotions had swept across Lang's craggy face—shock, fury, hurt, defiance, dismay, shame . . . How were these to be disentangled? And if he didn't know precisely what he felt now, as he was feeling it, how could he know it in ten years' time? Even his reaction at this moment I would have to simplify. In a sense, I would have to lie.

The chief prosecutor finished her statement, briefly answered a couple of shouted questions, then left the podium. The screen reverted to the aerial shot of Rhinehart's house, in its setting of woods, lake and ocean, as the world waited for Lang to appear.

Amelia muted the sound. Downstairs, the phones started ringing.

'Well,' said Kroll, 'there was nothing in *that* we weren't expecting.'

'Yes,' said Ruth. '*Well done.*'

Kroll pretended not to notice. 'We should get you to Washington, Adam, right away. My plane's waiting at the airport.'

Lang was still staring at the screen. 'When Marty said I could use his vacation house, I never realised how cut off this place was. We should never have come. Now we look as though we're hiding.'

'Exactly my feeling. You can't just hole up here, at least not today. I've made some calls. I can get you in to see the house majority leader at lunchtime and we can have a photo op with the secretary of state this afternoon.'

Lang dragged his eyes away from the television. 'I don't know about doing all that. It could look as though I'm panicking.'

'No, it won't. I've already spoken to them. They'll both say the meetings were fixed weeks ago, to discuss the Adam Lang Foundation.'

Lang frowned. 'What are we supposed to be discussing?'

'AIDS. Poverty. Climate change. Africa. Whatever you like. The point is to say: it's business as usual, I have my agenda, it's the big stuff, and I won't be diverted from it by these clowns pretending to be judges in The Hague.'

Amelia said, 'What about security?'

'The Secret Service will take care of it. We'll fill in the blanks in the schedule as we go along.'

'And the media?' said Lang. 'We'll need to respond soon.'

'On the way to the airport, we'll pull over and say a few words. I can make a statement, if you like. All you have to do is stand next to me.'

'No,' said Lang firmly. 'That really will make me look guilty. I'll have to talk to them myself. Ruth, what do you think about going to Washington?'

'I think it's a terrible idea. I'm sorry, Sid, but we've got to consider how this will play in Britain. If Adam goes to Washington, he'll look like America's whipping boy, running crying home to Daddy.'

'So what would you do?'

'Fly back to London. The British people may not like him much at the moment, but if there's one thing they like even less, it's interfering foreigners telling them what to do. The government will have to support him.'

Amelia said, 'The British government is going to cooperate fully with the investigation.'

'Oh, really?' said Ruth tartly. 'And what makes you think that?'

'I'm not thinking it, Ruth, I'm reading it. It's on the television. Look.'

The headline was running across the bottom of the screen: BREAKING NEWS: BRITISH GOVT 'WILL COOPERATE FULLY' WITH WAR CRIMES PROBE.

'How dare they?' cried Ruth. 'After all we've done for them!'

Josh said, 'With respect, ma'am, as signatory to the ICC, the British government is obliged under international law to "cooperate fully". Those are the precise words of Article 86.'

'And what if the ICC eventually decides to arrest me?' asked Lang quietly. 'Does the British government "cooperate fully" with that as well?'

'That's Article 59, sir.' Josh looked at his laptop again. '"A State Party which has received a request for a provisional arrest or for arrest and surrender shall immediately take steps to arrest the person in question."'

'Well, I think that settles it,' said Lang. 'Washington it is.'

Ruth folded her arms. 'I still say it will look bad,' she said.

'Not as bad as being led away in handcuffs from Heathrow.'

'At least it would show you had some guts.'

'Then why the hell don't you just fly back without me?' snapped Lang. 'I'll go where people want me. Amelia, tell the boys we're leaving in five minutes. Get one of the girls to pack me an overnight bag. And you'd better pack one for yourself.'

'Oh, but why don't you share a suitcase?' said Ruth. 'It will be so much more convenient.'

At that, the very air seemed to congeal. Even Kroll's little smile froze at the edges. Amelia hesitated, then picked up her notebook, rose in a hiss of silk and walked across the room. Her gaze was fixed straight ahead, her lips compressed. Ruth waited until she had gone, then slowly uncoiled her feet from beneath her and carefully pulled on her flat, wooden-soled shoes. She, too, left without a word. Thirty seconds later, a door slammed downstairs.

Lang flinched and sighed. He got up and collected his jacket from the back of a chair. Kroll stood and stretched. I put away my notebook.

'I'll see you tomorrow,' said Lang, offering me his hand. His eyes looked bruised and puffy. 'I'm sorry to abandon you. At least all this coverage should improve sales.'

I COULD HAVE GONE down to see them off. Instead I watched them leave on television. You can't beat sitting in front of a TV screen if you're after that authentic, firsthand experience. For example, it's curious how helicopter news shots impart to even the most innocent activity the dangerous whiff of criminality. When Jeff the chauffeur brought the armoured Jaguar round to the front of the house and left the engine running, it looked for all the world as if he were organising a Mafia getaway.

I had the same disorientating feeling I'd experienced the previous day, when Lang's statement started pinging back at me from the ether. On the television I could see one of the Special Branch men opening the rear passenger door, while down in the corridor I could hear Lang and the others preparing to leave. 'All right, people?' Kroll's voice floated up the staircase. 'Is everybody ready? OK. Remember: happy faces. Here we go.' The front door opened, and on the screen I glimpsed the top of the ex-prime minister's head as he took the few hurried steps to the car. As he ducked out of sight, his attorney scuttled round to the Jaguar's other side. At the bottom of the picture it said, ADAM LANG LEAVES MARTHA'S VINEYARD HOUSE. They know everything, these satellite boys, I thought, but they've never heard of tautology.

The entourage debouched in rapid single file from the house and headed for the minivan—Amelia in the lead, then the secretaries, the paralegals, and finally a couple of bodyguards. The long, dark shapes of the cars, headlights gleaming, pulled out of the compound and set off through the scrub oak. The helicopter tracked them and, as the noise of its rotors faded, something like peace returned to the house. I wondered where Ruth was. I stood at the top of the stairs and listened, but all and by the time I returned to the television, the coverage had shifted from aerial to ground level, and Lang's limousine was pulling out of the woods.

At the end of the track, a line of police was keeping the demonstrators corralled on the opposite side of the highway. The Jaguar's brake lights glowed and it stopped. The minivan swerved to a halt behind it. Suddenly, there was Lang, coatless, seemingly oblivious to the cold and to the chanting crowd, striding over to the cameras, trailed by three Special Branch men. I pointed the remote at the screen and pumped up the volume.

'I apologise for keeping you waiting so long in the cold,' Lang began. 'I just wanted to say a few words in response to the news from The Hague.'

He paused and glanced at the ground. The chant of 'Lang! Lang! Lang! Liar! Liar! Liar!' was clearly audible in the background.

'These are strange times,' he said and hesitated again, 'strange times'—and now at last he looked up—'when those who have always stood for freedom, peace and justice are accused of being criminals, while those who openly incite hatred, glorify slaughter and seek the destruction of democracy are treated by the law as if *they* are victims.'

'Liar! Liar! Liar!'

'As I said in my statement yesterday, I have always been a strong supporter of the International Criminal Court. I believe in its work. I believe in the integrity of its judges. That is why I do not fear this investigation. Because I have done nothing wrong.' He glanced across at the demonstrators. For the first time he appeared to notice the waving placards. The line of his mouth set firm. 'I refuse to be intimidated,' he said. 'I refuse to be made a scapegoat. I refuse to be distracted from my work combating AIDS, poverty and global warming. I propose to travel now to Washington to carry out my schedule as planned. Let me make one thing clear: as long as I have breath in my body, I shall fight terrorism wherever it has to be fought, whether it be on the battlefield or—if necessary—in the courts. Thank you.'

Ignoring the shouted questions—'When are you going back to Britain, Mr Lang?' 'Do you support torture, Mr Lang?'—he turned and strode away, his trio of bodyguards fanned out behind him.

I was surprised at how unmoved I felt. It was like watching some great actor in the last phase of his career, emotionally overspent, with nothing left to draw on but technique.

I waited until he was safely back in his gas- and bombproof cocoon, and then I switched off the television.

With Lang and the others gone, the house seemed desolate, bereft of purpose. I came down the stairs and followed the corridor round to the secretaries' office. The small room looked as if it had been abandoned in a panic. A profusion of papers and computer discs were strewn across the desk. It occurred to me then that I had no copy of Lang's manuscript to work on, but when I tried to open the filing cabinet it was locked.

I looked into the kitchen and called a hesitant 'Hello?' I stuck my head round the door of the pantry, but the housekeeper wasn't there.

With no idea which was my room, I had to work my way along the corridor, trying every door. The first was locked. The second was open, the room beyond it exuding the odour of aftershave; a track suit was thrown across the bed: it was obviously the bedroom used by Special Branch during the night shift. The third door was locked, and I was about to try the fourth when I heard the sound of a woman weeping. I could tell it was Ruth: even her sobs had a combative quality. *There are only six bedrooms in the main house*, Amelia had said. *Adam and Ruth have one each.* What a set-up this was, I thought as I crept away: the ex-prime minister and his wife sleeping in separate rooms, with his mistress just along the corridor. It was almost French.

Gingerly, I tried the handle of the next room. This one wasn't locked, and the aroma of worn clothes and lavender soap, even more than the sight of my old suitcase, established it immediately as McAra's former berth. I went in and closed the door softly. On the bed, someone had put a box. A yellow Post-it note said, *Good luck! Amelia.* I lifted the lid. MEMOIRS, proclaimed the title page, *by Adam Lang*. So she hadn't forgotten me after all, despite the exquisitely embarrassing circumstances of her departure. You could say what you liked about Mrs Bly, but the woman was a pro.

I recognised I was at a decisive point. Either I continued to hang around at the fringes of this floundering project, pathetically hoping that someone would help me. Or I could seize control of it myself, try to knock these 621 ineffable pages into publishable shape, take my 250 grand, and head off to lie on a beach somewhere until I had forgotten all about the Langs.

Put in those terms, it wasn't a choice. Steeling myself, I took the manuscript from its box and placed it on the table next to the window, opened my shoulder bag and took out my laptop and the transcripts from yesterday's interviews. I plugged in my laptop, switched on the lamp and contemplated the blank screen. Then I picked up McAra's manuscript to remind myself of how not to begin a ten-million-dollar autobiography:

> Langs are Scottish folk originally, and proud of it. Our name is a derivation of 'long', the Old English word for 'tall', and it is from north of the border that my forefathers hail. It was in the sixteenth century that the first of the Langs . . .

God help us! I ran my pen through it, then zigzagged a thick blue line through all the succeeding paragraphs of Lang ancestral history. Maddox's instruction was to begin the book with the war crimes allegations, which was fine by me, although it could serve only as a kind of long prologue. At some point, the memoir proper would have to begin, and for this I wanted to find a fresh and original note. I turned my attention to the transcripts. I knew what would make a perfect opening. I rested my fingers on the keys of my laptop, then started to type:

> I became a politician out of love. Not love for any particular party or ideology, but love for a woman who came knocking on my door one wet Sunday afternoon . . .

I carried on for a couple of hours, until about one o'clock or so, then I heard a very light tapping of fingertips on wood. It made me jump.

'Mister?' came a timid female voice. 'Sir? You want lunch?'

I opened the door to find Dep, the Vietnamese housekeeper, in her black silk uniform and slippers. She was about fifty, as tiny as a bird.

'That would be very nice. Thanks.'

'Here, or in kitchen?'

'The kitchen would be great.'

After she'd shuffled away, I turned to face my room. I couldn't put it off any longer. I unzipped my suitcase and laid it on the bed. Then, taking a deep breath, I slid open the doors to the closet and began removing McAra's clothes from their hangers—cheap shirts, off-the-peg jackets, chain store trousers. He had been a big fellow, I realised, as I felt all those supersize collars and great, hooped waistbands.

The possessions of the dead always get to me. Is there anything sadder than the clutter they leave behind? I reached up to the shelf above the clothes rail to pull down McAra's suitcase. I'd expected it to be empty but, as I took hold of the handle, something slid around inside. Ah, I thought. At last. The secret document.

I laid the case on the floor, knelt in front of it and pressed the catches. They flew up with a loud snap.

Inside was a large padded envelope addressed to M. McAra Esq., care of a post office box number in Vineyard Haven. A label on the back showed that it had come from the Adam Lang Archive Centre in Cambridge, England. I opened it and pulled out a handful of photographs and photocopies.

One of the photographs I recognised at once: Lang in his chicken outfit, from the Footlights Revue in the early 1970s. There were a dozen other production stills showing the whole cast, as well as a set of photographs of Lang punting, wearing a straw boater and a striped blazer, and at a riverside picnic, apparently taken on the same day. The photocopies were of various Footlights programmes and Cambridge theatre reviews, plus newspaper reports of the Greater London Council elections of May 1977, and Lang's original party membership card. When I saw the date on the card, I rocked back on my heels. It was from 1975.

I re-examined the package with more care, starting with the election reports. I saw now that they were from the news sheet of a political party—Lang's party—and he was actually pictured in a group as an election volunteer. His hair was long, his clothes were shabby. But that was him, all right, one of a team knocking on doors on a council estate. 'Canvasser: A. Lang.'

I was more irritated than anything. It certainly didn't strike me as sinister. I could see how it would have suited Lang to pretend he'd gone into politics only because he'd fancied a girl. It flattered him, by making him look less ambitious, and it flattered her, by making her look more influential than she probably was. But now the question arose: what was I supposed to do?

It's not an uncommon dilemma in the ghosting business, and the etiquette is simple: you draw the discrepancy to the author's attention and leave it to him to resolve it. Don't dictate, facilitate: that is our sacred rule. Obviously, McAra had failed to observe this. He must have had his suspicions about what he was being told, ordered up a parcel of research from the archives, then removed the ex-prime minister's most polished anecdote from his memoirs. I could imagine how that must have been received.

I turned my attention back to the Cambridge material. There was a strange kind of innocence about these faded *jeunesse dorée*, stranded in that lost valley somewhere between the twin cultural peaks of hippiedom and punk. The girls had long lacy dresses in floral prints, with plunging necklines. The men's hair was as long as the women's. In the only colour picture, Lang was holding a bottle of champagne in one hand and what looked very much like a joint in the other; a girl seemed to be feeding him strawberries, while in the background a bare-chested man gave a thumbs-up.

The biggest of the cast photographs showed eight young people grouped under a spotlight, their arms outstretched as if they had just finished a show-stopping routine. Lang was on the far right, wearing his striped blazer, a bow tie and a straw boater. There were two pretty girls in leotards, fishnet tights and high heels: one with short blonde hair, the other dark frizzy curls. Two of the men apart from Lang I recognised: one was now a famous comedian, the other an actor. A third man looked older than the others: a postgraduate researcher, perhaps. Everyone was wearing gloves.

Glued to the back was a typed slip listing the names of the performers, along with their colleges: G. W. Syme (Caius), W. K. Innes (Pembroke), A. Parke (Newnham), P. Emmett (St John's), A. D. Martin (King's), E. D. Vaux (Christ's), H. C. Martineau (Girton), A. P. Lang (Jesus).

There was a copyright stamp—*Cambridge Evening News*—in the bottom left-hand corner, and scrawled next to it in blue ballpoint was a telephone number, prefixed by the international dialling code. No doubt McAra, indefatigable fact hound that he was, had hunted down one of the cast. I wondered which one. On a whim, I took out my mobile and dialled the number. Instead of the familiar two-beat British ringing tone, I heard the single sustained note of the American. I let it ring for a long while. Just as I was about to give in, a man answered, cautiously.

'Richard Rycart.' The voice, with its slight colonial twang—'Richard Roicart'—was unmistakably that of the former foreign secretary. He sounded suspicious. 'Who is this?' he asked.

I hung up at once. In fact I was so alarmed that I threw the phone onto the bed. It lay there for about thirty seconds, then started to ring. I darted over and grabbed it—the incoming number was listed as 'withheld'—and switched it off. For half a minute I was too stunned to move.

I told myself not to rush to any conclusions. I didn't know for certain that McAra had written down the number. I checked the package, and saw that it had left the United Kingdom on January 3, nine days before McAra died.

It suddenly seemed vital to get every remaining trace of my predecessor out of that room. Hurriedly, I stripped the last of his clothes from the closet, upending the drawers of socks and underpants into his suitcase. I found no personal papers or books, and presumed they had been taken away by the police. From the bathroom I removed his razor, toothbrush and the rest of it. When all tangible effects of Michael McAra were crammed into the suitcase, I dragged it into the corridor and round to the solarium.

Once I'd recovered my breath, I headed back to his—my—our—room. I stuffed the photographs and photocopies back into the envelope and looked around for somewhere to conceal it. It had nothing to do with war crimes, but somehow it demanded to be hidden and, in the absence of any other bright idea, I resorted to the cliché of stuffing it underneath the mattress.

'Lunch, sir,' called Dep softly from the corridor. I wheeled round. I wasn't sure if she'd seen me, but then I wasn't sure it mattered. Compared to what else she must have witnessed in the house over the past few weeks, my own strange behaviour would surely have seemed small beer.

I followed her into the kitchen. 'Is Mrs Lang around?' I said.

'No, sir. She go Vineyard Haven. Shopping.'

She had fixed me a club sandwich. I sat on a tall stool at the breakfast bar and compelled myself to eat it while I considered what to do. Normally I would have forced myself back to my desk and continued writing. But for just about the first time in my career as a ghost, I was blocked. I'd wasted half the morning composing a charmingly intimate reminiscence of an event that couldn't have happened—because Ruth Lang hadn't arrived to start her career in London until 1976, by which time her future husband had already been a party member for a year.

Even the thought of tackling the Cambridge section, once regarded as words in the bank, led me to a blank wall. Who was he, this happy-go-lucky, politically allergic, would-be actor? What suddenly turned him into a party activist if it wasn't meeting Ruth? It made no sense to me. That was when I realised that our former prime minister was not a psychologically credible character. In the flesh, or on the screen, he seemed to have a strong personality. But somehow, when one sat down to think about him, he vanished.

I took out my cellphone and considered calling Rycart. But what was I supposed to say? 'Oh, hello, you don't know me, but I've replaced Mike McAra as Adam Lang's ghost. I believe he may have spoken to you a day or two before he was washed up dead on a beach.' I put the phone back in my pocket, and suddenly I couldn't rid my mind of the image of McAra's heavy body rolling back and forth in the surf. Did he hit rocks, or was he run up onto soft sand? What was the name of the place where he'd been found? Rick had mentioned it at his club in London. Lambert something-or-other.

'Excuse me, Dep,' I said to the housekeeper. 'Do you happen to know if there's a map of the island I could borrow?'

IT LOOKED TO BE about ten miles away, on the northwestern shore of the Vineyard. Lambert's Cove: that was it.

There was something beguiling about the names of the locations around it: Blackwater Brook, Uncle Seth's Pond, Indian Hill, Old Herring Creek Road. It was like a map from a children's adventure story, and in a strange way that was how I conceived of my plan, as a kind of amusing excursion. Dep suggested I borrow a bicycle—oh yes, Mr Rhinehart, he keep many, many bicycles, for use of guests—and that appealed to me as well, even though I hadn't ridden a bike for years, and even though I knew, at some deeper level, no good would come of it. More than three weeks had passed since the corpse had been recovered. What would there be to see? But curiosity is a powerful human impulse, and I was curious.

The receptionist at the hotel in Edgartown had warned me that a storm was forecast, and the sky was beginning to sag with the weight of it, like a soft grey sack waiting to split apart. Undeterred, I took Lang's windproof jacket from its peg in the cloakroom and followed Duc the gardener along the front of the house to the weathered wooden cubes that served as staff accommodation and outbuildings.

Duc stopped in front of the third cube and unlocked the big double doors. He dragged back one of them and we went inside. There must have been a dozen bicycles parked in two racks, but my gaze went straight to the tan-coloured Ford Escape SUV, which took up the other half of the garage. I had heard so much about it, had imagined it so often when I was coming over on the ferry, that it was quite a shock to encounter it unexpectedly.

Duc saw me looking at it. 'You want to borrow?' he asked.

'No, no,' I said quickly. 'A bike will be fine. It will do me good.'

The gardener watched me sceptically as I wobbled off on one of Rhinehart's expensive mountain bikes. I raised my hand to the Special Branch man in his little, wooden, sentry's hut, and that made me swerve towards the undergrowth. But I steered the machine back into the centre of the track, and once I got the hang of the gears I found I was moving fairly rapidly over the hard, compacted sand.

I pedalled up through the forest until I reached the T-junction where the track joined the highway. The anti-Lang demonstration had dwindled to just one man. He had erected some kind of installation on the opposite side of the road. Mounted on wooden boards, protected by sheets of plastic, were hundreds of terrible images, torn from magazines, of burned children, beheaded hostages and bomb-flattened neighbourhoods, interspersed with long lists of names, handwritten poems and letters. A banner ran across the top: FOR AS IN ADAM ALL DIE, EVEN SO IN CHRIST SHALL ALL BE MADE ALIVE. Beneath it was a flimsy shelter of wooden struts and more plastic, containing a folding table and chair. Sitting patiently at the table was the man I'd glimpsed that morning and couldn't remember. But I recognised him now: he was the military type from the hotel bar.

I came to an uncertain halt, conscious of him staring at me. Then, to my horror, he got to his feet.

'Just one moment!' he shouted, as I teetered out into the road. An oncoming car hit its horn. There was a blur of light and noise, and I felt the wind of it as it passed. When I looked back, the protester was standing in the centre of the road, staring after me, arms akimbo.

I cycled hard, conscious that I would soon start to lose the light, and the pumping of my legs kept me warm. I passed the airport and followed the perimeter of the state forest, then toiled on past the white clapboard houses and the neat New England fields. Just out of West Tisbury I stopped to check directions. A wind was getting up, and I almost lost the map. But I eased myself back onto the thin, hard saddle and set off again.

About two miles later the road forked and I turned left towards the sea. The track to the cove was similar to the approach to the Rhinehart place—scrub oak, ponds, dunes—but there were more houses here, mostly vacation homes, shuttered up for the winter. It started to rain at last—hard, cold pellets of moisture that exploded on my hands and face. One moment they were plopping sporadically in the pond, and the next it was as if some great aerial dam had broken and the rain swept down in torrents. I remembered why I disliked cycling: bicycles don't have roofs, windscreens or heaters.

The spindly, leafless scrub oaks offered no hope of shelter, but I couldn't see where I was going, so I dismounted and pushed my bike until I came to a low picket fence. I propped the bike against it, and ran up the cinder path to the verandah of the house. Once I was out of the rain, I leaned forward and shook my head to get the water out of my hair. Immediately a dog started barking and scratching at the door behind me. I'd assumed the house was empty—it certainly looked it—but a hazy white moon of a face appeared at the dusty window blurred by the screen door, and a moment later the door opened and the dog flew out at me.

I did my best to seem charmed by the hideous, yapping white furball, if only to appease its owner, an old-timer of not far off ninety to judge by the liver spots, the stoop and the still-handsome skull poking through the papery skin. He was wearing a well-cut sports jacket over a buttoned-up cardigan and had a plaid scarf round his neck. I made a stammering apology for disturbing his privacy, but he soon cut me off.

'You're British?' he said, squinting at me.

'I am.'

'That's OK. You can shelter. Sheltering's free.'

I guessed he was a retired professional and fairly well off—you had to be, living in a place where a shack with an outside lavatory would cost you half a million dollars.

'British, eh?' he repeated. He studied me through rimless spectacles. 'You anything to do with this feller Lang?'

'In a way,' I said.

'War crimes!' he said, with a roll of his head, and I caught a glimpse of flesh-coloured hearing aids. 'We could all have been charged with those! Maybe we ought to have been. I don't know. I guess I'll just have to put my trust in a higher judgment.' He chuckled sadly. 'I'll find out soon enough.'

I didn't know what he was talking about. I was just glad to be standing where it was dry. We leaned on the weathered handrail and stared out at the rain while the dog skittered dementedly on its claws around the verandah.

'So what brings you to this part of the Vineyard?' asked the old man.

There seemed no point in lying. 'Someone I knew was washed up on the beach down there,' I said. 'I thought I'd go and pay my respects.'

'Now *that* was a funny business,' he said. 'You mean the British guy a few weeks ago? No *way* should that current have carried him this far west. Not at this time of year.'

'What?' I turned to look at him. Despite his great age, there was something youthful about his sharp features and keen manner. He looked like an antique boy scout.

'I've known this sea most of my life. Hell, a guy tried to throw *me* off that damn ferry when I was still at the World Bank, and I can tell you this: if he'd succeeded, I wouldn't have floated ashore in Lambert's Cove!'

I was conscious of a drumming in my ears, but whether it was my blood or the downpour hitting the shingle roof I couldn't tell.

'Did you mention this to the police?'

'The police? Young man, I have better things to do with what little time I have left than spend it with the police! Anyway, I told all this to Annabeth. She's the one who was dealing with the police.' He saw my blank expression. 'Annabeth Wurmbrand,' he said. 'Mars Wurmbrand's widow. She has the house nearest the ocean. She's the one who told the police about the lights.'

'The lights?'

'The lights on the beach on the night the body was washed up.'

'What kind of lights?'

'Flashlights, I guess.'

'Why wasn't this reported in the media?'

'The media?' He gave another of his grating chuckles. 'Annabeth's never spoken to a reporter in her life!'

It seemed to me the rain had eased somewhat. 'Do you think you could point me in the direction of Mrs Wurmbrand's house?' I asked.

'Sure, but there's not much point in going there.'

'Why not?'

'She fell downstairs two weeks ago. Been in a coma ever since. Poor Annabeth. Ted says she's never going to regain consciousness. Hey!' he shouted, but by then I was halfway down the steps from the verandah.

'Thanks for the shelter,' I called over my shoulder. 'I've got to get going.'

'Well, tell your Mr Lang to keep his spirits up!' He gave me a trembling military salute and turned it into a wave. 'You take care now.'

I grabbed my bike and set off down the track. I didn't even notice the rain any more. About a quarter of a mile down the slope, in a clearing close to the dunes, was a big, low house surrounded by a wire fence. No lamps were lit, despite the darkness of the storm. That, I surmised, must be the residence of the comatose widow. Could she have seen *lights*? From the upstairs windows one would certainly have a good view of the beach. I leaned the bike against a bush and scrambled up the little path to the crest of the dune.

I'd already glimpsed what lay beyond the dunes from the old guy's house, but it was still a shock to clamber up and suddenly be confronted by that vista—that seamless grey hemisphere of scudding clouds and heaving ocean, the waves hurtling against the beach in a continuous, furious detonation. I wiped the rain out of my eyes, and thought of McAra alone on this immense shore—face down, glutted with salt water, his clothes stiff with brine and cold, carried in on the tide from Vineyard Sound, creeping higher up the beach until he grounded. And then I imagined him dumped over the side of a dinghy and dragged ashore by men with flashlights, who'd come back a few days later and thrown a garrulous old witness down her stairs.

A few hundred yards along the beach, a pair of figures emerged from the dunes and started walking towards me, dark and tiny and frail amid all that raging nature. I glanced in the other direction. The wind was whipping spouts of water from the surface of the waves and flinging them ashore.

What I ought to do, I thought, staggering slightly in the wind, is give all this to a journalist, some tenacious reporter from the *Washington Post*, some noble heir to the tradition of Woodward and Bernstein. I could see the headline. I could write the story in my mind.

> WASHINGTON—The death of Michael McAra, aide to former British prime minister Adam Lang, was a covert operation that went tragically wrong, according to sources within the intelligence community.

Was that so implausible? I took another look at the figures stumbling up the beach. It seemed to me they had quickened their pace. The wind slashed rain in my face and I wiped it away. I ought to get going, I thought. By the time I looked again they were closer still. One was short, the other tall. The tall one was a man, the short one a woman.

The short one was Ruth Lang.

I WENT HALFWAY DOWN the beach to meet her, amazed that she should have turned up. The noise of the wind and the sea wiped out our first exchanges. She had to take my arm and pull me down slightly, to shout in my ear.

'*I said*,' she repeated, and her breath was almost shockingly hot against my freezing skin, '*Dep told me you were here!*' The wind whipped her blue nylon hood away from her face and she tried to fumble for it, then gave up. She shouted something just as a wave exploded against the shore behind her. She smiled helplessly, waited until the noise had subsided, then cupped her hands and shouted, 'What are you doing?'

'Oh, just taking the air.'

'No—really.'

'I wanted to see where Mike McAra was found.'

'Why? You didn't even know him.'

'I'm starting to feel as if I did.'

'Where's your bike?'

'Just behind the dunes.'

'We came to fetch you back before the storm started.' She beckoned to the policeman, who was standing about five yards away, watching us—soaked, bored, disgruntled. 'Barry,' she shouted, 'bring the car round, will you, and meet us on the road? We'll wheel the bike up and find you.'

'Can't do that, Mrs Lang, I'm afraid,' he yelled back. 'Regulations say I have to stay with you at all times.'

'For God's sake!' she scoffed. 'Do you seriously think there's a terrorist cell at Uncle Seth's Pond? Go and get the car before you catch pneumonia.'

I watched his square, unhappy face, as his sense of duty warred with his desire for dryness. 'All right,' he said eventually. 'I'll meet you in ten minutes. But please don't leave the path or speak to anyone.'

'We won't, Officer,' she said with mock humility. 'I promise.'

He hesitated, then began jogging back the way he'd come.

'They treat us like children,' complained Ruth. 'I sometimes think their orders aren't to protect us so much as to spy on us.'

We climbed to the top of the dune and we both turned round automatically to stare at the sea. After a second or two, I risked a glance at her. Her pale skin was shiny with rain, her short dark hair flattened and glistening like a swimmer's cap. Her flesh looked hard, like alabaster. People said they couldn't understand what her husband saw in her, but at that moment I could. There was a tautness about her, a quick, nervous energy: she was a force.

'To be honest, I've come back here a couple of times myself,' she said. 'Poor Mike. He hated to be away from the city. He hated country walks. He couldn't even swim.' She brushed her cheeks with her hand.

'It's a hell of a place to end up,' I said.

'No it's not. When it's sunny, it's wonderful. It reminds me of Cornwall.'

She scrambled down the little footpath to the bike, and I followed her. When we reached it, she gazed intently at me, her dark brown eyes almost black in the fading light. 'Do you think his death was suspicious?'

The directness of the question took me unawares. 'I'm not sure,' I said, as I started wheeling the bike up the track. It was all I could do to stop myself telling her then what I'd heard from the old man. But I wasn't sure of my facts, and I didn't want to be on the receiving end of one of her scathing cross-examinations. So all I said was, 'I don't know enough about it. Presumably the police have investigated the whole thing thoroughly.'

'Yes. Of course,' she said, as we ascended through the scrub oak towards the road. 'They were very active at first, but it's gone quiet lately. I think the inquest was adjourned. They can't be that concerned—they released Mike's body last week and the embassy has flown it back to the UK.'

'Oh?' I tried not to sound too surprised. 'That seems very quick.'

'Not really. It's been three weeks. They did an autopsy. He was drunk and he drowned. End of story.'

'But what was he doing on the ferry in the first place?'

She gave me a sharp look. 'That I don't know. He was a grown man. He didn't have to account for his every move.'

We walked on in silence, passing the house where I'd sought shelter from the downpour. It appeared as deserted as when I'd first seen it.

Ruth said, 'The funeral's on Monday. He's being buried in Streatham. His mother's too ill to attend. I think perhaps I ought to go. One of us should put in an appearance, and it doesn't seem likely to be my husband.'

'I thought you said you didn't want to leave him.'

'It rather looks as though he's left me, wouldn't you say?'

She said no more after that, but pulled her hood up roughly, even though the rain had almost stopped, and walked on ahead, staring at the ground.

Barry was waiting for us at the end of the track in the minivan. He got out and opened the rear door. We manoeuvred the bike into the van, then he returned to his place behind the wheel and I climbed in beside Ruth.

We took a different route from the one I'd cycled, the road twisting up a hill away from the sea. The dusk was damp and gloomy, and the minivan's headlights fell on wild, almost moorland country. Ruth didn't speak for the whole of the journey. She turned her back slightly towards me and stared out of the window. But as we passed the lights of the airport, her cold hand moved across the seat and grasped mine. I didn't know what she was thinking, but I could guess, and I returned her pressure: even a ghost can show a little human sympathy from time to time.

SIX

The first thing I did when we got back was run a hot bath, tipping in half a bottle of organic bath oil (cardamom and ginger) I found in the bathroom cabinet. While that was filling, I drew the bedroom curtains and peeled off my damp clothes. Naturally, a house as modern as Rhinehart's didn't have anything so crudely useful as a radiator, so I left them where they fell, went into the bathroom and stepped into the tub.

Groaning with relief, I let myself slide down until only my nostrils were above the aromatic surface, and lay there like some basking alligator in its steamy lagoon for several minutes. I suppose that's why I didn't hear anyone knock on my bedroom door. Only when I broke the surface did I become aware of someone moving around next door.

'Hello?' I called.

'Sorry,' Ruth called back. 'I did knock. Just brought you some dry clothes.'

'That's all right,' I said. 'I can manage.'

'You need something that's been properly aired, or you'll catch your death. I'll get Dep to clean the others. Dinner's in an hour. Is that OK?'

'That's fine,' I said, surrendering. 'Thank you.'

When I heard the door click, I rose from the bath and grabbed a towel. On the bed, she had laid out a freshly laundered shirt belonging to her husband (it had his monogram, APBL, on the pocket), a sweater and a pair of jeans. Where my own clothes had been there was a wet mark on the floor.

There was something disconcerting about Ruth Lang. You never knew where you were with her. Sometimes she could be aggressive for no reason, and at others she was bizarrely overfamiliar, holding hands or dictating what you should wear.

I knotted my towel at my waist and sat down at the desk. I'd been struck before by how strangely absent she was from her husband's autobiography. That was one reason I'd wanted to begin the main part of the book with the story of their meeting—until I discovered that Lang had made it up. She was there on the dedication page—*To Ruth, and my kids, and the people of Britain*—but one had to wait another fifty pages until she appeared in person. I leafed through the manuscript until I reached the passage:

> It was at the time of the London elections that I got to know Ruth Capel, one of the most energetic members of the local association. I would like to say that it was her political commitment that drew me to her, but the truth is that I found her immensely attractive—small, intense, with very short dark hair and piercing dark eyes. She was a North Londoner, the only child of two university lecturers, and was, as my friends never tired of pointing out, much cleverer than I was! She had gained a First at Oxford in politics, philosophy and economics, then done a year's postgraduate research in postcolonial government as a Fulbright scholar. As if that were not enough to intimidate me, she had come top in the Foreign Office entrance examinations, although she later left to work for the party's foreign affairs team.
>
> Nevertheless, the Lang family motto has always been: 'Nothing ventured, nothing gained'. I managed to arrange for us to go canvassing together. It was then a relatively easy matter, after a hard evening's knocking on doors, to suggest a casual drink in a local pub. At first, other team members used to join us, but they soon became aware that Ruth and I wanted to be alone together. A year after the elections, we began sharing a flat, and when Ruth became pregnant with our first child, I asked her to marry me. Our wedding took place at Marylebone registry office in June 1979 and, after a blissful honeymoon in Hay-on-Wye, we returned to London, ready for the very different political fray following the election of Margaret Thatcher.

That was the only substantial reference to her.

I worked my way through the succeeding chapters, underlining places where she was mentioned. Her 'lifelong knowledge of the party' was 'invaluable' in helping Lang gain his safe parliamentary seat. 'Ruth saw the possibility that I might become party leader long before I did' was the promising opening of Chapter 3, but how she reached this prescient conclusion wasn't explained. She surfaced to give 'characteristically shrewd advice' when he had to sack a colleague. She shared his hotel suites at party conferences. She straightened his tie on the night he became prime minister. She went shopping with the wives of other world leaders on official visits. But for all that, hers was a phantom presence in the memoirs, which puzzled me, because she certainly wasn't a phantom presence in his life.

When I checked my watch I realised I'd already spent an hour going over the manuscript, and it was time for dinner. I contemplated the clothes she had laid out on the bed. I don't like wearing clothes that aren't my own, but these were cleaner and warmer than anything I possessed, and she had gone to the trouble of fetching them, so I put them on and went upstairs.

A log fire was burning in the stone hearth, and someone, presumably Dep, had lit candles all around the room. The security lights in the grounds had also been turned on, illuminating the gaunt, white outlines of trees. As I came into the room, a gust of rain slashed across the huge picture window.

Ruth was sitting on the same sofa, with her legs drawn up beneath her, reading the *New York Review of Books*. On the low table in front of her was a glass of what looked like white wine. She glanced up approvingly.

'A perfect fit,' she said. 'Now you need a drink.' She leaned her head over the back of the sofa and called in her mannish voice, 'Dep!' And then to me, 'What will you have?'

'What are you having?'

'Biodynamic white wine, from the Rhinehart Vinery in Napa Valley.'

'He doesn't own a distillery, I suppose?'

'Try it, it's delicious. Dep,' she said to the housekeeper, who had appeared at the top of the stairs, 'bring the bottle, would you, and another glass?'

I sat down opposite Ruth. She was wearing a long red woollen dress, and on her normally scrubbed-clean face was a trace of make-up. There was something touching about her determination to put on a show, even as the bombs, so to speak, were falling all around her.

'We'll eat in twenty minutes,' instructed Ruth as Dep poured me some wine, 'because first'—she picked up the remote control and jabbed it at the television—'we must watch the news. Cheers.' She raised her glass.

'Cheers,' I replied and did the same.

I drained the glass in thirty seconds. White wine: what *is* the point of it? Dep had left the bottle. I picked it up and studied the label. Apparently the vines were grown in soil treated in harmony with the lunar cycle, using manure buried in a cow's horn and flower heads of yarrow fermented in a stag's bladder. It sounded like the sort of suspicious activity for which people quite rightly used to be burned as witches.

'You like it?' asked Ruth.

'Subtle and fruity,' I said, 'with a hint of bladder.'

'Pour us some more, then. Here comes Adam. Christ, it's the lead story. I think I may have to get drunk for a change.'

The headline behind the announcer's shoulder read LANG: WAR CRIMES. I didn't like the fact that they weren't bothering to use a question mark any more. The familiar scenes from the morning unfolded: the press conference at The Hague, Lang leaving the Vineyard house, the statement to reporters on the West Tisbury highway. Then came shots of Lang in Washington, first greeting members of Congress in a glow of flashbulbs and mutual admiration, and then, more sombrely, Lang with the secretary of state. Amelia Bly was visible in the background.

'Adam Lang,' said the secretary of state, 'has stood by our side in the war against terror, and I am proud to stand by his side and offer him, on behalf of the American people, the hand of friendship. Adam. Good to see you.'

'Don't grin,' said Ruth.

'Thank you,' said Adam, grinning and shaking the proffered hand. He beamed at the cameras. He looked like an eager student collecting a prize on speech day. 'Thank you very much. It's good to see you.'

'Oh, for fuck's sake!' shouted Ruth.

She was about to press the remote when Richard Rycart appeared, passing through the lobby of the United Nations, surrounded by the usual bureaucratic phalanx. He seemed to swerve off his planned course and walked over to the cameras. He was a little older than Lang, just coming up to sixty. He'd been born in Australia, or some part of the Commonwealth, before coming to England in his teens. He had a cascade of dark grey hair, and his tanned and hook-prowed profile reminded me slightly of a Sioux Indian chief.

'I watched the announcement in The Hague today,' he said, 'with great shock and sadness.' I sat forward. This was definitely the voice I'd heard on the phone earlier in the day. 'Adam Lang was and is an old friend of mine—'

'You hypocritical bastard,' said Ruth.

'—and I regret that he's chosen to bring this down to a personal level. This isn't about individuals. This is about justice. This is about whether there's to be one law for the rich Western nations and another for the rest of the world. This is about making sure that every political and military leader knows that he will be held to account by international law. Thank you.'

A reporter shouted, 'If you're called to testify, sir, will you go?'

'Certainly I'll go.'

'I bet you will, you little shit,' said Ruth.

The news bulletin moved on to a report of a suicide bombing in the Middle East, and she turned off the television. Her mobile phone started ringing.

Ruth glanced at it. 'It's Adam, calling to ask how I think it went.' She turned that off as well. 'Let him sweat.'

'Does he always ask your advice?'

'Always. And he always used to take it. Until just lately.'

I poured us some more wine. 'You were right,' I said. 'He shouldn't have gone to Washington. It did look bad.'

'We should never have come *here*,' she said, gesturing with her wine to the room. 'And all for the sake of the Adam Lang Foundation. Which is what, exactly? A high-class displacement activity for the recently unemployed.' She leaned forward. 'Shall I tell you the first rule of politics?'

'Please.'

'Never lose touch with your base. You can reach beyond it—you've got to, if you're going to win. But if you lose touch with it altogether, you're finished. If those pictures tonight had been of him arriving in London—flying back to fight these absurd allegations—it would have looked magnificent! Instead of which—God!' She shook her head and gave a sigh of anger and frustration. 'Come on. Let's eat.' She pushed herself off the sofa.

The long table by the window had been laid for two, and the sight of Nature raging silently beyond the thick screen heightened the sense of intimacy: the candles, the flowers, the crackling fire. It felt slightly overdone. Dep brought in two bowls of clear soup, and for a while we clinked our spoons against Rhinehart's porcelain in self-conscious silence.

'How is it going?' she said eventually.

'The book? It's not, to be honest.'

'Why's that—apart from the obvious reason?'

I hesitated. 'Can I talk frankly?'

'Of course.'

'I find it difficult to understand him.'

'Oh?' She was drinking water now. Over the rim of her glass, her dark eyes gave me one of her double-barrelled-shotgun looks. 'In what way?'

'I can't understand why this good-looking eighteen-year-old lad who goes to Cambridge without the slightest interest in politics, and who spends his time acting and drinking and chasing girls, suddenly ends up a member of a political party. Where's that coming from?'

'Didn't you ask him?'

'He told me he joined because of you. That you came and canvassed him, and he was attracted to you, and he followed you into politics out of love. To see more of you. I mean, that I can relate to. It ought to be true.'

'But it isn't?'

'You know it isn't. He was a party member for at least a year before he even met you.'

'Was he?' She wrinkled her forehead. 'But that story he always tells about what drew him into politics—I do have a distinct memory of that episode, because I canvassed in the London elections of 1977, and I definitely knocked on his door, and after that was when he started showing up at party meetings regularly. So there has to be a grain of truth in it.'

'A grain,' I conceded. 'Maybe he'd joined in '75, hardly showed any interest for two years, then met you and became more active. It still doesn't answer the question of what took him into a political party in the first place.'

'Is it really that important?'

As Dep cleared away the soup plates, I considered Ruth's question.

'Yes,' I said when we were alone again, 'it *is* important. It means he isn't quite who we think he is. I'm not even sure he's quite who *he* thinks he is.'

Ruth frowned at the table and made minute adjustments to the placing of her knife and fork. 'How do you know he joined in '75?'

There seemed no reason not to tell her. 'Mike McAra found Adam's original party membership card in the Cambridge archives.'

'Those archives!' she said. 'They've got everything. Typical Mike, to ruin a good story by too much research.'

Dep came in with the main course—steamed fish, noodles and some kind of obscure, pale green vegetable that resembled a weed. I ostentatiously poured the last of the wine into my glass and studied the bottle.

'You want another, sir?' Dep asked.

'I don't suppose you have any whisky, do you?'

The housekeeper looked to Ruth for guidance.

'Oh, bring him some bloody whisky,' said Ruth.

Dep returned with a bottle of fifty-year-old Chivas Regal Royal Salute and a cut-glass tumbler. Ruth started to eat. I mixed myself a Scotch and water.

'This is delicious, Dep!' called Ruth. She dabbed her mouth with the corner of her napkin. 'Coming back to your question,' she said to me, 'there's no mystery. Adam always had a social conscience—he inherited that from his mother—and I know that after he left Cambridge and moved to London he became very unhappy. I believe he was actually clinically depressed.'

'Clinically depressed? Really?' I tried to keep the excitement out of my voice. Nothing sells a memoir like a good dose of misery.

'Put yourself in his place.' Ruth gestured with her laden fork. 'His mother and father were both dead. He'd left university, which he'd loved. Many of his acting friends had agents and were getting offers of work. But he wasn't. I think he was lost, and I think he turned to political activity to compensate. He might not want to put it in those terms—he's not one for self-analysis—but that's my reading of what happened.'

'So meeting you must have been very important for him. You had genuine political passion. And knowledge. And contacts in the party. You must have given him the focus to go forward.' I felt as if a mist were clearing. 'Do you mind if I make a note of this?'

'Go ahead. If you think it's useful.'

'Oh, it is.' I put my knife and fork together, took out my notebook and opened it to a new page. 'Marrying you was a real turning point.'

'I was certainly a bit different from his Cambridge girlfriends. Even when I was a girl I was always more interested in politics than ponies.'

'Didn't you ever want to be a proper politician in your own right?'

'Of course. Didn't you ever want to be a proper writer?'

It was like being struck in the face. 'Ouch,' I said.

'I'm sorry. I didn't mean to be rude. But you must see we're in the same boat, you and I. I've always understood more about politics than Adam. You know more about writing. But he's the star, isn't he? And our job is to service the star. It's his name that's going to sell the book, not yours. It was the same for me. It didn't take me long to realise that he could go all the way in politics. He had the looks, the charm. He was a great speaker. People liked him. Whereas I was a bit of an ugly duckling, with this gift for putting my foot in it. As I've just demonstrated.' She put her hand on mine again. 'I'm so sorry. I've hurt your feelings. I suppose even ghosts must have feelings?'

'If you prick us,' I said, 'we bleed.'

'You've finished eating? In that case, why don't you show me this research that Mike dug out? It might jog my memory. I'm interested.'

I went down to my room and retrieved McAra's package. By the time I returned upstairs, Ruth had moved back to the sofa. Fresh logs had been thrown on the fire and Dep was clearing away the dishes. I just managed to rescue my tumbler and the bottle of Scotch.

'Would you like dessert?' asked Ruth. 'Coffee?'

'I'm fine.'

'We're finished, Dep. Thank you.' She moved up, to indicate that I should sit next to her, but I pretended not to notice and took my place opposite her.

I opened the envelope and took out the photocopies of Lang's membership card and the articles about the London elections. I slid them across the table to her. She leaned forward to read, and I found myself staring into the surprisingly deep and shadowy valley of her cleavage.

'There's no arguing with that,' she said, putting the membership card to one side. 'That's his signature, all right.' She tapped the report on the canvassers in 1977. 'I recognise some of these faces. I must have been off that night, or I would have been in the picture. What else have you got there?'

There didn't seem much point in hiding anything, so I passed over the whole package. She inspected the name and address, and the postmark, then upended the envelope and tipped the contents out over the table.

I watched her pale, clever face as she sorted through the photographs and programmes. I saw the hard lines soften as she picked out a photograph of Lang in his striped blazer on a dappled riverbank.

'Oh, look at him,' she said. 'Isn't he pretty?' She held it up.

'Irresistible,' I said.

She inspected the picture more closely. 'It was another world, wasn't it? I mean, what was happening while this was being taken? Vietnam. The Cold War. The first miners' strike in Britain since 1926. The military coup in Chile. And what do they do? Get a bottle of champagne and go punting!'

'I'll drink to that.'

She picked up another photograph and looked at the back of it. 'What's this telephone number?'

I should have known nothing would escape her. I felt my face flush.

'Well?' she insisted.

I said quietly, 'It's Richard Rycart's.'

It was almost worth it just for her expression. She looked as though she'd swallowed a hornet. 'You've been calling Richard Rycart?' she gasped.

'*I* haven't. It must have been McAra.'

'That's not possible.'

'Who else could have written down that number?' I held out my cell-phone. 'Try it.'

She stared at me for a while, then reached over, took my phone and entered the fourteen digits. She raised it to her ear and stared at me again. About thirty seconds later a flicker of alarm passed across her face. She fumbled to press the disconnect button, and put the phone back on the table.

'Did he answer?' I asked.

She nodded. The phone began to ring again, throbbing along the surface of the table as if it had come alive.

'What should I do?' I asked.

'Do what you want. It's your phone.'

I turned it off. There was a silence, broken only by the roaring of the fire.

She said, 'When did you discover this?'

'Earlier today. When I moved into McAra's room.'

'Then you went to Lambert's Cove to look at where his body came ashore. Why did you do that?' Her voice was very quiet. 'Tell me honestly.'

'I'm not sure.' I paused. 'There was a man there,' I blurted out. I couldn't keep it to myself any longer. 'An old-timer, who's familiar with the currents in Vineyard Sound. He says there's no way a body from the Woods Hole ferry would wash up at Lambert's Cove this time of year. He also said that a woman who has a house just behind the dunes saw flashlights on the beach the night McAra went missing. But then she fell downstairs and is in a coma. So she can't tell the police anything.' I spread my hands. 'That's all I know.'

She was looking at me with her mouth slightly open. 'That,' she said slowly, 'is *all* you know. *Jesus*.' She started feeling around on the sofa, then flicked her fingers at me. 'Give me your phone.'

'Why?' I asked, handing it over.

'Isn't it obvious? I need to call Adam.' She held it in her palm, inspected it, and started entering his number with her thumb. Then she stopped.

'What?' I said.

'Nothing.' She was looking beyond me, over my shoulder, chewing the inside of her lip. Then she put the phone back down on the table.

'You're not going to call him?'

'In a while.' She stood. 'I'm going for a walk first. To clear my head.'

'I'll come with you.'

'No. Thanks, but I need to think things through on my own. You stay here and have another drink. You look as though you need one. Don't wait up.'

IT WAS BARRY I felt sorry for. No doubt he'd been downstairs with his feet up, looking forward to a quiet night in. And suddenly here was Lady Macbeth again, off on yet another of her walks, this time in the middle of a storm. I stood at the window and watched them cross the lawn. She was in the lead, as usual, her head bowed. The Special Branch man was still pulling on his coat.

I suddenly felt overwhelmingly tired. My legs were stiff from cycling. I felt shivery with an incipient cold. Even Rhinehart's whisky had lost its allure. She had said not to wait up, and I decided I wouldn't. I put the photographs and photocopies away in the envelope and went downstairs to my room. After I took off my clothes and switched off the light, sleep seemed to swallow me instantly, to suck me down through the mattress and into its dark waters, as if it were a strong current and I an exhausted swimmer.

I surfaced at some point to find myself alongside McAra, his large, clumsy body turning in the water like a dolphin's. He was fully clothed, in a thick black raincoat and heavy, rubber-soled shoes. *I'm not going to make it*, he said to me. *You go on without me*.

I sat up in alarm. I'd no idea how long I'd been asleep. The room was in darkness, apart from a vertical strip of light to my left.

'Are you awake?' said Ruth softly, knocking on the door. She had opened it a few inches and was standing in the corridor.

'I am now.'

'I'm sorry.'

'It doesn't matter. Hold on.'

I went into the bathroom and put on the white terry-cloth robe that was hanging on the back of the door, and when I returned to the bedroom and let her in I saw that she was wearing an identical robe to mine. It was too big for her. She looked unexpectedly small and vulnerable. Her hair was wet.

'What time is it?' I said.

'I don't know. I just spoke to Adam.' She seemed stunned, trembling.

'And?'

She glanced along the corridor. 'Can I come in?'

Still groggy from my dream, I turned on the bedside light. I stood aside to let her pass and closed the door after her.

'The day before Mike died, he and Adam had a terrible row,' she said, without preliminaries. 'I haven't told anyone this, not even the police.'

I massaged my temples and tried to concentrate. 'What was it about?'

'I don't know, but it was furious, and they never spoke again. Adam refused to discuss it. In light of what you've found out today, I felt I had to have it out with him once and for all.'

'What did he say?'

She sat on the edge of the bed and put her face in her hands. I sat down next to her. She was shaking from head to toe.

'He was having dinner with the vice president. He said he couldn't talk, but I said he bloody well had to, so he took the phone into the men's room. When I told him Mike had been in touch with Rycart just before he died, he didn't even pretend to be surprised.' She turned to me. 'He *knew*.'

'He said that?'

'He didn't need to. I could tell by his voice. He said we shouldn't say any more over the telephone. We should talk when he gets back.' She looked stricken. 'Dear God, help us—what has he got himself mixed up in?'

Something seemed to give way in her and she sagged towards me, her arms outstretched. Her head came to rest against my chest and she clung to me fiercely. My hands hovered an inch or two above her, then I stroked her hair and murmured words of reassurance I didn't really believe.

'I'm afraid,' she said in a muffled voice. 'I've never been frightened in my life before. But I am now.'

'Your hair's wet,' I said gently. 'Let me get you a towel.'

I extricated myself and went into the bathroom. When I returned, she'd taken off her robe and had got into bed, pulling the sheet up over her breasts.

'Do you mind?' she said.

'Of course not,' I said.

I turned off the light and climbed in beside her, and lay on the cold side of the bed. She rolled over and put her hand on my chest and pressed her lips very hard against mine, as if she were trying to give me the kiss of life.

WHEN I WOKE the next morning, I expected to find her gone. But in the dimness I could see her bare shoulder and her crop of black hair, and I could tell by her breathing that she was as awake as I was.

I lay motionless on my back, shutting my eyes periodically as some fresh aspect of the mess occurred to me. On the Richter scale of bad ideas, this surely had registered a ten. I let one hand travel crabwise to the bedside table, then brought my watch up close to my face. It was 7.14 a.m.

Cautiously, I slipped out of the bed and crept towards the bathroom.

'You're awake,' she said, without moving.

'I'm sorry if I disturbed you,' I said. 'I thought I'd take a shower.'

I locked the door behind me, turned the water up as hot and strong as I could bear, and let it pummel me—back, stomach, legs, scalp. The little room quickly filled with steam. Afterwards, when I shaved, I had to keep rubbing at my reflection in the mirror to stop myself from disappearing.

By the time I returned to the bedroom, she had put on her robe and was sitting at the desk, leafing through the manuscript. The curtains were still closed.

'You've taken out his family history,' she said. 'He won't like that. He's very proud of the Langs. And why have you underlined my name every time?'

'I wanted to check how often you were mentioned. I was surprised there wasn't more about you.'

'That's a hangover from the focus groups. In Downing Street, Mike used to say that every time I opened my mouth I cost Adam ten thousand votes.'

'I'm sure that's not true.'

'Of course it is. People are always looking for someone to resent. I often think my main usefulness, as far as he was concerned, was to serve as a lightning rod. They could take their anger out on me instead of him.'

'Even so,' I said, 'you ought not to be written out of history.'

'Why not? Most women usually are. Even the Amelia Blys of this world.'

'Well, then, I shall reinstate you.' I slid open the door of the closet so hard in my haste that it banged. I had to get out of that house, put some distance between myself and their destructive ménage à trois before I ended up as crazed as they were. 'I'd like to sit down with you, when you have the time, and do a long interview. Put in all the important occasions he's forgotten.'

'How very kind of you,' she said bitterly. 'Like the boss's secretary whose job is to remember his wife's birthdays for him?'

'Something like that. But as you say, I can't claim to be a proper writer.'

I put on a pair of boxer shorts, pulling them up under my dressing gown.

'Ah,' she said dryly, 'the modesty of the morning after.'

'A bit late for that,' I said, taking off the robe and reaching for a shirt.

Our former intimacy lay between us like a shadow. The silence lengthened, and hardened, until I felt her resentment as an almost solid barrier. I could no more have gone across and kissed her now than I could on the day we met.

'What are you going to do?' she asked.

'Leave.'

'That's not necessary as far as I'm concerned.'

'I'm afraid it is, as far as I am.' I pulled on my trousers.

'Are you going to tell Adam about this?'

'Oh, for God's sake!' I cried. 'What do you think?' I laid my suitcase on the bed and unzipped it. I started throwing in my clothes.

'Where will you go?' She looked as if she might be about to cry again.

'Back to the hotel. I can work much better there. I'm sorry. I should never have stayed in a client's house. It always ends—' I hesitated.

'With you fucking the client's wife?'

'No, of course not. It just makes it hard to keep a professional distance. Anyway, it wasn't *entirely* my idea, if you recall.'

'That's not very gentlemanly of you.'

I didn't answer. I carried on packing. Her gaze followed my every move.

'And the things I told you last night?' she said. 'What do you propose to do about them?'

'Nothing,' I said, stopping at last. 'Ruth, I'm his ghostwriter, not an investigative reporter. If he wants to tell the truth about what's been going on, I'm here to help him. If he doesn't, fine. I'm morally neutral.'

'It isn't morally neutral to conceal the facts if you know something illegal has happened—that's criminal.'

'But I don't know that anything illegal has happened. All I have is a phone number on the back of a photograph and gossip from some old man who may well be senile. If anyone has any evidence, it's you. That's the real question, actually: what are *you* going to do about it?'

'I don't know,' she said. 'Perhaps I'll write my own memoirs. "Ex-Prime Minister's Wife Tells All".'

I resumed packing. 'Well, if you do decide to do that, give me a call.'

She emitted one of her trademark full-throated laughs. 'Do you really think I need someone like you to enable me to produce a book?'

She stood up then, and tightened the belt round her robe. Then she turned and, in the practised manner of a prime minister's wife, pulled the nylon cord to open the curtains. 'I declare this day officially open,' she said. 'God bless it, and all who have to get through it.'

'Well,' I said, looking out, 'that really is the morning after the night before.'

The rain had turned to sleet and the lawn was covered with debris from the storm—small branches, twigs, a white cane chair thrown on its side. I could see Ruth's face quite clearly in the glass: watchful, brooding.

'I'm not going to give you an interview,' she said. 'I don't want to be in his bloody book, being patronised and thanked by him, using your words.' She turned and brushed past me. At the bedroom door she paused. 'He's on his own now. I'll get a divorce. And then *she* can do the prison visits.'

I heard her own door opening and closing. I folded the clothes she had lent me and laid them on the chair, and put my laptop into my shoulder bag. The only thing left was the manuscript. It sat on the table, three sullen inches of it—my millstone, my albatross, my meal ticket. I could make no progress without it, and I certainly couldn't face the embarrassment of staying here and running into Ruth every few hours. And hadn't the war crimes investigation changed the circumstances so completely that the old rules no longer applied? I put the manuscript into my suitcase, along with the package from the archive, zipped them up and went out into the corridor.

Barry was sitting in the chair by the front door. He gave me a look of weary disapproval, tinged with a sneer of amused contempt. 'Morning, sir,' he said. 'Finished for the night, have we?'

He knows, I thought. In a flash I saw his sniggering conversations with his colleagues, the log of his official observations passed to London, a discreet entry in a file somewhere. Feeling a thrust of fury and resentment, I marched past him and out of the house, then set off towards the track, only belatedly registering that high moral dudgeon offers no protection against stinging sleet. I took off my jacket and held it over my head, and considered how I was going to reach Edgartown. That was when the idea of borrowing the tan-coloured Ford Escape SUV popped helpfully into my mind.

How different the course of my life would have been if I hadn't gone running towards that garage, my jacket raised over me with one hand, the other dragging my little suitcase. The door was still unlocked from the previous day and the keys of the Ford were in the ignition—who worries about robbers when you live at the end of a two-mile track protected by six armed bodyguards? I heaved my case into the front passenger seat, put my jacket back on and slid behind the steering wheel.

I ran my fingertips over the Ford's unfamiliar controls. I don't own a car—I've never found much need, living alone in London—and on the rare occasions I hire one, it seems that another layer of gadgets has been added. There was a mystifying screen to the right of the wheel, which came alive when I switched on the engine. Pulsing green arcs were shown radiating upwards from Earth to an orbiting space station. As I watched, the pulse switched direction and the arcs beamed down from the heavens. An instant later, the screen showed a large red arrow, a yellow path and a great patch of blue.

An American woman's voice, soft but commanding, said, from somewhere behind me: *Join the road as soon as possible.*

I would have turned her off, but I couldn't see how. Conscious that the engine noise might soon bring Barry lumbering out of the house to investigate, I put the Ford into reverse and backed out of the garage. Then I adjusted the mirrors, switched on the headlights and the windscreen wipers, engaged drive and headed for the gate. As I passed the guard post, the scene on the satellite navigation monitor swung pleasingly, as if I were playing an arcade game, then the red arrow settled over the centre of the yellow path. I was away.

There was something oddly soothing about seeing all the little paths and streams, neatly labelled, appear at the top of the screen, then scroll down to the bottom and disappear. It made me feel as if the world were a safe and tamed place, its features tagged and stored in some celestial control room.

In two hundred yards, instructed the woman, *turn right*.

In fifty yards, turn right.

And then, *Turn right.*

The solitary demonstrator was huddled in his hut. He had a big old Volkswagen camper van parked nearby, and I wondered why he didn't shelter in that. I swung right, accelerating towards Edgartown. My disembodied guide was silent for the next four miles or so, and I forgot about her until, as I reached the outskirts of the town, she started up again.

In two hundred yards, turn left. Her voice made me jump.

In fifty yards, turn left.

Turn left, she repeated, when we reached the junction.

'I'm sorry,' I muttered and took a right towards Main Street.

Turn around when possible.

'This is getting ridiculous,' I said out loud and pulled over. I pressed various buttons on the navigator's console. The screen offered me a menu. One option was ENTER A NEW DESTINATION. Another was RETURN TO HOME ADDRESS. And a third—the one highlighted—was REMEMBER PREVIOUS DESTINATION.

I stared at it for a while, as the potential implications slowly filtered into my brain. Cautiously, I pressed SELECT.

The screen went blank. The device was obviously malfunctioning.

I turned off the engine and hunted around for instructions. Finding nothing I turned on the ignition. As the navigation system went through its start-up routine, I put the car into gear and headed down the hill.

Turn around when possible.

For the first time in my life I was confronted with the true meaning of the word 'predestination'. I had just passed the Victorian whaling church. Before me the hill dipped towards the harbour. I was not far from my old hotel. It was eight o'clock. There was no traffic on the road. The sidewalks were deserted. I carried on down the slope, past all the empty shops.

Turn around when possible.

Wearily, I surrendered to fate. I turned into a little street of houses and braked. The windscreen wiper thudded back and forth. I reversed out into Main Street and, with a thrilling screech of tyres, set off back up the hill. The arrow swung wildly, before settling contentedly over the yellow route.

Exactly what I thought I was doing I still don't know. I couldn't even be sure that McAra had been the last driver to enter an address. It might have been some other guest of Rhinehart's; it might have been Dep or Duc, or even the police. But it was in the back of my mind that if things started to get alarming, I could stop, and that gave me a false sense of reassurance.

Once I was out of Edgartown and onto Vineyard Haven Road, I heard nothing more from my heavenly guide for several minutes. I sat forward, peering into the grimy morning. The few approaching cars had their headlights on and were travelling slowly. Then the road bent sharply.

In two hundred yards, turn right.

In fifty yards, turn right.

Turn right.

I steered down the hill into Vineyard Haven, and then on to the flat, shabby area around the port. I turned a corner, and pulled up in a big car park. About a hundred yards away, across the rain-swept tarmac, a queue of vehicles was driving up the ramp of a ferry. The red arrow pointed me towards it.

On the navigation screen, the proposed route was inviting, like a child's painting of a summer holiday—a yellow jetty extending into the bright blue of Vineyard Haven Harbor. But the reality through the windscreen was uninviting: the sagging black mouth of the ferry, smeared at the corners with rust, and, beyond it, the heaving grey swell and the flailing hawsers of sleet.

Someone tapped on the glass beside me and I fumbled for the switch to lower the window. He was wearing dark blue oilskins with the hood pulled up, and a badge announced that he worked for the Steamship Authority.

'You'll have to hurry,' he shouted, turning his back into the wind. 'She leaves at eight fifteen. The weather's getting bad. There might not be another for a while.' He opened the door for me and almost pushed me towards the ticket office. 'You go pay. I'll tell them you'll be right there.'

I left the engine running and went into the little building. Even as I stood at the counter, I remained of two minds. Through the window I could see the car park attendant standing by the Ford, stamping his feet to ward off the cold. He saw me and beckoned at me urgently to get a move on.

'You going or what?' the elderly woman behind the desk demanded.

I sighed, took out my wallet and slapped down seven ten-dollar bills.

ONCE I'D DRIVEN up the clanking metal gangway into the dark, oily belly of the ship, another man in waterproofs directed me to a parking space. All around me, drivers were leaving their vehicles and squeezing through the narrow gaps towards the stairwells. The crewman indicated by a mime that I had to switch off the ignition. As I did so, the navigation screen died again. Behind me, the ferry's rear doors closed. The ship's engines started to throb, the hull lurched, and with a discouraging scrape of steel we began to move.

I felt trapped all of a sudden, sitting in the chilly twilight of that hold, with its stink of diesel and exhaust fumes, and it was more than just the claustrophobia of being below decks. It was McAra. I could sense his presence next to me. His dogged obsessions now seemed to have become mine.

I got out of the car and locked it, then went to find the bar on the upper deck. I relaxed in its warm, safe atmosphere, drinking coffee, until about half an hour later we passed Nobska Point Lighthouse and a loudspeaker instructed us to return to our vehicles. Then I went back down to the Ford.

By the time I emerged into the grey rain and wind of Woods Hole, the satellite screen was offering me its familiar golden path. I let the convoy of traffic carry me on Woods Hole Road to Main Street, and beyond. I had half a tank of fuel and the whole day stretched ahead of me.

In two hundred yards, at the circle, take the second exit.

I took it, and for forty-five minutes I headed north on a couple of big freeways, more or less retracing my route back to Boston. Could McAra have been heading to the airport? But as I let my mind fill with images of him meeting someone off a plane, I was directed west towards Interstate-95, and even with my feeble grasp of Massachusetts geography I knew I must be heading away from Logan Airport and downtown Boston.

I drove as slowly as I could for perhaps fifteen miles. The rain had eased, but it was still dark. I remember great swathes of woodland, interspersed with office blocks and gleaming factories. Just as I was beginning to think that McAra had been making a run for the Canadian border, the voice told me to take the next exit from the interstate, and I came down onto another six-lane freeway which, according to the screen, was the Concord Turnpike.

The woman spoke again. *In two hundred yards, take the next exit.*

I moved into the right-hand lane and came down the access road. At the end of the curve I found myself in a sylvan suburbia of big houses, wide drives and open lawns, almost every mailbox bearing a yellow ribbon in honour of the military. I believe it was actually called Pleasant Street.

A sign pointed to Belmont Center, and that was more or less the way I went, along roads that gradually became less populated as the price of the real estate rose. I passed a golf course and turned right into some woods. A red squirrel ran across the road in front of me and that was when, in the middle of what seemed to be nowhere, my guardian angel at last announced, in a tone of calm finality: *You have reached your destination.*

SEVEN

I pulled up onto the verge and turned off the engine. Looking around at the dense, dripping woodland, I felt a profound sense of disappointment. I wasn't sure exactly what I'd been expecting, but it was more than this.

I got out of the car and locked it. After two hours' driving I needed to fill my lungs with cold New England air. I walked down the wet lane for about fifty yards until I came to a gap in the trees. Set back from the road, a five-bar electric gate blocked access to a drive, which turned after a few yards and disappeared behind trees. Beside the gate was a metal mailbox with just a number on it—3551—and a stone pillar with an intercom and a code pad. A sign said, THESE PREMISES ARE PROTECTED BY CYCLOPS SECURITY. I hesitated, then pressed the buzzer. I glanced around. A small video camera was mounted on a nearby branch. I tried the buzzer again. There was no answer.

I stepped back, uncertain what to do. I noticed that the mailbox was crammed too full to close properly. With an apologetic shrug towards the camera, I pulled out a handful of mail. It was variously addressed to Mr and

Mrs Paul Emmett, Professor Emmett and Nancy Emmett. Judging by the postmarks, there was at least two days' worth uncollected. Some of the letters had been forwarded, with labels covering the original address. I scraped one of them back with my thumb. Emmett, I learned, was President Emeritus of something called the Arcadia Institution, in Washington, DC.

Emmett . . . Emmett . . . For some reason that name was familiar to me. I stuffed the letters back in the box and returned to my car. I opened my suitcase, took out the package addressed to McAra, and quickly found what I had vaguely remembered: P. Emmett (St John's) was one of the cast of the Footlights Revue, pictured with Lang. He was the oldest of the group, the one I'd thought was a postgraduate. Was this what had brought McAra all the way up here: yet more research about Cambridge? Emmett was mentioned in the memoirs, too, now I came to think about it. I picked up the manuscript and thumbed through the section on Lang's university days, but his name didn't appear there. Instead he was quoted at the start of the last chapter:

> Professor Paul Emmett of Harvard University has written of the unique importance of the English-speaking peoples in the spread of democracy around the world: 'As long as these nations stand together, freedom is safe; whenever they have faltered, tyranny has gathered strength.' I profoundly agree with this sentiment.

I don't know how long I sat there. I do remember that I was so bemused I forgot to turn on the Ford's heater, and it was only when I heard the sound of another car approaching that I realised how cold and stiff I had become. I saw a pair of headlights in the mirror, then a small Japanese car drove past me. A dark-haired woman was at the wheel, and next to her was a man of about sixty, wearing glasses and a jacket and tie. I couldn't imagine who else but the Emmetts would be travelling down such a quiet road. The car pulled up outside the entrance to the drive, and the man got out to empty the mailbox. He peered in my direction, and I thought he might come down and challenge me. Instead, he returned to the car, which moved out of my line of sight.

I stuffed the photographs and the page from the memoirs into my shoulder bag, gave the Emmetts ten minutes to open the place up and settle themselves in, then turned on the engine and drove up to the gate. When I pressed the buzzer, the answer came immediately.

'Hello?' It was a woman's voice.

'Is that Mrs Emmett?'

'Who is this?'

'I wondered if I could have a word with Professor Emmett.'

'Do you have an appointment?'

'It's about Adam Lang. I'm assisting him with his memoirs.'

'Just a moment please.'

I knew they'd be studying me on the video camera. I tried to adopt a suitably respectable pose. When the intercom crackled again, it was an American male voice that spoke: resonant, fruity, actorish.

'This is Paul Emmett. I think you must have made a mistake.'

'You were at Cambridge with Mr Lang, I believe?'

'We were contemporaries, yes, but I can't claim to know him.'

'I have a picture of the two of you together in a Footlights revue.'

There was a long pause. 'Come on up to the house.'

An electric motor whined, and the gate opened. As I followed the drive, the big, three-storey house appeared through the trees: a central section of grey stone flanked by wings of white-painted wood. The windows were arched and had slatted shutters. Steps led up to a pillared porch, where Emmett himself was waiting. I parked next to the Emmetts' car, and got out, carrying my bag.

'Forgive me if I seem a little groggy,' said Emmett after we'd shaken hands. 'We just flew in from Washington. I normally never see anyone without an appointment. But your mention of a photograph stimulated my curiosity.'

He dressed as precisely as he spoke. His spectacles had fashionable tortoiseshell frames, his bright red tie had a motif of pheasants in flight, and there was a matching silk handkerchief in his breast pocket.

He couldn't keep his eyes off my bag. I knew he wanted me to produce the photograph right there on the doorstep. But I waited, and kept on waiting, so that eventually he had to say, 'Fine. Please, do come in.'

The house had polished wood floors and an uninhabited chill about it. I could hear his wife on the telephone in another room, and a grandfather clock ticking loudly on the landing.

Emmett closed the front door behind us. 'May I?' he said.

I took out the cast photograph and gave it to him. He pushed his glasses up onto his silvery thatch of hair and wandered over to the hall window.

'Well, well,' he said, holding the monochrome image up to the weak winter light, 'I have literally no recollection of this.'

'But it *is* you?'

'Oh, yes. I was on the board of the Yale Dramatic Association in the sixties. Quite a time, as you can imagine.' He shared a complicit chuckle with his youthful image. 'I thought I'd maintain my theatrical interests when I went over to Cambridge for my doctoral research. Alas, after only a term, pressure of work put an end to my Footlights career. May I keep this?'

'I'm afraid not. But I'm sure I can get you a copy.'

'Would you? That would be very kind.' He turned it over and inspected the back. '*Cambridge Evening News*. You must tell me how you came by it.'

'I'd be happy to,' I said. The big clock ticked back and forth a few times.

'Come into my study,' he said.

I followed him into a room straight out of Rick's London club: green wallpaper, floor-to-ceiling books, library steps, brown leather furniture. One wall was devoted to memorabilia: citations, prizes, photographs. I took in Emmett with Bill Clinton and Al Gore, with Margaret Thatcher and Nelson Mandela. A German chancellor. A French president. There was also a picture of him with Lang, a grin-and-grip at what seemed to be a cocktail party.

He saw me looking. 'The wall of ego,' he said. 'We all have them. Do take a seat. I'm afraid I can only spare a few minutes.'

I perched on the unyielding brown sofa while he took the captain's chair.

'So,' he said. 'The picture.'

'I'm working with Adam Lang on his memoirs.'

'You said. Poor Lang. It's a bad business, this posturing by the ICC. If they continue to behave so foolishly, they will merely make Lang a martyr and a hero, and thus'—he gestured graciously towards me—'a best seller.'

'How well do you know him?'

'Lang? Hardly at all. You look surprised.'

'Well, for a start, he mentions you in his memoirs.'

Emmett appeared genuinely taken aback. 'What does he say?'

'It's a quote, at the start of the final chapter.' I pulled the page from my bag. '"As long as these nations"—that's everyone who speaks English—"stand together, freedom is safe; whenever they have faltered, tyranny has gathered strength." Then Lang says, "I profoundly agree with this sentiment."'

'Well, that's decent of him,' said Emmett. 'And his instincts as prime minister were good, in my judgment. But that doesn't mean I know him.'

'And then there's that,' I said, pointing to the wall of ego.

'Oh, *that*.' Emmett waved his hand dismissively. 'It was taken at a reception at Claridge's, to mark the tenth anniversary of the Arcadia Institution.'

'The Arcadia Institution?' I repeated.

'A little organisation I used to run. The prime minister graced us with his presence. It was purely professional.'

'But you must have known Adam Lang at Cambridge,' I persisted.

'Not really. One summer term, our paths crossed. That was it.'

'Can you remember much about him?' I took out my notebook.

Emmett eyed it warily. 'No one's mentioned the Cambridge connection between us in all these years. I've barely thought about it myself until this moment. I don't think I can tell you anything worth writing down.'

'But you performed together?'

'In one summer revue. There were a hundred members, you know.'

'So he made no impression on you?'

'None. Obviously if I'd known he was going to become prime minister, I'd have taken the trouble to get to know him better.'

'Can I show you something else?' I said, taking out the other photographs. Now that I looked at them again, it was clear that Emmett featured in several. Indeed, he was unmistakably the man on the summer picnic, giving a thumbs-up behind Lang's back, while the future prime minister did a Bogart with his joint and was fed strawberries and champagne.

I reached across and handed them to Emmett, who pushed up his glasses again so that he could study the pictures with his naked eyes.

'Oh my,' he said. 'Is that what I think it is? Let's hope he didn't inhale.'

'But that is you standing behind him, isn't it?'

'I do believe it is. And I'm on the point of issuing a stern warning to him on the perils of drug abuse. Can't you just sense it forming on my lips?' He gave the pictures back to me. 'Does Mr Lang really want these published in his memoirs? If so, I'd prefer it if I weren't identified. My children would be mortified. They're so much more puritanical than we were.'

'Can you tell me the names of any of the others? The girls, perhaps?'

'I'm sorry. That summer is just a blur, a long and happy blur. The world may have been going to pieces around us, but we were making merry.'

'You must have been lucky,' I said, 'given you were at Yale in the late sixties, to avoid being drafted to Vietnam.'

'You know the old saying: "If you had the dough, you didn't have to go." I got a student deferment. Now,' he said, picking up a pen and opening a notebook. 'You were going to tell me where you got those pictures.'

'Does the name Michael McAra mean anything to you?'

'No. Should it?' He answered just a touch too quickly, I thought.

'McAra was my predecessor on the Lang memoirs,' I said. 'He was the one who ordered the pictures from England. He drove up here from Martha's Vineyard to see you nearly three weeks ago and died a few hours afterwards.'

'Drove up to see *me*?' Emmett shook his head. 'I'm afraid you're mistaken.'

'The vehicle McAra was driving had your address programmed into its navigation system.'

'Well, I can't think why that should be the case.' Emmett stroked his chin and seemed to weigh the matter carefully. 'No, I really can't. And even if it's true, it doesn't prove he actually made the journey. How did he die?'

'He drowned.'

'I'm very sorry to hear it. I've never believed the myth that death by drowning is painless, have you? I'm sure it must be agonising.'

'The police never said anything to you about this?'

'No. I've had no contact with the police whatsoever.'

'Were you here that weekend? January the 11th and 12th?'

Emmett sighed. 'A less equable man than I would start to find your questions impertinent.' He went over to the door. 'Nancy!' he called. 'Our visitor wishes to know where we were on the weekend of the 11th and 12th of January. Do we possess that information?'

He stood holding the door open and gave me an unfriendly smile. When Mrs Emmett appeared, he didn't bother to introduce me.

She was carrying a desk diary. 'That was the Colorado weekend,' she said and showed the book to her husband.

'Of course it was,' he said. 'We were at the Aspen Institute.' He flourished the page at me. '"Bipolar Relationships in a Multipolar World".'

'Sounds fun.'

'It was.' He closed the diary with a snap. 'I was the main speaker.'

'You were there the whole weekend?'

'*I* was,' said Mrs Emmett. 'I stayed for the skiing. Emmett flew back on Sunday, didn't you, darling?'

'So you could have seen McAra,' I said to him.

'I could have, but I didn't.'

'Just to return to Cambridge—' I began.

'No,' he said, holding up his hand. 'Please. If you don't mind, let's *not* return to Cambridge. I've said all I have to say on the matter. Nancy?'

She jumped when he addressed her. 'Emmett?'

'Show our friend here out, would you?'

As we shook hands, he said, 'I am an avid reader of political memoirs. I shall be sure to get hold of Mr Lang's book when it appears.'

'Perhaps he'll send you a copy,' I said, 'for old times' sake.'

'I doubt it very much,' he replied. 'The gate will open automatically. Be sure to make a right at the bottom of the drive. If you turn left, the road will take you deeper into the woods and you'll never be seen again.'

MRS EMMETT closed the door behind me before I'd even reached the bottom step. I could sense her husband watching me from his study window as I walked across the damp grass to the Ford. At the bottom of the drive, while I waited for the gate to open, the wind moved suddenly through the trees on either side, laying a heavy lash of rainwater across the car. Unnerved, I pulled out into the empty road and headed back the way I had come.

Turn around where possible.

I stopped the Ford, grabbed the navigation system in both hands and twisted and yanked it. It came away from the front panel with a satisfying twang of breaking cables, and I tossed it into the passenger foot well.

Nature, I discovered, mingles an unexpected element of anger in with fear. My instinct at that moment was not to run; it was to get back at the supercilious Emmett. So instead of trying to find my way back to the interstate, I followed the road signs to Belmont, a sprawling, leafy, wealthy town of terrifying cleanliness and orderliness. I cruised along the wide boulevards until at last I came to something that resembled the middle of town. This time, when I parked my car, I took my suitcase with me.

I was on a road called Leonard Street, a curve of shops with coloured canopies. It offered me various things I didn't need—a real-estate agent, a jeweller, a hairdresser—and one thing I did: an Internet café. I ordered coffee and a bagel and took a seat away from the window. I put down my case, clicked on Google and typed in 'Paul Emmett' + 'Arcadia Institution'.

ACCORDING to www.arcadiainstitution.org, the Arcadia Institution was founded in August 1991 on the fiftieth anniversary of the first summit meeting between Prime Minister Winston Churchill and President Franklin D. Roosevelt, at Placentia Bay in Newfoundland. The institution had offices in London and Washington, and its aim was 'to further Anglo-American relations and foster the timeless ideals of democracy and free speech for which our two nations have always stood'. This was to be achieved 'through seminars, policy programmes, conferences and leadership development initiatives', and through the funding of ten annual Arcadia Scholarships, for postgraduate research into 'cultural, political and strategic subjects of mutual interest to Britain and the United States'.

Paul Emmett was the institution's first president and CEO, and the website usefully offered his life in a paragraph: born Chicago 1949; graduate of Yale University and St John's College, Cambridge (Rhodes scholar); lecturer in international affairs at Harvard University, 1975–79, and Howard T. Polk III Professor of Foreign Relations, 1979–91; thereafter the founding head of the Arcadia Institution; President Emeritus since 2007; publications included *Whither Though Goest: The Special Relationship 1940–1956*, and *The Triumphant Generation: America, Britain and the New World Order*.

I clicked on the Arcadia board of trustees, then laboriously entered their names, together with Adam Lang's, into the search engine. Steven D. Engler, former US defence secretary, had praised Lang's courage on the op-ed page of the *New York Times*. Lord Leghorn, former British foreign secretary, had made a hand-wringing speech in the House of Lords, regretting the situation in the Middle East but calling the prime minister 'a man of sincerity'. Raymond T. Streicher, former US ambassador to London, had been vocal in his support when Lang flew to Washington to pick up his Presidential Medal of Freedom.

I was starting to weary of the whole procedure until I typed in 'Arthur

Prussia, of the Hallington Group'. I got a one-year-old press release:

> LONDON—The Hallington Group is pleased to announce that Adam Lang, the former prime minister of Great Britain, will be joining the company as a strategic consultant.
>
> Arthur Prussia, Hallington's president and CEO, said: 'Adam Lang is one of the world's most respected and experienced statesmen, and we are honoured to be able to draw on his well of experience.'
>
> Adam Lang said: 'I welcome the challenge of working with a company of such global reach, commitment to democracy, and renowned integrity.'

The Hallington Group rang only the faintest of bells, so I looked it up. It had 600 employees, twenty-four worldwide offices, a mere 400 investors, mainly Saudi, and $35 billion of funds at its disposal. Its subsidiaries manufactured cluster bombs, mobile howitzers, interceptor missiles, tanks, tank-busting helicopters, nuclear centrifuges, aircraft carriers. It owned a company that provided security for contractors in the Middle East, and another that carried out surveillance operations and data checks worldwide. Two members of its main board had been senior directors of the CIA.

I know the Internet is the stuff a paranoiac's dreams are made of. But I also know the wisdom of the old saying that a paranoiac is simply a person in full possession of the facts. I typed in 'Arcadia Institution' + 'Hallington Group' + 'CIA', clicked on a story from the *Washington Post*, headed HALLINGTON JET LINKED TO CIA 'TORTURE FLIGHTS', and scrolled down to the relevant part:

> The Hallington Gulfstream Four was clandestinely photographed—minus its corporate logo—at the Stare Kiejkuty military base in Poland, where the CIA is believed to have maintained a secret detention center, on February 18. This was two days after four British citizens—Nasir Ashraf, Shakeel Qazi, Salim Khan, and Faruk Ahmed—were allegedly kidnapped by CIA operatives from Peshawar, Pakistan. Mr Ashraf is reported to have died of heart failure after the interrogation procedure known as 'water boarding.'
>
> Between February and July of that year, the jet made 51 visits to Guantánamo and 82 visits to Washington Dulles International Airport as well as landings at US air bases in Germany. The plane's flight log also shows visits to Afghanistan, Morocco, Dubai, Jordan, Italy, Japan,

Switzerland, Azerbaijan, and the Czech Republic.

A spokesman for Hallington confirmed that the Gulfstream had been frequently leased to other operators but insisted the company had no knowledge of the uses to which it might have been put.

Water boarding? I had never heard of it. It sounded harmless enough, a kind of healthy outdoor sport. I looked it up on a website.

Water boarding consists of tightly binding a prisoner to an inclined board so that the victim's feet are higher than the head. Cloth or cellophane is used to cover the prisoner's face, onto which the interrogator pours a continuous stream of water. Although some liquid may enter the victim's lungs, it is the psychological sensation of being under water that makes water boarding so effective. A gag reflex is triggered, the prisoner feels himself to be drowning, and almost instantly begs to be released. CIA officers who have been subjected to water boarding as part of their training have lasted an average of fourteen seconds before caving in. Al-Qaeda's toughest prisoner, and alleged mastermind of the 9/11 bombings, Khalid Sheikh Mohammed, won the admiration of his CIA interrogators when he lasted two and a half minutes before begging to confess.

Water boarding can cause severe pain and damage to the lungs, brain damage due to oxygen deprivation, limb breakage and dislocation due to struggling against restraints, and long-term psychological trauma. According to an investigation by ABC News, the CIA was authorized to use water boarding in mid-March 2002, and recruited a cadre of fourteen interrogators trained in the technique.

I sat back in my chair and thought of various things. I thought, especially, of Emmett's comment about McAra's death—that drowning wasn't painless but agonising. It had struck me at the time as an odd thing to say. I flexed my fingers and typed in a fresh search: 'Paul Emmett' + 'CIA'.

Immediately, the screen filled with results: articles by Emmett that happened to mention the CIA; articles by others about the CIA that also contained references to Emmett; articles about the Arcadia Institution in which the words 'CIA' and 'Emmett' featured. I must have gone through thirty or forty in all, until I came to one that sounded promising. The web page, from a site called spooks-on-campus.org, quoted Senator Frank Church's Select Committee report on the CIA, published in 1976:

> The Central Intelligence Agency is now using several hundred American academics . . . who, in addition to providing leads and making introductions for intelligence purposes, occasionally write books and other material to be used for propaganda purposes abroad.

Beneath it was a hyperlinked list of twenty names, among them Emmett's. When I clicked on it, I felt as though I had fallen through a trap door.

> Yale graduate Paul Emmett was reported by CIA whistleblower Frank Molinari to have joined the Agency as an officer in 1969 or 1970, where he was assigned to the Foreign Resources Division of the Directorate of Operations. (Source: *Inside the Agency,* Amsterdam, 1977)

'Oh no,' I said quietly. 'No, no. That can't be right.'

I must have stared at the screen for a full minute. Then I turned off the computer, took a final sip of coffee, picked up my suitcase and put a ten-dollar bill on the table. I walked briskly up the street towards the Ford, and once I was behind the wheel I locked myself in.

I took out the photographs again and flicked through them until I came to the one of Lang and Emmett onstage together. I turned the picture over, and the more I considered the number scrawled on the back, the more obvious it seemed that there was only one course of action open to me. The fact that I would, once again, be trailing in the footsteps of McAra could not be helped.

I took out my mobile phone, scrolled down to where the number was stored and called Richard Rycart.

This time, he answered within a few seconds.

'So you rang back,' he said quietly. 'I had a feeling you would, whoever you are. Not many people have this number.' He waited for me to reply. 'Well, my friend, are you going to stay on the line this time?'

'Yes,' I said, but I didn't know how to begin. I kept thinking of Lang, of what he would think if he could see me talking to his would-be nemesis. I was breaking every rule in the ghosting guidebook. I was in breach of the confidentiality agreement I'd signed. It was professional suicide.

'I tried to call you back a couple of times,' he said, with a hint of reproach.

'I know.' I found my voice at last. 'I'm sorry. I found your number written down somewhere. I didn't know whose it was. I called it on the off chance. It didn't seem right to be talking to you.'

'Why not?'

I took the plunge. 'I'm working for Adam Lang. I—'

'Don't tell me your name,' he said quickly. 'Don't use any names. Keep everything nonspecific. Where exactly did you find my number?'

His urgency unnerved me. 'On the back of a photograph.'

'What sort of photograph?'

'Of my client's days at university. My predecessor had it.'

'Did he, by God?' Now it was Rycart's turn to pause.

'You sound shocked,' I said.

'Yes, well, it ties in with something he said to me.'

'I've been to see one of the people in the photograph. I thought you might be able to help me.'

'Where are you? Without being too specific?'

'In New England.'

'Can you get to the city where I am, right away? Where I work?'

'I suppose so,' I said doubtfully. 'I have a car. I could drive.'

'No, don't drive. Flying's safer than the roads.'

'That's what the airlines say.'

'If I was in your position,' whispered Rycart fiercely, 'I wouldn't joke. Go to the nearest airport. Catch the first available plane. Text me the flight number, nothing else. I'll arrange for someone to collect you when you land.'

'But how will they know what I look like?'

'They won't. You'll have to look out for them.'

I started to raise a fresh objection, but it was too late. He had hung up.

I DROVE OUT of Belmont without any clear idea of the route I was supposed to take. I kept my eyes open for signs to Boston and eventually crossed a big river and joined the interstate, heading east.

It was not yet three in the afternoon, but already the day was darkening. Up ahead, the lights of the big jets fell towards Logan like shooting stars. Logan Airport, for those who have never had the pleasure, sits in the middle of Boston Harbor, approached from the south by a long tunnel. As the road descended underground, I asked myself whether I would really go through with this. When I rose again, nearly a mile later, I still hadn't decided.

I followed the signs to the long-term car park and was just reversing into a bay when my phone rang. The incoming number was unfamiliar. I almost didn't answer. When I did, a voice said, 'What on earth are you doing?'

It was Ruth Lang.

'Working,' I said.

'Really? You're not at your hotel. They told me you hadn't even checked in.'

I flailed around for an adequate lie. 'I went to New York to see John Maddox, to talk about the structure of the book, in view of'—a tactful euphemism was needed—'the changed circumstances.'

'I was worried about you,' she said. 'I've been thinking about what we discussed last night, and the more I go over things, the more worried I get. Adam keeps calling and I keep not answering. When will you be back?'

'I'm not sure.'

'Tonight?'

'I'll try.'

'Do, if you can.' She lowered her voice. 'It's Dep's night off. I'll cook.'

'Is that supposed to be an incentive?'

'You rude man.' She laughed, then rang off without saying goodbye.

I tapped my phone against my teeth. The prospect of a confiding fireside talk with Ruth, perhaps to be followed by a second round in her vigorous embrace, was not without its attractions. I could call Rycart and tell him I'd changed my mind. Undecided, I took my case out of the car and wheeled it through the puddles towards the waiting bus. Once I was aboard, I cradled it next to me and studied the airport map. At that point yet another choice presented itself. Terminal B—the shuttle to New York and Rycart—or Terminal E—international departures and an evening flight back to London? I hadn't considered that before. I had my passport. I could simply walk away.

I got off at Terminal B, bought my ticket, sent a text message to Rycart, and caught the US Airways Shuttle to New York.

WE TOUCHED DOWN at LaGuardia at six minutes past six—I checked my watch—and by twenty past I was heading into the busy arrivals hall. I scanned the bewildering array of faces, wondering if Rycart himself had turned out to greet me. The usual lugubrious drivers were waiting, holding the names of their passengers against their chests. Rycart had implied that I'd recognise the right person when I saw him, and I did, and my heart almost stopped. He was standing apart from the others—wan-faced, dark-haired, tall, heavyset, early fifties, in a badly fitting chain-store suit—and he was holding a small blackboard on which was chalked *Mike McAra*. Even his eyes were as I had imagined McAra's to be: crafty and colourless.

He nodded to my suitcase. 'You OK with that.' It was a statement, not a question, but I didn't care. I'd never been more pleased to hear a New York accent in my life. He turned on his heel and I followed him out of the hall.

He brought round his car, and as I struggled to get my case into the back seat he stared straight ahead, discouraging conversation. Not that there was much time to talk. Barely had we left the perimeter of the airport than we were pulling up in front of a big, glass-fronted hotel overlooking Grand Central Parkway. He shifted his heavy body round in his seat to address me.

'If you need to make contact, use this,' he said, giving me a brand-new cellphone, still in its plastic wrapper. 'The chip inside has twenty dollars' worth of calls on it. Turn your old phone off. Pay for your room in advance, with cash. Have you got enough? It'll be about three hundred bucks.'

I nodded.

'You have a reservation for one night.' He wriggled his wallet out from his back pocket. 'This is the card you use to guarantee the extras. The name on it is the name you register under. Use a UK address that isn't your own. Pay for any extras in cash. This is the telephone number you use to make contact.'

'You used to be a cop,' I said. I took the credit card and a torn-out strip of paper with a number written on it, both warm from the heat of his body.

'Don't use the Internet. Don't speak to strangers. And especially avoid any women who might try to come on to you.'

'You sound like my mother.'

His face didn't flicker. We sat there for a few seconds. 'Well,' he said impatiently. He waved a meaty hand at me. 'That's it.'

As I went through the revolving door into the lobby, I checked the card. 'I have a reservation,' I said to the desk clerk, 'in the name of Clive Dixon.'

I was on the clerk's computer, and my card was good. The room rate was $275. I filled out the reservation form and gave as my false address the number of Kate's terraced house in Shepherd's Bush and the street of Rick's London club. When I said I wanted to pay in cash, he took the notes as if they were the strangest things he had ever seen.

I declined to be assisted with my bags, took the elevator to the sixth floor and stuck the electronic keycard into the door. My room had a view across Grand Central Parkway to the East River. I opened the minibar. I didn't even bother to find a glass, but drank straight from the miniature bottle.

It must have been twenty minutes and a second miniature later that my new telephone suddenly glowed blue and purred ominously. I answered it.

'It's me,' said Rycart. 'Are you alone?'

'Yes.'

'Open the door, then.'

He was standing in the corridor, his phone to his ear. Beside him was the driver who had met me at LaGuardia.

'All right, Frank,' said Rycart to his minder. 'I'll take it from here. You keep an eye out in the lobby.'

He pocketed his phone as Frank plodded back to the elevators. Rycart was what my mother would have called 'handsome, and knows it': a striking profile, narrow-set blue eyes and that swept-back waterfall of hair the cartoonists loved. He looked a lot younger than sixty. As he came into the room, he nodded at the empty bottle in my hand. 'Tough day?'

'You could say that.' I closed the door.

He went straight over to the window and drew the curtains. 'My apologies for the location,' he said, 'but I tend to be recognised in Manhattan. Especially after yesterday. Did Frank look after you all right?'

'I've rarely had a warmer welcome.'

'I know what you mean, but he's a useful guy. Ex-NYPD. He handles security for me. I'm not exactly popular right now, as you can imagine.'

'Can I get you something to drink?'

'Water would be fine.' He prowled around the room while I poured him a glass. He checked the bathroom, even the closet.

'What is it?' I said. 'Do you think this is a trap?'

'It crossed my mind. Let's face it, you do work for Lang.'

'I met him for the first time on Monday,' I said. 'I don't even know him.'

Rycart laughed. 'Who does? I worked with him for fifteen years, and I don't have a clue where he's coming from. Mike McAra didn't, either, and he was with him from the beginning.'

'His wife said more or less the same thing to me.'

'Well, there you go. If someone as sharp as Ruth doesn't get him—and she's married to him, for God's sake—what hope do the rest of us have? The man's a mystery. Thanks.' Rycart took the water. He sipped it thoughtfully, studying me. 'But you sound as though you're starting to unravel him.'

'I feel as though I'm the one who's unravelling, quite frankly.'

'Let's sit down,' said Rycart, patting my shoulder, 'and you can tell me all about it.'

The gesture reminded me of Lang. A great man's charm. They made me feel like a minnow swimming between sharks. I sat down carefully in one of the two small armchairs. Rycart sat opposite me.

'So,' he said. 'How do we begin? You know who I am. Who are you?'

'I'm a professional ghostwriter,' I said. 'I was brought in to rewrite Adam Lang's memoirs after Mike McAra died. I know nothing about politics. It's as if I've stepped through the looking glass.'

'Tell me what you've found out.'

I hemmed and hawed. 'Perhaps you could tell me about McAra first.'

'If you like.' Rycart shrugged. 'What can I say? Mike was the consummate professional. Everyone expected Lang would fire him when he became leader and bring in his own man. But Mike was too useful. He knew the party inside out. What else do you want to know?'

'What was he like, as a person?'

'As a *person*? Well, he had no life outside politics, so Lang was everything to him. He was obsessive, a detail man. Almost everything Adam wasn't, Mike was. Maybe that was why he stayed on, right through Downing Street and out again, long after the others had cashed in and gone to make money. No fancy corporate jobs for our Mike. He was very loyal to Adam.'

'Not that loyal,' I said. 'Not if he was in touch with you.'

'That was only at the very end. You mentioned a photograph. Can I see it?'

When I fetched the envelope, his face had the same greedy expression as Emmett's, but when he saw the picture he couldn't hide his disappointment.

'Is this it?' he said. 'Just a bunch of privileged white kids doing a song-and-dance act?'

'It's a bit more interesting than that,' I said. 'For a start, why's your number on the back of it?'

Rycart gave me a sly look. 'Why exactly should I help you?'

'Why exactly should *I* help *you*?'

We stared at one another. Eventually he grinned, showing large, polished white teeth. 'You should have been a politician,' he said.

'I'm learning from the best.'

He bowed modestly, thinking I meant him, but it was Lang I had in mind. Vanity was his weakness, I realised. I could imagine how deftly Lang would have flattered him, and what a blow his sacking must have been to his ego.

'If you double-cross me,' he said, 'you'll pay for it. And if you doubt my willingness to hold a grudge and eventually settle the score, ask Adam Lang.'

'Fine,' I said.

He patrolled up and down in front of the bed. 'This ICC business,' he said, 'it's only hit the headlines in the past week, but I've been pursuing this thing for *years*. Iraq, rendition, torture, Guantánamo—what's been done in this so-called war on terror is illegal under international law, just as much as anything that happened in Kosovo or Liberia. The hypocrisy is nauseating.'

He seemed to realise he was starting on a speech he'd made too many times before and checked himself. He took a sip of water. 'Anyway, I could sense the political climate changing. But what I needed was just one piece of evidence that would meet the legal standard of proof, and I didn't have it.

'Then suddenly, just before Christmas, there it was. It came through the post, no covering letter. "Top Secret: Memorandum from the Prime Minister to the Secretary of State for Defence". It was five years old, written when I was still foreign secretary, but I'd no idea it existed. A directive from the British prime minister for these four poor bastards to be snatched off the streets in Pakistan by the SAS and handed over to the CIA.'

'A war crime,' I said.

'A war crime,' he agreed. 'A minor one, OK. But so what? In the end, they only got Al Capone for tax evasion. I carried out a few discreet checks to make sure the memo was authentic, then I took it to The Hague in person.'

'You'd no idea who it came from?'

'Not until my anonymous source called and told me. And just you wait till Lang hears who it was.' He leaned in close to me. 'Mike McAra!'

Looking back, I suppose I already knew it. But to see Rycart's exultation at that moment was to appreciate the scale of McAra's treachery.

'*He* called *me*! Can you believe that?'

'When did he call?'

'About three weeks after I first got the document. The 8th of January? The 9th? Something like that. "Hello, Richard. Did you get the present I sent you?" I almost had a heart attack. Then I had to shut him up quickly. Because of course the phone lines at the UN are all bugged.'

'Are they?' I was still trying to absorb everything.

'Oh, completely. The National Security Agency monitors every word. We're briefed to use disposable mobile phones, avoid mentioning specifics and change our numbers as often as possible—that way we can at least keep a bit ahead of them. So I gave Mike a brand-new number I'd not used before and asked him to call me straight back.'

'Ah,' I said. 'I see. He must have scribbled the number on the back of the photograph he was holding at the time.'

'And then he called me,' said Rycart. 'It struck me that he didn't sound his usual self. You asked me what he was like. Well, he was a tough operator. Adam relied on Mike to do the dirty work. He was sharp, businesslike, almost brutal, especially on the phone. My private office used to call him the McHorror. But that day, I remember, his voice was flat. He sounded broken. He said he'd just spent the past year in the archives in Cambridge, working on Adam's memoirs, going over our whole time in government, getting disillusioned with it all. He said that that was where he'd found the memorandum about Operation Tempest. But that was just the tip of the iceberg, he said. He'd just discovered something much more important, something that made sense of everything that had gone wrong while we were in power.'

I could hardly breathe. 'What was it?'

Rycart laughed. 'Well, I did ask him that, but he wouldn't tell me over the phone. He wanted to meet me to discuss it face-to-face. The only thing he would say was that the key to it could be found in Lang's autobiography, if anyone bothered to check, that it was all there in the beginning.'

'Those were his exact words?'

'Pretty much. He said he'd call me in a day or two to fix a meeting. But I heard nothing, then about a week later it was in the press that he was dead. And nobody else ever called me on that phone, because hardly anyone had that number. So you can imagine why I was so excited when it started ringing again. And now I think you should tell me exactly what the hell is going on.'

'I will. One more thing, though. Why didn't you tell the police?'

'Discussions at The Hague were at a delicate stage. If I'd told the police that McAra had been in contact with me, they'd have wanted to know why. It would have got back to Lang, and he'd have made some kind of pre-emptive move against the ICC. Besides, I thought it was accepted that Mike had killed himself, because he was depressed, drunk, or both. I'd only have confirmed what they already knew. He was certainly in a poor state when he rang me.'

'And I can tell you why,' I said. 'What he'd just found out was that one of the men in that picture with Lang at Cambridge—the picture McAra had in his hand when he spoke to you—was an officer in the CIA.'

Rycart stopped pacing. He turned towards me. 'He was *what*?'

'His name is Paul Emmett.' Suddenly I couldn't get the words out fast enough. I was desperate to unburden myself—to let someone else try to make sense of it. 'He later became a professor at Harvard. Then he went on to run something called the Arcadia Institution. Have you heard of it?'

'Of course I've heard of it, and I've always steered well clear of it, precisely because I've always thought it had CIA written all over it.' Rycart sat down. He seemed stunned.

'But is that really plausible?' I asked. 'Would someone join the CIA, then immediately be sent off to do postgraduate research in another country?'

'I'd say that's highly plausible. What better cover could you want? And where better than a university to spot the future best and brightest?' He held out his hand. 'Show me the photograph again. Which one is Emmett?'

I pointed Emmett out. 'I've no proof. I just found his name on one of those paranoid web sites. They said he joined the CIA after he left Yale, which must have been about three years before this was taken.'

'Oh, I can believe it,' said Rycart, studying him intently. 'What's really suspicious is that he should have known Lang.'

'No,' I said, 'what's *really* suspicious is that a matter of hours after McAra tracked down Emmett to his house near Boston, he was found washed up dead on a beach in Martha's Vineyard.'

AFTER THAT I told him everything I'd discovered. I told him about the tides and the flashlights on the beach at Lambert's Cove. I told him about Ruth's description of McAra's argument with Lang on the eve of his death, and about Lang's reluctance to discuss his Cambridge years, and the way he'd tried to conceal that he'd become politically active immediately after university rather than two years later. I described how McAra had turned up details that destroyed Lang's account of his early years. That was presumably what he meant when he said that the key to everything was in the beginning of Lang's autobiography. I told him how the satellite navigation system in the Ford had taken me to Emmett's doorstep, and how strangely Emmett had behaved. And the more I talked, the more excited Rycart became.

'Just suppose,' he said, pacing up and down again, 'that it was Emmett who originally suggested to Lang that he should think about a career in politics. What year did he join?'

'Nineteen seventy-five.'

'That would make perfect sense. Remember what Britain was like in '75? The security services were out of control, spying on the prime minister. The economy was collapsing. There were strikes, riots. It wouldn't be a surprise if the CIA had recruited a few bright young things and encouraged them to make their careers in useful places—the civil service, the media, politics. It's what they do everywhere else, after all.'

'But not in Britain, surely,' I said. 'We're an ally.'

Rycart looked at me with contempt. 'Of course they were active in Britain! They still are. They have a head of station in London and a huge staff. I could name half a dozen MPs right now who are in regular contact with the CIA. In fact—' He stopped pacing. 'That's a thought!' He whirled round to look at me. 'Does the name Reg Giffen mean anything to you?'

'Vaguely.'

'Reg Giffen—Sir Reginald Giffen, later Lord Giffen, now dead Giffen, thank God—spent so long making speeches in the House of Commons on behalf of the Americans, we used to call him the member for Michigan. He announced his resignation as an MP in the first week of the 1983 general election campaign, and it caught everyone by surprise, apart from one very enterprising and photogenic young party member, who just happened to have moved into Giffen's constituency six months earlier.'

'And who got the nomination to become the party's candidate,' I said, 'and who then won one of the safest seats in the country when he was only thirty.' The story of Lang's rise was legendary. 'But you can't really think the CIA asked Giffen to help fix it so that Lang could get into parliament.'

'Use your imagination! Imagine you're Professor Emmett, back in Harvard, writing unreadable bilge about the alliance of the English-speaking peoples. Haven't you got potentially the most amazing agent in history on your hands? A man already being talked about as a future party leader? A possible prime minister? Aren't you going to persuade the Agency's powers that be to do everything they can to further his career? I was already in parliament when Lang arrived. I watched him streak past all of us.' He scowled at the memory. 'Of course he had *help*. He had no real connection with the party. We couldn't begin to understand what made him tick.'

'Surely that's the point of him,' I said. 'He didn't have an ideology.'

'He may not have had an ideology, but he sure as hell had an agenda.' Rycart sat down again. He leaned towards me. 'OK. Here's a quiz for you. Name me one decision that Adam Lang took as prime minister that wasn't in the interests of the United States of America.'

I was silent.

'Come on,' he said. 'Name one thing he did that Washington wouldn't have approved of. Let's think.' He held up his thumb. 'One: deployment of British troops to the Middle East, against the advice of just about every senior commander in our armed forces and all our ambassadors who know the region. Two'—up went his right index finger—'failure to demand any quid pro quo from the White House in terms of reconstruction contracts for British firms. Three: the stationing on British soil of an American missile defence system that does nothing for our security—that in fact makes us a more obvious target for a first strike and provides protection only for the US. Four: the purchase, for fifty billion dollars, of an American nuclear missile system that we call "independent" but that we couldn't fire without US approval. Five: a treaty that allows the US to extradite our citizens to stand trial in America but doesn't allow us to do the same to theirs. Six: collusion in the illegal kidnapping, torture, imprisonment and even murder of our own citizens. Seven—'

'All right,' I said, holding up my hand. 'I get the message.'

'I have friends in Washington who were *embarrassed* by how much support Lang gave and how little he got in return.' Rycart laughed ruefully and shook his head. 'You know, I'm almost relieved to discover there might be a rational explanation for what we got up to while he was prime minister. If he was working for the CIA it makes sense. So now,' he said, patting my knee, 'the question is: what are we going to do about it?'

I didn't like the sound of that first person plural.

'Well,' I said, wincing slightly, 'I'm in a tricky position. I have a legal obligation not to divulge anything I hear in the course of my work to a third party.'

'It's too late to stop now.'

I didn't like the sound of that, either.

'We don't actually have any proof,' I pointed out. 'We don't even know for sure that *Emmett* was in the CIA, let alone that he recruited Lang. I mean, how is this relationship supposed to have worked after Lang got into Number Ten? Did he have a secret radio transmitter hidden in the attic?'

'Contact could be managed easily enough,' said Rycart. 'Emmett was always coming to London, because of Arcadia. It was the perfect front. In fact, I wouldn't be surprised if the whole institution wasn't set up as part of the covert operation to run Lang. The timing would fit.'

'But there's still no *proof*,' I repeated, 'and short of Lang confessing, or Emmett confessing, or the CIA opening their files, there never will be.'

'Then you'll just have to get some proof,' said Rycart flatly.

'What?' My mouth sagged; my everything sagged.

'You're in the perfect position,' Rycart went on. 'He trusts you. He lets you ask him whatever you like, even record his answers. You can confront him with the allegation. He'll deny it, but the mere fact you're laying the evidence in front of him will put the story on the record.'

'No it won't. The discs are his property.'

'The discs can be subpoenaed by the war crimes court, as evidence of his direct complicity with the CIA rendition programme.'

'What if I don't make any recordings?'

'In that case, I'll suggest to the prosecutor that she subpoenas *you*.'

'What if I deny the whole story?'

'Then I'll give her this,' said Rycart, and opened his jacket to show a small microphone clipped to his shirt, with a wire trailing into his inside pocket.

'Frank is recording every word down in the lobby. Oh, don't look so shocked. Did you expect me to come to a meeting with a complete stranger, who's working for Lang, without taking precautions? Except you're not working for Lang any more.' He smiled, showing again that row of teeth, more brilliantly white than anything in nature. 'You're working for me.'

EIGHT

After a few seconds I started to swear, fluently and indiscriminately. I was swearing at Rycart and at my own stupidity, at Frank and at whoever would one day transcribe the disc. I was swearing at the war crimes prosecutor, at the court, the judges, the media. And I would have gone on for a lot longer if my telephone hadn't started to ring—the one I'd brought from London. Needless to say, I'd forgotten to switch it off.

'Don't answer it,' warned Rycart. 'It'll lead them straight to us.'

I looked at the incoming number. 'It's Amelia Bly. It could be important.'

'Amelia Bly,' repeated Rycart, his voice a blend of awe and lust. 'I haven't seen her for a while.' He hesitated. 'If they're monitoring you, they can fix your location to within a hundred yards, and this hotel is the only building where you're likely to be.'

The phone continued to throb. 'To hell with it,' I said. 'I'm not taking orders from you.' I pressed the green button. 'Hi,' I said. 'Amelia.'

'Good evening,' she said crisply. 'I have Adam for you.'

I mouthed, 'It's Adam Lang,' at Rycart and waved my hand to warn him against speaking. An instant later the familiar, classless voice filled my ear.

'I was just speaking to Ruth,' he said. 'She tells me you're in New York.'

'That's right.'

'So am I. Whereabouts are you?'

'I'm not sure exactly, Adam. I haven't checked in anywhere yet.'

'We're at the Waldorf,' said Lang. 'Why don't you come over?'

'Hold on a second, Adam.' I pressed MUTE and turned to Rycart. 'He wants me to go over and see him at the Waldorf.'

'It'll look odd if you don't go,' Rycart said. 'Tell him yes, then hang up.'

I pressed MUTE again. 'Hi, Adam,' I said, trying to keep the tension out of my voice. 'That's great. I'll be right over.'

Rycart passed his finger across his throat.

'What brings you to New York, in any case?' asked Lang.

'I wanted to see John Maddox.'

'Right. And how was he?'

'Fine. Listen, I've got to go now.'

Rycart's throat slashing was becoming ever more urgent.

'We've had a great couple of days,' continued Lang, as if he hadn't heard me. 'The Americans have been fantastic. You know, it's in the tough times that you find out who your real friends are.'

Was it my imagination, or did he freight those words with extra emphasis for my benefit?

'Great. I'll be with you as fast as I can, Adam.'

I ended the call. My hand was shaking.

'Well done,' said Rycart. 'How did he sound?'

'Cheerful.'

'Well, we'll just have to do something about that, won't we?' He was on his feet, retrieving his coat from the bed. 'We have about ten minutes to get out of here. Get your stuff together.'

I gathered up the photographs and put them back in the case.

The elevator down to the lobby stopped at every floor, and Rycart grew more and more nervous.

'We mustn't be seen together,' he muttered as we stepped out at the ground floor. 'You hang back. We'll meet you in the car park.'

Frank was already on his feet, and the two of them set off without a word. I took my time crossing the lobby, circling the groups of chattering guests, keeping my head down. There was something so ludicrous about this whole situation that, as I joined the crush at the door, I found myself smiling. It was like a Feydeau farce: each scene more far-fetched than the last, yet a logical development of it. I stood in line until my turn came, and that was when I saw Emmett, or thought I did, and suddenly I wasn't smiling any more.

The hotel had one of those big revolving doors, with compartments that hold five or six people, who are obliged to shuffle forward like convicts on a chain gang. I was in the middle of the outgoing group, which is probably why Emmett didn't see me. He had a man on either side of him, and they were in the compartment that was swinging into the hotel.

We came out into the night and in my anxiety to get away I stumbled. My suitcase toppled onto its side and I dragged it along as if it were a stubborn dog. Across the parking lot a pair of headlights came on, then drove straight at me. The car swerved and the rear passenger door flew open.

'Get in,' said Rycart.

The speed with which Frank accelerated away served to slam the door shut after me and threw me back in my seat.

'I just saw Emmett,' I said.

Rycart exchanged looks in the mirror with his driver. 'Are you sure?'

'No.'

'Did he see you?'

'No.'

'Are you sure?'

'Yes.'

We sped down the access road and pulled into the heavy traffic heading towards Manhattan.

'They could have followed us from LaGuardia,' said Frank.

'Why did they hold back?' asked Rycart.

'Could be they were waiting for Emmett to make a positive ID.'

Up to that point, I hadn't taken Rycart's amateur tradecraft too seriously, but now I felt a fresh surge of panic.

'Listen,' I said, 'I don't think it's a good idea for me to go and see Lang right now. Assuming that was Emmett, Lang must have been alerted to what I've been doing. He'll know I've shown Emmett the photographs.'

'So? What do you think he's going to do about it?' asked Rycart. 'Drown you in his bathtub at the Waldorf-Astoria?'

'Yeah, right,' said Frank. His shoulders shook with amusement. 'As if.'

I felt sick, and despite the freezing night I lowered the window. The wind was blowing from the east, gusting off the river, carrying on its cold, industrial edge the sickly tang of aviation fuel. I can still taste it at the back of my throat whenever I think of it. That, for me, will always be the taste of fear.

'Don't I need a cover story?' I said. 'What am I supposed to tell Lang?'

'You've done nothing wrong,' said Rycart. 'You're just following up your predecessor's work. You're trying to research his Cambridge years. Don't act so guilty. Lang can't know for sure that you're on to him.'

'It's not Lang I'm worried about.'

We lapsed into silence. The night-time Manhattan skyline came into view.

'Close the window, would you?' said Rycart. 'I'm freezing to death.'

I did as he asked. 'What about the car?' I said. 'It's still at Logan Airport.'

'You can pick it up in the morning.' After a long moment, Rycart turned to look at me. 'I know Lang thinks it's personal,' he said, 'but it's not. All right, there's an element of getting my own back, I'll admit. But if we carry on licensing torture—well, what will become of us?'

'I'll tell you what will become of us,' I said savagely. 'We'll get ten million dollars for our memoirs and live happily ever after.' Once again, my nervousness was making me angry. 'You do know this is pointless, don't you? In the end he'll just retire over here on his CIA pension and tell you and your bloody war crimes court to go screw yourselves.'

'Maybe he will. But he'll be an exile. He won't be able to travel anywhere in the world, not even the handful of countries that don't recognise the ICC, because there'll always be a danger that his plane may have to put in somewhere with engine trouble or to refuel. And that's when we'll get him.'

I glanced at Rycart. He was staring straight ahead, nodding slightly.

'Or the political climate may change here one day,' he went on, 'and there'll be a public campaign to hand him over to justice. I wonder if he's thought of that. His life is going to be hell.'

'You almost make me feel sorry for him.'

Rycart gave me a sharp look. We crossed the Triborough Bridge, the tyres thumping on the joints in the road like a fast pulse.

'I feel as though I'm in a tumbril,' I said.

The journey downtown took us a while. Each time the traffic came to a stop, I thought of making a run for it. But where would I go?

'If you're that worried, we can arrange to have a fail-safe signal,' said Rycart. 'You can call me using the phone Frank gave you, let's say at ten past every hour. We don't have to speak. Just let it ring a couple of times. If you miss making the call, I won't do anything the first time. If you miss a second, I'll call Lang and tell him I hold him personally responsible for your safety.'

'Why is it that I don't find that very reassuring?'

We were almost there. I could see the Waldorf's entrance on the opposite side of Park Avenue. The area in front of the hotel was cordoned off by concrete blocks. I counted half a dozen police motorcycles waiting, four patrol cars, two large black limousines, a small crowd of cameramen and a slightly larger one of curious onlookers. My heart began to accelerate.

Rycart squeezed my arm. 'Courage, my friend. He's already lost one ghost in suspicious circumstances. He can hardly afford to lose another.'

'This can't *all* be for him, surely?' I said in amazement. 'Anyone would think he was still prime minister.'

'It seems I've only made him even more of a celebrity,' said Rycart. 'OK, good luck. We'll talk later. Pull over here, Frank.'

Frank stopped briefly on the corner of East Fiftieth Street to let me out, then eased deftly back into the traffic. The last view I ever had of Rycart was of the back of his silvery head dwindling into the Manhattan evening.

I was on my own.

I crossed the great expanse of road, yellow with taxis, and made my way past the crowds and the police. None of the cops challenged me; seeing my suitcase, they must have assumed I was just a guest checking in. I went through the Art Deco doors, up the grand marble staircase and into the Babylonian splendour of the Waldorf's lobby. I went over to one of the concierges at the front desk and asked him to call Amelia Bly's room.

There was no reply. He hung up, frowning, and was just starting to check his computer when, from the interior of the hotel, across the immense expanse of the golden lobby, came a wedge of security men, Special Branch and Secret Service, with Lang enclosed among them, marching purposefully. Behind him walked Amelia and the two secretaries. Amelia was on the phone. I moved towards the group. Lang swept by me, his eyes fixed straight ahead. As he began descending the staircase, Amelia saw me. She appeared flustered.

'I was just trying to call you,' she said as she went by. She didn't break step. 'There's been a change of plan,' she said over her shoulder. 'We're flying back to Martha's Vineyard now.'

'Now?' I hurried after her. 'It's rather late, isn't it?'

We started descending the stairs.

'Adam's insisting. I've managed to find us a plane.'

'But why now?'

'I've no idea. Something's come up. You'll have to ask him.'

Lang had already reached the entrance. The bodyguards opened the doors and his broad shoulders were suddenly framed by a glow of halogen light. The reporters' shouts, the fusillade of camera shutters, the rumble of the Harley-Davidsons—it was as if someone had rolled back the doors to hell.

'What am I supposed to do?' I asked.

'Get into the back-up car. I expect Adam will want to talk to you on the plane.' She saw my look of panic. 'Is there something the matter?'

Now what am I supposed to do? I wondered. Faint? Plead a prior engagement? I seemed to be trapped on a moving walkway.

'Everything seems to be happening in a rush,' I said weakly.

'This is nothing. You should have been with us when he was PM.'

We emerged into the tumult of noise and light. The door to Lang's limousine was open. He paused briefly to wave at the crowd, then ducked inside.

Amelia took my arm and propelled me towards the second car. 'Go on!' she shouted. 'Don't forget, we can't stop if you're left behind.'

She slipped in beside Lang, and I found myself stepping into the second limo, next to Alice and Lucy. They shifted cheerfully along the bench seat to make room for me. A Special Branch man climbed in the front, next to the driver, and then we were away, with an accompanying *whoop whoop* from one of the motorbikes.

In different circumstances, I would have relished that journey: the Harley-Davidsons gliding past us to hold back the traffic; the pedestrians turning to watch as we hurtled by; the noise of the sirens; the flashing lights; the speed; the *force*. I can think of only two categories of human being who are transported with such pomp and drama: world leaders and captured terrorists.

We flew over the Fifty-ninth Street Bridge like gods, reaching LaGuardia a few minutes later. We drove past the terminal building, through an open metal gate and directly onto the tarmac, where a big private jet was being fuelled. It was a Hallington plane, in its dark blue livery, with the corporate logo—the Earth with a circle girdling it—painted on its high tail. Lang's limousine swerved to a halt and he was the first to emerge. He dived through the doorway of the mobile body-scanner and up the steps into the Gulfstream without a backward glance. A bodyguard hurried after him.

As I clambered out of the car I felt almost arthritic with anxiety. It took an effort simply to walk over to where Amelia was standing. The night air shook with the noise of jets coming in to land.

'Now that's the way to travel,' I said, trying to sound relaxed.

'They want to show him they love him,' said Amelia. 'And no doubt it helps to show everyone else how they treat their friends.'

Security men with metal wands were inspecting all the luggage. I added my suitcase to the pile.

'He says he has to get back to Ruth,' she continued, gazing up at the plane. 'There's something he needs to talk over with her.' Her voice was puzzled. She was almost talking to herself.

One of the security men told me to open my suitcase. I unzipped it and held it up to him. He lifted out the manuscript to search underneath it.

Amelia was so preoccupied, she didn't even notice. 'It's odd,' she said, 'because Washington went so well.' She stared vacantly towards the runway.

'Your shoulder bag,' said the security man.

I handed it to him. He took out the package of photographs. For a moment I thought he was going to open it, but he was more interested in my laptop.

'Perhaps he's heard something from The Hague,' I suggested.

'No. It's nothing to do with that. He would have told me.'

'OK, you're clear to board,' said the guard.

'Don't go near him just yet,' Amelia warned, as I passed through the scanner. 'Not in his present mood. I'll take you back to him if he wants to talk.'

I climbed the steps.

The cabin was configured to take ten passengers, two each on a couple of sofas that ran along the side of the fuselage, and the rest in six armchairs that faced one another in pairs, with tables between them. It looked like an extension of the Waldorf's lobby: gold fittings, polished walnut and creamy leather. Lang was in the armchair nearest the tail, gazing out of the window. The Special Branch man sat on a nearby sofa. A steward in a white jacket was bending over the former prime minister. I couldn't see what drink he was being served, but I could hear the clink of ice against cut glass. It sounded as if Lang had given up tea in favour of a stiff whisky.

The steward saw me staring and came down the gangway towards me. 'Can I get you something, sir?'

'Thanks. Yes. I'll have whatever Mr Lang is having.'

I was wrong: it was brandy.

By the time the door was closed, there were twelve of us on board: three crew (pilot, copilot and steward) and nine passengers—two secretaries, four bodyguards, Amelia, Lang and me. I sat with my back to the cockpit so that I could keep an eye on my client. Amelia was directly opposite him. The engines started to whine, then the Gulfstream shuddered slightly, and the terminal building seemed to drift slowly away. I could see Amelia's hand making emphatic gestures, but Lang continued to stare out at the airfield.

Someone touched my arm. 'Do you know how much one of these things costs?' It was the policeman who'd been in my car on the drive from the Waldorf. He was in the seat across the aisle. 'Have a guess.'

I shrugged. 'Ten million dollars?'

'*Forty* million dollars.' He sounded triumphant. 'Hallington has *five*.'

'Makes you wonder what they can possibly use them all for.'

'They lease them out when they don't need them.'

'Oh, yes, that's right,' I said. 'I'd heard that.'

The noise of the engines increased and we began our charge down the runway. I imagined the terrorist suspects, handcuffed and hooded, strapped into their leather armchairs as they lifted off from some red-dusted military airstrip near the Afghan border, bound for eastern Poland. The plane seemed to spring into the air, and I watched the lights of Manhattan spread to fill the window, then slide and tilt, and finally flicker into darkness as we rose into the cloud. It felt as though we were climbing blindly for a long time, but then the gauze fell away and we came up into a bright night.

After the plane levelled off, Amelia came down the aisle towards me, her hips swaying with the motion of the cabin. 'He's ready to have a word,' she said. 'But go easy on him. He's had a hell of a couple of days.'

He and I both, I thought, as I grabbed my shoulder bag.

'You haven't got long,' she warned. 'This flight's only a hop. We'll be starting to descend any minute.'

IT CERTAINLY WAS A HOP. I checked afterwards. Only 260 miles separate New York City and Martha's Vineyard, and the cruising speed of a Gulfstream G450 is 528 miles per hour. The conjunction of these two facts explains why the disc of my conversation with Lang lasts a mere eleven minutes.

His eyes were closed as I approached him, his glass still held in his outstretched hand. He had removed his jacket and tie and eased off his shoes, and was sprawled back in his seat like a starfish. At first I thought he'd fallen asleep, then I realised his eyes were narrowed to slits and he was watching me. He gestured with his drink towards the seat opposite him.

'Hi, man,' he said. 'Join me.' He opened his eyes fully, yawned and put the back of his hand to his mouth. 'Sorry.'

'Hello, Adam.' I sat down. I had my bag in my lap. I fumbled to pull out my notebook, the minirecorder and a spare disc. If Lang had so much as raised an eyebrow I would have put the recorder away again. But he didn't appear to notice. He must have gone through this ritual many times. In the recording you can hear the exhaustion in his voice.

'So,' he said, 'how's it going?'

'It's going,' I said. 'It's certainly going.' When I listen to the disc, my register's so high from anxiety, it sounds as though I've been sucking helium.

'Found out anything interesting?' There was a gleam of something in his eyes. Contempt? Amusement?

'This and that. How was Washington?'

'Washington was great, actually.' There's a rustling noise on the disc as he straightens in his chair. 'I got the most terrific support everywhere—on the Hill, of course, as you probably saw, but also the vice president and the secretary of state. They're going to help me in every way they can.'

'And is the bottom line that you'll be able to settle in America?'

'Yes. If worst comes to worst, they'll offer me asylum, certainly. Maybe even a job of some kind, as long as it doesn't involve overseas travel. But it won't get that far. They're going to supply something much more valuable.'

'Really?'

Lang nodded. 'Evidence.'

'Right.' I hadn't a clue what he was talking about.

'Is that thing working?' he asked.

There is a deafening clunk as I pick up the recorder. 'Yes, I think so. Is that OK?' With a thump, I replace it.

'Sure,' said Lang. 'I just want to make sure you get this down, because we can use this, as an exclusive for the memoirs.' He leaned forward.

'Washington is prepared to provide sworn testimony that no UK personnel were directly involved in the capture of those four men in Pakistan.'

'Really?' *Really? Really?* I wince every time I hear the sycophancy in my voice. The fawning courtier. The self-effacing ghost.

'You bet. The director of the CIA himself will provide a deposition to the court in The Hague, saying that this was an entirely American covert operation, and he's even prepared to let the actual officers who were running the mission provide evidence in camera.' Lang sat back and sipped his brandy. 'How's Rycart going to make a charge of war crimes stick now?'

'But your memorandum to the Ministry of Defence—'

'That's genuine,' he conceded with a shrug. 'It's true, I can't deny that I urged the use of the SAS. And the British government can't deny that our special forces were in Peshawar at the time of Operation Tempest. And we also can't deny that it was our intelligence services that tracked down those men to the particular location where they were arrested. But there's no proof that we passed that intelligence on to the CIA.' Lang smiled at me.

'But we did?'

'There's no proof that we passed that intelligence on to the CIA.'

'But if we did, surely that would be aiding and abetting—'

'There's no proof that we passed that intelligence on to the CIA.'

He was still holding his smile, albeit now with a crease of concentration in his brow, as a tenor might hold a note at the end of a difficult aria.

'Then how did it get to them?'

'That's a difficult question. Not through any official channel, that's for sure. And certainly it was nothing to do with me.' There was a long pause. His smile died. 'Well,' he said. 'What do you think?'

'It sounds a bit'—I tried to say it diplomatically—'technical.'

'Meaning?'

My reply on the disc is so slippery, so sweaty with nervous circumlocutions, it's enough to make one laugh out loud.

'Well . . . you know . . . you admit you wanted the SAS to pick them up—no doubt for, you know, understandable reasons—and the Ministry of Defence—as I understand it—hasn't been able to deny they were involved, presumably because they were, in a way, even if . . . even if they were only parked in a car round the corner. And apparently . . . British intelligence gave the CIA the location where they could be picked up. And when they were tortured, you didn't condemn it.' The last line was delivered in a rush.

'Sid Kroll was very pleased with the commitment given by the CIA,' Lang said coldly. 'He believes the prosecutor may even have to drop the case.'

'Well, if Sid says that—'

'But fuck it,' said Lang suddenly. He banged his hand on the table. 'I don't regret what happened to those four men. If we'd relied on the Pakistanis we'd never have got them. We had to grab them while we had the chance, or they'd have gone underground, and the next time we'd have known anything about them would've been when they were killing our people.'

'You really don't regret it?'

'No.'

'Not even the one who died under interrogation?'

'Oh, him,' said Lang dismissively. 'He had an undiagnosed heart problem. He could have died getting out of bed one morning.'

I said nothing. I pretended to make a note.

'Look,' said Lang, 'I don't condone torture, but let me just say this. First, it does actually produce results—I've seen the intelligence. Second, having power, in the end, is all about balancing evils and, when you think about it, what are a couple of minutes of suffering for a few individuals compared to the deaths—the *deaths*, mark you—of thousands. Third, don't try telling me this is unique to the war on terror. Torture's always been part of warfare. The difference is that in the past there were no media around to report it.'

'The men arrested in Pakistan claim they were innocent,' I pointed out.

'Of course they claim they were innocent! What else are they going to say?' Lang studied me closely, as if seeing me properly for the first time. 'I'm beginning to think you're too naive for this job.'

I couldn't resist it. 'Unlike Mike McAra?'

'Mike!' Lang laughed. 'Mike was naive in a different way.'

The plane was beginning to descend quite rapidly now. I could feel the pressure change in my ears, and I had to pinch my nose and swallow hard.

Amelia made her way down the aisle. 'Is everything all right?' she asked. She must have heard Lang's outburst of temper; everyone must have.

'We're just doing some work on my memoirs,' said Lang. 'I'm telling him what happened over Operation Tempest.'

'You're recording it?' said Amelia.

'If that's all right,' I said.

'Be careful,' she told Lang. 'Remember what Sid Kroll said—'

'The tapes will be yours,' I interrupted, 'not mine.'

'They could still be subpoenaed.'

'Stop treating me as though I'm a child,' said Lang abruptly. 'I know what I want to say. Let's deal with it once and for all.'

Amelia permitted herself a slight widening of her eyes and withdrew.

'Women!' muttered Lang. He took another gulp of brandy, and it occurred to me that our former prime minister was slightly drunk. I sensed this was my moment.

'In what way,' I asked, 'was Mike McAra naive?'

'Never mind,' muttered Lang. He nursed his drink, his chin on his chest, brooding. He jerked up again. 'I mean, take all this civil liberties crap. You know what I'd do if I were in power again? I'd say, OK then, we'll have two queues at the airports. On the left, we'll have queues to flights on which we've done no background checks on the passengers, no profiling, no biometric data, nothing that infringed anyone's precious civil liberties, used no intelligence obtained under torture. On the right, we'll have queues to the flights where we've done everything possible to make them safe. People can make their own minds up which plane they want to catch. Wouldn't that be great? To sit back and watch which queue the Rycarts of this world would *really* choose to put their kids on, if the chips were down.'

'And Mike was like that?'

'Not at the beginning. But Mike discovered idealism in his old age. I said to him—it was our last conversation, actually—I said, if our Lord Jesus Christ was unable to solve all the problems of the world when he came down to live among us—and he was the son of God!—wasn't it a bit unreasonable of Mike to expect me to have sorted out everything in ten years?'

'Is it true you had a serious row with him? Just before he died?'

'Mike made certain wild accusations. I could hardly ignore them.'

'May I ask what kind of accusations?'

On the disc, the pause that followed is quite short, but at the time it seemed endless, and Lang's voice when it came was deadly quiet.

'I'd prefer not to repeat them.'

'Were they to do with the CIA?'

'Surely you know,' said Lang bitterly, 'if you've been to see Paul Emmett?'

And this time the pause is as long on the recording as it is in my memory.

Delivered of his bombshell, Lang gazed out of the window and sipped his drink. When at last he turned back to me, there wasn't anger in his expression, merely a great weariness.

'I want you to understand,' he said with heavy emphasis, 'that everything I did, both as party leader and as prime minister—everything—I did out of conviction, because I believed it was right.'

I mumbled a reply. I was in a state of shock.

'Emmett claims you showed him some photographs. May I see?'

My hands shook as I removed them from the envelope and pushed them across the table. He flicked through the first four quickly, paused over the fifth—the one that showed him and Emmett onstage—then went back to the beginning and started looking at them again, lingering over each image.

He said, without raising his eyes, 'Where did you get them?'

'McAra ordered them up from the archive. I found them in his room.'

Over the intercom, the copilot asked us to fasten our seat belts.

'Odd,' murmured Lang, 'the way we've all changed so much yet also stayed the same.' He squinted at one of the riverbank pictures. It was the girls who seemed to fascinate him the most. 'I remember her,' he said, tapping the picture. 'And her. She wrote to me, when I was prime minister. Ruth was not pleased. Oh, God,' he said, and passed his hand across his face. 'Ruth.' For a moment, I thought he was about to break down, but when he looked at me his eyes were dry. 'What happens next? Is there a procedure in your line of work to deal with this sort of situation?'

Patterns of light were very clear in the window now. I could see the headlamps of a car on a road.

'The client always has the last word about what goes in a book,' I said. 'Always. But, obviously, in this case, given what happened . . .'

On the disc, my voice trails away, and then there is a loud clunk as Lang leans forward and grabs my forearm.

'If you mean what happened to Mike, then let me tell you I was appalled by that.' His gaze was fixed on me; he was putting everything he had left into the task of convincing me, and I'll freely confess, despite everything I'd discovered, he succeeded: to this day, I'm sure he was telling the truth. 'If you believe nothing else, you must believe that his death had nothing to do with me. I shall carry that image of Mike in the morgue until my own dying day. I'm sure it was an accident. But let's say, for the sake of argument, it wasn't.' He tightened his grip on my arm. 'What was he thinking of, driving up to Boston to confront Emmett? He'd been around politics long enough to know you don't do something like that, not when the stakes are this high. In a way, he did kill himself. It was a suicidal act.'

'That's what worries me,' I said.

'You can't seriously think that the same thing could happen to you,' he said. 'You need have no fears on that score. I can guarantee it.'

I guess my disbelief must have been obvious.

'Oh, come on, man!' he said urgently. Again, the fingers clenched on my flesh. 'There are four policemen travelling on this plane with us right now! What kind of people do you think we are?'

'Well, that's just it,' I said. 'What kind of people *are* you?'

We were coming in low over the treetops. The lights of the Gulfstream gleamed across dark waves of foliage.

I tried to pull my arm away. 'Excuse me,' I said.

Lang let go of me and I fastened my seat belt. He did the same. He glanced out of the window at the terminal, then back at me, appalled.

'My God, you've already told someone, haven't you?'

I could feel myself turning scarlet. 'No,' I said.

'You have.'

'I haven't.' On the disc I sound as feeble as a child caught red-handed.

He leaned forward again. 'Who have you told?'

Looking out at the dark forest beyond the perimeter of the airport, where anything could be lurking, it seemed like the only insurance policy I had.

'Richard Rycart,' I said.

He must have known then that it was the end of everything. In my mind's eye I see him still, like one of those condemned apartment blocks, moments after the demolition charges have been exploded: for a few seconds, the façade remains bizarrely intact, before slowly beginning to slide. That was Lang. He gave me a long blank look, then subsided back into his seat.

The plane came to a halt in front of the terminal building.

AT THIS POINT, at long last, I did something smart.

As Lang sat contemplating his ruin, and as Amelia came hurrying down the aisle to discover what I'd said, I had the presence of mind to eject the disc from the recorder and slip it into my pocket. In its place I inserted the blank. Lang was too stunned to care and Amelia too fixated on him to notice.

'All right,' she said firmly, 'that's enough for tonight.' She lifted the empty glass from his unresisting hand and gave it to the steward. 'We need to get you home, Adam. Ruth's waiting at the gate.' She reached over and unfastened his seat belt, then removed his suit jacket from the back of his seat. She held it out ready for him to slip into. 'Adam?'

He rose to obey, gazing vacantly towards the cockpit as she guided his arms into the sleeves. She glared at me over his shoulder.

At the front of the plane, the door had opened and three of the Special Branch men were disembarking. A blast of cold air ran down the cabin. Lang walked towards the exit, preceded by his fourth bodyguard, Amelia at his back. I stuffed my recorder and the photographs into my shoulder bag and followed them. The pilot had come out of the cockpit to say goodbye and I saw Lang advance to meet him, his hand outstretched.

'That was great,' said Lang vaguely, 'as usual. My favourite airline.' He shook the pilot's hand, then leaned past him to greet the copilot and the waiting steward. 'Thanks. Thanks so much.' He turned to us, still smiling his professional smile, but it faded fast; he looked stricken. The last bodyguard was already halfway down the steps. There was just Amelia, me and the two secretaries waiting to follow him off the plane. Standing in the lighted glass window of the terminal I could just make out the figure of Ruth. She was too far away for me to judge her expression.

'Would you mind just hanging back a minute?' he said to Amelia. 'And you, too?' he added to me. 'I need to have a private word with my wife.'

'Is everything all right, Adam?' asked Amelia. I suppose she loved him too much not to know that something was terribly wrong.

'It'll be fine,' said Lang. He touched her elbow lightly, then gave us all a slight bow. 'Thank you, ladies and gentlemen, and good night.'

He ducked through the door and paused at the top of the steps, glancing around, smoothing down his hair. Amelia and I watched him from the interior of the plane. He was just as he was when I first saw him—still, out of habit, searching for an audience to connect with, even though the floodlit concourse was deserted, apart from the waiting bodyguards, and a ground technician in overalls, working late, no doubt eager to get home.

Lang must have seen Ruth waiting at the window, because he suddenly raised his hand in acknowledgment, then set off down the steps, gracefully, like a dancer. He reached the tarmac and had gone about ten yards towards the terminal when the technician shouted out, 'Adam!' and waved. The voice was English, and Lang must have recognised the accent of a fellow countryman because he suddenly broke away from his bodyguards and strode towards the man, his hand held out. And that is my final image of Lang: a man always with his hand held out. It is burned into my retinas—his yearning shadow against the expanding ball of bright white fire that suddenly engulfed him, then there was only the flying debris, the stinging grit, the glass, the furnace heat and the underwater silence of the explosion.

NINE

I saw nothing more after that initial flash of brilliant light; there was too much glass and blood in my eyes. The force of the blast flung us all back. Amelia, I learned later, hit her head on the side of a seat and was knocked unconscious, while I lay across the aisle in darkness and silence for what could have been minutes or hours. I felt no pain, except when one of the terrified secretaries trod on my hand with her high heel in her desperation to get out of the plane. But I couldn't see, and it was also to be several hours before I could hear properly. Eventually, I was given a wonderful shot of morphine that burst like warm fireworks in my brain. Then I was airlifted by helicopter with all the other survivors to a hospital near Boston.

Throughout the next day or two, as I lay in my hospital room, my face bandaged, a policeman on guard in the corridor outside, I ran over recent events in my mind, and felt certain that I would never leave that place alive. But nothing happened. While I was still blinded, I was gently questioned by a Special Agent Murphy from the Boston office of the FBI about what I could remember about Lang's assassination. The next afternoon, when the bandages were removed from my eyes, Murphy returned. He looked like a muscular young priest in a 1950s movie, and this time he was accompanied by a saturnine Englishman from MI5, whose name I never quite caught—because, I assume, I was never meant to.

They showed me a photograph. My vision was still bleary, but I was able to identify the crazy man I had met in the bar of my hotel and who had staged that lonely vigil at the end of the track from the Rhinehart compound. His name, they said, was George Arthur Boxer, a former major in the British army, whose son had been killed in Iraq and whose wife had died six months later in a London suicide bombing. In his unhinged state, Major Boxer had held Adam Lang personally responsible, and had stalked him to Martha's Vineyard just after McAra's death had been reported in the papers. He had studied tactics for suicide bombing on jihadist web sites. He had rented a cottage in Oak Bluffs, brought in supplies of peroxide and weedkiller and turned it into an explosives factory. He would have known when Lang was returning from New York, because he would have seen the bombproof car heading to the airport to meet him. How he had got onto the airfield nobody was quite sure, but it was dark, there was a four-mile perimeter fence, and the experts had always assumed that four Special Branch men and an armoured car were sufficient protection.

But there was a limit to what security could do against a determined suicide bomber, said the man from MI5. I got the impression everyone was slightly relieved by the way things had worked out: the British, because Lang had been killed on American soil; the Americans, because he'd been blown up by a Brit; and both because there would now be no war crimes trial, no unseemly revelations, and no guest who has overstayed his welcome, drifting around the dinner tables of Georgetown for the next twenty years.

Agent Murphy asked me about the flight from New York and whether Lang had expressed any worries about his personal security. I said truthfully that he hadn't.

'Mrs Bly,' said the MI5 man, 'tells us you recorded an interview with him during the final part of the flight.'

'No, she's wrong about that,' I said. 'I had the machine in front of me, but I never switched it on. It wasn't really an interview, in any case. More of a chat.'

'Do you mind if I take a look?'

'Go ahead.'

My shoulder bag was on the nightstand next to my bed. The MI5 man took out the minirecorder and ejected the disc. I watched him, dry-mouthed.

'Can I borrow this?'

'You can keep it,' I said. 'How is Amelia, by the way?'

'She's fine.' He put the disc into his briefcase. 'Thanks.'

'Can I see her?'

'She flew back to London last night.' I guess my disappointment must have been evident, because the MI5 man added, with chilly pleasure, 'It's not surprising. She hasn't seen her husband since before Christmas.'

'And what about Ruth?' I asked.

'She's accompanying Mr Lang's body home right now,' said Murphy. 'Your government sent a plane to fetch them.'

'He'll get full military honours,' added the MI5 man. 'A statue in the Palace of Westminster, and a funeral in the Abbey if she wants it. He's never been more popular than since he died.'

'He should have done it years ago,' I said. They didn't smile. 'And is it really true that nobody else was killed?'

'Nobody,' said Murphy, 'which was a miracle, believe me.'

'In fact,' said the man from MI5, 'Mrs Bly wonders if Mr Lang didn't actually recognise his assassin and deliberately head towards him, knowing something like this might happen. Can you shed any light on that?'

'It sounds far-fetched,' I said. 'I thought a fuel truck had exploded.'

'It was certainly quite a bang,' said Murphy, slipping his pen into his inside pocket. 'We eventually found the killer's head on the terminal roof.'

I WATCHED LANG'S FUNERAL on CNN two days later. My eyesight was more or less restored. I could see that it was tastefully done: the Queen, the prime minister, the US vice-president and half the leaders of Europe; the coffin draped in the Union Jack; the guard of honour; the solitary piper playing a lament. Ruth looked very good in black, I thought. During a lull in proceedings, there was even an interview with Richard Rycart. Naturally, he hadn't been invited to the service, but he paid a moving tribute from his office in the United Nations: a great colleague . . . a true patriot . . . we had our disagreements . . . remained friends . . . my heart goes out to Ruth and the family . . . as far as I'm concerned the whole chapter is closed.

I found the mobile phone he had given me and threw it out of the window.

The next day, when I was due to be discharged from hospital, Rick came up from New York to say goodbye and take me to the airport.

'Do you want the good news or the good news?' he said.

'I'm not sure your idea of good news is the same as mine.'

'Sid Kroll just called. Ruth Lang still wants you to finish the memoirs, and Maddox will give you an extra month to work on the manuscript.'

'And the good news is?'

'Don't be so goddamn snooty about it. This is a really hot book now. This is Adam Lang's voice from the grave. You don't have to work on it here any more; you can finish it in London. You look terrible, by the way.'

'His "voice from the grave"?' I repeated incredulously. 'So now I'm to be the ghost of a ghost?'

'Come on, the situation is rich with possibilities. You can write what you like, within reason. Nobody will stop you. And you liked him, didn't you?'

I had been thinking about that ever since I came round from the sedative. Worse than the pain in my eyes and the buzzing in my ears, worse even than my fear that I would never emerge from the hospital, was my sense of guilt. Despite what I'd learned, I couldn't work up any resentment against Lang. I was the one at fault. It wasn't just that I'd betrayed my client, it was the sequence of events my actions had set in motion. If I hadn't gone to see Emmett, Emmett wouldn't have contacted Lang to warn him. Then maybe Lang wouldn't have insisted on flying back to Martha's Vineyard that night to see Ruth. Then I wouldn't have had to tell him about Rycart. And then, and then . . . ? It nagged away at me as I lay in the darkness. I just couldn't erase the memory of how bleak he had looked on the plane at the very end.

Mrs Bly wonders if Mr Lang didn't actually recognise his assassin and deliberately head towards him, knowing something like this might happen . . .

'Yes,' I said to Rick. 'Yes, I did like him.'

'There you go. You owe it to him. Besides, there's another consideration.'

'Which is what?'

'Sid Kroll says that if you don't fulfil your contractual obligations and finish the book, they'll sue your ass off.'

AND SO I RETURNED to London, and for the next six weeks I barely emerged from my flat, except once, early on, to go out for dinner with Kate. The manner of Adam Lang's death seemed to have silenced even her hostility, and I suppose a kind of glamour attached to me as an eyewitness. I had turned down a score of requests to give interviews, so she was the first person, apart from the FBI and MI5, to whom I described what had happened. I wanted to tell her about my final conversation with Lang. But as I was about to broach it, the waiter came over to discuss dessert, and when he left she announced she had something she wanted to tell me, first.

She was engaged to be married.

I confess it was a shock. I didn't like the other man. You'd know him if I mentioned his name: craggy, handsome, soulful. He specialises in flying briefly into the world's worst trouble spots and flying out again with moving descriptions of human suffering, usually his own.

'Congratulations,' I said.

We skipped dessert. Our relationship ended ten minutes later with a peck on the cheek on the pavement outside the restaurant.

'You were going to tell me something,' she said. 'I'm sorry I cut you off. I didn't want you to say anything . . . too personal . . . before I—'

'It doesn't matter,' I said.

'Are you sure you're all right? You seem . . . different.'

'I'm fine.' I held open the door of her cab for her. I couldn't help overhearing that the address she gave the driver wasn't hers.

After that, I withdrew from the world. I spent my every waking hour with Lang, and now that he was dead, I found I suddenly had his voice. It was more a Ouija board than a keyboard that I sat down to every morning. If my fingers typed out a sentence that sounded wrong, I could almost physically feel them being drawn to the DELETE key.

The basic structure of the story remained McAra's sixteen chapters. My method was to retype his manuscript completely, and in the process of passing it through my brain and fingers, to strain it of my predecessor's lumpy clichés. I made no mention of Emmett, of course, cutting even the anodyne quote of his that had opened the final chapter. The image of Adam Lang I presented to the world was very much the character he'd chosen to play: the regular guy who fell into politics almost by accident. I took up Ruth's suggestion that Lang had turned to politics as solace for his depression when he first arrived in London. In my telling of his story, Lang's political involvement really got going only when Ruth came knocking at his door two years later. It sounded plausible. Who knows? It might even have been true.

I started writing *Memoirs by Adam Lang* on February 10 and promised Maddox I'd have it done, all 160,000 words, by the end of March. That meant I had to produce 3,400 words a day, every day. I had a chart on the wall and marked it up each morning. I was like Captain Scott returning from the South Pole: I had to make those daily distances, or I'd fall irrevocably behind and perish in a white wilderness of blank pages. It was a hard slog, especially as almost no lines of McAra's were salvageable, except, curiously, the very last one in the manuscript, which had made me groan aloud when I read it on Martha's Vineyard: *Ruth and I look forward to the future, whatever it may hold.* Read that, you bastards, I thought, as I typed it in on the evening of March 30: read that, and close this book without a catch in your throat.

I added 'The End' and then, I guess, I had a kind of nervous breakdown.

I DISPATCHED ONE COPY of the manuscript to New York and another to the office of the Adam Lang Foundation in London, for the personal attention of Mrs Ruth Lang—or, as I should more properly have styled her by then, Baroness Lang of Calderthorpe, the government having just given her a seat in the House of Lords as a mark of the nation's respect.

I hadn't heard anything from Ruth since the assassination. I'd written to her while I was in hospital, one of over 100,000 correspondents reported to have sent their condolences, so I wasn't surprised to get a standard printed reply. But a week after she received the manuscript, a handwritten message arrived on the red-embossed notepaper of the House of Lords:

> *You have done all that I ever hoped you wd do—and more! You have caught his tone beautifully & brought him back to life—all his wonderful humour & compassion & energy. Pls come & see me here in the HoL when you have a spare moment. It wd be great to catch up. Martha's V seems a v long time ago, & a long way away! Bless you again for yr talent. And it is a proper book!!*
>
> *Much love, R*

Maddox was equally effusive, but without the love. The first printing was to be 400,000 copies. The publication date was the end of May.

So that was that. The job was done.

It didn't take me long to realise that I was in a bad state. I'd been kept going, I suppose, by Lang's 'wonderful humour & compassion & energy', but once he was written out of me, I collapsed like an empty suit of clothes. Rick had insisted we wait until the Lang memoirs were published before negotiating new contracts, so I had no work to go to. I was afflicted by a horrible combination of lethargy and panic. When I did summon the energy to get out of bed, I moped on the sofa in my dressing gown, watching daytime television. I didn't eat much. I stopped opening my letters and answering the phone. I didn't shave. I left the flat for any length of time only on Mondays and Thursdays, to avoid seeing my cleaner, then I either sat in a park, if it was fine, or in a nearby greasy café if it wasn't; it mostly wasn't.

And yet, paradoxically, at the same time I was also permanently agitated. I fretted absurdly about trivialities—where I'd put a pair of shoes, or if it was wise to keep all my money with the same bank. This nerviness made me feel physically shaky, often breathless, and it was in this spirit, late one rainy night, about two months after I finished the book, that I made what to me, in my condition, was a calamitous discovery.

I'd run out of whisky and had ten minutes to get to the little supermarket on Ladbroke Grove before it closed. I grabbed the nearest jacket and was halfway down the stairs when I realised it was the one I'd been wearing when Lang was killed. It was torn and bloodstained. In one pocket was the recording of my final interview with Adam, and in the other the keys to the Ford Escape SUV.

The car! I had forgotten all about it. It was still parked at Logan Airport! It was costing eighteen dollars a day! I must owe *thousands*!

To you, no doubt—and indeed to me, now—my panic seems ridiculous. But I raced back up those stairs with my pulse drumming. It was after six in New York and Rhinehart Inc. had closed for the day. There was no reply from the Martha's Vineyard house, either. In despair, I called Rick at home and, without preliminaries, began gabbling out the details of the crisis. He listened for about thirty seconds, then told me roughly to shut up.

'This was sorted out weeks ago. The guys at the car park called the cops, and they called Rhinehart's office. Maddox paid the bill. Now listen, my friend. It seems you've got a nasty case of delayed shock. I know a shrink—'

I hung up.

When I finally fell asleep on the sofa, I had my recurrent dream about McAra, the one in which he floated fully clothed in the sea beside me and told me he wasn't going to make it: *You go on without me*. This time, a wave took McAra away, until he became only a dark shape in the distance, face down in the foam. I waded towards him and, with a supreme effort, rolled him over, then suddenly he was staring up naked from a white slab, with Adam Lang bending over him.

The next morning I left the flat early and walked down the hill to the tube station. It wouldn't take much to kill myself, I thought. One swift leap out in front of the approaching train, then oblivion. Much better than drowning. But it was only the briefest of impulses, not least because I couldn't bear the idea of someone having to clean up afterwards. Instead I boarded the train and travelled to the end of the line at Hammersmith, then crossed the road to the other platform. Motion, that's the cure for depression, I decided. You have to keep moving. At Embankment I changed again for Morden. We passed through Balham and I got off two stops later.

It didn't take me long to find the grave. I remembered Ruth had said the funeral was at Streatham Cemetery. I looked up his name and a groundsman pointed the way towards the plot. I passed stone angels, mossy cherubs and crosses garlanded with marble roses. But McAra's contribution was characteristically plain. Merely a slab of limestone with his name and dates.

It was a late spring morning, drowsy with pollen and petrol fumes. I squatted on my haunches and pressed my palms to the dewy grass. I felt a current of relief pass through me, as if I'd closed a circle, or fulfilled a task.

That was when I noticed, resting against the stone, half obscured by the overgrown grass, a small bunch of shrivelled flowers. A card was attached, written in an elegant hand, just legible after successive downpours: *In memory of a good friend and loyal colleague. Rest in peace, dear Mike. Amelia.*

WHEN I GOT BACK to my flat, I called her on her mobile number. She didn't seem surprised to hear from me.

'Hello,' she said. 'I was just thinking about you.'

'Why's that?'

'I'm reading your book—Adam's book.'

'And?'

'It's good. No, actually, it's better than good. It's like having him back. There's only one element missing, I think.'

'And what's that?'

'Oh, it doesn't matter. I'll tell you if I see you. Perhaps we'll get the opportunity to talk at the reception tonight.'

'What reception?'

She laughed. '*Your* reception, you idiot. The launch of your book. Don't tell me you haven't been invited.'

It took me a second or two to reply. 'I don't know whether I have or not. To be honest, I haven't checked my post in a while.'

'You must have been invited.'

'Don't you believe it. Authors tend to be funny about having their ghosts staring at them over the canapés.'

'Well, the author isn't going to be there, is he?' she said. She wanted to sound brisk, but she came across as desperately hollow and strained. 'You should go, whether you've been invited or not. In fact, if you haven't, you can come as my guest. My invitation has "Amelia Bly plus one" on it.'

The prospect of returning to society made my heartbeat start to race.

'But don't you want to take someone else? What about your husband?'

'Oh, him. That didn't work out, I'm afraid. I hadn't realised quite how bored he was with being my "plus one".'

'I'm sorry to hear that.'

'Liar,' she said. 'I'll meet you at the end of Downing Street at seven o'clock. The party's just across Whitehall. I'll only wait five minutes, so if you decide you do want to come, don't be late.'

After we hung up, I went through my weeks of accumulated mail. There was no invitation to the party. There was, however, a copy of the finished book. On the cover was a photograph of Lang, looking debonair, addressing a joint session of the US Congress. The photographs inside did not include any of the Cambridge ones that McAra had discovered; I hadn't passed them on to the picture researcher. I flicked through to the acknowledgments, which I had written in Lang's voice:

> This book would not exist without the dedication, support, wisdom and friendship of the late Michael McAra, who collaborated with me on its composition from the first page to the last. Thank you, Mike—for everything.

My name wasn't mentioned. Much to Rick's annoyance, I'd forgone my collaborator credit. I thought it was safer that way. The expurgated contents and my anonymity would, I hoped, serve as a message to whoever might be paying attention that there would be no further trouble from me.

I soaked in the bath for an hour that afternoon and contemplated whether to go to the reception. As usual, I spun out my procrastination for hours. I told myself I still hadn't made up my mind as I shaved off my beard, and as I dressed in a dark suit and white shirt, and as I went out into the street and hailed a taxi, and even as I stood on the corner of Downing Street at five minutes to seven; it wasn't too late to turn back. Across the broad, ceremonial boulevard of Whitehall, I could see the cars and taxis pulling up outside the Banqueting House, where I guessed the party must be taking place.

I kept looking for Amelia, up the street towards Horse Guards, and down it again to the Palace of Westminster. When Big Ben finished chiming the hour, there was still no sign of her. But then I felt a touch on my sleeve and turned to find Amelia standing behind me. She had emerged from the sunless canyon of Downing Street in her dark blue suit, carrying a briefcase. She looked older, faded. We exchanged polite hellos.

'Well,' she said, 'here we are.'

'Here we are.' We stood awkwardly, a few feet apart. 'I didn't realise you were back working in Number Ten,' I said.

'I was only on attachment to Adam. The king is dead,' she said, and suddenly her voice cracked.

I put my arms round her and patted her back, as if she were a child who had fallen over. I felt the wetness of her cheek against mine. When she pulled back, she opened her briefcase and took out a handkerchief.

'Sorry,' she said. She blew her nose. 'I keep thinking I'm over it, then I realise I'm not. You look terrible,' she added. 'In fact, you look—'

'Like a ghost?' I said. 'Thanks. I've heard it before.'

She checked herself in the mirror of her powder compact and carried out some swift repairs. 'Right,' she said, shutting it with a click. 'Let's go.'

We walked up Whitehall, through the crowds of spring tourists.

'So, were you invited in the end?' she asked.

'No, I wasn't. Actually, I'm rather surprised that you were.'

'Oh, that's not so odd,' she said, as we crossed the road. 'She's won, hasn't she? She's the grieving widow. Our very own Jackie Kennedy. She won't mind having me around. I'm hardly a threat, just a trophy in the victory parade.'

The moment we stepped inside I knew it was a mistake. Amelia had to open her briefcase for the security men. My keys set off the metal detector and I had to be searched. In the great open space of the Banqueting House, we were confronted by a roar of conversation and a wall of turned backs. I didn't know a soul.

Deftly, I seized a couple of flutes of champagne from a passing waiter and presented one to Amelia. 'I can't see Ruth,' I said.

'She'll be in the thick of it, I expect. Your health,' she said.

We clicked glasses. Champagne: even more pointless than white wine, in my opinion. But there didn't seem to be anything else.

'It's Ruth, actually, who is the one element missing from your book, if I had to make a criticism.'

'I know,' I said. 'I wanted to put in more of her, but she wouldn't have it.'

'Well, it's a pity.' Drink seemed to embolden the normally cautious Mrs Bly. She leaned in close to me, giving me a familiar lungful of her scent. 'I adored Adam, and I think he had similar feelings for me. But I was under no illusions: he'd never have left her. He told me that during that last drive to the airport. They were a complete team. He knew he'd have been nothing without her. She was the one who understood power. She was the one who originally had the contacts in the party. In fact, she was the one who was supposed to go into parliament, did you know that? Not him. That isn't in your book.'

'I didn't know.'

'Adam told me about it once. It isn't widely known—at least I've never seen it written up anywhere. But apparently his seat was originally all lined up for her, only at the last minute she stood aside and let him have it.'

I thought of my conversation with Rycart. 'The member for Michigan,' I murmured.

'Who?'

'The sitting MP was a man called Reg Giffen. He was so pro-American he was known as the member for Michigan.' Something moved uneasily inside my mind. 'Can I ask you a question? Before Adam was killed, why were you so determined to keep that manuscript under lock and key?'

'I told you: security.'

'But there was nothing in it. I know. I've read every word a dozen times.'

Amelia glanced around. Nobody was paying us any attention. 'Between you and me,' she said quietly, 'we weren't the ones who were concerned. It was the Americans. I was told they passed the word to MI5 that there might be something early on in the manuscript that was a threat to national security.'

'How did they know that?'

'Who's to say? But immediately after Mike died, they requested we take care to ensure the book wasn't circulated until they'd had a chance to clear it.'

'And did they?'

'I've no idea.'

I thought again of my meeting with Rycart. What was it he claimed McAra had said to him on the telephone, just before he died? *The key to everything is in Lang's autobiography—it's all there at the beginning.*

Did that mean their conversation had been bugged?

I sensed that something important had just changed, but I couldn't quite grasp what it was. I needed to get away to somewhere quiet, to think things through. But already I was aware that the acoustics of the party had changed. The roar of talk was dwindling. People were shushing one another. A man bellowed pompously, 'Be quiet!' and I turned round. At the side of the room, opposite the windows, not far from where we were standing, Ruth Lang was waiting patiently on a platform, holding a microphone.

'Thank you,' she said. 'Thank you very much. And good evening.' She paused, and a great stillness spread across three hundred people. She took a breath. There was a catch in her throat. 'I miss Adam all the time. But never more than tonight. Not just because we're meeting to launch his wonderful book, and he should be here to share the joy of his life story with us, but because he was so brilliant at making speeches, and I'm so terrible.'

I was surprised at how professionally she delivered the last line, how she built the emotional tension, then punctured it. There was a release of laughter. She seemed much more confident in public than I remembered her.

'Therefore,' she continued, 'you'll be relieved to hear I'm not going to make a speech. I'd just like to thank a few people. I'd like to thank Marty Rhinehart and John Maddox for not only being marvellous publishers, but also being great friends. I'd like to thank Sidney Kroll for his wit and his wise counsel. And I'd like to thank in particular, and especially, Mike McAra, who tragically also can't be with us. Mike, you are in our thoughts.'

The great hall rang with a rumble of 'hear hear'.

'And now,' said Ruth, 'may I propose a toast to the one we really need to thank?' She raised her glass. 'To the memory of a great man and a great patriot, a great father and a wonderful husband—to Adam Lang!'

'To Adam Lang!' we boomed in unison, then we clapped, and went on clapping, while Ruth nodded graciously to all corners of the hall, including ours, at which point she saw me and blinked, then recovered, smiled, and hoisted her glass to me in salute.

She left the platform quickly.

'The merry widow,' hissed Amelia. 'Death becomes her, don't you think?'

'I have a feeling she's coming over,' I said.

'Shit,' said Amelia, draining her glass. 'In that case I'm getting out of here. Would you like me to take you to dinner?'

'Amelia Bly, are you asking me on a date?'

'I'll meet you outside in ten minutes.'

Even as she moved away, the crowd before me seemed to part, and Ruth emerged, looking very different from the last time I had seen her: glossy haired, smooth-skinned, slimmed by grief, and designer clad in something black and silky. Sid Kroll was just behind her.

'Hello, you,' she said. She took my hands in hers and mwah-mwahed me, brushing her thick helmet of hair briefly against each of my cheeks.

'Hello, Ruth. Hello, Sid.'

I nodded to him. He winked.

'I was told you couldn't stand these kinds of parties,' she said, still holding my hands and fixing me with her glittering dark eyes, 'or else I would have invited you. Did you get my note?'

'I did. Thanks.'

'But you didn't call me!'

'I didn't know if you were just being polite.'

'Being polite!' She briefly shook my hands in reproach. 'Since when was

I ever polite? You must come and see me.' And then she did that thing that important people always do to me at parties: she glanced over my shoulder. And I saw in her gaze a flash of alarm, followed by a barely perceptible shake of her head. I detached my hands, turned round and saw Paul Emmett. He was no more than five feet away.

'Hello,' he said. 'I believe we've met.'

I swung back to Ruth. I tried to speak. 'Ah,' I said. 'Ah—'

'Paul was my tutor,' she said calmly, 'when I was a Fulbright scholar at Harvard. You and I must talk.'

'Ah—'

I backed away. I knocked into a man who shielded his drink and told me cheerfully to watch out. Ruth was saying something earnestly, and so was Kroll, but my ears were buzzing and I couldn't hear them. I saw Amelia staring at me and I waved my hands feebly, and then I fled from the hall, across the lobby and out into the hollow, imperial grandeur of Whitehall.

IT WAS OBVIOUS when I got outside that another bomb had gone off. I could hear the sirens in the distance, and a pillar of smoke was rising from behind the National Gallery. I set off at a run towards Trafalgar Square and barged in front of an outraged couple to seize their taxi. Avenues of escape were being closed off all over central London. We turned into a one-way street, to find the police sealing the far end with yellow tape. The driver flung the cab into reverse, jerking me onto the edge of my seat, where I stayed throughout the rest of the journey, clinging to the handle by the door, as we dodged through the back routes north. When we reached my flat I paid him double the fare.

The key to everything is in Lang's autobiography—it's all there at the beginning.

I grabbed my copy of the finished book, took it over to my desk, and started flicking through the opening chapters. I ran my finger swiftly down the centre of the pages, sweeping my eyes over all the made-up feelings and half-true memories. My professional prose, typeset and bound, had rendered the roughness of a human life as smooth as a plastered wall.

Nothing.

I threw it away in disgust. What a worthless piece of junk it was, what a soulless commercial exercise. For the first time I recognised something honest in the plodding earnestness of the original.

I opened a drawer and grabbed McAra's manuscript, tattered from use and in places barely legible beneath my crossings-out and overwritings.

'Chapter 1. Langs are Scottish folk originally, and proud of it . . .' I remembered the deathless beginning I had cut so ruthlessly in Martha's Vineyard. Come to think of it, every single one of McAra's chapter beginnings had been particularly dreadful. I hadn't left one unaltered. I searched through the loose pages, the bulky manuscript fanning open and twisting in my clumsy hands like a living thing.

'Chapter 2. Wife and child in tow, I decided to settle in a small town where we could live away from the hurly-burly of London . . . Chapter 3. Ruth saw the possibility that I might become party leader long before I did . . . Chapter 4. Studying the failures of my predecessors, I resolved to be different . . . Chapter 5. In retrospect, our general election victory seems inevitable, but at the time . . . Chapter 6. Seventy-six separate agencies oversaw social security . . . Chapter 7. Was ever a land so haunted by history as Northern Ireland . . . Chapter 8. Recruited from all walks of life, I was proud of our candidates in the European elections . . . Chapter 9. As a rule, nations pursue self-interest in their foreign policy . . . Chapter 10. A major problem facing the new government . . . Chapter 11. CIA assessments of the terrorist threat . . . Chapter 12. Agent reports from Afghanistan . . . Chapter 13. In deciding to launch an attack on civilian areas, I knew . . . Chapter 14. America needs allies who are prepared . . . Chapter 15. By the time of the annual party conference, demands for my resignation . . . Chapter 16. Professor Paul Emmett of Harvard University has written of the importance . . .'

I took all sixteen chapter openings and laid them out across the desk in sequence. *The key to everything is in Lang's autobiography—it's all there at the beginning.*

The *beginning* or the *beginnings*?

I was never any good at puzzles. But when I went through the pages and circled the first word of each chapter, even I couldn't help but see it—the sentence that McAra, fearful for his safety, had embedded in the manuscript: 'Langs Wife Ruth Studying In Seventy-six Was Recruited As A CIA Agent In America By Professor Paul Emmett of Harvard University.'

TEN

I left my flat that night, never to return. Since then a month has passed. As far as know, I haven't been missed. There were times, especially in the first week, sitting alone in my scruffy hotel room—I've stayed in four by now—when I was sure I had gone mad. I ought to ring Rick, I told myself, and get the name of his shrink. I was suffering from delusions. But then, about three weeks ago, after a hard day's writing, I heard on the midnight news that the former foreign secretary Richard Rycart had been killed in a car accident in New York City, along with his driver.

I knew after that there was no going back.

Although I've done nothing but write and think about what happened, I still can't tell you precisely how McAra uncovered the truth. I presume it started in the archives, when he came across Operation Tempest. He was already disillusioned with Lang's years in power, unable to understand why something that had started with such promise had ended in such a bloody mess. When he stumbled on those Cambridge photographs, it must have seemed like the key to the mystery. But McAra would have known that Ruth was a Fulbright scholar at Harvard, and it would have taken him ten minutes on the Internet to discover that Emmett was teaching her specialist subject on the campus in the mid-seventies.

He also knew that Lang rarely made a decision without consulting his wife. Adam was the brilliant political salesman, Ruth the strategist. She was the one that had the brains, the nerve and the ruthlessness to be an ideological recruit. McAra can't have known for sure, but I believe he'd put together enough of the picture to blurt out his suspicions to Lang during that heated argument on the night before he went off to confront Emmett.

I try to imagine what Lang must have felt when he heard the accusation. Dismissive, I'm sure; furious also. But a day or two afterwards, when he went to the morgue to identify McAra—what did he think then?

Most days I have listened to the disc of my final conversation with Lang.

The key to everything is there, I'm sure, but always the whole story remains tantalisingly out of reach. Our voices are thin but recognisable.

ME: Is it true you had a serious row with him? Just before he died?
LANG: Mike made certain wild accusations. I could hardly ignore them.
ME: May I ask what kind of accusations?
LANG: I'd prefer not to repeat them.
ME: Were they to do with the CIA?
LANG: Surely you know, if you've been to see Paul Emmett?
[A pause, lasting seventy-five seconds]
LANG: I want you to understand that everything I did, both as party leader and as prime minister—everything—I did out of conviction, because I believed it was right.
ME: [Inaudible]
LANG: Emmett claims you showed him some photographs. May I see?

I fast-forward to the part where he lingers over the girls at the picnic on the riverbank. He sounds inexpressibly sad.

'I remember her. And her. She wrote to me once, when I was prime minister. Ruth was not pleased. Oh, God, Ruth—'
'Oh, God, Ruth—'
'Oh, God, Ruth—'

I play it over and over again. It's obvious from his voice, now that I've listened to it often enough, that his concern is entirely for his wife. She must have called him late that afternoon in a panic to report I'd been to see Emmett and shown him some photographs. She would have needed to talk to him face-to-face as soon as possible—the whole story was threatening to unravel—hence the scramble to find a plane. God knows if she was aware of what might be waiting for her husband on the tarmac. Surely not, is my opinion, although the questions about the lapses in security that allowed it to happen have never been fully answered. But it's Lang's failure to complete the sentence that I find moving. 'What have you done?' is surely what he means to add. 'Oh, God, Ruth—what have you done?' This, I think, is the instant when the days of suspicion abruptly crystallise in his mind, when he realises that McAra's 'wild accusations' must have been true after all, and his wife of thirty years is not the woman he thought she was.

No wonder I was the one she suggested should complete the book. She had plenty to hide, and must have been confident that the author of Christy Costello's hazy memoir would be the least likely person to discover it.

I would like to write more, but this will have to do, at least for the present. As you can appreciate, I don't care to linger in one place too long. Already I sense that strangers are starting to take too close an interest in me. My plan is to parcel up a copy of this manuscript and give it to Kate. I shall put it through her door in about an hour's time, before anyone is awake, with a letter asking her not to open it but to look after it. Only if she doesn't hear from me within a month, or if she discovers that something has happened to me, is she to read it and decide how best to get it published. She will think I'm being melodramatic, which I am. But I trust her. She will do it. If anyone is stubborn enough and bloody-minded enough to get this thing into print, it is Kate.

I wonder where I'll go next. I can't decide. I know what I'd *like* to do. It may surprise you. I'd like to go back to Martha's Vineyard. It's summer there now, and I have a peculiar desire to see those wretched scrub oaks in leaf and to watch the yachts go skimming out full-sailed from Edgartown across Nantucket Sound. I'd like to return to that beach at Lambert's Cove and feel the hot sand beneath my bare feet, watch the families playing in the surf and stretch my limbs in the warmth of the clear New England sun.

This puts me in something of a dilemma, as you may appreciate, now that we reach the final paragraph. Am I supposed to be pleased that you are reading this, or not? Pleased, of course, to speak at last in my own voice. Disappointed, obviously, that it probably means I'm dead. But then, as my mother used to say, I'm afraid in this life you just can't have everything.

ROBERT HARRIS

Home: Berkshire
Relaxation: walking the dog in the country
Favourite book: *1984* by George Orwell

RD: When did the inspiration for *The Ghost* first come to you?

RH: A long time ago, maybe fifteen years, just after I'd finished *Fatherland*. I liked the idea of writing something—at first I thought a stage play rather than a novel—using the character of a ghostwriter, who would be licensed to ask questions of some powerful person. The obvious next step would be that he (or she) would discover something about their client which they weren't supposed to know.

RD: What stopped you putting pen to paper back then?

RH: There were two aspects I could never properly resolve: firstly, who would this 'powerful person' be? An ex-prime minister? An aspiring presidential candidate? A hugely rich businessman? And then, where would the book be set? Locations are important to me, and I could never decide where this one would be.

RD: And what eventually got you started?

RH: The decisive moment for me came about two years ago, when I heard a radio interview with someone who was trying to take Tony Blair to the International Criminal Court and have him prosecuted for war crimes. That immediately gave me the central character—a former British prime minister—and a location, the USA, which is where such a figure would have to go in order to seek sanctuary from arrest. So, to that extent the couple in the novel were suggested by the Blairs. But I genuinely maintain that they are fictional characters, and that once one gets beyond the superficial similarities, this is obvious.

RD: What comes first in your writing, plot or character?

RH: First comes an idea. Then characters begin to evolve out of the landscape of that idea. And then, finally, characters dominate: plot is simply a function of what these people might do, or be. Everything has to flow from their personalities, otherwise it will not be emotionally engaging, or plausible.

RD: The book has a lot of humour, was that fun to write?

RH: It was great fun. I liked the character of the narrator—his slightly desperate humour

—and it was a delight to be able to use his voice. My greatest regret as a writer is that I've never been able to include as many jokes as I'd like. This time I could.

RD: Did you visit Martha's Vineyard as part of your research?

RH: Yes. My agent in the US offered to introduce me to his godmother, who has a house on Martha's Vineyard, and she turned out to be Rose Styron, widow of writer William, who probably knows as much about the place as anyone. She knew all the Kennedy brothers and the Clintons and could get me into any location. She was marvellously helpful. When I wasn't with her, I wandered around on my own. I love seaside resorts out of season. This was in December. The place was deserted. It was the perfect backdrop for the story I wanted to tell.

RD: Can you tell us about your experiences when you went on the campaign trail with Tony Blair in 1997?

RH: I was a columnist on the *Sunday Times*, and knew Tony Blair reasonably well. He asked if I'd like to travel around with him during the campaign—much to Alastair Campbell's fury—and so I was given a ringside seat. I flew with him on his private jets and helicopters, I was with him before and after his speeches, I was standing next to him on election night in his sitting room when the exit polls announced that he was going to become prime minister with a landslide majority. It was a great privilege and I'll always be grateful to him for it. Not many journalists, let alone novelists, get that close to a successful politician at the climactic moment of his career.

RD: How does British political life today compare with that of ancient Rome, which you wrote about in your previous novel, *Imperium*?

RH: It was much more exciting in Rome, obviously, but it is astonishing how close the parallels are: the electioneering, the speeches, the importance of the law courts, and the perennial questions of liberty versus security, order versus anarchy, empire versus democracy. One gains a double benefit in writing about the past, conjuring up how things might have been, and at the same time acquiring a different perspective on the present.

RD: What is the best thing about being a successful writer?

RH: Freedom. Within reason, I can write what I like and spend as long doing it as is necessary. That is a luxury beyond price.

RD: Is there anything that you would change about yourself?

RH: A lot, from physical appearance through to my tone deafness, my hopelessness at languages, my allergy to sport. But I guess these are me, and made me a writer.

RD: What is the best piece of advice you've been given?

RH: I like Lloyd George's dictum: 'Never apologise, never explain.'

SACRIFICE

S.J.BOLTON

On Shetland, on a sunny day, the dark myths and lore of ancient times are easy to dismiss as so much superstitious nonsense. But the truth is, the old stories—including the strange legend of the Kunal Trows—have never disappeared completely from local minds. Beneath the surface of everyday life they still hold sway.

1

The corpse I could cope with. It was the context that threw me.

We who make our living from the frailties of the human body accept, almost as part of our terms and conditions, an ever-increasing familiarity with death. For most people, an element of mystery shrouds the departure of the soul from its earthly home of bone, muscle, fat and sinew. For us, the business of death and decay is gradually but relentlessly stripped bare, beginning with the introductory anatomy lesson and our first glimpse of human forms under white sheets in a room gleaming with clinical steel.

Over the years, I had seen death, dissected death, smelt death, weighed and probed death, even heard death (the soft, whispery sounds a corpse can make as fluids settle) more times than I could count. I'd become accustomed to death. I just never expected it to jump out and yell 'Boo!'

Someone asked me once, during a pub-lunch debate on the merits of various detective dramas, how I'd react if I came across a real live body. I'd known exactly what he meant and I'd told him I didn't know. But I'd thought about it from time to time. Would professional detachment click in, prompting me to check for vitals, make mental notes of condition and surroundings? Or would I scream and run?

And then came the day I found out.

It was just starting to rain as I climbed into the mini-excavator I'd hired that morning. The drops were gentle, almost pleasant, but a dark cloud overhead told me not to expect a light spring shower. It might be early May but, this far north, heavy rain was still an almost daily occurrence. It struck me that digging in wet conditions might be dangerous, but I started the engine even so.

Jamie lay on his side about twenty yards up the hill. Two legs, the right hind and fore, lay along the ground. The left pair stuck out away from his body, each hoof hovering a foot above the turf. Had he been asleep, his pose would have been comic; dead, it was grotesque. Swarms of flies were buzzing around his head. A magpie perched on the fence nearby, his gaze shifting from Jamie to me.

Goddamn bird wants his eyes, I thought, his beautiful, tender brown eyes. I wasn't sure I was up to burying Jamie by myself, but I couldn't just sit by and watch while magpies turned my best friend into a takeaway.

I put my right hand on the throttle and pulled it back to increase the revs. I felt the hydraulics kick in and pushed both steering sticks. The digger lurched forward. As it climbed the hill, I calculated quickly. Jamie was a fair-sized horse, fifteen hands and long in the back, and I would need a big hole, maybe an eight-foot cube. That was a lot of earth, the conditions were far from ideal and I was no digger driver. I expected Duncan home in twenty-four hours and I wondered if it might, after all, be better to wait. On the fence post the magpie smirked and did a cocky little side-step shuffle. I clenched my teeth and pushed the controls forward again.

Two yards away I stopped and jumped down. I knelt beside Jamie and stroked his black mane. Jamie, beautiful Jamie, as fast as the wind and as strong as a tiger. His great, kind heart had finally given up and the last thing I was ever going to be able to do for him was dig a bloody great hole.

I climbed back into the digger, raised its arm and lowered the bucket. It came up half full of earth. Not bad. I swung the digger round, dumped the earth, swung back and performed the same sequence again. This time, the bucket was full of dark brown soil. When we first came here, Duncan joked that if his new business failed, he could become a peat farmer. It covers our land to a depth of between one and three yards, and it was making the job heavy work.

After an hour, the rain clouds had fulfilled their promise and my muddy hole was around six feet deep. I'd lowered the bucket and was scooping forward when I felt it catch on something. I raised the arm, climbed out of the cabin and walked to the edge of the hole. A large object, wrapped in fabric stained brown by the peat, had been half pulled out of the ground by the digger. I jumped down into the hole to look.

Suddenly the day became quieter and darker. I could no longer feel the wind and even the rain seemed to have slackened. Nor could I hear clearly the crackle of the waves breaking on the nearby bay.

The fabric was linen, and from the frayed edges appearing at intervals I could see that it had been cut into twelve-inch-wide strips and wrapped round the object like a bandage. One end of the bundle was relatively wide, but then it narrowed down immediately before becoming wider again. I'd uncovered about three and a half feet, but more remained buried.

Crime scene, said a voice in my head; a voice I didn't recognise, never having heard it before. *Don't touch anything, call the authorities.*

Get real, I replied. *You are not calling the police to investigate a bundle of old jumble or the remains of a pet dog.*

I was crouched in about three inches of mud and raindrops were running off my hair and into my eyes. Glancing up, I saw that the grey cloud overhead had thickened. At this time of year the sun wouldn't set until at least 10 p.m. but I didn't think we were going to see it again today.

I looked back down. I tried not to think about Egyptian mummies, but what I'd uncovered so far looked distinctly human in shape. I tried to run my finger in between the bandages. They weren't shifting and I knew I couldn't loosen them without a knife. That meant a trip back to the house.

Climbing out of the hole proved to be a lot harder than jumping in, and I felt a flash of panic when my third attempt sent me tumbling back down again. The idea that I'd dug my own grave and found it occupied sprang into my head like a punch line missing a joke. On my fourth attempt I cleared the edge and jogged back down to the house. At the back door I realised that my Wellingtons were covered with wet, black peat. We have a small shed at the back of our property. I went in, pulled off my boots, replaced them with a pair of old trainers, found a gardening trowel and returned to the house.

I took a serrated vegetable knife from the cutlery drawer in the kitchen. Then I walked back to . . . my mind kept saying *gravesite.*

Hole, I told myself firmly as I jumped back in. It's just a hole.

The earth was soft and I didn't have to dig for long before I'd uncovered another ten inches of the bundle. I took hold of it round the widest part and pulled gently. With a soft slurping noise the last of it came free.

I reached for the end of the bundle I'd uncovered first and tugged at the linen to loosen it. Then I inserted the tip of the knife and, holding tight with my left hand, drew the knife upwards.

I saw a human foot.

I didn't scream. In fact, I smiled. Because my first feeling as the linen fell away was one of relief: I must have dug up a tailor's dummy, because human skin is never the colour of the foot I was looking at. I let out a huge breath and started to laugh.

Then stopped. Because the skin was the exact same colour as the linen that had covered it and the peat it had lain in. I reached out. Indescribably cold: undoubtedly organic. Moving my fingers gently I could feel the bone structure beneath the skin. Real after all, but stained a dark brown by the peat. The slender foot was a little smaller than my own and the nails had been manicured. I'd found a woman. In her twenties or thirties, I guessed.

I looked at the rest of the linen-wrapped body. At the spot where I knew the chest would be was a large patch, roughly circular in shape and about fourteen inches in diameter, where the linen changed colour, becoming darker, almost black. Somehow, I couldn't stop myself from making another cut. I pulled the dark cloth apart to see what was beneath.

Even then I didn't scream. On legs that didn't feel like my own I stood up and backed away to the side of the pit, then turned and leapt. Clambering out, I was surprised by the sight of the dead horse. I had forgotten Jamie. But the magpie had not. He was perched on Jamie's head, digging furiously. He looked up, guiltily; then, I swear, he smirked. A lump of shiny tissue, dripping blood, bulged from his beak: Jamie's eye.

That was when I screamed.

I SAT BY JAMIE, stroking his lovely auburn coat and waiting.

When I could no longer bear to look at him, I raised my head and looked out across the sea inlet known as Tresta Voe. Voes, or drowned valleys, are a common feature of this part of the world, dozens of them fraying the coastline like fragile silk. I was on the Shetland Islands, probably the most remote part of the British Isles. About a hundred miles from the northeastern tip of Scotland, Shetland is a group of around a hundred islands. Fifteen are inhabited by people; all of them by puffins, kittiwakes and other assorted wildlife.

When we first stood together on this spot, Duncan wrapped his arms round me and whispered that, long ago, a terrible battle was fought between massive icebergs and ancient granite rocks. Shetland, a land of sea caves, voes and storm-washed cliffs, was its aftermath. At the time, I liked the story, but now I think he was wrong; I think the battle goes on. In fact, sometimes I think that Shetland and its people have spent centuries fighting the wind and the sea . . . and losing.

It took them twenty minutes. The white car with its distinctive blue stripe and Celtic symbol was the first to pull into our yard. The police car was followed by a large, black, four-wheel-drive and a silver Mercedes sports car. Two uniformed constables got out of the police car, but it was the occupants of the other cars that I watched as the group headed towards me.

The Mercedes driver looked far too tiny to be a policewoman. Her hair was very dark, brushing her shoulders and layered around her face. As she drew closer I saw that she had fine, small features, hazel-green eyes and perfect skin the colour of caffè latte. She wore new, green Hunter boots, a spotless Barbour coat and crimson wool trousers.

Beside her the man from the four-wheel-drive looked enormous, at least six three, and broad across the shoulders. He too wore a Barbour and green Wellingtons but his were scuffed. His hair was thick and gingery-blond and he had the high-coloured, broken-capillaried complexion of a fair-skinned person who spends a lot of time outdoors. I stood up when they approached.

'Tora Guthrie?' he asked, looking down at Jamie.

'Yes,' I said, when he'd looked up at me once more. 'And I think you might be more interested in that one.' I indicated the hole. The woman was already standing at the edge, staring down.

The big policeman looked into my pit, then turned back to me.

'I'm Detective Inspector Andy Dunn of the Northern Constabulary,' he said. 'This is Detective Sergeant Dana Tulloch. She'll take you inside now.'

'ABOUT SIX MONTHS,' I said, wondering when I was going to stop shivering.

We were in the kitchen, Detective Sergeant Tulloch and I sitting at the pine table, a WPC standing in the corner of the room. Normally, our kitchen is the warmest room in the house, but it didn't feel so today. The constable had made us coffee and the hot mug between my hands helped a little.

DS Tulloch was typing away on a tiny notebook computer in between shooting questions at me. I'd changed out of my wet clothes and everything I'd been wearing had been bagged and carried out to one of the waiting cars.

'Five or six months,' I repeated. 'We moved here in December last year.'

'Why?' she asked. I'd already noticed her soft, sweet east-coast accent. She wasn't from Shetland.

'Beautiful scenery and a good quality of life,' I replied, wondering what it was about her that was annoying me. Nothing specifically to complain of: she had been polite, professional, if a little cold. She was economical with language, not a word escaping her lips that wasn't strictly necessary. I, on the other hand, was talking too much and getting edgier by the minute. This tiny, pretty woman was making me feel oversized, badly dressed, dirty and—of all things—guilty.

'And it's one of the safest places to live in the UK,' I added, with a mirthless smile. 'At least, that's what it said on the job ad.'

Detective Sergeant Tulloch was looking at me. There was a glint in her eyes that I couldn't identify. She was either pissed off or amused.

'My husband is a shipbroker,' I went on. 'He used to work at the Baltic Exchange in London. Around the middle of last year he was offered a senior partnership in a business up here. It was too good to turn down.'

'Bit of an upheaval for you. Long way from the South of England.'

I bowed my head, acknowledging the truth of what she said. I was a long way from the gentle, fertile hills of Wiltshire where I'd grown up; a long way from the dusty, noisy streets of London, where Duncan and I had lived for the past five years; a long way from parents, brothers, friends.

'For me, perhaps,' I said at last. 'Duncan was brought up on Unst.'

'Beautiful island. Do you own this house?'

I nodded. Duncan had put in an offer on one of several visits he'd made last year to sort out the details of his new business. Thanks to a trust fund he'd come into on his thirtieth birthday, we hadn't needed a mortgage. The first time I'd seen our new home was when it was already ours, and we'd followed the removal vans along the A971. I'd seen a large, stone-built house, about a hundred years old. Sash windows looked out over Tresta Voe at the front and the hills of Weisdale at the back. When the sun shone, the views were stunning. There was plenty of land for our horses; plenty of room inside for the two of us and anyone else who might happen to come along.

'Who did you buy it from?'

Realising the significance of the question, I came out of my little day-dream. 'I'm not really sure,' I admitted. 'My husband handled it.'

She said nothing, just raised her eyebrows.

'I was working out my notice in London,' I added, not wanting her to think me one of those women who leave all the financial stuff to the men-folk, even though I am. 'But I do know that no one had lived here for quite some time. The previous owners were some sort of church trust, I think.' I'd taken so little interest. I'd been busy at work, completely unenthusiastic about the move. I'd just nodded at what Duncan told me and signed where he'd asked. 'Yes, definitely something to do with the church,' I said, 'because we had to sign an undertaking that we'd behave appropriately.'

Her eyes seemed to get darker. 'Meaning?'

'Well, daft things, really. We had to promise that we wouldn't use it as a place of worship of any kind; that we wouldn't turn it into a drinking or gambling house; and that we wouldn't practise witchcraft.'

I was used to people being amused when I told them that. DS Tulloch looked bored. 'Would such a contract be enforceable, legally?' she asked.

'Probably not. But as we don't practise witchcraft, it's never really been an issue.'

'I'm glad to hear it,' she said, without a smile.

The room seemed to be getting colder and my limbs were stiffening up. I stretched, stood up and turned to the window.

Behold the crime scene: more police had arrived, including several wearing jumpsuits that appeared to have been made from white plastic bin-liners. A tent had been erected over my excavations and red-and-white-striped tape stretched the length of our barbed-wire fence. I turned back.

'But given the state of the corpse out there, maybe someone around here dabbles in the black arts.'

She sat up, lost her bored look. 'What do you mean, Dr Guthrie?'

'You should wait for the post-mortem. I could be wrong. The pelvic region is my speciality, not the chest. Oh, and it's Miss Hamilton. I'm a consultant surgeon. We are addressed as Mr or Miss, not Dr. And Guthrie is my husband's name. I'm registered under my own.'

'I'll try to remember that. In the meantime, we need to do something about that horse. The Scientific Support Unit will be arriving soon. They'll need to sweep the entire area. We may be here for weeks. We can't work round a rotting carcass.'

I think it was her choice of words, accurate but insensitive, that caused the tight ball to materialise in my chest, the one that tells me I'm mad as hell.

'I'll bury him myself,' I said firmly.

'As I'm sure you're aware, burying your own horse has been illegal for several years,' she said. I glared back at her. Of course I was bloody aware: my mother had been running a riding school for the last thirty years. But I was not about to argue with Sergeant Tulloch about the prohibitive cost of having a horse taken away on Shetland. Nor was I going to tell her about my (admittedly very sentimental) need to keep Jamie close.

Tulloch stood up and walked to the telephone. 'Would you like to make the arrangements,' she said, 'or should I?'

I honestly think I might have hit her at that point. Fortunately for us both, before Tulloch could lift the receiver, the phone rang. To my increasing annoyance, she answered it, then held it out. 'For you,' she said.

'You don't say!' Giving her my best glare, I grabbed the phone and turned my back on her. A voice I'd never heard before started talking.

'Miss Hamilton, Kenn Gifford here. We have a twenty-eight-year-old patient. Thirty-six weeks pregnant. She arrived about fifteen minutes ago, haemorrhaging badly. Foetus showing signs of mild distress.'

I willed myself to focus. Who the hell was Kenn Gifford? Couldn't place him at all. One of the house officers, maybe, or a locum?

'Who is she?' I said.

Gifford paused. I could hear paper being shuffled. 'Janet Kennedy.'

I swore under my breath. I'd been keeping a close eye on Janet. She was about three stone overweight, had a placenta praevia and, to cap it all, was a rhesus negative blood group. Placenta praevia means that the placenta has implanted in the lower, rather than the upper, part of the uterus, blocking the baby's exit. It is a major cause of haemorrhage in the final two months. Janet was booked in for a Caesarean six days from now but had gone into labour early. I looked at the clock. It was five fifteen. I thought for a second.

I took a deep breath. 'Get her into theatre. We need to anticipate intra-operative bleeding so let the blood bank know. I'll be twenty minutes.'

The line went dead, just as I remembered that Kenn Gifford was the Chief Consultant Surgeon and Medical Director at the Franklin Stone Hospital, Lerwick. In other words, my boss. He'd been on sabbatical for the past six months and, although he'd approved my appointment, we'd never met. Now he was about to watch me perform a difficult procedure with a serious possibility the patient might die.

And there I'd been, thinking the day couldn't possibly get any worse.

2

Twenty-five minutes later I was gowned up, scrubbed and heading for Theatre 2 when a house officer stopped me.

'We don't have enough blood,' the young Scotsman said. 'The bank's got only one unit of AB negative. We've ordered more but the helicopter can't take off at the moment. The wind's too strong.'

What the hell else was going to go wrong?

I glared at him, then pushed my way into theatre just as a huge man in air-force-blue cotton scrubs made the final incision into Janet's uterus.

'Suction,' he said. He took a tube from the attendant scrub nurse and inserted it to drain off the amniotic fluid.

In spite of the mask and theatre hat he wore, I could see at once that Kenn Gifford was exceptional-looking; not handsome, quite the opposite in fact, but striking all the same. The skin I could see above the mask was fair, but the theatre was hot and now his colour was high. His eyes were small, deep set, and of an indeterminate colour, perhaps grey.

He saw me and stepped back, gesturing me forward with his head. A screen had been set up to shield Janet and her husband from the gorier aspects of the operation. I looked down, determined to think about the job in hand. Gifford stood uncomfortably close, just behind my left shoulder.

'I'll need some fundal pressure,' I said, and he moved round to face me.

I went through the usual checklist in my head, noting the position of the baby, location of the umbilical cord. I put my hand under the baby's shoulder and eased gently. Gifford began to push on Janet's abdomen as my other hand slipped in round the baby's bottom. My left hand moved upwards to cup the head and neck, and then gently I lifted the mucus-covered, blood-smeared little body out of his mother and into his life. I felt that second of sheer emotion—of triumph, elation and misery all at once—that makes my eyes water and my voice tremble. Maybe one day I'll get so used to bringing new life into the world that it will cease to affect me. I hope not.

The baby began to scream and I allowed myself to smile, to relax for a second, before I handed him to Gifford—who had been watching me very closely—and turned back to Janet to clamp and cut the cord.

'What is it? It is all right?' came her voice from behind the screen.

Gifford took the baby to the Kennedys, allowing them a few moments to cuddle and greet their son before the weighing and testing began. My job was to take care of the mother.

Janet had lost a lot of blood, more than we were able to replace, and was still bleeding. Immediately after delivery the anaesthetist had given her Syntocinon, the drug routinely administered to prevent postpartum haemorrhage. In most cases it worked. In a very few it didn't. This was going to be one of the few. I delivered the placenta, then called my boss over.

'Mr Gifford.'

He crossed the room and we stood a little back from the Kennedys.

'We have only one unit of AB negative in stock,' I said. 'She's still haemorrhaging. She can't lose any more.'

Cursing under his breath, he stepped closer to Janet and looked at her. Then at me. He nodded. We walked round the screen. John Kennedy was holding his son, beaming. His wife, on the other hand, did not look well.

'Janet, can you hear me?' I asked.

She turned and made eye contact.

'Janet, you're losing too much blood. The drug we've given you to stop the bleeding hasn't worked and you're getting very weak. I need to perform a hysterectomy.'

Her eyes widened in shock.

'Now?' her husband said, his face draining pale.

I nodded. 'Yes, now. As soon as possible.'

He looked at Gifford. 'Do you agree with this?'

'Yes,' said Gifford. 'I think your wife will die if we don't.'

Pretty blunt, even by my standards, but I couldn't argue with him.

The Kennedys looked at each other. Then John spoke to Gifford again. 'Can you do it?'

'No,' he said. 'Miss Hamilton will do it better than I can.'

I somehow doubted that, but it wasn't the place to argue. A nurse arrived with the consent forms. I took a deep breath and got to work.

TWO HOURS LATER, Janet Kennedy was weak but stable, the wind had dropped and the blood she badly needed was on its way. She was probably going to be OK.

Gifford had stayed in theatre throughout the hysterectomy. He might have pretended absolute confidence when speaking to the Kennedys but he'd kept a pretty close eye on me. Once the operation was over, he'd left the theatre, at least trusting me to close by myself. But I wasn't really sure whether he'd been satisfied with me or not.

As I stood at my office window, waiting for the blood to arrive, the phone rang. I walked over to my desk.

'Miss Hamilton, this is Stephen Renney.'

'Hello,' I said, thinking, Renney, Renney, I should know that name.

'I heard you'd been called in. If you're not too busy, there's something you can help me with. Any chance of you popping down?'

'Of course,' I said. 'Anything I need to bring?'

'No, no, just your expertise. Call it professional pride, but I want to hand over a complete report when the big boys get here. I've got a suspicion which could be important and I don't want a couple of smart-arses from the mainland waving it in my face tomorrow morning like some big discovery.'

I had no idea what he was talking about but I'd heard it all before. So reluctant were the islanders to be thought inferior to their mainland counterparts that they created a climate of excellence, even overachievement, as the norm. I called it the Collective Chip on the Shetland Shoulder.

'I'm on my way,' I said. 'What room are you in?'

'One oh three,' he replied. A room on the ground floor.

I put the phone down and made my way downstairs. I found room 103 and pushed open the double doors. On the other side were DI Dunn, DS

Tulloch and Kenn Gifford. Also a small, bespectacled man with thinning hair whom I knew I'd seen before. Feeling like a complete idiot, I finally remembered that Stephen Renney was the hospital's locum pathologist.

Room 103 was the morgue.

THE SMALL MAN came forward, holding out a bony hand.

'Miss Hamilton, Stephen Renney. I'm so grateful. I've just been explaining that, in the interests of completeness, I really do need—'

The doors opened again and a porter wheeled in a trolley. We all had to stand back against the wall to let him past.

'Why don't we go into your office for a moment, Stephen?' Gifford said.

Stephen Renney's office was small, windowless and absurdly tidy. Two orange plastic chairs were placed in front of his desk. He waved his hand at them, glancing from DS Tulloch to me, then back to the detective sergeant. She shook her head. I remained standing, too.

'This is entirely inappropriate,' Tulloch said to her inspector, gesturing towards me. She was probably right, but I don't like being described as inappropriate; it tends to put my back up.

'Miss Hamilton isn't under suspicion, surely?' said Gifford, smiling at me. I was intrigued to see that he wore his blond hair unusually long for a man, especially a senior surgeon. His eyebrows and lashes were the same pale colour as his hair. 'She's only been here six months,' he went on. 'From what you tell me, our friend next door is headed for the British Museum. What's your best guess, Andy? Bronze Age? Iron Age?' He was smiling, not quite pleasantly. I had the feeling that Andy Dunn wouldn't know his Bronze Age from his Iron from his Stone, and that Gifford knew it.

'Well, actually . . .' Renney said, quietly, as if afraid of Gifford.

'Something like that,' agreed Dunn, and I was struck by how alike he and Gifford were: huge, fair-skinned, rather ugly blond men, and also by how many island men I could think of who resembled them. It was as though the islands' gene pool had been undisturbed since the Norwegian invasions.

'Wouldn't be the first to be found up here,' Dunn was saying. 'Peat bogs are notorious.'

'We saw Tollund Man once,' said Gifford. 'Do you remember that trip to Denmark in the lower sixth, Andy? Absolutely incredible. Came from the

Pre-Roman Iron Age but you could see the stubble on his chin, wrinkles on his face, everything. Perfect preservation.'

I wasn't remotely surprised to hear that Gifford and Dunn had been high-school contemporaries. Shetland was a small place.

'Maybe we can hang on to it,' said Dunn. 'Be good for tourism.'

'Oh, for God's sake!' I snapped. 'Correct me if I'm wrong, but as far as I'm aware, women in the Pre-Roman Iron Age didn't paint their toenails.'

Dunn looked as though I'd slapped him. Tulloch's mouth twitched briefly. Gifford stiffened but I couldn't read his expression.

Stephen Renney seemed relieved. 'That's what I've been trying to tell you. This is not an archaeological find. There are traces of nail varnish on her toenails and her fingernails. Plus some very modern dental work.'

Gifford sighed deeply. 'OK, what can you tell us, Stephen?' he asked.

Renney cleared his throat. 'What we have,' he began, 'are the remains of a female, aged between twenty-five and thirty-five. The peat has tanned her skin but I'm pretty certain she was Caucasian. I'm also as certain as it's possible to be that death wasn't due to natural causes.'

Well, there was an understatement if ever I'd heard one.

'What then?' asked Gifford.

Dr Renney glanced at me. 'The victim died from massive haemorrhage when her heart was cut out of her body.'

Gifford's head jerked; his face blanched. 'Jesus!' he said.

The two officers didn't react. Like me, they'd already seen the body.

Having got the worst over, Renney seemed to relax a little. 'A series of slashes, ten or twelve in all, with a very sharp instrument,' he said. 'I'd say a surgical instrument, or maybe a butcher's knife.'

'Through the rib cage?' said Gifford. It was a surgeon's question. I could think of no surgical instrument that would cut straight through a rib cage. Neither could he, judging by the way his eyebrows had knitted together.

Renney shook his head. 'The rib cage was opened first,' he said. 'Forced open with some sort of blunt instrument, I'd say.'

Saliva was building at the back of my mouth. The orange plastic chair in front of me started to look very inviting.

'Could the heart have been used again?' asked Dana Tulloch. 'Could she have been killed because someone needed her heart?'

I watched DS Tulloch, following her train of thought. One heard of such things: of people being abducted and their organs forcibly removed. It happened, but in faraway countries where human life was cheap. Not here.

'My guess is not,' Renney said. 'The inferior vena cava and the pulmonary veins were quite neatly removed. But the pulmonary trunk and the ascending aorta were badly hacked about. I'd say someone with a rudimentary knowledge of anatomy, but not a surgeon.'

'I'm off the hook then,' quipped Gifford.

Tulloch glared at him. I bit my lip to stop a nervous giggle slipping out.

'I've done a few quick tests and there are very high levels of Propofol in her blood,' continued Renney. He looked at DI Dunn. 'She was almost certainly very heavily anaesthetised when it happened.'

'Thank goodness for that,' said Tulloch.

'I also found evidence of trauma round her wrists and ankles,' continued Renney. 'I'd say she was restrained for quite some period before death.'

I'd done with being macho. I stepped forward and sat down.

'OK, so we know the how,' said Gifford. 'Any thoughts on the when?'

'Yes, exactly. When did she die? When was she buried? Very interesting questions, because with peat the normal process of decay is thrown into the air.' Stephen Renney seemed to be enjoying himself. 'You see, in a typical peat bog you have the combination of cold temperature, the absence of oxygen—which is essential for most bacteria to grow—and the antibiotic properties of organic materials, including humic acids, in the bog water.'

'I'm not sure I'm following you, Mr Renney,' said DS Tulloch. 'How can organic materials slow down decomposition?'

Renney beamed at her. 'Well, take sphagnum moss. When the putrefactive bacteria secrete digestive enzymes, the sphagnum reacts with the enzymes and immobilises them in the peat, bringing the process to a halt.'

'You're very well informed, Stephen,' said Gifford.

I swear I saw Stephen Renney blush at that point.

'Well, the thing is, I'm a bit of an archaeologist in my spare time. Sort of an amateur Indiana Jones. Part of the reason why I took this job. The wealth of sites on these islands is, well . . . anyway, I've had to learn quite a bit about the nature of peat bogs. Every time there's a dig I go along and volunteer.'

I'd risked a sneaky glance back at DS Tulloch, wanting to see how she took the comparison of the mouselike Stephen Renney with Harrison Ford. There was no hint of amusement on her face.

'But nail varnish was around for most of the last century,' said DI Dunn. 'She could still have been down there for decades?'

'Well, no, I don't think so,' said Renney. 'You see, although soft tissue can be well preserved by peat bogs, the same doesn't apply to bone or teeth. In a peat bog, the inorganic component of the bone, the hydroxyapatite, is dissolved away by the humic acids. What's left is the bone collagen, which then shrinks into itself and deforms the original outline of the bone. I've taken bone samples and examined her teeth and there's no trace of this process happening. So I'd say she can't have been buried for more than five years.'

'Looks like you could be a suspect after all, Miss Hamilton,' drawled Gifford, behind me. I decided to ignore that.

Renney looked up at him in alarm. 'No, no, I really don't think so. When I heard the body was coming I ran a quick Internet check on Miss Hamilton's village, Tresta, to find out if the area has a history of bog finds. It hasn't, as a matter of fact, but I did find something very interesting.'

He waited for us to respond. I wondered which of us would.

'What would that be?' asked Gifford, impatient now.

'A massive sea storm took place in the area in January 2005. The tidal defences were breached and the whole area was flooded for several days.'

I nodded. Duncan and I had been told about it when we bought the house. It had been described as a one-in-a-thousand-year event and we hadn't let it worry us.

'How would that be relevant?' I asked.

'If a bog gets flooded,' replied Renney, 'its tissue-preserving abilities become impaired. If our subject was in the ground when that storm occurred, I would expect her to be in a much poorer condition than she is.'

'Two and a half years,' mused Gifford. 'Narrows the field down.'

'I also had a look at her stomach contents,' Renney continued. 'She'd eaten, a couple of hours before she died. There were traces of meat and cheese, some possible remains of grains, maybe from wholemeal bread. Also, something else, that took me a while to identify.'

He paused; no one spoke but this time our unwavering attention must have been enough for him.

'I'm pretty certain they're strawberry seeds. But these are unusually small. Which suggests . . .'

'Wild strawberries,' said Gifford quietly.

'Exactly,' said Renney again. 'Tiny wild strawberries. They can be found all over the islands but have a very short season. Less than four weeks.'

'Late June, early July,' said Gifford.

'Early summer 2005,' I said, thinking I'd misjudged Stephen Renney. He was self-important and irritating but a very clever man nonetheless.

'Or early summer 2006,' said DS Tulloch.

'Yes, possibly. The key will lie in the tanning process. Our subject was completely coloured. The time it took for the acids to seep through the linen and stain the corpse will be crucial. I intend to get onto it this evening.'

'Thank you,' said Tulloch, sounding as though she meant it.

Wild strawberries. She had eaten wild strawberries and then, a few hours later, someone had cut out her heart. I started to feel sick and wanted to go. Unfortunately, I'd yet to play my part.

'What do you need me for, Dr Renney?' I asked.

'I need to check something with you. Something in your area.'

'Was she pregnant?' asked Tulloch quickly.

Renney shook his head. 'No; that I could have spotted myself. Our victim had given birth,' he said. 'What I can't tell you, and I'm hoping Miss Hamilton can, is how shortly before death it occurred.'

'The uterus swells during pregnancy,' I explained, 'and then starts to contract again immediately after delivery. If the swelling is still in evidence, it means she gave birth within a couple of weeks of her death.'

'Are you happy for Miss Hamilton to examine the body?' asked Renney.

DS Tulloch's eyes shot to her boss. He glanced at Gifford.

'Is Superintendent Harris coming over to take charge?' asked Gifford.

Andy Dunn frowned and nodded. 'For the next couple of days,' he said.

Of course, I had no idea who Superintendent Harris was, but I assumed some bigwig from the mainland. I guessed that DI Dunn and DS Tulloch were shortly to find themselves sidelined.

'Can't hurt to know,' said Gifford. 'Are you OK to do this, Tora?'

I had never felt less OK in my life.

I nodded. 'Of course. Let's get on with it.'

WE GOWNED AND SCRUBBED UP, the five of us, each witnessing that the others had followed procedure. We put on gloves, masks and hats and followed Stephen Renney into the examination room.

She lay on a steel trolley in the centre of a white-tiled room. Her linen shroud had been cut clean away, leaving her naked. She looked like a statue, a beautiful brown statue. I found myself wandering up towards her head.

She'd been pretty, her features dainty and regular. Her hair was very long; so long it trailed over the sides of the trolley, twisting in long spirals. It was the sort of hair I'd dreamed of having as a child. I started to find it hard to look at her face and moved down the body.

Although I'd attended post-mortems in the past, I don't think anything could have prepared me for the damage I was looking at.

On her abdomen Dr Renney had made a Y-shaped incision to enable examination of her internal organs, and this had been crudely sewn up, but the pathologist carried no responsibility for the more extensive damage to her chest area. There was a deep wound between her breasts, roughly oval in shape and about two inches long, where I guessed the blunt instrument had been inserted. I tried to imagine the force needed to inflict such a blow and was glad Dr Renney had told us what he had about Propofol. A jagged tear stretched vertically from the wound in both directions, reaching close to her neck and down almost to her waist, where the forcing open of the rib cage had torn her skin. I swallowed hard.

The room had fallen silent. I realised everyone was waiting for me.

'It's here,' said Renney, from behind me. He was holding a steel dish. He carried it over to the worktop and I followed.

Bracing myself, I lifted the uterus onto the scales. Fifty-three grams. Dr Renney offered me a ruler. I measured the length and the breadth at its widest, superior level. An incision had already been made and I opened it. The cavity was large and the muscular layers thicker and more defined than you would find in a woman who had never gone to full-term pregnancy.

I turned to Stephen Renney. 'Yes,' I said. 'She gave birth between a week and ten days before death. Difficult to be more precise.'

He smiled, delighted to have been proved right. 'There is one other thing the officers should see. Will you help me turn her?'

Gifford caught my eye. 'I'll do it,' he said, stepping forward.

He walked to the head of the trolley and slid his gloved hands beneath her shoulders. Stephen Renney held her round the hips, counted down, 'Three, two, one, turn,' and she was lifted up and turned. We could see her slender back, freckled shoulders, curved buttocks. No one spoke. The two police officers stepped closer to the trolley and—I couldn't help it—I did too.

'What the hell are they?' asked Gifford at last.

Three symbols had been carved into the victim's back: the first between her shoulder blades, the second across her waist and the third along her lower back. The first reminded me a little of the Christian fish symbol. The second consisted of two triangles lying on their sides with their apexes touching—how a child might draw an angular bow on a kite string. The third was just two straight lines, the longest running diagonally from just above the right hip bone to the cleft of her buttocks and the second crossing it diagonally. Each measured about six inches at its longest dimension.

'Very shallow wounds,' said Renney, the only one of us not transfixed by what we were looking at. 'Made with an extremely sharp knife.'

'While she was alive?' asked Tulloch.

Renney nodded. 'Oh yes. I'd say a day or two before she died.'

'Which would explain the need for restraint,' said Dunn.

'But what *are* they?' asked Gifford again.

'They're runes,' I said.

Everyone turned to me. Gifford twisted his head as if to say, Come again.

'Viking runes,' I elaborated. 'Some sort of ancient script brought over by the Norwegians. I have five in my cellar at home. Carved into some stone. My father-in-law identified them. He knows a lot about local history.'

'Do you know what they mean?' asked Tulloch.

'Haven't a clue,' I confessed.

'Would your father-in-law know what they mean?' asked Tulloch.

I nodded. 'Probably. I'll give you his number.'

'SO, WHAT HAPPENS NEXT?' Kenn Gifford asked, as the four of us walked back down the corridor towards the hospital entrance.

'We start combing the missing-persons lists,' replied Dunn. 'We get the nail varnish tested, find out where that batch was sold. Same with the linen.'

'With DNA and dental records, and what we know about her pregnancy, it shouldn't take long to find out who she is,' replied Tulloch. 'Fortunately, we have a relatively small population up here to work with.'

'Of course, she might not be from the islands at all,' said Inspector Dunn. 'We might be just a convenient dumping ground for a body.'

'With respect, sir, I'm sure she was local,' said Tulloch. 'Why would anyone travel out here to bury a body? Why not just dump it at sea?'

At that moment, my pager and Gifford's went off simultaneously. Janet Kennedy's blood had arrived. The two officers thanked us and left, heading for the airport to meet the mainland team.

AN HOUR LATER, all had gone well and I was back in my office, trying to summon up the energy to go home. I was standing at the window, watching banks of cloud roll in from the sea. I had a sharp, stabbing muscle-pain between my shoulder blades and I reached back with both hands to massage it.

Two hands, warm and large, dropped onto my shoulders. Instead of nearly jumping out of my skin, I relaxed and slid my hands forward.

'Stretch your arms up, high as you can,' commanded a familiar voice. I did what I was told. Gifford pushed down on my shoulders, rotating backwards and down. It was painful. I felt the urge to protest, as much at the impropriety as at the physical discomfort. I said nothing.

'Now, out to the sides,' he said. I reached out, as instructed. Gifford wrapped his hands round my neck and pulled upwards. I wanted to object but found I couldn't speak. He twisted once to the right and released me.

I spun round. The pain was gone, my shoulders were tingling and I felt great, like I'd slept for twelve hours.

'How'd you do that?' I took a step back.

He grinned. 'I'm a doctor. Drink?'

I felt myself blush. Suddenly unsure of myself, I looked down at my watch: 6.45 p.m.

'There are things I need to talk to you about,' said Gifford. 'Besides, you look as though you need one.'

'You got that right.' I found my coat and followed him out. As I locked my office I wondered how he'd managed to open the door and cross an uncarpeted room without my hearing him. Come to think of it, how come I hadn't noticed his reflection in the window? I must have been in a daydream.

TWENTY MINUTES LATER we'd found a window seat in the inn at Weisdale. The view of the voe was grey: grey sea, grey sky, grey hills. On Shetland, spring arrives late and sulking, like a teenager forced to attend church.

'I'd heard you didn't drink,' said Gifford, as he put a large glass of red wine down in front of me. He sat and ran his fingers through his hair, sweeping it up and back, away from his face.

'I didn't,' I replied, picking up the glass. 'That is, I don't usually. Not much.' Truth was, I used to drink as much as anyone, until Duncan and I started trying for a family. Then I'd taken the pledge. But my resolution had weakened of late. It's just so easy to tell yourself that one small glass won't hurt and then, before you know it, one glass becomes half a bottle and another developing follicle is seriously compromised. Sometimes I wish I didn't know so much about how the body works.

'I think you have a pretty good excuse,' said Gifford. 'Have you read Walter Scott's *Ivanhoe*?'

I shook my head. The classics had never really been my thing.

Gifford picked up his drink, a large malt whisky. While his attention was elsewhere I allowed myself to stare. His face was a strong oval, the dominant feature being his nose, which was long and thick, but perfectly straight and regular. He had a generous mouth, rather well drawn, plump and curved with a perfect Cupid's bow. He certainly couldn't measure up to Duncan, but there was something about him all the same.

He turned back to me. 'Nasty thing to happen,' he said. 'Are you OK?'

He'd lost me. 'Umm, finding the body, getting dragged into the post-mortem, or being deprived of *Ivanhoe*?' I queried.

Around us the pub was getting busy—mainly men, mainly young: oil workers seeking company more than drink.

Gifford laughed. 'You remind me of one of the characters,' he said. 'How are you settling in?'

'OK, thanks. Everyone's been very helpful.' They hadn't, but this didn't seem like the time to grouse. 'I saw the film. Do you mean the woman played by Elizabeth Taylor?'

'You're thinking of Rebecca. No, I meant the other one, Rowena.'

'Oh,' I said, waiting for him to elaborate. He didn't.

'Quite an experience you've had,' he said.

'Can't argue with that.'

'It's over now.'

'Tell that to the army digging up my field.'

He smiled. He was making me incredibly nervous. It wasn't just his size; I am tall myself and have always sought the company of big men. There was something about him that was just so there.

'I stand corrected,' he said. 'It'll be over soon.' He drank. 'What made you go into obstetrics?'

When I got to know Kenn Gifford better, I realised that his brain works twice as fast as most people's, flitting from one topic to another like a hummingbird dipping into this flower, then that, then back to the first. His speech follows suit. I got used to it after a while, but at this first meeting, especially in my keyed-up state, it was disorientating.

'I thought the field needed more women,' I said, sipping my drink.

'How horribly predictable. You're not going to give me that tired old cliché about women being gentler and more sympathetic, are you?'

'No, I was going to use the one about them being less arrogant, less bossy and less likely to jump on their dictatorial high horse about feelings they will never personally experience.'

'You've never had a baby. What makes you so different?'

I was drinking too quickly. I made myself put my glass down. 'OK, I'll tell you what did it for me. In my third year I read a book by some big obstetrical cheese. There was a whole load of bunkum in it, mainly about how all the problems women experience during pregnancy are due to their own small brains. But the bit that really got me was his dictum that new mothers should wash their breasts before and after each feed.'

Gifford was smiling now. 'And that's a problem because . . .?'

'Do you have any idea how difficult it is to wash your breasts?' From the corner of my eye, I saw someone glance in our direction. 'New mothers can feed their babies ten times or more in twenty-four hours. So, twenty times a day, they're going to strip to the waist, lean over a basin of warm water, give them a good lather, grit their teeth when the soap stings the cracked nipples, dry off and then get dressed again. And all this when the baby is screaming with hunger. I just thought: I don't care how technically brilliant this man is, he should not be in contact with stressed and vulnerable women.'

'I agree. I'll have breast-washing taken off the postnatal protocols.'

'Thank you,' I said, feeling myself starting to smile in response.

'Everyone seems highly impressed with you,' he said, leaning closer.

'Thank you,' I said again. It was news to me, but nice news all the same.

'Be a shame for you to be thrown off course so early.'

And the smile died. 'What do you mean?'

'Finding a body like that would unsettle anyone. Do you need to take a few days off? Visit your parents, maybe?'

Time off hadn't even occurred to me. 'No, why should I?'

'You're handling it well, but you have to be traumatised. If you need to talk about it, it's better that you do so away from here.'

'Better for whom?' At last, the real reason for our cosy little chat.

Gifford lowered his voice. 'Tora, this is no ordinary murder. If you want someone dead, you slit their throat or put a pillow over their face. You don't do what was done to that poor lass. It all smacks of ceremonial killing.'

'Some sort of cult thing?' I asked, remembering my taunts to Dana Tulloch about witchcraft.

'Who knows? It's not my place to speculate.' Gifford sat upright. 'Let the police do their job. Andy Dunn is no fool and DS Tulloch is the brightest button I've seen in the local police for a long time. My job, on the other hand, and yours, is to make sure the hospital continues to function calmly and that a ridiculous panic does not get a hold on these islands.'

I could see the first prickles of a beard jutting through his chin. I made myself look back up into his eyes, but it was making me uncomfortable; his stare was a little too intense. Green. His eyes were now a deep olive green.

'I need you to put the experience behind you now. Can you do that?'

'Of course,' I said, because I didn't have a choice. He was my boss, after all. I knew, though, that it wasn't going to be easy.

He leaned back in his chair. 'Tora,' he said. 'Unusual name. Sounds like it should be an island name, but I can't say I've heard it before.'

'I was christened Thora,' I said, telling the truth for the first time in years. 'As in Thora Hird. When I got brave enough, I dropped the H.'

'Damnedest thing I ever saw,' he said. 'I wonder what happened to the heart.'

I leaned back too. 'I wonder what happened to the baby.'

3

'Tora, what the hell were you thinking of?'

Our sitting room was gloomy. The sun appeared to have called it a day and Duncan hadn't bothered with the light switch. He was sitting in a battered old leather chair, one of our 'finds' from our bargain-hunting days around Camden Market when we were first married. I stood in the doorway, looking at his outline, not seeing his face properly in the shadows.

'Trying to bury a horse by yourself,' he went on. 'Do you know how much those animals weigh? You could have been killed.'

I'd already thought of that. A moment's carelessness, a tumbling earth mover and it could have been me lying on the steel trolley today.

'You're home early,' I said, pointing out the obvious.

'Andy Dunn phoned me. Thought I should get back here. Jesus! Have you seen the state of the field?'

I turned my back on Duncan and walked through to the kitchen. I tested the weight of the kettle and flicked the switch. Beside it stood our bottle of Talisker. The level seemed to have gone down considerably. But then again, I'd just come from the pub myself, hadn't I? Who was I to get preachy?

A movement behind me made me jump. Duncan had followed me into the kitchen. 'Sorry,' he said, putting his arms round me. 'It was a bit of a shock. Not quite the welcome home I'd expected.'

Suddenly, it all seemed more manageable. Duncan, after all, was on my side. I turned round so that I could put my arms round his waist and drop my head against his chest.

'I tried to phone,' I said lamely.

He let his chin drop so that it rested on the top of my head. It was our favourite hug pose, familiar, comforting. 'I'm sorry about Jamie,' he said.

'You hated Jamie,' I replied, nuzzling into his neck and thinking that one of the best things about Duncan was that he was so much taller than I.

'Only because he repeatedly tried to bring about my demise.'

I looked up at him and was struck, for the millionth time, by how bright blue his eyes were. And by how gorgeous a contrast they made with his pale skin and spiky black hair. 'What are you talking about?'

'Well, let me think. How about the time he got spooked at some cyclists on Hazledown Hill, leapt into the air, spun round, shot across the road in front of the vicar's new convertible and took off down the hill with you yelling "Pull him up, pull him up!" at the top of your voice.'

'He didn't like bikes.'

'Wasn't too keen on them myself after that.'

I laughed, something I couldn't have imagined myself doing just half an hour earlier. Nobody has ever been able to make me laugh the way Duncan can. I fell in love with Duncan for a whole host of reasons: the way his grin seems just a little too wide for his face; the speed at which he can run; the fact that everyone likes him and he likes everyone, me most of all. But it was the laughing that kept me in there.

He tightened his arms round me. 'I'm still sorry.'

'I know. Thanks.'

He pushed me away from him and we made eye contact. He ran his hand down my cheek. 'Are you OK?' He wasn't talking about Jamie any more.

I nodded. 'I think so.'

'Want to talk about it?'

'I don't think I can. What they did to her, Dunc . . .' I couldn't go on, couldn't talk about what I'd seen. But that didn't mean I could stop thinking about it. I wasn't sure I would ever be able to stop thinking about it.

Women in the first few days after childbirth—especially their first childbirth—are intensely vulnerable, often physical and emotional wrecks. To take a woman in this state, pin her down and carve up her flesh was the most unspeakable act of callousness I'd ever imagined.

He shushed me and held me close again. We stood, not talking, for what felt like a long time.

'The police will want to talk to you,' I said, straightening up.

Duncan's arms dropped to his side. 'They already have.' He walked over to the fridge and opened the door. He squatted down, peering inside.

'When?' I asked.

'Did it all over the phone,' he said. 'Dunn said he shouldn't need to bother me again. She was almost certainly buried before we came here.'

'They were asking about the previous owners.'

'Yeah, I know. I said I'd drop the deeds off at the station tomorrow.' Duncan stood up again. He carried a plate on which sat a half-eaten chicken carcass to the table. 'Tor, we need to try and forget about it now.'

Twice in two hours someone had told me that.

'Dunc, they're digging up the field. They're looking for more bodies. I don't know about you, but I'm going to find that a bit difficult to ignore.'

Duncan shook his head as he sliced into a red pepper. 'There aren't any more bodies and they'll be finished by the end of tomorrow.'

'How can they possibly know that?'

'They have instruments that can pick up the heat given off by decomposing flesh, apparently. Like metal detectors.'

Except any bodies out there were buried in peat. They weren't decomposing. 'I thought they'd have to dig up the whole field.'

'Apparently not. The wonders of modern technology. They've already done one sweep and found nothing. They'll do another tomorrow, just to be sure, then they're out of here.'

'Detective Sergeant Tulloch thought they'd be here for some time.'

'Yes, well, reading between the lines, I think the sergeant has a tendency to get a touch overenthusiastic. Bit too anxious to make her mark.'

Which hadn't been the impression I'd had of Dana Tulloch.

'You seem to have got very chummy with DI Dunn in one phone call.'

'Oh, we know each other from way back.'

I should have known. I felt annoyed that Duncan had been given far more information than I had, purely on the strength of being a fellow islander.

We sat down. I buttered some bread. Duncan served himself a large helping of cold chicken. I helped myself to salad and a piece of cheese.

'Were there any reporters when you got home?' I asked. By the time I'd arrived, just before nine, the place had been deserted apart from one solitary copper standing guard.

Duncan shook his head. 'Nope. Dunn's trying to keep a lid on the whole thing. Thinks it might be bad for tourism.'

'Jesus, not again. I had the same thing from Gifford. Bad for hospital PR. This isn't the people's republic of Shetland. You are remotely answerable to the outside world.'

Duncan had stopped eating and was looking at me. 'Gifford?'

'My new boss. He's back. I met him just now.'

Duncan stood up and poured an inch of neat Talisker into a glass. He drank, looking out of the window.

'Can't help thinking there's a story here,' I said.

Duncan didn't answer.

'Anything I need to know?' I tried.

Duncan muttered something that included more than one expletive. He doesn't often swear. By this stage I was shamefully curious.

He turned. 'I'm going for a bath,' he said as he left the room.

I made myself wait ten minutes before I followed him. I wandered back into our sitting room and switched on the TV just as the late news was starting. If I'd been hoping for a starring role I'd have been disappointed. The last item was a twenty-second piece about the discovery of a corpse in some peat land several miles outside Lerwick. DI Andy Dunn, standing outside Lerwick police headquarters, had said the minimum possible while still using words. He did, though, finish with a speculative comment about the possibility of an archaeological find. I guessed the recording had been made before we'd met Stephen Renney. It was an obvious attempt to play down the situation but I assumed he knew what he was doing.

When I went upstairs, Duncan was in the bath with his eyes closed. He'd filled the tub so full that water was trickling down the overflow pipe. I knew from experience that the temperature would be pretty close to forty degrees. About a year ago, before the sperm tests, I'd wondered if Duncan's hot baths were behind our failure to conceive. The effect of hot water on sperm is well known. But the results were normal.

I leaned against the basin. Duncan made no sign of knowing I was there.

'You can't just leave it at that, you know. I have to work with the man. We're probably expected to entertain him and his wife for dinner.'

'Gifford isn't married.'

I felt a jolt of something like relief mixed with alarm. Had I been hinting? And if I had, had Duncan spotted it?

'What is it?' I tried again.

Duncan opened his eyes but didn't look at me. 'We were at secondary school together. I didn't like him. The feeling was mutual.'

'Is that it?' I said.

Duncan sat up. He looked me up and down, and held out the loofah to me. It looked like some sort of kinky invitation. If I picked it up, we would have sex. If I didn't, I was rejecting him and would have to deal with sulks for the next couple of days. I thought for a second. My period was due any day but it was worth a try. I reached out for the loofah. Duncan leaned forward towards the tap, exposing his sleek, strong back.

'I prefer my handmaidens naked,' he said.

With one hand, I started to rub the loofah up and down his back. With the other, I unfastened the buttons of my shirt.

AFTER DUNCAN AND I had made love, I slept deeply. Until something woke me. I lay in the half-light of our bedroom, listening to Duncan's steady breathing beside me. Otherwise silence. I listened hard. Nothing.

I looked at the clock: 3.15 a.m., and about as dark as it ever got on Shetland during the summer, which wasn't very. I got up and walked to the window. Slowly, trying not to make a sound, I pulled up the blind.

I could make out just about everything: white police tent; red-and-white-striped tape; sheep in the neighbouring field; Charles and Henry, wide awake, with their heads poking over the fence. Horses are nosy. If they see someone close by, they hurry over for a better look. So who were they looking at?

Then I saw the light.

It appeared inside the police tent, a faint brightness shining briefly behind the canvas, then disappearing, then flashing again. Flash, sweep, flicker.

Something stroked my bare hip. Then Duncan's warm body pressed against me from behind. His hands slid round my waist.

'There's someone in the field,' I said. 'In the tent.'

'Can't see anything,' he said, nuzzling the place behind my ear.

'Well, you won't. You're not looking.' I pushed his hands away.

'It'll be the police,' he said. 'Dunn said they'd be leaving someone here overnight.'

'I suppose.'

We stood staring out into the darkness, but the light didn't appear again.

'Did they hurt her?' asked Duncan quietly after a minute or two.

I turned in surprise, glared at him. 'They cut out her heart.'

Duncan's pale face drained. Instantly I regretted being so brutal.

'Dunn didn't tell you that? I'm sorry . . .' I began.

He rubbed his hands over his face. 'Jesus, what a mess.'

There didn't seem to be an answer to that, so I said nothing. Duncan made no move to go back to bed and neither did I. After a while I started to feel the chill. I closed my eyes and leaned against him, seeking warmth.

Duncan wrapped his arms round me and said, 'Tor, would you consider adoption?'

I opened my eyes. 'You mean a baby?' I asked.

He squeezed one buttock. 'No, a walrus. Of course I mean a baby.'

Well, he'd certainly taken me by surprise. I hadn't thought about adoption, hadn't considered we were anywhere near that stage.

'It's just there's a good programme on the islands. It's not difficult to adopt here. A newborn, I mean. Not a screwed-up teenager.'

'How can Shetland have more babies than anywhere else?' I asked.

'I don't know. I just remember it being discussed when I lived here before. Maybe we're more old-fashioned about single mothers.'

It was possible. On the whole, moral standards in Shetland seemed comparable with what they'd been in the rest of the UK some twenty or thirty years ago. Maybe this was a real possibility.

Then Duncan took hold of me round the waist.

'Of course,' he said, 'we could just keep trying.'

LERWICK IS A GREY stone town on the eastern coast of the main island, a short channel hop from the island of Bressay. Like the rest of the islands' townships, it isn't noted for its architecture: the granite buildings are simple and functional but rarely beautiful. For the most part, two storeys are thought ample by the practical islanders—maybe they worry about high winds—but in the older parts of town and around the harbour a few three-storey, even four-storey houses can be seen. They seem to represent a rare flash of ambition, or defiance, on the part of the islanders.

Gazing at a rain-washed Lerwick from my office window, I found myself stifling a yawn. I hadn't slept well. I'd been restless, my head full of the woman I'd found. What had happened to her was appalling, and I was appalled . . . but I was angry too. Because I'd wanted to plant snowdrops on

Jamie's grave to remind me of the time he tried to eat some, and now I'd never be able to do that because some sick bastard had chosen our land to bury his dirty work on. And Jamie had been carted off to the knackers' yard.

I had seen my last morning appointment but I had a ward round in twenty minutes. Immediately afterwards I had to drive north and catch a ferry to the island of Yell for my monthly visit. I'd meet the island's midwife and hold a clinic for the eight women currently pregnant there.

The car park was below my window. Without really thinking I found myself searching for Gifford's silver BMW. Let the police do their job, he'd said. He was right, of course. But I still had eighteen minutes to kill.

Back at my desk I accessed the hospital's intranet site. It wasn't long before I had the file I wanted: a list of every baby born on the islands since records had been computerised. If Stephen Renney was right about the strawberry seeds, the woman's baby had to have been born in the summer of 2005. I highlighted the section between March and August and pressed print. I collected five printed sheets of A4 and spread them out on my desk. If she was a local woman, and if her labour had been medically managed, then my friend from the field was one of the names in front of me. It would just be a matter of checking whether each woman on the list was still alive.

A normal year on Shetland sees between 200 and 250 births and 2005 had been pretty typical with 227. Of these 140 had been delivered between March and August. I turned back to my screen and opened up a few individual files, looking for a Caucasian woman between twenty-five and thirty-five years of age. Just about every file I opened fitted the bill. There were a few teenage mothers, one or two older ones who could probably be discounted, two Indian women and one Chinese. Most of the women I was looking at would remain potentials.

My mind started wandering, in the way minds do when they come up against a brick wall. Out of nowhere, I heard Duncan talking about more babies being available for adoption on Shetland than in other parts of the UK. I wondered how I could check quickly.

I left the hospital's intranet site and accessed the Internet, typing General Register Office for Scotland into the search engine. When the site appeared, I called up the latest annual report. I'm not great with stats, but even for me it was clear. Teenage pregnancy rates were quite low on the islands. In fact, for the year I was looking at, they had been nearly 40 per cent lower than in the rest of Scotland. Wherever Duncan's glut of babies was coming from, it wasn't from our teenage mothers.

I went back to my list of 2005 babies, wondering how 140 names could be narrowed down. Most Shetlanders live on the main island and consequently most births take place here at the Franklin Stone Hospital. As I went down the list, I saw the occasional appearance of one or other of the smaller islands—Yell, Unst, Bressay, Fair Isle, Tronal, Unst again, Papa Stour.

Tronal? Now that was a new one on me. All the other islands I knew. They all had medical centres, resident midwives and regular antenatal clinics, presided over by yours truly. But Tronal I'd never even heard of, let alone visited. And yet it appeared four times. That probably meant between six and eight births a year, more than some of the other smaller islands. I made a mental note to find out about Tronal as soon as I could.

The list also gave the name and age of the mother; the date, time and place of delivery; the sex, weight and condition (i.e. live or stillbirth) of the baby. And something else. The initials KT appeared at the end of several entries. I tried to think of any condition or obstetric outcome that might be abbreviated to KT and couldn't.

I glanced at my watch. Time up. I was gathering up my things when there was a knock on the door.

'Yes, hello!' I called out.

The door opened and I looked up to see DS Tulloch in a crisp, slate-grey trouser-suit. Not a crease in sight.

'Good morning,' she said. 'Got a minute?'

'I have a ward round,' I said. 'But we're supposed to run ten minutes late.'

She raised her eyebrows. I was starting to hate it when she did that.

'It's written into our contract,' I went on. 'Creates the impression of being busy and important; stops the patients getting too demanding.'

She didn't smile.

'I understand my field will be cleared today after all,' I said.

'Yes, I understand that too,' she replied, walking over to my desk. She picked up the list. 'I came for this,' she said.

I held out my hand. 'I can't just pass over patient information. I have to ask you to put it down.'

She looked at me, put the papers back down on my desk and carried on reading them. I reached out. She held up a hand to stop me.

'Most of this is a matter of public record. I can get it elsewhere. It just seemed quicker to come to you. I thought you might want to help.'

Well, she had a point. She and I were supposed to be on the same side. I picked up the list anyway. 'I really should check before I—'

'Tora,' she said, using my name for the first time. 'I've spent ten years in the police force. But nothing could have prepared me for what we saw on the autopsy table last night. I want to get my team making phone calls to check these women are alive and busy looking after their two-year-old children. And I really want to do that now.'

I handed her the list. Her face softened as she took it from me.

'You can discount the ones who had Caesarean sections,' I said, wondering why I hadn't thought of it before. 'She didn't have a scar.' Well, not that sort of scar.

'Anything else?' she asked.

I shook my head. 'Have the Inverness pathologists finished yet?'

She didn't reply, and I looked pointedly at the list in her hand.

'Pretty much,' she said. 'We've also spoken to some experts on the impact of peat on organic material like linen. Dr Renney was spot-on about spring or summer 2005 being the time she died. This list is important.'

She thanked me and made for the door. 'Can I pop round to your house later?' she asked, glancing back. 'I need to see your runes.'

I suppressed a smile and nodded. I told her I'd be home about six.

My clinic on Yell overran and there was a queue for the return ferry. When I finally arrived home, Dana Tulloch's sports car was parked in my yard. I'd forgotten she was coming. I glanced at my watch. Damn! I'd kept her waiting nearly three hours. I got out of the car just as she climbed out of hers.

'I'm so sorry,' I said. 'Have you been here all this time?'

'Course not,' she said. 'When you didn't arrive at six I started making phone calls. I came back about ten minutes ago.'

She followed me inside and we went straight to the cellar, accessed via eight stone steps leading down from the kitchen.

'Good Lord,' she said, as we reached the bottom and I turned on the solitary light bulb. 'You'd never dream all this was beneath your house, would you?' She pulled a torch out of her bag and walked forward.

Our cellar is probably the most interesting feature of our property. It's older and larger than the house, and in places shows the remains of fire damage, so we surmised that the original house was destroyed some time ago, and had been considerably grander than our own. I led Dana through an archway into the biggest room and stopped in front of the north-facing wall.

'A fireplace?' she said. 'In a cellar?'

It had puzzled us too, but there it was. A fully functional fireplace with stone grate and chimney flue. A stone lintel had been fixed into the wall above the hearth and it was on this that the five runes had been carved.

'All different,' Dana said. With a small digital camera she took several photographs.

'Did you phone my father-in-law?' I asked.

She shook her head. 'Haven't needed to yet,' she replied. 'Found a book in the library at Lerwick.'

She finished her photographs and looked towards the stone archway that led to the rest of the cellars.

'Mind if I look around?' she asked.

'Be my guest,' I said. 'Mind if I get something to eat?'

She shook her head and turned away.

When she appeared ten minutes later, I was tucking into a microwaved portion of pasta with cream and ham. I pointed to the chair opposite mine. 'I made you a cup of tea.' I'd also put some local shortbread on the table.

She glanced at her watch, looked uncertain for a second, then sat down. She picked up the tea and gulped down a piece of shortbread in two bites.

'What do you know about the history of this property?' she said.

I shrugged. 'Very little. My husband handled the purchase. Didn't he bring the deeds over to the station this morning?'

'He did. But they don't tell us much. Some sort of church or religious building used to be here. It was demolished to make way for this house.'

'So what about the runes?' I asked.

She leaned down and pulled from her bag a notebook and a small, blue leather-bound book, with the title *Runes and Viking Script* printed in gold on the front. She turned the book round for me. On the inside front cover were pictured twenty-five runes: simple, mainly angular symbols, with descriptive names like Disruption, Standstill, Gateway.

'I don't get it,' she said. 'There are only twenty-five of them. Each one appears to have a distinct meaning of its own. How can they form any sort of alphabet and make words? There just aren't enough characters.'

I flipped through the book. 'I think it works a bit like the Chinese alphabet,' I said. 'Each character has a principal meaning but also several sub-meanings. And when you use two or more together, each one impacts upon the others to create a unique meaning. Does that make sense?'

'Yes,' she said. 'But there are over two thousand Chinese characters.'

'Maybe the Vikings didn't talk much.'

She opened her notebook and showed me a drawing of the three runes we'd seen on the victim. 'So what we have here,' she said, 'are the runes for Separation, Breakthrough and Constraint. What's that all about then?'

I looked from her notes to the textbook. On the next page the runes were reproduced again, this time with their Viking names. The fishlike symbol was Othila, meaning Separation, the kite bow was Dagaz, meaning Breakthrough, and the diagonal, swordlike rune was Nauthiz, meaning Constraint. On the page opposite, lesser meanings for each rune were listed. Othila also meant Property, Native Land, Home; Dagaz meant Day, God's Light, Prosperity; Nauthiz meant Need, Cause of Human Sorrow, Hardship.

'Separation of significant internal organ from rest of body?' I suggested, not entirely seriously. 'Breakthrough . . . umm, breaking through the chest wall to reach the heart? Constraint . . . well, she was constrained, wasn't she? The bruises round her ankles and wrists . . .' I tailed off and shook my head. 'What about the ones downstairs?'

She pressed a button on her camera and pulled up the photograph she'd taken. There were five symbols inscribed along the lintel.

'An arrow pointing upwards,' I said.

Dana flicked to the back page of the book. 'Teiwaz,' she said, 'meaning Warrior and Victory in battle.'

'Next up looks like a slanted letter F.' I reached over and indicated it on the page. 'There, what does it say?'

'Ansuz,' she replied, 'meaning Signals, God and River Mouth.'

'Our third symbol of the evening is a flash of lightning.'

'Sowelu. Wholeness, the Sun.' She looked up again.

'Next we have an upturned table called Perth, meaning . . . aah! Initiation.'

She frowned. 'I always worry when I hear that word.'

'Know what you mean. And, finally, a crooked letter H, called Hagalaz, meaning Disruption and Natural Forces.'

'Warrior, Signals, Wholeness, Initiation, Disruption,' Dana summarised.

We both made mystified faces.

'You need to talk to Duncan's dad. Maybe it's a question of context.'

'Who needs to talk to my dad?' said a voice from the doorway.

Duncan had crept up on us. He stood there, grinning, and I felt my stomach tensing the way it always did when Duncan was in the presence of a pretty woman who wasn't me. They had a way of softening around him: their skin would blush, eyes shine, bodies instinctively lean towards him. I braced myself for Dana to respond in the time-honoured way, but to my surprise she didn't. They exchanged a few pleasantries, she ascertained that he knew nothing more about runes than I did, and then she left.

4

'Go on, go,' I urged, as Henry moved into top gear. I rose out of the saddle and leaned forward as he pounded along the beach.

My favourite place to ride on Shetland was a half-moon beach, where dusky-pink, grass-tufted cliffs rose like the sides of a pudding basin around a bay of deepest turquoise. As I thundered along, spray blurred my vision and all I could see was colour: emerald grass, turquoise sea, pink sand and the soft, robin's-egg blue of the distant ocean.

I turned Henry and we walked back through the surf. Blissful emptiness of mind disappeared and reality came tumbling back.

Thursday was my regular day off. I was expected to stay near a phone in case of emergency but otherwise I was free to relax. Some hope.

For a start, something was worrying Duncan but he wasn't telling me about it. His new business was proving harder to settle into than he'd expected and the hours he was working were as long as mine but he was doing it six, sometimes seven days a week. The couple of times I'd mentioned babies his face had tightened and he'd changed the subject just as soon as he could. He hadn't spoken about adoption again. That morning, he'd left on a three-day trip back to London for meetings with clients.

Second, I wasn't performing well at work. Nothing had gone wrong yet, but I was clumsy both in theatre and in the delivery room. I was pretty certain that no one, either on the medical team or among the patients, actually liked me. And it was my fault. I couldn't relax and be natural. Either I was stiff and cold or I made inappropriate jokes, getting glassy-eyed stares in response.

Third, I was itching to know what was happening in the murder investigation. A team had come over from Inverness, but most of them had gone home and Dunn and Tulloch were, once again, in charge. I'd thought about calling Dana but didn't much fancy the inevitable rebuff I'd get. I'd made a point of catching the main news each evening for the last few days but had learned nothing. There had been some coverage in the local press and on Shetland TV, but far less than I'd expected. Nobody from the media had tried to interview me. Nobody at work had bothered to ask about it. For God's sake, I'd wanted to yell. We dug up a body four days ago, not ten miles from here. Does nobody care? I had wondered if Gifford's oblique warning to me in the pub that night had been repeated across the hospital: Don't discuss the grisly murder that has taken place among us, because that will be bad for the social and economic health of the islands.

And then there was Kenn Gifford.

I'd met him just four days ago, and since then he'd been on my mind a lot more than he had any business to be. I'd been married for five years and of course Gifford wasn't the first man I'd found attractive during that time. It had never been a problem. I have this simple test. I say to myself, 'Tora, however amiable, however pleasing to the eye he may be, can he honestly measure up to Duncan?' And the answer has always been the same: never in a million years. But with Gifford it wasn't quite so clear-cut.

All in all, I had quite a lot to think about.

Henry, perhaps picking up on my mood, started to skitter about. A guillemot flew close and he shied, backing into the water, bucking and kicking.

I tightened the reins and pulled him up sharply. 'Pack it in!' I snarled.

I pulled him round so that he was facing up the beach and out of the sea. He sidestepped and backed up further. I kicked him onwards and he shot forwards, just as I saw a man standing on the cliff top, staring down at us.

The cliffs were to the east of us, the sun was still low, and the man was little more than a shadow blocking out a fraction of the early-morning light. He was tall and broad and his hair, long and loose, seemed to gleam like gold. The sun was hurting my eyes and I closed them for a second to shut out the brightness. When I opened them again the man was gone.

I urged Henry away from the surf and put him into an active walk along the beach. It was two miles to home and I still had Charles to ride.

CHARLES WAS IN NO STATE to be ridden. Missing Henry and with no Jamie to keep him calm, he'd panicked, jumped a fence into the next field, stumbled on the uneven ground and fallen into the stream that runs down our land. In slipping he'd dislodged an old barbed-wire fence and wrapped it round his left hind leg. His eyes were rolling and his grey coat was dark with sweat.

I untacked Henry as fast as I could and pushed him into the field. Hearing Charles's panic he rushed up to the fence and started calling out to him. Horses have a particular whinnying cry when they're distressed that pierces your heart. Charles's cries doubled in volume and he started to kick.

I knew I'd never get the wire off Charles without some sort of wire cutter, so I turned and ran back into the house. I was wearing an ancient pair of green Hunter Wellingtons and they were caked in mud from the last time I'd worn them—Jamie's aborted burial day. The dried mud flaked off over the carpet as I rushed upstairs to the spare room at the top of the stairs where Duncan kept his tools. I rummaged frantically through the toolbox, pulled out a pair of cutting pliers, raced downstairs and back outside.

I found Henry preparing to jump the fence to join Charles in the stream. He needed to be tied up but the time it would take me to find a head-collar and catch him just couldn't be spared. Blood was running down Charles's leg, and I thought he'd probably done irreparable damage to it. Surely I wasn't about to lose a second horse in as many weeks?

Forcing myself to move slowly, I approached Charles. He was using his front legs in a scrambling motion to try to propel himself out of the gully, but every effort pushed the sharp prongs of the wire deeper into his flesh.

I tried to calm him. 'Steady, steady, steady, whoa now, steady.' I looked down at the three strands of wire connecting Charles to the fence. If he would let me approach, I might be able to cut through the wire.

I jumped down into the gully and Charles glared, swinging round to face me. Talking gently, I moved forward. If he sprang, I could be pinioned beneath two very powerful forelegs; if he fell, I'd be crushed. I was tempted to give up and ring the vet. Yet I knew that if there were to be any possibility of saving Charles, I had to get him loose immediately.

I moved forward again as Charles reared on his trapped hind leg. He fell forward and I moved again before he could recover. Crouching in the ditch, willing myself to ignore the half-ton of muscle and bone poised above me, I squeezed the pliers round the first thick strand of wire. It snapped, and Charles chose that moment to kick out with both hind legs. The remaining wire dug deep into his fetlock and he screamed and reared again. This time those murderous forelegs were above me and coming down fast.

'Stay where you are,' said a voice.

I froze.

Charles's forelegs came down with a thud on the bank and he sobbed. Believe me—that's what he did. A tanned, freckled arm covered in fine golden hairs was wrapped round his neck and two enormous hands were gripping his mane, holding him still. It was impossible. No man is strong enough to hold a panicking horse, without reins, but Gifford was doing it.

As I lay, half in and half out of the ditch, unable to move a muscle, I watched Gifford stroke Charles's mane, whispering softly. Charles was trembling, still visibly distressed, but otherwise perfectly still. This was my chance to cut the two remaining strands of wire. Yet I still couldn't move.

'Cut them, now,' said Gifford, without moving from his close embrace of the horse. His left hand was still clutching Charles's mane, his right was stroking his neck; short, quick, firm strokes.

I turned. Lying on my stomach, I pushed myself forward, closer to Charles's hind leg. Gifford resumed his low chanting. Shutting my mind to what could, at any moment, come slamming down on top of me, breaking my back and rendering me crippled at the very least, I reached forwards, clamped the pliers round the closest piece of wire and cut it. Without stopping to think I reached for the second wire and squeezed. It broke with a high-pitched zinging sound that seemed to echo around the voe.

'Get out of there,' called Gifford and I rolled, over and over, until I judged I was far enough away to be safe.

I looked back to see that Gifford had pulled Charles out of the ditch and was struggling to hold him still. Free at last of the painful brace, Charles just wanted to bolt, but Gifford was having none of it. He hung close round Charles's neck, muttering in his ear all the while. After a minute or two, Charles admitted defeat. He drooped, seeming to lean against Gifford.

It was, quite simply, incredible. I'd heard, of course, of people with uncanny abilities to calm animals. I'd seen the film *The Horse Whisperer*, but I'd never seen anything like it in real life.

Gifford let go, and Charles cantered off towards the fence, where Henry had been watching the whole incident with increasing impatience. Charles slowed to a walk. He was lame but still able to put weight on the damaged limb. I started to hope that it wasn't going to be too bad after all.

'How'd you do that?' I asked, without taking my eyes off Charles. 'He wouldn't let me near him.'

'You were more afraid than he was,' replied Gifford. 'He could sense that. I wasn't scared and I wasn't standing for any nonsense.'

It made sense. Horses are herd animals, following without question a strong leader—equine or human. Horses like to know who is boss.

'And I used a bit of hypnosis. Just to calm him down.'

That made no sense. I turned to look at Gifford.

'Animals are very susceptible to hypnosis,' he said. 'Especially horses.'

'You're kidding me,' I said, although he looked perfectly serious.

'You're right, I'm kidding you. Now, painkillers and a tetanus jab.'

'I'll call the vet,' I said.

'I'm talking about you,' said Gifford, running his hand up my right arm towards the shoulder. The pain was as sharp as it was surprising; either Charles had kicked me without my noticing, or I'd fallen on a sharp stone.

'Let's go in,' he said. 'I'll see what I've got in my bag.'

Gifford's car was parked in our yard and he took his bag from the boot as we walked past. In the kitchen I took off my riding helmet and sat down at the table, acutely conscious of the debris from breakfast and that my hair needed washing. I probably didn't smell too good, either. Gifford turned on the tap and let it run till the water steamed. I unbuttoned my shirt and wriggled out of the sleeve. As he started to bathe my arm I assessed the damage. Most of my upper arm was starting to bruise. There was a nasty scratch, which was bleeding and hurt like hell, but it didn't look too deep.

Gifford dressed the wound and gave me a tetanus jab. Finally, he offered me painkillers and I took them gratefully.

He looked at his watch. 'I have surgery in twenty minutes.' He started to pack away his things.

'What are you doing here?'

He laughed. 'Thank you, Mr Gifford, for saving my life, not to mention that of my horse.' He closed his bag.

'Put my bad manners down to shock. Why are you here?'

'I wanted to talk to you away from the hospital.'

And there was my heartbeat, skipping away on a roller-coaster ride of its own. I just knew there was bad news coming.

'Oh?'

'There've been complaints.'

'About me?'

He nodded.

'From whom?'

'Doesn't matter. I told them I'm highly impressed with what I've seen so far and that I have every intention of keeping you on the team. But that you are in a new environment and they need to cut you some slack for a while.'

'Thank you,' I said, feeling no better.

'Don't mention it.' He lifted his bag. 'You need to make the effort, too. Your technical skills are all there but you don't handle people that well.'

That pissed me off, big time. Probably because I knew he was telling the truth. I stood up. 'If you have a problem with my performance at work there are procedures you need to follow. You don't need me to tell you that.'

Gifford wasn't intimidated. 'Oh, get over yourself. We can do it by the book if you want. It will take an immense amount of time and the end result will be no different, except there'll be a damaging paper trail on your file. See you tomorrow.'

He turned and was gone, leaving me alone with a very sore arm and my self-esteem in tatters.

TEN MINUTES LATER the vet had been summoned and the pain in my arm had faded to an ache. I sat on the fence, watching Charles hobble around, knowing there was nothing more I could do for him but reluctant to leave him by himself. I found the pliers and used them to cut several strands of wire from the broken fence posts. I gathered it up and carried it back to the yard, then I took the pliers inside.

God damn Gifford for a patronising, manipulative bastard. Over the years I'd learned to recognise this kind of crude but highly effective professional one-upmanship. I was tempted to dismiss it as obnoxious power play. On the other hand, I've always known that I'm not popular: I don't have the gift of making small talk, I don't smile easily and I have quite a way with the clumsy remark and the ill-timed joke. I am a perfectly competent doctor; I work hard and never knowingly carry out a dishonourable act, but because of a lack of surface charm, I'm doomed to be disliked by those around me.

On the third stair up there was a gold ring.

I stood, staring at it. It was a wide band, with some sort of pattern etched round the upper and lower circumferences, and it was caked in dried mud.

I bent to pick it up. Some of the mud flaked away, a sizable piece with a definite indentation along one side. I sat down and took off one of my boots. Hunter boots have a distinctive pattern on the underside and the piece of mud that had fallen away from the ring seemed a pretty good match. The ring must have spent the last few days stuck to the underside of my boot. My running up the stairs had dislodged it.

I felt a bolt of panic. I'd been wearing these boots when I'd found the body last Sunday. The police forensics team had taken away the trainers I'd replaced them with, but I'd forgotten all about the boots.

It's what they were looking for in the field the other night.

Suddenly, I felt nervous. If someone had been looking for it, then whoever killed her was still on the islands. I stood up, listening for sounds in the house, as though someone might be creeping up on me even now. Then I walked back into the kitchen and locked the back door. I went to the sink and ran about two inches of lukewarm water. I dropped the ring into it, waited a few seconds then rubbed it between my palms. I dried it on a tea towel and, without really thinking, slipped it onto the third finger of my left hand. It wouldn't go past the knuckle.

The body I'd seen on the morgue trolley was that of a slim woman. Was I now looking at her ring? Well, whatever the case, I had to let Dana Tulloch know immediately. Naturally, she'd be furious with me. Not only had I carried a crucial piece of evidence away from a crime scene, delaying its discovery by several days, but I'd even washed away the surrounding mud.

I put the ring down on the kitchen worktop and crossed to the phone. As I started to dial, the sun flashed in through the window, making the ring gleam. I replaced the receiver and picked up the ring again. There was an inscription inside. Too easy, I thought. I held it up to the light. It was engraved in virtually indecipherable italic script. The first letter was J, the second H or maybe N. Then there was a K followed by what could have been a C or a G. Then there were four numbers: a four, a five, a zero and a two. If they were the initials of the marrying couple and the wedding date, and if the ring had come from my friend, then we'd identified her.

I found the phone book. There were twenty registration districts on Shetland. I dialled the number for the Lerwick office. It was answered immediately. I told the woman who I was, stressing my position of seniority at the hospital. As usual, it worked; she became interested, eager to help.

'We've found a piece of jewellery. I think it's a wedding ring,' I explained. 'It has an inscription that looks like a date and some initials. You may be able to help trace its owner. You keep records of weddings, don't you?'

'All weddings in Lerwick, yes. Did the wedding take place in the town?'

'I'm not sure, I think so. I don't have a name, though.'

'Well, you could come along and look up all the weddings that took place on that particular day and see if your initials match any of them. Our hours are ten a.m. till one p.m. and then two till four.'

I glanced at the clock. The vet was due any second but I had nothing planned for the rest of the day that couldn't wait.

'Thank you,' I said. 'I'll be along this afternoon.'

TWO HOURS LATER I arrived at the registry office in Lerwick. The vet had been and gone. Charles was going to be fine: lame for a few days, but then good as new. The news had softened my fury with Gifford. He might have given my confidence a kicking but at least he'd saved my horse.

Before leaving home I'd phoned DS Tulloch and left a brief message on her voicemail, telling her I'd found something that might be connected to the murder and that I'd drop it by the station on my way into town. I hadn't been specific. I'd put the ring in a sterile bag and enclosed it, with a brief note, in a large brown envelope. When I'd arrived at the station Dana was still out, so I left it, marked for her attention, at the front desk.

Marion, the woman I'd spoken to on the phone, led me to a computer. Taking a Post-it note out of my bag I double-checked the date: May 4, 2002. I found the right year and scrolled down until I came to the 4th of May and immediately spotted a possibility. Kyle Griffiths married Janet Hammond at St Margaret's Church. I scribbled down the details.

'Found anything?'

I jumped before I could help it, then took a deep breath and told myself not to look guilty or apologise. I turned round.

Dana Tulloch, as usual, was immaculately dressed, in black trousers, red top and an obviously expensive plaid jacket.

She pulled up a chair beside me. I showed her my scribble. She nodded.

'I'll get it checked,' she said. She reached into her bag and pulled out the clear plastic wallet I'd left at the station earlier. The ring gleamed inside it. 'When did you find it?' she asked.

'This morning,' I said. 'Late morning.'

'How sure can you be that it came out of the same patch of ground?'

'I can't,' I said. 'But I haven't worn those Wellingtons since Sunday.'

'They should have been given to the SSU.'

I couldn't remember what the SSU was, but I knew I was in trouble.

'Slipped my mind,' I said truthfully. 'I was traumatised.'

'And you washed it.' She shook her head. 'It's all far from ideal.'

'I'm sure the woman missing her heart would agree with you.'

Dana sighed and leaned back in her chair. 'You really shouldn't be here.'

I looked her straight in the eye. 'I dug her up. I have an interest.'

'I know. But you should let us do our job.' She stood up. 'I spoke to your father-in-law,' she went on. 'He said the book I had was as good an authority as I was going to get. He was sorry he couldn't be more help.'

I stood too. 'There are eight more registration districts on the southern part of the mainland,' I said.

She looked at me. 'And?'

'I have no plans for the rest of the day. From here, I'm going to Walls, then to Tingwall. I expect to be done by about five and I'll probably be in the mood for a drink in the Douglas Arms. Tomorrow I'm back at work and no longer available to act as your unpaid personal assistant. If I were you, I'd make the most of it.'

I walked out of the office, feeling rather spitefully pleased at doing something of which I knew the police and my boss would disapprove.

BY FIVE FIFTEEN I was back in Lerwick. I walked into the dim interior of the Douglas Arms and spotted Dana sitting alone at a table in one of the darker corners, gazing at the screen of her laptop computer. I bought myself a drink and sat down beside her.

'Come here often?' I asked.

She looked up and frowned. 'Anything?' she said, looking pissed off.

I opened my notebook. 'One more possibility,' I said. 'A Kirsten Georgeson, aged twenty-six, married a Joss Hawick at St Magnus's Church in Lerwick. How about you?'

'Three districts, no matches,' she said. 'And I checked out the one you found earlier. Janet Hammond is living in Aberdeen, very much alive.'

'Well, good for her.'

'Quite.' She wiggled the mouse around on the table and a new screen appeared: the list of births on the islands I'd given her three days earlier. 'The team have almost finished checking this,' she said. 'The ones in the right age and ethnic groups are almost all accounted for. It looks as though she wasn't a local woman, after all.'

I now understood why she looked annoyed. Her boss was about to be proved right and she wrong. 'That throws it wide open.'

'Oh yes.'

There was a rush of cold air as the door opened and a group of men from one of the rigs came in. Noise levels in the pub leapt up.

'What do you know about Tronal?' Dana asked.

'An island,' I said. 'Four women on the list gave birth there.'

Dana nodded. 'Two of whom we haven't been able to trace yet. So yesterday, DI Dunn and I took a trip. It's about half a mile off the coast of Unst, privately owned. They have a state-of-the-art maternity hospital there, run by a charitable trust, with links to the local adoption agency.' She appeared to enjoy the look of amazement on my face. 'They offer, and I'm quoting now, a "sensitive solution to unfortunate and ill-timed pregnancies".'

'Hang on . . . but . . . where do these women come from?'

She shook her head. 'All over the UK, even overseas.'

'Don't such women just have terminations?'

'Tronal does those as well. But they say some women have ethical difficulties with abortion, even in this day and age.'

I was still struggling with the idea of a maternity facility I knew nothing about. 'Who provides obstetric support?'

'They have a resident obstetrician. A Mr Mortensen. Fellow of your—what do you call it—Royal College?'

I nodded, but was far from happy. A Fellow of the Royal College of Obstetricians and Gynaecologists? For fewer than a dozen births a year? 'What happens to the babies?' I asked, wondering whether Duncan had been thinking about Tronal when we'd talked about adoption the other night.

'Most are adopted here on the islands,' said Dana, confirming my guess.

'And you think the woman in my field could have been a Tronal woman? Maybe a mother who changed her mind about giving up her baby?'

'It's possible. The only women outstanding from your list gave birth there.'

I fell silent then, wondering why I'd been told nothing about Tronal. It was a few seconds before I realised Dana was talking to me and I had to ask her to repeat herself.

'What does KT mean? It appeared on your list seven times.'

I'd forgotten about that. 'I don't know,' I had to confess. 'I'll check it out tomorrow.'

She fell silent again. I realised I needed the loo.

When I returned, she was staring at her computer screen, at what appeared to be an online telephone directory.

'What's up?' I said.

She looked at me. 'I need to go and check out the Hawicks, the ones who got married on May the 4th, 2002. I think this ring could be a red herring. I want to get it out of the equation.'

'Want some company?' I ventured, not expecting that she would say yes.

She frowned, then nodded. 'Yes, thank you. That would be good.'

WE TOOK HER CAR. The Hawick family lived at Scalloway, the old capital of the Shetlands, about six miles west of Lerwick and a much smaller town. The road was quiet and we arrived in fifteen minutes.

'Second on the right,' I instructed, looking at a map Dana had given me.

We turned into the street where a J. Hawick lived. It ran directly along the coastline on the south side of the town. The moment we left the car, the wind raced towards us like a battle charge, and it whipped up and tangled our hair as we waited on the doorstep of the house. When Mr Hawick opened the door, we must have looked like two dishevelled mermaids.

From his physique and his hair colour, I guessed Joss Hawick to be in his mid to late thirties, but his face suggested someone a good decade older. His white work shirt was slightly grey and hadn't been well ironed.

Dana showed her ID and introduced herself and me.

Hawick looked only mildly interested and not remotely concerned: like a man with nothing left to lose. 'What can I do for you?' he asked.

Dana explained about the ring and its engraving. Before she'd even finished speaking he was shaking his head.

'Sorry, Sergeant, wasted trip. Now if you'll excuse me.'

He began to back away; the door started to close on us.

Dana was having none of that. 'Sir, this is important. Are you certain that your wife is not missing a ring? Could we just check with her?'

'Sergeant, my wife is dead.'

Dana flinched, but I wasn't surprised. The drawn, empty look that Joss Hawick wore is invariably seen on the faces of the bereaved.

'I'm so sorry.' I spoke for the first time. 'Did she pass away recently?'

'Three years this summer.'

'Had you been married long?'

'Just two years,' he said. 'Last Friday would have been our anniversary.'

I thought quickly. Today was Thursday, May the 10th. Friday, six days ago, had been the 4th. But the year didn't fit. This man's wife had died in 2004, not 2005. Because of the flood, Renney had been certain our victim hadn't been in the ground longer than two years.

'Mr Hawick.' It was Dana this time. 'The inscription on the ring refers to May the 4th, 2002. Was that your wedding day?'

Angry now, he looked from Dana to me. 'What's this about?' he demanded.

We were inside. His house, bright and trendily furnished, looked like the home of a young, affluent couple, but layers of dust lay on the mantelpiece and the windowsill, and the rug hadn't been vacuumed any time recently. He'd offered us a drink, which we'd declined, and had left the room to get himself one. Glancing around, I noticed a photograph in a pewter frame on the mantelpiece. A younger, happier Joss Hawick beamed at the camera. At his side, white veil billowing around her head, was his wife. Kirsten Hawick had been a tall, attractive woman—with long red hair, falling in ringlets almost to her waist. I looked quickly at Dana. She'd seen the photograph already. She frowned at me, her unspoken instruction clear: Keep quiet!

Hawick came back and sat down on a chair opposite us. That was one large Scotch he carried and it didn't look diluted.

'I'm sorry for your loss, sir,' Dana began.

He turned to me and I felt a stab of alarm. 'Why are you here? Are you about to tell me the hospital did something wrong?'

Dana spoke quickly. 'Miss Hamilton has been at the hospital five months. She knows nothing about your wife's death. May I ask you some questions?'

He nodded. And drank.

'Could you just confirm your wife's maiden name?'

'Georgeson,' he said. 'Kirsten Georgeson.' He drank again.

I glanced at Dana. If she was as worried as I was, she wasn't showing it. I knew that the first suspect in a murder case is always the spouse. What I'd taken for grief on Joss Hawick's face might actually be guilt, and fear of being found out. The names fitted—KG and JH—and the date. But there was still the discrepancy of the year of her death.

'May I ask how and where she died?' Dana asked.

He looked at me again. 'In hospital,' he said. 'In your hospital.' He made it sound like an accusation. 'She'd been in a riding accident. Her horse was hit by a lorry just a couple of miles north of here. She was still alive when they got her to hospital but with very severe brain damage and a broken neck. We switched the machines off after three hours.'

'Who treated her?' I asked.

'I can't recall his name,' he replied. 'But he said she had absolutely no chance of recovery. Are you about to tell me he was wrong?'

'No, no,' I said hurriedly. 'Nothing like that. I do need to ask you something else, though, and I am truly sorry to add to your grief. Did your wife have a baby shortly before she died?'

He flinched. 'No,' he said. 'We were planning a family, but Kirsten was a good rider. She wanted to compete for a few years before giving up.'

Joss Hawick was pretty convincing. But he had to know I could check his story out in minutes.

Dana stood up. I stood too. We went to the front door.

'One thing puzzles me,' Hawick said as Dana and I stood in the doorway.

'What's that, sir?'

'You said you'd found a ring. It can't be Kirsten's.'

'Why not?'

'It *was* inscribed, but I knew it was tight on her finger and I didn't want it forced off. I asked that she be buried wearing it.'

I couldn't help it. 'Where?' I said. 'Where was she buried?'

He looked surprised and a little disgusted, as though the question was in poor taste. Which it was—but hell, I had an excuse.

'St Magnus's Church,' he said. 'Where we were married.'

'WE SHOULD HAVE brought two cars,' said Dana. 'Damn!'

She started the engine and drove 500 yards down the road, until we were just out of sight. I fumbled in my bag and found my cellphone. Within minutes a taxi was on its way to us. Dana pulled out a notebook and started scribbling. I glanced at the page and read: *Kirsten Hawick, née Georgeson. Died summer 2004. Head injury. Franklin Stone Hospital.*

'He's lying,' I said. 'It's her.'

'Possibly.'

'You saw the photograph. How many women have hair that long? It's got to be her.'

'Tora, calm down. It was a small photograph. We can't be sure.' She scribbled something else. 'This is my mobile number,' she said, tearing the page out and handing it to me. 'Get to the hospital as soon as you can and check it. Don't speak to anyone else. I'll stay here until I hear from you.'

I nodded. 'Will you be OK?'

'Of course. I'm just going to sit in my car and watch.'

The taxi arrived shortly afterwards and I was off.

FIFTY MINUTES LATER I called her. She answered on the first ring.

'It's me,' I said. 'Can you talk?'

'Go ahead.'

I took a deep breath. 'Everything he told us is true.'

Silence. I thought I could hear the wind whistling around Scalloway Voe.

'What now?' I said.

She thought for a moment. 'I need to drop by the station. Go home. I'll see you there.'

It was just after eight in the evening and the Franklin Stone was still busy. I hoped I wouldn't bump into anyone I knew as I left the building. I was seriously disturbed and I'm not a good liar at the best of times.

Kirsten Hawick had to be the woman in my field. Death hadn't changed her much. That delicate, white skin had been tanned by the peat, but her face had still been the perfect oval that I'd seen in the photograph.

Yet I'd just called up her hospital medical records. She had indeed been admitted on 18 August 2004, presenting with severe head trauma and multiple fractures of her upper spine. She'd been pronounced dead at 7.16 p.m. and her body released for burial two days later.

I stopped at the front desk to borrow a street map from the night porter. St Magnus's Church, I found, wasn't far from the hospital.

I WAS GLAD it was still light when I arrived at St Magnus's. I had to park on the main road and walk down a narrow street, and after dark I'm not sure I'd have found the courage. The area was deserted. Tall, granite buildings towered overhead. Converted to offices, they were empty for the evening.

I found my way into the small, walled churchyard, and followed an overgrown path to the more recent graves at the back. It took me five minutes to find it. A large, granite headstone, the carving simple:

KIRSTEN HAWICK

1975–2004

A MOST BELOVED WIFE

The mound of earth had been flattened and planted with spring bulbs. Some of the daffodils were still in bloom; others had dried, their petals shrivelled and orange. They needed to be deadheaded. I knelt down and, because I really couldn't think of anything else to do, started knotting the stalks. When I'd finished the grave looked neater.

'Touching,' said a voice.

I spun round to see two men standing over me. Two tall men. The setting sun was directly behind them and for a second I wasn't sure who they were. Then, with a sinking heart, I recognised both. I stood up, determined to brazen it out. I pointed at the grave.

'So, who do you reckon is down here?' I said.

Andy Dunn looked back at me like I was a difficult child. 'Kirsten Hawick is buried here,' he said. 'Joss Hawick is extremely distressed. He'll probably make a formal complaint.'

'I can't imagine what about,' I snapped. 'He was handled with extreme sensitivity and the visit was perfectly legitimate. There was every chance that the ring—the one I found on my land—was his wife's.'

'How's your horse?' asked Gifford, interrupting my train of thought.

'Please, Kenn,' said Dunn, sounding tired.

I ignored Gifford and looked at Andy Dunn. 'I saw her photograph this evening. It's the same woman. How else do you explain the fact that a ring, bearing the date of their wedding and their initials, was found in my field?'

'Tora.' It was Gifford now. 'You saw the corpse only twice. The first time it was covered in peat and you were in shock. The second time was on an autopsy table and, frankly, you didn't look at her face that much.'

I looked at Gifford. His eyes seemed larger and brighter than I remembered. For the first time that evening I started to have doubts.

'I knew Kirsten Hawick,' he went on. 'I'd have recognised her. She was nearly your height. A good five inches taller than the corpse you found.'

I shook my head, but what he was saying was plausible.

He reached out and put a hand on my shoulder, speaking quietly. 'Two doctors, a nurse and her husband were present when the machines were turned off. Kirsten Hawick died in our hospital.'

I wasn't giving in easily. 'Then her body was stolen. Probably from the hospital morgue. Someone stole the body because they wanted her heart.'

They looked at me like I was deranged.

'The woman in your field had just had a baby,' said Gifford. 'Kirsten Hawick had never been pregnant.'

Well, I had to admit, he had me there. Plus, according to Dr Renney, the heart had been removed while the victim was still alive, not post-mortem.

'And the timing just doesn't fit,' added Dunn, imitating Gifford's gentle tones. 'I've checked with the Inverness pathology team. The woman from your field could not have been dead since 2004.'

I looked down at the grave. 'There's one way to know for sure.'

Dunn glared at me. 'Don't even think about it. We are not about to start exhuming graves. Do you have any idea how much distress that causes?'

Gifford's hand left my shoulder and slid down my arm, my sore arm. I had to grit my teeth not to flinch. 'This is exactly what I was afraid of. Tora, I want you to think again about taking some time off.'

I shook my head. There were some difficult deliveries coming up and the hospital needed me.

'OK.' He glanced at Andy Dunn, as if to say, I've done my best. 'I'd like to see you in the morning. Can you be in by eight?'

I nodded, feeling like a delinquent teenager whose parents were being just too understanding.

Gifford smiled at me. 'Come on. I'll walk you to your car.'

Andy Dunn followed us in silence as we walked down the path and left the churchyard. As I drove away, I could see them both in the rearview mirror, standing in the road and watching me.

WHEN I ARRIVED HOME, a shadowy figure was huddled on my doorstep. I shrieked as it moved towards me.

'It's OK, it's only me.' Dana stepped out into the light.

Even as I knew there was nothing to worry about, my nerve endings felt as though someone had administered a thousand tiny electric shocks.

'We arranged to meet here, remember?' she prompted.

'Yes, but . . . you obviously haven't seen your DI this evening.'

'Of course I've seen him. Why, have you?'

I nodded. 'He found me in St Magnus's churchyard. At Kirsten's grave.'

Her eyebrows shot up. 'Did he, now?'

'He explained everything. He and Kenn Gifford.'

She looked at me with both amusement and pity on her face. 'And you fell for it? Tora Hamilton, you are not the woman I took you for.'

5

'I saw her grave, Dana, it's just not possible.'

We were sitting at my kitchen table, doors locked, blinds drawn. I was tired and had an uncomfortable sense of being drawn back into something I'd been happy to leave behind just half an hour ago. We were drinking hot, strong coffee. I'd offered red wine but Dana had shaken her head. 'We need to think,' she'd said. Scary word: we. Suddenly, we were accomplices, working against clear instructions from our superiors.

'Everything is possible,' she said now. 'I just can't see how they did it.'

'Who exactly are *they*? You're talking about my boss. He's a Fellow of the Royal College of Obstetricians and Gynaecologists, for heaven's sake. There were other people in the room when the machines were turned off.'

I stood up to make a sandwich. I got out the ham, butter and bread.

'Does it strike you as odd that the two of them should follow you to the churchyard? How did they know you'd gone there? And why would it bother them?' Dana stopped, thought for a second. 'Do I sound paranoid?'

I glanced over my shoulder. 'Only totally.'

'Thanks.' To her credit, she managed a smile.

'Welcome.' I bent down once more, fumbling in the back of the fridge for the mayonnaise. When I straightened up she was serious again.

'There's something I want you to do,' she said.

'What?'

She reached into a briefcase and pulled out a folder of thin, green cardboard. From inside she removed a sheet of black and white transparent film.

'This is a dental X-ray that was taken of our corpse. My team have been checking it against records of women on the missing-persons list. No matches so far, although obviously not all records are available to us.'

'What do you want me to do?'

'I have nagged and pleaded, but DI Dunn will not even consider asking Joss Hawick to release his wife's dental records for comparison.'

I really couldn't see where she was going with this. 'So . . .'

'You should be able to find them. There was an IT pilot scheme carried out here a year ago, and all the islands' NHS dental records were computerised. There's a dental unit attached to your hospital. Kirsten's records will probably be on the hospital computer system. You can access them.'

'I'm not a dentist,' I said lamely.

'You've studied anatomy. You know how to read X-rays. You'd have a better chance of seeing a match than I would. Will you do it?'

I didn't know. Following a hunch was one thing, asking someone you barely knew to carry out an illegal search was another.

'If there's no match, that's it,' she said. 'The ring is a red herring and we waste no more time on it.'

It was worth it, surely, to be able to close the chapter. I could prove to Dana that the corpse was not Kirsten and that would be the end of it.

'OK, I'll do it tomorrow.'

I'M NOT SURE at what point in the night I started to suspect that there was someone in the room with me. I can't explain how I knew; I just did. When you habitually sleep with a partner, you develop a sense of the closeness of the other and, upon waking, a dozen triggers remind you in an instant that he is still there: the scent of skin, the sound of breathing, the extra warmth another body creates. The otherness beside you is comfort and familiarity.

This was neither comfortable nor familiar. The presence I could sense was alien, intrusive, predatory. I lay there, unable to move a muscle. I'm not sure how much time passed: it felt like for ever; it was probably only a minute or two. Then the lightest movement of air passed across my cheek, the atmosphere in the room changed and I found myself sitting up.

The room was dark, much darker than normal. I looked all around, struggling to make everything out, to see into the deepest shadows. There was nothing and no one in the room that shouldn't be there.

Then I noticed that the bedroom door was slightly ajar. Strange though it may seem, I cannot sleep when there are doors open around me. Duncan laughs at me, but the doors to the corridor and to our bathroom have to be closed before I go to sleep.

I made myself climb out of bed as I tried to remember what we are supposed to do in these situations. Make a noise or be silent? Pick up the phone and loudly pretend to call the police? I walked to the door and eased it open. The corridor was empty. Downstairs something scraped along a wooden floorboard.

I ran back into the bedroom, pulled open the wardrobe door and reached up to the top shelf. My fingers touched what I was searching for and I pulled it down. I checked the bolt was set and held it out in front of me, the way I'd seen people do on television. Then I stepped out along the corridor and paused at the top of the stairs. I was carrying a humane horse-killer, a crude, inefficient weapon of iron and copper. It had belonged to my grandfather and had been designed to put down injured or very old horses by firing a four-inch iron bolt directly into their brains. It was completely ineffective unless the target was close enough to touch, but having a weapon, even this one, gave me the courage to walk down the stairs.

Our front door was at the bottom. I checked quickly: still closed and locked. I pushed open the door to the dining room and looked around. Nothing that I could see.

Down the hall came the sound of something breaking, footsteps running, a door being pulled open. I ran into the kitchen, fumbling for the light switch as I went. A glass vase, which I'd left too close to the edge of the worktop, had smashed into a thousand pieces on the slate floor. The back door was open and the cold night air was pushing its way into the room. I ran across, slammed it shut, turned the key and pulled both bolts into place.

As I turned to the phone, I noticed something.

I stopped moving, even stopped breathing. I absolutely could not take my eyes off what lay in front of me. For a second or two I even thought I'd lost my mind. I grabbed the phone. Then I ran, out of the kitchen, across the hall and into the downstairs lavatory. I slammed the door behind me, pulled the bolt and sank to the floor. Fighting back nausea, I phoned the police.

FOR THE TWENTY MINUTES it took them to arrive, I barely moved. I couldn't stop shaking. Every few minutes nausea reared up but thankfully always stopped short of making me chuck. I phoned Duncan's mobile but he'd switched it off. I didn't leave a message. What the hell would I say?

Eventually I heard cars pulling into the yard and made myself get up to answer the door. Andy Dunn took one look at me and ordered me into the sitting room with a WPC. A blanket materialised and I sat, shivering, trying to answer the questions that she and a detective constable put to me. From the kitchen I heard Dunn's sharp intake of breath, the blasphemous exclamation of the sergeant accompanying him. Then I heard Dunn on the radio:

'Yeah, we've got a break-in. Some sort of organ left on the kitchen table. Looks like a heart . . . yeah, looks human . . .'

I pushed myself up, ignored the protests of the two officers and walked into the kitchen. The heart hadn't been touched. It lay, glistening, in a pool of blood. The smell was strong, metallic, sickening.

'I don't think it's human,' I said.

Dunn stopped talking into the radio, muttered something about getting back and switched it off. 'You don't?' he said.

I shook my head. 'I thought it was, at first. But I've had time to think about it . . .' The truth was, I still wasn't sure. 'Mammalian hearts are all very similar in structure,' I went on. 'There's an outside chance it's the heart of a big adult male. Over six foot and powerfully built. But if I was putting money on it, I'd say it came from a large pig.'

The relief in the room was almost strong enough to reach out and touch. I was ordered back into the other room and questioned again. More police arrived. They dusted for fingerprints, walked the perimeter of the property with dogs and removed the heart. There was no sign of any break-in.

Eventually, Dunn came to join me on the sofa.

'You need to get some rest now,' he said gently. 'I'm leaving a couple of constables in the house for the rest of the night. You'll be perfectly safe.'

'Thank you,' I managed.

'Duncan's back on Saturday, right?'

I nodded.

'You might want to find somewhere else to stay tomorrow. This is almost certainly some sort of sick practical joke but whoever got in here did so without breaking in. A change of locks probably isn't a bad idea.'

I nodded again.

He gave my arm a feeble pat, then he got up and left. I went upstairs thinking that, as practical jokes go, it was the least funny I'd ever heard of. Besides, it didn't feel like a joke to me. It felt like someone was trying to scare the shit out of me.

'TOR, I FOUND THE RING.'

'What? You did what?'

It was 7.45 the next morning; I was running late and driving too fast. Duncan had called to say he had an extra meeting scheduled—a really important one—and wouldn't be home till Saturday evening. He'd sounded so excited about the potential deal, so fired up, that I couldn't bring myself to tell him about what had happened the night before. I'd be OK for another night. I could always sleep at the hospital.

So instead, I'd told him about all the stuff that had happened the previous day: finding the ring on my boot, checking the registers and visiting both the Hawick family home and the graveyard. I'd even told him about my plans to carry out an illicit search of dental records. He'd listened patiently until I'd just about done, then dropped his bombshell.

'I found it,' he was saying, 'months ago, before you came out. I was laying concrete in the bottom field to put the fence posts in. I saw it lying on a pile of earth. I must have dug it up. I threw it into my toolbox and forgot about it.'

And suddenly, it all made sense: the ring had been in Duncan's toolbox. I'd dislodged it when I'd been looking for something to cut the wire round Charles's leg and it had landed on the stair. It had been nowhere near my Wellington and—more importantly—nowhere near the grave. The ring was a red herring after all.

'But how did it get there?' Red herring or not, it still didn't add up.

'Good question. Assuming it really is the wedding ring of the woman who died. Is it possible it wasn't? How clear was the inscription?'

'Not very.' I hadn't even been completely sure about the letters. Only the date was clear, and several weddings had taken place that day.

'Tor, you're not really going to check dental records, are you? At best it's a waste of time and at worst illegal. Don't get involved any more.'

It's not often Duncan asks me to do something.

'No, of course not. You're right.' I meant it, too. It had gone far enough.

'Good girl. I'll see you tomorrow. Love you.'

He hadn't said that in a long time. By the time I was ready to respond, he'd hung up.

I was on the edge of Lerwick now and drove quickly to the hospital. I glanced at the car clock. I was going to be ten minutes late.

Kenn Gifford was waiting for me in my office, looking out of the window, already dressed in blue surgical scrubs, his long hair in a ponytail.

'How are you feeling?' he asked, turning round.

'Been better,' I replied. 'Sorry I'm late. Duncan phoned.' I told Gifford about Duncan finding the ring. When I'd finished, he nodded.

'I'll call Joss Hawick. If he wants to pursue the matter he can call into the police station to identify it. If it is his wife's ring, it looks like we have a pilfering problem—a particularly distasteful one, at that, if someone is robbing the morgue. I'm sorry all this is happening, Tora, it can't be easy settling in with all these distractions. Can I get you a coffee?'

'Thanks,' I said.

He walked over to the coffee-maker in the corner and poured two cups.

'Do you have some sort of master key?' I asked.

He turned round, a steaming mug in each hand, and raised his eyebrows.

'I lock my office in the evening but you managed to find your way in and organise breakfast. Do you have croissants baking as well?'

'No, I don't have a master key. The cleaner was in here when I arrived and let me stay and make coffee. Just thought you might need it.' He handed me a mug. 'DI Dunn came by earlier,' he said. 'He wanted Stephen Renney to confirm that the heart wasn't human.'

'And . . .?' I prompted.

'From a pig,' he said.

'Is he still going with his practical-joke theory?'

Gifford nodded. 'I think he's right, don't you? Why would the killer, assuming he's still around, take such a risk? Supposing you'd seen him?'

Then I'd be dead right now.

'Andy's done his best to keep details under wraps,' continued Gifford, 'but this is a small place. Any number of people might know that you found the body, about the missing heart. As jokes go it's not particularly tasteful but there are some very odd people around.'

'Is he making progress with the murder investigation?' I asked.

'The victim matches no one on the local missing-persons list,' he said. 'Andy has his team combing similar lists for the rest of the UK. Sooner or later they should get results.'

'You'd think so, but . . .' I stopped. He'd known Dunn since school, he'd known me for a matter of days. Where did I think his loyalty would lie?

'But what?' he prompted.

'He just doesn't seem to be taking it terribly seriously. First the body was an archaeological find, then the victim couldn't possibly be local, and then last night was a practical joke. It's like he's playing it down all the time. Dana Tulloch thinks so too. She hasn't said anything, but I can tell.'

Gifford was frowning at me. 'Tora, I'm probably breaking all sorts of professional confidences, but there's something you need to know about Sergeant Tulloch. This is not her first sergeant's job. She was a sergeant in Dundee. She also did a spell in Manchester. Neither job worked out. I get the impression this is her last chance in the force.'

I was amazed. 'But, she's just so . . . competent.'

'Oh, she's bright enough. IQ off the stratosphere. One of the reasons she's lasted so long. But there are other problems.'

'Such as?' I didn't like this, talking behind her back.

'I'd say she shows signs of obsessive compulsive disorder. I think there've been eating problems in the past; she's still very slim. And she has a compulsive interest in order and appearance. Look at the way she dresses. Have you ever seen her less than immaculate? How does she afford that on a police sergeant's salary? And her Mercedes looks like she just drove it out of the showroom.' He walked over to my window.

'What are you saying?'

'She's believed to be seriously in debt,' he said to the seagulls outside. Then he turned round to me again. 'And she can't work as part of a team. She's secretive. Drives Dunn up the wall and makes her very unpopular.'

I remembered her actions the previous evening, working with me rather than any of her colleagues, not letting them know what she was up to. It had seemed odd at the time. And that was before her accusations against Gifford and Dunn, or her persuading me to carry out an illegal search of confidential records. Oh great, my new best friend was a fruit-cake!

'Dana Tulloch needs professional help, in my view,' said Gifford. 'You, on the other hand, need to come to terms with what's happened and move on.'

'You mentioned that before.'

'And it bears repeating.' He looked at his watch. 'Time marches on. I'd better go. You have a clinic this morning?'

I nodded. A busy one. He was in the doorway when I called him back. 'Kenn, what does KT mean?'

He turned. 'Excuse me?'

'KT. I found it on the system, recorded against births in summer 2005.'

Light seemed to dawn. 'Oh yes, I asked that too. It's Keloid Trauma.'

'What?' I knew only that the word 'keloid' referred to an overgrowth of fibrous tissue forming a thickened or pronounced scar.

'There was a study here a while ago. There's a genetic condition up here that results in severe scarring after perineum tearing in childbirth. When the next child comes along it can cause problems. Hence, Keloid Trauma.'

'Sounds like something I should watch out for,' I said, relieved that KT, at least, was a mystery I could cross off the list.

I THANKED MY LUCKY STARS for a busy clinic that morning and for the fact that this isn't a job you can do with your mind elsewhere. For four hours I monitored foetal heartbeats, checked for excess sugar in urine and examined abdomens. After a sandwich lunch, I headed down to theatre. By six o'clock I was exhausted, but the thought of going home didn't hold enormous appeal. I found I was really missing Duncan. We had to try to use this weekend as a chance to reconnect, somehow.

Dana hadn't phoned and I was relieved. I had decided I wasn't going to do what she'd asked. I no longer believed the woman buried in my field was Kirsten Hawick, and any more digging on my part could get me into serious trouble. I picked up a pile of midwives' time sheets that needed checking, read through the first and scribbled my signature at the bottom.

If you're not getting close, why is someone trying to scare you?

I stopped, pen in midair. Then looked down. My briefcase was by my desk. I reached into it and pulled out the green folder.

I'd promised Duncan.

I shoved the folder back down and closed the case. Last night had been a joke, a sick prank, nothing more. I bent to the time sheets again.

They entered your house and watched you while you were asleep. Sound like a joke to you?

I put down my pen and looked at my case again.

Can't hurt, can it, to rule Kirsten out once and for all?

I pulled the black and white film from the folder and placed it on top of white paper on my desk. There was a noise outside, someone walking past. I got up, meaning to lock the door, and found that my office keys weren't in my handbag. Leaving keys at home is hardly a first for me so, thinking nothing of it, I took a spare set from the desk drawer and used them. Sitting back down again, I looked at the X-ray. It was what is known as a panoramic radiograph, showing every tooth present in the mouth.

Permanent dentition consists normally of thirty-two teeth. I counted thirty-one: fifteen uppers, sixteen lowers, only two molars in the upper right quadrant rather than three. There was a crown in the upper left quadrant, also a malformed root above one of the premolars in the upper right quadrant; it had a distinctive distal curvature. Most of the teeth were regular, but there was a slight gap in the bottom right-hand side, between the first and second premolar. I was no dentist, but I was pretty certain I'd be able to make an intelligent comparison of this film with any others that might be relevant.

I found the hospital's intranet site and tried to access the dental department. And found myself tripped at the first hurdle. As a consultant I have access to pretty much the entire site, but the dental unit requested a password.

I took a puce-coloured folder from my cupboard, tucked the X-ray inside it and walked to the recently opened dental unit. I was still wearing my scrubs and I made sure my consultant's badge was visible.

I pushed through the double doors and forced my best smile onto my face. The nurse/receptionist looked up. The name on her badge said Shirley. She didn't smile back or look at all pleased to have a visitor.

'Hi! We haven't met. I'm Tora Hamilton.' I held up my badge. 'Obstetrics,' I added, somewhat unnecessarily. 'Are you new too?'

She nodded. 'Just three months,' she responded in a Shetland accent.

So far, so good. I leaned forward, trying for a friendly, confidential manner. 'The thing is, I've got a bit of an embarrassing problem.'

Suddenly, she looked interested.

'My predecessor left my office in a bit of a shambles and I'm trying to sort it out. I've just come across what appear to be some dental records, but no indication of whom they might belong to. Now, I don't want to get Dr McLean into trouble, what with him just retired and everything, but these things shouldn't just be left around, should they? They're confidential?'

She nodded. 'Aye, they are.'

'The thing is, I have an idea whose they might be. If we could just check, I can leave them with you and you can file them where they belong.'

'You can call up the records yourself, you know.'

'I know, but I haven't got all my passwords sorted out yet.'

She appeared to have a brainwave. 'Is all you need the password then?'

I tried to look puzzled. 'I guess,' I said. 'Do you know it?'

'Sure,' she said and scribbled something down.

Willing myself not to snatch, I reached out and took the Post-it note. I read what she'd written and then looked at her for confirmation.

She smiled. 'Dr McDouglas's favourite film.'

'Mine too,' I replied, not entirely untruthfully. I thanked her and left.

BACK IN MY OFFICE, I wasn't sure whether I was terrified at what I'd done or delighted by my own cleverness. Shirley would almost certainly tell her boss what had happened. Even if it didn't get back to Gifford, I could face some difficult questions from Dr McDouglas.

My screen still showed the Homepage of the dental department. I typed in 'Terminator' and waited. Then I was in. I found patient records and typed in 'Kirsten Hawick'. There was nothing there.

I thought for a bit. Kirsten hadn't been married that long when she died. Maybe she hadn't got round to changing her name on all her records. I typed in Kirsten Georgeson and there she was: age, address, brief medical history, records of visits, invoices for non-NHS treatment. And her X-rays.

The comparison wasn't as easy as I'd expected. The X-ray taken during the post-mortem was just one film scanning from one side of the mouth to the other. Those produced during dental appointments tend to be taken in sections from inside the mouth. I had six small X-rays to compare with one large one. I started off in the top left corner, the section that I guessed would be easiest to distinguish. I was looking for a crown. Nothing.

Then I tried the bottom right corner for a small gap. Again nothing. I was as sure as I could be that the X-ray taken of the corpse didn't match the dental records of Kirsten Hawick. I'd known already, of course, but now even Dana would have to accept defeat. It wasn't her.

I started thinking. Dana had told me that all Shetland's NHS patients' records were on this central data base. If my friend buried in the field was an island woman and an NHS patient, her records were here for me to find.

I switched to the Internet and called up the site of the Scottish Census.

The 2004 Census was the most recent available and it told me that the number of women on the islands aged between twenty and thirty-four was 2,558: an impossible number to check.

Good, that's settled then, let's go and get some rest.

Could it be narrowed down? I went back to the dental data base, pressed the button for data sort and put in my criteria: female patients, resident on the islands, aged between sixteen and thirty-four. The system wouldn't let me specify a narrower age band. Then I was looking at a list of 1,700 names. Still an impossible search. I got up and crossed to the coffee machine.

OK, think, tired brain, think . . . Of course! I shot back to my desk and scanned the list of search criteria. Yes! There it was: date of last appointment. My friend had been dead since early summer 2005; I had to get rid of all the women who'd attended the surgery since, say, September 2005. It took a few seconds then . . . sixty-three women left on the list.

It was a manageable—if lengthy—search. It was already seven thirty and I was shattered. On the other hand, by tomorrow morning my unauthorised hacking would have been discovered, so I had to make it worth while.

In my desk drawer was a copy of the print-out I'd given Dana at the start of the week: the list of women who'd given birth on the islands during the spring and summer of 2005. I began to compare the two lists, looking for a woman who had given birth that summer and, simultaneously, ceased regular dental checkups. Thirty minutes and two cups of coffee later I was pretty certain there were no matches.

There was really no getting round the birth issue. The woman had had a baby and any woman who had done so on the islands that summer had to be on my list. Maybe she had visited a dentist privately. Unfortunately, I would have to go through the sixty-three records or I'd never know for sure.

The phone rang. I picked it up. 'Hello.'

'It's Dana. Are you OK?'

'I'm fine, just tired.'

'I have just had the devil of a row with my inspector. I can't believe no one called me last night. You must have been out of your wits.'

'Something like that,' I confessed. 'I *was* a bit surprised not to see you.'

'I'm supposed to be in charge of this investigation. Can you believe what the official line is? I wasn't called out because there was no direct link to the case. What happened last night was just somebody's idea of a joke.'

'You don't go along with that theory then?' I said.

'Are you kidding me? What are you up to right now?'

I explained about my examination of Kirsten Hawick's records, and drawing a blank. Then I told her about my plans to go through the rest.

'How many more do you have to look at?' she asked.

'Sixty-three,' I told her.

'I'm coming in to help,' she said.

I stood up, peered out of the window. Gifford's car was still there.

'No, you'll be far too conspicuous. I'll call when I'm done.'

'Thanks, Tora, I mean it. Look, let me give you my address and home phone number. Come round, it doesn't matter what time.'

I scribbled the details down and she was gone.

I called up the first set of X-rays.

TWO HOURS LATER, I'd ruled out twenty-two of the names on the list. Needing sustenance, I locked my office and went down to the canteen. I piled my tray high with fatty carbohydrates and added a Diet Coke. I ate like a robot, then went back to my office.

Another hour and a half, another two cups of coffee, and either something was going wrong with the hospital electrics or I was seriously in need of sleep, because the room had grown decidedly dimmer. I looked up at the neon strips above me. The light just wasn't what it had been a couple of hours ago. I looked back at the screen. The X-ray image had blurred into a confused mass of shapes and shading. Words were indistinguishable. I had eighteen more records to check, but it just wasn't possible. I'd print them off, go find a bed and read through them in the morning.

I selected the print field and pressed the print command. From the printer at the other side of the room came a shrill, persistent beeping sound. Great! As invariably happens when it's important, it was out of paper. I started to get up and couldn't. I just about managed to push the keyboard out of the way before my head hit the desk.

THE NEXT THING I remember was my mobile ringing. I raised my head and gasped out loud: there were demons in my skull, beating a tattoo on my brain. And someone had broken my spine; nothing less could cause this amount of pain. What the hell was wrong with me?

Without moving, I managed to locate my mobile in the pocket of my jacket. I looked at the screen. It was Dana. I switched the phone off.

Then I remembered what I'd been doing. I pressed a key and the screen sprang to life. There was nothing there. I was looking at the desktop wallpaper. I grabbed the mouse and flicked round the screen, in case the dental records were minimised somewhere. They couldn't have just disappeared.

Except they had. I clicked on the dental department's section of the site and once again it requested a password. I typed in 'Terminator'.

Access denied.

I looked round my office, as though the answer might lie on my walls, my desk. The room was tidy, nothing out of place. Except . . .

My desk was never that tidy. Papers were stacked up neatly. The cup I'd been drinking from was over by the sink. It had been rinsed out. I hadn't done that. I crossed to the light switch and flicked. The lights flashed on. Functioning normally. Which was a whole lot more than could be said for me.

I staggered to the sink and poured a cup of water. In my bag I found some of the painkillers Gifford had given me the other day and I swallowed two gratefully. I leaned against the sink, waiting for the pain in my head to subside. My watch said 04:26. I'd been asleep for over four hours.

I started to walk back to my desk and a flashing button on the printer caught my eye. Without really thinking about it, I took a few sheets of paper from the cupboard and slid them into the empty paper tray.

The machine whirred into life and started sending out printed sheets. I picked the first one up. It was an X-ray of the upper left quadrant and the second molar had been crowned. I picked up the next sheet. It showed the central and lateral incisors. The placement looked right. I picked up the next sheet. Then the next. I counted the teeth. Then, for the first time, I looked at the patient's name at the top of the page.

Melissa Gair.

I wanted to weep. I wanted to scream my triumph to the rooftops.

I flicked through the print-outs that followed. I saw her birth date and calculated her age: thirty-two. I saw that she'd been married and had lived in Lerwick. She'd had dental appointments roughly every six months going back ten years or so. Her last one had been just before Christmas 2003.

Which, of course, didn't quite fit. My head started to hurt more as I struggled to work out why. The woman in my field was Melissa Gair; the records matched exactly. Yet why would a woman who attended her dentist religiously suddenly stop a good eighteen months before her death? Unless she'd left the islands temporarily, coming back only to meet an untimely end.

I grabbed my list of women who had given birth on the islands and scanned it quickly. No, Melissa Gair had not given birth here. She'd had her baby off the islands and then returned less than two weeks afterwards.

I picked up the phone and dialled Dana's mobile number but got an unobtainable tone. Then I thought of one more thing I could check. I turned back to my computer and went into the main hospital records. I put Melissa's name into the search facility, not really expecting to find anything. She'd been a healthy young woman and might never have been admitted.

Her name appeared. I opened the file, read it through once, then again, checking and double-checking the dates. My headache was back with a vengeance and I think only the certain knowledge that I was a split second from throwing up kept me motionless in my seat. Had I moved, it would have been to ram my fist directly into the computer screen.

6

I saw no other traffic on the way over to Dana's house, which was a good thing, because I'd probably have collided with it. I parked in the car park that I assumed was closest to her house and climbed out of the car. I staggered like a drunk down a flight of steps and a steep, cobbled slope. It was an hour or so before dawn, and though the sky in the east had lightened, the narrow streets of The Lanes were still drenched in shadows.

The Lanes are one of the oldest areas of Lerwick, popular with tourists and much sought-after as trendy, town-centre homes. The buildings rise up to three and four storeys on either side of the narrow, sloping alleys. And when the light is poor and no one else is around, they are decidedly eerie.

Three times I'd tried Dana on her mobile but had got no response. At first, I'd assumed she'd gone to bed, but now that seemed unlikely. I'd found her door and had been banging on it for several minutes. She wasn't home, and I was in no fit state to drive anywhere else. I climbed slowly back up to my car. On the back seat were my coat and an old horse blanket. I wrapped them both round me, and was asleep in seconds.

IT WAS NEARLY DAWN when the tapping on the window woke me. I was cold, stiff and acutely aware that the moment I moved I would regret it. But there was nothing else for it. Dana's incredulous face was staring down at me and I had to move. I sat up. Oh boy, so much worse than I'd expected. I reached for the lock and then Dana opened the door.

'Tora, I've been at your house half the night. I've been seriously—'

I waved her away, turned and vomited over the rear wheel of my car.

The next thing I remember is being half led, half carried, through Dana's front door, across some polished oak floorboards, and deposited on her sofa. While she went into the kitchen, I tried to steady my nausea by focusing on her living room. It was exactly as I would have expected: immaculately tidy and undoubtedly expensive. A flat-screen TV was fastened to one wall and there was a Bang & Olufsen stereo system under the window. Dana came back with some tea and toast and sat down on a footstool in front of me.

'Ready to tell me what happened to you?'

'I worked half the night, spent the rest of it in a car,' I managed. The tea was scalding and totally wonderful.

She looked at me, then down at herself. Her linen trousers and pink cotton shirt were creased but clean, and her skin looked daisy-fresh.

'So did I,' she said. She had a point.

'First, I need to tell you—I found a match,' I said, watching the glint leap into her eyes.

'My God, well done! Who was she?'

I took another gulp of tea. 'Melissa Gair,' I said. 'Aged thirty-two. An island woman, from Lerwick, married to a local man.'

Dana clenched her fist and made a little stabbing action with it. 'So why wasn't she reported missing? Was she on your list of 2005 deliveries?'

'No, she wasn't. She was already dead.'

She stared at me. 'Come again,' she said.

'I checked her hospital records. She was admitted on September the 29th, 2004, with a malignant breast tumour that was subsequently found to have spread to her lungs, back and kidneys. Her GP had spotted a lump just a couple of weeks earlier during a routine examination. She was transferred to Aberdeen for treatment but it didn't work. She died on October the sixth.'

'Fuck!' I hadn't heard Dana swear before.

'You can say that again,' I said.

She did. She got up and walked across the room. Then she turned and looked at me. 'How sure are you about those dental records?'

'You need to have a dentist look at them, but I'm sure they were the same.'

'Could there have been two Melissa Gairs living in Lerwick?'

I shook my head. 'The birth dates were identical. And blood groups.'

'Shit!' And she was off again, pacing the room and swearing. 'OK, OK.' She came back to sit on her footstool. 'Now tell me what happened to you.'

I told her that, for the second time in two nights, someone had bypassed locked doors, not to mention considerable hospital security, to force their way into my presence. That it was possible I had been drugged.

'We need to get you to a doctor.' She saw the look on my face and allowed herself to smile. 'We need to do some blood tests or something.'

'Already done. I took some bloods before I left the hospital. They're in my office fridge; I'll send them off on Monday. But until we know for certain, can we keep quiet about this? It's only going to be a distraction.'

Dana nodded slowly but her eyes were dull and unfocused. I recognised the sign that she was thinking hard. I hated to leave her with such a bombshell, but knew I couldn't carry on any longer. I stood up.

'Dana, I'm sorry, but I really need to get home.'

She looked up sharply. 'Will Duncan be there?'

'No,' I said, surprised. 'He's not back till this evening.'

'You're safer here. Use the spare bedroom. When we know he's back I'll sign your release papers.'

I didn't move. I hardly knew this girl. I was far from sure I trusted her. She must have read my face because her own expression sharpened.

'What?' she said.

I sat back down. I told her everything Gifford had said about her.

She listened, her eyebrows flickering once or twice. When I'd finished, her mouth tightened. 'My father died three years ago,' she said. 'I lost my mother when I was fifteen and have no siblings so I inherited the whole of his estate. I bought the car, the house and the things you can see around you. It's nice to have some money but I'd much rather have my dad.'

She took a deep breath. 'I did not leave Manchester in disgrace. I left with an excellent record. I transferred to Dundee because I wanted to work in Scotland. I left Dundee because I began a relationship with another officer—a much more senior one—and we agreed it wasn't good for the force.'

She stood up. 'As for not fitting in here, well, they got that bit right. These islands are run by a powerful clique of big blond men who all went to the same schools and whose families have known each other since the Norwegian invasions. Just think about it, Tora—the doctors you know at the hospital, the head teachers, the police force, the local councils . . .'

I didn't need to think about it. I'd noticed how many islanders fitted into the same distinctive physical type. 'Oh, the place is crawling with Vikings.'

'I am not in debt, nor am I anorexic,' Dana continued. 'I eat quite a lot but I work out most evenings. And yes, I shop a lot, too. It's called displacement activity. I don't particularly like it here and I miss Helen.'

'Helen?' I said stupidly.

'DCI Helen Rowley. The officer in Dundee with whom I was—am still, when we get the chance—having a relationship. Helen is my girlfriend.'

And no, I admit, I had definitely not seen that one coming.

'Now, you can stay down here and help me do some pretty arduous police work, you can go home and risk someone disturbing your rest for a third time in three days, or you can go upstairs and get some sleep.'

Not really too difficult a decision. I turned to leave the room.

WHEN I WOKE, it was to the sound of voices. Two voices, to be precise: Dana's and that of a man. I sat up. The blind in Dana's spare bedroom was drawn, but behind it I could see bright sunshine. I felt groggy and aching, but the horrible nausea had gone.

I sat down to slip on my shoes and looked around me. Bookshelves lined one wall. The desk in the corner held a computer and printer, and beside the monitor stood a framed photograph of Dana in graduation robes.

I walked softly downstairs, but Dana and her guest must have heard me coming because silence heralded my arrival into the room below. First a man, then Dana, stood as I walked in. The man was in his early forties, slightly above average height, with pale blue eyes and thick, carrot-coloured hair turning to grey. He was smartly dressed and attractive.

'This is Stephen Gair,' said Dana.

I turned to Dana in astonishment.

'Melissa's husband,' she added, quite unnecessarily.

He held out his hand. 'How are you feeling now?'

'Mr Gair knows you've been working all night,' said Dana. 'We've been waiting for you to wake up before . . .' She looked at him, uncertain.

'Before we go to get my wife's X-rays checked,' said Stephen Gair.

Dana relaxed visibly.

I said, 'Has Dana told you . . .?' What on earth *had* Dana told him?

'Shall I summarise?' he offered.

I nodded, thinking: What kind of talk was that for a man who'd just been given such devastating news?

'Last Sunday,' he began, 'a body was found on your land. The body was that of a young woman who was murdered—rather brutally, I understand—in the early summer of 2005. You've been using your position at the hospital to conduct a comparison of dental records. You believe you've found a match in the dental records of my late wife, Melissa. Am I right so far?'

'Absolutely,' I said, wondering what Stephen Gair did for a living.

'Except my wife died of breast cancer in October 2004. She'd been dead for months, possibly the better part of a year, by the time the murder took place. So the body on your land cannot be her. How am I doing?'

'You're cooking on gas,' I said, borrowing an expression of Duncan's.

Gair smiled. 'Thanks,' he said.

'Trouble is, the X-rays match,' I said. 'There's no getting round that. If she'd been my wife, I'd want to know why.'

The smile faded. 'I *do* want to know why,' he said.

Dana spoke quickly. 'Shall we go? Tora, are you OK to go straight away?'

'Of course,' I said. 'Where are we going?'

We were going to the hospital dental unit. Dana drove me, Stephen Gair followed behind. It took us ten minutes to get there and, when we did, three cars were already parked in the car park. I was not in the least bit surprised to see Gifford's silver BMW and DI Dunn's black four-wheel-drive. Stephen Gair got out of his car and started to walk towards the entrance.

'He's dodgy,' I said.

'He's senior partner in the biggest firm of solicitors in Lerwick.'

'Oh, well, there you go. Do you think he tipped off the fuzz?'

'What do you watch on TV? And no, I think that was probably Dentist McDouglas. You might want to muffle that schoolgirl sense of humour of yours for the next hour.'

'Right you are, Sarge,' I said, as we headed for the swing doors.

'Your actions are reprehensible, Miss Hamilton,' said Dr McDouglas, a tall, thin, arrogant man whom I'd disliked on first sight. 'You might do things differently where you come from, but I assure you, in Scot—'

'With all due respect, Dr McDouglas,' I interrupted, 'my actions are not our primary concern right now. If I'm wrong, you can instigate a formal complaint. But if I'm right, then so much shit is going to hit the fan that any complaint against me will, frankly, get lost in the general hysteria.'

'Your use of profanities offends me deeply,' the sour, Presbyterian tooth-puller spat back at me.

'Yeah, well digging up mutilated corpses offends me deeply. Can we get on with it, please?'

'We're not getting on with anything. Not without the proper authority.'

'I agree,' said Andy Dunn.

I pointed at Stephen Gair. 'There's your proper authority. Mr Gair says he is prepared to release his wife's X-rays for examination.'

'I think it would help to see exactly what we're dealing with here,' said Gifford. 'Who's got the X-rays?'

'Kenn,' said Andy Dunn, 'this is really not—'

'I have,' said Dana, ignoring her boss. From her bag she pulled the folder I'd given her that morning. She took out the large panoramic film taken in the hospital morgue and then the half-dozen smaller shots that I'd printed off the dental intranet site the night before.

'What do you think, Richard?' said Gifford.

Richard McDouglas looked at the films on his desk, a frown of concentration crinkling his brow. After about five minutes, he shook his head.

'I can't see it,' he said. Sighs of relief all round the table.

Oh, for heaven's sake! 'Dr McDouglas,' I said quickly. 'Could you look at the second molar in the upper left quadrant on the panoramic radiograph? Would you say that molar has been crowned?'

He nodded. 'It would appear so.'

'Now look at the same tooth on your own X-rays.' I pushed the relevant film towards him. 'There, has that tooth been crowned?'

He nodded again, but didn't speak.

'Now, please look in the upper right quadrant. Is there a molar missing?'

'Difficult to say. Could be one of the premolars.'

'Whatever.' I pushed another film in front of him. 'This is the corresponding quadrant for Mrs Gair's X-rays. Is there a molar or premolar missing?'

He counted the teeth. 'Yes, there is.'

Gifford leaned forward. I was about to play my trump card.

'Dr McDouglas, could you please look at the root of this tooth.' I pointed to a tooth on the panoramic X-ray. 'It has a distinctive curvature. Would you say it's mesial or distal?'

He pretended to study it but the answer was obvious.

'The curvature is distal.'

'And this one.' I indicated the same tooth on Melissa's X-ray.

He stared down. 'Miss Hamilton is correct,' he said eventually. 'There are sufficient similarities to merit a proper investigation.'

Stephen Gair pointed to the panoramic, then looked at Gifford. 'Are you saying this is my wife? That my wife is in your morgue? What is going on?'

'OK, that's it,' said Andy Dunn. 'We're going down to the station. Mr Gair, can you come with us, please.'

At that moment, my beeper sounded. I excused myself and went into the hallway to make a call. One of my patients was nearing the end of the second stage of labour and the baby was showing signs of distress. The midwife thought an emergency Caesar might be needed. I went back in and explained.

'I'll give you a hand,' said Gifford. 'Catch up with you later, Andy.'

He had the doors open and me out of there before anyone had time to object. Once outside, he strode ahead. It was difficult to keep up as we crossed the car park and walked up the flagged path to the main door of the hospital. Gifford still hadn't said a word as we turned left past A&E and carried on towards the maternity unit. At the stairs he turned and started to climb.

'I thought you were coming to give me a hand,' I said.

He stopped and looked at me. 'I needed to get away. There are things I have to do. Come and see me when you're done.'

KENN GIFFORD'S OFFICE came as something of a surprise, reminding me of private consulting rooms I'd visited during my student days: heavy, striped curtains, brown studded leather armchairs and a reproduction desk. The desk had just a closed laptop computer and a solitary manila file on it.

Gifford had his back to the door. He was leaning forward, elbows on the window ledge, staring out over the buildings towards the ocean. I didn't knock, just pushed the already open door. He turned.

'How'd you get on?' he asked.

'It's a girl,' I answered, crossing the carpet to the middle of the room.

'Congratulations.' He stood there looking at me, the picture of self-possession. I was close to throwing the biggest tantrum of my life.

'What the hell are you lot playing at? I want an explanation.'

His response was a weary smile. 'Don't we all,' he said. He ran both hands over his face, sweeping his hair back and up. 'I can tell you what's happened while you've been in delivery. Will that do?'

'It's a start.'

He nodded towards a chair. I sat down.

'Detective Superintendent Harris is on his way over from Inverness, to take control. Andy Dunn came here twenty minutes ago to collect details of the doctors and nurses who treated Mrs Gair. Three are being interviewed. The other two are being tracked down. Mrs Gair's GP is also at the station.'

'What about you?'

He smiled again. 'When Mrs Gair was admitted, I was on extended leave in New Zealand. She'd been dead five days by the time I got back.'

I thought about what he was telling me. Was it possible that whatever was going on here, Kenn Gifford had no part in it?

'The pathologist who carried out her post-mortem is on sick leave in—'

'Wait a sec,' I interrupted him. 'Stephen Renney didn't do it?'

Gifford shook his head. 'Stephen's been with us only about eight months. He's covering for our regular guy—Jonathan Wheeler. Sergeant Tulloch is at this moment flying to Edinburgh to interview Jonathan. The report seems pretty thorough, though.' He gestured to the file on his desk. 'Want to see it?'

I took the file and flicked through it. 'So how, exactly, does a woman who died of cancer three years ago end up in my field?'

'My best guess is that someone, for reasons of their own, stole her body from the morgue. An empty coffin—or a weighted one—got cremated.'

'But she didn't die in October 2004. According to the pathologists, she died nearly a year later.'

'Her body was put in the peat nearly a year later. What if she was kept in a deepfreeze for several months?'

'She'd had a baby. A corpse in a freezer can't gestate a baby to full term.'

'Well, there my theory hits an obstacle, I admit. I just have to hope that you and Stephen Renney got it totally wrong.'

'We didn't,' I whispered.

'Melissa Gair was pregnant.'

'She was?'

'I spoke to her GP. Forty minutes ago. Before the police picked him up.'

'You mean you warned him.'

'Tora, get a grip. I've known Peter Jobbs since I was ten years old. He's as straight as an arrow, trust me.'

I decided to let that one pass. 'So, what did he tell you?'

'She went to see him in September 2004, concerned about a lump in her left breast. She also suspected she was in the very early stages of pregnancy. Peter arranged a consultation with a specialist in Aberdeen, but two weeks later—three days before her appointment—she was admitted to hospital in great pain. The initial X-rays showed extensive spread of the cancer. She was transferred to Aberdeen. They did an open-and-shut and brought her back here. They upped her pain relief and she died a few days later.'

Open-and-shut refers to a surgical procedure cut short following the discovery of an inoperable condition.

'Poor Melissa.'

He nodded agreement. 'Thirty-two years old.'

Except . . . 'No, fuck it.' I was on my feet again and shouting. I couldn't believe I'd nearly fallen for that shit. 'Melissa did not die of cancer. Melissa died when someone took a chisel, forced open her rib cage, hacked through several arteries and pulled her heart, probably still beating, from her body.' I was breathing too fast and starting to feel light-headed. 'And a whole load of wankers are lying about it. Probably you, too.'

'Tora.' Gifford came towards me and put his hands on my shoulders.

I felt an immense flood of warmth wash into me. We looked at each other. Slate, his eyes were the colour of slate. I found my breathing slowing down to fall into sync with his. The fuzziness in my head faded.

'Feeling better?' asked Gifford.

I shook my head, but more out of stubbornness than honesty.

Gifford lifted a hand and stroked it down over my head. It came to rest on the bare skin of my neck. I took a step closer, dropped my head and stared at the fabric of his shirt, knowing the situation had strayed way beyond the bounds of what was appropriate and that I really needed to snap out of it.

'Tora, I'm going to have to suspend you on full pay for a fortnight.'

I backed away. 'You are kidding me.'

He said nothing. He wasn't kidding.

'You can't do that. I've done nothing wrong.'

He laughed and walked back over to the window, turning his back on me.

'Technically,' he said to my reflection in the windowpane, 'you've done quite a lot wrong. You've interfered in a police investigation, you've broken any number of hospital regulations and you've disregarded instructions from me.' He turned round again. 'But that isn't why you're suspended.'

'Why, then?'

'One, if you stay, you'll carry on as you have been and I can't protect you for ever. Two, as you so eloquently put it over in the dental unit, the shit is going to hit the fan here in the next few days and I don't want you seen as the cause of all that. You won't be able to work here if everyone dislikes you.'

'They won't like me more for running away. Hell, if you tell them I'm suspended, they might even think I'm involved.'

'I'll tell them you're deeply upset by what's been going on. You'll be the object of sympathy, not resentment. Three, I want you where you're safe.'

I had completely forgotten, amidst the heady rush of discovery and vindication, that—to use a cop-show cliché—there was a killer about.

He had stepped forwards and was holding me again, upper arms this time. 'You need some serious time off,' he said. 'You're white as a sheet, and your pupils look like you've taken drugs. I can't have you working in a hospital.'

I had taken drugs, albeit unwittingly. Was it really so obvious? Or did Gifford know more than he was letting on? I wondered again how anyone could bypass my locked office door. He himself had done it the previous morning, claiming a cleaner had let him in, but . . .

There was a rush of cold air through the room as the door was pushed open. Gifford was no longer looking at me but at whoever was standing in the doorway. I spun round and my day was complete. It was Duncan.

'Hands off my wife, Gifford,' he said calmly. His face looked anything but calm.

For a moment, my boss's hands remained on my arms and then the warmth was gone. I moved forwards, away from him and towards my husband, who was not, it had to be said, looking particularly pleased to see me.

'What kept you?' said Gifford.

'Delayed flight,' replied Duncan, glaring back at him. Then he took a step into the room and looked around. He gave a short, unpleasant laugh. 'What are you—a Harley Street gynaecologist?'

'Glad you like it,' said Gifford. 'But my predecessor designed this room.'

Beside me, I sensed Duncan stiffen.

'What? Did he never invite you in?' said Gifford.

I looked from one man to the other. 'What's going on?' I said.

Gifford turned to me. 'My predecessor. Medical director here for fifteen years. Something of a mentor for me. Give him my regards, won't you?'

I looked at Duncan.

'Wake up, Tor,' he said irritably. 'He's talking about Dad.'

OK, really not keeping up here. 'But your father worked in Edinburgh.'

Duncan had told me his father was an anaesthetist, and that he'd worked away from home, coming back only at weekends.

'He came back,' said Duncan, 'round about the time I went to university. Where's your car?'

'Parked outside Sergeant Tulloch's house,' said Gifford. 'Safe enough—one would hope.'

I FELL ASLEEP minutes after Duncan started driving. I jerked awake when he braked hard to avoid a stray sheep. We were not on the road home.

'Where are we going?' I asked.

'Westing,' he replied. Westing was his parents' home on Unst.

I thought for a moment. 'Who's looking after the horses?'

'Mary said she'd come over.'

I nodded. Mary was a local girl who helped me with the horses on my busy days. She knew them well and they knew her. They'd be fine. I closed my eyes again and drifted off. I woke briefly during the ferry crossing to Yell.

'Gifford phoned you, didn't he?' I asked. 'He told you about the break-in at the house the other night.'

Without looking at me, Duncan nodded. It gave me an uncomfortable feeling. Duncan and Gifford might dislike each other but they were working together to manage me.

It doesn't take long to drive up Yell and by nine o'clock we were on the last leg of the journey.

Duncan is an only child. One who arrived relatively late into the marriage. One might have thought he would be all the more precious, all the more loved because of that, but that didn't seem to be the case. While his mother, Elspeth, was as doting as one would expect an older mother of an only son to be, there was no comfortable familiarity in their relationship. Polite seemed to best summarise it.

The relationship between Duncan and his father was easier to describe. It was formal, courteous and, to my mind, distinctly cold. It wasn't that they didn't talk. They talked quite a lot—about Duncan's work, the economy, current affairs, life on the islands—but they never touched on the personal. They never went sailing together, or sneaked off to the pub while his mother and I were preparing dinner, and they never, ever quarrelled.

On the fifteen-minute ferry journey from Yell to Unst I asked, 'Did your dad retire early?' I had no idea how old Richard was but he barely looked seventy. Yet he hadn't worked in all the time I'd known him.

'Ten years ago,' he replied, looking straight ahead.

'Why?' I asked. Perhaps he'd left under some sort of cloud.

Duncan shrugged, still looking at me. 'He had other things to do. And he'd groomed his successor.'

'Gifford.'

Duncan was silent.

'What is it between you two?' I said.

Then he turned towards me. 'Do I need to ask *you* that?'

For a moment the face looking back at me was not one I recognised.

The ferry docked and the heavy ramp slammed down. Duncan muttered something under his breath, but I didn't dare ask him to repeat himself.

7

Unst, lying on the same latitude as southern Greenland, is home to around 700 people and 50,000 puffins. The most northerly of all the inhabited British islands, it measures roughly twelve miles long and five miles wide, with one main road, the A968, running from the southwestern ferry port at Belmont up to Norwick in the northeast.

Two miles after leaving the ferry we turned left along a single-track road and started to drive up and down the shore-edged hills. At the end of the road you find the handful of buildings that is Westing, and the cold, grand, granite house that is Duncan's family home.

Elspeth hugged Duncan and pressed her cold cheek against mine. Richard shook hands with his son and nodded to me. They led us into their large, west-facing sitting room. I walked over to the window. The sun was setting in a violet sky. Behind me, a short silence fell, then I heard the sound of a cork being pulled. There was movement beside me and I turned. It was Richard, holding out a glass of red wine. He stood beside me and looked out. The sun had disappeared behind the cliffs of Yell but, in doing so, had draped them in light. They looked as if they had been carved from bronze.

'The loveliest and loneliest place on earth,' said Richard, and he seemed to be voicing my thoughts.

I took a gulp of wine. It was excellent. Richard led me to an armchair near the fire and Elspeth scurried forward with a loaded plate. I surrendered myself to their hospitality and ate and drank gratefully.

Half an hour later, while Duncan and his father were discussing the state of the roads on the island, I excused myself and went upstairs to our room. I pulled my mobile out of my bag and checked messages. There were three from Dana and I felt a glimmer of affection for her. She, at least, was not part of the general conspiracy to get me out of the loop. I knew my mobile wouldn't work too well this far north so I used the land line in the bedroom. She answered on the second ring.

'Thank God, Tora, where are you?'

'Serving exile in the Siberian wastelands.'

'Come again?'

I explained and she said, 'Well, at least you'll be safe up there.'

Why did everyone keep going on about my safety. It was unnerving.

'Can you tell me what's been happening?'

'Of course. I just got back from Edinburgh. I went to interview a Jonathan Wheeler. He's the regular pathologist at your place. Been on sick leave for a few months.'

'Yes, I've heard of him. What did you find out?'

'Well, it didn't help that he'd obviously been warned I was coming. Your friend Gifford needs banging up for obstructing justice, if you ask me, not that that's likely to happen, given that he and my inspector are old buddies. Anyway, Wheeler remembered the case and was pretty forthcoming. It all seemed to square with what we'd been told. Young woman with malignant lumps one breast and extensive spread of the cancer through major organs. I'll tell you what didn't fit, though. Apparently Melissa Gair was pregnant when she first went to her GP. Early stages. Even Stephen Gair didn't know.'

'Gifford told me.'

There was a sharp intake of breath. 'Bloody man's a menace. Anyway, by the time of the post-mortem, three weeks later, she wasn't pregnant.'

'Lots of pregnancies fail to develop,' I said. 'Melissa could have had a very early miscarriage between her visit to the GP and being admitted to hospital. Given the invasive nature of the cancer, I'd say that was pretty likely.'

There was silence, while Dana processed the information.

'Dana,' I continued. 'Maybe the woman who was admitted to hospital with cancer, who died there, wasn't Melissa Gair. Maybe records got mixed up.'

'We thought of that. But her GP is adamant that Melissa came to see him. He'd known her for years. The hospital staff didn't know her personally but I've shown them photographs and they're all pretty sure it was her.'

'So were Stephen Renney and I wrong? Was I wrong about the dental records?' I couldn't believe it, but it seemed the only possible explanation.

'No, you weren't. We've had another dentist look at the records. The body in the morgue is definitely Melissa. And another post-mortem was carried out. She'd most certainly had a baby. They also found a small lump in her left breast. It's being tested, but they think it wasn't malignant.'

I was quiet for a moment. 'We're going round in circles,' I said eventually.

'Tell me about it.'

'So what happens next?'

'No one seems to know. The hospital staff and the GP have all gone home. So has Stephen Gair.'

'You let them go?'

Even over the phone line I could feel Dana's frustration. 'Tora, who is our suspect? What do we charge them with? We have several members of the medical profession all saying the same thing: a woman called Melissa Gair was admitted with acute breast cancer in September 2004. She died in hospital. Everything was done by the book. We can't even begin to start constructing a case against them.'

I couldn't think of anything to say. Then I could. 'Life insurance. How much was she insured for?'

'I'm checking Gair's finances but probably not enough to pay off all the other people as well. The other thing is that Stephen Gair has identified the body in the morgue as his wife. Would he make a positive identification if he was involved in foul play?'

'Tor, are you OK?' Duncan was standing at the bottom of the stairs, shouting up at me.

'I have to go,' I said to Dana. 'I'll call you.'

DUNCAN HAD HIS BACK to the peat fire. His parents sat close by. Even in May the air on Unst had a distinct chill to it. Duncan, I noticed, had finished the wine and moved on to Lagavulin, a smoky single highland malt.

'Who were you calling?' he asked.

'Dana,' I said.

Duncan closed his eyes briefly. 'I do wish you'd leave it,' he said softly, in a tone that suggested he knew I wouldn't.

I saw Elspeth glance at Richard, but neither asked what it was, exactly, I was supposed to leave. I guessed they already knew.

Behind Duncan's shoulder I spotted something that I suppose I must have seen several times, but had never really thought about before. I walked over.

The fireplace in the sitting room of Richard and Elspeth's house is huge. It must measure six feet in length and be about four feet deep. A granite lintel runs across the top of the hearth, supported on either side by stone pillars. Carved into the lintel were shapes I recognised from our own fireplace: an upright arrow, a crooked letter F, a zigzag like a flash of lightning. They were repeated several times, sometimes appearing upside-down, sometimes like a mirror image.

'You've spoken to Sergeant Tulloch yourself, Richard,' I said, tracing with one finger the shape of the rune I was pretty certain meant Initiation. 'She needed your advice on some runes carved on the body I found.'

Out of the corner of my eye I saw Elspeth wince.

'Yes, I remember,' said Richard. 'She'd found a book on the subject. I told her I had nothing to add to the interpretation offered by the author.'

I couldn't believe my father-in-law had nothing useful to say on a subject so integral to the islands' history. Was he joining the conspiracy to keep Tora's little nastiness under wraps? I realised that if Melissa's murder was connected to the hospital, Richard Guthrie might have a strong interest in covering the facts.

'These are the same as the carvings in our cellar,' I said, wondering how Richard would deal with a straight question. 'What do they mean?'

Richard joined me at the hearth and I had to steel myself not to step backwards. He was a tall man, built on a very large frame. His physical presence, along with a formidable intellect, made him immensely intimidating.

'Nobody really knows,' he said. 'They date back thousands of years and the original meanings have almost certainly been lost. The book Sergeant Tulloch had offered one set of interpretations. Others exist too. You simply take your pick.' As though bored with the subject, he sighed and moved towards the door. 'Now, if you'll all excuse me, I'm going to bed.'

'Good idea,' said Elspeth, getting to her feet.

'YOU DON'T LOOK much like your dad,' I said, as Duncan started to undress.

'You've said that before,' he replied, his voice muffled by the sweater he was pulling over his head.

'He's much bigger, for a start,' I said. 'And wasn't he blond?'

'Maybe I take after my mother,' said Duncan, unbuttoning his jeans. He was still annoyed with me.

I thought about it. Elspeth was short and, not to put too fine a point on it, dumpy. There was no immediate resemblance to Duncan that I could think of, but the flow of genes is notoriously unpredictable.

'Are you going to shower before you come to bed?' asked Duncan.

At last I'd found someone honest enough to admit I smelt like a skunk in mating season.

I showered for a long time, and when I got back to the bedroom Duncan was asleep. Five minutes later, mere seconds before I too drifted off, it occurred to me that while Richard Guthrie might bear little resemblance to his son, he bore quite a lot to Kenn Gifford.

I WAS WOKEN BY LIGHT, lots of it, flooding the room and coaxing me out of sleep. The curtains of our east-facing window were open, and Duncan stood by the bed, fully dressed, with a steaming mug of tea.

'You awake?'

I looked at the tea. 'Is that for me?'

'Yup.' He put it down on the bedside table.

'I'm awake.' I was amazed at how much better I felt.

Duncan sat down on the bed. 'Wanna come sailing?' he asked.

'Now?'

'Bacon sandwiches in the clubhouse,' he tempted.

I thought about it. Spend the morning hanging around the house, searching for polite things to say to Elspeth, or . . .

Twenty-five minutes later we were at the Uyea clubhouse, where we'd left our Laser 2 dinghy for the summer, tucking into bacon sandwiches and looking out over Uyea Sound to the island of—

'My God, that's it!' I said, between mouthfuls.

'What?' mumbled Duncan. He was already fastening his life jacket.

'Tronal,' I said. 'There's a maternity clinic there. And an adoption centre.'

'Come on,' said Duncan, getting to his feet. 'We have an hour and a half before it pours down.'

Directly above us the sky was blue, but out over the ocean low clouds hung ominously. The wind was strong, about a force five, and coming in an easterly direction. Duncan was right, the storm was on its way.

'It can't be much more than a quarter of a mile away,' I said, my eyes still fixed on Tronal as we pushed the dinghy down the slipway. 'Can we go?'

'No, we can't,' Duncan replied. 'For a start it's private land, and the navigation's a bugger. There are rocks that'll rip the hull off before we get near.'

As we sped away from the jetty, with Duncan at the helm and me controlling the jib, I realised I must have seen Tronal a dozen times without really registering it. In the early-morning light, against the blue backdrop of sky, I could see the tops of buildings behind a ridge. No other obvious signs of life.

The wind was perfect and the dinghy was tearing along, but starting to keel over. Duncan signalled to me to put the trapeze out, and a few minutes later I was skimming just inches above the water, at a speed that felt like flight. We bounced high on a few rogue waves and the spray stung my eyes. Beneath me, the sea looked like a shimmering mass of diamonds.

'Ready about,' called Duncan, and as I prepared to tack I saw that we were now only yards from Tronal. A crumbling stone wall rimmed the lower reaches of the land and, just a foot or so outside it, a barbed-wire fence. Some twenty yards up the hill I saw a woman. I wondered if she was one of the unhappy souls about to give up her baby.

'Lee-ho!' called Duncan, and the dinghy turned to head southwest.

Given the strong winds and the approaching storm, Duncan had chosen to steer us not out towards the North Sea but into the more sheltered waters that lay between Unst to the north, Yell to the west and Fetlar in the south. But the boat was keeling hard, even though I was fully out on the trapeze, and the wind seemed to have picked up.

'Get back in,' Duncan yelled at me, none too soon, and I started to pull myself back towards the marginally greater comfort of the boat.

At that moment, there was a deafening crack. Thunder, I thought. The storm's an hour ahead of schedule. Then I heard a loud tearing noise and a cry of warning from Duncan. I was thrown up in the air and came down in the cold waters of Bluemull Sound.

Several feet above me I could see sunlight and clear, sparkling water. I kicked hard and broke through the surface. I coughed over and over, with no time in between to take in more air. I started to go down again.

Although I was wearing a life jacket, it wasn't inflated. Forcing myself not to panic, I fumbled for the red pull toggle. I had only to tug on it and the jacket would automatically fill with air, propelling me to the surface. Except I couldn't find the damn thing!

I knew I had to stay calm, so I gave up and kicked for the surface again. This time I managed to control the coughing just long enough to breathe in. All I could see were the short, aggressive waves that bounced around me. No sign of the boat. Nor of Duncan.

I gave up on the toggle and fumbled for the air inlet that allows you to inflate a life jacket manually. I found it easily enough, ripped off the stopper and started to blow. After sixteen blows I was exhausted and the life jacket was not inflating. I had to admit defeat.

I sobbed aloud and tried to yell but I could barely hear my own voice above the wind. I turned round in the water and caught sight of the boat, little more than a white speck, a quarter of a mile, maybe more, further up Bluemull Sound. Its sails were dragging in the water and it looked as though the mast was gone. There was no sign of Duncan.

I thought quickly. Unst or Yell? Unst looked closer but the cliffs are steeper and far less forgiving than those on the neighbouring island. I turned for Yell and started swimming.

Several minutes later, the wind got up, the rain became heavier and I'd made no progress through the water. I guessed I was swimming against the current. I looked around again, hoping to see a passing fishing boat, a cliff walker, anyone. That's when I saw, not ten yards away and barely visible against the water, a broken-off chunk of wooden pallet. I swam for it, gripped it tight and started to kick. It kept me afloat.

I know exactly how long I spent in the water because I always wear a waterproof watch when sailing. The watch enabled me to set little targets for myself. I would swim for ten minutes, then rest for two, timing it to the second. The pallet kept me afloat, the watch kept me sane, and my legs, strong from years of daily horse-riding, kicked me back to land.

It took three hours and twenty minutes to swim the quarter-mile from where the dingy capsized to Yell: the equivalent of about sixteen lengths of a twenty-five-metre swimming pool, and if it seems wimpishly slow, remember that swimming pools do not, as a rule, have tides, currents, freezing temperatures or heavy rain pelting down on you. But eventually it was over, and at ten minutes to twelve I collapsed onto the beach.

Death from exposure was still on the cards, though, and I had to get moving. I pulled myself to my feet and looked around. Ahead of me was a cliff, not massively high but a cliff nonetheless. The beach was very narrow, and behind a thin causeway there was a small lake. Two streams fed it, running down from the cliff top, and I realised they offered my best route up.

I started upwards. The stream I was following had cut out numerous little ledges and gullies over the years, and climbing wasn't difficult. But I was barefoot. My sailing boots had filled with water and I'd kicked them off in the Sound. After a few minutes my feet were bleeding.

Before I reached the top I saw a car drive past, not thirty yards away from me, but the driver was staring straight ahead. I kept on going and collapsed at the roadside. The rain was striking my face like a whip with a thousand tiny lashes, and I was shivering violently and my head throbbed, but by 12.15 I hadn't seen another car and had no choice but to start walking.

I walked along the road until I came to Gutcher, from where the Yell–Unst ferry leaves, and stumbled into the café by the pier.

'Dat in traath!' said the woman behind the counter at the sight of me. 'Da lassie is haff drunned.' There were two other people in the café, a boy of about ten and his mother. They said nothing, just stared.

They brought me a phone but I couldn't dial the number. I couldn't even remember it, but I managed to tell them who I was and they put the call through. It seemed to take a long time and all the while I was bracing myself for the news of my husband's death.

DUNCAN WAS NOT DEAD. Duncan came racing into the café an hour later, a little whiter in the face than normal but otherwise perfectly OK. Later, I learned that the dinghy hadn't capsized, just broached violently, then righted itself. Duncan had managed to cling to the tiller and remain on board, but the dinghy was uncontrollable and heading for the cliffs. He'd inflated his life jacket—working perfectly, thank you—and prepared to bail. Then he'd had the good fortune to be spotted by a passing boat: the owner of a salmon farm on Unst returning from an early-morning check on his offshore cages. The two of them had spent the next hour looking for me. In the face of a steadily worsening storm, Duncan had eventually been persuaded to return to Unst and call out the coastguard. By the time the phone call from the Yell café reached the Guthrie home, I had been missing for nearly four hours.

I don't remember much about the journey back to Westing. Just that Richard drove and I sat in the back, huddled close to Duncan.

VOICES WOKE ME. Duncan was shouting. I'd never heard raised voices in that house before. I turned to look at the clock. It was a little past seven in the evening. I sat up and felt OK so I climbed out of bed.

The door was slightly ajar. I could hear Richard now, arguing. I moved out into the corridor and hovered uncertainly at the top of the stairs.

The door to Richard's study was open and Duncan appeared in the doorway. 'I've had enough,' he said firmly. 'I want out. I'm getting out!' Then he was gone: along the corridor, through the kitchen and out of the back door.

I moved down the steps. Four steps down, I realised that Richard wasn't alone in his study. Elspeth was with him. They were arguing too, but very quietly. Another step down and I realised she was pleading with him.

'It's unthinkable,' said Richard.

'He's in love,' said Elspeth.

'He can't do it. He can't just walk away from everything he has here.'

I froze, one hand gripping the banister; then, forcing myself to move, I retreated on legs that were suddenly shaky again, one step . . . two . . . three. At the top I ran to the guest room and climbed back into bed. I pulled the quilts up over my head, waiting for the trembling to slow down.

Duncan was going to leave me? Of course, I knew things hadn't exactly been great between us for some time. I'd put it down to the stress of the move and our difficulties in starting a family. Now it seemed it was much more. What I'd seen as a bad patch, he'd recognised as the end. He was baling out.

Try as I might, I couldn't find any other explanation for what I'd just heard. Duncan was going to leave me. Duncan was in love with someone else. What the hell was I going to do? I had a job here. I couldn't just up and leave after six months. I could wave goodbye to any future consultant's post if I did that. I'd only come to this godforsaken place to be with Duncan. How was I ever going to have a baby now?

My tears, when they came, were hot and stinging. My headache was back with a vengeance, so I got up to see what I could find in the bathroom. There was nothing in the cabinet, nor in the toilet bag that Duncan had packed for me. Duncan's bag lay next to mine on the window ledge. I looked inside. A soggy blue flannel, razor, toothbrush, ibuprofen—thank God—and another packet of pills. I picked them up without really thinking about it and read the label: Desogestrel. Desogestrel is a synthetic hormone, known to reduce levels of testosterone in the male body and thus inhibit the production of sperm. For several years it's been used in clinical trials aimed at perfecting a male contraceptive pill. Although not yet available as a prescriptive medicine, it would only be a matter of time.

Duncan, it seemed, was ahead of the game. And I'd discovered the reason why, after two years of trying, I'd been unable to get pregnant.

8

'I'll be back by Wednesday, Thursday at the latest,' said Duncan.

'OK,' I replied, without turning round. I'd pulled an armchair over to the window and was looking out across the moor behind the house. The rain had stopped but there were heavy clouds overhead, their long shadows clutching the moor like the claws of a miser grasping something precious.

'We'll be home for next weekend,' he continued. 'Maybe try and get the garden sorted out.'

'Whatever,' I said.

Duncan knelt down beside me. I felt a tear roll down my cheek, but if I carried on staring straight ahead he wouldn't be able to see it.

'Tor, I can't take you with me. Dad says you're not fit to travel and I've back-to-back meetings for the next few days. I wouldn't be able to look—'

'I don't want to come,' I said.

He took hold of my hand. I let him but didn't return the pressure.

'I'm sorry, honey,' he said. 'I'm really sorry about everything you're going through.'

I'll bet you are, I thought, but I couldn't bring myself to say it. I couldn't say the few bitter words that would bring everything out into the open.

He hung around for another few minutes and then, kissing me on top of the head, he left. I heard the car engine start up and then fade away as he drove down the cliff road towards the ferry.

I forced myself to get up, knowing I couldn't stay in the house all day, obsessing about Duncan and my uncertain future. Official invalid or not, I was going out for a walk. I dressed and went downstairs. Luckily, only Elspeth was in the kitchen. Richard might have tried to stop me going out.

For the first half-mile I followed the coast road south. When it veered inland towards the village of Uyeasound, I took a detour to St Olaf's Kirk at Lund, one of the few remaining Norse churches on the island. It's a popular tourist spot, mainly for the views it offers over Bluemull Sound. But that day I was alone as I walked round the ruin and looked out across Lunda Wick.

All around me, perched on stones, launching themselves from rocks, sliding and bouncing on the wind, were hundreds of sea birds: kittiwakes, gannets, fulmars, terns and skuas. As I watched, a frenetic excitement seemed to grow in their midst. Then, almost as one, they dived straight into the wick, and hurled themselves among a shoal of sand eels. There was a whirl of feathers, a blizzard of sleek bodies as they fought and feasted.

I was wondering if I had the energy to walk into Uyeasound for a coffee when I noticed the large standing stone, not ten yards from the road. I wandered over to it, more for the purpose of filling time than anything else. The stone was smooth—except for the shapes that had been carved into it. Not the same markings exactly, but similar enough for me to be pretty sure I'd find them among the runic alphabet in Dana's leather-bound library book.

I set off down the road again. Ten minutes later, my mobile rang.

It was Dana. 'I heard about the accident. Are you OK?'

'I'm fine,' I said, because that's what you always say, isn't it? 'How could you possibly have heard . . .?' The line started to crackle and I stood still.

'. . . at the station saw the coastguard report and recognised the name. Look, can I do anything? Do you want me to come up?'

I was touched. And I would have given anything to have her company, but

I knew it would have been ridiculously selfish. Dana had far too much to do.

'Thanks, but the outlaws are looking after me. Anything new?'

'Sort of. I've been talking to Melissa Gair's GP again. He told me that, while the lump in Melissa's breast was worth checking out, it hadn't unduly worried him at the time. At the worst, he'd thought it would be a malignant tumour in the very early stages. He'd been amazed, he said, to hear about her death so soon afterwards.'

The wind was getting up; I pulled my jacket collar higher round my neck. I lost Dana for a few seconds and then she was back again.

'. . . and I went to see Stephen Gair at home yesterday. Nice place. Met his new wife and a child they say is hers from a previous relationship. A little boy about two years old. Stephen's officially adopted him. Connor looks a lot like his new stepdad. And they seem very close.'

I couldn't see how Stephen Gair's family life was remotely relevant.

'He has carrot-coloured hair, gorgeous fair skin and very fine features. His mother, on the other hand, is quite dark.'

I thought for a moment. Light dawned. 'Blimey!' I said.

'Quite.'

She started crackling again so I told her, without being sure she could hear me, that I would phone her that evening. I carried on into Uyeasound.

I found the coffee shop easily enough. A couple of hikers sat at one of the tables. That left three tables free. I sat down, pulled a ball-point pen out of my coat pocket and started to doodle on a paper napkin. And think.

I'd been wondering what had happened to the dead woman's baby. Had Dana now found that baby? Well, if Stephen Gair was bringing up his own son by Melissa but passing him off as the child of his new wife, he had to have been involved in Melissa's death. There was no getting round that one.

'Ye writin' to da trowie folk?'

I jumped. A waitress had appeared and was looking down at the napkin. I'd drawn several of the runes I remembered from the standing stone.

'Oh,' I said, 'they're runes. From the standing stone.'

She nodded. 'Aye, da trowie marks.'

'Sorry, but what's trowie?'

She grinned at me, showing bad teeth. 'Da trows,' she said. 'Da grey folk.'

It was a new one on me. 'I thought they were runes. Viking runes.'

She nodded and seemed to lose interest. 'Aye. Dey say dey came fra da Norse lands. What'll I get ye?'

I ordered a sandwich and coffee and she disappeared into her kitchen. Trow, trowie? I wrote it down, guessing at the spelling. Who were the trows? And why would they carve their marks on Melissa's body?

I waited for her to come back but the café was filling up. When she brought my order, she plonked it down and turned to another table. I could come back later, or find a library. Now that was a thought: I had access to the best library on Unst. Always assuming I could navigate the librarian.

I WAS LUCKY. Richard was still out and Elspeth only too happy to be left alone all afternoon. By five o'clock, I knew more about the history of Shetland than I'd ever wanted to.

Though geographically closer to Scotland, the Shetland Isles had been part of a Norse earldom from the eighth century until the late fifteenth. The dialect was still heavily interspersed with Norse words, many of which had been adapted and localised. The word 'trow' being a case in point.

Trow, I discovered, was an island corruption of the Scandinavian word 'troll'. According to legend, when the Vikings had arrived for a spot of rape and pillage, they hadn't come alone—they'd brought the trows: cheerful, happy people, who lived in splendid caverns in the ground, were fond of good food, drink and music, but hated anything connected to religion. Humans took care not to offend them on account of their supernatural abilities. They had powers to charm and hypnotise, and liked to lure away humans, particularly children and pretty young women. They also had the gift of making themselves invisible.

I found stories of trows stealing into homes at night-time, to sit round the fireside and help themselves to silver, and of islanders leaving gifts of fresh water and bread out for their trowie visitors. I learned that trows were powerless when confronted with iron. It was all quite harmless, entertaining stuff. Until I got to the Unst versions of the stories. Then things took a decidedly darker turn.

I read, for example, that the numerous tiny hillocks around the islands were believed to be trow graves; the creatures, it seemed, believed that if their bodies didn't lie in 'sweet, dark earth', their souls would wander and turn malicious. Even today, it was claimed, an islander, discovering disturbed ground on his land, wouldn't investigate, in case he uncovered a trowie grave and set loose an evil spirit. I am not remotely a superstitious person, but as I read that something cold pressed itself against my spine.

Whenever the trows stole an object, I read, they left in its place a replica, known as a stock. When they stole a person, they left a semblance. I looked 'semblance' up in a dictionary of folklore: 'a wraith-like creature', it said, 'little more than a ghost, but bearing a strong resemblance to a human'.

In relation to Unst, I found no stories of mischievous, hobbit-like creatures. Instead, there were several brief references to the Kunal Trow, or King Trow: human in appearance but with great strength and considerable supernatural powers, including that of hypnosis. In one book the Kunal Trows were described as a race of males, unable to beget female children. To reproduce, they stole human women, leaving behind semblances in their place. Babies born of these unions were always strong, healthy sons. And yet nine days after giving birth, the mothers died.

I found several references to a book by an islander, Jessie Saxby, generally considered to be the expert on the Unst Kunal Trow. I was sure Richard would have a copy of the Saxby book but it wasn't anywhere obvious.

Well, it was all very interesting, but it wasn't getting me any closer to interpreting my runes or trowie marks.

Richard had told me that one could find different interpretations of the runes. I scanned his study. The walls were lined, floor to ceiling, with shelves. The west wall contained his Shetland collection, including the works on folklore that I'd been skimming. The lower shelves were piled high with box files, each one neatly labelled in Richard's tiny handwriting. At the bottom of a pile I found a box labelled *Runic Scripts and Alphabet*. At that moment the door opened.

I made myself turn slowly and smile. Richard stood in the doorway.

'Can I help you find something?' He'd been out walking and brought the smell of the moors with him. He was still wearing his coat.

'Maybe something light,' I replied. 'In case I have trouble sleeping.'

'Mrs Gaskell is probably the closest I have to Mills and Boon,' he said.

I stood up. 'You never mentioned that you worked at the Franklin Stone.'

He didn't flinch. 'Would you have been interested?'

I stared at him, more than ready for a fight. 'Did you get me my job? Did you put in a good word for me with your protégé?'

'No,' he said simply. I was sure he was lying.

'Why do Kenn Gifford and Duncan hate each other? What happened?'

His eyes narrowed. 'Kenn doesn't hate Duncan. I doubt he gives him much thought at all.' He shrugged, as if the matter was too trivial to be of interest. 'Duncan can be childish sometimes.' His eyes fixed on the pile of books I'd left on the carpet. 'My books are carefully arranged. I find it difficult if someone displaces them. I'll be happy to find you anything you need.'

I bent down and picked up the scattered books.

'Leave them, please. Elspeth has made tea.' I knew he wasn't going to budge until I left, so I walked out.

THE NEXT MORNING, Richard left early. For a retired man he spent a lot of time out of the house, and I realised I had no idea what he did. Shortly after breakfast, Elspeth left too, on a shopping trip. She asked if I'd like to go with her but I truthfully pleaded a headache and tiredness and, after fussing a bit, she went. I waited for the sound of her car engine to fade and made straight for Richard's study, only to find the door locked.

I stood behind it for a moment, steaming. Then I ran upstairs. In my handbag I knew I'd find a few hairgrips. I grabbed four from the debris at the bottom and started bending them into shape.

I grew up with three brothers, in a Wiltshire farmhouse three miles from the nearest village. After school they were my only companions. Consequently, I understand rugby, I can name every bug and insect that crawls on British soil, I can perform some pretty impressive stunts on a skateboard and, coming to the point now, I can pick a lock.

It took me fifteen minutes. Inside the study, I went straight for the box file I'd noticed the evening before. It contained six copies of a magazine called *Ancient Scripts and Symbols*, some photocopied pages from books and several dozen sheets of coarse paper on which the runic symbols had been hand-drawn with explanatory paragraphs by each.

Three runic symbols had been carved into Melissa Gair. One was like a child's drawing of the bow on a kite string. I flicked through the sheets. There it was: the angular fish shape, called Othila or Fertility. It was described as the symbol for Womanhood and Childbirth. Scanning through the pages, I found Dagaz. The translation offered was Harvest and its primary meanings were listed as Fruitfulness, Abundance, New Life. The third rune had been two crossed lines. I found it: Nauthiz, or Sacrifice. Its meanings were listed as Pain, Deprivation, Starvation.

What a difference. With Dana's library book, we'd interpreted the three runes as meaning Separation, Breakthrough and Constraint, and had seen little significance at all. According to Richard's script, the runes seemed decidedly more apt: Fertility—a woman able to bear children; Harvest—the new life emerging from her body; Sacrifice—the price she has to pay. Very disturbingly I'd learned that my father-in-law knew about the meaning of the runes carved on Melissa's body and had chosen to keep quiet.

Something started niggling at me. There was more there if only I could see it, something new, something in the meaning of the words.

On a desk in a far corner stood a fax machine and photocopier. I took the sheets of paper over to it, copied them and tucked the copies into the pocket of my jeans. Then I replaced the originals, put back the box file and left the room, taking a few minutes to relock the door behind me.

I had to call Dana. She didn't answer her mobile or her home phone. Through directory enquiries I found the number of Lerwick police station, but got her voicemail. While I was wondering what to do next, the phone rang.

'It's McGill. Tell Mr Guthrie his son's boat has been retrieved. It's down at my yard. I need to know what he wants me to do now.'

I promised to pass on the message and got the address of the boatyard. I'd put the receiver down before I realised it was really up to me to deal with it. The boat belonged to Duncan and me. *Duncan and me.* How much longer would I be able to say 'Duncan and me'? I felt tears rushing up. No. Not now. I couldn't deal with it yet.

I phoned Dana's voicemail again and explained about the new runic meanings I'd found and about the local woman calling them the trowie marks. I quickly ran through the various stories about trows and Kunal Trows and suggested she investigate any island cults with links to ancient legends. I didn't mention Richard. It might be nothing more than bloody-mindedness on his part and, when it came to it, I was a bit reluctant to shop my husband's father.

BORROWING ELSPETH'S BICYCLE, I rode to Uyeasound and found the boatyard. A red-faced, red-haired islander in his late teens told me McGill had gone out for half an hour and led me to our Laser, lying against a wall. A chunk of the bow was missing, the port side badly dented and scraped.

The lad shifted from one foot to the other. 'Insurance job, is it?'

I looked at him. 'Sorry?'

'Are ye plannin' an insurance claim?' he muttered.

'I suppose so,' I said. 'Why?'

'Thing is,' he said, without looking at me. 'Thing is, I wouldn't. We've had a lot just lately. Boat accidents. They always send someone, the insurance company. They investigate, you see. Find out what really happened.'

'What do you mean?' I said. 'The mast broke.'

Then he gave me that half-pitying, half-amused look we all use when we know someone is lying to us. And they know that we know.

Except I didn't.

I walked over to the boat. It was upturned but there was room to lift it and I did. I shoved it hard and it turned over. Now I was looking at the cockpit. Just an eight-inch stump remained where the mast had been. Most of the rigging was gone too.

The boy was beside me now. He pointed to the mast stump. 'You make an insurance claim and you're going to end up in court,' he said. 'No one will believe that snapped. It was sawn through, to nearly halfway.'

I MADE IT BACK into town and headed out along the B9084, sick to the stomach at what I'd just learned. Our sailing accident had been nothing of the kind. The dinghy had been sabotaged. I remembered my life jacket that hadn't inflated and felt worse still. At the Belmont pier I had to wait the ten agonising minutes it took for the ferry to arrive. I had to get off Unst.

The ferry arrived. The waiting cars drove on and I followed. As the air filled with a pungent smell of diesel, soft rain started to fall. I pulled my coat collar up and hunched forward, fixing my eyes on Yell.

I had too much time to think, on that long journey back to the main island. Someone wanted me dead. I didn't need to ask why. I'd unearthed what was meant to stay hidden. Without my search through the dental records, who would have dreamed of linking a mutilated corpse with a death from cancer? Without an identity the crime would never have been solved, but thanks to yours truly, someone had cause to fear. And now so did I.

From leaving the boatyard to arriving back on the main island, my thoughts remained resolutely selfish. Then I remembered Dana. She had been as persistent and determined as I. If someone wanted me out of the way, she was a target too and I had to warn her. Trouble was, I didn't have my mobile. I'd left it at Richard and Elspeth's house. I realised that I hadn't spoken to Dana since late yesterday morning. I'd tried and failed the previous evening to find her and again this morning. It hadn't worried me at the time but it was worrying me now.

Back on the main island I rode to Mossbank, a small town on the east coast, where I had fifteen minutes to spare before the last bus of the day left. I folded Elspeth's bicycle and tucked it into the luggage rack, and when the bus set off I was able to rest for an hour and eat a sandwich. By the time we arrived back in Lerwick I had a plan.

First, find Dana. I had to fill her in with what I'd learned since being on Unst and I had to warn her. Second, get off the islands. Go home briefly, collect clothes and important personal papers and get to the airport. Catch the first plane to London, then a train to Mum and Dad's house. Third, get some career-focused advice on what my options were if I left the Franklin Stone. Four . . . I didn't really have a Four. Find a good divorce lawyer, maybe.

We pulled into Lerwick bus station just after four o'clock. I got off, unfolded the bicycle, and set off for Dana's house.

By the time I turned into the car park my chest was starting to feel tight and my head woozy. But I was cheered by the realisation that Dana was home. Or at least, her car was. My own car was where I'd left it.

I left the bike leaning against my car and ran down the flight of steps and along the narrow, sloping alley leading to he house. I banged on the door. The noise seemed to echo inside, as though the house was empty. I banged again.

'I've been knocking for ten minutes.'

I spun round. I hadn't heard anyone approach but Andy Dunn was right behind me. Too close.

'If she's in, she can't hear us,' he said. 'When did you last talk to her?'

I couldn't reply. He took a step closer and put his hands on my shoulders. I wanted to shrug him off and run away, but I couldn't move. He had very deep-set eyes, a dull blue in colour. The skin around them was deeply lined.

'Miss Hamilton, are you OK? Do you need to sit down?'

I felt myself relax a little. 'I'm fine, thank you. I need to see Dana.'

He didn't ask why. 'So do I,' he said. 'Please. When did you last talk to her?'

'Yesterday morning,' I replied. 'I've left several messages.'

'Stand back,' he ordered. I did and then watched as he backed away for several paces then charged the door at a run. His shoulder connected and the door buckled under the force and crashed inwards.

'Wait here.' He disappeared inside the house. I was aware of DI Dunn moving swiftly through the downstairs rooms, and a rhythmic thumping noise, loud in my ears, that I couldn't place at the time but I think now must have been the sound of my own heartbeat.

Dunn ran upstairs. I heard doors slamming. Silence. I started to pray.

Then his footsteps, thudding down the stairs. He jumped the last three, strode across the small hallway and looked directly into my eyes. Much of the colour seemed to have drained from his face and there was sweat on his temples. For a second, maybe longer, he just stared at me. I don't remember seeing his lips move but I was sure I heard his voice anyway.

You can go upstairs now. Look in the bathroom.

I stepped into the house. I heard the click and crackle of a radio and Dunn's voice, urgent and unsteady, behind me. I started to climb the stairs.

'Hey!' he yelled, and then there were footsteps running back into the house. I'd reached the landing and had pushed open the bathroom door.

Footsteps, running up the stairs. Heavy breathing. Dunn was behind me, his hands on my shoulders. 'What are you doing?' he said gently.

'I need to check for vitals.'

He must have seen some sense in that because he let me go. I took a step forward and leaned over the bathtub. I picked up Dana's left arm. It was pale and slender, like that of a child, and blood was no longer pumping from the three-inch gash that stretched diagonally across her wrist. I knew I would feel no pulse. One glance at her face had told me that. I hadn't even needed to look at her face. From the moment I'd hammered on the door of her house and heard emptiness inside, I'd known.

My vision was blurring. I could no longer make out the tiled walls of Dana's bathroom. Just Dana herself, like a beautiful statue, and the blood.

WHEN I CAME ROUND, my first thought was that I was still in the house and DI Dunn was leaning over me. Then I realised the eyes were more slate-grey than blue-grey and that the hair was dull blond with no hint of ginger.

'What did you give me?' I managed.

'Diazepam,' Gifford said. 'You were pretty wired up when they brought you in. Had me worried for a while.' Diazepam is a mild sedative. If he was telling the truth, I'd be woozy for a couple of hours but otherwise OK. I decided to put it to the test by sitting up. Harder than expected.

'Easy.' He wound the handle that lifts a hospital bed into a sitting position. Then he checked my pulse, took my blood pressure, shone a light into my eyes and pronounced me basically sound.

'I'm so sorry,' said Gifford. 'I guess we never really know what's going on in someone else's head.'

'I guess not.'

'She was under a lot of stress. Had been unhappy for a long time.'

'I know. I just wish . . .'

'There was nothing you could have done. When suicides are determined, nothing will stop them. You know that.'

I nodded. I knew that.

'I spoke to Duncan. He's coming back tomorrow morning.'

I looked at him. 'I might . . . I think I'll go to my parents' for a few days. Will that be OK, do you think?'

'I'm sure it will,' he said. 'DI Dunn needs to speak to you. I told him to wait till morning. I'm keeping you here overnight.'

I nodded again. 'Thank you.'

Gifford wound my bed back down and I closed my eyes.

I WAS STARTLED by voices outside the door, and braced myself to feign sleep.

'At least she's on hand if she's needed,' said a voice, one I recognised as belonging to one of the student midwives.

'Can't see it happening,' said an older woman. 'I've never seen a healthier batch of babies.'

The midwives moved on and I sank back into my pit of self-pity.

Gradually, over the past few days, Dana had gone from being someone I didn't much like to someone I trusted without question, a friend. Until, some time while I'd been scurrying around the islands like a panic-stricken rabbit, she had lain down in a bath of her own blood.

I opened my eyes. Thank the Lord for chattering midwives. I knew what had been bothering me since that moment in Richard's study when I'd learned that one of the symbols on Melissa's body meant Harvest. I knew what I had to look for next.

I found my clothes and dressed quickly. It was a quarter to nine and the hospital would be quietening down for the night. Unnoticed, I walked from my room, through the ward and out into the corridor.

I needed a computer but couldn't risk going to my office. In an office two doors down from my own I switched on the desktop. My password was still valid, and after a couple of minutes I was in the system.

'Batch' was the word the midwife had used that had struck a chord with me while I lay in my room. I was looking for a batch.

In Richard's study, I'd found an interpretation of Melissa's runes that had finally started to have some meaning. But one of them still hadn't made much sense. I could see where the artist (shall we call him?) was coming from with Fertility and Sacrifice, but Harvest? It seemed likely that 'harvest' was a reference to the baby. But how often do you come across a harvest of one? The word harvest conjures images of fruitfulness and plenty.

I already knew that at least one other young woman had met an untimely death in 2004, the year Melissa had supposedly died: Kirsten Hawick, who'd been hit by a lorry while out riding her horse. Her wedding ring had been found in my field. I'd never truly accepted that as coincidence.

Melissa hadn't died in 2004. While I couldn't begin to imagine how it had been achieved, her earlier death had to have been faked. So had the same thing happened to Kirsten and maybe other women too?

The first thing I had to find out was how many female deaths were recorded in 2004 and I accessed the General Register Office for Scotland on the Internet. After a bit of poking around, I had it: a table covering deaths that had occurred on Shetland between 1983 and 2006, grouped by age.

In 2004, the year Melissa's and Kirsten's deaths had been recorded, there had been 106 female deaths on the islands. Scanning across the row I found that, as you'd expect, the majority of them fell into the older age groups, from age 65 upwards. At the lower end of the scale, of course, deaths were far less common. But in this particular year, twelve young women had died between the ages of 20 and 35. Seemed like quite a lot to me.

I looked next at 2005. Only six women in the corresponding age bracket had died. In 2006, the latest year for which stats had been collected, there had been only four such deaths.

I went back in time. In 2003, two women in the age range had died. The year 2002 had been a particularly good one for young women, with no deaths recorded. In 2001, on the other hand, eleven deaths were recorded.

I went further back, as far as the table did, to 1983. I'm no statistician but even I could see a pattern emerging. Every three years a significant blip appeared in the female death rates. Now, what the hell did that mean?

I'd gone looking for one batch; I'd found eight. At least eight years in which the female death rate leapt way above the norm. And if some of these deaths were suspicious, how could some very senior people at this hospital not be involved? Whatever Gifford claimed about being in New Zealand when Melissa was admitted, he still ran the place. I decided I needed more details. Who were these dead women? How had they died?

I left the Internet, went into the hospital's own records and called up details of mortalities for 2004. There were 106 female deaths in total that year. Fortunately, the list included a name and a date of birth. It took about thirty minutes, but eventually I had my list of twelve women aged between 20 and 35 who died that year. I scribbled their names, ages and cause of death on a notepad I found on the desk.

Melissa Gair	*32*	*breast cancer*
Kirsten Hawick	*29*	*riding accident*
Heather Paterson	*28*	*suicide*
Kate Innes	*23*	*breast cancer*
Jacqueline Ross	*33*	*eclampsia*
Rachel Gibb	*21*	*car accident*
Joanna Buchan	*24*	*drowning*
Vivian Elrick	*27*	*suicide*
Olivia Birnie	*33*	*heart disease*
Laura Pendry	*27*	*cervical cancer*
Caitlin Corrigan	*22*	*drowning*
Phoebe Jones	*20*	*suicide*

I looked back to the list I'd printed off the General Register. A crude calculation told me that every three years, six or seven more women than usual were dying. Was it remotely possible to fake that number of deaths; to spirit these women away, keep them alive for a further year, before murdering them? And—big question coming up—had they, like Melissa, given birth shortly before death?

A harvest of babies. At last I'd said it.

OK, think. If these women were being abducted, they had to be kept somewhere secure and out-of-the-way but local. Somewhere with medical facilities, where babies could be delivered . . . Jesus! It was obvious.

I started typing again and brought up the obs and gynae pages I'd produced the day after I'd found Melissa: the details of all births on the islands between March and August 2005—the time Melissa's baby would have been born. I printed it off and highlighted every birth that had taken place on Tronal. I was looking for six or seven; I found four. It was too few to suggest an easy answer, yet Tronal was the ideal place: remote enough to offer privacy, with a modern maternity facility and its own resident obstetrician. I remembered what Stephen Renney had said about Melissa being anaesthetised before she was killed, and realised, with a sinking heart, that it also had a qualified anaesthetist well within commuting distance.

Oh Christ!

Suddenly I was sure Richard was involved in the facility on Tronal. He had to be; that was where he went when he left the house most days. Probably his protégé, Kenn Gifford, too, if the deaths were being faked at the Franklin Stone. And Dana and I had both had our doubts about Andy Dunn. One of them had tried to murder me. And they would try again.

I switched off the computer, gathered up the papers and grabbed my jacket from the back of the chair. Somehow, I had to get back to Dana's house to collect my car. I made my way out of the hospital and started to walk through the car park. Then I stopped. And almost laughed.

My car was parked in the area reserved for hospital staff. My keys were still in my pocket. Someone had even put Elspeth's bicycle in the back.

It was too late to leave the islands that night. But I needed some clothes and a sleeping-bag, in case I ended up spending the night in my car. I parked a quarter of a mile down from our house, pulled Elspeth's bicycle out of the back and cycled up the hill. I walked round the house once, peering into all the downstairs windows, but it seemed empty. I was jumpy all the same. I slipped inside and ran upstairs, found a holdall and threw my sleeping-bag and some clothes into it. Granddad's humane horse-killer went in too.

I stood in the doorway of our bedroom and it occurred to me that I might never see this room, this house again. It was only polite to leave a note.

On our dresser was a photograph of Duncan and me on our wedding day. He was tall and elegant in full morning dress. I was draped in cream lace and, for once in my life, looking feminine. I'd always loved that photograph. I picked it up, dropped it and stamped down hard with my right foot. Should get the message across.

I carried my stuff to the door and bent to pick up the mail. I was planning to dump it in the living room but one item caught my attention, a lilac envelope with *Tora* handwritten on the front. I opened it, took out a heavy gold key and read the short note, the first I'd ever received from beyond the grave.

Tora—Just spoke to your mum-in-law. She's concerned about you.
Your message very helpful. Things are starting to come together.
Assume you're heading back here. Don't stay home by yourself.
Come to my house. Let yourself in and wait.
Worried about you! Get in touch soon, please.—Dana

She'd put both the date and time of writing in the top corner. Twelve noon that day. I realised it would be crucial in establishing time of death and that I ought to hand it over to the police immediately.

Somehow I managed to balance everything on the bike and cycle back to where my car was parked. It started to rain as I set off back to Lerwick. Once I got to The Lanes, I drove past Dana's usual car park and headed for the next one along.

The front door had been repaired—quick work, guys—but the key still worked. Dana's hallway seemed still, silent. I walked through to the kitchen.

The room was spotless. Without really thinking what I was doing, I crossed to the fridge and opened it. The salad tray was full. A giant tub of apricots sat on one shelf, several cheeses on another. Natural yoghurt by the bucketful, two litres of skimmed milk, a litre of cranberry juice, a bottle of white wine, a row of organic eggs—Dana had been shopping.

I thought about eating but knew I couldn't. I closed the fridge door and left the kitchen. One step at a time, I retraced the last journey I'd made in this house, thinking, if only . . . If only I hadn't panicked on Unst; if only I'd stolen Elspeth's car instead of her bicycle, I'd have been back on the main island in a couple of hours, I could have been here before Dana . . .

The bathroom was spotless. The bath had been scrubbed. The small pink splashes on the tiles had gone. I backed out and pulled the door shut.

I walked past Dana's bedroom. I was heading for her spare room, where I'd slept briefly a few days earlier and which I knew doubled as a study.

Her desk was practically empty. I knew she kept her case notes in a folder but there was no sign of it in the room. I pulled open the desk drawer and counted twenty folders in hanging files. Each was labelled: *House*, *Car*, *Investments*, *Pension*, *Insurance* . . . and so on. I closed the drawer. I was probably wasting my time. Anything pertaining to the case would have been removed already by the police. I remembered a computer from my previous visit but it was gone now. Only a printer remained. And a pile of books stacked neatly to one side.

The top one caught my eye: *Shetland Traditional Lore* by Jessie Saxby, a book I'd found several references to in Richard's study. I flicked open the hard cover and saw that it was a library book, very recently taken out. Dana had taken my comments about local cults seriously. The book held a lot of Post-it notes. I sat on the bed and started to read.

There were stories of mass graves being discovered, stories of women being imprisoned on rocks. I lost all track of time as I read on, learning more and more about the strange and sometimes ghastly history of the islands. One story I found particularly chilling concerned a young man who went fishing one day, leaving his wife and new baby in the care of an old island woman. Neglecting her charges in favour of tea and gossip in a neighbour's house, the nurse returned at twilight to see a man dressed in grey leaving the house. Rushing inside, the nurse found a 'distraught wraith' and a 'dead changeling' in place of the mother and child; the trows had taken both mother and baby and left semblances in their place. For hours the wraith sat huddled on the bed, mourning her dead child, before dying herself. There were numerous other stories with the same theme.

Of course, I didn't believe in semblances. If deaths had been faked in order to conceal kidnappings—which was basically what all these stories boiled down to—then it had been achieved by natural means. I wasn't going down any supernatural route.

Trouble was, I wasn't going down any route. The words were starting to jump around on the page and I was done with thinking for one day. I put the book down and allowed my eyes to close.

IN MY DREAM, I closed the door on Duncan and the sound of wood slamming into the door frame rang out around the house. I woke up. It hadn't been a dream. Someone had entered the house, and was moving around downstairs.

I was back in the nightmare world of five nights ago. He'd come back. He'd found me. What the hell was I going to do? Where could I hide?

I felt beneath me. The bed was a divan. There was no wardrobe in the room. Nowhere someone of my size could hope to go unnoticed.

Escape was the only option. I got up and went to the window. The handle wouldn't move. Of course Dana would lock her windows. I looked closer. It was double-glazed. Breaking it might be possible but would make too much noise. I had to go down. Get past him somehow.

I reached into my holdall and rummaged around until I found the extra bit of protection I'd brought from home. Grasping it tight in my right hand I walked to the door, pressed the handle softly and opened it. I crossed the carpeted landing. At the top of the stairs I paused and listened.

Faint sounds were coming from behind the closed kitchen door. I peered over the banister. There were two doors leading from Dana's kitchen, not counting the external back door: the first, the one I was looking at, led into the hall; the second into the living room. I was planning to go that way, throw something back into the hall to distract whoever it was, then slip through the kitchen and out of the back door. Once outside I could climb the garden wall and run like hell back to the car.

Five more steps, six. My right hand was sticky with sweat. I checked the trigger. Loosened the safety catch.

The bottom step creaked.

I crossed the hall and into Dana's living room. I stopped. Listened. My right hand was up now, in front of me, but it was shaking.

Then something hit me square in the back and I went down hard.

9

I lay on the floor, the side of my head pressed against Dana's oak floorboards, my right hand empty.

The weight pressing me down moved. I jabbed my elbow back hard and heard someone grunt. Then that solid weight was on me again. My right arm was being twisted behind me. I squirmed and bucked and kicked.

'Police! Keep still!'

Yeah right! One of the hands holding my right arm was released, presumably to grab a hold of my left hand and get cuffs on me. But he wasn't strong enough to hold me with one arm.

I took a large breath and twisted round. The figure on top of me slipped sideways. I was on my feet. So was my opponent. In the darkness I could make out a tall figure with short, fair hair and neat, regular features. I now knew who I'd been scrapping with.

'Who the hell are you?' she said.

'Tora Hamilton,' I answered. 'A friend of Dana's. She gave me a key. I've been helping Dana with one of her cases.'

The woman seemed to relax. 'She told me.'

I was breathing normally again. My head had stopped spinning.

'I'm truly, truly sorry,' I said, hearing my voice crack.

Detective Chief Inspector Helen Rowley stared at me for a long time.

'Can you believe she killed herself?' she asked me, so softly I could barely make out the words. She wasn't really expecting an answer.

I said the first thing that came into my head. 'Have you seen the fridge?'

Helen's eyes glinted in surprise. 'What are you talking about?'

'You think Dana would stock a fridge before taking her own life? The Dana I knew—if she planned to kill herself—would have put the contents in the wheelie bin and cleaned the fridge with Dettol,' I said. 'Oh, and she'd have taken back her library books as well.'

Helen took a step back and fumbled against the wall. The room filled with light and I could see her properly. She wore a padded green jacket and baggy combat-style trousers. She was tall, almost my height, with a clean jaw line and brown eyes, and her hair wasn't short, it was pulled back in a plait. She looked around, then sank onto one of Dana's sofas.

'About four years ago, I spent some time working with failed suicides,' I continued, sitting down opposite Helen. 'They have various reasons, come from various circumstances, but they have one thing in common.'

Helen had curled herself forward, arms crossed in front of her body, hands gripping her upper arms. 'What's that? Despair?'

'I guess. But the word I was going to use was emptiness. These people look into their future and see nothing, believe they have nothing to live for.'

She looked at me. 'And that wasn't Dana?'

I leaned closer. 'No way was it Dana. There was just too much going on in her life. She was determined to get to the bottom of this case. She was worried, angry—but not empty. She wrote a note to me this morning. I'll show it to you. It's not the note of a suicide.'

'They told me she'd been struggling to fit in, not relating to her colleagues, missing her old force . . . missing me.' Her voice was unsteady.

'Probably all true. But not nearly enough.'

'She phoned me yesterday evening. She was worried, she wanted my help, but you're right, she didn't sound . . .'

We were still, for a while, and silent. I was wondering whether I should offer to make tea when she spoke again.

'This house is so like her. She could make homes beautiful. Her flat in Dundee was the same. You should see my place. Total mess.'

'Mine too,' I agreed, but inside I was getting edgy again. My relief at finding Helen was giving way to anxiety. I needed Helen functioning, not grieving and helpless.

'What the hell is that?' she said, looking at the floor.

I followed her gaze. 'A humane killer,' I said. 'For putting horses down.'

For a second I thought she was going to laugh. 'Is it legal?'

I shrugged. 'Used to be. Back in the 1950s.'

She stood up, retrieved the gun and put it on the top of a dresser. When she came back and sat down again, the skin around her eyes was blotched pink but I could see she was a long way from breaking down.

'So who killed her?' she asked.

'I'm not sure. But it was almost certainly someone connected to the case she was investigating. I think Dana was close to finding something out. Me too. I think someone tried to kill me, a couple of days ago.'

I told her about the sailing accident, the sawn-off mast. When I'd finished she was silent.

'I need your help,' I said. 'To find out what's going on here.'

She shook her head. 'You need to let the police handle that.'

'No! That's just it. The police will not handle it. Dana knew that. That's why she didn't trust her colleagues. There is something very, very wrong up here and somehow the police are involved.'

She sighed and then leaned back. 'I'm listening,' she said.

'This is going to sound a bit weird,' I began.

TWENTY MINUTES LATER I finished. A glance at the clock told me it was a quarter past midnight. Helen got up and left the room. I could hear her rustling about in the kitchen. After a minute or two she came back with two glasses of white wine.

'You were right,' she said, sitting down. 'That did sound weird.'

I gave her a shrug and a goofy half-smile. Well, I had warned her.

'Trolls?' she said, giving me an *are you serious?* look.

I sipped my wine. It was good: crisp and clean. 'Well, no. Obviously not real trolls. But some sort of cult that's based on an old island legend.'

Helen looked down at the notes she'd been making. 'OK, let's put Shetland folklore to one side and concentrate on what we know. You dug up a body in your field that has been positively identified as that of Melissa Gair. She'd been dead about two years, and shortly before her death she'd had a baby.'

I nodded.

'The complication comes because Melissa Gair is supposed to have died almost a year earlier. We have a woman who died twice. The earlier death was well documented and witnessed. The second death has the edge, of course, because it has a body to back it up.' She took a sip of her wine.

'Bit of a tricky one,' I agreed.

'You're telling me. Now, because of a ring found in your field, you started to think that more than one woman might have been murdered.'

I nodded again.

'So, you looked up mortality statistics on the islands.' She picked up the notes I'd made at the hospital. 'And they indicate—I admit—a pattern. Every three years, the death rate among young females increases. OK, now we move from fact to theory. You theorise that every three years a number of these women were abducted. Their deaths were faked, and they were held somewhere against their will for a whole year. Your best guess is this island called Tronal. During that time they were . . . impregnated?' She grimaced.

'Or they could have been in the early stages of pregnancy when they were taken,' I said. 'Like Melissa was.'

'And you think that while they were being held prisoner they had babies. Then they were killed and buried in your field.'

'Yes, that's what I think happened. It's exactly like legend,' I rushed on. 'The Kunal Trows steal human wives. Nine days after their sons are born—it's always a son because they're a race of males—the mothers die. Melissa was killed a week to ten days after giving birth.'

'Whoa . . . Is it remotely possible to fake death in a modern hospital?'

'Not so long ago I'd have said definitely not. Now I think it could be. But quite a lot of people would have to be involved: several of the medical staff, an administrator, definitely the pathologist. I'm not sure you could fool a trained medic, but a layman, especially a distressed relative . . . if there was a lot of fuss, plenty of distractions . . . and if the patient was very still, maybe heavily drugged into a coma-like state.'

Helen was whirling the wine round in her glass, staring at the patterns it made. She was giving nothing away but I sensed she was listening.

'And I think they use hypnosis,' I went on, reckoning, in for a penny . . .

She stopped whirling. 'Hypnosis?' she said.

'Hypnosis isn't hokum,' I said quickly. 'Plenty of psychiatrists practise it. You can alter someone's perception by planting ideas in their head. I think it just possible that a grieving relative could be shown an apparently lifeless body and be led to believe that person was dead.'

'Are there drugs that do that—make someone look dead?' Helen asked.

'Absolutely. Just about any sedative, if you take enough of it, will drop the blood pressure so low that finding a peripheral pulse would be all but impossible. It's risky, but a skilled anaesthetist could probably manage it.'

'How much of this did you discuss with Dana?' she asked.

'I didn't get a chance. But I left messages. I told her of the trow legends. And I know she took me seriously because she has a book upstairs.'

'I'm not dismissing the stats you found, but I'm struggling with this trow business,' Helen said. 'We still have only one body. Let's work with that.' She stood up. 'Come on, let's see what Dana has to say about all this.'

I looked up at her stupidly. What was she planning, a séance?

'Let's go and check her computer. I know her passwords.'

I shook my head. 'Her desk is empty. The police took it.'

'Oh, you think?' she said, and turned to go upstairs.

IN THE MAIN BEDROOM, Helen hopped up onto a chair in front of the large oak wardrobes and opened the middle of three cupboards that ran along the top. Then she handed down a small canvas suitcase trimmed with red leather. Inside was a small laptop computer that I recognised immediately.

Helen grinned at me. 'The desktop belonged to the Force. This was her own. Really sensitive stuff she only ever put on here.'

She carried it through to the spare room and fiddled around with leads. As the screen sprang to life, I glanced towards the window.

'Helen. You should know the police are almost certainly looking for me.'

She looked up.

'They want to question me about what happened here today—I mean yesterday. I sort of checked myself out of hospital earlier. Unofficially.'

'Do they know you have a key to this house?'

I shook my head. 'They'll probably work it out. We need to get a move on.'

I joined her at the computer. We were looking at a list of case folders, each one numbered. Helen clicked on the most recent, and it opened up.

It contained a number of files. The first was named Missing Persons. The second was named Babies, and had sub-files called Franklin Stone deliveries and Tronal deliveries. Then came Financial Records. In that section was a series of names, several of which I recognised: Andrew Dunn, Kenn Gifford, Richard Guthrie, Duncan Guthrie, Tora Hamilton. Not Stephen Gair, though; he had a filing section all to himself.

'Spouse is always the first suspect,' said Helen, opening up the Gair file.

There were a few personal details: his education, early years practising, the dates of his two marriages, to Melissa in 1999, then to an Alison Jenner in 2005. Most of it, though, was related to Gair's firm of solicitors: Gair, Carter, Gow, based in Lerwick but with offices in Oban and Stirling. Much of their business seemed to come from handling commercial contracts for the larger local oil and shipping companies. I noticed, with no real surprise, that they were legal advisers to the hospital.

Gair, Carter, Gow had numerous accounts with the First National Bank of Scotland. Each of its branches had a commercial account and a deposit account; after a few minutes of ploughing through statements it was clear that the firm held substantial reserves. There were also six client accounts.

'How the hell did Dana get all this stuff?' I asked.

'Dana did her PhD in software creation. She had a particular expertise when it came to hacking into financial institutions.'

'She got all this illegally? How? How did she do it?'

Helen sighed. 'Tora, I don't know. But my guess is that when she moved here, she would have opened accounts for herself in every bank and financial institution on the island. She'd have visited them frequently, getting to know the staff, copying down account numbers and sort codes. She'd have tried to work out passwords by watching people type on their keyboards. And she'd have known how to bypass most security systems.'

Well, Dana the villain. Who would have thought it?

'But doesn't information obtained illegally jeopardise an investigation?'

'Only if you try to use it. Once Dana knew what was going on, she'd have found proof using normal routes. OK, look, Dana has flagged this client account for the last last financial year. Shiller Drilling. Heard of them?'

'Vaguely. I think it's one of the larger oil companies.'

'Looks to me like Shiller Drilling were realising quite a lot of assets that year,' she went on. 'Look . . .' Helen pointed out the first three account entries that Dana had highlighted.

11 April TRF	Shiller Drilling sale: Minnesot.ranchland	$75,000.00
15 June TRF	Shiller Drilling sale: Boston.prop	$150,000.00
23 June TRF	Shiller Drilling sale: Dubai.seafront	$90,000.00

There were many more, all apparently relating to income from land and property sales. At the bottom, Dana had added a highlighted note: NB: Total year's incomings—$9.075 million, Cross Reference 3.

Helen called up the search facility and typed in 'Cross Reference 3'. Another page of figures filled the screen. Helen flicked to the bottom of the page. 'Manganate Minerals Inc. Annual Report and Accounts.' Dana had cross-referenced Gair, Carter, Gow's client account with the annual report of a . . . mineral company?

Helen drummed her fingers on the desk. Then she flicked the screen back up. 'Of course, Manganate whatsit is a group holding company. Shiller Drilling is part of the group.'

She was right. Shiller Drilling was there, tucked away in the left-hand column, headed 'Income from Land and Property Sales'. Helen traced her finger horizontally across the screen. According to the annual report, Shiller Drilling had sold $4.54 million of land and property that year.

'And what would you expect that to be?' Helen asked.

'Just over nine million dollars?' I ventured, remembering Dana's note.

'Clever girl,' said Helen. 'So, Gair, Carter, Gow's client account shows nearly four and a half million dollars of income from overseas land and property sales that isn't on the client company's annual report. So where is that money really coming from?'

'Different accounting period?'

'Good point.' She started flicking again and in a few seconds we had bank statements for the Shiller Drilling client account for the previous financial year. Another footnote from Dana: NB: Total year's incomings—$10.065 million, Cross Reference 2.

Putting 'Cross Reference 2' into the search facility took us to another of Manganate's annual reports. Again, the report showed far less income from overseas land and property sales than did the solicitors' client account.

We did it once more. Dana had gone back just three years. The story was the same. I started looking down the columns of numbers and text notes. The law firm's statement showed debit as well as credit entries; as sales of land and property were completed, the proceeds were transferred into client bank accounts, most of which were referenced by name.

'Any point adding up all the debits to Shiller Drilling?' I asked.

'Can't hurt,' said Helen. 'I need to pee.'

Helen got up and I scanned the debit column. And spotted something. Not all the debits had the same bank account reference. The money was being directed to two different accounts. I made a note of both reference numbers.

The lavatory flushed and I heard Helen going downstairs. I opened the file on Andy Dunn and went straight to his bank account. Helen returned carrying two glasses of water.

'He likes to live well,' she muttered, sitting down beside me. The same thing had occurred to me too. Substantial payments went out each month: to a car leasing company, a wine merchant, overseas flights. The size of his monthly mortgage payments made me blink.

'What would an inspector earn up here?' I asked.

'Not that much,' said Helen. 'And where's that coming from?' She was pointing to a credit entry for £5,000. We flicked back through the months. There were several entries for similarly substantial sums. Each carried a reference number, presumably of the bank account that the money had been transferred from: CK0012946170.

'Hang on a minute,' I said. I went back to the Gair, Carter, Gow's client account, scrolled through until I found the right place, then pointed at the screen. 'Look, I thought I recognised it. It's the same number.'

There it was, CK0012946170. The first two letters had made me think of Calvin Klein. We checked the column of figures. There were twelve transfers from the Gair, Carter, Gow client account to the CK reference number, totalling some £2.5 million.

'This isn't good,' said Helen to herself.

'Am I following this?' I said. 'We have unaccounted-for millions coming in from overseas. Stephen Gair is directing a good proportion of them to this bank account and then Andy Dunn is getting a monthly pay-out from it.'

'Looks that way,' said Helen.

'You should check Gifford,' I said. 'If there's stuff going on at the hospital, he has to be involved.'

She nodded, took the mouse and opened up the file on Kenn Gifford.

'Spartan,' she said. She was right. The statement I was looking at was short and simple. The salary came in monthly—substantially more than mine—and then two-thirds of it went out again to a savings account. He took out a largish sum in cash each month and that was it; no standing orders, direct debits or monthly payments of any kind—well, just the one: £1,000 came into his account regularly every month: reference number CK0012946170.

Helen flicked open the file on Richard Guthrie and went straight to his current bank account. Dana had flagged two entries: the first a credit payment of £2,000 from the same numbered bank account that Gifford and Dunn were receiving money from; the second another incoming payment of £2,000, referenced Tronal Med Salary. I'd been right. Richard Guthrie was practising at the Tronal Maternity Clinic.

'I really need to check your husband out,' said Helen.

'I know.'

She opened up Duncan's file and found his bank account. I was finding it harder to breathe. I watched as Helen flicked through the pages, seeing the same entry repeated month after month: £1,000. Guess the reference number.

Helen looked at me, put her hand on my shoulder. 'Are you OK?'

I nodded, although I was far from OK.

'There's something else,' she said. 'Late last year. Does this mean anything to you?' She pointed to an entry in early December.

A huge sum of money had come into Duncan's account from the CK bank account before going out again just days later.

'We bought the house the first week in December. That's how much we paid. Duncan told me the money came from a trust fund.'

'Your husband uses a telephone bank,' she said in a gentle voice, as though dealing with an invalid. 'Do you know his security details?'

I thought about it. He'd never actually told me, but I'd heard him on the phone to the bank dozens of times. His memorable date was 12 September 1974, my birthday; his memorable address was 10 Rillington Place, a sick joke that only he found funny. I knew his mother's maiden name: McClare. It was only his password I struggled with. I ran through the names of family members, best mates from university, even pets, but came up with nothing.

'It's pointless anyway,' I said. 'They'll never believe I'm Duncan Guthrie.'

'Lower your voice.'

I dropped it an octave. 'They'll never believe I'm Duncan Guthrie,' I said in a ridiculous imitation of a man.

'Speed it up and hold your nose, like you have a cold.'

'Oh for God's sake, you do it!'

Helen exhaled through her nose, like a mother at the end of her patience with a particularly tiresome toddler.

'Osprey,' I said, realising my little outburst had made me feel better. 'His first boat was an Osprey. That's it.'

'Ready to have a go?' she said, picking up the phone. 'We really need to know exactly where that money is coming from.'

I took the phone from her and dialled the number of the bank. When I gave Duncan's name the girl asked, 'From your password, Mr Guthrie, can I take the third letter number?

Fifteen seconds later I was through security. 'I've been going through my account; first time for months, to be honest, and I've got myself a bit confused about some of the monthly retainers I get from clients. There's one referenced CK0012946170. Can you confirm where that comes from?'

A short pause. 'That payment is referenced from the Tronal Maternity Clinic. Is there anything else I can help you with?'

'No. Thank you, that's great. Thank you very much for your help.'

I put the phone down. 'Tronal,' I said. 'It's all about Tronal.'

Helen's eyes flickered over my shoulder to the window. She jumped up, switched out the light and crossed the room to the window. I didn't like what I could see on her face. I got up too. Three police cars had pulled up just below us on Commercial Street, lights flickering but sirens turned off.

'Can't help thinking that's something to do with you,' said Helen.

She pushed past me, back to the desk. She shut down the laptop and folded it up. Then she looked over her shoulder. 'Do you have a car?'

I nodded and she led the way as we fled the house. We went out through the back door just as we heard hammering on the front. She locked the door, then we set off down the garden and scrambled over the wall into the back lane. We ran along it, climbed a short flight of steps, ducked left through a stone archway into the car park, and ran to my car.

I was pulling out of the car park when in my rearview mirror, I saw lights flick on upstairs in Dana's house.

'They'll expect us to head for the airport,' said Helen. 'They'll be watching the road south.'

She was right, and even if we made it to Sumburgh, we could hardly just park and wait for the first plane. Well before daybreak, the people who were looking for me would have every airport, every ferry port covered. And there are few roads on Shetland, so disappearing into a labyrinth of back streets was not an option. If we were to avoid being picked up in the next hour we had to get off the roads.

'I can't get a helicopter out here until morning,' Helen said. She was drumming her fists against the dashboard, obviously thinking hard. 'And I can't start flinging accusations around about a senior police officer without a lot more proof than we have already. We need more time.' She looked at her watch. 'It's almost two. Can you hide us for three or four hours?'

I thought of going home: not good, the first place they'd look. I thought of going back to the hospital: plenty of quiet areas this time of night but I'd almost certainly be recognised.

'Can you ride?' I asked.

FIFTEEN MINUTES LATER I was parking, for the second time that night, some way down the hill from our house. Charles and Henry heard us coming and trotted over to the fence. They were perfectly amenable to being tacked up. I was a bit anxious about Charles's leg, but it seemed to be healing well, and as long as we took it easy I felt that it should hold up.

Dana's laptop, our money and Helen's mobile went into two saddlebags; everything else we had to leave behind. I helped Helen onto Henry, then climbed onto Charles. The horses were excited about the prospect of a moonlight outing and skittered about. Helen sat rigid, her knuckles white against the reins. As we set off I felt a pang of misgiving; riding at night isn't a recommended activity for an inexperienced rider.

I was able to guide us through a field and out of Tresta before we turned onto the main road, which was probably just as well, because I don't think I'd appreciated what a racket the hoofs of two large horses make on a tarmac surface. Fortunately, Charles was walking well forward, excited about his first real exercise in a week, but setting a good pace that Henry was happy to follow. I wanted to get off the road as quickly as I could, but I didn't dare risk it until Helen felt more confident. I could hear her swearing to herself as Henry's hoofs slid on smooth tarmac or clattered against loose stones.

As we moved east we lost much of our light. The moon disappeared behind a cloud and the hills seemed to close in around us. Neither Helen nor I had much night vision yet, and even the horses were struggling.

We rounded a bend, and to our left the hill became a cliff, towering above us. To our right, the land fell away, down towards Weisdale Voe. In spite of the twinkling lights down at the water's edge, the land around us felt hostile.

We walked on, and I tried to make sense of what we'd discovered: huge sums entering Stephen Gair's business accounts from unknown sources, much of it being distributed to prominent men on the islands, including my own husband. What sort of activity could generate such large amounts?

As we turned off onto a smaller road, Henry drew level with Charles.

'Where are we going?' Helen asked, having to shout above the sound of the hoofs. It was a good sign that she felt relaxed enough to talk.

'We're heading north through the Kergord valley to Voe,' I answered. 'A friend of mine has a couple of horses there. She'll keep these two in her field until I can arrange to have them collected.'

'Is there road all the way?' she asked hopefully.

'No. We've got about half a mile of this road, then a farm track for another three-quarters. Then we're in open country. Should take a couple of hours.'

'We should have brought food.'

I too was starving. I'd last eaten about twelve hours ago, I reckoned: a sandwich on the bus. I regretted my squeamishness over Dana's fridge.

Ahead of us reared dark shapes, rare enough in this landscape to seem strange. They were trees: the Kergord plantations, covering about eight to nine acres in total and the only woodlands I'd seen on the Shetlands. A flapping and cawing above us made both horses jump. Rooks whirled in the sky, scolding us for waking them.

We'd reached the farm track and were forced to slow down in order to navigate round a cattle grid. After this we broke into a trot and after a while I judged Helen was relaxed enough to talk again.

'Well, I guess millions of pounds don't usually appear from nowhere without something dodgy going on. Any idea what?'

Helen risked taking her eyes off the path ahead. 'I've been thinking about that,' she said. 'I wonder if they're selling babies. Maybe to wealthy couples from overseas, countries where private adoption is the norm. Most of the money we saw seemed to be coming from the United States.'

The same thought had occurred to me, but it didn't seem possible. 'According to the records, only about eight babies are born there every year,' I said. 'They'd need more, wouldn't they, to generate that sort of income?'

'Less than ten babies, huh? A maternity clinic on a private island for less than ten babies a year? Seem likely to you?'

'No,' I said. That had never seemed even remotely likely.

We'd reached the end of the farm track and were in open country. On either side the hills loomed high above us, deep shadows against a charcoal sky. We were about as far from the sea as it is possible to get on Shetland—which isn't far, three or four miles at most—and the scents had become those of land rather than sea, the musty dampness of peat, the ripeness of fresh vegetation. Every now and again the moon appeared from behind a cloud and in its light the ground sparkled as though showered with broken glass. We were walking over flints gripped tight by the land.

We came to a stream that we had to cross. As I urged Charles over, he tugged his head forward and bent to drink. Henry copied him.

'Is this water drinkable?'asked Helen.

'Well, these two seem to think so,' I said, jumping down.

Helen followed suit and the four of us drank the ice-cold, slightly peaty-flavoured water. Helen washed her face, I splashed copious amounts over my head and felt better immediately. Still starving hungry, though.

Out of the corner of my eye I saw something moving towards us; something too large to be a sheep. I cried out, every nerve-ending in my body prickling. Helen was beside me in a second. Then we both relaxed. The one shape had become several and they were all heading our way. They were a dozen or more native Shetland ponies. Spotting two strangers of their own kind, the herd had come up to say hello. They seemed not remotely perturbed at finding two humans as well.

'You know it could catch on,' I said, watching Henry rub muzzles with a grey mare that could only have been nine hands high.

'What could?' said Helen.

'Mounted police on the Shetlands,' I said. 'There's a whole mass of terrain that's totally inaccessible by road and no shortage of native livestock.'

'Worth thinking about,' agreed Helen. 'Course, we'd need to rethink the height rule. How many of these ponies do you have up here?'

'Not sure anyone knows. They breed like rabbits, apparently. A lot are sold—to pet centres, model farms, that sort of place. And they're exported all over the wor—' I stopped, realising what I was saying.

'Like Shetland babies?' asked Helen.

'Possibly,' I said, 'except where are they all coming from?'

Helen frowned, appeared to think for a moment. 'Let's just say,' she said at last, 'that Stephen Gair, Andy Dunn, Kenn Gifford . . . all the men whose records we checked . . .'

'It's OK,' I interrupted. 'You're allowed to mention Duncan.'

She gave me a half-smile. 'Suppose they're all involved, making a packet of money from it, and Melissa Gair found out, threatened to go to the police. That would be motive enough, wouldn't it, to get her out of the way?'

'I guess.'

'But why fake her death and keep her alive for so long?'

'Because Stephen Gair knew she was pregnant. He wanted his child.'

I explained Dana's theory about the boy Stephen Gair called his stepson being, in fact, his own son by Melissa. Helen seemed to shrink a little inside herself at the mention of Dana, but managed to hold it together.

'Hell of a risk,' she said. 'And why cut out her heart? Why those weird symbols on her back? Why bury her in your field, for God's sake?'

'Because they have to be buried in sweet, dark earth,' I whispered, not really intending that she should hear.

She gave me a look. 'Are we back to trolls again? I can't do trolls right now. We need to get moving.' She gathered up her reins and lifted her foot to the stirrup. Then she stopped. 'Listen,' she hissed.

I listened. Soft whinnying from the ponies, whistling of the wind. And something else. Something low, regular, mechanical. Something insistent; something approaching.

'Shit!' Helen started pulling Henry towards a steep overhang of rock at the valley's edge. 'Come on,' she urged.

I reached the outcrop a few seconds after Helen. We backed close to the rock, pulling the horses up against us. We tried to keep them still as we waited for the helicopter to approach.

'They found your car,' said Helen. 'Does everyone know you have horses?'

I thought about it. Duncan, of course, but he was off the islands. Gifford! Gifford knew. And Dunn, of course. And Richard. Yes, just about everyone.

The helicopter was close now and we could see the searchlight illuminating the valley. I tightened my hold on Charles. The Shetlands didn't like the noise and, seeking security in numbers, had all followed us to the overhang.

'Skit! Scram! Get out of here!' hissed Helen. 'Little buggers are going to draw attention to us.'

'I should have untacked the horses when we first heard it,' I said. 'No one would think twice about finding two untacked horses out here.'

Helen shook her head. 'They'll have surveillance equipment. They'll be able to spot body heat. Actually, these little tykes might save the day.'

The Shetlands seemed to fear the light more than the noise. As it grew closer they broke cover, scattering across the valley, seeking the safety of darkness. The chopper swerved and followed them just as the light touched on Henry's brown tail. A stallion set off south at a gallop, most of the herd veering round to follow him, and the chopper went too, increasing the panic among the animals. The herd turned, so did the chopper. It began to circle; the light edged closer. But then it rose higher in the sky and moved north.

Charles and Henry started to fidget, but Helen and I hardly dared move as the noise of the helicopter's engine faded.

'I can't believe we got away with that,' I said, when it felt safe to breathe.

'They saw movement and body heat but assumed it was the ponies.'

We mounted and set off again. The tension of the last few minutes seemed to have sapped me of energy. It was all I could do to point Charles in the right direction and urge him forward.

'How much further do we have to go?' asked Helen.

'Another forty-five minutes,' I guessed.

At that moment the world around us changed.

We'd been travelling through a landscape of shadows, of cliffs topped with scrubby vegetation, silhouetted against a deep indigo sky. Of subtle hues there was an endless variety; of real colour there was none.

And then a great draper in the sky unleashed a roll of finest green silk; it hung in the air, stretching as far as we could see, shifting and gleaming, changing constantly, giving off and reflecting back a light that was all its own. The sky grew blacker around it. Trees and rock formations were thrown into harsh relief as the draper shook his cloth, the silken sky rippled, and shades of pale green I'd never dreamed of danced before us.

'Oh my God,' whispered Helen. 'What is it?'

From the northwest came a soundless explosion of colour, as though heaven had thrown open a window, allowing awe-stricken mortals below a glimpse of the treasures beyond. Cascading down came beams of silvery green, of a rich deep violet, and of the warmest, softest, rosiest pink you could imagine. It was colour so incredibly rich, and yet so fine that through it we could still see the stars.

And so we joined the ranks of the few privileged souls who, thanks to a lucky coincidence of time, geography and atmospheric conditions, have been permitted to glimpse the aurora borealis.

'The northern lights,' I said. 'The Inuits called them gifts from the dead.' Then, surprised at the sentimental depths to which my normally cynical nature could plummet, I added, 'I think Dana sent them.'

'Thank you,' whispered Helen, and I knew she wasn't talking to me.

10

Shortly before three thirty we arrived at my friend's livery yard in Voe. The stable block was empty but I could see her two horses peering at us from a nearby field. I ran my hands over Charles's injured leg. It had held up but he would need a few days' rest. I found buckets and gave both horses a long drink and an armful of hay. Then I untacked them, released them into the field and carried the saddles and bridles over to the tack room. The key was where I expected to find it, beneath a flower tub.

My friend's tack room doubles as an office and there was a phone line. I pointed it out to Helen, closed the door behind us and headed straight for a drawer in the desk. I was in luck. Half a packet of Jaffa Cakes, a nearly full box of Maltesers and three tubes of Polo mints. I divided the bounty and we ate ravenously for five minutes. Feeling slightly better but still sore and weary, we plugged in Dana's laptop.

There was only room for one at my friend's cramped desk so Helen took the chair and I settled myself onto a straw bale and leaned against the stone wall of the tack room. I didn't think I'd ever been on a less comfortable seat, but I allowed my eyes to close and was asleep in seconds.

'TORA.'

Didn't want to wake up. Knew I had to.

'Tora!' Firmer this time. Like Mum on a school day.

I pushed myself up. Helen was standing over me. She had one bag slung over each shoulder. The tack-room door was open and it was light outside.

'We have to leave,' she said.

I stood up, drank some water. Then I scribbled a note to my friend and walked out into the sunlight. Helen locked up behind me and replaced the key. We went out through the yard gate and started to walk down the road.

'Where are we going?' I asked. I looked at my watch: 5.30 a.m.

'Pub at the bottom,' Helen replied. 'Chopper can land in the car park.'

In spite of everything I was impressed. She was going to get us out of here. I'd be safe. I could rest. We could work it all out.

The helicopter that touched down in the pub car park was small, black and yellow, not unlike the one the medical team used in emergencies. The pilot signalled to Helen, and we ran towards it. Helen opened the door, I jumped into the back seat and she followed, closing the door behind her. We were in the air, heading south, before either of us could fasten our seat belts.

Helen had said nothing but I guessed we were going to Dundee, where she was based. On her own patch she would have the best use of resources and be better able to look after me if Dunn and his gang came after me.

I watched the coastline go by. In the early sun the sea sparkled and the white of the foam had turned to silver. The first time I saw Duncan he'd been surfing and was walking out of the water, board tucked under one arm, his wet hair gleaming black. I had thought him way out of my league, but later that night he'd found me. I'd thought myself the luckiest girl in the world. So what did that make me now? There were a dozen questions that I really didn't want answers to, but I just couldn't get them out of my head. How deep did Duncan's involvement go?

Soon Dundee drew nearer and I prepared myself for descent. Instead, the pilot banked sharp right and headed west. I watched the Grampian peaks sail below us, some capped with snow, some with heather; I saw glinting sapphires of lochs and deep, thick forests. When we could see the sea again the helicopter at last started to go down.

We put down on a football field. Fifty yards away sat a blue and white police car. Helen yelled something at the pilot and then jumped out. I followed. The constable in the police car started the engine.

'Morning, Nigel,' said Helen.

'Morning, Ma'am,' he replied. 'Where to first?'

'The harbour, please,' replied Helen.

We drove through a small, grey-stone town I recognised as Oban, where we stopped just short of the pier, for no reason I could see, and got out. Helen led me to one of the small stalls that lined the seafront.

'Do you like seafood?' she asked.

'I guess,' I said, thinking that a good chuck-up might get rid of the nausea.

Helen pointed out a bench overlooking the sea and I sat down. A few minutes later she sat down beside me, handing me a large mug of coffee, several white paper napkins and a grease-stained paper bag.

'Lobster bap,' she said smugly. 'Fresh caught this morning.'

It was an incredible breakfast: the bitter, rich strength of the coffee worked like medicine. And the lobster, rich and sweet, every mouthful a feast. Helen and I ate like we were racing and, by a fraction of a second, I won. I'd have given anything to have stayed there, drinking coffee as the sun rose in the sky. But I knew Helen hadn't brought me to Oban just for breakfast.

As though reading my mind, she looked at her watch. 'Seven forty-five,' she said. 'I'd say that's a respectable enough time for house calls.'

Back in the car she turned to me. 'OK, listen good, because we'll be there in a minute. While you were in the land of nod last night, I had another look at Gair, Carter, Gow's bank accounts.' We'd left the harbour and were winding our way through Oban's residential streets. 'When I was going through the commercial account for their Oban branch, something stood out.'

We turned into a cul-de-sac of newish detached houses. 'Here we are, Ma'am,' said Nigel. 'Number fourteen.'

'Thanks, give us a minute,' said Helen. 'Three payments from the Oban commercial account to something called the Cathy Morton Trust. What got my attention was their size—they amounted to half a million in sterling in total—and the timing. Three payments, in September and October 2004. The second of them on October the 6th, 2004.'

I said nothing, waiting for the punch line. Helen looked disappointed; I'd obviously missed something.

'So I got on the Internet and called up a national police register. Only one Cathy Morton in Oban and this was her last known address. Come on.'

We got out of the car and walked to the front door. Helen knocked. The door was opened by a man in his late thirties, dressed in a suit and a blue shirt open at the neck. A small boy in Spider-Man pyjamas peered at us from round the door frame. Another child, a girl this time, joined him.

Helen flashed her badge and introduced me. 'Mr Mark Salter?' she asked.

The man's head jerked forward.

'We need to talk to you and your wife. May we come in?'

Salter muttered something about getting his wife up and disappeared upstairs. We went into the living room. The TV was tuned into CBeebies. The kids, aged about seven and three, seemed mesmerised by us.

'Hi!' said Helen, addressing the boy. 'You must be Jamie.' The boy said nothing. Helen tried the girl. 'Hello, Kirsty.'

Kirsty, a cute little thing with porcelain skin and bright-red hair, turned and ran from the room. Mark Salter returned with his wife. Over one shoulder she held a small baby, about four weeks old. Kirsty clung to her legs.

'I'm Caroline Salter,' she said.

Helen glanced at the children and lowered her voice as she looked at Caroline Salter. 'I need to talk to you about your sister.'

The woman reached down and pulled Kirsty firmly away from her legs. 'Come on, you two, breakfast.'

She looked at her husband. He led the children from the room, switching off the TV as he went and closing the door behind him.

'My sister is dead,' she said, lowering herself onto one of the sofas.

Helen nodded. 'I know, I'm very sorry.' She looked round at the other sofa and raised her arm in a 'May we?' gesture.

The Salter woman nodded and Helen and I sat down.

'How are the children doing?' asked Helen.

Something in the woman's face softened. 'OK,' she said. 'They still have their bad days. It's harder for Jamie. Kirsty barely remembers her mum.'

Helen gestured towards the baby. 'This one is yours?' she said.

Caroline nodded.

'He's gorgeous,' said Helen. Then she turned to me. 'Miss Hamilton here is an obstetrician. Brings little ones like that into the world all the time.'

Caroline sat up straighter and the wariness gave way, just a fraction, to interest. I made myself smile.

The door opened, Mark Salter came back into the room and sat next to his wife. Beside me, Helen stiffened. Female empathy time was over.

'When did your sister become ill?' asked Helen.

Caroline looked at her husband. He made a thinking face.

'She had a breast tumour removed about five years ago,' he said. 'Christmas time. Jamie was just a toddler. Then she was OK for a while.'

'But the cancer came back?'

Caroline nodded. 'Early in 2004. Cathy was pregnant so she wouldn't have chemotherapy. By the time Kirsty was born it had spread too much.'

'The doctors weren't able to remove it?' I asked.

'They tried,' Caroline said, her eyes moist. 'She had an operation but it wasn't successful. She had chemo, but in the end just pain relief.'

'She lived here with you?' asked Helen.

Caroline nodded again. 'She couldn't manage the children. She couldn't do anything at the end. She was just in so much pain . . .'

She started to cry and the baby squawked in protest. Mark Salter took the opportunity to play the annoyed husband.

'Oh great! We really don't need this right now. Are you through yet?' He didn't do it terribly well. He looked more afraid than angry.

'Not quite, sir,' said Helen, who hadn't been convinced either. 'I want to ask you about the Cathy Morton Trust. I assume you're both trustees.'

Mark nodded. 'Yes, us two and our solicitor, Stephen Gair,' he replied.

'When did Cathy meet Mr Gair?'

Husband and wife looked at each other.

'I want to know what this is about,' he began.

'I think you know already, Mr Salter. It's about the money your sister-in-law received from Mr Gair.'

'It's not our money,' said Caroline. 'It's for the kids.'

Mark Salter stood up. 'We've nothing more to say. I'd like you to leave.'

Helen stood up too. 'Mr Salter, at this moment I have no reason to suspect you or your wife of any wrongdoing. But I can and will arrest you for obstruction of justice if you don't start cooperating.'

There was silence for a moment. Then Helen sat down again. Salter hovered for a second, then lowered himself back down beside his wife.

'Did Cathy make a will?' asked Helen.

Caroline nodded. 'In June. She was very ill. She knew by then she wasn't going to be around for too long.'

'And Stephen Gair drew it up for her?'

'Yes. She'd met him about a year earlier. When she sold her house. They went out for a while. Dinner when he was in town, weekends away. She didn't tell us much about it because—'

'He was married,' said Helen.

Caroline nodded.

I wanted to scream at her to tell us what she knew. 'What happened in September 2004? He came to see her, didn't he?'

'They knocked on the door one day. Asked to see her. They said they knew she was ill but it was important.'

'They?' asked Helen.

'Stephen Gair and the other man. He talked like a doctor. I took them up to see her. It was hard for her, talking to anyone, but she made a big effort.'

'What did they talk about?'

'They made her an offer.' This time Mark was talking. 'We told her she didn't need to do it, that we would take care of the kids.'

'What was the offer?'

'That she would take part in a trial of a cancer drug. She'd have to go away, to a hospital on the Shetlands where the trial was taking place. They said there was no guarantee she'd respond to the drug but there was a chance. In return, the drug company would set up a trust fund for the children. The money is released monthly for things like school uniforms for Jamie and child care for Kirsty. We get none of it.'

I looked round the room, at the leather sofas, the stereo equipment.

'And Cathy agreed to this?'

'Yes,' said Caroline, 'she agreed. It was the worst thing for her, worrying about the kids, about what would happen to them.'

'I do understand,' said Helen. 'What happened next?'

'Stephen Gair set up the trust fund, making Mark and me trustees. The first instalment was paid and they came for her a couple of days later.'

'Who came?'

'That man, the doctor, in an ambulance. And a nurse.

'When did you see her again?'

Caroline shook her head. 'We didn't. She died just over a week later.'

'Where was the funeral?'

'There wasn't one,' said Mark. 'Gair said it had been part of the arrangement that Cathy's body would be used for medical research.'

'Did you talk to her ever?'

'We didn't have a number,' said Mark. 'Stephen Gair phoned us most evenings with a report. Kept saying she was comfortable but very drowsy with the drugs. Not able to talk on the phone.'

'Can you remember the date she died?' asked Helen.

'October the 6th,' said Caroline. Helen was looking at me, to see if I'd finally got it. I had. October 6 was the day Melissa was supposed to have died.

'We weren't happy that she could just disappear like that,' said Mark. 'We wanted to talk to her doctors, find out about her last days. But Gair wouldn't take our calls. Then the bloke we'd thought was a doctor came round.'

'Go on.'

'I was on my own in the house,' said Caroline, 'and he pretty much threatened me. Said we had to stop pestering Mr Gair. Cathy hadn't been harmed by the drugs and would have died anyway. He implied that if we wanted to keep the money we'd have to keep quiet.'

'We had to think about the kids,' said Mark. 'Nothing was going to bring Cathy back. We had to think about their future.'

'I wasn't happy, though,' said Caroline. 'I threatened to call the police.'

'What did he say?'

'He said he *was* the police.'

No one spoke for a few moments. Then Helen turned once more to Caroline. 'Do you have a photograph of your sister, Mrs Salter?'

Caroline got up still clutching the baby. She crossed the room, opened the top drawer of a dresser and fumbled inside. Then she returned to Helen and gave her a photograph. Helen looked at it for a second and handed it to me.

Stephen Gair's arms were round a pretty young woman in a green sweater. The likeness between Melissa and Cathy was unmistakable: similar age and build; long red hair; fair skin; fine, small features.

There'd been a semblance after all.

STEPHEN GAIR HAD had an incredible stroke of luck. Needing to get rid of his wife, he'd known a terminally sick woman who bore a strong resemblance to her. Terrified for the future of her young children, Cathy Morton had allowed herself to be moved to a new hospital where, spaced out with painkillers, she wouldn't have known what was going on around her. And who was there to suspect she wasn't who a respected local solicitor said she was? None of the medical staff who had treated Cathy had known Melissa; Cathy's sister and brother-in-law hadn't been allowed to visit; Melissa's parents hadn't been told she was in hospital. Even if someone had met Melissa once or twice, he or she could have been fooled by the sight of a cancer-ridden Cathy in a hospital bed. And Cathy had died just days after being admitted.

I imagined the funeral, the church full of Melissa's friends and relatives, deeply shocked by her sudden death. Which of them could have dreamed the body in the coffin heading for the furnace wasn't Melissa at all? That Melissa, still very much alive, was . . . somewhere else? Where had she been for the nine months between Cathy's death and her own? And what the hell had happened to her in that time?

When the helicopter landed at Dundee, Helen gave me a quick smile and disappeared into a waiting car. Another car took me to the police station, where a member of Helen's team, an inspector, came to interview me.

I told him the whole story, from finding the body to meeting the Salters. I told him about Kirsten Hawick, who'd been killed in a riding accident, and about my finding the ring that had every appearance of being hers; about someone breaking in to my house and my office; about the pig's heart on my kitchen table; about my suspicions that I'd been drugged. I told him about my sabotaged boat and useless life jacket; about my belief that Dana had been murdered because she'd found out too much. I described the evidence of financial irregularities and about my escape with Helen through the dark Shetland landscape. Then I went through it all again. And again.

An hour and a half later we stopped. I was brought lunch. Then he came back. More questions. Another hour and he leaned back in his chair.

'Who knew you planned to go sailing that morning, Miss Hamilton?'

'We didn't plan it,' I replied, knowing I was stalling. 'It was a last-minute thing. But lots of people know we keep a boat there.'

'Do you keep your life jackets there too?'

I couldn't look at him. 'No,' I said. 'We keep them at home. In the attic. Duncan would have picked them up from home before we set off.'

He frowned, stared down at his notes for a while, then looked back up. 'Whose idea was it to go sailing? Who thought of it?'

'Duncan's,' I said. 'It was Duncan.'

WHEN WE HAD FINISHED, Helen entered the room. She'd changed into a tailored black trouser-suit and an emerald-green silk top. Her hair had been washed and wound up on the top of her head. She looked nothing like the woman I'd ridden across country with the night before.

'Ready to go back?'

Back? To the islands? Early that morning, I'd watched them disappear over the horizon and I'd told myself that that part of my life was finished.

'Do I have a choice?' I asked, knowing what the answer was going to be.

'Not really. You can eat on the way.'

She was silent as we drove to the helipad. I had a hundred questions but I didn't know where to start and, if I'm honest, I was a little afraid to. Helen wasn't my fellow fugitive any more; she was a senior police officer, probably in charge of a very serious investigation. And I was a principal witness.

When the driver was parking she said, 'Stephen Gair has confessed.'

I sat bolt upright in my seat. 'You're kidding me? He just admitted it?'

She nodded. 'He's been in custody since midday. It took two hours and then he cracked.'

'What? I mean, what exactly has he confessed to?'

'Well, everything. Selling babies to the highest bidder, for one thing. He says he worked with several unscrupulous adoption agencies overseas. Whenever a wealthy couple appeared they were told about a way of short-cutting the system for a price. It was all done by blind auction on the Internet.'

Our driver got out of the car. He waved to the pilot, who nodded back, and the chopper's blades started to turn.

'George Reynolds, the director of social services, is in Lerwick nick, helping us with our inquiries. He's denying all knowledge, but if the babies went overseas with adoption papers, his department must be involved.'

'Who actually took them overseas?'

'A nursing agency. They claim they didn't know anything was illegal.'

'And Gair admits substituting Cathy for his wife at the hospital?' The noise of the helicopter's engines was increasing and I had to raise my voice.

'Yep. Insists she was very well treated, that her illness followed its natural course and that in no way can he be held responsible for her death. He also says no one at the hospital knew anything about it.'

'So who was the doctor who helped him, the one who later claimed to be a policeman? The one Caroline met?'

'He insists there was no accomplice. Says Caroline was confused.'

'She didn't sound confused to me.'

'No. She's at Lerwick now. We've got an identity parade lined up.'

'And Melissa?'

Helen held up one finger at the pilot. 'Gair admits killing her. She found out about the adoptions and threatened to go to the police. He says he kept her in your cellar. A forensic team's been there for the last few hours.'

'You're kidding me,' I whispered.

'He'd handled the probate for the last owner and knew the house was empty. He even had a set of keys. He says he kept Melissa tied up and heavily drugged and once she'd given birth he killed her.'

'He couldn't have done that without help. He's covering for someone.'

'Probably. He says he carved the symbols on her back. Got the idea from some markings around your fireplace. He can't remember what he did with the heart. Says he was under a great deal of stress at the time. He's also admitting that Connor, the little boy he calls his stepson, is his own child. And Melissa, not Alison his new wife, was his mother.'

'Dana was right.'

Beside me, Helen took a sharp breath. 'Well, we can DNA test, prove it conclusively, one way or another. Look, don't worry. A few more hours, maybe days and he'll tell us everything. Right now, we need to move.'

IT TOOK US JUST OVER an hour to get back. Helen spent the time reading and making notes, her body language giving very definite *don't ask me now* signals and I didn't want to push her. But shit . . .

First thing that occurred to me, as the helicopter took off, was that we'd never have made it to this point if Stephen Gair hadn't agreed to have his wife's dental records examined. Why the hell had he done that? Had he deliberately played along, knowing the system was in place to protect him; that he had friends who could get him off the hook?

And in spite of what Helen had just told me about Gair's confession, I knew it wasn't over. Why the hell was I going back to Shetland?

We landed in a field close to Lerwick police station and the noise dimmed enough for Helen and me to be able to talk.

'There's a car here, waiting to take you home to collect whatever you need. Then we'll put you in a hotel for the night. I'm not sure when we'll need you at the station so just sit tight.'

'Are you in charge now?'

'No, Detective Superintendent Harris is. But I'm officially advising and observing. We're going by the book from now on, I promise you.' She looked at me. 'There is something you need to know. A lot of people are in custody tonight, and will stay that way until we're convinced they had nothing to do with all this. I'm afraid your husband is one of them.'

I nodded. I'd expected that. I even welcomed the news. The last thing I could deal with just then was a confrontation with Duncan.

'Also, your father-in-law and your boss from the hospital. You may well be needed at work over the next few days.'

She was right. The hospital couldn't afford to lose me and Gifford.

We climbed down. Helen squeezed my shoulder and stepped into one of the waiting cars. A woman constable introduced herself and led me to a second car. A male constable was driving. As we set off on the twenty-minute drive that would take me home, I wondered what I was going to do with my evening, stuck in a strange hotel in Lerwick.

The car pulled up at the front of the house.

'Do you want me to come in with you?' asked the WPC.

'No, thank you. I'll be fine. It won't take long.'

I walked to the front door and found my key. The hall was in darkness and the house had that still, cold feel that houses assume when they've been empty for a while. I walked down the hall to the kitchen, registering but not appreciating the significance of the beam of light shining out from under the door. I pushed the door open.

Duncan and Kenn Gifford were sitting together at the kitchen table, our bottle of Talisker standing open and nearly empty between them.

11

I almost yelled but knew the officers outside would never hear me. Duncan moved towards me, the picture of a distraught husband overwhelmed with relief at seeing his wife again.

'Tor, thank God . . . I was trying your mobile all yesterday. Everybody was worried about you.'

I took a sharp step back and held up both hands in front of me.

Duncan looked confused, but he stopped. 'Are you OK?'

'No, I am not OK.' I started to edge round the kitchen, closer to the worktop. 'I am a long way from being OK.' I grabbed the cook's knife I'd spotted lying on the kitchen counter.

Duncan looked horrified, Kenn vaguely amused.

'Tor . . .' Duncan moved forward again.

'If either of you tries to touch me, I will slice you up. Got that?' I yelled.

He was still two feet away but I'd made my point. He stepped back.

'I've got it,' said Gifford, who hadn't moved. He picked up his drink and raised it to his lips. 'How about you, Dunc?'

Dunc? Since when were these two on pet-name terms?

'Why don't you get Tora a glass?' said Gifford.

'There are two police officers outside,' I said.

'Well, they can't drink on duty,' said Gifford. 'I think you should both sit down. If it makes you feel better, Tora, invite your two friends in.'

I looked from one to the other: my husband, almost shaking with anxiety; my boss, the picture of calm. 'I was told you two were in custody.'

'We were,' said Gifford. 'Got released about an hour ago. Our friends at the station found no charges for us to answer.'

'You helped Stephen Gair substitute a terminally sick woman for his wife,' I said to Gifford. 'You helped him keep Melissa Gair prisoner—here, in our cellar—for eight months. You kept her alive and delivered her baby and then killed her, you inhuman bastard!'

Gifford flinched. 'When Cathy Morton died at our hospital I was in New

Zealand,' he said. 'The police have checked my flight details and the people I stayed with. I never saw Caroline Salter in my life until I took part in an identity parade this afternoon. Had she picked me out, I wouldn't be here.'

'Somebody helped Gair. He couldn't have done it alone.'

'No, I don't think he could. But he wasn't helped by us. Neither of us had anything to do with what's being going on up on Tronal.' Gifford had lowered his voice almost to a whisper. I found myself staring into his eyes, wanting to believe him. I made myself look away.

'You wanted me dead, though,' I said to Duncan.

'The idiot at the boatyard got it wrong, Tor.' Duncan was still hovering, wanting to come towards me, not quite daring to. 'The mast collapsed but it didn't break clean off. After I was picked up, the boat got caught around some salmon cages. The salvage team had to saw through the mast to get it clear. McGill's boy jumped to conclusions. No one's trying to kill you.'

'Will you pack it in? You had a chopper searching the moors for me last night, for God's sake.'

'We were worried about you. You bailed out of hospital with a whole load of diazepam in your system. For all we knew you were heading for the nearest cliff top to go flying with the puffins.'

'Someone killed Dana. Dana did not kill herself.'

I wasn't sure any more about Gifford's involvement, or that Duncan had tried to kill me, but if I had just one truth to hold on to, it was that.

And then Gifford took my breath away.

'Probably not.' He glanced at Duncan. 'Caroline Salter identified Andrew Dunn as the man who accompanied Gair when he visited Cathy. Dunn was involved in the adoption scam; he almost certainly conspired to kill Melissa and may well have killed Dana too. But you may never be able to prove it.'

I knew that any second now I was going to start sobbing. I picked up Gifford's glass and drained it. The Scotch hit the back of my throat like a blow but it helped. I wasn't going to cry just yet.

'How . . . how did he . . .?'

Gifford poured another drink. Same glass. 'DI Dunn is a police officer with—how shall I put it?—a few unusual skills.'

Something clicked. 'He hypnotised her, made her slash her own wrists.'

Gifford nodded. 'Probably,' he said.

I looked at Duncan. He gave me a sympathetic twitch of the lips. I turned back to Gifford. 'You can do it too.'

He waited for a second before inclining his head forward in acknowledgment. 'It's a sort of passed-down-through-the-generations thing.'

At that moment, we all jumped at a sudden noise. Someone was banging on the front door. At the same time the telephone started ringing. We looked at each other, not sure what to respond to first. Then I got up and walked to the front door. Behind me I could hear Duncan answering the phone.

'Are you all right?' The WPC was on the doorstep, her colleague behind her. 'We've been told not to leave you alone.'

I nodded. 'I'm fine. Come on in.'

I led the officers to our living room. 'Can you wait here for a bit? There's something I need to finish.'

As I returned to the kitchen, Duncan was holding out the phone. I took it.

'Tora, I've only just been told.' Helen was speaking fast. 'About your husband being released. Are you OK?'

'I'm fine. Don't worry. Your constables are in the next room.'

'Well, for God's sake keep them there. I can't get away right now. Gair has admitted that Andy Dunn helped him kill Melissa.'

Duncan and Gifford were watching me. 'Andy Dunn killed Dana,' I said.

The line was silent for a few seconds. 'I can't deal with that right now. I'll get back to you.' She hung up and I replaced the receiver.

'Dunn hasn't been seen since about eleven p.m. last night,' said Gifford. 'The Salter woman had to identify his photograph. They think he's left the islands. Until he's found, you need to be careful.'

I sat down, trying to figure something out. Then I remembered. 'You two are receiving money from Tronal,' I said, turning to Duncan. 'If neither of you was involved with the maternity clinic, why are you on the payroll?'

'Looks like we've no secrets left, buddy,' said Gifford. 'Will you tell her or shall I? By the way, I'm starving. Is anyone planning on eating tonight?'

As Gifford got up and crossed the room, I waited for Duncan to tell me the last big secret.

'Eight people get a monthly income from Tronal,' he said eventually. 'In addition to the staff, of course. Kenn and I, Dad, Gair and Dunn. And three others you probably don't know.'

'Why?' I demanded.

'We own it. We bought shares around ten years ago, long before I met you. It was in financial trouble, we bailed it out. My trust fund was part of the loan. It was paid back in time to buy the house.'

They owned the clinic? And knew nothing about what had been going on up there? Was I seriously expected to believe this?

'The Tronal clinic has been around for a long time,' continued Duncan. 'This business with Gair, it's just like . . . the rotten branch of a tree. Tronal has helped a lot of women in its time, a lot of local families.'

Gifford had opened our fridge door. Finding nothing in there, he turned back. 'Most babies born there are adopted normally and legally,' he said. 'Most people who work at the clinic probably knew nothing about what Gair and Dunn were up to. I'm pretty certain Richard didn't.'

'I still don't understand why you bailed it out. Why did you care?'

Kenn opened a cupboard. 'Christ, have you two even heard of supermarkets?' He gave up and came back to the table.

'Because we were born there,' said Duncan. 'We were both Tronal babies. Adopted by island families.'

I stared at Duncan. 'Elspeth and Richard aren't your parents?'

'Elspeth couldn't have children,' said Duncan. A shadow crossed his face. 'Richard could,' he added, looking at Gifford.

'Richard is my father,' said Gifford.

I found I had nothing to say.

'Richard and Elspeth tried for several years to have a family,' explained Gifford. 'During that time, when I guess their relationship was under some strain, Richard had an affair with a house officer at the hospital. She had her baby on Tronal and put him—me—up for adoption by the Giffords. Three years later, Elspeth agreed to adopt too. Duncan was four months old.'

'Why didn't they adopt you?' I asked Gifford.

'Elspeth doesn't know about me. I didn't know who my genetic father was myself till I was sixteen. I wasn't surprised though.'

No, I bet he hadn't been. Why hadn't I thought of it before? I'd seen the strong likeness between Richard and Kenn, the antipathy between Duncan and Kenn, the cool formality between Duncan and his parents, but I hadn't put it all together. Poor Duncan. Poor Kenn, come to think of it. What a mess.

AN HOUR LATER, I was still at home. I'd found I really couldn't cope with a night in a strange hotel. The WPC, whose name was Jane, was sleeping in one of our spare rooms, at Helen's insistence. Duncan was firmly consigned to another. It wasn't that I didn't believe everything he'd told me. I wanted to check it all out, but actually, the more I thought about it the more convinced I became that I finally had most of the answers.

I took a long shower and cleaned my teeth. It felt good to be back in a bathroom. Then I caught sight of Duncan's toilet bag on the shelf. No, I didn't have all the answers yet, after all.

I walked across the corridor and pushed open the door of the spare room. Duncan was lying on the bed, face downcast. He brightened at the sight of me, until he saw the packet I was holding up.

'Anything you want to say?' I asked.

He stood up. 'How about I'm sorry?'

I shook my head. 'Not nearly good enough.' I stepped into the room. 'Do you have any idea what it's been like for me this past year?'

Duncan, to his credit, could no longer look me in the eye.

'I have to see, talk to, touch pregnant women every working day of my life. I have to hold every newborn baby, and each time I hand one over to its mother, I want to collapse on the floor and sob, Why, why isn't it me? Why is it that every other woman in the world can do this and I can't? Except I can, can't I? All this pain has been totally unnecessary.'

By the time I finished I was yelling. I threw the packet at him.

'That shit isn't even licensed in the UK. Who got them for you? Daddy or Big Brother? You know what? I don't give a toss any more. And by the way, I know you're planning to leave me and thank God for that.'

I walked out, slamming the door behind me, and caught sight of Jane at the top of the stairs. I went back into my room and closed the door.

Well, sleep didn't seem like a possibility any more. I wondered how I was going to get through the rest of the night.

The bedroom door opened.

'I don't want to hear it,' I said.

'There's a reason my birth mother put me up for adoption,' said Duncan.

'You're confusing me with someone who gives a damn,' I replied.

'She had multiple sclerosis,' continued Duncan. 'She was already ill when she had me. She knew she would deteriorate quickly.'

I said nothing but my posture must have betrayed that I was listening.

'I know I carry the gene,' said Duncan. 'There's a good chance I'll get ill myself. There's a fifty per cent chance I'll pass the gene on to any children.'

I turned. The skin round Duncan's eyes had turned red and blotchy. His eyes were shining. I'd never seen him cry before. How little we really know the people around us. He risked coming further into the room.

'I know I should have told you. I'm really sorry I didn't.'

'Why? Why didn't you tell me?'

'I have no excuse. Except that when I met you you showed no interest in having a family. When you weren't working you were riding. You were going to be a consultant by the time you were thirty-five and win the Badminton Horse Trials. I couldn't see how children could fit into that lifestyle.'

What he was saying was true, but he was describing the person I'd been eight years ago. 'I changed. The lifestyle changed. We talked about kids. Ad nauseam. You said you wanted them too.'

'I do. They just can't be mine.'

'I should have known this. I had all those tests. And all that time—'

'I knew that if we moved up here we could adopt. A newborn. Maybe more than one.' He sat down on the bed next to me. 'Women can love adopted babies. The maternal bond doesn't rely upon a blood link. Neither does the paternal one.'

'Oh, because you and your folks are just so close.'

He shook his head. 'Not a good example. I know a lot of adoptees. They're adored, precious children. They bring huge happiness.'

'You still don't get it, do you? It wasn't just any baby, it was *your* baby. A little boy with dark blue eyes and long limbs and hair that never lies flat. I used to talk to that baby, tell him stories about what we'd all do together when he was born. He even had a name.'

'What was his name?'

'It doesn't matter.'

'It matters. What was his name?'

'Duncaroony,' I managed.

For a moment I thought Duncan was laughing. Then I realised he wasn't. We sat together, side by side, as the night got darker.

SOME TIME IN THE NIGHT, Duncan and I declared a truce. There remained a lot of unfinished business, but neither of us had the energy to resume hostilities just yet. As for the future, I wasn't sure. Duncan had told me that the fight I'd overheard on Unst had been about his desire to leave Shetland, that Elspeth had been referring to me when she'd said he was in love. He'd declared that no power on earth would make him leave me. The jury was still out, though, on whether I was staying—with him, in the job, on the islands; I didn't know. I was taking it one day at a time. Because, in spite of everything, I still loved him.

The next day I phoned my friend in Voe, thanked her for taking care of Charles and Henry and made arrangements to collect them that evening. Then I went to work, my suspension having expired with the knowledge that the hospital was in the clear. I did the ward round, ignoring curious looks from the staff, then went upstairs to prepare for afternoon clinic.

'Hey!'

I looked up from my desk. 'Hey yourself!'

Helen stood in the doorway. I realised I was ridiculously pleased to see her.

'Coffee?' I offered as she came in. She nodded and I got up to pour it out.

'Are you OK?' she asked, and from the way she was looking at me, I started to think that she might have something to tell me.

'I'm fine,' I said, stalling for time, because I wasn't sure I wanted to hear whatever it was. 'Duncan and I sorted a few things out and here I am, back at work. Is Duncan . . .? I mean . . .'

'Is he in the clear? I think so. His story about being a shareholder checks out and he doesn't seem to have set foot on Tronal for years. The Franklin Stone and Mr Gifford seem out of it as well. You heard about Dunn, I take it.'

'I did. Is he still missing?'

'Yep. We've alerted all the air and ferry ports but . . .'

'Could be well away by now?'

She nodded. 'Right, the good news is, the field where you discovered the body has been thoroughly swept this morning. Ground-penetrating radar across the length and breadth of it. I really don't think there's anything down there, Tora. It'll take a few more days. But nothing has been found so far.'

I was silent.

'So, no more worries about little men with a silver fixation?' she said.

I had the grace to look abashed. 'Guess the stress was getting to me the other night.'

She smiled back. But the slightly wary, nervous look was still there.

'There's something else, isn't there? Something not so good?'

'I'm afraid so. Stephen Gair hanged himself. He was found shortly after five this morning.'

I stood up. 'How could that have happened? What did you do, give him some rope to practise tying knots with?'

She held up her hand. 'Take it easy. It will be fully investigated. These things happen. I know they shouldn't, but they do. He just wasn't considered a suicide risk.'

'I guess it's really over then?' I said.

'You're kidding! This Tronal business will keep us going for years.'

'What do you mean?'

'That place is an unholy hotchpotch of legitimate business and the illegal trading of infants. We have to trace all Tronal's adopted babies. Trouble is, we can see the money coming in but they're all cash transfers that will be hellishly hard to trace to source. We may suspect which agencies were involved, but they're hardly going to admit it. Everyone we've spoken to so far at this end, including George Reynolds at social services, is denying any knowledge of overseas adoptions—whether for money or not. And there's no evidence of any significant number of babies being born here.'

'But Gair admitted it. He said he was selling babies over the Internet.'

'True, but apart from the money and the word of a now-dead man, we really have no evidence.' She put her mug down. 'I'm on my way to Tronal now. I'll call you later, Tora.'

When Helen had left, I washed up the coffee things and went downstairs. A couple of my third-trimester ladies were kind enough to say they'd missed me at the last clinic. But the Tronal business was still preying on my mind, so as soon as we broke for lunch I grabbed a sandwich and went back up to my room. From my bag I dug out the pieces of paper that had started it all: the record of deliveries for the Shetland District Health Authority.

Once again, I counted up the Tronal deliveries. Four. Four in a six-month period meant around six to ten a year. If around half a dozen were adopted locally, that just didn't leave enough to sell overseas and make any sort of money. There must be more babies being born there than were recorded on my stats. But how could a birth not be registered?

I started going through the list one more time.

The first thing that jumped out at me were those blessed initials. KT. Keloid Trauma. It had made a certain sort of sense the way Gifford had explained it but it wasn't a term I'd come across before. I started checking all the KT entries again. April 1, a baby boy, born on Papa Stour. Then, on the May 8, another boy, born here at the Franklin Stone. On May 19, a third boy. Then on June 6, Alison Jenner had had a little boy on Bressay; later in June another delivery at the Franklin Stone. They were all boys. Not a single girl among them. Race of males.

Hang on a minute. Alison Jenner. That name meant something. Where had I heard that before? Jenner, Jenner, Jenner. Shit, it had gone.

STEPHEN RENNEY was in his windowless office, eating a sandwich and drinking Fanta from a can. He sensed me standing in his doorway, looked up and motioned to a chair. I took it.

'I wanted to ask you something. About Dana Tulloch's post-mortem.'

'I didn't carry out Miss Tulloch's post-mortem, Miss Hamilton,' he said. 'And I don't think the report's come through just yet. I can check for you.'

'So who did?' I demanded, manners out the window.

He frowned at me. 'I never actually saw Miss Tulloch. She was taken to Dundee. I understand her next of kin, a policewoman, requested the transfer. The PM was carried out in Dundee.'

'Of course, I'm sorry.' Helen hadn't mentioned it, but there was no real reason why she should.

'Is there anything else I can help you with?'

I shook my head, thanked him and left.

Back in my room I made fresh coffee, sat down at my desk—and remembered who Alison Jenner was. She was Stephen Gair's second wife. Gair had admitted that his son, Connor, was Melissa's child, not Alison's. So why was Alison's name on the list of Shetland births—with the KT reference?

I found the entry again. Alison Jenner, forty, gave birth to a boy, 8lb 2oz, on June 6. Surely that couldn't be coincidence. Either Gair had been lying about Connor being Melissa's, or the entry referred to Melissa's son.

I double-checked the number of entries with the KT initials after them. There were seven that summer. I pulled up the corresponding list for the subsequent period, from September 2005 through February 2006. No KT entries. Then I went back, to the previous winter. Nothing. I kept on going back until I spotted them again. In summer 2002 there were five entries with KT after them, born in various centres around the islands, all baby boys.

A tightness was forming in my chest. The whole of 2001 was clear; so was 2000. In the summer of 1999 there were six KT entries. Boys.

I went back to 1980 and the pattern was unmistakable. Every three years, between four and eight baby boys had their deliveries recorded as KT.

Every three years, the female death rate on Shetland made a modest but unmistakable blip. The following summer, some unusual little boys were born. KT had nothing to do with Keloid Trauma. That was a smoke screen. The condition probably didn't even exist. KT stood for Kunal Trow.

I flicked back to the earliest year the computerised records showed: 1975. I needed to go further back. I stood up, on legs that felt none too steady, walked along the corridor to the service lift and went down to the basement.

Most hospital archives are a mess and these were no exception. Everything was in cardboard boxes, stacked several high on steel shelving. The labels were mostly turned to the front. It took a few minutes to locate the box I needed. Inside were ledgers, handwritten records of births. I found the year I was looking for, 1972. On July 25, there it was. Elspeth Guthrie, aged thirty-five, on the island of Unst, a baby boy, 7lb 15oz. KT.

I could think of only one reason for falsifying birth records to record the adoptive mother as the birth mother: something was so badly wrong with the real birth that it would bear no investigating. Duncan's birth mother had been killed. Just like Melissa had been, just like all the others had been.

Every three years, island women were being bred in captivity like farm animals and then slaughtered. I wondered whether the legends of the trows had given some maniac the idea in the first place, or whether the stories had sprung from real events taking place in the islands over the years, known about but never openly acknowledged.

I pushed myself to my feet, put the lid back on the box and lifted it back onto the shelf. I tucked the ledger under my arm and headed for the stairs.

How the hell were they doing it? How do you spirit away a live woman, and convince all her relatives that she's dead? They couldn't use semblances for all of them. It wasn't feasible. The Cathy/Melissa switch had to have been a special case. I was back to hypnosis and drugs, to the involvement of enough people to make sure the procedures were never questioned.

But I still hadn't found out where Stephen Gair had been getting his babies from. The numbers involved, an average of just two per annum, still seemed far too few to attract the sort of revenues Helen and I had found. Plus, the babies I could name—Duncan, Kenn Gifford, Connor Gair—had all been adopted locally. Money might have changed hands but it couldn't explain the massive amounts that were coming in from overseas. No, the babies being sold were coming from another source.

Back in my office I poured myself another mug of coffee. The phone rang and I picked up the receiver. It was Helen. I couldn't tell her yet. I needed to get my head together first.

'Where are you?' I said.

'Just leaving Tronal. Boy, the wind's getting up. Can you hear me?'

A flash of panic so sharp it was painful. I'd forgotten Helen was going to Tronal. 'Are you OK? How was it?'

'Tora, I'm fine. The clinic was quiet. Only a few women, a couple of babies. We're staying on Unst and going back in the morning. Look, I wanted to ask you something. Something personal. Is now a good time?'

'Of course,' I said.

'Thing is, I have to start thinking about Dana's funeral.'

Dana's funeral. I closed my eyes and found myself in the midst of a sad, solemn gathering. We were in an ancient church, softly lit by tall white candles. I could smell the incense that drifted down from the high altar.

'I know you hadn't known her very long,' came Helen's voice from a distance, 'but . . . I think . . . well, I think you made quite an impression. On me too, come to that. It would mean a lot if you could be there.'

Dana's flowers would be white: roses, orchids and lilies; stylish and beautiful, like the woman herself. The back of my throat started to hurt. Tears were rolling down my cheeks. 'Of course. Do you have a date in mind?'

Helen's voice had deepened. 'No. I'm still waiting to hear from your place about when they can let her go.'

And the vision froze. 'She's still here? In the hospital?'

'Just for a little while. I have to go. I'll see you.'

She was gone. I blinked hard. My face was wet but my eyes were clear. I could see again. And, praise the Lord, I could think again.

I grasped, in that moment, the true meaning of the word epiphany. Because I'd just had one. There was much I still didn't get, but I understood one thing with perfect and absolute clarity. Sorry, Helen, couldn't oblige after all. I was not going to be one of Dana's mourners. This was one funeral I was going nowhere near.

Because Dana wasn't dead.

12

An hour and a half later, I drove onto the Yell ferry. It wasn't quite eight o'clock but it was going to be the last crossing of the evening: there were dark clouds overhead and a storm was threatening.

Just before leaving the hospital I'd phoned home. Duncan hadn't answered and I left a message that I would be working late. I added that I loved him, partly because it was true and partly because I wasn't sure I was ever going to be able to say it to him again.

I'd taken out one small insurance policy. I'd put the ledger from the basement, several computer print-outs and a scribbled note in a brown envelope. On my way out of Lerwick, I'd dropped by Dana's house and left it where Helen would find it. If I didn't come back, she'd know where I'd gone and why.

Helen and her team were staying on Unst that night. The Tronal people would be wary, watching the north and northeastern approaches to the island; any boats setting off from Unst would be spotted in good time. I could not hope to approach the island stealthily from that direction.

So I wasn't going to try.

The ferry docked and I was off again. At Gutcher on Yell there is a small sailing club, affiliated to its neighbouring club on Unst. I had a key that I knew would get me into the shed that passed as a clubhouse. Once in there, I'd break into the cupboard that held spare boat keys. That was the easy bit.

After that, I'd have to rig up an unfamiliar boat in the dark, sail it single-handed in winds that were verging on storm conditions, in waters I barely knew, towards an area of notoriously treacherous navigation. Even that wasn't the hard bit.

I parked in the empty car park. The clubhouse was in darkness. It took just a few seconds to break into the cupboard and find the right keys. I took some waterproofs and a life jacket and made my way down to the jetty.

I found the vessel I was looking for—a sports boat owned by a friend of Duncan's. I climbed aboard and unlocked the cabin. I fixed the jib in place and threaded the sheets, attached the mainsail and released the kicker.

Duncan's friend had local charts on board and I studied them. I would sail directly southeast for about a mile, hidden behind a small, uninhabited island called Linga. Once I cleared Linga, I would head west towards Tronal.

Telling myself it was now or never, I released the stern line, started the engine and reversed slowly out of the marina.

The sky was thick with cloud and darkness was falling fast. Soon I was in the channel between Linga and Yell. Every couple of seconds we slammed into a wave and its freezing particles came hurtling over the bow. I was soon soaked. On either side land rose up like dark shadows. The engine was a small one; I had to sail. I started to haul up the mainsail. Immediately the boat began to heel. I unfurled the jib and pulled it out halfway. The sail filled, the boat accelerated away and I switched off the engine.

Within minutes the boat speed was up to seven knots and it was heeling at a thirty-degree angle. I was braced against the side of the boat as we slammed into waves that felt like brick walls. But I was making progress.

All too soon, I'd reached the southernmost tip of Linga and had to leave the shelter of the channel. I turned the boat to port and altered the sails. The wind was now coming over the port stern. The sails filled and my speed picked up. Eight and a half knots. At this rate I'd be at Tronal in no time.

And what the hell was I going to find there?

Helen had stuck to the facts, which only took us so far. They took us to Tronal being the centre of a scheme involving the illegal sale of babies, to Stephen Gair being head of the operation, assisted by Dunn and others. They took us to Melissa being murdered to protect the operation.

But the facts didn't explain her strange, ritualistic burial, or why Gair risked holding her prisoner for long enough for their baby to be born. They didn't explain Kirsten's wedding ring being found in my field. Nor the regular rise in the female death rate, followed a year later by a batch of baby boys, illegally registered as the birth children of their adoptive mothers.

To explain all that, you had to take a giant leap of faith, which Helen had been unable to do, but at which I had finally arrived. Here, on Shetland, legend lived. The trows of so many island stories were real.

History offers countless examples of the self-proclaimed master race. That had to be what I was dealing with now: a group of men who believed themselves intrinsically superior to the rest of us, and subject not to ordinary laws but to a code of their own. In this remote corner of the world, a few dozen island men were operating their own private kingdom. Running the police, the local government, the health service, the schools, they had control over every aspect of island life, automatically assuming the best jobs, making themselves rich with a complex mixture of legal and illegal trading. It was the Masons meets the Mafia. With an extra bit of nastiness thrown in.

I asked myself why these men couldn't just leave it at that: marry and mate like other men and enjoy the fruits of their little fiefdom. Why did they have to kidnap, rape and murder the mothers of their sons? That dreadful process, I guessed, would go to the very heart of their distinctness.

Boys born into the trow community would face a stark choice—accept what they were, or leave and risk the destruction of everything they'd been taught to value. I knew now that Duncan had no desire to leave me; it was the life he wanted out of. I understood why he'd seemed depressed about the move back to Shetland, in spite of the huge advantages it offered; why our relationship had been under such strain. Duncan was fighting the forces that had drawn him back to the islands. My heart went out to him.

A mass of darkness ahead of me was growing blacker, more solid than the night around it. I thought I could even see small lights. I was nearing Tronal.

I furled the jib and the boat slowed by a couple of knots. The depth gauge read fifteen metres, fourteen . . . Waves were breaking on the shore. Ten metres, nine . . . I was about to turn the boat so that I could drop the sails when I spotted rocks off the port side. The starboard side looked clear but I'd have to turn the boat round nearly 300 degrees and I wasn't sure I had the speed any more. I looked again to port: more rocks. I was in five metres of water, four, three . . . I reached forward, pulled up the keel and released the mainsail. Then I held on tight to the stick. The wind was behind us and the boat continued forward until a scraping sound under the hull and a massive jerk forward told me we'd hit the beach.

I pulled the anchor from its locker, walked up the beach and wedged it behind a small rock. I tugged on a small rucksack I'd brought with me and set off towards the lowest point on the cliff. At the edge of the beach I began to climb. The pebbles gave way to thin soil, clumps of grass and coarse, springy heather. I was breathing heavily when I reached the top. A barbed-wire fence ringed the upper part of the island, but with the aid of a small pair of pliers from the boat I'd soon cut a way through. After that there was a stone wall, about waist high. I climbed over, found a stone that had fallen and placed it on top of the wall as a rough marker of where I'd cut the wire.

Keeping low, I looked around me. Tronal is a small, oval island, roughly a kilometre long and a third of a kilometre wide, with three stubby promontories at its southeastern edge. It is fifty metres above sea level at its highest point, pretty much where I was crouching. Looking north I could see the lights of Tronal's tiny marina. A single pier jutted out from the small natural harbour. Several boats, including a large white cruiser, were moored there.

From the harbour a rough single-track road led to the only visible buildings. Almost in the centre of the island, the terrain rose and then dipped, forming a natural hollow in which the buildings nestled. I dropped lower and started making my way towards them. After about fifteen minutes I could see lights not too far away. I climbed the ridge and lay down on the coarse, prickly grass. Below me, not fifteen metres away, was the clinic.

It was a one-storey stone building surrounding a square and with a central courtyard. A gated archway in the northwestern elevation gave vehicular access. The gates stood open. Dormer windows appeared at regular intervals along the roof, six to a side. Only a few lights shone from the building itself, but small lights were set along the surrounding gravel paths. I set off again, keeping a good distance away, to inspect the building.

Moving south away from the gates I found a row of dark rooms. On the southeastern side, several windows had blinds up and lights on. There were men inside. Three, maybe four, were in some sort of common room. Another two were in a large kitchen. Some of the men wore jeans and sweaters, a couple were dressed in white surgical scrubs. They stood around, chatting, drinking from mugs. One of the men was smoking, his cigarette held out of an open window. My watch told me it was just after ten o'clock. A normal hospital would be quietening down for the night. No sign of that here.

I crouched low, thinking about video surveillance, security lights, alarms. If this building were the prison I believed it to be, it would surely have all of those. Turning another corner, I saw a row of outbuildings about ten metres away from the clinic. I planned to hide behind them.

I must have been about six metres from the sheds when there came a terrifying explosion of sound: the manic barking of large dogs. I dropped to the ground, curling instinctively into the tightest ball I could manage.

The barking grew in intensity, claws scratched against wood, animals yelped in their urgency to tear me apart. The cacophonous din continued, but nothing happened. With relief I realised the dogs were locked up.

I crawled back the way I'd come, towards the common room and kitchen. As my scent faded, the dogs calmed. The television in the common room was on and several of the men were gathered round it. The kitchen was empty, the smoker's window still open.

Glancing round, I saw a tall bush. I ran behind it, unhooked my rucksack and pulled off my waterproofs. Underneath were the scrubs I'd been wearing all day. I pulled a cap onto my head and tucked my hair inside it. Then I ran forward and climbed into the kitchen.

The volume of the TV next door was turned up loud and I was pretty certain no one had heard me. I crossed the kitchen and gently opened the door. The corridor was empty and I set off left, away from the common room. Looking up, I could see cameras tucked away in the corner between wall and ceiling. I hoped they weren't being monitored.

I walked slowly, silently, alert for the slightest noise. Along the wall on my right were windows looking across the courtyard to another lit and windowed corridor. On my left were rooms. Most had closed doors, one with light shining under that I passed by quickly. Two had open doors and I glanced inside: the first was an office; the second was some sort of meeting room.

At the end of the corridor I found a flight of stairs, and climbed them. At the top was a narrow, windowless corridor, lit by dim spotlights. I counted six doors along my right-hand side. Each had a small shuttered window.

I slid back the first shutter. The room beyond was dark but I could make out a narrow, hospital-style bed, a chair and a small TV mounted on the wall. Someone lay in the bed but the covers were pulled high and I couldn't tell whether the someone was young or old, male or female, dead or alive.

I moved on to the next window. Same set-up. Except this time, as I watched, the figure in the bed turned over and settled down again.

The next room was empty; so was the fourth.

There was light in the fifth room. A woman wearing a dressing gown sat in the armchair, reading a magazine. She looked up and we made eye contact. Then she dropped her magazine, pushed herself up out of the chair, and came towards the door. She was pregnant. Every nerve ending I had was on fire, but I knew if I ran now the game would be up. She opened the door.

'Hello,' she said.

All I could do was stare back. Her eyes narrowed.

'Sorry,' I managed. 'Long day, four hours in theatre, brain not really functioning any more. How are you feeling?'

She relaxed and stepped back, inviting me into her room. I went in, closing the door behind me and pulling the window shutter across.

'I'm OK,' she said. 'Bit nervous. Are we still OK for tomorrow?'

I forced myself to smile at her. 'Haven't heard anything to the contrary.'

'Thank Christ. I just want it to be over. I really need to get back to work.'

A termination. This woman, at least, was here voluntarily.

'Have I seen you before?' she was asking me.

I shook my head. 'Don't think so. I've been away for a week,' I said. 'Just back on duty this afternoon. I haven't managed to look at your notes yet. Have there been complications?'

She sighed. 'Just about everything you can think of. Blood pressure sky high; sugar and protein in my urine; traces of a viral infection in my blood. Though why that should stop you going ahead is beyond me.'

It was beyond me too. Something was starting to feel very wrong. I glanced at the notes pinned to the foot of her bed, found her name.

'Emma, can I have a quick look at your tummy?'

She lay on the bed and pulled her dressing gown open. She was a striking-looking woman, probably in her late twenties: tall, with vivid blonde hair, large brown eyes and perfect teeth. I started to press my hands gently on her abdomen. Immediately something kicked back. I glanced up at Emma but her face had tightened. She wouldn't make eye contact.

I finished my examination and picked up her notes. On the second page I found what I was looking for. LMP: November 3, 2006. Emma was sitting up now and watching me. Her eyes looked cautious.

'Emma, it says here your last menstrual period was on November the 3rd. Which would make you . . . about twenty-seven, twenty-eight weeks?'

She nodded again, more slowly. 'Don't tell me now it's a problem. I've—'

'No, no . . .' I held up both hands. 'Please don't be concerned. As I said, I'm just catching up. I'll let you get some rest now.'

She seemed to relax a little. I gave her a last smile and left the room.

Back in the corridor I leaned against the wall, needing a moment to clear my head. After the twenty-fourth week, termination is only legally permitted in the UK if there's medical evidence that the woman's health would be seriously threatened by continuing with the pregnancy, or if the child is expected to be born severely handicapped. In Emma's notes I'd found no valid reason why the procedure was being carried out so late.

Moving on, I pulled the next shutter back an inch and looked through. The woman inside (no, girl—she couldn't have been more than sixteen) was sitting up in bed watching television. She looked pregnant, although I couldn't be sure. I moved on and turned the corner.

I passed six rooms, all of them empty, and turned another corner. The first three rooms on the next corridor were empty, but the third looked ready to receive a patient. I stepped inside. The bed was neatly made. White towels were folded on the armchair. A nightdress lay at the foot of the bed. It looked like a room in an exclusive private hospital. Except for the four metal shackles chained to each corner of the bed.

I backed out and pulled the door towards me, then opened the door of the next room. The woman on the bed couldn't have been more than twenty-five. She had brown hair and thick, dark eyelashes, the willowy slenderness of the young. She lay on her back, breathing evenly, her legs straight and close together, her arms by her sides. I guessed she'd been sedated. I wandered to the foot of the bed but there were no notes, just a name: Freya. The shackles on her bed hung loose. I tiptoed out.

The woman in the next room looked older, but she too lay in an unnaturally still state of sleep on the narrow bed. Her name was Odel and her feet, though not her arms, were manacled. Odel? Freya? Who were these two women? How had they arrived here? Did they have families grieving for them, believing them dead? Neither showed any sign of being pregnant. I wondered where they'd been hidden that day, during Helen's visit.

I pushed open the last door, noticing, as I did so, the pyjamas folded neatly on the armchair. They were white linen, with a scallop pattern round the collar, cuffs and ankles. They were laundered, pristine, showing no trace of the blood that had turned them a soft pink the last time I'd seen them. I turned to the bed, then walked over and stared down at the face on the pillow. In spite of everything I'd been through, in spite of the danger I was still in, such a wave of joy hit me that it was all I could do not to dance round the room. I forced myself to be calm and reached under the covers.

Two days ago I'd arrived at Dana's house, exhausted and scared, dreading that something terrible had happened to her. I would have been putty in the hands of a skilled hypnotist. Planting ideas in my head must have been child's play for Andy Dunn. I'd been stupid not to think of it before.

Dana's wrists were dressed with fine white bandages. Her wrists had been cut, but probably only superficially. I hadn't felt a pulse in Dana's bathroom—whatever drug she'd been given had made her peripheral pulse undetectable—but I could feel one now, strong and regular.

I'd assumed Dana had been taken to the hospital, but she'd been brought here. For what? To be part of this summer's breeding programme?

I bent down. 'Dana. Can you hear me? It's Tora. Dana, can you wake up?'

Nothing, not even a flicker. This was not a normal sleep.

A door slammed and footsteps were coming down the corridor. Voices were talking, softly but urgently. I crossed to the bathroom and pulled open the door. There was a lavatory, washbasin and shower cubicle. No window. I opened the door of the cubicle, jumped in and crouched down. If someone entered the room, they couldn't help but see me. I would just have to hope.

The footsteps stopped. The door to Dana's room opened.

'What do you think?' asked a voice that sounded remarkably like that of my father-in-law. I realised my luck had run out.

'Well . . . she's bright, healthy, good-looking,' answered the voice I knew better than any other in the whole world. 'Seems . . . a bit of a waste,' he continued, and I didn't know whether I was going to scream or be sick.

'Exactly,' said the voice of Detective Inspector Andrew Dunn. 'Why the hell go to the risk of getting another one?'

I sat in the shower cubicle, shivering so violently it hurt.

'This was an unforgivable risk,' came an unfamiliar voice. 'You were told to get rid of her, not bring her here.'

'Yeah, well, sorry about the reality check,' snapped Dunn, 'but even I can't hypnotise someone into slashing their own wrists.'

'She's half Indian,' said the unknown man. 'We don't pollute the blood.'

'Oh, for God's sake,' spat Dunn. 'What is this—the Middle Ages?'

'Robert is right,' said my father-in-law. 'She isn't suitable.'

My husband spoke again. 'All right, what do we do with her, then?'

'We'll take her in the boat with the other two,' answered Richard. 'When we're far enough out, I'll slip her over the side.'

'I need a leak,' said Duncan. 'Won't be a sec.'

The bathroom door opened and Duncan came into the room. He walked to the basin and leaned over it.

'And what do we tell the girlfriend?' asked Dunn.

'We send her a coffin,' said Richard. 'Leave it till the last minute, day of the funeral if we can. No big deal, we've done it before.'

'OK, then, settled. Now, what else do we have to do?'

Duncan turned on one of the taps and splashed water over his face. He sighed deeply and straightened up. A second later we made eye contact.

'Patients in one and two, we don't have to worry about,' replied Richard. 'Standard adoptions, likely to deliver in the next week. The Rowley woman spoke to both of them today. I shouldn't think she'll want to bother again.'

Duncan had turned to face me. I braced myself for him to shout out, alert the others or, even worse, to laugh. All he did was stare.

Then he put one finger to his mouth. He glared at me as he left the room, pulling the door firmly closed behind him.

'A cargo of three, then, Richard. Sure you'll be OK on your own? Don't want to leave it till dawn?'

'No, I want to be well away before there's any chance of the police coming back. Right, I'm going downstairs. There's work to do.'

Footsteps faded away down the corridor. Had they all gone? Could I risk moving? What the hell was Duncan going to do? Dana's room was silent. I pushed myself up. Then the bathroom door opened and Duncan reappeared.

'What the hell are you doing here?' he hissed at me. 'You idiot, you stupid idiot!' He opened the door of the cubicle. 'How did you get here?'

I couldn't reply. Couldn't do anything but stare at him. He waited a split second before reaching in and shaking me. 'Did you come by boat?'

I was able to nod.

'Where is it?'

'Beach,' I managed.

'We need to get you back to it. Now.' He started to drag me out of the room. Then he grasped me close and put one hand over my mouth.

I could hear footsteps returning along the corridor and a clanging, whirring sound. The door to Dana's room slammed open. A trolley was wheeled inside. I heard footsteps moving around the room, a countdown, 'Three, two, one, lift . . .' and there was a soft thud. Then I heard the trolley being pushed out of the room. From the next room along the corridor came similar, if fainter, sounds. Then the footsteps and the sound of the wheels faded.

Duncan let out a noisy breath, then spun me round to face him. I'd never seen him so angry. Except it wasn't anger. He was afraid.

'Tora, you have got to get a hold of yourself or you are going to die. Do you understand what I'm—? No, don't you dare cry.' He pulled me close. 'Listen, baby, listen,' he whispered. 'I can get you out of the clinic but then you have to get back to the boat. Get as far from the island as possible then get on the radio to your policewoman friend. Can you do that?'

I didn't know. But I think I nodded. Duncan opened the bathroom door. Dana's room was empty. He walked to the door and looked out. Then he grabbed my hand and pulled me into the deserted corridor. We rounded a corner, ran down a short, fourth corridor and made it to the stairs. We could hear nothing below so risked running down to the bottom.

Duncan pulled me along another corridor, past an open door to a small operating suite. The next door was closed; its window showed only darkness. Another door, light beyond the glass. Duncan stopped and I peered through. As far as I could make out, there was no one inside. At least . . . Pulling my hand out of Duncan's grasp I pushed open the door and went inside.

I was in a neonatal intensive-care unit. The air was warm and heavy with the hum of electronic equipment. Several of the machines emitted beeping sounds every few seconds. I'd worked in some well-equipped facilities in my time but never seen such a concentration of the latest equipment.

'Tora, we don't have time.' Duncan was tugging at my shoulder.

There were ten incubators. Eight of them were empty. I walked across the room, no longer caring if someone found us. I had to see.

The infant in the incubator was female. She was about eleven inches long and, I guessed, would weigh around three pounds. Her skin was red, her eyes tightly closed and her head, tucked inside a knitted pink cap, seemed unnaturally large for her tiny, emaciated body. I moved to the next incubator. Duncan followed, no longer trying to stop me. This baby was male, even smaller than the girl, but his skin was the same dark, blotchy red. A ventilator was breathing for him, a monitor gave a continual reading of his heartbeat and a tiny blue mask covered his eyes to protect them from the light.

I knew now where Stephen Gair had been getting his babies from. I knew why Helen had been able to find no paper trail of the babies that had been adopted overseas. The babies Duncan and I were looking at would need no formal approval, no paperwork, because officially they did not exist.

They were aborted foetuses—that were still alive.

13

In recent years, enormous progress has been made in the care of babies born extremely prematurely. Not long ago, a baby born at twenty-four weeks would have been expected to die within minutes of birth. Now, such babies have a good chance of survival, and have been known to grow into normal, healthy children. Every day that a foetus remains in its mother's uterus, it grows more viable. By twenty-eight weeks, its chances are excellent.

The next day, Emma's twenty-eight-week foetus would be delivered and rushed into one of these incubators. Emma's 'termination' had been delayed by five days. I guessed that was standard practice with all the women who came here seeking late terminations. It would allow a little more time for the foetus to grow; it would also enable the team to administer steroid drugs to encourage foetal lung development.

I turned to Duncan. 'How long have you known?'

His eyes held mine steadily. 'About the premature babies? Only a few weeks. The rest since I was sixteen. We get told on our sixteenth birthdays. That's why I left Shetland, went away to university, and didn't come back even for a weekend. I've never set foot on this island before tonight, I swear.'

Duncan was a good liar. I'd learned that in the last few days. But somehow, I didn't think he was lying now.

'But we did come back. You wanted to come back. Why?'

'I did not want to come back,' he spat at me. 'They threatened to kill you if I didn't. I had to take those fucking pills. If I'd got you pregnant they'd have c—'

He couldn't finish. But he didn't have to. 'Cut out my heart?' I asked.

He nodded. I could see the huge purple shadows under his eyes. For the first time, I understood what Duncan had been going through.

'Your mother didn't have MS?'

'My mother was perfectly healthy. Until they got their hands on her.'

I reached out for his hand. 'What the hell are we going to do?'

'You are going to get back on your boat, just as I told you.'

'You too. Come with me.'

He shook his head. 'If I come with you, those women will die. Richard will drop them all over the side. He'll claim he was out on an all-night fishing trip, and who's going to prove otherwise? Tor, you can't imagine the influence these people have. Even if we're allowed to live, no one will believe us. We need Dana and the others alive.'

He was right, of course. 'What are you going to do?'

'I'm going down to the harbour to get on that boat with Richard. I'll wait until we're out at sea and whack him on the back of the head. Then I'll sail to Uyeasound. With luck, your friend Helen will be there to meet me.'

'I love you so much,' I said.

Somehow, he managed to smile. Then he pulled me across the room to a door at the far end. We stood listening. Nothing. He opened the door and we went into a corridor, at the end of which was an external door. He pushed it open. A rush of cold air came in as he leaned out and looked all around. I could hear voices but none of them seemed close.

'The dogs are locked up,' Duncan said, 'and most of the staff will be moving the women down to the boat. Go as fast as you can.'

I hesitated. Then Duncan pushed me out of the clinic and I ran.

I made for the ridge, and when I reached it I dropped low, catching my breath. Then I set off again, retracing my footsteps. I found the rucksack I'd left earlier and pulled on my waterproofs, then followed the cliff path to the marker stone I'd left on the wall. I climbed over, squeezed through the gap in the barbed wire and crept down the cliff path. A loose rock went tumbling beneath me and I froze. Below, where I guessed the boat would be, a light flashed on. A beam of light crept round the rocks. I flattened myself against the cliff. After a minute or two, the torch was switched off.

Slowly, carefully, I started to climb back up the cliff. My boat had been discovered. They would be looking for me. I might manage to hold them off until dawn, but once the daylight came back there'd be nowhere to hide. And they had dogs. If they set the dogs loose . . .

There was only one other way off the island I could think of. I set off again, running almost due north. Once I reached the track I kept as close to it as I dared for the half-mile or so that took me to the other side of the island. When I reached the little harbour I saw that the motor launch was still moored up to the pier. Its cabin lights were on and, from the bubble of water at its stern, I knew its engine was running.

The wind was still ferocious, but some of the dark clouds had blown away, allowing a small moon to shine through. I ran down to the pier and crouched low by the side of the launch. It was fastened by lines at the bow and the stern. I crept to the nearest cabin hatch and peered through. It was the main cabin. There was a helm, control panel and radio, a small teak-fitted living area with tiny galley, a chart table and three further doors leading off. No sign of Richard. I moved on and looked through the hatch of a small sleeping cabin. Dana lay on the bunk, motionless, but she wasn't alone. I could see a polished black brogue and a few inches of charcoal-grey trouser fabric. Thank God, Duncan was already on board. As gently as I could, I pulled myself up and swung my leg over the guardrail. The boat rocked only a fraction.

'Someone up there?' called my father-in-law from below.

I looked around frantically for a hiding place. On the cabin roof was a folded awning, used to protect the cockpit from spray. I climbed up, lay down and burrowed into its folds.

The boat rocked as Richard climbed the companionway steps. I could see nothing, but knew he would be at the top of the steps, less than two feet away, looking around, puzzled to see no one. I held my breath.

Below, the boat's radio burst into crackling, static life. '*Arctic Skua*, come in, *Arctic Skua*. Base here.' Richard climbed back down the steps. The radio crackled again: I thought I heard the word 'basement' and a couple of expletives but I couldn't be sure. Then Richard spoke.

'Right, I understand. I'll be careful. I'm setting off now. *Arctic Skua* out.'

Below me, Richard was moving again. A cabin door opened and shut, then I heard him heading up to the cockpit. He climbed heavily, onto the seat and then the deck. I heard him walk forwards and then the sliding sound of the bowline being released. As the boat swung round, Richard walked back towards the stern. He must have unfastened the stern line, because the boat drifted swiftly away from the pier. Then he strode through the cockpit and down the steps. I heard the engines revving and the boat swung round to starboard. I looked up, trying to get my bearings. We were heading east down the Skuda Sound, out into the North Sea.

Richard wasn't sparing the engines. We sped along at seven or eight knots, the bow of the boat rising and dipping in the waves.

When was Duncan going to make his move? I got up and lowered myself onto the deck. I reached inside my rucksack, found what I was looking for and tucked it into the front pocket of my waterproofs.

Now we were heading south, and the boat slowed as around us loomed dark, menacing shapes. I'd never been this far east of the islands and I didn't know that some of the oldest rocks in Shetland can be found here: stacks of granite, echoes of the cliffs that towered here millions of years ago.

After ten minutes we left them behind and Richard picked up speed. Still no sign of Duncan. I moved along the deck to the cockpit. Glancing down the companionway, I could see Richard at the helm. Hoping he wouldn't turn round, I raised the lid of the portside locker and looked inside: several knots of rope. I chose the shortest and closed the lid. Then I moved across the cockpit, stepped into the companionway and put my foot on the top step.

Richard didn't move.

Holding the guardrail with my free hand, I lowered myself onto the next step down. Then the next. The third step was damp and my trainer slipped a fraction. It made a faint squeaking sound.

'Good evening, Tora,' said Richard quietly.

ALL THE WIND went out of me and I sat down, hard, on the steps. He turned and we looked into each other's eyes. I'd expected anger, exasperation, maybe even a cruel sort of triumph. What I saw was sadness.

He pulled back the throttle, and reached over and switched on the autopilot. Then he took a step towards me. 'I wish you hadn't,' he said.

'I suppose Emma gave me away?' I asked, praying that was the case. If Emma had told them, they might not know I'd met up with Duncan. Richard might not know he was on board. Where the hell was he, anyway?

'Yes, she mentioned your visit. And then it was a simple matter of checking video footage to confirm it was you. You've been very brave, my dear.'

I jumped down into the cabin. Richard took a step back.

'OK, less of the "my dears"; you and I have never been close, nor are we likely to be in future, given where you're going. I think the GMC might have a few questions about the services you offer at that clinic of yours. That's when the police have finished with you.'

Richard stiffened. 'Please don't presume to preach at me. We help women out of difficult situations. We provide childless couples with hope for the future. And we save dozens of babies who would otherwise be murdered before birth. Because of us they will have a good life, with parents who love and want them. We are preservers of life.'

I couldn't believe he was seriously trying to take the moral high ground. 'And Dana? Are you planning on preserving her life?'

He seemed to shrink a little into himself. 'Sadly, no. That's out of my hands. I hear she was a fine young woman. I'm sorry she had to get involved.' Then he pulled himself up again. 'Although, frankly, if anyone's responsible for Miss Tulloch's death, it's you. If you hadn't meddled in the investigation, she'd never have learned enough to put her life in danger.'

'Out of your hands? It's your hands that will be weighting her down and throwing her overboard.'

Richard shook his head, as though dealing with an unreasonable child. 'This is so typical of you, Tora. You can't reason your way out of an argument, so you resort to abuse. Is it any wonder we've never been close?'

'Shut up! I can't believe you're preaching to me about saving lives. You tried to kill me last Sunday. You sabotaged my boat and my life jacket.'

'Actually I knew nothing about that.'

'Stop lying. You're about to kill me. The least you can do is tell the truth.'

'He isn't lying. I sawed through the mast.'

I whipped round. Stephen Gair stood in the doorway of the port cabin.

'What do you have to do to get some decent kip round here?' His face was crumpled, slightly red. My eyes dropped to his feet. Black brogues.

'You look like you've seen a ghost, Tora,' he said, smiling sleepily.

I DROPPED THE ROPE and backed up against the chart table. Gair stepped to one side and leaned against the steps. No way out.

I took hold of the zip on the pocket of my waterproofs and started to inch it down. 'Don't tell me,' I said, 'reports of your death have been exaggerated. Where's Duncan?'

'Duncan had a change of heart. He won't be joining us tonight.'

I looked at Richard. 'What have you done with Duncan?' I demanded.

Richard leaned over and fumbled on the shelf that ran round the cabin's interior. He straightened up again and I saw a hypodermic in his hand.

'And no one's about to kill you,' continued Gair, when he'd done yawning. 'At least, not any more. You're going back to Tronal.'

I stared at him, not sure what he meant. Then I got it; as a strong, cold hand took a grip on my heart, I got it.

'I think one or two people might just notice I'm gone,' I managed.

Gair shook his head, seemingly unable to take the grin off his face. 'That boat you stole will be found drifting some time in the next couple of days. Traces of your blood will be discovered on the deck. People will assume you had an accident and went overboard.'

'If it's all the same to you,' I said, 'I'd just as soon you drowned me now.'

Gair's eyes dropped to my stomach. 'Sorry, love, you and your little friend are far too valuable.'

'What are you talking about?'

'You're pregnant, Tora. Congratulations.' His grin got even wider.

'What?' For a second I was so amazed I forgot to feel afraid.

'In the club, up the duff, bun in the oven. Richard, is she pregnant?'

I risked a glance at my father-in-law.

'I'm afraid you are, Tora,' he said. 'I took a blood sample last Sunday while you were sedated. There were significant levels of hCG. I guess Duncan got careless with his medication.'

Human chorionic gonadotrophin, or hCG, is the hormone produced by the body of a pregnant woman. Blood tests pick it up just days after conception.

It didn't occur to me to doubt what they were saying. I'd felt like shit for days: nausea and exhaustion are classic symptoms of early pregnancy, but I'd put them down to stress. I was pregnant. After two years of trying and failing, I was finally pregnant. I was carrying Duncan's child and these guys—these monsters—thought they were going to take it away from me.

'How did you get into my office?' I said, feeling a surge of hatred for Gair as I remembered the drugs I'd unwittingly taken the night I'd discovered Melissa's identity. Even as I spoke, I realised how he'd done it. Gair had stolen my office keys the night he left the pig's heart in our house.

'Pick up that rope and tie up Richard,' I said, gesturing to the rope I'd dropped minutes before. 'Do it properly and he won't get hurt.'

'And why would I do that?' Gair asked, a terrifying emptiness in his eyes.

I pulled my hand out from my pocket. 'Because a four-inch iron bolt ramming into your brain is going to hurt a bit.'

Gair glanced down, looking, to my immense satisfaction, slightly less sure of himself. 'What the hell is that?'

'My grandfather's humane horse-killer. Except you're not going to think it very humane when it's pressed up against your temple.'

'Tora, please put that down,' Richard said. 'Someone's going to get hurt.'

'You are so right,' I said. 'And it isn't going to be me.'

Gair moved towards me. I jerked my hand up. He danced back and came at me the other way. I jabbed the weapon at him and he jumped back again. He moved left then right, feinting attacks, diving back at the last second. He was taunting me, trying to unnerve me, and it was working. He was also gradually moving round the cabin, forcing me to turn my back on Richard.

I spun round and jumped away from Gair, to Richard's other side. Richard reached for me and I ducked. Then I grabbed him by the neck of his pullover and pushed the gun up against the side of his face. If I pulled the trigger now I would miss his brain but still make a hell of a mess.

'Don't move. Don't move an inch. Either of you.'

Gair froze. He held his hands in the air and stood poised, ready to leap, eyes glinting with excitement.

'Tora,' gasped Richard. 'Others are coming, they'll be here any second.'

'Good,' I spat, knowing the news was anything but good. 'There are one or two things I'd like to say to Andy Dunn, not to mention my boss.'

'Kenn isn't one of us,' Richard said softly, as though breaking bad news. 'I can see why you might think so; he certainly looks the part, but he isn't.'

I released the pressure I'd been applying to Richard's face. 'How come?' I demanded. 'How come Duncan is but Kenn isn't?'

'I loved his mother,' said Richard. 'When it came to it, I couldn't hurt her. I helped her escape. She's lived in New Zealand for the past forty years.'

'Kenn knows nothing about this?'

Richard shook his head. 'He knows his mother. I helped them make contact a few years ago. But no, he's not one of us. It's a great shame. He is an exceptional man, very gifted. What he would have achieved if . . . Well, it doesn't do to dwell on these things. My fault, of course. I let myself get involved. It won't happen again.'

I could see Gair making impatient movements.

'You were never intended to be part of this,' continued Richard. 'Elspeth and I are fond of you. We know Duncan loves you. A year from now you could have adopted a baby. It could even have been Duncan's baby. You weren't supposed to be harmed.'

'Unlike the poor child's mother, of course. Did I meet her tonight? Which one was it to be? Odel or Freya?'

'This is getting us nowhere,' said Gair, and leapt at us.

I swung the gun up as he came crashing down on me. I pulled the trigger, felt the bolt connect, then the gun was knocked from my hand as we fell.

For a second I lay stunned, pinned to the cabin floor by Gair's weight.

'Be careful with her, for heaven's sake,' said Richard. 'We don't want to lose that baby.'

'Richard, will you take care of the boat? God knows where we are.'

I heard Richard move, then the revs of the boat increased and we turned. I heard the crackle of the ship's radio.

Gair was wearing a crumpled grey business suit, no doubt the same one he'd been wearing when he'd been arrested; when he'd swallowed the sedatives so that he'd have no peripheral pulse when he faked death by hanging. A dark stain on his right shoulder was spreading slowly, but if he felt any pain he wasn't showing it. His eyes searched along the cabin floor until he spotted the gun. His weight shifted as he raised himself up and reached out. Then he leaned back over me, pushed the humane killer against my left thigh and looked into my eyes. He smiled as he pulled the trigger, and my world exploded in a mass of white-hot pain.

14

I couldn't see, couldn't hear, couldn't breathe. The boat swerved.

'. . . the hell are you doing?' I heard Richard calling out from some great distance away. 'She'll bleed to death before we can get her back.'

'Then fix it, Doctor. I'll drive the boat.'

Marginally, the pain was receding, leaving my head, my chest, my abdomen, and concentrating in the fleshy part of my upper thigh. The blackness in my head faded a little and I could see again. And hear again: a terrifying noise filled the cabin and I realised it was me—screaming. Richard picked me up and lay me on the bunk in the starboard cabin, beside the still form of a woman. Freya, even through the pain I recognised her. Then he took hold of both my hands and pressed them against the wound.

'Push hard,' he instructed. 'You know what will happen if you don't.'

Only too well. Gair had most likely hit an artery and I was in big trouble. Crimson fluid was pumping from my leg and I could feel the strength draining from me. Gair's voice drifted back. He was on the radio.

Richard was back. He pushed my hands away and started wrapping something round my leg. He pulled tight, then tighter. I looked down—the white of the bandages was already soaked scarlet.

Gair was giving the coordinates of our position. Reinforcements were on their way. I had lost. I was going back to Tronal, to spend the next eight months chained and drugged, while a new life grew inside me. A life I had longed for, prayed for. And now it was to be my death. I wondered whether Duncan would be allowed to live. Or whether he was already dead.

Richard twisted me so that my head rested on Freya's shoulder, then propped my left leg against the wall, allowing gravity to do its job.

'Why?' I managed. 'Why do you kill us? Why do you hate your mothers?'

He held my hand in both of his. 'We have no choice,' he said. 'It's what makes us who we are.' He leaned closer. 'But never think we hate the women who bear our children. We don't. We honour their memories, miss them all our lives. They made the ultimate sacrifice for their sons.'

'Their lives,' I whispered.

'Their hearts,' he said.

Oh God, please God, no.

Richard sat down on the bunk beside me. He was still holding my hand. 'When I was nine days old,' he said, 'I drank the blood of my mother's heart.'

He paused, giving me a moment to understand what he was saying. I couldn't speak. I could only stare at him.

'It was given to me in a bottle,' he went on, 'along with the last of her milk. Of course, I knew nothing of it at the time; it was much later, on my sixteenth birthday, that I learned of . . . shall we say, my extraordinary heritage?'

I swallowed hard; concentrated on taking deep breaths.

'You can imagine the shock. I'd grown up with my father and his wife, a woman I loved very much. The horror of what they were telling me, of what had been done to the woman who . . . I think it was just about the darkest day of my life. But at the same time, it was the start of my life, of understanding who I really was. I already knew I was special, brighter by far than any other child in the class. I was a gifted musician and I could speak four languages, two of them I'd taught myself. I was stronger, faster and more able in just about everything I did. And I was never ill.'

I found my voice. 'You were just lucky; a fortunate combination of genes. It had nothing to do with . . .'

'And I had other powers too, stranger powers. I'd discovered I could make people do what I wanted, just by suggestion.'

'Hypnosis.'

'Yes, that's what some of the younger ones like to call it.'

I shook my head. I wasn't buying it, but I couldn't find words to argue.

'I was introduced to two other boys who'd already turned sixteen. They were just like me, just as strong, just as clever. I was told about four others, a few months younger, who were the rest of my peer group. And I met six older boys who had just turned nineteen. They knew what we were going through, had been through it themselves three years previously.'

'Every three years,' I said.

He nodded. 'Every three years, between five and eight boys are born. We have just one son, in our lifetimes, one son who will become one of us.'

'Trows?' I wanted to scoff, tried to scoff, but it was hard.

He frowned. 'Kunal Trows,' he corrected. Then he half smiled. 'So many stories, so much nonsense: little grey men who live in caves and fear iron. Yet tucked away inside all legends, a kernel of truth can be found.'

'All those women. All those deaths. How do you do it?'

'The key is having people in the right places. Once a woman has been identified, we watch her closely. We may stage an accident, or her GP might discover an illness. Once she's in hospital, a high dose of something like Midazolam is typically given to slow the metabolism right down so the life-support machines automatically sound the alarm. If relatives are present, the medical team make a show of trying to save the patient, but fail. The unconscious woman is taken to the morgue, where our people are on standby to take her to Tronal. The pathologist produces a report and a weighted coffin is either buried or incinerated. Naturally, we encourage cremation.'

'Naturally. What about Melissa?'

'Melissa was a special case. Like you, never intended to be part of all this. She went through Stephen's computer files one night. Her mistake, of course, was in confronting him, telling him what she knew. At first, we planned to eliminate her, but she'd told Stephen she was pregnant and he didn't want to lose the child. It was his idea to substitute the other woman, the one from Oban. I was against it. Too many complications. But we'd run out of time.'

'Why do you bury the women? Why not just burn them?'

'It's against our beliefs. Our mothers lie in what for us is sacred ground. It's the way we honour them.'

'And Duncan? Duncan did this too? Drank . . .'

Richard nodded. 'He did. So did his father and his grandfather before him, and my father and grandfather and great-grandfather. We are the Kunal Trows, stronger and more powerful than any other men on earth.'

He stood up to return to the main cabin. I was so tired. I wanted nothing more than to slip into unconsciousness. And I knew that if I did so I would die. I had to keep talking.

'You're not special,' I said. 'It's all in your head.'

Richard's voice fell. 'You have no idea of the powers we have. Influence and wealth you couldn't even dream of.'

'Richard,' called Gair, 'I think I can hear an engine. I need to go up top and signal. Can you take the helm?'

Richard started to turn. 'Believe me if you can, my dear. It will make the next few months easier.'

He turned and left the cabin, closing the door. I felt a moment of surprise that he hadn't sedated me. Maybe he thought the pain and blood loss would be enough to keep me immobile. I looked up at my leg. Blood was no longer pumping out and it was possible the artery wasn't severed after all. I risked lowering it, then raised myself up so that I was sitting on the bunk. The bleeding increased but not alarmingly.

It would be just about impossible to get the better of Richard and Gair, injured as I was, but I had to try. While they were separated, Gair on deck, Richard driving the boat, I had the best chance.

I tried standing up. A stab of pain shot through my leg. I took deep breaths, counted to ten, waited for the pain to subside. Then I stepped forwards. Another stab of pain, not so bad this time. I inched forwards until I reached the door. I turned the handle and pulled. The door opened silently.

Richard was alone in the main cabin, standing at the wheel, peering ahead. We'd reached another mass of stacks and the navigation was tricky.

I needed a weapon. Granddad's horse gun lay on a shelf at the far side of the cabin but I'd never be able to reach it without Richard seeing me. I checked the shelves that ran round the cabin and found where the boat tools were kept. I slipped my hand down. It was like a life-or-death game of jackstraws—dislodge one without moving the others or making a sound. Amazingly, I managed to extract some sort of pliers, thick steel, about twelve inches long. They would do. I limped forwards, arm above my head.

Of course, Richard saw my reflection in the cabin windows. He spun round, catching my arm, pushing it down behind my back. With my free hand, I pushed at his chest then, in desperation, clawed at his eyes. He hit me, just once, a heavy blow across the temples. My legs gave way under me, but as I toppled I grabbed his sweater and took him with me.

We landed heavily, he on top of me. He pushed himself up. I grabbed his ear lobe and he yelled with pain. Then he hit my arm hard and I had to let go, but with my other hand I went for his eyes again. He sat up, straddled me, pinning me down. With one hand, he grabbed my right wrist and held fast. With the other, he reached for my throat.

Knowing it could be the last sound I ever made, I screamed.

Richard's hand wrapped round my neck and squeezed. I thrashed my head from side to side but his grip wasn't budging. I tore at the hand holding my throat, dug my nails into skin, tried to wrench it away.

Richard was no longer looking at me. He wasn't capable of looking me in the eyes as he throttled me. I think I took a small measure of comfort from that as the darkness grew.

Then he convulsed—just once—and his grip relaxed, releasing the pressure on my throat. My lungs started pumping, desperate for air.

Richard fell towards me. I managed to raise both hands to fend him off and he fell face down on the floor of the cabin. A circle of blackness stained the thick white hair on the back of his head and a small bubble of blood rose from the wound. Tearing my eyes away, I looked at the figure kneeling above him. There was a thud as the humane killer, the iron bolt stained with blood, fell to the floor. Eyes met mine, eyes dazed with drugs. Then I saw a gleam of intelligence and Dana's lips stretched into a smile.

'Can you understand me?' I whispered, feeling myself smile in response.

She nodded, but didn't seem able to speak.

'Stephen Gair is up there,' I said, gesturing towards the cockpit. 'Can you watch the steps? Let me know if he appears?'

She nodded again, and I stood up, picked up the horse gun and reloaded the bolt. Then I limped over to the helm. Seeing no immediate hazards ahead, I flicked the boat onto autopilot. Then I switched the radio to channel 16.

'Mayday, mayday, mayday,' I said as loudly as I dared. 'This is motor launch *Arctic Skua*, *Arctic Skua*. We are in Shetland waters, travelling south down the eastern coast of Tronal island. Six people on board, two injured. We require urgent medical and police assistance.'

There was a crackle of static. No response. I glanced round. Dana's eyes hadn't left the companionway steps. I could hear footsteps above us.

'Mayday, mayday, mayday,' I repeated. 'We need help urgently.'

It was close to hopeless. Even if anyone were listening, they would never get to us in time. The second Tronal boat would be here any second.

Gair's face appeared upside-down in the companionway. He was lying on the cabin roof, staring down at us. 'I'm opening the seacocks, Tora,' he sneered. 'You'll have about ten minutes before the boat sinks like a stone. If you want to save your three friends, you come up top now.'

His face disappeared. I staggered to the companionway and pulled myself up the steps. Gair was bent over the anchor locker at the bow. He saw me, straightened up and moved towards me.

I stood my ground. He was wounded too, though not as badly as I, and I still had the gun. I wasn't giving in just yet. He climbed onto the cabin roof and stood there, legs apart for balance, towering above me. In his right hand Gair held a short length of chain. He swung it round and it crashed against the cabin roof. Then he caught hold of the other end with his left hand and pulled it tight. He stood at the edge of the cabin roof, poised to leap down.

Just off the port bow loomed a massive shape, for a split second almost as terrifying as the man about to leap at me. A granite stack, dangerously close. I dropped the gun and reached my right hand back through the spokes of the steering wheel, stretching up and back, towards where I knew the instruments must be. My fingers felt buttons and I began pressing. I had no idea what they were, I just had to hope.

Gair raised himself on tiptoe. I reached high again, grabbed a spoke at the top of the wheel and pulled down as hard as I could.

The boat responded; one of the buttons I'd pressed had disengaged the autopilot and I was in control of the helm. Travelling at speed, the launch almost tipped over under the force of the abrupt turn. I heard Dana cry out. Gair staggered, almost slipped, grasped for something to steady himself and then miraculously regained his balance.

Just as we hit the twenty-foot-high granite stack.

As the boat swerved, I'd fallen to the floor of the cockpit; the force of the impact threw me against the wheel, jarring my shoulders. I watched Stephen Gair fly towards me. His eyes held mine and in that moment I saw fury, then fear, as he sailed through the air and crashed against the steering wheel. I heard a crack that I knew must be bone breaking and I made myself turn to face him as he collapsed over the wheel. Then the freewheeling motion of the boat sent him over again, to land slumped in the stern.

I took hold of the wheel and dragged myself up. Gair was starting to move. Bracing myself against the wheel I kicked out, my foot connected and he slid backwards. His hand shot out and grabbed my ankle. I held the wheel with both hands, lifted my other foot and jumped on his wrist. He let go and slid further back and I kicked him again. I pushed one last time with both feet, then I fell down into the stern as he slid overboard.

I don't know how long I knelt there, staring down at the wash, before I realised the boat was spinning out of control. I crawled back into the cockpit and switched the engines off. Their sound faded into the night. The boat was still moving with the wind and the tide, but no longer careering around madly. I collapsed. That was it, absolutely it, nothing more I could do.

Dana's face appeared in the companionway. She saw me and then disappeared. I wondered if she'd fallen. Then something was pushed over the top of the companionway steps. A tangle of canvas straps and metal. It was a life jacket. I watched and another appeared. Then a third.

'Tora, come on. Get one of these things on yourself.'

I could barely hear Dana's voice. I crawled round the wheel and across the cockpit floor to the steps, trying not to think about my throbbing leg.

A hand appeared, a woman's arm. I reached out and grabbed it. I had no strength but I held on and a woman collapsed over the top of the steps. Her dark hair fell forwards, covering her face. I pulled again and heard Dana grunt as she pushed from below. The dark-haired woman came up over the steps and landed on top of me. I pushed her to one side. It was Freya, the younger of the two women I'd seen in the clinic.

I heard Dana's voice calling 'Tora', saw a movement at the steps, more hands on the rails. Odel was climbing up by herself. She looked weak, barely able to focus, and I guessed Dana was pushing her up. I reached out for her hand as she staggered into the cockpit.

Somehow I managed to stand up and stumble to the steps. I reached out and helped Dana climb out. As the wind hit her she started shivering violently. Below, I could see the cabin floor was underwater. It was rising fast.

Dana's eyes met mine. 'Life jackets,' I gasped, looking at Freya and Odel.

Sensible, practical Dana was already wearing hers. I managed to pull one over my head and fasten the metal buckle, and she helped me pull jackets over the other two. Then I inflated them and switched on the rescue lights.

Water was breaking over the stern now and spray was soaking us, filling the cockpit every few seconds, hastening our descent. There was no time for the life raft even if I could find it. We struggled to our feet.

Odel was able to stand, and between us we supported Freya. I climbed on to the seat and then the side deck. Dana followed, then Odel and we dragged up Freya. We stumbled our way to the stern of the rocking boat until we were all standing, looking down at the motionless propeller. I unclipped the rail and held tight to one of the stanchions.

'We have to jump,' I shouted. 'I'll give the signal.'

Dana nodded. Odel was struggling to keep her eyes open but Dana wrapped one arm tightly round her and grasped a stanchion with the other.

I lowered myself onto the top step. Waves were now washing over my feet. I turned and nodded to Dana.

'After three,' she gasped. 'One, two, three, go!'

We leapt through the air and hit the silky smooth welcome of the ocean. Stars sparkled all around us as we sank lower and the blackness below reached up its arms and carried us down. I felt no cold, no pain, no fear.

I was filled with a sense of peace, of finality; it wasn't so bad after all, this dying business, just sinking into silent, velvet-soft darkness.

Then the ancient laws of physics kicked in and the air in our jackets began to rise upwards, taking us with it. The surface broke around our faces like shattering glass and the salty night air leapt into my lungs. I reached out for Dana, found her hand and thought I saw the glint of her eyes as they met mine. Odel and Freya were just dark shapes in the water.

I could hear engines and knew that someone was close. I tried to summon up fury that we'd been through so much, only to be picked up by the second Tronal boat, but couldn't do it. I didn't care.

A second later we were bathed in light.

WHEN I OPENED my eyes again, I started screaming.

I was in a small, cream-painted room, with flower prints on the walls and a door opening onto a private bathroom. I was back on Tronal, chained to a narrow hospital bed. My screams echoed through the building.

The door slammed open and a nurse ran in, followed by a young doctor. They stood at my bedside, making soothing noises, trying to settle me back down again. I looked down at my wrists. No shackles encircled them. I tried to move my legs. One of them moved easily, the other was too stiffly wrapped in bandages. No sign of chains. There was another bed in the room, but I couldn't see who was in it; the nurse was standing in the way.

The doctor was holding my arm, a syringe in his hand.

I tugged free and hit him. 'No drugs. Don't you dare drug me!' I yelled.

'Sounds like she means it,' said a voice I knew. We all turned.

Kenn Gifford stood in the doorway. The others stepped back.

'Where am I?' I said.

'The Balfour,' replied Gifford. 'On Orkney. DCI Rowley and I thought you might all prefer to be off Shetland for a while.'

'Duncan,' I gasped, ready to start screaming again.

Gifford gestured across the room, a small smile on his face. The nurse had moved and I could see the man in the bed next to my own. Ignoring the pain, I pushed my legs over the side of the bed until I was standing.

Gifford put an arm round my waist and half steered, half carried me to Duncan's bed. My husband's eyes were open but dull. I reached out to stroke the side of his face. His entire head was bandaged. I didn't take my eyes off him as Gifford settled me back down on my own bed.

'He took a nasty blow to the head,' said Gifford.

'Will he be OK?' I asked.

'We think so. He needed a craniotomy, but it was all fairly straightforward. They'll keep him sedated for another twelve hours or so.'

Gifford sat down on the bed. The doctor and nurse left the room.

'Dana and the others? They're here?'

He nodded. 'Dana discharged herself a couple of hours ago. Alison and Collette are still here. Both doing fine.'

For a second I wasn't with him. Then I had it. Freya and Odel: of course.

'Alison and Collette,' I repeated. 'Tell me about them.'

'Collette McNeil is thirty-three,' he said. 'She's married with two young children and lives just outside Sumburgh. A month ago she dropped the kids at school as usual and walked the dog along the cliff tops. She was approached by some men. Next thing she can remember is waking up on Tronal. Everyone assumed she fell over the cliff. Alison Rogers was a tourist, exploring the islands on her own. She can't remember what happened, she's pretty traumatised, but she was seen getting on the ferry from Fair Isle three weeks ago. No one saw her arrive. She was presumed drowned.'

'They couldn't afford bodies to be found this summer,' I said.

Kenn frowned at me.

'Stephen Renney isn't one of them,' I said. 'He's only been at the hospital a few months. They couldn't risk faking a death at the hospital this year.'

Gifford fell silent. We listened to the sounds in the corridor outside, to Duncan's breathing. 'Look, that's enough now. You need to rest.' As he made to leave the room I felt panic rising again.

'No drugs, no sedatives, not even painkillers. Promise me,' I said.

Gifford held up both hands. 'I promise,' he said, walking back.

'You're not one of them, are you? They said you're not one of them.'

'Take it easy. No, I'm not. You're both perfectly safe. I won't leave you.'

'I'm so tired,' I said.

He bent over and kissed me on the forehead. I managed to smile at him as he sat down in the chair beside me, but it was Duncan's face I was looking at as my eyes slowly closed.

Epilogue

A skylark had woken us, just as the silvery light of early dawn was beginning to soften and turn gold. Before breakfast we walked along the cliff tops, watching the waves break on the rocks below and hordes of sea birds bustle about building nests, preparing for imminent parenthood. The day was unseasonably warm for late May. Walking home along the roadside, we could hardly see the grass beneath the thick rug of primroses. Shetland was at its most beautiful. And a small army of English police officers were searching our land for the remains of Kirsten Hawick.

Duncan and I sat on the flagged area at the back of the house. Even from a distance we could see they meant business this time. Metres of tape criss-crossed the length and breadth of our field, held in place by tiny metal pegs. The officers, working in teams of three, were systematically checking square after square after square: measuring, probing, digging. They'd found nothing so far. But the world's media, who'd been camped on our doorstep for the past week, seemed to have swollen in ranks this morning. A sense of grim expectation hung in the air.

Two weeks had passed since our adventures on Tronal. My leg was healing well; Duncan had made a near complete recovery. We'd been incredibly lucky. My detour to Dana's house that night had saved our lives. Helen had instructed one of her constables to collect something she'd left behind there. He found the envelope and, on her instructions, opened it. Hearing what I was up to (and, I'm told, cursing nonstop for the following two hours), Helen sent a dozen officers back to Tronal. They had found Duncan locked in the basement. Helen had directed the operation herself from on board a police helicopter, the same one that picked us out of the water.

And then the fun really began.

Twelve island men, including the staff of the Tronal clinic, several hospital personnel, Dentist McDouglas, DI Andy Dunn and two members of the local police force, are being held in custody on various charges, including murder, conspiracy to murder, kidnapping and actual bodily harm, to name just a few. Superintendent Harris of the Northern Constabulary has been suspended from duties pending an internal inquiry. Duncan tells me that these men are the tip of the iceberg and I don't doubt him for a second.

Stephen Gair is still missing. Whether he's alive or dead, we have no idea. Richard's funeral is to be held on Unst tomorrow. The launch sank, that night, in relatively shallow water and his body was easily recovered. Half of Shetland is expected to turn up to honour Richard's memory, but Duncan and I will not be among them. There are still faint bruises round my neck; I can't pretend to grieve for the man who put them there.

Duncan's motivation is more complex. He is struggling to deal with how close he came to becoming one of them.

So Kenn will be our proxy tomorrow. We've seen quite a lot of him the last couple of weeks. He's formed a habit of turning up unannounced, usually at mealtimes. He still flirts disgracefully, but only when Duncan is in the room. It was Kenn, we discovered, who performed the surgery that removed a clot from Duncan's brain.

The Tronal Maternity Clinic has closed for good. The two infants I saw that night have been transferred to a neonatal unit in Edinburgh and are both doing well. Their birth mothers will be traced. What their legal relationship will be to the babies they thought they'd aborted, who can say?

Collette McNeil and Alison Rogers are both pregnant as a result of their stay on Tronal. The pregnancies were achieved by doctors inserting sperm directly into their uterine cavities. Lawyers are currently arguing over whether, technically, that constitutes rape. Collette is planning a termination. Alison is thinking of keeping the baby.

I turned at the sound of footsteps on gravel. Dana had made it through the press barricade and was walking towards us. She was wearing jeans and a large shapeless sweater, her hair scraped back in a ponytail. I hadn't seen her since the night we all leapt into the ocean together.

'Thought you were in Dundee. On sick leave,' I said.

She pulled up a wooden chair and sat down. 'Supposed to be,' she agreed. 'Bored to death. Flew back this morning.'

'I think you might be in trouble,' said Duncan, who was looking towards the top of the field. We both followed his eye line. Helen, in a white jumpsuit, had stopped work and was staring down at us.

I turned back to Dana, risked a smile, saw its pale reflection on her face.

'How are you feeling?' she asked, her eyes dropping to my stomach.

'Dreadful,' I replied, 'but that's normal.'

We fell silent, and I was thinking that the only remotely normal thing about my pregnancy was the little creature at the centre of it. A midwife had scanned me yesterday. Duncan and I had held hands, tears streaming down both our faces, as we watched a shapeless little blob with a very strong heartbeat, totally oblivious to what had been going on around it.

'And I suppose we're hoping for . . . a girl?' said Dana tentatively. I heard Duncan give a soft laugh and it seemed like a very good sign.

A sudden noise grabbed my attention. On the fence that ran the length of the field were a group of pale grey birds with forked tails, black heads and red beaks. They were arctic terns, come back from their long winter in the Southern Hemisphere. Hoping to nest in our field, as was their usual custom, they were frustrated at the sudden human invasion. They jumped around on the fence, circled overhead, yelling down at the police officers to be off and find somewhere else to dig, didn't they know this was breeding ground?

'I think they've found something,' said Dana.

My attention snapped away from the birds. 'Where?'

'That group near Helen. Tall man with sandy hair. Woman with thick-rimmed glasses. Near the reed bed.'

I watched. The small group Dana was talking about became the focus of activity up on the field. One by one, other white-clad officers stepped closer.

'They're very close to where I found Melissa,' I said, in a small voice.

Nobody spoke. Up in the field four men started digging in earnest.

'We should go inside,' said Duncan.

THE PERFECTLY PRESERVED, peat-stained bodies of four women were eventually found on our land: Rachel Gibb, Heather Paterson, Caitlin Corrigan and Kirsten Hawick. All were names I knew; I'd seen them on my computer screen the night I met Helen. Each had had her heart cut out. Each had three runic symbols carved into the flesh of her back: Othila, meaning Fertility; Dagaz, the rune for Harvest; and Nauthiz: Sacrifice.

The search has been called off now, much to my dismay, because I know there must be two more bodies buried somewhere; seven KT boys were born a year after these women supposedly died. So the bodies will stay out there. They may lie in the Shetland earth for all time, along with all the other women who have disappeared without trace on these islands over the centuries. Or they may turn up out of the blue one day when someone, too ignorant to know better, dares to disturb the ground.

The terns have found somewhere else to build their nests now. We don't blame them: we're going to do the same.

S.J. BOLTON

Born: Darwen, Lancashire
Most inspirational writer: Stephen King
One wish: that life carries on as it is now

RD: When did you start writing fiction?

SJB: I was twelve. My heroine, a young girl called Charlotte, was the most boring prig ever to hit the page. Luckily that book didn't last beyond the first 1,000 words.

RD: You had a top PR job in the financial sector of the City before writing *Sacrifice*, your first novel. What made you change career?

SJB: I just felt that that phase of my life was coming to an end. I'd been putting ideas together for some time, but it's hard to write fiction after working long office hours.

RD: Where do you get your ideas from—and do you hate being asked that question?

SJB: No, I'm still at the stage of being fascinated by how ideas spring up. I have this theory that ideas are like love in the Wet Wet Wet song (all around us) and that we all encounter lots in the course of the day. If I hit a blank wall, I usually take Lupe, our lop-eared lurcher out for a walk. I don't know whether it's the steady rhythm of walking, or the fresh air, but something always clears my head and lets the ideas flow again.

RD: Once you began to write, did all your thoughts come together easily?

SJB: Yes, one night I went off to bed, put my laptop on my lap and the words poured out. I'm one of those people who have an imaginary life going on inside the head. It's like having two parallel worlds that exist side by side.

RD: Have you always enjoyed reading scary books yourself?

SJB: Ever since I was a child I've loved 'the dark side', but for a long time I felt a little ashamed of that aspect of myself. Then one day I was reading a nonfiction book by Stephen King, in which he was talking about what inspired him, and he said something I'll never forget: 'I was born with a love of the night and the unquiet coffin'. It was such a relief to know that I wasn't the only person who felt that way.

RD: At what point did the Shetlands Islands become the setting for *Sacrifice*?

SJB: Originally I wanted to base the story on a German legend and I went to the library in Aylesbury, close by our home, to research German and Scandinavian mythology. I didn't find much, but I did come across the fascinating legend of the Shetland Kunal Trows, a race of supernatural males who stole human wives in order to perpetuate their species. It fitted in perfectly with my ideas.

RD: Did you spend time in Scotland researching the islands?

SJB: No. I had such a strong image in my head of what it must be like that I didn't want reality to cloud it. I used photographs, Ordnance Survey maps and the Internet, but the Shetland of *Sacrifice* is the Shetland of my imagination—a remote, wild, fabulous place of incomparable beauty and dark secrets. In the final stages of writing, though, I did go there and found that it was very close to what I had imagined.

RD: Is your heroine, Tora, based on you?

SJB: If only! I suspect in Tora I've created the woman I'd liked to have been. In all honesty, though, I think I gave her a lot of my own faults.

RD: She enjoys riding and she's a competent sailor. Does the same go for you?

SJB: I love horses, but I'm not particularly good at riding. My husband and my son both ride, though, and we could definitely enjoy a family trek together. And we do go sailing. But I'm not brave like Tora. I'm always imagining what might go wrong.

RD: Are you writing a new novel?

SJB: I've just finished my first draft. This book's all about snakes.

ᚠᚢᚦᚨᚱᚲ . . . READING THE RUNES

J.R. Tolkien made many readers aware of runes, which he used on maps in *The Hobbit* and in the *Lord of the Rings* trilogy. These, and the three runic symbols etched onto the corpse in *Sacrifice*, probably had their origins in early Bronze Age carvings.

A runic alphabet, known as futhark, was developed by ancient Germanic peoples and used by the Scandinavians and Anglo-Saxons. It was named after the first six letters, or glyphs *(see above)*: f, u, th, a, r , k.

From the beginning, runes took on a ritual function. There were runes and spells to influence the weather, the tides, crops, love and healing; runes of fertility, cursing and removing curses, birth and death. Runes were carved on amulets, drinking cups, battle spears, over the lintels of dwellings and onto the prows of Viking ships. The Vikings believed that the runes were a gift from the Norse god Odin, possessing divine, magical powers.

By Roman times runes generally took the form of painted pebbles, often carried in a pouch and used for divination.

The Man in the Picture
Susan Hill

Have you ever seen an image of Venice at carnival time and been mesmerised by the blank, masked faces?

When Dr Theo Parmitter first set eyes on just such an 18th-century painting of revellers beside a canal, he was enthralled by what he saw. He bought it at auction, unaware of the strange way in which it would come to haunt his life . . .

PROLOGUE

The story was told to me by my old tutor, Theo Parmitter, as we sat beside the fire in his college rooms one bitterly cold January night. There were still real fires in those days, the coals brought up by the servant in huge brass scuttles. I had travelled down from London to see my old friend, who was by then well into his eighties, hale and hearty and with a mind as sharp as ever, but crippled by severe arthritis so that he had difficulty leaving his rooms. The college looked after him well. He was one of a dying breed, the old Cambridge bachelor for whom his college was his family. He had lived in this handsome set for over fifty years and he would be content to die here. Meanwhile a number of us, his old pupils from several generations back, made a point of visiting him from time to time, to bring news and a breath of the outside world. For he loved that world. He loved the gossip—to hear who had got what job, who was succeeding, who was tipped for this or that high office, who was involved in some scandal.

But I should not like to give the impression that this was a sympathy visit to an old man from whom I gained little in return. On the contrary, Theo was tremendous company, witty, acerbic, shrewd, a fund of stories that were not merely the rambling reminiscences of an old man. He was a wonderful conversationalist—people, even the youngest fellows, had always vied to sit next to him at dinner in hall.

I had done my best to entertain him most of the afternoon and through dinner, which was served to us in his rooms. It was the last week of the vacation and the college was quiet. We had drunk a bottle of good claret, and we were stretched out comfortably in our chairs before a good fire. But the winter wind, coming as always straight off the Fens, howled round and occasionally a burst of hail rattled against the glass.

Our talk had been winding down gently for the past hour. I had told all my news, we had set the world to rights between us, and now, with the fire blazing up, the edge of our conversation had blunted. It was delightfully cosy sitting in the pools of light from a couple of lamps and for a few moments I had fancied that Theo was dozing.

But then he said, 'I wonder if you would care to hear a strange story?'

'Very much.'

'Strange and somewhat disturbing.' He shifted in his chair. He never complained of it but I suspected that the arthritis gave him considerable pain. 'The right sort of tale for such a night.'

I glanced across at him. His face, caught in the flicker of the firelight, had an expression so serious—I would almost say deathly serious—that I was startled.

'Make of it what you will, Oliver,' he said quietly, 'but I assure you of this, the story is true.' He leaned forward. 'Before I begin, could I trouble you to fetch the whisky decanter nearer?'

I got up and went to the shelf of drinks, and as I did so, Theo said, 'My story concerns the picture to your left. Do you remember it at all?'

He was indicating a narrow strip of wall between two bookcases. It was in heavy shadow. Theo had always been known as something of a shrewd art collector with some quite valuable old-master drawings and eighteenth-century watercolours, all picked up, he had once told me, for modest sums when he was a young man. I went over to the picture he was pointing out.

'Switch on the lamp there.'

Although it was a somewhat dark oil painting, I now saw it quite well. It was of a Venetian carnival scene. On a landing stage beside the Grand Canal and in the square behind it, a crowd in masks and cloaks milled around among entertainers—jugglers and tumblers and musicians—and more people were climbing into gondolas; others were already out on the water, the boats bunched together, with the gondoliers clashing poles. The picture was typical of those whose scenes are lit by flares and torches that throw an uncanny glow, illuminating faces and patches of bright clothing and the silver ripples on the water, leaving other parts in deep shadow. I thought it had an artificial air but it was certainly an accomplished work.

I switched off the lamp and the picture, with its slightly sinister revellers, retreated into its corner of darkness again.

‘I don’t think I ever took any notice of it before,’ I said now, pouring myself a whisky. ‘Have you had it long?’

‘Longer than I have had the right to it.’ Theo leaned back into his deep chair so that he too was now in shadow. ‘It will be a relief to tell someone. I have never done so and it has been a burden. Perhaps you would not mind taking a share of the load?’

I had never known him sound so deathly serious, but of course I did not hesitate to say that I would do anything he wished, never imagining what taking, as he called it, ‘a share of the load’ would cost me.

ONE

Theo Parmitter’s Story

‘My story really begins some seventy years ago, in my boyhood. I was an only child and my mother died when I was three. I have no memory of her. Nowadays, of course, my father might well have made a decent fist of bringing me up himself, at least until he met a second wife, but times were very different then and, although he cared greatly for me, he had no idea how to look after a boy scarcely out of nappies, and so a series of nurses and then nannies were employed. They were all kindly and well-meaning enough, all efficient, and though I remember little of them, I feel a general warmth towards them and the way they steered me into young boyhood.

‘My mother had a sister, married to a wealthy man with considerable land and properties in Devon, and from the age of seven or so I spent many idyllic holidays with them. I was allowed to roam free, I enjoyed the company of local boys—my aunt and uncle had no children but my uncle had an adult son from his first marriage, his wife having died giving birth—and of the surrounding tenant farmers, villagers, ploughmen and blacksmiths, grooms, hedgers and ditchers. I grew up healthy and robust as a result of spending so much time outdoors. But when I was not about the countryside, I was enjoying a very different sort of education indoors. My aunt and uncle were cultured people, widely and well read and with a splendid library. I was allowed the run of this as much as I was allowed the run of the estate and I followed their example and became a voracious reader.

'My aunt was also a great connoisseur of pictures. She loved English watercolours but also had a taste for the old masters and, though she could not afford to buy paintings by the great names, she had acquired a good collection of minor artists. Her husband was more than happy to fund her passion, and seeing that I showed an early liking for certain pictures about the place, Aunt Mary jumped at the chance of bringing someone else up to share her enthusiasm. She began to talk to me about the pictures and to encourage me to read about the artists, and I very quickly understood the delight she took in them and had my own particular favourites. I loved some of the great seascapes and also the watercolours of the East Anglia school, the wonderful skies and flat fens—I think my taste in art had a good deal to do with my pleasure in the outside world. I could not warm to portraits or still lifes—but nor did Aunt Mary and there were few of them about. She encouraged me to be open to everything, not to copy her taste but to develop my own, and always to wait to be surprised and challenged as well as delighted by what I saw.

'I owe my subsequent love of pictures entirely to Aunt Mary and those happy, formative years. When she died, just as I was coming up to Cambridge, she left me many of the pictures you see around you now and others, too, some of which I sold in order to buy different ones—as I know she would have wished. She would have wanted me to keep my collection alive, to enjoy the business of acquiring new when I had tired of the old.

'In short, for some twenty years or more I became quite a picture dealer, going to auctions regularly and, in the process of having fun at the whole business, building up more capital than I could ever have enjoyed on my academic salary. In between my forays into the art world, of course, I worked my way slowly up the academic ladder, establishing myself here in the college and publishing the books you know.

'I have sketched in my background and you now know a little more about my love of pictures. But what happened one day you could never guess and perhaps you will never believe the story. I can only repeat what I assured you of at the start. It is true.'

TWO
Theo Parmitter's Story

'It was a beautiful day at the beginning of the Easter vacation and I had gone up to London for a couple of weeks, to work in the Reading Room of the British Museum and to do some picture dealing. On this particular day there was an auction, with viewing in the morning, and from the catalogue I had picked out a couple of old-master drawings and one major painting that I particularly wanted to see. I guessed that the painting would go for a price far higher than I could afford but I was hopeful of the drawings and I felt buoyant as I walked from Bloomsbury down to St James's in the spring sunshine. The magnolias were out, as were the cherry blossoms and, set against the white stucco of the eighteenth-century terraces, they were gay enough to lift the heart. Not that my heart was ever down. I was cheerful and optimistic when I was younger—indeed, in general I have been blessed with a sunny and equable temperament—and I enjoyed my walk, keenly anticipating the viewing and the sale. There was no cloud in the sky, real or metaphorical.

'The painting was not, in fact, as good as had been made out and I did not want to bid for it, but I was keen to buy at least one of the drawings, and I also saw a couple of watercolours that I knew I could sell on and I thought it likely that they would not fetch high prices. I marked them off in the catalogue and went on wandering around.

'Then, slightly hidden by a pair of rather overpowering religious panels, that Venetian oil of the carnival scene caught my eye. It was in poor condition, it badly needed cleaning and the frame was chipped in several places. It was not, indeed, the sort of picture I generally liked, but there was a strange, almost hallucinatory quality about it and I found myself looking at it for a long time and coming back to it, several times. It seemed to draw me into itself so that I felt a part of the night-time scene, lit by the torches and lanterns, one of the crowd of masked revellers, or of the party boarding a gondola and sailing over the moonlit canal and off into the darkness under an ancient bridge.

'I stood in front of it for a long time, peering into every nook and cranny of the palazzi with their shutters opening here and there onto rooms dark save for the light of a branch of candles or a lamp, the odd shadowy figure just glimpsed in the reflected light. The faces of many of the revellers were of the classic Venetian type, with prominent noses, the same faces that could be seen as Magi and angels, saints and popes, in the great paintings that filled Venice's churches.

'The sale began at two and I went out into the spring sunshine to find some refreshment before returning to the auction rooms, but as I sat in the dim bar of a quiet pub, through the windows of which the sun lanced here and there, I was still immersed in that Venetian scene. I knew, of course, that I had to buy the picture. I could barely enjoy my lunch and became agitated in case something happened to prevent my getting back to the rooms to bid, so I was one of the first there. But for some reason, I wanted to be standing at the back, away from the rostrum, and I hovered close to the door as the room began to fill. There were some important pictures and I caught sight of several well-known dealers. No one knew me.

'The painting I had at first come to bid for was sold for more than I had expected, and the drawings quickly went beyond my means, but I was almost successful in obtaining a fine Cotman watercolour that came immediately after them. I secured a small group of good seascapes and then sat through one stodgy sporting oil after another—fat men on horseback, huntsmen, horses with docked tails giving them an odd, unbalanced air, horses being held by bored grooms; on and on they went and up and up went the sea of hands. I almost dozed off. But then, as the sale was petering out, there was the Venetian carnival scene, looking dark and unattractive now that it was out in the open. There were a couple of halfhearted bids and then a pause. I raised my hand. No one took me on. The hammer was just coming down when there was a slight flurry behind me and a voice called out. I glanced round, surprised and dismayed that I should have last-minute competition, but the auctioneer took the view that the hammer had indeed fallen on my bid and there was an end to it. It was mine for a very modest sum.

'The palms of my hands were damp and my heart was pounding. I have never felt such an anxiety—indeed, it was close to a desperation—to obtain anything and I felt oddly shaken, with relief and also with some other emotion I could not identify. Why did I want the picture so badly?

'As I went out of the saleroom towards the cashier's office to pay for my purchases, someone tapped me on the shoulder. I turned and saw a stout, sweating man carrying a large leather portfolio case.

'"Mr . . . ?" he asked.

I hesitated.

"I need to speak with you urgently."

'"If you will forgive me, I want to get to the cashier's office ahead of the usual queue . . ."

'"No. Please do not."

'"I beg your pardon?"

'"You must listen to what I have to say first. Is there somewhere we can go so as not to be overheard?" He was glancing around him as if he expected a dozen eavesdroppers to be closing in on us and I felt annoyed. I did not know the man and had no wish to scurry off with him to some corner.

'"Anything you have to say to me can surely be said here. Everyone is busy about their own affairs. Why should they be interested in us?" I wanted to secure my purchases, arrange for them to be delivered to me, and be done.

'"Mr . . ." He paused again.

'"Joiner," I said curtly, giving him the alias I used for bidding, as all dealers do.

'"Thank you. My name is not relevant—I am acting on behalf of a client. I should have been here earlier but I encountered a road accident and I was obliged to stay and speak to the police; it made me too late, I . . ." He took out a large handkerchief and wiped his brow and upper lip but the beads of sweat popped up again at once. "I have a commission. There is a picture . . . I have to acquire it. It is absolutely vital."

'"But you were too late. Bad luck. Still, it was hardly your fault—your client cannot reasonably blame you for witnessing a road accident."

'He looked increasingly uncomfortable and was sweating even more. I made to move away but he grabbed me and held me by the arm so fiercely that it was painful. "The last picture," he said, his breath foetid in my face, "the Venetian scene. You obtained it and I must have it. I will pay you what you ask, with a good profit; you will not lose. It is in your interests after all; you would only sell it on later. What is your price?"

'I wrenched my arm from his grip. "There is none. The picture is not for sale."

'"Don't be absurd man; my client is wealthy; you can name your price. Don't you understand me?—*I have to have that picture.*"

'I had heard enough. I turned on my heel and walked away from him. But he was there again, pawing at me, keeping close to my side. "You have to sell the picture to me."

'"If you do not take your hands off I will be obliged to call the porters."

'"My client gave me instructions . . . It has taken years to track the picture down. I have to have it."

'We had reached the cashier's office, where there was now a considerable queue of buyers waiting to pay. "For the last time," I hissed at him, "let me alone. I have told you: I want the picture and I intend to keep it."

'He took a step back and, for a moment, I thought that was that, but then he leaned close to me and said, "You will regret it. I have to warn you. You will not want to keep that picture." His eyes bulged, and the sweat was running down his face now. "Do you understand? Sell me the picture. It is for your own good."

'It was all I could do not to laugh in his face but, instead, I merely shook my head and turned away to stare at the grey cloth of the jacket belonging to the man in front of me as if it were the most fascinating thing in the world.

'I dared not look round again but by the time I had left the cashier's window having paid for my purchases, including the Venetian picture, the man was nowhere to be seen.

'I was relieved and dismissed the incident from my mind as I went out into the sunshine of St James's.

'It was only later that evening, as I was settling down to work at my desk, that I felt a sudden, strange frisson, a chill down my spine. I had not been in the least troubled by the man—he had clearly been trying to make up some tale about the picture to convince me I should let him have it—nevertheless, I felt uneasy.

'Everything I had bought at the auction was delivered the next day and the first thing I did was take the Venetian picture across London to a firm of restorers. They would clean it expertly, and either repair the old frame or find another. I also took one of the other pictures to have a small chip made good and because picture restorers work slowly, as they should, I did not see the paintings again for some weeks, by which time I had returned here to the Cambridge summer term that was in full swing.

'I brought all the new pictures with me. I was in my London rooms too infrequently to leave anything of much value or interest there. I placed the rest with ease, but wherever I put the Venetian picture it looked wrong. I have never had such trouble hanging a painting. Because I had such trouble finding the right place for it, in the end I left the painting propped up there, on the bookcase. And I could not stop looking at it. Every time I came back into these rooms, it drew me. I spent more time looking at it—no, into it—than I did with pictures of far greater beauty and merit. I seemed to need it, to spend far too much time looking into every corner, every single face.

'I did not hear any more from the tiresome pest in the auction rooms, and I soon forgot about him entirely.'

'JUST ONE CURIOUS THING happened around that time. It was in the autumn of the same year, the first week of Michaelmas term and a night when the first chills of autumn had me ring for a fire. It was blazing up well, and I was working at my desk in a circle of lamplight, when I happened to glance up for a second. The Venetian painting was directly in my sight and something about it made me look more closely.

'Cleaning had revealed fresh depths, and much more detail was now clear. I could see far more people crowded on the path beside the water, and gondolas and other craft laden with revellers, some masked, others not, on the canal. I had studied the faces over and over again, and each time I found more. People hung out of windows and over balconies; more were in the dim recesses of rooms in the palazzi. But now, it was only one figure that caught my eye and stood out from all the rest, near the front of the picture. I did not think I had noticed the man before. He was not looking at the lagoon or the boats, but rather away from them and out of the scene—he seemed, in fact, to be looking at me, and into this room. He wore clothes of the day but plain ones, not the elaborate fancy dress of many of the carnival-goers, and he was not masked. But two of the revellers close to him wore masks and both appeared to have their hands upon him, one on his shoulder, the other round his left wrist, almost as if they were trying to pull him back. His face had a strange expression, as if he were at once astonished and afraid. He was looking away from the scene because he did not want to be part of it, and at me—at anyone in front of the picture—with what I can only describe as pleading. But for what?

'The shock was seeing a man's figure there at all when I had previously not noticed it. I supposed that the lamplight, cast on the painting at a particular angle, had revealed the figure clearly for the first time. Whatever the reason, his expression distressed me and I could not work with my former deep concentration.

'In the night I woke several times and, once, out of a strange dream in which the man in the picture was drowning in the canal and stretching out his arms for me to save him. So vivid was the dream that I got out of bed and came in here, switched on the lamp and looked at the picture. Of course nothing had changed. The man was not drowning though he still looked at me, still pleaded, as if trying to get away from the two men who had their hands on him.

'I went back to bed. And that, for a very long time, was that. Nothing more happened. The picture stayed propped up on the bookcase for months until eventually I found a space for it there, where you see it now.

'I did not dream about it again. But it never lessened its hold on me, its presence was never anything but powerful, as if the ghosts of all those people in that weirdly lit, artificial scene were present with me, forever in the room.

'SOME YEARS PASSED. The painting did not lose any of its strange force but of course everyday life goes on and I became used to it. I often spent time looking at it though, staring at the faces, the shadows, the buildings, the dark rippling waters of the Grand Canal, and I also vowed that one day I would go to Venice. I have never been a great traveller, as you know; I love the English countryside too much and never wanted to venture far from it during vacations. Besides, in those days I was busy teaching here, performing more and more duties within the college, researching and publishing a number of books and continuing to buy and sell pictures.

'Only one odd thing happened concerning the picture during that period. An old friend, Brammer, came to visit me here. I had not seen him for some years and we had a great deal to talk about but at one point, soon after his arrival and while I was out of the room, he started to look round at the pictures. When I returned, he was standing in front of the Venetian scene and peering closely at it.

'"Where did you come by this, Theo?"

'"Oh, in a saleroom some years ago. Why?"

'"It is quite extraordinary. If I hadn't . . ." He shook his head. "No."

'I went to stand beside him. "What?"

'"When do you suppose it was painted?"

'"It's late eighteenth century."

'He shook his head. "Then I can't make it out. You see, that man there . . ." He pointed to one of the figures in the nearest gondola. "I . . . I know—knew him. That's to say it is the absolute likeness of someone I knew well. We were young men together. Of course it cannot be him . . . but everything—the way he holds his head, the expression—it is quite uncanny."

'"With so many billions of people born and all of us only having two eyes, one nose, one mouth, I suppose it is even more remarkable that there are not more identical people."

'But Brammer was not paying me any attention. He was too absorbed in scrutinising that one face. It took me a while to draw him away from it and to divert him back to our earlier conversation, and several times over the next twenty-four hours he went back to the picture and would stand there, an expression of concern and disbelief on his face.

'There was no further incident and, after a while, I put Brammer's strange discovery, if not out of, then well to the back of, my mind.

'Perhaps, if I had not been the subject of an article in a magazine, more general than academic, some years later, there would have been nothing else and so the story, such as it was, would have petered out.

'I had completed a long work on Chaucer and it happened that there was a major anniversary that included an exhibition at the British Museum. There had also been an important manuscript discovery relating to his life. The general press took an interest and there was a gratifying amount of attention given to my beloved poet. I was delighted. I had long wanted to share the delights his work afforded with a wider public and my publisher was pleased when I agreed to be interviewed.

'One of the interviewers who came to see me brought a photographer and he took several pictures in these rooms. If you would care to go to the bureau and open the second drawer, you will find the magazine article filed there.'

THREE

Theo was a meticulous man—everything was filed and ordered. I had always been impressed, coming in here to tutorials and seeing the exemplary tidiness of his desk. It was a clue to the man. He had an ordered mind. In another life, he ought to have been a lawyer.

The cutting was exactly where he had indicated. It was a large spread about Theo, Chaucer, the exhibition and the new discovery, highly informed and informative, and the photograph of him, which took up a full page, was not only an excellent likeness of him as he had been some thirty years previously, but a fine composition in its own right. He was sitting in an armchair, with a pile of books on a small table beside him, his spectacles on top. The sun was slanting through the high window and lighting the whole scene quite dramatically.

'This is a fine photograph, Theo.'

'Look though—look at where the sun falls.'

It fell onto the Venetian picture, which hung behind him, illuminating it vividly and in a strange harmony of light and dark. It seemed to be far more than a mere background.

'Extraordinary.'

'Yes. I confess I was quite taken aback when I saw it. I suppose by then I had grown used to the picture and I had no idea it had such presence in the room.'

I looked round. Now, the painting was half hidden, half in shade, and seemed a small thing, not attracting any attention. The figures were a little stiff and distant, the light rippling on the water dulled. It was like someone in a group who is so retiring and plain that he or she merges into the background unnoticed.

What I saw in the magazine photograph was almost a different canvas, not in its content, which was of course the same, but in—I might almost say—in its attitude.

'Odd, is it not?' Theo was watching me intently.

'Did the photographer remark on the picture? Did he deliberately arrange it behind you and light it in some particular way?'

'No. It was never mentioned. He fussed a little with the table of books, I remember . . . making the pile regular, then irregular . . . and he had me shift about in the chair. That was all. I recall that when I saw the results—and there were quite a number of shots of course—I was very surprised. I had not even realised the painting was there. Indeed . . .' He paused.

'Yes?'

He shook his head. 'It is something, to be frank, that has played on my mind ever since, especially in the light of . . . subsequent events.'

'What is that?'

But he did not answer. I waited. His eyes were closed and he was quite motionless. I realised that the evening had exhausted him, and after waiting a little longer in the silence of those rooms, I got up and left, trying to make my exit soundless, and went away down the dark stone staircase and out into the court.

IT WAS A STILL, clear and bitter night with a frost and a sky thick and brilliant with stars, and I went quickly across to my own staircase to fetch my coat. It was late but I felt like fresh air and a brisk walk. The court was deserted and there were only one or two lights shining out from sets of rooms.

The night porter was already installed in his lodge with a fire in the grate and a great brown pot of tea.

'You mind your step, sir, the pavements have a rime on them even now.'

I thanked him and went out through the great gate. King's Parade was deserted, the shops shuttered. A solitary policeman on the beat nodded to me as I passed him. I was intent on both keeping warm and staying upright as the porter had been right that the pavements were slippery.

But quite without warning, I stopped because a sense of fear and oppression came over me like a wave of fever, so that a shudder ran through my body. I glanced round but the lane was empty. The fear I felt was not of anyone or anything, it was just an anonymous, unattached fear and I was in its grip. It was combined with a sense of impending doom, a dread, and also with a terrible sadness, as if someone close to me was suffering and I was feeling that suffering with them.

I am not given to premonitions and, so far as I was aware, no one close to me, no friend or family member, was in trouble. I felt quite well. The only thing that was on my mind was Theo Parmitter's strange story, but why should that have me, who had merely sat by the fire listening to it, so seized by fear?

I no longer wanted to be out tramping the streets alone and I turned sharply. There must have been a patch of frost exactly there for I felt my feet slither away from under me and fell heavily on the pavement. I lay winded and shaken but not in pain, and it was at that moment that I heard, a little distance away to my left, a cry and a couple of low voices. After that came the sound of a scuffle and then another desperate cry. It seemed to be coming from the direction of the Backs and yet, in some strange sense that is hard to explain, to be not *away* from me at all but here, at my hand, next to me. It is very difficult to convey a clear impression because nothing was clear, and I was also lying on a frozen pavement and feeling anxious in case I had injured myself.

If what I had heard was someone being set upon in the dark and robbed, then I should get up and either find the victim and go to his aid or warn the policeman I had seen a few minutes before. It was just after midnight, not a night for strollers, other than fools like me. It then came to me that I was in danger of being attacked myself. I had my wallet in my inner pocket and a gold watch on my chain. I was worth a villain's attack.

I pulled myself hastily to my feet. I was unhurt apart from a bash to the knee—I would be stiff the next day—and looked quickly round but there was no one about.

Had I imagined the noises? No, I had not. In a quiet street on a still and frosty night, when every sound carries, I could not have mistaken what I heard for wind in the trees, or in my own ears. I had heard a cry, and voices, and even a splash of water, yet the riverside was some distance away and hidden by the walls and gardens of the colleges.

I went back to the main thoroughfare and caught sight of the policeman again, trying the door handles of shops to check that they were secure. Should I go up to him and alert him? But if I had heard the robbers, he, only a few yards away in a nearby street, must surely have heard them too, yet he was merely continuing down King's Parade with his steady, measured tread.

A car turned down from the direction of Trinity Street and glided past me. A cat streaked away into a dark slit between two buildings. My breath smoked on the frosty air. There was nothing untoward about and the town was settled for the night.

The oppression and dread that had enshrouded me a few minutes earlier had lifted, almost as a consequence of my fall, but I did not feel comfortable in my own skin and by now I was also thoroughly chilled, so I made my way back to the college gate as briskly as I could, my coat collar turned up against the freezing night air.

The porter, still ensconced by his glowing fire, wished me good night. I replied, and turned into the court.

All was dark and quiet but light shone from one of the same two windows I had noticed when I went out, and now from another on the far left-hand row. Someone must have just returned. In a couple of weeks, term would have begun and then lights would be on all round.

I stood for a moment looking, remembering the good years I had spent within these walls, the conversations late into the night, the japes, the hours spent sweating over an essay or boning up for Part One. I would never want to be like Theo, spending all my years here, however comfortable the college life might be, but I had a pang of longing for the freedoms and the friendships.

It was then that my eye was caught by one light, the original one, going out, so that now there was only one room with a light on, on the far side, and it was automatic for me to glance up there.

What I saw made my blood freeze.

Whereas before there had been a blank, now a figure was in the room and close to the window. The lamp was to one side of him and its beam was thrown onto his face, and the effect was startlingly like that of the Venetian picture. Well, there was nothing strange about that—lamplight and torchlight will always highlight and provide sharply contrasting shadows in this way. No, I was transfixed because the man was looking directly at me and I could have sworn I recognised him, not from life but from the picture. He bore such an uncanny resemblance to one of the faces that I would have sworn in any court that they were one and the same. But how could this possibly be? It could not, and besides, the figure was some distance from me. There are only so many combinations of features, as Theo himself had said.

But it was not the mere resemblance that struck me so, it was the expression on the face. I had particularly noticed this face in the picture because it was a fine depiction of decadence, of greed and depravity, of malice and loathing, of every sort of inhuman feeling and intent. The eyes were piercing and intense, the mouth set into a sneer of arrogance. It was a mesmerisingly unpleasant face and it had repelled me in the picture as much as it horrified me now. I had glanced away, but now looked up again at the window. The face had gone and after another couple of seconds the light went out and the room was black. The whole court was now in darkness, save for the lamps at each corner, which cast a comforting pool of tallow light onto the gravel path.

I came to, feeling numb with cold and chilled with fear. The sense of dread and imminent doom had returned and seemed to wrap round me in place of my coat. But, determined not to let these feelings get the better of me, I went across the court and up the staircase of the rooms from which the light had been shining. I remembered them as being the set a friend of mine had occupied, and found them without trouble.

I stood outside the door and listened closely. There was a silence so absolute that it was uncanny. Old buildings generally make some sound, creaking and settling back, but here it was as still and quiet as the grave. After a moment, I knocked on the outer door, though without expecting any reply, as the occupant would now be in the bedroom and might well not have heard me.

I knocked again more loudly, and when again there was no answer, I turned the door handle and stepped inside the small outer lobby. The air was bitterly cold here, which was strange as no one would be occupying rooms on such a night without having heated them. I hesitated, then went into the study.

'Hello,' I said in a low voice.

There was no response and after I had repeated my 'Hello' I felt along the wall for the light switch. The room was empty of anything, apart from a desk and chair, one armchair beside the cold and empty grate and a bookcase without any books in it. There was an overhead light but no lamp of any kind. I went through to the bedroom. There was a bed, stripped of all linen. Nothing else.

Obviously, I had mistaken the rooms and I left, and made my way to the second set adjacent to them, the only others on the upper level of this staircase—each one had two sets up and a single, much larger, set on the ground floor, and the pattern was the same on three sides of this, the Great Court.

I knocked and, hearing only silence in response again, went into this set of rooms too. They were as empty as the first—emptier indeed since here there was no furniture other than the bookcases, which were built into the wall. There was also a smell of plaster and paint.

I thought that I would go across to the night porter and ask who normally occupied this staircase. But what purpose would that serve? There were no undergraduates in residence, these sets had not been used by fellows for many years and, clearly, decoration and maintenance were underway.

I cannot possibly have seen a lamp lit and a figure in any of these windows.

But I knew that I had.

I went, thoroughly shaken now, down the staircase and across the court to the guest set in which I was staying. There, I poured myself a large slug of the Scotch I had and downed it in one. I followed it with another, which I took more slowly. I then went to bed and, in spite of the whisky, lay shivering for some time before falling into a heavy sleep. It was filled with the most appalling nightmares, through which I tossed and turned and sweated in horror, nightmares filled with strange flaring lights and the shouts of people drowning.

I woke hearing myself cry out and, as I gathered my senses, I heard something else, a tremendous crash, as of something heavy falling. It was followed by a distant, muffled cry, as if someone had been hit and injured.

My heart was pounding so loudly in my ears, and my brain was still swirling so with the dreadful pictures, that it took me a moment to separate nightmare from reality, but when I had been sitting upright with the lamp on for a few moments, I knew that what I had seen and the voices of the people drowning had been unreal and merely part of a disturbing nightmare, but that the crashing sound and the subsequent cry most certainly had not.

Everything was quiet now but I got out of bed and went into the sitting room. All was in order. I returned for my dressing gown, and then went out onto the staircase but here, too, all was still and silent. No one was occupying the adjacent set but I did not know if a fellow was in residence below. Theo Parmitter's rooms were on a different staircase.

I went down in the dark and icy cold and listened at the doors below but there was absolutely no sound.

'Is anyone there? Is everything all right?' I called, but my voice echoed oddly up the stone stairwell and there was no answering call.

I went back to bed, and slept fitfully until morning, mainly because I was half frozen and found it difficult to get warm and comfortable again.

When I looked out of the window a little after eight, I saw that a light snow had fallen and that the fountain in the centre of the court had frozen solid.

I was dressing when there was a hurried knock on the outer door and the college servant came in looking troubled.

'I thought you would want to know at once, sir, that there's been an accident. It's Mr Parmitter . . .'

FOUR

'There is really no need to trouble a doctor. I am a little shaken but unhurt. I will be perfectly all right.'

The servant had managed to get Theo into his chair in the sitting room, where I found him, looking pale and with an odd look about his eyes that I could not read.

'The doctor is on his way so there's an end to it,' I said, nodding approvingly at the servant, who had brought in a tray of tea and was refilling a water jug. 'Now, tell me what happened.'

Theo leaned back and sighed, but I could tell that he was not going to argue further.

'You fell? You must have slipped on something. We must get the maintenance people to check . . .'

'No. It is not their concern.' He spoke quite sharply.

I poured us both tea and waited until the servant had left. I had already noticed that the Venetian picture was no longer in its former place.

'Something happened,' I said. 'And you must tell me, Theo.'

He took up his cup and I noticed that his hand was shaking slightly.

'I did not sleep well,' he said at last. 'That is not unusual. But last night it was well after two before I got off and I slept very fitfully, with nightmares and general disturbance.'

'I had nightmares,' I said. 'Which is most unusual for me.'

'It is my fault. I should never have started on that wretched story. Anyhow, I was in such discomfort and sleeping so wretchedly that I knew I would be better off up and sitting in this chair. It takes me some time to get myself out of bed and stirring and I had heard the clock strike four when I made my way in here. As I came up to that wall on which the picture hung, I hesitated for a split second—something made me hesitate. The wire holding the painting snapped and the whole thing crashed down, glancing my shoulder so that I lost my balance and fell. If I had not paused, it would have hit me on the head. There is no question about it.'

'What made you pause? A premonition, surely?'

'No, no. I daresay I was aware, subliminally, of the wire straining and being about to break. But the whole incident has shaken me a little.'

'I'm sorry—sorry for you, of course, but I confess I am sorry that I will not hear the rest of the story.'

Theo looked alarmed. 'Why? Of course, if you have to leave . . . But I wish that you would stay, Oliver. I wish that you would hear me out.'

'Of course I will. I could hardly bear to be left dangling like this, but perhaps it would be better for your peace of mind if we let the whole thing drop.'

'Most emphatically it would not! If I do not tell you the rest I fear I shall never sleep well again. Now that it is buzzing in my mind it is as disturbing as a hive of angry bees. Do you now have to return to London?'

'I can stay another night—indeed it would be time well spent. There are some things I can usefully look at in the library while I am here.'

There was a tap on the door. The doctor arrived and I told Theo I would see him later that day, if he was up to talking, but that he must on no account disobey any 'doctor's orders'—the tale could wait. It was of no consequence. But I did not mean that. It was of more consequence now than I dared admit. Enough things had happened both to unnerve me and to convince me that they were connected, though each one taken alone meant little. I should say that I am by no means a man who jumps readily to outlandish conclusions. I am a scholar and I have been trained to require evidence, though as I am not a lawyer, circumstantial evidence will sometimes satisfy me well enough. I am also a man of strong nerve and sanguine temperament, so the fact that I had been disturbed is noteworthy. And I now knew that Theo, too, was disturbed and, above all, that he had begun to tell me the story of the Venetian picture, not to entertain me but to unburden himself, to share his fears with another human being, one not unlike him in temperament, who would bring a calm, rational mind to bear upon them.

But although my reason told me that the falling picture was a straightforward event and readily explained, my shadowy sense of foreboding and unease told me otherwise.

I SPENT MOST OF THE DAY in the library working on a medieval psalter and then went into the town to have tea in the Trumpington Street café I often frequented and which, in term-time, was generally full of steam and the buzz of conversation. Now it was almost deserted and I sat eating my buttered crumpets in a somewhat chill and gloomy atmosphere. I had hoped to be cheered up by human company but even the shopping streets were quiet—it was too cold for strollers and anyone who had needed to buy something had done so speedily and returned to the warmth and snugness of home.

I would be doing the same tomorrow, and although I loved this town, in which I had spent some supremely happy years, I would not be sorry when this particular visit was over. It had been an unhappy and an unsettling one. I longed for the bustle of London and for my own comfortable house.

I returned to the college and, because I felt in need of company, went to dine in hall with half a dozen of the fellows. We made cheerful conversation and in typical Cambridge fashion, finished off a good bottle of port in the combination room, so that it was rather late by the time I went across the court and up the staircase to my rooms. I found an anxious message awaiting me from Theo, asking me to go and see him as soon as I was free.

I had managed to blow away the clinging cobwebs of my earlier low and anxious mood and I was now apprehensive about hearing any more of Theo's story. Yet he had all but begged me to go and hear him out, for his peace of mind depended upon it, and I felt badly about leaving him alone all day. So, I hurried out and down the staircase.

THEO WAS LOOKING BETTER. He had a small glass of malt whisky beside him, a good fire and a cheerful face and he enquired about my day in a perfectly easy manner.

'I'm sorry I was occupied and didn't get along here earlier.'

'My dear fellow, you're not in Cambridge to sit with me day and night.'

'All the same . . .'

I sat down and accepted a glass of the Macallan. 'I have come to hear the rest of the story,' I said, 'if you feel up to it and still wish to tell me.'

Theo smiled.

The first thing I had looked for on coming into the room was the picture.

It had been re-hung in its original position but it was in full shadow, the lamp turned away and shining on the opposite wall. I thought the change must have been made deliberately.

'What point had I reached?' Theo asked. 'I can't for the life of me remember.'

'Come, Theo,' I said quietly, 'I rather think that you remember very clearly, for all that you dropped off to sleep and I left you to your slumbers. You were coming to an important part of the story.'

'Perhaps my falling asleep was a gesture of self-defence.'

'At any rate, you need to tell me the rest or both of us will sleep badly again tonight. You had just shown me the article in the magazine, in which the picture appeared too prominently. I asked you if the photographer had placed it deliberately.'

'And he had not. So far as I was aware he had paid it no attention and I certainly had not done so. But there it was, one might say, dominating the photograph and the room. I was surprised but nothing more. And then, a couple of weeks after the magazine appeared, I received a letter. I have it still and I looked it out this morning. It is there, on the table beside you.'

He pointed to a stiff, ivory-coloured envelope. I picked it up. It was addressed to him here in college in violet ink, in an elaborate, old-style hand, and postmarked Yorkshire, some thirty years previously.

Hawdon
by Eskby
North Riding of Yorkshire

Dear Dr Parmitter,

I am writing to you on behalf of the Countess of Hawdon, who has seen an article about you and your work in the —Journal and wishes to make contact with you with regard to a painting hanging in the room in which you appear photographed. The painting, an oil of a Venetian carnival scene, is of most particular and personal interest to Her Ladyship.

Lady Hawdon has asked me to invite you here as there are matters to do with the picture that she needs most urgently to discuss.

The house is situated to the north of Eskby and a car will meet your train from the railway station at any time. Please communicate with me as to your willingness to visit Her Ladyship and offer a date, at your convenience. I would stress again that because of Her Ladyship's frail health and considerable agitation on this matter, an immediate visit would suit.

Yours,

John Thurlby, Secretary

'And did you go?' I asked, setting the letter down.

'Oh yes. Yes, I went to Yorkshire. Something in the tone of the letter meant that I felt I had no choice. Besides, I was intrigued. I was younger then and up for an adventure. I went off as soon as term ended, within a couple of weeks.'

He leaned forward and poured himself another whisky and indicated that I should do the same. I caught his expression in the light from the fire as he did so. He spoke lightly of a jaunt to the North. But a haunted and troubled look had settled on his features that belied the cheerfulness of his words.

'I do not know what I expected to find,' he said, after sipping his whisky. 'I had no preconceived ideas of Hawdon or of this Countess. If I had . . . You think mine is a strange story, Oliver. But my story is nothing, it is merely a prelude to the story told me by an extraordinary old woman.'

FIVE
Theo Parmitter's Story

'Yorkshire proved dismal and overcast on the day I made my journey. I changed trains in the early afternoon when rain had set in, and although the scenery through which we passed was clearly magnificent in decent weather, now I scarcely saw a hundred yards beyond the windows—no great hills and valleys were visible but merely lowering clouds over dun countryside. It was December, and dark by the time the slow train arrived, panting uphill, at Eskby station. A handful of other passengers got out and disappeared quickly into the station passageway. The air was raw and a damp chill wind blew into my face as I came out into the forecourt, where two taxis and, at a little distance away, a large black car were drawn up. The moment I emerged, a man in a tweed cap slid up to me through the murk.

'"Dr Parmitter." It was not a question. "Harold, sir. I'm to take you to Hawdon."

'Those were the only words he spoke voluntarily, the entire way, after he had put my bag in the boot and started up. He had automatically put me in the back seat, though I would have preferred to sit beside him, and as it was pitch dark once we had left the small town, which sat snugly on the side of a hill, it was a dreary journey.

'"How much farther?" I asked at one point.

'"Four mile."

'"Have you worked for Lady Hawdon many years?"

'"I have."

'"I gather she is in poor health?"

'"She is."

'I gave up, put my head back against the cold seat leather and waited, without saying any more, for the end of our journey.'

'WHAT HAD I EXPECTED? A bleak and lonely house set above a ravine, with ivy clinging to damp walls; a moat filled with stagnant water? An aged and skeletal butler, wizened and bent, and a shadowy, ravaged figure gliding past me on the stairs?

'Well, the house was certainly isolated. We left the main country road and drove for well over a mile, at a guess, over a rough single track, but at the end it broadened out suddenly and I saw great iron gates ahead, standing open. The drive bent, we veered quite sharply to the right and over a low stone bridge, and, peering through the darkness, I could see an imposing house with lights shining out from several of the high upper windows.

'We drew up on the gravel and I saw that the front door, at the top of a flight of stone steps, stood open. Light shone out from here too. It was altogether more welcoming than I had expected and bore not the slightest resemblance to the House of Usher, whose fearsome situation I had been remembering.

'I was greeted by a pleasant-faced butler, who introduced himself as Stephens, and taken up two flights of stairs to a splendid room whose long, dark red curtains were drawn and in which I found everything I could have wanted to pass a comfortable night. It was a little after six o'clock.

'"Her Ladyship would like you to join her in the drawing room at seven thirty, sir. If you would ring the bell when you are ready I will escort you down."

'"Does Lady Hawdon dress for dinner?"

'"Oh yes, sir." The butler's face was impassive but I heard a frisson of disdain in his voice. "If you do not have a dinner jacket . . ."

'"Yes, thank you, I do. But I thought it best to enquire."

'It had been only as an afterthought that I had packed the jacket and black tie, as I have always found it best to be over- rather than under-prepared. I had now no idea at all what to expect from the evening ahead.'

'STEPHENS CAME PROMPTLY to lead me down the stairs and along a wide corridor lined with many large oil paintings, some sporting prints and cabinets full of curiosities, including masks, fossils and shells, silver and enamel. We walked too quickly for me to do more than glance eagerly from side to side but my spirits had lifted at the thought of what treasures there must be in the house and which I might be allowed to see.

'"Dr Parmitter, M'Lady."

'It was an extremely grand room with a magnificent fireplace, in front of which was a group of three large sofas on which lamplight and the light of the fire were focused. There were lamps elsewhere in the room, on small tables and illuminating pictures, but they were turned down low. There were a number of fine paintings on the walls: Edwardian family portraits, hunting scenes, groups of small oils. At the far end of the room I saw a grand piano.

'There was nothing decaying, dilapidated or chilling about such a drawing room. But the woman who sat on an upright chair with her face turned away from the fire did not match the room in warmth and welcome. She was extremely old, with the pale, parchment-textured skin that goes with great age; skin like the paper petals of dried honesty. Her hair was white and thin, but elaborately combed up onto her head and set with a couple of glittering ornaments. She wore a long frock of some green material on which a splendid diamond brooch was set, and there were diamonds about her long, sinewy neck. Her eyes were deep set but were not the washed-out eyes of an old woman: they were a piercing, unnerving blue.

'She did not move except to reach out her left hand to me, her eyes scrutinising my face. I took the cold, bony fingers, which were heavily, even grotesquely, jewelled, principally with diamonds but also with a single, large chunk of emerald.

'"Dr Parmitter, please sit down. Thank you for coming here."

'As I sat, the butler reappeared and offered champagne. I noticed that it was an extremely fine vintage and that the Countess was not drinking it.

'"This is a very splendid house and you have some wonderful works of art," I said.

She waved her hand slightly.

"I presume this is a family home of some generations?"

'"It is." There was a dreadful silence and I felt this was going to be a tricky evening. The Countess was clearly not one for small talk, I still did not know exactly why I had been summoned and, in spite of the comfort and beauty surrounding me, I felt awkward. Then she said, "You cannot know what a shock I received on seeing the picture."

'"The Venetian picture? Your secretary mentioned in his letter to me . . ."

'"I know nothing of you. I do not customarily look at picture papers. It was Stephens who chanced upon it and brought it to my attention. I was considerably shaken, as I say."

'"May I ask why? What the picture has to do with you—or perhaps with your family? Clearly it is of some importance, for you to ask me here."

'"It is of more importance than I can say. Nothing else in life matters to me more. *Nothing else.*" Her gaze held mine as a hand might hold another in a grip of steel. I could not look away and it was only the voice of the silent-footed butler, who appeared behind us and announced dinner, that broke the dreadful spell.

'The dining room was high-ceilinged and chill and we sat together at one end of the long table, with silver candlesticks before us and the full paraphernalia of china, silver and glassware for an elaborate dinner. I wondered if the Countess sat in such state when she dined alone. I had offered her my arm across the polished floors into the dining room and it had been like having the claw of a bird resting there. Her back was bent and she had no flesh on her bones. I guessed that she must be well into her nineties.

'Sitting next to me, she seemed more like a moth than a bird, and I noticed that she was made up with rouge and powder and that her nails were painted. She had a high forehead behind which the hair was puffed out, a beaky, bony nose and a thin line of mouth. Her cheekbones were high and I thought that, with the blue of her eyes and with flesh on her distinguished bones, she might well have been a beauty in her youth.

'A plate of smoked fish was offered, together with thinly sliced bread and chunks of lemon, and a bowl of salad was set in front of us. I filled my mouth full, partly because I was hungry but also in order not to have to talk for a few moments. A fine white Burgundy was poured and the dinner proceeded in a stately way. The Countess spoke little, save to give me some scraps of information about the history of the estate and the surrounding area, and to ask me a couple of cursory questions about my own work. There was no liveliness in her manner. She ate little, broke up a piece of bread into small fragments and left them on her plate, and seemed tired and distant. I was gloomy at the thought of spending the rest of the evening with her and frustrated that the point of my journey had not been reached.

'At the end of dinner, the butler came to announce that coffee was served in the "blue room". The Countess took my arm and we followed him down the long corridor again and into a small, wood-panelled room. I barely felt the weight of her fingers as the pale bones rested on my jacket, the huge emerald ring looking like a carbuncle.

'The blue room was partly a library, though I doubt if any of the heavy, leather-bound sets of books had been taken down from the shelves for years. But there was a long polished table, on which were set out several large albums, and also the magazine with the article about me, spread open. The butler poured coffee and a further glass of water for the Countess, helped her to a chair at the table before the books, and left us. As he did so, he turned the main lights down a little. Two lamps shone onto the table at either side of us and the Countess motioned for me to sit beside her.

'She opened one of the albums, and I saw that it contained photographs, with names, places and dates written neatly beneath in ink. She turned several pages over carefully without explanation, but at last came to a double spread of wedding photographs from seventy or more years ago, sepia pictures with the bridegroom seated, the bride standing, others with parents, the women draped in lace and wearing huge hats, the men moustached.

'"My wedding, Dr Parmitter. Please look carefully." She turned the album round. I studied the various groups. The Countess had indeed been a very beautiful young woman, even as she stood unsmiling, as was the way in such photographs then, and I admired her long face with its straight nose, pretty mouth, pert chin.

'"Does nothing strike you?"

'It did not. I looked for a long time but knew no one, recognised nothing.

'"Look at my husband."

'I did so. He was a dark-haired young man, the only male who was clean-shaven. His hair was slightly waved at the sides, his mouth rather full. He had a handsome face of character but not, I would say, rare character. "I confess I do not know him—I recognise no one save yourself."

'She turned her eyes on me now and her face wore a curious expression, partly of hauteur but also of a distress I could not fathom. "Please . . ."

'I glanced down again at the photograph and, in that split second, had an extraordinary flash of—what? Shock? Recognition? Revelation? It must have shown clearly on my face, for the Countess said, "Ah. Now you see."

'I had seen—and yet *what* had I seen? I now knew that there was something very familiar, intimately familiar, about a face—but which face? Not hers, not that of . . . No. His face. Her young husband's face. I knew it, or a face very like it. It was as though I knew it so well that it was the face of a member of my own family, a face I saw every day, a face with which I was so very familiar that I was, if you understand me, no longer aware of it.

'Something was in the shadows of my mind, out of reach, out of my grasp, hovering but incomprehensible. I shook my head.

'"Look." She had taken up the magazine and was gazing at it, then she slid it across the table to me, one long thin finger pointing down.

'There was a brief instant when what I saw made me experience a wave of shock so tremendous that I felt rising nausea and the room seemed to lurch crazily from side to side. What had been at the back of my mind came to the very front of it and clicked into place. Yet how could I believe what I was seeing? How could this be?

'The Venetian picture was very clear in the magazine photograph, but even if it had not been, I knew it so well, so thoroughly, that I could not have been mistaken. There was, you remember, one particular scene within the scene. A young man, on the point of stepping into one of the boats, was being held by the arm and threatened by another person and his head was turned to look into the eyes of whoever was viewing the picture with an expression of desperate terror and of pleading. Now, I looked at it and it was vivid: the face of the young man being persuaded into the boat was the face of the Countess's husband. There was no doubt about it. The resemblance was absolute. The two young men did not share a similar physiognomy. They were one and the same.

'She was staring at me intently.

'"My God," I whispered. I struggled for words, tried to grab hold of sanity. There was, of course, a sensible, a rational explanation.

'"So your husband was a sitter for the artist." As I said it, I knew how ridiculous it was.

'"The picture was painted in the late eighteenth century."

'"Then—this is a relative? One you perhaps have only just discovered? This is an extraordinary family likeness."

'"No. It is my husband. It is Lawrence."

'"Then I do not understand."

'She was leaning over the photograph, gazing at the picture and at the face of her young husband, with an intensity of longing such as I had never seen.

'I waited. Then she said, "I would like to return to the drawing room. Now that you have seen this . . . I can tell you what there is to tell."

'"I would like to hear it. But I have no idea how I can help you."

'She put out her hand for me to assist her up. "We can make our own way. We have no need of Stephens."

'Once more, the thin, weightless hand rested on my arm and we walked the length of the corridor, now in shadow as the wall lamps had been dimmed, so that the pictures and cabinets receded into darkness except when the gilt corner of a frame glowed eerily in the tallow light.

SIX
The Countess's Story

'"I was married when I was twenty. I met my husband at a ball and we experienced a *coup de foudre.* Few people are lucky enough to know that thing commonly called love at first sight. Few people really know and understand its utterly transforming power. We are the fortunate ones. Such an experience changes one entirely and for ever.

'"He was several years older than me, in his early thirties. But that did not matter. Nothing mattered. My parents were a little concerned—I was young, and I had an elder sister who should, in the natural order of these things, have been married before me. But they looked upon Lawrence with favour, nevertheless. There was only one thing to trouble us. He had been on the verge of an engagement. He had not proposed but there was an understanding. If he and I had not met that evening, it is sure that there would have been an engagement and a marriage and naturally the young woman in question was bitterly hurt. These things happen, Dr Parmitter. I had no reason to feel in any way to blame. Nor, perhaps, had he. But of course he felt a great concern for the girl and I—when I was eventually told—I felt as great a guilt and sorrow as a girl of twenty in the throes of such a love could be expected to feel. What usually happens in these cases is that one party suffers for a time from hurt pride and a broken heart, both of which are eventually healed, generally by the arrival of another suitor.

'"In this instance, it was otherwise. The young woman, whose name was Clarissa Vigo, suffered so greatly that I believe it turned her mind. I had not known her at all prior to this but I was assured that she had been a charming, gentle, generous young woman. She became a bitter, angry, tormented one whose only thought was of the injury she had suffered and how she could obtain revenge. Of course, the best way was to destroy our happiness. That is what she set her mind to and what consumed her. Much of this was kept from me, at least at first, but I learned afterwards that her family despaired of her sanity to the extent that they had her visited by a priest!

'"This was not the parish vicar, Dr Parmitter. This was a priest who undertook exorcisms. He was called both to houses under the influence of unhappy spirits and to persons behaving as if they were possessed. I believe that is how the young woman was treated. But he came away, he said, in despair. He felt unable to help her because she would not allow herself to be helped. Her bitterness and desire for retribution had become so strong that they possessed her entirely. They became her reason for living. Whether that is what you would class as demonic possession I do not know. I do know that she set out to destroy. And she succeeded in the most terrible way. Her determination grew stronger and with it her power to do harm. She was indeed possessed. And anger and jealousy are terrible forces when united together with an iron will.

'"But to begin with I was unaware of any of this. Lawrence referred only briefly and somewhat obliquely to her, and of course I was obsessed and possessed in my turn—by an equally single-minded and powerful love.

'"My time and energies were entirely consumed by Lawrence and our forthcoming marriage. All that is perfectly usual. I was not an unusual young woman, you know. Two things happened in the weeks before our marriage. I received an anonymous letter. It was unsigned and I did not know who had sent it. Not then. It was full of poison. Poison against me, against Lawrence, bitter, vindictive poison. It contained a threat, too: to destroy our future; to bring about pain and shock and devastating loss. I was terrified by it. I had never known hatred in my happy young life and here it was, directed at me, hatred and the desire—no, more, the determination—to harm. For several days I kept the letter locked in my writing desk. It seemed to sear through the wood. I seemed to smell it, to feel the hatred that emanated from it every time I went near, so that in the end I tore it into shreds and burned it in the hearth. I tried to put it out of my mind.

'"We were to be married the following month and naturally wedding presents began to arrive at my parents' house—silver, china and so forth—and I was happily occupied in unpacking and looking at it all, and in writing little notes of thanks. And one day—I remember it very clearly—along with some handsome antique tables and a footstool, a picture arrived. There was a card with it, on which was written the name of the painter, and a date, 1797. There was also a message: *To the Bride and Bridegroom. Let what is begun be completed*, in the same hand as the malign letter.

'"I hated the picture from the moment I first saw it. Partly because it came from someone who wished us harm. But it was more than that. I did not know much about art but I had grown up among delightful pictures that had come down through my family on my mother's side, charming English pastoral scenes, still-life oils of flowers and fruit, innocent, happy things. This was a dark, sinister painting. If I had known the words 'corrupt' and 'decadent' then, I would have used them to describe it. As I looked at the faces of those people, at the eyes behind the masks and at the strange smiles, the suggestions of figures in windows, in shadows, I shuddered. I felt uneasy, I felt afraid.

'"But when Lawrence saw the picture he had nothing but praise for it. He found it interesting. When he asked me who had sent it, I lied. I said that I had mislaid the card. I could certainly not have expressed to him any of my feelings about the picture—they were so odd, even to me, so unlike anything I had ever experienced.

'"Two secrets. Not a good way to begin a marriage, you may feel. But what else should I have done? I had had so little experience of the world and of different kinds of people. I had had a happy and a sheltered upbringing. So it was not until a day or two before our wedding that I understood who had sent both the anonymous letter and the picture, and then only when I chanced to see an envelope addressed to Lawrence in the same handwriting. I asked him who had sent it and he told me, of course, that it was from the young woman he might have married. I remember his tone of voice, as if he were holding something back, as if he were trying not to make anything of the letter. It was just some snippet of information he had asked for many months before, he said, and changed the subject. I was not worried that he had any feelings for her. I was worried because I knew at once that he, too, had received a letter full of hatred and ill-will, that he wanted to protect me, that the woman was the sender of the picture. I did not ask him. I did not need to. But once all of these things fell into place, I was more than ever afraid. Yet of what? I disliked the picture—it repelled me, made me shudder. But it was just a picture. We could hang it in some distant corner of our house, or even leave it wrapped and put it away.

'"Our wedding was a happy occasion. Everyone was happy—our families, our friends. We were happy. Only one person in the world was not but naturally she did not attend and on that day no one could have been further from our thoughts.

'"I did as best I could to put the incidents and the painting out of my mind and we began our married life. Six weeks after the wedding, Lawrence's father, the Earl of Hawdon, died very suddenly. Lawrence was the eldest son and I found myself, not yet even twenty-one years old, the mistress of this large house with a husband thrust into the running of a huge estate. We had taken a short honeymoon on the south coast and planned a longer tour the following spring. Now, perhaps we would never undertake it.

'"I have said that my father-in-law died suddenly—quite suddenly and unexpectedly. He had been in the best of health, he was an energetic man—and he was found dead at his desk one evening after dinner. A stroke. Of course we believed the medical men. One must. What reason was there to doubt them?

'"I have now to tell you something which I expect you to disbelieve. At first you will disbelieve it. I would ask you to go across to the bureau in the far corner of this room and look at the framed photograph that stands there."

'I crossed the long, silent room, leaving the Countess, a tiny, wraithlike figure, hunched into her chair in the circle of lamplight, and entered the shadows. But there was a lamp on the bureau, which I switched on. As I did so, I caught my breath.

'I saw a photograph in a plain silver frame. It was of a man in middle age, sitting at this same desk and half turning to the camera. His hands rested on the blotter that was in front of me now. He had a high forehead, a thick head of hair, a full mouth, heavy lids. It was a good face, a strong, resolute face of character, and a handsome one too. But I was transfixed by it because I knew it. I had seen it before, many times.

'*I had lived with that face.*

'I looked back to the old woman, again sitting with her eyes closed.

'But she said, her voice making me start, "So now you see."

'My throat was dry and I had to clear it a couple of times before I could answer her, and even when I did so, my own voice sounded strange and unfamiliar. "I see, but I scarcely know what it is that I do see."

'But I did know. Even as I spoke, of course I knew. I had known the instant I set eyes on the photograph. And yet . . . I did not understand.

'I returned to my chair opposite the old woman.

'"Please refill your glass."

'I did so thankfully. After I had downed my whisky and poured a second, I said, "Now, I confess I do not understand but I can only suppose this is some hoax . . . The painting cannot be of its date, of course, there is some trick, some faking? I hope you will explain."

'I had spoken in a falsely amused and over-loud tone and as the words dropped into the silent space between us, I felt foolish. Whatever the explanation, it was not a matter for jest.

'The Countess looked at me with disdain. "There is no question of either a hoax or a mistake. But you know it."

'"I know it."

'Silence. I wondered how this great house could be so silent. In my experience old houses are never so, they speak, they have movements and soft voices and odd footfalls, they have a life of their own, but this house had none.'

SEVEN
The Countess's Story

'"Nothing happened immediately. My father-in-law was dead and we were thrown into the usual business that surrounds a death—and my husband found himself pitched into a wholly new life with all its responsibilities. We had not even moved into the small house at the far side of the estate that was to have been our married home, and now we found ourselves forced to take over this house instead. We had barely unpacked our wedding presents and there was no place for most of them here. Lawrence and his mother of course were shocked and still in deep mourning. I was sad but I had known my father-in-law so little. I wandered about this great place like a lost soul, trying to get to know each room, to find a role for myself, to keep out of everyone's way. It was on these wanderings, a week after we had moved in, that I finally came upon the Venetian picture. It had been put with some other items into one of the small, rarely used sitting rooms on the first floor. The room smelled of damp and had an empty, purposeless air. The curtains hung heavy, the furniture seemed ill-chosen.

'"The picture faced me as I went into the room. And . . . and it seemed to me that it drew me to it and that every face within it looked into mine. I cannot describe it better. Every face. I wanted to leave the room at once, but I could not; the picture drew me to itself as if every person painted there had the strength to reach out and pull me towards them. As I approached it, some of the faces receded, some disappeared completely into the shadows.

'"But one face was still there. It was a face at a window. There was a palazzo with two lighted windows and with open shutters and a balcony overlooking the Grand Canal. In one of those lighted rooms, but looking out as if desperate to escape, even to fling himself over the balcony into the waters below to get away, there was a man, turned towards me. His body was not clearly depicted—his clothes seem to be only sketched in hastily, almost as an afterthought. But his face . . . It was the face of my father-in-law, so lately, so suddenly dead. It was his exact likeness save that it wore an expression I had never seen him wear, one full of fear and desperation. Horror? Yes, even horror. I knew that I had not only never noticed his likeness in the picture before but that, absolutely and unmistakably, *it had not been there.*

'"You can imagine that scene, Dr Parmitter. I was alone in a remote room of this house that was home and yet could not have felt less like a home to me, and looking into the terrified face of my dead father-in-law trapped inside a picture. I felt nauseous and faint, and I remember grabbing hold of a chair and holding on to it while the ground dipped and swayed beneath me. What should I do? How could I bring my husband here to see the picture?

How could I begin to tell him what I had so far kept to myself? Only two people knew anything of this—I myself and the woman, Clarissa Vigo. I was faced with something I did not understand and was poorly equipped to deal with.

'"I dared not touch the picture, or I would have taken it down and turned it face to the wall, or carried it up to one of the farthest attics and hidden it there. But I doubted if many people came into this fusty little room. On leaving it, I discovered that the key was in the lock, so I turned it and put the key in my pocket. Later, I slipped it into a drawer of my dressing table.

'"The following weeks were too busy and too exhausting for me to think much about the picture, though I had nightmares about it and I preferred not to go down the corridor leading to the small sitting room but would always take a long detour. My mother-in-law was in mourning and great distress and I had to spend time with her, as of course Lawrence was occupied from dawn till dusk in taking up the reins of the estate. She was a kindly but not very communicative woman and my memories are mainly of sitting in this drawing room or in her small boudoir, turning the pages of a book that I never managed to read or glancing through country magazines, while she sat with crochet on her lap, her hands still, staring ahead of her. And I carried a dreadful and bewildering secret within me. I had never before quite understood that once a thing is known it cannot be unknown. Now I did. Oh, I did.

'"I became even thinner and Lawrence once or twice commented that I looked pale or tired. He came to me one day saying that he wanted us to get away, though it could only be for ten days at most, and that we would travel down through France and Italy, by train to Venice. He was so pleased, so anxious for me to be well and happy. I should have welcomed it all. We had barely spent any time alone together and I had never travelled. But when he told me that we were to visit Venice I felt a terrible sensation, as if someone's hand had squeezed my heart so tightly I could not breathe.

'"But there was nothing I dared say, nothing I could do. I had to endure in silence.

'"Before we left, we were invited to a very large dinner at the house of a neighbour in the county and, as we were seated, I looked up to see that opposite me, exactly opposite, so that I could not avoid her gaze, was

Clarissa Vigo. She was a remarkably beautiful woman and she was also beautifully dressed. I was not clever at dressing. I wore simple clothes, which Lawrence always preferred, and did not like to stand out. Clarissa stood out and I sat across the table feeling both inferior and afraid. Her eyes kept finding me out, looking over the silver and the flowers, challenging me to meet her gaze. When I did it made me tremble. I have never known such hatred, such malevolence. I tried to ignore it, but she was there, watching, filled with loathing and a terrible sort of power. She knew. She knew that she had power over me, over us. I felt ill that evening, ill with fear.

'"But it passed. She did not speak a word to me. It was over.

'"A week later, we left for our trip to Europe.'

'"I WILL NOT TAKE you step by step with us down through France and the northern part of Italy. We were happy, we were together, and the strains and responsibilities of the past months receded. We could pretend to be a carefree, married couple. But a dark shadow hung over me, and even as I was happy, I dreaded our arrival in Venice. I did not know what would or could happen. Many times, I told myself severely that my fears were groundless and that Clarissa Vigo had no power over either of us.

'"Dr Parmitter, I have read that everyone who visits Venice falls in love with that city, that Venice puts everyone under her spell. Perhaps I was never going to be happy there, because of the painting and of what I had seen, but I was taken aback by how much I disliked it from the moment we arrived. I marvelled at the buildings, the canals and the lagoon. And yet I hated it. It seemed to be a city of corruption and excess, an artificial place, full of darkness and foul odours. I looked over my shoulder. I saw everything as sinister and threatening and, as I did so, I knew that an unbridgeable chasm had opened between Lawrence and myself, for he loved the city, adored it, said he was never happier.

'"I could only follow him and smile and remain silent. The days passed so slowly, and all the time I was in a state of dread. My love for my dear husband had turned to a passionate, fearful clinging desire to possess and keep. I did not want to let him out of my sight, and when he was within it, I looked and looked at him in case I forgot him. How strange that must sound. But it is true. I was possessed by fear.

'"We were to be there for five nights and the blow fell on the third. I fell asleep in the afternoon. I found Venice enervating and my fear exhausting. I could not help myself and, while I slept, Lawrence went out. He liked simply to wander in and out of the squares and over the bridges, looking, enjoying.

'"When I woke he was in the room and smiling with delight. He had bumped into friends, he said. I would never believe it, except that one always did meet everyone one knew in Venice. They lived here for several months of the year, and had a palazzo on the Grand Canal. Tomorrow night, there was a mini-carnival, with a masked ball. They were to go, they would be taking a party. We were to join them. Costumiers would be visited, costumes and masks hired, he had arranged an appointment in an hour's time.'

'"HOW CAN I CONVEY to you the fearfulness of that place? It was a narrow dark shop in one of the innumerable alleyways and reached a long way back. The walls were festooned with costumes, masks and hats, all of them, I was told, traditional to carnivals and balls in Venice for hundreds of years and none of them to me pretty or beautiful or fun, every one sinister and strange. One could dress as a weeping Jew, a satyr, a butcher, a king with his sceptre or a man with a monkey on his shoulder; as a peasant girl with a baby, a street ruffian or a masquerader on stilts; as Pantaloon, Pulcinello or the plague doctor. As a woman I had less choice and Lawrence wanted me to wear silk and lace and taffeta with an ornate, jewelled mask, but I preferred to go as the peasant girl with her child in a basket: I could not have borne to dress up any more elaborately, though I was still obliged to take a mask on its ribboned stick.

'"Lawrence hired a great black cloak and tricorn hat, and his mask was black and covered in mother-of-pearl buttons. He had long shiny boots too. He was thrilled, excited, like a child going off to a party. I was in a fever of dread. I could not prevent my bouts of sudden trembling and I saw that my face was deathly pale. I prayed for the whole thing to come and go quickly, because I somehow felt sure that when it had gone, so would whatever it was that I feared be gone too.

'"It was a hot night and I was nauseated by the smell of the foetid canals, whose slimy black water seemed to me full of all the filth and scum of the city. There were the smells of oil and smoke from the flares and, from street food vendors, smells of hot charred meat and peculiar spices. The ballroom of the palazzo was packed with people and noise and I found it strange and sinister not being able to see faces, not to know if people were old or young or even man or woman. But there was good food and drink and I revived myself by eating fruit and sweetmeats and drinking some sparkling wine, and then I danced with Lawrence and the evening seemed, if not very pleasurable, at least less frightening than I had feared. The time passed.

'"I was almost enjoying myself, almost relaxed, when it was announced that we were to leave the palazzo and go down into the streets, to parade through the squares to the light of flares, watched by the citizens from their windows, joined by passers-by—the whole celebration would move out to become part of the city. Apparently this was usual. The people expected it. There was then a great exodus, a rush and general confusion, during which I became separated from my husband. I found myself pushed along beside a Pulcinello and a priest and a wicked old witch, as we crowded down the great staircase and streamed outside. The torches were flaring. I can see them now, orange and smoking against the night sky. You can see the scene, Dr Parmitter. You have seen it often enough. The light glancing on the dark waters. The waiting gondolas. The crowds pressing forward. The masks. The eyes gleaming. The lights in the other buildings along the Grand Canal. You have seen it all.

'"What happened next I can barely believe or bring myself to tell. You may dismiss it. Any sane person would. I would not believe it. I do not believe it. But I know it to be true.

'"We were outside the palazzo on the landing stage. Some of the crowd had already gone on into the streets on that side of the canal—we could hear the laughter and the cries. People were leaning out of windows now, looking down on us all. The gondolas were lining up waiting to take us out onto the canal, over to the other side, up to the Rialto Bridge . . . Occasionally they bumped together and rocked and the reflection of their lamps also rocked wildly, sickeningly, in the churning water. I was standing a yard or two from Lawrence when suddenly I heard my name called. I turned my head. The strange thing was that I responded even though it was my maiden name I heard. Who here knew my former name? The voice had come from behind me, but when I looked round I saw no one I knew—not everyone was still masked, but every face was strange in one way or another.

'"And then I thought I saw not a face, but only the eyes, of someone I recognised. They were the eyes of Clarissa Vigo, looking out from a white silk mask with silver sequins below a great plume of white feathers. How could I know? I knew.

'"I tried to move through the throng to get closer to her, but someone swung towards me and I had to avoid them or I would have been knocked over. When I looked again the white-masked woman had gone.

'"The gondoliers were crying out and the water was splashing over the wooden landing stage and someone was trying to get me to go on board. I would not go alone, of course; I wanted only to go if my husband would too—and indeed, I would infinitely have preferred not to embark on one of the gondolas and slink off across that dark and sinister water. I drew back and then I started to look for Lawrence. I made my way down the side of the building and over the narrow bridge that led into a square. But the revellers had moved far on. I could not even hear them now, and the cobbled square was in almost total darkness. I retreated and now there was panic in my search. Lawrence was not on the landing stage and I was as certain as I could be that he would never have crossed the canal without me. I thought I should return inside the palazzo and look for him there. I was frightened. I had seen the woman; I had heard her whisper my name. I had dreaded this night, this place, and now I was dry-mouthed with fear.

'"But as I tried to make my way to the open doors of the palazzo, I heard a commotion behind me and then a shout. It was my husband who was shouting to me but I had never heard his voice sound like it. He was shouting in alarm—no, in terror, in horrible fear. I pushed forward and managed to reach the edge of the wooden landing stage. The last gondola laden with revellers was pulling away and I searched it for a glimpse of my husband but there was no one dressed like him. Most of the people had gone. A few stood, apparently uncertain if another gondola would come up and unable to decide if they wanted to go aboard if it did.

'"I went back into the palazzo. The great rooms were deserted apart from some servants who were clearing the last of the feast. I spoke no Italian, but I asked if they had seen my husband and went on asking. They smiled, or gestured, but did not understand. Everyone else had gone.

'"I found my cape and left. I ran through the squares, into the main piazza, ran like a mad, demented creature, calling Lawrence's name. No one was about. A beggar was lying in an alleyway and snarled at me; a dog barked and snapped as I ran past. I reached our hotel in a state of frenzy, yet I was sure there might still be an innocent explanation, that Lawrence would be there, waiting. But he was not. I roused the entire hotel and was in such distress that after pressing a glass of brandy to my lips, the proprietor called the police.

'"Lawrence was never found. I stayed on in Venice for sixteen days beyond the original date for our departure. The police search could hardly have been more thorough but nothing came to light. No one had seen him, no one else had heard his voice that last time. No one remembered anything. It was concluded that he had accidentally slipped into the canal and drowned, but his body was never discovered. He had simply vanished.

'"I returned home. I was in such a state of distress that I fell ill and for two or three weeks the doctors feared for my life. I remember almost nothing of that terrible time but sometimes, in the midst of feverish dreams, I heard my husband crying out, felt that he was just beside me, that if I reached out my hand I could save him. All through this time, something would slide towards my conscious mind but then dodge out of my grasp, as happens when a particular name eludes one. Through feverish days and the storms of my nightmares, it was there, just out of reach.

'"I recovered slowly. I was able to sit up, then to be taken into the garden room to benefit from the sunshine during the afternoon. I asked time and time again for news of Lawrence but there never was any. My mother-in-law was sunk into a profound, silent depression and I barely saw her.

'"And then I discovered, as I was beginning to feel stronger, that I was expecting a child. My husband was the last of the line and the title would have died out with his death—if indeed he were dead. Now, if I had a son, title, estates, house would be secure. I had a reason to live. My mother-in-law rallied too.

'"The nightmares loosened their hold and became strange dreams with only intermittent horrors. But in the middle of one night I woke suddenly, because what had been hovering just out of reach had come cleanly into my mind. It was not a thought or a name, it was an image, and as I recognised it, I felt icy cold. My hands were stiff so that I could hardly move my fingers but I managed to get into my dressing robe, to find the key in my dressing table and to leave my bedroom and make my way slowly down the long, dark, silent corridors of the house. The portraits and sporting prints seemed to loom towards me in the light of the small torch I had brought, for I did not want to switch on any lights and, indeed, did not know where half of the switches might be found.

'"The farther I walked down through this little-used end of the house, the stronger was the image in my mind. I felt ill, I felt weak, I felt afraid, yet I had no choice but to see this dreadful thing through.

'"There were no sounds at all. My slippered feet barely seemed to make any impression on the long runner of carpet down the middle of the corridor. I had a sensation of being watched and not so much followed as accompanied, as if someone were close to my side the whole way, making sure I did not weaken and turn back. Oh, it was a dreadful journey. I shudder when I remember it, as I often, so often, do.

'"I reached the door of the small sitting room and turned the key. It smelled of old furniture and fabrics that had been sealed in against any fresh air and light. But I did not want to be here with only my torch, and when I found the switch, the two lamps, with their thin light, came on and I saw the picture again. And as I saw it, I realised that in the mustiness I could smell something else, a hint of something sharp and distinctive. It took me a second or two to work out that it was fresh oil paint. I looked around everywhere. Perhaps this room was used after all, perhaps one of the servants had been here to repair or repaint something, though I could see no sign of it. Nor were there any painting materials or brushes lying about.

'"I looked at the painting.

'"At first, it seemed exactly as before. It reminded me starkly of that horrible evening and of the masks and costumes, the noise, the smell, the light from the torches and of losing my husband among the crowd. Some of the costumes and masks were familiar but they are traditional, they have been on display on such occasions in Venice for hundreds of years.

'"And then, in a corner, almost hidden in the crowd, I saw the head of someone wearing a white silk mask with white plumes and the eyes of Clarissa

Vigo. It was the eyes that convinced me I was not imagining anything. They were the same staring, brilliant, malevolent eyes, full of hatred but also now with a dreadful gloating in them. They seemed to be both looking straight into me and to be directing me elsewhere. How could eyes look in two places at once?—at me and at . . .

'"I followed them. I saw.

'"Standing up at the back of a gondola was a man wearing a black cloak and a tricorn hat. He was between two other heavily masked figures. One had a hand on his arm, the other was somehow propelling him forwards. The black water was choppy beneath the slightly rocking gondola. The man had his head turned to me. The expression on his face was ghastly to see—it was one of abject terror. He was trying to get away. He was asking to be saved. He did not want to be in the clutches of those others.

'"It was unmistakably a picture of my husband, and the last time I had seen the Venetian painting *it had not been there*—of that I was as sure as I was of my own self. My husband had become someone in a picture painted two hundred years before. I touched the canvas with one finger but it was clean and dry. There was no sign that anything had been painted onto it or changed at all recently and, in any case, I could no longer smell the oil paint that had been so pungent moments before.

'"I was faint with shock and distress, so that I was forced to sit down in that dim little room. I could not explain what had happened, but I knew that an evil force had caused it and knew who was responsible. Yet it made no sense. It still makes no sense.

'"One thing I did know, and it was with a certain relief, was that Lawrence was dead—whether 'buried alive' in this picture or buried in the Grand Canal, he was dead. Until now I had hoped against hope that one day I would receive a message telling me that he had been found alive. Now I knew that no such message could ever come.

'"I remember little more. I must have made my way back to my room and slept, but the next day I woke to the picture before my eyes again and I made myself go back to look at it. Nothing had changed. In such daylight as filtered between the heavy curtains and half-barred windows of the sitting room, which overlooked an inner courtyard, I saw the face of my husband looking out at me, beseeching me to help him."

EIGHT
Theo Parmitter's Story

'She was silent for a long time. I think she had exhausted herself. We sat on opposite one another not speaking, but I felt a closeness of understanding and I wanted to tell her of my own small experiences in the presence of the Venetian picture, of how it often troubled me.

'I was wondering if I should simply get up and make my way to my room, leaving any further conversation until the following day when she would be more refreshed, but then the blue eyes were open and on my face as the Countess said, "I must have that picture," in such a fierce and desperate tone, that I started.

'"I do not understand," I replied, "how it left your hands and eventually came into mine."

'Her old face crumpled and tears came then, softening the glare of those brilliant blue eyes.

'"I am tired," she said. "I must ask you to wait until tomorrow. I do not think I have the strength to tell you any more of this terrible story tonight. But I am spurred on by the thought that it will soon be over and I will be able to rest. It has been a long, long search, and it is almost at an end. It can wait a few more hours."

'I was unsure exactly what she meant but I agreed that she should rest as long as she wished and said that I was at her disposal the next day. She asked me to ring the bell for Stephens, who appeared at once to show me to my room. I took her hand for a moment as she sat, like a bird, deep in the great chair and, on an impulse, lifted it to my lips. It was like kissing a feather.

'I slept badly. The wind blew, rattling the catches every so often, and episodes of the strange story the Countess had told came back to me and I tried hopelessly to work out some rational explanation for it all. I would have dismissed her as old and with a failing mind had it not been for my own experiences with the picture. I was uneasy in that house and her story had disturbed me profoundly. I knew only too well the fierce power of jealousy, which fuels a passion to be avenged. It does not happen very often but when it does and a person has their love rejected and all their future hopes betrayed for another, rage, pride and jealousy are terrible forces and can do immeasurable harm. Who is to say that they could not do even these evil supernatural deeds?

'My own part in all of this was innocent. I had nothing to fear from the jilted woman who, in any case, was presumably long dead. Yet as I lay tossing and turning through that long night, it seemed as if I was indeed being possessed by something unusual—for there grew in me an absolute determination to keep the Venetian picture. Why I should now so desperately want it, I did not know. It had caused me trouble and anxiety. I did not need it. But, just as when I had been approached by the sweating, breathless man after the sale, desperate that I sell it to him for any amount of money I cared to name, I again felt a stubbornness I had never known. I would not sell then, and I would neither sell nor give back the painting to the Countess. I felt almost frightened of my resolution, which made no sense and which seemed to have taken hold of me by dint of some outside force. For of course she had brought me here to ask for the painting. What other reason could there be? She could not have simply wanted to tell her story to a stranger.

'I did not see her until late the following morning and occupied myself by taking a long walk around the very fine parkland and then by enjoying the excellent library. I met no one other than a few groundsmen and maids cleaning the house and the latter scurried away like mice into holes on seeing me. But, a little after eleven, the silken-footed Stephens materialised and told me that coffee and the Countess awaited me in the morning room.

'He led me there. It was a delightful room, furnished in spring yellows and light greens and with long windows onto the gardens, through which the sun was now shining. It is extraordinary how a little sunshine and brightness will lift both the aspect of any room and one's spirits on entering it. My tiredness and staleness from the sleepless night lifted and I was glad to see the old Countess, still looking small and frail but with rather more colour and liveliness.

'I began to make remarks about the grounds, but she cut me short.'

NINE
The Countess's Story

'"There is only a little more to tell. I gave birth to a son, Henry. This family has always alternated the names of the male heirs—Lawrence and Henry, for many generations. All was well. I kept the door of the small sitting room locked and the key, in its turn, locked in my dressing table, and from that first terrible night I did not go into it again.

'"My mother-in-law lived here and my son grew up. Gradually, I became used to my state and to this house being my home—and naturally I adored my only son, who looked so very like his father.

'"At his coming-of-age, we gave a great party—neighbours, tenants, staff. That is traditional. It would have been a happy occasion—had it not been for the arrival, with a party from another house, of the woman Clarissa Vigo. When I set eyes on her . . . well, you may imagine. But one has to be civil. I was not going to spoil my only son's most important day.

'"And so far as I was aware, nothing untoward occurred. The party proceeded. Everyone enjoyed it. My son, a fine young man, took over his duties with pride.

'"But I had reckoned without the powers of evil. On that evening, Clarissa Vigo took my son. I mean that. She took him by force of persuasion, she seduced him, however you wish to describe what happened. He was lost to me and to everything else here. He was under her influence and her sway and he married her.

'"Clearly she had been planning this for years. Within six months of that terrible day, my mother-in-law was dead and I had been dismissed from here, given a small farmhouse on the farthest side of the estate and a few sticks of furniture. I had an inheritance of a personal income from my husband, which could not be taken from me, but otherwise I had nothing. This house was barred to me. I did not see my son. Her reign was absolute. And then the plunder began—things were removed, sold, thrown away and otherwise disposed of: things she did not care for, and without a word of protest from my son. She took charge of everything. She had what she had wanted and schemed for, for so many years. The Venetian picture was among the things she got rid of and I knew nothing of it.

'"The final tragedy came five years later. She and my son went out hunting, as they did almost every day throughout the winter. My husband had never hunted—he loathed field sports, though he allowed shooting of vermin on the estate. He was a gentle man, but she stamped upon any streak of gentleness there may have been in his son. As they jumped a fence in the wood that November day, she fell and was killed outright, and in the crashing fall disturbed a decayed tree, which was uprooted and came down, killing another horseman and injuring my son.

'"He lived, Dr Parmitter. He lived, paralysed in every limb, for seven years. He lived to regret bitterly what he had done, to regret his marriage, to come out from under her possession and to ask me to forgive him. Of course I did so without hesitation and I returned to live here and to care for him until he died.

'"I made it my work to restore the house and everything in it to the way it had been, and to undo every single change she had made, to throw out every hideous modern thing with which she had filled this place. I brought back the servants she had dismissed. It was my single-minded determination to obliterate her from Hawdon and to leave it in as near the state in which I had first seen it as I could. I was helped by the loyal people here, who flocked back, and by friends and neighbours who sought out so many items and brought them back here, over time.

'"But one thing I could never trace. The Venetian picture mattered to me because . . . because my husband was trapped there. My husband lived—lives—within that picture.

'"I sought after it for years," the Countess continued, "and then it was found for me in an auctioneer's catalogue. I commissioned someone to attend the sale and buy it for me no matter what it cost. But as you know, things went wrong at the last minute, you bought it because my representative was not there and you would not sell it to him afterwards. That was your privilege. But I was angry, Dr Parmitter. I was angry and distressed and frustrated. I wanted that picture, my picture, and I have continued to want it for all these years. But you had disappeared. We could not trace the buyer of the picture."

'"No. In those days, I dealt rather a lot and I bid and bought under aliases—all dealers do. The auction houses of course know one's true identity but they never disclose that sort of information."

'"You were Mr Thomas Joiner and Mr Joiner was never to be found. And so the matter rested. Of course I continued to hope, and friends and searchers continued to keep their eyes and ears open, but my picture had vanished together with Mr Joiner."

'"Until you chanced to see my photograph in a magazine."

'"Indeed. I cannot begin to describe to you my feelings on seeing the picture there—the sense of an ending, the realisation that at last, at long last, my husband would in a very real sense return home to me."

'In a macabre comparison, it flashed through my mind that, to the Countess, wanting the picture back was like wanting to receive an urn full of his cremated ashes. Whatever had happened, to her he was as present in the Venetian painting as he would have been in some funereal jar.

'"I invited you here with the greatest of pleasure," she said now. "And I felt that you had every right to hear the full story and to meet me, to see this place. I could have employed some envoy—and hope that it was a more efficient one than the last time—but that was not the way I wanted to bring about a conclusion to this most important business."

'"A conclusion?" I said with feigned innocence. Inside me I could feel determination, that absolute and steadfast steel resolve. It was unlike me. The man you know as Theo Parmitter would most likely have not so much sold back but given back the Venetian painting. But something had possessed me there. I was not the man you knew and know.

'"I mean to have my picture. You may name your price, Dr Parmitter."

'"But it is not for sale."

'"Of course it is for sale. Only a fool would refuse to sell when he could name his price. You have been a dealer in pictures."

'"No longer. The Venetian picture and all the others I have chosen to keep are my permanent collection. I value them quite beyond money. As I said, it is not for sale. I would be happy to provide you with a very good photograph. I would be glad for you to visit me in Cambridge to see it at any time to suit you. But I will never sell."

'Two points of bright colour had appeared on her high cheekbones and two points of brightness in the centre of her already piercing blue eyes. She was sitting upright, straight-backed, her face a white mask of anger.

'"I think that perhaps you do not understand me clearly," she said now. "I will have my picture. I mean it to come to me."

'"Then I am sorry."

'"You do not need it. It means nothing to you. Or only in the sense that it pleases you as a decoration on your wall."

'"No. It means more than that. You must remember that I have had it for some years."

'"That is of no consequence."

'"It is to me."

'There was a long silence, during which she stared at me unflinchingly. Her expression was quite terrifying. She had not struck me in any case as a warm woman, though she had spoken of her sufferings and her feelings and I had sympathised with her. But there was a cold ruthlessness, a passionate single-mindedness about her now that alarmed me.

'"If you do not let me have the picture, you will live to regret your decision, regret it more than you have ever regretted anything."

'"Oh, there is little in my life that I regret, Countess." I kept a tone of lightness and good humour in my voice which I most assuredly did not feel.

'"The picture is better here. It will be quite harmless."

'"How on earth could it be anything else?"

'"You have heard my story."

'I stood up. "I regret that I must leave here today, Countess, and leave without acceding to your request. I found your story interesting and curious and I am grateful to you for your hospitality. I hope you may live out your days in this beautiful spot with the peace of mind you deserve after your sufferings."

'"I will never have peace of mind, never rest, never be content, until the picture is returned to me."

'I turned away. But as I walked towards the door, the Countess said quietly, "And nor will you, Dr Parmitter. Nor will you."

TEN

'You will feel better for having told all this to me,' I said to Theo. He had his head back, his eyes closed, and when he had finished speaking, he had drained his whisky glass and set it down.

It was late. He looked suddenly much older, I thought, but when he opened his eyes again and looked at me there was something new there, an expression of relief. He seemed very calm.

'Thank you, Oliver. I am grateful to you. You have done me more good than you may know.'

I left him with a light heart and took a turn or two around the college court. But tonight, all was quiet and still, there were no shadows, no whisperings, no footsteps, no faces at any lighted windows. No fear.

I slept at once and deeply, and I remember praying, as I dropped down into the soft cushions of oblivion, that Theo would do the same. I thought it most likely.

I WOKE in the small hours of the morning. It was pitch black and silent but, as I came to, I heard the chapel clock strike three. I was sweating and my heart was racing. I had had no nightmares—no dreams of any kind—but I was in a state of abject fear. I got up and drank water and lay down again, but immediately I was seized with the need to go down and check on Theo. The message in my head would not be ignored or dismissed.

I rinsed my head under the cold tap and vigorously rubbed it dry to try to get some grip on myself and think rationally, but I could not. I was terrified for Theo. The story he had told me was vivid in my mind and although unburdening himself of it had clearly eased his mind greatly, I sensed that in some terrible way it was unfinished, that there would be more strange, dark happenings.

I could not rest. I went down the dark staircase and along to Theo's set. I put my head to the door and listened intently but there was no sound at all. I waited, wondering if I should knock, but it was bitterly cold and I had only a thin dressing gown. I turned to go but, as I did so, it occurred to me that Theo might well not lock his door. He was old and unable to move far, and was looked after well by the college. I did not know how he would summon help if he were ill and could not reach the telephone.

I reached out my hand to try the door. As I touched it, there was a harsh and horrible cry from within, followed by a single, loud crash.

I turned the knob and found that the door was indeed unlocked. I pushed my way in and switched on the lights.

Theo was lying on his back in the entrance to the sitting room, in his nightclothes. His face was twisted slightly to the left, his mouth looked as if he were about to speak. His eyes were wide open and staring and they had in them a look I will never forget to my dying day: a look of such horror, such terror, such appalled realisation and recognition that it was dreadful to see. I knelt down and touched him. There was no breath, no pulse. He was dead. For a second, I assumed that the crash I had heard was of his own fall, but then I saw that on the floor, a few yards away from him, the Venetian picture lay. The wire, which I knew had been strong and firm the previous evening, was intact, the hook on the wall in its place. Nothing had snapped or broken, and Theo had not knocked against it—he had not reached it before he fell.

There were two things I knew I had to do. Obviously, I had to call the lodge, wake the college, set the usual business in motion. But before I did that, I had to do another thing: I dreaded it but I also felt I owed this last favour to my old tutor; I had to find out. I lifted up the picture and took it into the study, where I propped it on the bookcase and turned the lamp directly onto it.

I drew in my breath and looked at the picture, knowing what I would find there.

But I did not. I searched every inch of that canvas. I looked at every face, in the crowd, in the gondolas, in the windows, in corners, down alleyways barely visible. There was no Theo. No face remotely resembled his. I saw the young man I took to be the Countess's young husband, and the figure in the white silk mask with the plume of white feathers which I supposed was Clarissa Vigo. But of Theo, thank God, thank God, there was no image. In all probability, he had woken, felt unwell, got up and had his fatal stroke or heart attack. In crashing to the ground, he had shaken floor and walls—he was a heavy man—and the picture had been disturbed and fallen also.

Breaking out into a sweat again, but this time of relief, I went to the telephone on Theo's desk and dialled the night porter.

IT WAS a desperately sad few days and I missed Theo greatly. The college chapel was packed for his funeral, the oration was one of the best I had ever heard, and afterwards everyone spoke fondly of him. I was still shocked, my mind still full of our last hours together. From time to time, one thing came to my mind to trouble me: I was pretty sure that Theo's death had nothing to do with the story he had told me, with the Venetian picture. Yet I could not forget the look on his dead face, the horrified expression in his eyes, the way his arm was outstretched. The picture had fallen, and although there was a perfectly sensible explanation for that, it worried me.

I left Cambridge with a heavy heart. I would never again sit in those rooms, talking over a fire and a whisky, hearing his sound views on so many subjects, his humorous asides and his sharp, but never cruel, comments on his fellows. But I could not remain sad or troubled for long. I had work to get back to but, even more, I had Anne.

I had told Theo in the first few minutes after my arrival that I was engaged to be married to Anne Fernleigh—not a fellow scholar in medieval English but a barrister—beautiful, accomplished and fun, a few years younger than I was. The perfect wife. Theo had wished me well and asked that I take her to meet him soon. I had said that I would. And now I could not. It cast a shadow. Of course, one wants two people one cares for to meet and to care for one another in turn.

I had told her of Theo's death, of course—the reason that I had stayed on longer than planned—and now, as we sat in her flat after a good dinner, I told her in turn the story of the Venetian picture and of the old Countess.

She listened intently but, at the end, smiled and said, 'I'm sorry I won't meet your old tutor for I have a feeling I would have liked him, but I can't say I'm sorry not to be meeting the picture. It sounds horrible.'

'It's rather fine, actually.'

'Not the art—I'm sure you may be right. The story. The whole business of . . .' She shuddered.

'It's a tale. A good one, but just a tale. It needn't trouble you.'

'It troubled him.'

'Oh, not so very much. It was a story he wanted to tell over a whisky and a good fire on a cold night. Forget it. We've more important things to discuss. I have something I want to ask you.'

Since Theo's sudden death, I had had one thought: I do not know why, but it seemed very important to me that instead of marrying the following summer, planning everything in a leisurely way and making a fuss of it, we should marry now, straight away.

'I know it will mean we marry quietly, without all the razzmatazz, and perhaps that will disappoint you. But I don't want us to wait. Theo's death made me realise that we should seize life—and he was a lonely man, you know. No family other than a Cambridge college. Oh, he was contented enough but he was lonely and a college full of strangers, however warmly disposed, is not a wife and children.'

To my surprise, Anne said she had no problem at all about giving up plans for a lavish wedding and being married quietly, with just our family and closest friends, as soon as it could be arranged.

'It isn't the money you spend and the fuss you make—a marriage is about other things that are far more serious and lasting. Think of that poor old Countess—think of the wretched other woman. We are very fortunate. We should never forget it.'

I never would. I never will. I could not have been happier and I had a good feeling that Theo would have agreed and approved. I felt his benign presence hovering about us as we made our preparations.

The only hesitation I had was when Anne determined that, even though work meant we could not now take the long honeymoon in Kenya that we had planned, we should manage a long weekend away. She asked if we might spend it in Venice.

'I went once when I was fourteen,' she said, 'and I sensed something magical but I was too young to know what it was—I think one can be too young for Venice.'

'Well perhaps we should save it for a longer visit in that case,' I said, 'and go down to the south of France.'

'No, it won't be warm enough there yet. Venice. Please?'

I SHOOK OFF any forebodings and made the booking. Superstitions and stories were not going to cast their long shadow over the first days of our marriage and I realised that in fact I was greatly looking forward to visiting the city again. Venice is magical. Venice is like nowhere else, in the real world or the worlds of invention.

I remembered the first time I visited it, as a young man taking a few months out to travel, and emerging from the railway station to that astonishing sight—streets that were water. The first ride on the vaporetto down the Grand Canal. The first glimpse of San Giorgio Maggiore rising out of the mist. The first sight of the pigeons rising like a ghostly cloud above the cathedral in St Mark's Square, and of those spires touched with gold and gleaming in the sun. Walks through squares where all you heard were the sounds of footsteps on stone because there were no motor vehicles, hours spent at café tables on the quiet Giudecca, the cry of the fish sellers in the early morning, the graceful arch of the Rialto Bridge, the faces of the locals with those memorable, ancient Venetian features—the prominent nose, the hauteur of expression, the red hair.

The more I thought about the city, the more my pulse quickened with the anticipation of seeing it again, and this time with Anne. Venice filled my dreams and was there when I woke. I found myself searching out books about the city—the novels by Henry James and Edith Wharton and others that caught the moods so vividly. Once or twice, I thought about Theo's picture and its strange story, but now I was merely intrigued, wondering where the tale had originated and how long ago. When we got back, I meant to look up Hawdon and the Countess's family. Perhaps we would even take a few days in Yorkshire later in the year. The real settings of stories always hold a fascination.

Anne and I were married two weeks later, on a day of brilliant, warm sunshine—surely a good omen. We had a celebratory lunch with our families and a couple of friends—I wished Theo could have been there—and by late afternoon, we were en route for our honeymoon in Venice.

ELEVEN

To give myself something to do while I wait here, I write what I am beginning to fear must be the end of this story. I can barely hold the pen. I am writing to give myself something to do in these long and dreadful hours when all hope is lost and yet I still must hope, for once hope is extinguished, there is nothing else left.

I am sitting in the room of our hotel. I write and I do not understand what I am writing or why but they say that a fear, like a nightmare, +written down is exorcised. Writing should calm me as I wait. When I stop writing, I pace up and down the room, before returning to this small table in front of the window. The telephone is at my right hand. Any moment, any moment now, it will ring with the news I am desperate to hear.

How do I describe what happened? How to explain something for which there is no explanation? I can as soon convey the pain I am feeling.

But I must, I have to. I cannot let the story remain unfinished or I shall go mad. For now it is my story, mine and Anne's; we have somehow become a part of this horrible nightmare.

We had been less than twenty-four hours in the city when Anne discovered that there was, as there so often is, a festival in honour of one of Venice's hundreds of saints, with a procession, fireworks, dancing in the square.

I said that we would go but that I was adamant that if there was to be any dressing-up, any tradition of wearing masks, we would not join in. I did not believe in Theo's story and yet it, together with the strange things that had happened to me in Cambridge and his subsequent death, had made me anxious and suspicious. It was irrational but I felt that I needed to stay on the side of good luck, not court the bad.

The first hour or two of the festival was tremendous fun. The streets were full of people on their way to join the procession; the shops had some sort of special cakes baking and the smell filled the night air. There were drummers and dancers and people playing pipes on every corner, and many of the balconies had flags and garlands hanging from them. I am trying to remember how it felt to be light-hearted, full of happiness, walking through the city with Anne, such a short time ago.

St Mark's Square was thronged and there was music coming from every side. We walked along the Riva degli Schiavoni and back, moving slowly with the long procession and, as we returned, the fireworks began over the water, lighting the sky and the canal in greens and blues, reds and gold. Showers of crystals and silver and gold dust shot up into the air; the rockets soared. It was spectacular.

We walked along the canal, in and out of the alleys and squares, until we came down a walk between high buildings again to a spot facing the bridge.

The jetty was thronged with people. All of those who had been processing must have been there and we were pushed and jostled by people trying to get to the front beside the canal, where the gondolas were lined up waiting to take people to the festivities on the opposite bank. The fireworks were still exploding in all directions so that every few minutes there was a collective sigh of wonder from the crowd. And then I noticed that some of them were wearing the costumes of the carnival: the old woman, the fortune teller, the doctor, the barber, the man with the monkey, Pulcinello and Death with his scythe mingled among us, their faces concealed by low hats and masks and paint, eyes gleaming. I was suddenly stricken with panic. I had not meant to be here. I wanted to leave urgently, to go back to our quiet square. I turned to Anne.

But she was not at my side. Somehow, she had been hidden from me by the crowd. I pushed my way urgently between bodies, calling her name. I turned to see if she was behind me. And as I turned, the blood stopped in my veins. My heart itself seemed to cease beating. My mouth was dry and my tongue felt swollen and I could not speak Anne's name.

I glimpsed, a yard or two away, a figure wearing a white silk mask studded with sequins and with a white plume of feathers. I caught her eyes, dark and huge and full of hatred.

I struggled to my left, towards the alleyway, away from the water, away from the gondolas rocking and swaying, away from the masks and the figures and the brilliant lights of the fireworks that kept exploding and cascading down again towards the dark water. I lost sight of the woman and when I looked back again she had gone.

I ran then, ran and ran, calling out to Anne, shouting for help, screaming in the end as I searched frantically through all the twists and turns of Venice for my wife.

I came back to the hotel. I alerted the police. I was forced to wait to give them Anne's description. They said that visitors to Venice get lost every day, especially in a crowd, that until it was daylight they had little hope of finding her but that she would be most likely to return here on her own, or perhaps in the care of someone local, that perhaps she had fallen or become ill. They tried to reassure me. They left, telling me to wait here for Anne.

But I cannot wait. I have to leave this wretched story and go out again; I will go mad unless I find her. Because I saw the woman, the woman in the white silk mask with the white plumes, the woman in the story, the woman desperate for revenge. I believe in her now. I have seen. Why she would want to harm Anne I have no idea, but she is a destroyer of happiness, one whose desire to haunt and hurt even death cannot stop.

I will do whatever is necessary—and perhaps I am the only person who can—to put an end to it all.

TWELVE
Anne's Story

It is left to me, Anne, to end this story. Will there be an ending? Oh, there has to be, there must. Such evil surely cannot retain its power for ever?

In the crowd of people on the landing stage beside the water, I had felt myself at first jostled and pushed by a number of people who were trying to surge forward—indeed, I feared for a child at the very edge of the canal and pulled her away in case she fell in. I almost lost my own balance, but I felt a hand on my arm, helping me to right myself. The only unnerving thing was that the hand gripped me so hard it was painful and I had to wrench myself to get away. I caught a glimpse of someone, of a malevolent glance that made me shudder, and saw a hand reach out again towards me. But then I was being taken along by the crowd trying to go in the opposite direction, away from the water, and I let myself go with them, up the narrow walk between the high houses and onto one of the bridges over a side canal.

The procession re-formed, a band began to play and we were all walking together to the music, towards the Rialto and over it and on and on, and I felt myself caught up in the scene, laughing and clapping and occasionally looking back at the fireworks still bursting into the night sky. It was exhilarating, it was fun. I was unaware of where we were walking but felt quite happy, confident that, in a short time, I would separate myself from the others and turn back.

But for one reason or another I did not and then we were far away, the band still playing, children banging toy drums, through streets, across bridges, into squares. The Venice I knew was left far behind. And then I slipped on an uneven stretch of the pavement and fell, and in doing so, put my weight on my arm. I heard a crack and felt the pain. I let out a cry. Someone stopped. Someone else shouted. People bent over me. I was surrounded, helped, and everyone was jabbering in fast Italian that I could not understand. I was suddenly and violently sick and the sky whirled and then it was coming down on my head.

There is little else to tell. I was taken into a nearby house and a doctor was fetched. I had not, he decided, broken my arm; I had bruised it badly and cut my hand, and they looked after me very kindly. I was bandaged and given painkillers and an injection against infections. By now, it was two in the morning and I wrote down and gave to one of those looking after me my name and the telephone number of the hotel. But I felt nauseous again and the doctor insisted that I should lie down and sleep, that everything would be done. I would be moved the next morning.

I did sleep. The pain in my arm and hand did not wake me for some hours, and by then I was feeling better in myself and able to drink some good strong coffee and eat a soft bread roll with butter.

What happened next made me laugh. I wonder, when I will laugh again?

I was coaxed into a wheelchair belonging to the grandmother of the family and trundled through the streets of Venice in the morning sunshine, my bandaged arm resting proudly on my lap, back to our hotel and my husband.

Except that Oliver was not there. He had gone out to search for me again, they said; he had slipped past the night porter in the early hours, distraught. At first, no one reported having seen him but, later that day, the police, who had switched from looking for me to looking for him with some irritation towards accident-prone visitors, told me that a gondolier, up early to wash out his craft, reported having seen a man answering to Oliver's description. He had been walking between two men who had their hands on his arms and seemed to be making him get into another gondola, farther up the jetty, against his will. I dismissed this, saying that it could not have been Oliver. Oliver would have been alone.

The police took it more seriously but could see no reason at all, if it had been Oliver with the two men, why he should have been taken anywhere against his will. He did not look rich, our hotel was not one of the grandest, his wallet was still in the room, and the watch he always wore was a plain steel one without great value.

I did not buy any theories of kidnap, ransom or the Mafia. The Italian police seem obsessed with all three but I knew they were far from the mark.

I knew. I know.

I read the story Oliver had left. I read everything twice, slowly and carefully; I crawled over it, if you like, looking for a message, an explanation.

I CAME BACK to London alone. That was a fortnight ago. Nothing happened. There was no news. In the first few days the Venetian police telephoned me. The inspector spoke good English.

'Signora, we have revised our opinion. This man the *gondoliere* saw with the others . . . we think it is not probable to be your husband, after all. Our theory is now, he slip and fall into the Grande Canale. He was out in the dark; the ground there is often wet.'

'But you would have found his body?'

'Not yet, not found yet. But yes, the body will be washed up later or sooner and we will call you at once.'

'Will I have to come to identify him?'

'*Si*. I am very sorry but yes, it is necessary.'

I thanked him and then I wept. I wept until my body ached, my throat was sore and I had no tears left. And I dreaded having to travel back to Venice to see Oliver's dead—drowned—body, when the time came.

I decided I must go back to work, if only in the office. I must have something to occupy my mind and it was a relief to sit reading through complex, dry, legal phraseology for hours at a time. If my thoughts turned to Venice, the black filthy waters of the Grand Canal, the next flight I would take there, I went out and walked for miles through London, trying to tire myself out.

Two days ago, I had walked from Lincoln's Inn back to our flat. My arm still ached a little and I thought I would take some strong painkillers and try to sleep. The phone was switched through to my office, and when I left there, to my mobile, so I knew I had not missed a call from the police.

The porter in our mansion block told me that he had taken in a parcel and put it upstairs, outside the door. I was not expecting anything and it was with some distress that I saw the label addressed to Oliver. Taped to the outside of the parcel was an envelope—the whole had been delivered by courier.

I took it inside, took off my coat and riffled through the other post, which was of no interest. There was nothing for Oliver.

And so I peeled the envelope from the parcel and opened it. I did not believe, by then, you see, that Oliver would ever return to open it. Oliver was dead. Drowned. Before long I would see that, with my own eyes.

The letter was from a firm of solicitors in Cambridge. It enclosed a cheque for a thousand pounds, left to Oliver by his old tutor, Theo, 'to buy himself a present'. I had to wipe the tears from my eyes before reading on, to learn that the letter came with an item that Dr Parmitter had also left to Oliver in his will.

It is very strange, but, as I began to cut off the brown paper, I had no idea as to what the item could possibly be. I should have known, of course I should. I should have taken the whole package, unopened, down to the incinerator and burned it, or taken a knife and slashed it to shreds.

Instead, I simply undid the last of the wrapping paper and looked down at the Venetian picture.

And as I did so, as my heart contracted and my fingers became numb, I smelled, quite unmistakably, the faintest smell of fresh oil paint.

Then, I began the frantic search for my husband.

He was not hard to find. Behind the crowd in their masks and cloaks and tricorn hats, behind the gleaming canal and the rocking gondolas and the flaring torches, I saw the dark alley leading away, and the backs of two large men, heavy and broad-shouldered, cloaked in black, their hands on a man's arms, gripping them. The man was turning his head to look back and to look out, beyond the world of the picture, to look at me, and his expression was one of terror and of dread. His eyes were begging and imploring me to find him, follow him, rescue him. Get him back.

But it was too late. He was like the others. He had turned into a picture. It took me a little longer to find the woman and then it was only the smallest image, almost hidden in one corner, the gleam of white silk, the sparkle of a sequin, the edge of a white-plumed feather. But she was there. Her arm was outstretched, her finger pointed in Oliver's direction, but her eyes were looking, like his, at me, directly at me, in hideous triumph.

I dropped into a chair before my legs gave way. I had only one hope left. That by taking Oliver, as she had taken the others, surely, surely to God the woman had satisfied her desire for revenge. Who is left? What more can she do? Has she not done enough?

I do not know. I will not know, though I cannot say 'never'. I will live with this fear, this dread, during all the years ahead until the child I have learned I am expecting, grows up. All I do now is pray—and it is always the same prayer—a foolish prayer, of course, since the die is already cast.

I pray that I will not have a son.

SUSAN HILL

Born: Scarborough, February 5, 1942
Home: Suffolk
Website: www.susan-hill.com

RD: You grew up in Scarborough. Do you have any memories that are especially evocative of that time?

SH: The sea, the sea, the sea! The beautiful coastline. Of being an only child, so inventing imaginary companions when I wasn't at school.

RD: Your first novel, *The Enclosure*, written when you were in the sixth form at grammar school in Coventry, was published in 1961. What was your reaction, and did it change you, or your ambitions?

SH: It will sound boastful but I wasn't surprised. I knew the only thing I could do and wanted to do was write and I just believed the story would be published. I was far more surprised and excited at that point about getting a place to read English at King's College, London. It didn't change my ambitions, it just confirmed them.

RD: When you were in London, you met many famous literary figures like T.S. Eliot and W.H. Auden. Do you have any strong recollections of them?

SH: Auden, how gracious he was to a young writer—asked me to sit next to him on the floor and we talked . . . T.S.Eliot, how incredibly happy he seemed with his then fairly new second wife . . . and how they both looked *exactly* like their photos, which is rare.

RD: After graduation, you went to work as the books page editor for Coventry's local newspaper. Did you enjoy that? And why were you sacked?

SH: I enjoyed it, but I only did it because I needed a job while I was writing a new book. It was very, very good professional experience though, working to a deadline and an exact length. It stood me in good stead for the next forty-odd years of reviewing. I was sacked just because a new editor came in. New broom, swept clean. I wasn't the only one.

RD: Is it true that you were first drawn to Suffolk, where you now live, because of composer Benjamin Britten's work, and that you often went to his home town of Aldeburgh for weeks at a time in the winter to do your writing?

SH: Absolutely. I would never have heard of Aldeburgh had it not been for B.B., whose imaginative world influenced mine so much. I owe him everything.

RD: How did you first meet your husband, Shakespeare professor Stanley Wells? And was it love at first sight, or at first meeting?

SH: No to the last. He grew on me. We met at someone's dinner . . . A bit of match-making, I suspect.

RD: And you now have two daughters, one of whom is at college in America. How do you feel about the prospect of them leaving home?

SH: The elder one left when she was eighteen, really. She's now married. She had been at boarding school, and after that they never really live at home. The younger one is reading for a degree at Queen Mary College, London, but got a scholarship from there to do her second year at Berkeley [University of California]. She is there now. It's strange without her but they come back . . . And I love the house to myself and less washing.

RD: Was there anything in particular that inspired *The Man in the Picture*? Maybe a painting of Venice?

SH: No. Nothing. It just came into my head. The best stories always do.

RD: Your most famous ghost story is, of course, *The Woman in Black*, which is still running as a play in London's West End. And you've written others. What attracts you to the supernatural? And have you ever seen a ghost, or had any strange, inexplicable experiences yourself?

SH: Writing novels is, par excellence, telling stories—or should be. The rest comes second. The ghost story form is a great one for a writer as it depends on atmosphere, which I have always loved creating. No, I've never seen a ghost. Yes, experiences, but more spiritual than ghostly, and I wouldn't want to talk about them.

RD: You recently started a writing course on your website and it has already attracted over a thousand would-be writers. What was your motivation?

SH: My own small publishing company, Long Barn Books, gets so many manuscripts from writers who, with a lot of help, could produce something good. I also looked at writing-course syllabuses and they seemed dull, samey, and were all trotting out similar statements as though they were fact—when they are not. I felt a lot of people were being misled and, after forty-five years, I think I have some things to teach and can explode a lot of pretentious myths. I don't do pretentious.

RD: Can you come up with three adjectives that describe you?

SH: Laid back (not an adjective!). Warm. Direct.

RD: And who, alive or dead, would you invite to dinner if you could?

SH: Virginia Woolf. J.K. Rowling. Stephen Fry. Prince Charles. Dickens. Sarah Brown (i.e. Mrs Gordon). All at once would be fun.

JOSEPH
FINDER

POWER PLAY

Jake Landry, a middle manager at
troubled Hammond Aerospace, is a taciturn guy
with a gift for keeping his head down.
When he receives an unexpected invitation
to join a retreat for high-ranking executives
in the backwoods of British Columbia,
he resigns himself to a week of
grinding tedium.
And then, suddenly, all hell
breaks loose.

Prologue

If you've never killed someone, you really can't imagine what it's like. You don't want to know. It leaves you with something hard and leaden in the pit of your stomach, something that never dissolves.

Most people, I'm convinced, just aren't wired to take a human life. I'm not talking about some sniper with a thousand-yard stare. I'm talking about normal people.

I remember reading once how during World War II maybe 85 per cent of the soldiers never even fired at the enemy. These were heroes, not cowards, yet they couldn't bring themselves to aim at a fellow human being and pull the trigger.

I understand that now.

But what if you don't have a choice?

I was standing at the end of a splintery wooden dock in the pale moonlight, the turbulent ocean at my back, blue-black and flecked with grey foam. On either side of me was rock-strewn beach.

And right in front of me, a man was pointing a gun at me, a matt black SIG-Sauer 9mm.

'Boy, you're full of surprises, aren't you?' he said.

I just looked at him.

He shook his head slowly. 'Nowhere to run, you know.'

He was right, of course. There really was nowhere to run. There was nowhere to swim, either.

I took a long, slow breath. 'Who says I want to run?'

I could smell the seaweed, the tang of salt in the air, the rot of dead fish.

'Just put your hands up, Jake,' he said, 'and come back inside. I don't want to hurt you. I really don't.'

I was surprised he knew my name, and I was even more surprised by the gentleness in his voice, almost an intimacy.

I didn't answer, didn't move.

'Come on, now, let's go,' he said. 'Hands up, Jake, and you won't get hurt. I promise.' The crash of the waves on the shore was so loud I had to strain to make out his words.

I nodded, but I knew he was lying. My eyes strayed to the left, and then I saw the crumpled body on the sand. I felt my chest constrict. I knew he'd killed the guy, and that if it were up to him, I'd be next. It wasn't up to him, though.

I don't want to do this, I thought. *Don't make me do this*.

He saw my eyes move. There was no point in trying to stall for time any more: he knew what I'd just seen. And he knew I didn't believe him.

Don't make me kill you.

'Jake,' he said, in his lulling, reasonable voice. 'You see, you really don't have a choice.'

'No,' I agreed, and I felt that hard lump forming in the pit of my stomach. 'I really don't.'

Chapter 1

'We got trouble.'

I recognised Zoë's voice, but I didn't turn round from my computer. I was too absorbed in a news report on the website AviationNow.com. A competitor's new plane had crashed a couple of days ago, at the Paris Air Show. My boss was there and so I'd heard all about it. At least no one was killed.

And at least it wasn't one of ours.

I picked up my big black coffee mug—THE HAMMOND SKYCRUISER: THE FUTURE OF FLIGHT—and took a sip. The coffee was cold and bitter.

'You hear me, Landry? This is serious.'

I swivelled slowly round in my chair. Zoë Robichaux was my boss's admin. She had dyed copper hair and a ghostly pallor. She was in her mid-twenties and did a lot of club-hopping. If the dress code at Hammond allowed, I suspected she'd have worn studded black leather every day, black fingernail polish, probably got everything pierced.

'Mike called. From Mumbai.'

'What's he doing in India? He told me he'd be back in the office today for a couple of hours before he leaves for the offsite.'

'Yeah, well, Eurospatiale's losing orders all over the place since their plane crashed.'

'So Mike's lined up meetings at Air India instead of coming back here,' I said. 'Nice of him to tell me.'

Mike Zorn was an executive vice-president and the programme manager in charge of building our brand-new wide-bodied passenger jet, the H-880, which we called the SkyCruiser. Four VPs and hundreds of people reported to him. But Mike was always selling the hell out of the 880, which meant he was out of the office far more than he was in.

So he'd hired a chief assistant—me—to make sure everything ran smoothly. Crack the whip if necessary. His jack-of-all-trades and UN translator, since I have enough of an engineering background to talk to the engineers in their own geeky language, and can talk finance with the money people, as well as talk to the shop-floor guys in the assembly plant who distrust the lardasses who sit in the office revising and revising the damned drawings.

Zoë looked uneasy. 'Sorry, he wanted me to tell you, but I kind of forgot. Anyway, the point is, he wants you to get over to Fab.'

The fabrication plant was the enormous factory where we were building part of the SkyCruiser. 'Why?' I said. 'What's going on?'

'I didn't quite get it, but the head QA guy found something wrong with the vertical tail. And he just, like, shut down the whole production line.'

I groaned. 'That's got to be Marty Kluza.' The lead Quality Assurance inspector was a famous pain in the butt. But he'd been at Hammond for fifteen years, and he was awfully good at his job, and if he wouldn't let a part leave the factory, there was usually a good reason for it.

'I don't know. Anyway, like everyone at headquarters is totally freaking, and Mike wants you to deal with it. Now.'

I RACED OVER in my Jeep. The fabrication plant was only a five-minute walk from the office building, but it was so immense—a quarter of a mile long—you could spend twenty minutes walking round to the right entrance.

Whenever I walked across the factory floor—I came here maybe every couple of weeks—I was awestruck by the sheer scale. It was an enormous hangar big enough to contain ten football fields. The vaulted ceiling was 100 feet high. There were miles of catwalks and crane rails.

The place was like the set of some futuristic sci-fi movie. There were more machines than people. Robotic fork-lifts zoomed around silently, carrying huge pallets of equipment and parts in their jaws. The autoclave, basically a pressure cooker, was 30 feet in diameter and 100 feet long. The automated tape layers were as tall as two men, with spidery legs like the extraterrestrial creature in *Alien*, extruding yards of shiny black tape.

Visitors were always surprised by how quiet it was here. That's because we rarely used metal any more—no more clanging and riveting. The SkyCruiser, you see, was 80 per cent plastic. Well, not plastic, really. We used composites—layers of carbon-fibre tape soaked in epoxy glue, then baked at high temperature and pressure. Like Boeing and Airbus and Eurospatiale, we used as much composite as we could get away with because it's a lot lighter than metal, and the lighter a plane is, the less fuel it's going to use. Everyone likes to save money on fuel.

Also like Boeing and the others, we don't really build our own planes any more. We mostly assemble them from parts built all over the world.

But here in Fab, we made exactly one part of the SkyCruiser: an incredibly important part called the vertical stabiliser—what you'd call the tail.

One of them was suspended from a gantry crane and surrounded by scaffolding. And underneath it I found Martin Kluza, moving a handheld device slowly along the black skin. Kluza was heavyset, around fifty, with a pink face and a small white goatee on his double chin. He looked up with an expression of annoyance.

'What's this, I get the kid? Where's Mike?'

'Out of town, so you get me. Your lucky day.'

'Oh, great.' He liked to give me a hard time.

'Hey,' I shot back at him, 'didn't you once tell me I was the smartest guy in the SkyCruiser Programme?'

'Correction: excluding myself,' Marty said.

'I stand corrected. So I hear we've got a problem.'

'I believe the word is "catastrophe". Check this out.' He led me over to a video display terminal on a rolling cart, tapped quickly at the keys. A green blob danced across the screen, then a jagged red line slashed through it.

'See that red line?' he said. 'That's the bond line between the skin and the spars, OK? About a quarter of an inch in.'

'Cool,' I said. 'Looks like you got a disbond, huh?'

'That's not a disbond,' he said. 'It's a kissing bond.'

'Kissing bond,' I said. 'Gotta love that phrase.' That referred to when two pieces of composite were right next to each other, no space between, but weren't stuck together.

'I put one of them through a shake-table vibe test to check out the flutter and the flex/rigid dynamics, and that's when I discovered a discrepancy in the frequency signature.'

'If you're trying to snow me with all this technical gobbledegook, it's not going to work.'

He looked at me sternly for a few seconds, then realised I was giving him attitude right back. 'We're going to have to scrap every single one.'

'You can't do that, Marty.'

'You want these vertical stabilisers flying apart at thirty-five thousand feet with three hundred people aboard? I don't think so.'

'There's no fix?'

'If I could figure out where the defect is, yeah. But I can't.'

'Maybe they were overbaked? Or underbaked?'

'Landry.'

'Contaminants?'

'Landry, you could eat off the floor here.'

'Maybe you got a bad lot of Hexocyte.' That was the epoxy adhesive film they used to bond the composite skin to the understructure.

'The supplier's got a perfect record on that.'

'Will you scan this bar code? I want to check the inventory log.' I handed him a tag I'd taken from a roll of Hexocyte adhesive film. He took it over to another console, scanned it. The screen filled up with a series of dates and temperatures.

I walked over to the screen and studied it for a minute or so.

'Marty,' I said, 'I'm going to take a walk down to Shipping and Receiving.'

'You're wasting your time,' he said.

I FOUND THE SHIPPING CLERK smoking a cigarette in the outside loading area. He was a kid around twenty, with a wispy blond beard. He wore Oakley mirrored sunglasses, baggy jeans and a black T-shirt that said NO FEAR.

The kid looked like he couldn't decide whether he wanted to be surfer dude or gangsta. I felt for him. During the eighteen months I'd once spent in juvie—the Glenview Residential Center in upstate New York—I'd known kids far tougher than he was pretending to be.

'You Kevin?' I said, introducing myself.

'Sorry, dude, I didn't know you weren't supposed to smoke back here.' He threw his cigarette to the asphalt and stamped it out.

'I don't care about that. You signed for this shipment of Hexocyte on Friday at one thirty-six.' I showed him a print-out of the log with his signature. He took off his sunglasses, studied it with a dense, incurious expression.

'Yeah, so?'

'You left early last Friday afternoon?'

'But my boss said it was cool!' he protested. 'Me and my buddies went down to Topanga to do some shredding—'

'It rained all weekend.'

'Friday it was looking awesome, dude—'

'You signed for it and you pulled the temperature recorder and logged it in, like you're supposed to. But you didn't put it in the freezer, did you?'

He looked at me for a few seconds.

'You picked a lousy weekend to screw up, Kevin. Heat and humidity—they just kill this stuff. There's a reason it's shipped packed in dry ice, right from the Hexocyte factory to here. That's also why they ship it with a temperature sensor, so the customer knows it was kept cold from the minute it left the factory. That's an entire week's work down the tubes. Dude.'

The sullen diffidence had suddenly vanished. 'Oh, shit.'

'Do you know what would have happened if Marty Kluza hadn't caught the defect? We might have built six planes with defective tails. And you have any idea what happens to a plane if the tail comes apart in flight?'

'Oh, shit, man. Oh, shit.'

'Don't ever let this happen again.' My cellphone started ringing.

He gave me a confused look. 'You're not telling my boss?'

'No. He'd fire you. But I'm thinking that you'll never forget this as long as you live. Am I right?'

Tears came to the kid's eyes. 'Listen, dude—'

I turned away and answered my cell.

It was Zoë. 'Hank Bodine wants to see you.'

'Hank Bodine?'

Bodine, an executive vice-president of Hammond Aerospace and the president of the Commercial Airplanes Division, was not just my boss. He was, to be precise, my boss's boss's boss. 'What for?'

'How the hell do I know, Landry? Gloria, his admin, just called. He says he wants to see you now. It's important.'

'But—I don't even have a tie.'

'Yeah, you do,' she said. 'In your bottom drawer. It's in there with all those packages of instant ramen noodles. Now you'd better move it.'

I'D MET HANK BODINE a number of times, but I'd never actually been to his office, on the top floor of the Hammond Tower in downtown Los Angeles. Usually I saw him when he came out to El Segundo, where I worked.

I waited outside Bodine's office for a good twenty minutes, flipping through old copies of *Aviation Week & Space Technology*. I kept adjusting my rumpled tie and thinking how stupid it looked with my denim shirt and jeans. Everyone here at Hammond world headquarters was wearing a suit.

Finally, Bodine's admin, Gloria Morales, showed me in to Bodine's office, a vast expanse of chrome and glass.

He didn't get up to shake my hand or anything. He sat in a high-backed leather desk chair behind the huge slab of glass that served as his desk. There was nothing on it except for a row of scale models of all the great Hammond aeroplanes—the wide-bodied 818, the best-selling 808, the flop that was the 828, and of course my plane, the 880.

Bodine was around sixty, with silver hair, deep-set eyes beneath heavy black brows, a high forehead, a big square jaw. If you'd met him only briefly, you might call him distinguished-looking. Spend more than two minutes with him, though, and you'd realise he was a bully—a big, swaggering man with a sharp tongue who was given to explosive tirades.

Bodine leaned back, folding his arms, as I sat in one of the low chairs in front of his desk. I'm not short—just over six foot—but I found myself looking up at him as if he were Darth Vader. I had a feeling the set-up was one of Bodine's tricks to intimidate his visitors. Sunlight blazed in through the floor-to-ceiling glass behind him so I could barely make out his face.

'What's the holdup at Fab?'

'A bonding problem in the vertical stabiliser,' I said. 'It's taken care of.'

Was that why I was here? I braced myself for a barrage of questions, but he just nodded. 'OK. Pack your bags. You're going to Canada.'

'Canada?' I said.

'The offsite. The company jet's leaving from Van Nuys in five hours.'

'I don't understand.' The annual leadership retreat, at some famously luxurious fishing lodge in British Columbia, was only for the top guys at Hammond—the twelve or so members of the 'leadership team'.

'Yeah, well, sorry about the short notice, but there you have it. Should be plenty of time for you to pack a suitcase. Make sure you bring outdoor gear. Don't tell me you're not the outdoors type.'

'I do OK. But why me?'

His eyes bored into me. 'Jesus Christ, guy, didn't you hear about the Eurospatiale disaster?'

The crash at the Paris Air Show, he meant. 'What about it?'

'Right in the middle of the aerial demonstration, the pilot was forced to make an emergency crash landing. An inboard flap ripped off a wing and landed smack-dab on the runway at Le Bourget near Mr Deepak Gupta, the chairman and managing director of Air India. Almost killed the guy.'

'OK.' That I hadn't heard.

'Mr Gupta didn't even wait for the plane to crash,' he went on. 'Pulled out his mobile phone and called Mike and said he was about to cancel his order for thirty-four Eurospatiale E-336 planes. Wanted to talk business as soon as the show was over.'

'That's about eight billion dollars' worth of business,' I said, nodding.

'Right. I told Mike not to leave Mumbai until he gets Mr Gupta's signature on the letter of intent. I don't care how sick of curry he gets.'

'OK.'

He pointed at me with a big, meaty index finger. 'Lemme tell you something. It wasn't just one damned E-336 that crashed at Le Bourget. It was Eurospatiale's whole programme. And Air India's just the first penny to drop. This is a no-brainer.'

'OK, but the offsite—'

'Cheryl wants someone who can talk knowledgeably about the 880.'

Cheryl Tobin was our new CEO and his boss. She was the first female CEO in the sixty-year history of Hammond Aerospace and, in fact, our first female top executive. She'd been named to the job four months before, after the legendary James Rawlings had dropped dead on the golf course at Pebble Beach. Bodine must have been as stunned as everyone else when the board of directors voted to hire not just an outsider—from Boeing, our biggest competitor—but a woman. Ouch. Because everyone thought the next CEO was going to be Hank Bodine.

'But there's plenty of others who can.' Granted, I probably knew more about the plane than anyone else in the company. But that didn't make any difference: I wasn't a member of the executive team. I was a peon.

Bodine came forward in his chair, his eyes lasering into mine. 'You're right. But Cheryl wanted you. Any idea why that might be?'

'I've never talked to Cheryl Tobin in my life,' I said. 'She doesn't even know who I am.'

'Well, for some reason, you've been asked to go. It's not optional.'

'Then I'm flattered to be invited.' A long weekend in a remote lodge in British Columbia with the twelve or thirteen top executives of Hammond Aerospace? I would have preferred a root canal. Anaesthesia optional.

His phone buzzed, and he picked it up. 'Yeah. I'm on my way,' he said into the mouthpiece. He stood up. 'Walk with me. I'm late for a meeting.'

He bounded out of his office with the stride of an ex-athlete—he'd played football at Purdue years ago, I'd heard—and I lengthened mine to keep up.

'One more thing,' he said. 'Before we reach the lodge, I want you to find out why that plane crashed in Paris. I want Mike to have every last bit of ammo we can get to trash Eurospatiale and sell some SkyCruisers.'

The executive corridor was hushed and carpeted, the walls mahogany and lined with vintage aeroplane blueprints in black frames.

'I doubt I can call Eurospatiale and ask them, Hank.'

'Are you always this insubordinate?'

'Only with people I'm trying to impress.'

He laughed once, a seal's bark. 'You're ballsy. I like that.'

We stopped right outside the executive conference room. I sneaked a glance inside. One entire side of the room was a floor-to-ceiling window overlooking downtown LA. Ten or twelve people were sitting in tall leather chairs at a huge O-shaped conference table made of burnished black wood. The only woman among them was Cheryl Tobin, an attractive blonde in her early fifties wearing a crisp lavender suit with crisp white lapels.

Bodine looked down at me. He was a good four inches taller than me and probably seventy pounds heavier. He narrowed his eyes. 'I'll be honest with you. You weren't my choice to fill in for Mike. Cheryl's going to ask you all sorts of questions about the SkyCruiser. And I just want to make sure you're going to give her the right answers.'

I nodded. *The right answers*. What the hell did that mean?

'Look, I don't want any trouble from you this weekend. We clear?'

'Of course.'

'Good,' he said, putting his hand on my shoulder. 'Just keep your head down and stay in your own lane, and everything should work out OK.'

I wondered what he was talking about, what kind of 'trouble' he was referring to.

Then again, I don't think Hank Bodine had any idea, either.

RIGHT AFTER LEAVING Hank Bodine's office, I drove the twenty miles to my apartment in El Segundo to grab some clothes. I don't travel much for work but my dog, Gerty, understood at once what the black suitcase meant. She put her head down between her paws with a stricken, panicked look.

When I broke up with Ali a year or so ago, the first thing I did was get a dog. I went to the animal shelter and adopted a golden retriever. For no good reason I named her Gertrude. Gerty for short.

Gerty was all skin and bones when she first moved in, but she was beautiful, and she took to me right away. She was also sort of a headcase: she followed me everywhere I went in the apartment, couldn't be more than two or three feet away at any time. She'd follow me into the bathroom if I didn't close the door. Gerty was needy, and extremely clingy, but no more so than some of the women I'd gone out with since Alison Hillman.

Sometimes I wondered whether her last owner had abandoned her because she was so clingy or whether she got that way because she'd been abandoned.

'Chill,' I said.

Dogs are underrated as girlfriend-substitutes, I think. Gerty never complained when I came home late from work. She didn't mind eating the same thing day after day. And she never asked me if I thought she looked fat.

I didn't know what to pack. 'Outdoor gear', Hank Bodine had said, whatever that meant. I collected a couple of pairs of jeans, my old hunting jacket, a pair of boots. Then I looked up the resort online, saw how high-end it was, and threw in a pair of khakis and a fancy pair of shoes for dinner, just in case. I changed into a blazer and tie to wear on the corporate jet.

Then there was the question of what to do with Gerty for the four days I'd be gone. I called a bunch of my friends, who all begged off. They knew about Gerty.

This could be a major problem, I realised, because I really didn't want to board Gerty at a kennel. I glanced at my watch, realised I had about two hours before I had to be at Van Nuys Airport. Just enough time to race over to the office and download the latest files on the 880 and try to find out what caused the crash of the Eurospatiale plane in Paris.

As long as I got Hank Bodine what he wanted, I figured, everything would go fine.

Chapter 2

On the short drive over to the office, I kept thinking about that strange meeting with Hank Bodine. Why had the CEO of the Hammond Aerospace Corporation put me on the 'guest list' for the offsite? She didn't even know who I was.

And what trouble was Bodine afraid I might cause? If he wanted to make sure I gave her the 'right answers', then what were the wrong ones?

As soon as I got to my cubicle, I ploughed through my emails while copying files onto a flash drive. One was from the Office of the CEO, concerning the importance of ethics and 'a culture of accountability' at Hammond. I saved that one to read later. Meaning: probably never.

Zoë was watching me. 'So what'd Bodine want?'

'He told me I'm going to the offsite in Canada.'

'Get out! For what, to carry their luggage?'

I gave her a look, then went back to copying files. 'Cheryl Tobin specifically requested me,' I said with a straight face. 'To stand in for Mike.'

'Uh-huh. Like she even knows who you are.'

'Not by name, exactly,' I admitted. 'She wanted someone who could talk knowledgeably about the 880.'

'And you're the best they could come up with?'

This was why Zoë and I got along so well. Since she worked for Mike, not for me, she could pretty much say whatever she wanted to me without fear of getting fired.

'Don't you have work to do?' I said.

'So you actually agreed to do it.'

I gave her another look. 'Think I had a choice? It wasn't a request. It was an order. So, I gotta ask you a huge favour.'

She looked at me warily.

'Would you mind taking my dog?' I said.

'Gerty? I'd love to. It's like rent-a-dog. I get a dog for a couple of days, then return it when it stops being fun.'

'You're the best.' I handed her the keys to my apartment. 'One more favour?'

Her look was suspicious.

'Bodine wants to know how the Eurospatiale crash happened.'

'The wing fell off or something.'

'A little piece of the wing, Zoë, called the inboard flap. The question is, why? It's a brand-new plane.'

'You want *me* to find out?'

'Email some of the journalists on the good aviation websites—ask them if they've heard anything. Rumours, whatever—stuff they might not have reported. And try to grab some photos. There were a bunch of photographers in the crowd taking pictures of the aerial demo. I'll bet you when that piece hit the tarmac, someone shot some close-ups.'

'Why does Bodine care?'

'He says he wants Mike to have all the dirt on Eurospatiale he can get.'

'When do you need it? By the time you get back from Canada?'

'Actually, Bodine wants the info before we get there.'

'That doesn't give me much time, Landry. Mike needs me to do a spreadsheet for him. I could get to it in a couple of hours.'

'That should work if there's Internet access on the company plane.'

'There is. Just make sure you do it before you get to the lodge.'

'Why?'

'The place is off the grid. No cellphones, no BlackBerrys, no email, nothing. It's so remote they don't have land-line phones. And Cheryl's not even letting anyone use the Internet or the manager's satellite phone. She wants everyone to be offline.'

'Sounds great to me. But those guys are all going to go apeshit.'

'And you're actually going to have to talk to them.'

'Not if I can help it.'

'You don't get it, do you? That's the whole *point* of these stupid offsites. Team-building and morale-building exercises and outdoor sports. It's all about breaking down barriers and getting people who don't like each other to become friends.'

Going kayaking together was supposed to make all those supercompetitive EVPs into friends? 'Somehow I don't think it's going to make Bodine like Cheryl Tobin any better.'

Zoë gave me a long, cryptic look, then moved closer. 'Listen, Jake. Not to be repeated, OK?'

'OK.'

'So, there's this chick, Sophie, works in Corporate Security?'

'Yeah?'

'I ran into her at a club on North Vine last night, and she told me she'd just finished doing this top-secret job for the general counsel's office.'

She paused, as if unsure whether to keep going. I nodded, said, 'OK.'

'Going into people's email accounts,' she continued, 'and archiving their email and sending it to some law firm in Washington, DC.'

'For what?'

'She didn't know. They just told her to do it. She knew it meant something serious was going on. Some kind of witch hunt, maybe.'

'Everyone's email?'

She shook her head. 'Just a few of the top officers.' She waited a few seconds. 'Including Hank Bodine.'

'Really?' That *was* interesting. 'You think Cheryl Tobin ordered it?'

'Wouldn't surprise me.'

I thought for a few seconds. I'd heard that one of the reasons the board of directors had brought in an outsider to run Hammond was to clean house. There were all sorts of rumours of corruption, of bribes and slush funds. But to be honest, our business is sort of known for that. 'No wonder Bodine wanted to know if I was a buddy of Cheryl Tobin's.'

'If I were you, I'd be careful,' Zoë said. 'Four days of all that face time with the corporate bigwigs, I'm afraid you might speak your mind and lose your job. Those guys aren't going to take crap from you.'

'No?'

'No. You may know dogs, Landry, but you don't know the first thing about wolves. It's a dominance thing.'

AS I CRUISED DOWN the 405 Freeway to Van Nuys, making unusually good time, a police cruiser came out of nowhere: blue strobe lights whirling, siren whooping. My stomach clenched. *Damn it, was I speeding?*

But then the cop raced on past me, chasing down some other poor sucker, leaving me with only an afterimage burnt on my retina and a memory of a time I rarely thought about any more.

THE COURT OFFICIAL took me into the courtroom in handcuffs.

I wore a white button-down dress shirt, which was too big on me—sixteen years old, lanky, not yet broad-shouldered—and the label made my neck itch. The official, a squat, potbellied man, took me over to the long wooden table next to the public defender who'd been assigned to me. He waited until I sat down before he removed the cuffs.

The courtroom was stuffy and overheated, smelt of perspiration and cleaning fluid. I glanced at the attorney, a well-meaning woman with a tangle of frizzy brown hair. She gave me a quick, sympathetic look that told me she wasn't hopeful.

My heart was pounding. The judge was a black woman who wore tortoise-shell reading glasses on a chain round her neck. She was whispering to the clerk. I stared at the nameplate in front of her: THE HONOURABLE FLORENCE ALTON-WILLIAMS.

Finally, the judge turned towards me, peered over her half glasses. She cleared her throat. 'Mr Landry,' she said. 'There's a Cherokee legend about a young man who keeps getting into trouble because of his aggressive tendencies. The young man goes to see his grandfather, and says, "Sometimes I feel such anger that I can't stop myself." And his grandfather, who's a wise tribal elder, says, "I used to be the same way. You see, inside of you are two wolves. One is kind and peaceful, and the other is mean and angry. The mean wolf is always fighting the good wolf." The boy thought for a moment, then said, "But, Grandfather, which wolf will win?" And the old man said, "The one you feed."'

She picked up a manila folder, flipped it open. A minute went by. My mouth had gone dry, and I was finding it hard to swallow.

'Mr Landry, I have found you guilty of criminally negligent homicide.' The public defender next to me inhaled slowly. 'You should thank your lucky stars that you weren't tried as an adult. I'm remanding you to a limited-secure residential facility—that is, juvenile detention—for eighteen months. And I can only hope that by the time you've completed your sentence, you'll have learned which wolf to feed.'

HAMMOND AEROSPACE had four corporate jets, all of which were kept at the company's own hangar at Van Nuys Airport, about twenty-five miles northwest of downtown LA. It was farther from Hammond headquarters than LAX, but since it didn't service commercial flights it was quicker and easier to get into and out of.

Not that I'd ever flown on a corporate jet before—whenever I travelled for work, I flew commercial. The company planes were only for the elite.

I parked my Jeep in front of the low-slung terminal building and grabbed my suitcase from the back. The jet was parked on the tarmac, very close by.

This was the biggest and fanciest plane in our corporate fleet, a brand-new Hammond Business Jet with the Hammond logo painted on the tail. It glinted in the sun as if it had just been washed. It was a thing of beauty.

No one had told me where I was supposed to go when I got to the airport. But I could see, through the plate-glass windows of our 'executive terminal', a cluster of guys who looked like Hammond execs, so I wheeled my suitcase up to the building and walked in.

The passenger lounge was designed to resemble a 1930s airport, with marble-tiled floors and leather couches. It reminded me of one of those fancy airport 'clubs' for first-class passengers, the kind of place you sometimes catch a fleeting glimpse of as you trundle by. Out there in the overcrowded airport, you're dodging speeding electric passenger carts and being jostled on the moving walkway, while inside the Ambassador's Club or the Emperor's Club well-dressed passengers are clinking flutes of champagne and scarfing down beluga on toast points.

I looked around. There were ten or so men here. They all resembled one another. Their ages ranged from early forties to maybe sixty, but they all looked vigorously middle-aged, virile and prosperous. They had a certain gladiatorial swagger.

Also, unlike me, none of them was wearing a tie. Or even a blazer. They were all dressed casually—cargo shorts or trousers, golf shirts, Patagonia shells, North Face performance tees. Brand names all over the place.

I sure hadn't received the memo.

A couple of them were wandering around, talking to themselves, wearing Bluetooth earpieces. Hank Bodine was standing near the entrance talking to someone I didn't recognise.

Since he was the only one here I knew, I figured I should go up to him and say hi. I couldn't help feeling like the new kid in grade school, peering around the cafeteria at lunch, holding my tray, looking for a familiar face so I could sit down. The same way I'd felt when I'd arrived at Glenview, when I was sixteen.

So I left my suitcase near the door and tentatively approached Bodine. 'Hey, Hank,' I said.

Before he had a chance to reply, a tall, wiry guy came up and clapped him on the shoulder. This was Kevin Bross, the EVP of Sales in the

Commercial Airplanes Division. He had a long, narrow face and a nose that looked like it had been broken a few times. Probably playing football: Bross was another Big Ten football jock—he'd played at Michigan State.

'There he is,' Bross said to Hank Bodine.

Bross didn't even seem to notice me standing there. 'You read that bull-shit email Cheryl sent around this morning?' he said in a low voice. 'All that crap about "guiding principles" and "a culture of accountability"?' I couldn't believe he was dissing the CEO so brazenly.

Bodine smiled, shook his head, unreadable. 'Guess we didn't have any guiding principles before. You know Jake Landry?'

'How's it going?' Bross said without interest. He gave me a quick, perfunctory glance before turning back to Bodine. 'Where's Hugo?'

'He should be here any second,' Bodine said. 'Flying in from DC.'

'So Cheryl didn't fire him yet, huh?'

'Cheryl's not going to fire Hugo,' Bodine said quietly. 'Though by the time she gets done with him, he'll probably *wish* he got fired.'

I knew they were talking about Hugo Lummis, the senior VP of Hammond's Washington Operations. In plain English, he was our chief lobbyist on Capitol Hill. Before Hammond hired him, he'd been a deputy secretary of defence under George W. Bush, and before that he'd been chief of staff for some important Republican congressman. He was on back-slapping terms with just about everyone in Congress who counted.

There were rumours around the company that he'd done something funky, possibly illegal, to land Hammond a big Air Force contract a few months ago. Now I wondered whether that was why Zoë's friend from Corporate Security had been ordered to search through Bodine's emails.

'She's just gonna let him twist slowly in the wind, huh?' Bross said.

Bodine leaned close to Bross and spoke in a low voice. 'What I hear, she's hired one of those big Washington law firms to do an internal corporate investigation.'

Bross stared. 'You're joking.'

Bodine just looked back.

I was sort of embarrassed to be standing there listening to their conversation. But I guessed that, to these guys, I was just some functionary so far down the totem pole I might as well have been below ground.

My cellphone rang. I took it out of my pocket and excused myself, though the two men barely realised I was leaving.

'Hey,' Zoë said. 'You having fun yet? Are you talking to anyone, or are you standing by yourself, too proud to hang with your superiors?'

'You got something for me, Zoë?' I had stepped outside the terminal building and was standing in the sun, admiring the gleaming Hammond plane.

'I just talked to a reporter from *Aviation Daily* about that plane crash. He said a composites problem caused the whatchamacallit to break off.'

'The inboard flap. What kind of composites problem, did he say? A joint?' I felt the sunshine warm my face.

'Do I look like an engineer to you? I can't even figure out my TiVo. Anyway, I took notes and put it in an email to you. I also attached some close-up shots of that piece of the wing.'

'Great, Zo. I'll download them after we board. Thanks.'

'*De nada*. Oh, and the *Aviation Daily* guy also told me that Singapore Airlines just cancelled their deal with Eurospatiale. Like, they totally freaked out over the crash.'

'Really?' That was a major contract. Almost as big as the Air India deal. 'Is that public information?'

'Not yet. The reporter just got the news himself, and he's about to put it on their website. You're, like, fifteen minutes ahead of the curve.'

'Hank Bodine's gonna squeal like a pig in a mud bath.'

'Hey, Jake, you know—you might want to tell him the good news yourself, start sucking up to all the big dogs. Especially since you're about to spend a long weekend with them.'

'OK, I'll break the news to Bodine. And thanks again. I owe you one.'

'One?' Zoë said. 'One *squared*, more like.'

'That's still one, Zoë.'

'Whatever.'

I clicked off and headed back inside.

A BIG, ROTUND bald man with jug-handle ears pushed through the glass doors of the terminal right in front of me. Someone called out to him, and he replied in a booming voice with a Southern accent, erupting in a big, rolling laugh. He started hailing people as if this was a frat party. His double chin jiggled. He wore a silvery-grey golf shirt stretched tight over a pot-belly.

This had to be the famous Hugo Lummis, our chief lobbyist. The man Cheryl Tobin was hanging out to dry, according to Kevin Bross.

He went right up to Bodine and Bross. Lummis checked his watch, a huge, extravagant-looking silver thing. Then Bross checked his watch, too, gold, just as big. They seemed to be concerned about the time, which I didn't quite get. Who cared what time we got to the offsite?

As I came over to Bodine's rat pack, Bross, who had a klaxon voice you could pretty much hear anywhere, said, 'IWC Destriero.'

Lummis rumbled something, and Bross went on, 'World's most complicated wristwatch. Seven hundred and fifty mechanical parts, seventy-six rubies. Perpetual calendar with day, month, year, decade and century.'

So they were comparing wristwatches. 'In case you forget which century you're living in, that it?' Lummis shot back.

'The moon-phase display is the most precise ever made,' Bross said.

'Excuse me,' I said. I tried to catch Bodine's eye, but he didn't see.

'How the hell can you tell the time on that thing?' Bodine said. 'I just want to know what time we're going to leave already.'

'No one's going anywhere until Cheryl shows up,' Lummis said. 'I guess she's gotta be fashionably late, being the CEO and all.'

'Nah,' said Bross, 'women are always running late. Like my wife—it's always hurry up and wait.'

Bodine was smiling faintly, neither joining in their mocking nor disapproving of it. 'Well, the plane's not gonna leave till she gets here,' he said.

Hugo Lummis noticed me, and said, 'We about ready to leave?'

'I—I don't know.'

He squinted at me, then guffawed. 'Sorry, young man, I thought you were a flight attendant.' The men around him laughed, too. 'It's the tie.'

I stuck out my hand. 'Jake Landry,' I said. 'And I'm not a pilot, either.'

He shook my hand, without introducing himself. 'You a new hire?'

'I work for Mike Zorn.'

'Cheryl wanted an expert on the 880,' Bodine explained.

'Hell, I've got *haemorrhoids* older than him,' Lummis said to the others, then added to me, mock-sternly, 'Remember, young fella, what happens in

Rivers Inlet stays in Rivers Inlet.' Everyone laughed uproariously, as if this were some kind of inside joke.

'Hank,' I finally said to Bodine. 'Singapore Airlines is in play.'

It took him a minute to realise I was talking to him, but then his eyes narrowed. 'Excellent. *Excellent*. How do you know this?'

'Guy at *Aviation Daily*.'

He nodded, rubbed his hands together briskly.

By then they were all staring at me. Kevin Bross said, 'They had eighteen 336s on order from Eurospatiale. That's five billion dollars up for grabs.'

Bodine said to Bross, 'Call George in Tokyo and tell him to touch skin with Japan Air and All Nippon. This is our big chance. A no-brainer. Get to 'em with a bid before the other guys move in.'

George Easter was the senior vice-president for Asia-Pacific Sales.

Bross nodded, then whipped out a handheld from its holster, a quick-draw BlackBerry cowboy. The tall EVP for Sales (Commercial) punched in numbers as he turned away.

I was about to tell Bodine about the suspected cause of the crash, but then I decided to read Zoë's email first so I'd know what I was talking about.

'Let's get this show on the road,' Bodine muttered, while Bross talked on his cell loud enough for everyone to hear. 'There's billions to be made in the next couple of weeks, and she's got us playing games in the woods.'

'Speak of the she-devil,' Lummis said, and we all turned to the door.

Cheryl Tobin, wearing the same lavender suit I'd seen her in earlier, entered the lounge. She bestowed a beatific smile on the assembled.

Right behind her came another woman, who I assumed was her administrative assistant. An elegant, auburn-haired beauty in a navy polo shirt and khaki slacks, holding a clipboard and moving with a dancer's grace.

It took me a few seconds to realise that I knew her. I drew a sharp breath.

Ali Hillman.

SHE DIDN'T SEE ME. She was immersed in conversation with Cheryl Tobin as the two of them swept into the room, parting a Red Sea of middle-aged men. An electric force field seemed to surround them, crackling and radiating through the room. Like it or not, this was the boss.

And—what?—her assistant? When we had been going out she worked in HR. Was she working for the CEO now? If so, when had this happened?

I felt the electrical charge, too, but of a different sort. It was the voltage generated by all sorts of little switches going off in my brain, circuits closing, thoughts colliding. We had gone out for a year and a half, and then sort of out of the blue she had initiated the breakup. She said she wasn't angry or anything, she just thought it was for the best. We wanted different things, that was all. 'Sometimes I think there's something frozen inside you, Landry,' she had said.

A month or so after the breakup I saw her in an Irish bar in downtown LA with some tall, good-looking guy, but since then I hadn't seen her in ages. I just assumed she was still a rising executive in HR.

I wish I could say I'd moved on to the next woman without looking back. The truth is, I knew that if I allowed myself to mope or obsess, I'd never get over her. I wasn't sure I ever would anyway.

And now Ali was working with, or for, Cheryl—you could tell from the body language—and she was probably going on the offsite, too.

For a moment it felt as if I were inside a freeze-frame: I couldn't hear or see anyone around me except for Ali.

I knew now who'd put me on the guest list for the offsite. One mystery solved. But it only created a new one. Why?

Yet before I could go up to her, she was gone. She said something to Cheryl and, holding a cellphone to her ear, disappeared down a corridor.

I heard Bodine mutter to Bross, 'Notice she said no staff, no assistants. Yet she brought one of hers.'

Cheryl worked the room like a master politician. She circulated among the twelve or so guys, smiling and touching them on the shoulder in a way that was warm but not too intimate.

Most of the men responded the way you'd expect. They gave her smiles that were too wide and too bright. They tried to suck up without being too transparent about it.

Not all of the guys, though. Hank Bodine's little clique seemed to be making a point of ignoring her. Kevin Bross said something under his breath to Bodine, who nodded. Then Bross turned and headed towards Cheryl. Not right towards her, but meandering in her general direction. As he got close, she must have said something—I couldn't hear—because he turned and smiled right at her.

'I admired your email this morning,' he said loudly.

Bodine and Lummis were watching the exchange from across the room.

I could see Cheryl's pleased smile. She said something else.

'No, I was really impressed,' Bross said. 'People need to be reminded about the culture of accountability. We all do.'

Cheryl smiled and touched his shoulder. Bross gave a sort of embarrassed smile. Then he turned and looked at Bodine and winked.

NOT UNTIL we all began boarding the plane did Ali see me.

She was at the top of the metal stairs leading into the jet, just behind Cheryl Tobin, as I started to climb the steps. She turned round and her eyes raked mine. Then, abruptly, she looked away.

'Ali?' I said.

But she entered the cabin without turning back.

Chapter 3

By the time I boarded, Ali was nowhere to be found, and I was left feeling as if I'd been kicked in the solar plexus. Or someplace a little lower.

She'd seen me, no question about that. And whether she'd put me on the guest list or not, she had to know I'd be here.

Why, then, the cold shoulder?

I assumed she'd gone off to work in the CEO's private lounge. It took all the restraint I could summon to keep from walking down there and asking her what was going on.

Instead, I took a seat in the main salon. Most of the seats were taken by the time I got there, but I found a chair off by itself, next to where Hank Bodine was holding court with Hugo Lummis, Kevin Bross and another guy I didn't know. I was close enough to hear them talking but I'd sort of lost interest in hearing them compare watches, as fun as that was, so I tuned out.

Anyway, my mind had been derailed. As much as I tried not to, I couldn't stop thinking about Ali. Seeing her after so long, I was like a parched man lost in the desert for weeks who'd just been given a thimbleful of water. My thirst hadn't been slaked; it had been whetted.

I thought about Ali, presumably sitting with Cheryl Tobin in the executive lounge, which included a private office, bedroom suite, exercise studio and a personal kitchen. Even among the superprivileged who got to fly on private corporate jets, there was first class. I loved that. You finally claw your way to the top only to find there's still one more rung above you.

The rest of us weren't exactly in steerage, though. The walls of the main salon were panelled in Brazilian mahogany. The floors were covered with antique-looking Oriental rugs. Huge, cushy, black leather club chairs were arranged in little 'conversation groups' around marble-topped tables. There was a burlwood stand-alone bar.

My chair swivelled and tilted. All around me was wide-open space. There was no seat six inches in front of mine that would tip back into my knees. Very nice. I could get used to this.

The Hammond Business Jet was far and away the best on the market, with the widest body and the largest cabin of any private corporate jet. Even configured as luxuriously as it was, it easily held twenty-five people.

The pitch we used to convince companies to spend fifty million bucks for one of our planes was that it wasn't simply a means of transportation. Oh, no. It was a productivity tool. It allowed an executive to make good use of his travel time. And a relaxed and refreshed executive could seal a deal much more effectively than his travel-worn counterpart.

Yeah, right. You can justify any obscene luxury on the grounds of productivity, I've found.

I took out my laptop and powered it on. I had to download the files Zoë had sent so I could try to get Bodine the answers he wanted—but I was finding it hard to concentrate.

I logged on to my email, opened Zoë's message and read it over twice. Then I opened the zipped folder containing eight high-resolution close-ups of the Eurospatiale crash. They were big files and took a while to download.

Meanwhile, I could hear Hugo Lummis saying to the others, in his booming

Southern accent: 'Uh-uh, no, *sir*. So I'm having dinner at Café Milano with the Secretary of the Air Force just last week, and he keeps talking about "the Great White Arab Tribe" and I finally say to him, "What in God's name are you talking about?" And he says, "Oh, that's just our nickname for *Boeing*." So how does Cheryl think we're supposed to compete with that kinda favouritism if we *don't* grease the skids a little?'

I looked at him, without meaning to, and Kevin Bross noticed my glance. He made a subtle hand gesture, and Lummis's voice died down.

After a while, I started smelling cigar smoke, and I looked over and saw Bodine and Lummis smoking a couple of big ugly stogies. Thick white tendrils of smoke wreathed their heads.

Two beautiful blonde flight attendants were circulating with trays of little Pellegrino bottles, taking drink orders.

When one of them finally came over to me, I decided to order a Scotch. Seeing Ali had set me back, I realised; I needed a drink.

Just then, someone made an announcement over the speakers that we'd be taking off shortly and asked us politely to fasten our seat belts. The idling engines roared to life—two Rolls-Royce Trent 1000 turbofan engines—and we began the takeoff roll. Seventy-five thousand pounds of thrust lifted us off the ground; but for all that power, you could barely hear any noise. This baby could go Mach 0.89, and even when it was cruising at max speed it was so solidly built that nothing ever squeaked or rattled.

I learned to fly when I was in college, wanted to be a pilot but was disqualified because my vision wasn't totally perfect. But at least I got to work with planes, and when I'm a passenger on a well-built plane, I'm always watching and listening, noticing things most people don't.

Once we started our ascent I turned back to my laptop and began studying the photos Zoë had sent. Something caught my attention and I enlarged the photo to the full size of my computer screen, then zoomed in on one small area of the picture. A piece of the plane's wing was lying on the asphalt. The inboard flap, I could tell right away.

I zoomed in still closer. I could see where the aluminium hinge had ripped out. It was pretty dramatic-looking, and sort of surprising, too.

The wings and the wing flaps on the Eurospatiale E-336 were made out of composite materials, just like our own SkyCruiser. But the hinges that attach the flaps to the wings are made of a high-grade 7075 aluminium.

And somehow those aluminium hinges had just ripped clean off the wing flap. How, I had no idea. I needed to do some research.

My Scotch arrived, in a cut-glass crystal tumbler on a silver tray, with a dish of warm mixed nuts. Next to it was a small envelope made from very thick, expensive-looking stock. It was blank on the outside. Inside was a note on matching paper. I recognised the handwriting at once. It said simply:

Landry—

Please come to the executive lounge as soon as you get this.

BE SUBTLE—A

I closed my laptop and got right up.

THE INNER SANCTUM—the CEO's private lounge—was even more opulent than the main salon.

The walls here were panelled in a rich, antique wood, though I knew they had to be veneers, since real wainscoting would be too heavy. The antique cabinets looked like family heirlooms (though not my family, of course, whose oldest piece of furniture had been Dad's BarcaLounger). A flat-screen TV hung on one wall, tuned to CNBC. In a corner was a steel-clad galley kitchen with an espresso machine.

And sunk down in the middle of one of the overstuffed couches, facing the door, was Ali. She was reading a folder, but she put it down when I entered.

'Landry.'

'There you are,' I said, as casually as I could manage, walking up to her. 'A private summons, huh? And I thought you'd forgotten who I was.'

'I'm so sorry about that. I really am. It's just really important for us to be discreet.' She got up off the sofa and put her arms round me. She had to stand on tiptoes to do it. 'Hey, I've missed you.'

'Me, too.'

If I was perplexed before, by this time I was totally confused. She looked even more beautiful. Ali was petite and slender—people tended to call her 'perky' or 'spunky', words she hated, because she thought they were all basically synonyms for 'short'. When we were going out, she wore her hair short. Now it was long and flowing, down to her shoulders. She'd done something to her eyebrows, too, made them sort of arched. She wore glossy lipstick. The old Ali didn't wear much make-up; she didn't need it. She was like a tomboy who'd grown up. The new Ali was willowy, elegant, polished.

I liked the old Ali better, even if the new one was more striking.

'You look good,' I said.

'Thanks. I like your jacket.'

'You got it for me.'

'I remember.'

'It's the only decent blazer I own.'

'No argument there. You did have the worst clothes.'

'I haven't changed.'

'That doesn't surprise me, Landry. You never liked change.'

'That hasn't changed either,' I said.

She smiled. She thought I was kidding.

'What's going on?' I said. 'You don't want these guys to figure out we used to be involved, is that it?'

'Yes. Sit down, Landry. We need to talk.'

'Words a guy never wants to hear.'

She didn't laugh. She didn't seem in a light-hearted mood. 'It's important,' she said.

I sat next to her on the couch.

'How long have you been working for Cheryl Tobin?' I said.

'Since about a month after she started. So, almost three months.'

'How'd that happen? I thought you were in HR.'

'Only we call it People now,' she said. 'Cheryl heard about how I brought in this fancy new information-systems programme to keep track of payroll and benefits, and she invited me to her office to talk. We just hit it off. She asked me to be her executive assistant in charge of Internal Governance, Internal Audit and Ethics.'

I could understand why Cheryl Tobin would have been impressed by Ali. She had what my dad used to call a 'smart mouth', only when it came from him, it wasn't a compliment. She was quick-witted; her mind cycled a lot faster than most. As a guy who tends to be better at listening than at speaking,

I always admired her ability to express herself at such lightning speed.

'Last time I checked, we already have an Office of Internal Governance.' I was never sure what the Office of Internal Governance did exactly—check that all the company procedures are followed, maybe.

'Sure. And an Office of Internal Audit. But she wanted me to directly oversee them.'

'Meaning she didn't trust them to do their job right without supervision.'

'You said it, not me.'

I nodded. She smelt great. She always smelt great. At least her perfume hadn't changed—something by Clinique, I remembered.

'Where's your boss?' I said.

She pointed at a set of leather-covered double doors a few feet away. Cheryl's private office, I assumed. 'On a call.'

'You like working for her?'

'I do.'

'Would you tell me if you didn't?'

'Landry,' she said. She tipped her head to one side, an expression I knew well, which meant: *How can you even ask?*

Ali never lied to me. I don't think she even knew how to be less than honest. Which was another thing I liked about her. 'Sorry.'

'If I didn't like it, I wouldn't do it,' she said. 'Cheryl's one of the most impressive women I've ever met. One of the most impressive *people* I've ever met. I think she's amazing.'

I wasn't going to ask her at that point if her boss was really as much of a bitch as everyone said. Probably wasn't the best time.

'And yes, I know how all these guys talk about her.' She waved in the general direction of the main salon. 'You think she doesn't know?'

'They're probably freaked out by having a woman running the show for the first time,' I said. 'Plus, they're nervous they'll get canned, too.'

She lowered her voice, leaned in closer to me. 'What makes you think she has that power? The board of directors won't let her fire any more vice-presidents without consulting them. Believe me, those guys know that.'

'You're kidding.'

'After her first round of management changes, riots almost broke out on the thirty-third floor. Hank Bodine went to one of his buddies on the board and had a little talk, and the board met in emergency session to limit her hiring-and-firing authority. It's outrageous.'

'If Bodine has so many buddies on the board, why didn't they make him CEO instead of her?'

She shrugged. 'Maybe he didn't have enough supporters on the board. Maybe they thought he'd be too much of a bully. Or maybe they wanted to bring in an outsider to try to clean up the mess here. But whatever the reason, it wasn't a unanimous vote, I know that. Plus, they all know how valuable Bodine is to Hammond, and they don't want to lose him. Which was a real risk when they passed him over. So a fair number of board members are watching closely to see if she screws up. And if she does, they'll get rid of her, believe me.'

'Does any of this have to do with why I'm here? Why *am* I here?'

'Well, Mike Zorn said no one knows more about the SkyCruiser than you. He said you're—how'd he put it?—a "diamond in the rough".'

Just then I was feeling more like a golf ball in the rough. 'But he didn't recommend me as his stand-in, did he?'

Ali hesitated. 'He did say you might be a little . . . junior.'

'Bodine was convinced that Cheryl put me on the list herself,' I said. 'She didn't, did she?'

'No, of course not,' said a voice from behind us. The leather-clad doors had opened, and Cheryl Tobin emerged. 'I'd never even heard your name before. But Alison tells me you can be trusted, and I hope she's right.'

SHE EXTENDED A HAND. I stood and shook it. Her handshake was firm, her hand icy cold.

'Cheryl Tobin,' she said. She didn't smile.

'Nice to meet you. Jake Landry.'

I'd never seen her up close. She was better-looking from a distance. Up close, she seemed all artifice. Her face was smooth and unlined, but unnaturally so, as if she'd had a lot of roadwork—Botox or plastic surgery. Her make-up was a little too thick, mask-like, and it cracked around her eyes. She gave me a steady, appraising look. 'Alison tells me good things about you.'

'All lies,' I said.

'Oh, Alison knows better than to lie to me. Sit, please.'

I sat down, more obedient than my golden retriever. She took a seat on the couch facing us, and said, 'I'll get right to the point. I'm sure you read my email.'

'Which one?'

She widened her eyes a bit. She was probably trying to raise her eyebrows, too, but Botox had frozen her forehead. 'This morning.'

'Oh, that. About the ethics. Yeah, it sounded nice.'

'Sounded nice?' she echoed, her voice as frosty as her handshake.

'I always thought that Enron had the finest code of ethics I ever heard,' I said, and immediately wished I'd kept my mouth shut.

She smiled with her mouth, though not the rest of her face. 'Quite the brown-noser, I see.'

'Not working, huh?'

'Not exactly.'

I shrugged. 'I guess that's the advantage to being a low-level flunky. I'm not a member of the team. You know what they say: the nail that sticks up gets hammered down.'

'Ah. So you don't stick up. That way you can say whatever you want.'

'Something like that.'

She turned to look at Ali. 'You didn't tell me what a charmer he is, Alison.'

Ali rolled her eyes, and said to me warningly, 'Landry.'

Cheryl leaned forward and fixed me with an intense stare. 'What I'm about to tell you, Jake, is not to be repeated.'

'OK.' I nodded.

'I have your word on this?'

'Yes.' What next: a pinkie swear, maybe?

'Alison assured me you could be trusted, and I trust her judgment. A few months ago I hired a DC law firm, Craigie Blythe, to conduct an internal corporate investigation into Hammond Aerospace.'

I nodded again. I didn't want her to know that I'd already overheard Bodine telling Bross about it. Or that Zoë's friend in Corporate Security had revealed how they'd been going through the emails of a few top officers in the company. I couldn't help thinking, though: for a brand-new CEO to launch an investigation of her own company—that was almost unheard of.

No wonder everyone hated her.

'Do you remember the trouble that Boeing got into a few years ago with the Pentagon acquisitions office?'

'Sure.' That was a huge scandal. Boeing's CFO had offered a high-paying job to the head of the Air Force acquisitions office if she'd throw a big tanker deal their way. The woman had power over billions of dollars in government defence contracts. She decided which planes and helicopters and satellites the Air Force would buy. 'Didn't the CFO go to prison?'

'That's right. So did the head of the acquisitions office. And Boeing's CEO was forced to resign. Boeing had to pay a massive settlement, lost a twenty-three-billion-dollar deal, and their reputation was damaged for years. I was at Boeing at the time, and I remember it well. So you can bet that I'm not going to let anything like that happen at Hammond—not on my watch.'

I just looked at her, not sure why she was telling me all this.

'I'm sure you've heard the rumours about something similar going on here,' she said. 'That *someone* at the Pentagon—presumably the current chief of acquisitions—was given a bribe by *someone* at Hammond.'

'To lock in that big transport plane deal we signed a few months back,' I said. 'Yeah, I've heard that.'

'At first I dismissed these reports as just sour grapes,' Cheryl said. 'You know, how in the world did a second-tier player like Hammond Aerospace beat out both Boeing and Lockheed? But after I got here, I was determined to make sure there was no truth in the rumours. Alison?'

Ali shifted on the couch so she could address both of us at the same time. 'The investigators at Craigie Blythe have already turned up some interesting things,' she said.

'Such as?'

'What looks like a pattern of improper payments, both here and abroad.'

'We're talking bribes, right?'

'Basically.'

'Who?'

'We don't have names yet. That's one of the problems.'

'Why don't you just lean on the Air Force acquisitions chief?'

Ali shook her head. 'This is a private investigation. We don't have subpoena power or anything like that.'

'So why don't you tip off the government and have them take over?'

'Absolutely not,' Cheryl broke in. 'Not until we know who at Hammond was involved. And we have prosecutable evidence.'

'How come?'

'It's tricky,' Ali said. 'Once the word spreads at Hammond, people will start destroying documents. Deleting evidence. Covering their tracks.'

Cheryl said, 'And the moment you bring in the US Attorney's Office it becomes a media circus. I saw that with Boeing. Their investigation will become front-page news, and it'll do immeasurable harm to the company. No, I want this inquiry completely nailed down before we turn it over to the government—names, dates, documents, everything.'

'Come on,' I said, 'you're telling me you have a team of lawyers flying in and poking around the company and no one's going to find out? I doubt it.'

'So far, everything's been done remotely,' Ali said. 'They've got computer forensics examiners going through back-up tapes of email and financial records. Huge amount of data.'

'Our in-house coordinator is our general counsel, Geoff Latimer, and he's been tasked with keeping everything under wraps,' said Cheryl. 'He's one of only four people at Hammond who know. Well, five, now, counting you.'

'Who else?' I said.

'Besides us and Latimer, just Ron Slattery.' That was the new CFO, whom Cheryl had brought over from Boeing. He was generally considered to be her toady, the only member of the executive council loyal to her.

'Oh, there's more than five who know about the investigation,' I said.

Ali nodded. 'The head of Corporate Security,' she said, 'and whoever he assigned to monitor email. And probably Latimer's admin, too.'

'More than that,' I said. 'The word's out. I heard Hank Bodine tell Kevin Bross about the investigation earlier.'

Cheryl gave Ali a penetrating look. 'I suppose that explains why he's suddenly being so circumspect in his emails and phone calls.'

He, I assumed, was Hank Bodine.

To me, she said, 'You were in Hank Bodine's office?'

'No, in the airport lounge. But I was in his office this morning.'

'Interesting. What was the reason he asked you there?'

'I think the real reason was to find out why you'd put me on the offsite list. He seemed awfully suspicious. He wanted to know if I knew you.'

'Was he aware that you and Ali are acquainted?' Cheryl asked.

I shook my head. 'I don't think so. He would have said something.'

For a few seconds she seemed to be watching the flat-screen TV.

'The "real reason",' she repeated softly. 'So there must have been an ostensible reason he asked to see you. A *cover* reason.'

I was impressed: she was awfully smart. 'He wanted me to find out why the E-336 crashed at the Paris Air Show. He said he wanted to give Mike Zorn ammunition against Eurospatiale to help him "trash" them.'

'As if Mike needs that,' she said, more to Ali than to me. Then, 'Do you know who Clive Rylance is?'

'Of course.' Clive Rylance was an executive vice-president and the London-based chief of Hammond's international relations. That meant he oversaw all eighteen of our in-country operations around the world.

'We know that Hank Bodine's planning to have a little chat with him at the lodge. About things he didn't want to put in an email. I want you to find out what they talk about.'

I stared at her. 'How?'

'Eavesdrop. Hang out at the bar with the rest of the guys. And feel free to badmouth me, if that helps you get in with them.'

I smiled, didn't know what to say to that.

'I assume you get along with Hank, don't you? You seem to be a real guy's guy.' She said it with obvious distaste, like I was a pervert.

'Get along?' I said. 'He barely notices me.'

'If he doesn't notice you, that's a good thing,' Cheryl said. 'You're not a threat to him. He's not likely to be as careful around you as he might be with a member of the leadership team.'

'You're asking me to spy,' I said.

She shrugged. 'Call it what you will. We need to know where to point the investigators. Also, I want to know whether he mentions Craigie Blythe. Or Hamilton Wender, our lead attorney there.'

I was momentarily confused. Hamilton Wender, Craigie Blythe—which was the law firm, and which was the lawyer? Finally, I said, 'That's it?'

'Jake,' Ali said, 'it would be really helpful if you could find out whether Bodine or any of the other guys are talking about the Pentagon bribe thing.

Even in some vague, indirect way. Because if we can narrow it down to certain individuals, maybe we can speed things up.'

'Anything that might indicate an illegal proffer of employment,' Cheryl put in. 'Any violation of policy that could conceivably get us in trouble. Any talk of "gifts" offered as inducements to secure deals.'

I didn't like this at all. What Cheryl was asking me to do sounded like nothing more than serving as her stool pigeon. I was beginning to wonder if all this high-flown talk about law firms was just a cover for turning me into her ratfink. I thought about it for a while, then said, 'Is this spy stuff supposed to come before the team-building exercises or after?'

Cheryl looked at me blankly. I could tell she wasn't impressed.

'You may not hear anything,' she said. 'Then again, you may overhear something that helps us crack the case.'

I remained silent.

'I'm sensing reluctance on your part,' she said.

Ali, I noticed, was avoiding my eyes.

'I'm a little uncomfortable with it, yes,' I admitted.

'I understand. But this could be a very good thing for you. An *opportunity*, if you take my meaning.'

I knew she was offering me her own kind of bribe. 'I don't know,' I said. 'Being a spy isn't really a skill set I was hoping to develop.'

'Are you saying you won't do this for me?'

'I didn't say that.' I stood up. 'I'll think about it.'

'I'd like an answer now,' Cheryl said.

'I'll think about it,' I repeated, and walked out.

I RETURNED TO MY SEAT and went back to inspecting the photos of the plane crash. Bodine and his buddies were still toking on their stogies. The cabin was dense with cigar smoke. My eyes started to smart.

And I thought about Cheryl Tobin and Ali and what they'd just asked me to do. It wasn't as if I felt any loyalty to Bodine or Lummis, but I didn't much like being recruited as a spy. On the other hand, I knew Ali wouldn't have asked me to do something that she didn't think was important. I was becoming convinced that there was a lot more going on than anyone was telling me.

By the time the plane landed, half an hour later, I'd gone from a low-level dread about the next four days to an uneasy suspicion that something bad was about to happen at the lodge.

I had no idea, of course.

Chapter 4

The King Chinook Lodge was built on the side of a steep hill, massive and rustic and beautiful. It was basically an overgrown log cabin, grand and primitive, probably a century old. The exterior was peeled logs, and the gaps between the logs were chinked with creosote-treated rope. It was two storeys, with a steeply pitched roof shingled in salt-silvered cedar. A large front porch connected to a wooden plank walkway that wound down the hillside to a weathered dock.

The lodge was located on the shores of an isolated body of water called Shotbolt Bay, off Rivers Inlet, on the coast of British Columbia, 300 miles north of Vancouver. The only way to reach it was by private boat, helicopter or chartered seaplane. When they said the place was remote, that was an understatement.

The Hammond jet had landed on the northwest tip of Vancouver Island, at Port Hardy Airport, where we transferred to a couple of small seaplanes. After a quick flight, we landed on the water in front of a simple dock. The sun was low in the sky, a huge ochre globe, and it glittered on the water.

We were met by a lanky guy around my age with a thick thatch of sandy-brown hair and clear blue eyes. He was wearing a dun-coloured polo shirt with KING CHINOOK LODGE stitched on the left breast. Greeting us with a big smile, he introduced himself as Ryan, and addressed everyone but me by name: obviously he remembered them from the year before. Or maybe he'd brushed up.

'How was your flight?'

'Flights,' Kevin Bross corrected him brusquely as he stepped onto the dock and walked past.

Hugo Lummis needed an assist onto the dock. He'd donned a pair of Ray-Ban Wayfarers and needed only a porkpie hat to look like one of the Blues Brothers.

'Fish biting?' he asked the guy.

'The chinook are staging right now,' said Ryan. 'I caught a forty-pounder yesterday, not two hundred feet from the lodge.'

Another two dun-shirted guys, who looked Hispanic, were pulling suitcases and crates of perishable foodstuffs from the back of the plane.

Lummis said, 'Last summer I caught a ninety-pounder with a Berkeley four-point-nine test line. I do believe that was a line-class record.'

'I remember,' Ryan said, nodding. Something very subtle in his expression seemed to indicate scepticism.

'This is one of the best sports-fishing lodges in the world,' Lummis boomed at me. 'World-class.'

I nodded.

'You fish?'

'Some,' I said.

'Well, it don't take a lot of skill out here. Just drop the line in the water. But reeling 'em in ain't for wussies. Chinooks—that's what they call the king salmon—they'll straighten out your hook, break your line, tow your boat sideways. Tough fighters. Am I right or am I right, Ryan?'

'Right, Mr Lummis,' Ryan said.

Lummis started waddling up the steps to the lodge.

'First time here?' Ryan said to me.

'Yep. Didn't bring any fishing gear, though.'

'No worries. We provide everything. And if you're not a fisherman, there's plenty of other things to do when you're not in your meetings or doing the team-building exercises, like hiking and kayaking.'

'I like fishing,' I said. 'Never gone salmon-fishing, though.'

'Oh, it's the best. Mr Lummis is right. We've got incredible trophy king salmon-fishing. Forty-pound salmon's average, but I've seen 'em fifty, sixty, even seventy pounds.'

'Not ninety?'

'Never seen one that big,' Ryan said. He didn't smile, but his clear eyes twinkled. 'Not here.'

THE LONG, DEEP PORCH was lined with rustic furniture—a long glider, a porch swing suspended by chains, a couple of Adirondack chairs—that all looked handmade, of logs and twigs. A different staff member held the screen door open for me as if he were a bell captain at a Ritz-Carlton, and I entered an enormous, dimly lit room.

I was immediately hit by the pleasant smells of woodsmoke and mulled cider. Once my eyes adjusted to the light, I realised I'd never seen a fishing lodge like this before. It was the kind of place you might see in some big spread in *Architectural Digest* titled 'The World's Most Exclusive Rustic Hideaways'. The so-called great room had walls of rough-hewn timber and the floors were wide cedar planks, mellow and worn. At one end was a three-tiered fireplace made from river stone, almost twenty feet wide and thirty feet high. Above it was a giant rack of six-point elk antlers. On another wall was a huge bearskin. More tree-branch furniture here, but the couches and chairs were plump and overstuffed and upholstered in kilim fabric.

Our luggage had been collected in the centre of the room and was being carried off by staff. We were the last load of passengers to arrive. Everyone else from our party seemed to have checked in to their rooms.

A man with a clipboard came up to me. He was middle-aged, balding, had reading glasses round his neck. He shook my hand. 'I'm Paul Fecher, the manager. You must be Mr Landry.'

'Good guess,' I said.

'Process of elimination. We've got three new people, and two of them are women. Welcome to King Chinook Lodge.'

'Nice place you got here.'

'Glad you like it. If there's anything at all I can get you, please let me or any of our staff know. I think you've already met my son, Ryan.'

'Right.' The kid down at the dock.

'Our motto here is, the only thing our guests ever have to lift is a fishing rod. Or a glass of whisky. But the whisky's optional.'

'Later, maybe,' I said.

He looked at his watch. 'Well, you've got a while before you all get together for the cocktail party and the opening banquet. Some folks are taking naps. Couple of guys are working out in our gym downstairs. And if you just want to take it easy, we've got a traditional wood-fired cedar sauna.' He gestured over to a bar at one end of the room, where Lummis was drinking with Clive Rylance, the executive vice-president of international relations. 'And, of course, the bar's always open.'

'I'll keep that in mind.'

'Now, you're in the Vancouver Room with Mr Latimer.'

Geoffrey Latimer, the general counsel, was supposed to be a total stiff, strait-laced and humourless. He was also the one coordinating the internal investigation for Cheryl. That was an interesting choice.

'Room-mates, huh?'

'There's twelve of you, and only seven guest rooms. You'll enjoy it. Take you back to summer camp.' I never went to summer camp.

After I did the maths, I said, 'So not everyone gets a room-mate?'

'Well, your new CEO, of course, gets her own suite.'

'Of course.' That meant that Ali got her own room, too.

Sharing a room with one of these guys. What a blast.

YEAH, JUST LIKE summer camp. Except that some of the campers got suites with Jacuzzis.

As I climbed the stairs, I glanced into one of the suites. Its door was open, and I could see that the room was pretty big. Ali was in there, unpacking her suitcase. She looked up as I passed by, gave me a smile.

'So, you get your own room, huh?'

She shrugged. 'Yeah, well, Cheryl—'

'And I thought you'd be sharing a room with Hank Bodine.'

'Yeah, right. Why don't you come in for a second?'

I did, and she closed the door behind me. I felt that tingle of anticipation down below that I used to get when we were alone behind closed doors together, but of course I banished all those impure thoughts from my mind.

'You think it's safe?' I said, taking a seat in a rustic, tree-branch chair. 'I thought you didn't want any of the guys to know we're friends.'

'Just make sure no one sees you walk out of here.'

I liked the furtive thing. It was kind of sexy, actually. 'I sure wouldn't want anyone to think we were having an affair.'

She gave a faint smile as she took a seat in a chair next to me. 'Listen, about that meeting with—on the plane. You seemed a little pissed off.'

'A little put off, maybe. Being a ratfink for the boss isn't exactly the career path I had in mind at Hammond.'

'But that's not what she's asking you to do,' Ali said, looking uneasy. 'Just keep your eyes and ears open, that's all.'

'So why do I get the feeling she's got an ulterior motive? She's got the board of directors looking for an excuse to get rid of her, and Hank Bodine stirring up trouble like some deposed shah, right? But now he and his buddies suspect their email is being monitored, so wouldn't it be convenient to press some junior guy into service as your own private informer?'

I could see the flush in her porcelain skin, and I knew right away I'd struck a nerve. I'd forgotten how transparent her emotions were.

She shook her head. 'She can handle any crap those guys throw at her, believe me. This is about flushing out evidence of a crime, and protecting the company from a huge legal nightmare.'

'And if that ends up with Hank Bodine wearing an orange jumpsuit and handcuffs, doing the perp walk, so much the better.'

'I wouldn't mind it. Admit it, you wouldn't, either.'

'I don't really give a damn about the guy, frankly.'

'The point is, if he or Hugo Lummis or anyone else in the company bribed a Pentagon official to get a contract, it's going to blow up in our faces. Just like it did at Boeing.'

I paused. 'Is this important to you?'

'Uh-uh, Landry. Don't do this for me.'

'Oh, come on, Ali,' I said. 'You know that's why you brought me in. You knew I would never say no to you. Given our history.'

She stared at me for a few very long seconds. 'Given our history,' she said softly, 'I was taking a big risk you'd tell us both to go to hell. I suggested you to Cheryl because you're the only one I trust.'

I didn't know what to say, so I said nothing. She looked down, then suddenly brushed her hand along my trouser leg, down my outer thigh. 'You've got dog hair all over your trousers.'

I felt a jolt, even though I knew she didn't mean anything by it. 'I should probably buy a lint brush,' I said.

She smiled as if secretly amused by something. 'You still going out with that cheap blonde with the big tits?'

'Which one?'

'The one I saw you out to dinner with at Sushi Masa.'

'Oh, her. No, that's over.' I tried not to show my surprise. I didn't know she'd seen me out on a date. Was I hearing jealousy in her voice?

She nodded. 'I thought you hate sushi.'

'I'm not really into blondes, either.'

'You seemed to be into both that night. You know how many times I tried to get you to go to that place?'

'You should take it as a sign of respect that I felt safe enough with you to reveal my true, deep inner dislike of raw fish. So, are you in a relationship these days?'

'It's been too crazy at work. You?'

I nodded.

'But not a blonde.'

'Oh, this one's a blonde too, actually.'

'Huh. What's her name?'

'Gerty. Short for Gertrude.'

'Sounds real sexy. What does she do?'

'Loves to run. And eat. Loves to eat. She'd never stop if I didn't limit her to two meals a day.'

'Are we talking eating disorder here?'

'Nah, it goes with the breed.'

She gave me a playful punch, but it landed hard. A strong girl. 'So, you're still working for Mike Zorn.'

'Of course. He's a nice guy. It's a good job.'

'I bet you still have that junky old Jeep, don't you?'

'Still drives great.'

'Probably didn't even replace that front right quarter panel, did you?'

'Doesn't affect the ride,' I said.

She smiled, conceded the point. Then she said, 'You never congratulated me, by the way. On my new job.'

I arched my eyebrows. I can do that. I haven't had Botox.

'Right,' she said. 'I'd forgotten about Jake-speak. No need to say what you know I know you know, right? Like, obviously you're happy for me, why should you say it out loud? Why waste words?'

'Talk's overrated,' I said. 'Of course I'm happy for you.'

We fell silent for a few seconds, then I asked her, 'Look, is this going to be—complicated for us?'

'Complicated? You mean, because we used to sleep together?'

'Oh, right—we did, didn't we?'

'I don't think it'll be complicated, do you?'

I shook my head. Of course it would. How could it not? 'Not at all,' I said. 'So, when we run into each other in the next couple of days are we supposed to pretend that we've never met?'

She thought for a moment. 'Maybe we've seen each other around. But we don't know each other's names. We've never been introduced.'

'Gotcha,' I said, thinking how much I liked being around her. Looking at her. Being in her presence. Inhaling her smell.

She stood up. 'I should get back to work. I have to go over Cheryl's remarks with her. So, just be careful leaving here, OK?'

I nodded, got up, and went over to the door. I opened it slowly, just a crack. I looked out, saw no one in the hall. Then I slipped out—and saw a couple of guys standing a few feet away at the top of the landing, whispering. On the other side of the door, where I hadn't seen them.

I recognised both of them, though I'd never met either. One was the corporate controller, John Danziger. He was tall and lean and broad-shouldered, around forty, with thinning blond hair and grey-blue eyes. The other was the treasurer, Alan Grogan, around the same age and height. He had thick dark brown hair touched with grey, hazel-green eyes, a wide mouth, a sharp chin and an aquiline nose.

As soon as Danziger noticed me, he stopped whispering. Grogan turned round, gave me a sharp look, and the two men parted abruptly, without another word, walking in separate directions.

THE DOOR to the Vancouver Room was open. The walls and ceiling were unpainted, rough-hewn pine boards; the floorboards, smooth wideboard pine. All the furniture—the two large beds, armoire, dresser and desk—was rustic. Big puffy down comforters on the beds. A window overlooked the ocean.

Geoffrey Latimer was already in there, unpacking. He looked up as I entered. Around fifty, he had warm, sincere brown eyes, the trusting eyes of a child. Greying light brown hair, perfectly Brylcreemed and parted on the side. His face was reddened and chafed, like he had psoriasis or something. 'I don't believe we've met,' he said. 'Geoff Latimer.'

He shook my hand, his grip firm and dry. His fingernails looked bitten. He was thin and wore chinos and a striped golf shirt. He gave off the faint whiff of Old Spice, which reminded me, unpleasantly, of my father.

'Jake Landry. I'm filling in for Mike Zorn.'

He nodded. 'Those are big shoes to fill.'

'Do my best.'

'Don't let the turkeys get you down. They're just middle-aged frat boys.'

I gave him a blank look.

'Lummis and Bross and those guys. They're bullies, that's all.'

I was surprised he'd even noticed. 'It's no big deal,' I said.

He turned back to his suitcase, working methodically, transferring impeccably folded clothes from a battered old suitcase to dresser drawers.

'You'll see the same posturing when it comes to the team-building exercises,' he said. 'Those guys are always competing with each other. Who can climb higher or pull harder. They don't want you showing them up, climbing higher or pulling harder.'

I smiled. Latimer was shrewder and more insightful than I'd expected. I knew he was coordinating the internal corporate investigation, but I wasn't sure whether he knew that I'd been asked to help. So I decided I'd better wait for him to bring it up.

I unzipped my suitcase and started unpacking, too. My clothes were a jumbled mess. I'd tossed them in there in about five minutes. I noticed him take a handful of syringes out of the suitcase, an orange plastic kit, a couple of vials, and put them all in a dresser drawer. I didn't say anything. He was either a heroin addict or a diabetic. Diabetic seemed more likely.

He looked over at me. 'That all you brought?'

I nodded.

'Travel light, huh?' Latimer said. 'You married, Jake?'

'Nope.'

'Planning on it?'

'No danger of it happening anytime soon.'

'Hope you don't mind me saying, but you should. You need a stable home life if you want to make it in business, I've always thought. Wife and kids—it anchors you.'

'I just drink,' I said.

He looked at me keenly for a second.

'I'm kidding,' I said. 'You got kids?'

He nodded, smiled. 'A daughter. Twelve.'

'Nice age,' I said, just because that seemed like the thing to say.

His smile turned rueful. 'It's a terrible age, actually. In the course of a month I went from a guy who couldn't do anything wrong to a guy who can't do anything right. A loser. Uncool.'

'Can't wait to have kids, myself,' I said with a straight face.

WE CHANGED INTO dinner clothes. Latimer's boxer shorts were white with green Christmas trees and red candy canes on them. 'Christmas gift from my daughter,' he said sheepishly. He was scrawny, with a smooth, milky-white belly and spindly legs.

He put on grey dress slacks, a white button-down shirt. When he'd finished changing, he took out an iPod.

'Don't know if you're a gadget guy like me, but here's my latest toy,' he said proudly. 'Ever see one of these?'

Not one that old, actually. 'Sure.'

'My daughter got it for me. I've even learned how to download music. You like show tunes?'

I shrugged. 'Sure.' I hate show tunes.

'Feel free to borrow it whenever. I've got *Music Man* and *Carousel* and *Kismet*. You know, I've always thought that so much of what goes on in the business world is like a musical. A stage play. A pageant.'

'Never thought of it that way.'

'Much of it's about how we perceive things, more than what's really going on. So Hank and Hugo and all those guys look at you and think you're a kid, too young to know anything. Whereas in truth, you could be every bit as smart or qualified as any of them.'

'Yeah, maybe. So what happens tonight?'

'The opening-night banquet. Cheryl gives a talk. The facilitator gives a run-down on the team-building exercises. I talk at dinner tomorrow night.'

'What's your talk about?'

'Ethics and business.'

'In general, or at Hammond?'

He compressed his lips, zipped up his suitcase, and placed it neatly at the back of the clothes closet. 'Hammond. There's a win-at-any-cost culture in this company. An ethical rottenness, sort of a hangover from Jim Rawlings's hard-charging style. Cheryl's doing what she can to clean it up, but . . .'

Latimer was a real type: the clothes, the hair, the packing, everything conservative and by the book. A real rules-loving guy. But I was surprised to hear him criticise our old CEO. Rawlings had, after all, named Latimer general counsel. They were said to have been close.

'What's she doing to clean it up?' I said.

He hesitated, but only for a second or two. 'Making it clear she won't tolerate any malfeasance.'

'You think Rawlings encouraged that sort of stuff?'

'I do. Or he'd look the other way. There was always this feeling that, you know, there's Boeing and there's Lockheed; and then there's us. The predator and the prey. We were the little guy. We had to do whatever it took to survive. Even if we had to play dirty.'

He was silent for a moment. He seemed to be staring out at the ocean.

'The big guys play dirty sometimes, too,' I said.

'Lockheed cleaned up their act quite some time ago,' Latimer said. 'I know those guys. Boeing—well, who knows? But even if Boeing plays dirty, that doesn't justify our doing it. This is something Cheryl's really concerned about. She wants me to rattle some cages.'

'That's not going to make you very popular around here.'

He sighed. 'A little late for that. I'm probably going to ruin some people's dinners tomorrow night. No one wants to hear doom-and-gloom stuff. But you've got to get their attention somehow.'

He went quiet again for a while. Then he said, 'Look at this,' and beckoned me to the window.

The sun was low on the horizon, a fat orange globe. The ocean shimmered. At first I didn't know what he was calling my attention to—the sunset, maybe? Then I noticed a dark shape moving in the sky. An immense bald eagle was dropping slowly towards the water.

'Watch.'

With a sudden, swift movement, the eagle swooped down and snatched something up in its powerful talons: a glinting silver fish. *Predator and prey*. 'Boy, talk about symbolism,' I said.

Latimer turned to look at me, puzzled. 'What do you mean?'

Maybe he wasn't all that insightful after all.

'Then again, it's just a fish,' I said.

GEOFF LATIMER announced that he was going downstairs and invited me to join him, but I told him, vaguely, that I had a couple of things to finish up. When he'd left the room, I pulled out my laptop to take another look at those photos of the crash that I'd downloaded on the flight over.

Theoretically, I guess, I was doing it because Hank Bodine had asked me to. But by then I'd become curious myself. A brand-new plane crashes—at an air show, of all places—you can't help wondering why.

According to one of the reports Zoë had sent me, the E-336 had made maybe twenty test flights before the show. Twenty test flights—that was nothing. That was brand spanking new.

So there had to be something wrong with the plane, and I knew that the Eurospatiale consortium sure as hell wasn't going to admit it. They'd blame the weather or pilot error or whatever.

All I could tell from examining the photographs was that the hinges had ripped out of the composite skin of the flap. But why? The hinges were cut into the flap and glued on with a powerful epoxy adhesive. They sure as hell weren't supposed to rip out. After twenty years, maybe. Not after twenty short hops between Paris and London.

For a couple of minutes I stared at the damaged flap, until something itched at the back of my mind. A possible explanation. I zoomed in as close as I could before the photograph disintegrated into pixels. Yes. At that resolution I could see quite clearly the cracks at the stress concentration points. And the telltale swelling in the composite skin. 'Brooming', it was called. It happened when moisture somehow got into the graphite epoxy, which had a nasty habit of absorbing water like a sponge. And that could happen for a number of reasons, none of them good.

Such as a design flaw in the plane itself.

Which was the case here, I was convinced.

I knew now why the plane had gone down, and I was certain Hank Bodine wouldn't want to hear the explanation.

Unless . . .

Unless, say, he already knew the cause and wanted me to find it out for myself. But I couldn't see any possible logic in that. I wondered whether Cheryl knew more about the crash than she'd let on. Was it possible, I wondered, that she already knew what I'd just found out?

With a sinking feeling, I realised, that as much as I wanted to steer clear of the power struggle between Cheryl Tobin and Hank Bodine, I was already deeply embroiled in it.

I went downstairs to find Bodine and tell him what I'd learned.

Chapter 5

As I came down the stairs I heard loud voices and raucous laughter emanating from the bar. Hugo Lummis was clutching a tumbler of something brown and seemed to have a real buzz on. He was talking to a guy I recognised as Upton Barlow, the chief of Hammond's Defence Division.

Barlow was tall, with sloped shoulders, looked like an athlete. Deep lines were etched round his mouth, a stack of parallel lines carved into his forehead. He had receding grey hair, little black eyes like raisins, a pursed mouth.

The two of them seemed to be trading travel horror stories. They were both members of the million-mile frequent-flier club, and it sounded like they didn't much like Europe.

'Good luck finding an ice machine in your hotel,' Lummis said. 'Ask for Coke and you get it as warm as a bucket of spit.'

'You can't even watch the news in your hotel room,' Barlow said. 'You put on CNN, and it's all *different*. You get, like, a forty-five-minute report on *Nairobi* or *Somaliland* or something.'

'Why don't you join us, fella?' Lummis said to me.

I hesitated for an instant. Having a drink with these old goats was just about the last thing I wanted to do.

But then I reminded myself that the two guys at the bar were exactly who I should be hanging out with. Both of them schemed night and day to sell planes to the Air Force and were willing to do anything to make the sale. If a bribe had really been made to someone in the Pentagon they'd have to be two of the key players.

Upton Barlow picked up on my silence, and said, 'Aw, he doesn't want to sit with us old farts.'

'Sure, that would be great,' I said, walking down the bar and sitting on the stool next to him. I introduced myself.

'I'm sure I've got emails from you,' Barlow said, shaking my hand. 'Mike Zorn's assistant, right?'

'That's right.' I was surprised he remembered who I was.

'But Mike's not going to be here, is he?'

I started to answer, but he turned away to greet someone else who'd just come down the stairs. It was Clive Rylance, an intense-looking, dark-haired man who looked as if he'd been carved out of granite. He had a square jaw and a heavy beard that he probably had to trim twice a day.

'Well, if it isn't Clive Rylance, international man of mystery,' Barlow said jovially.

Rylance put one hand on Lummis's shoulder and, with the other, reached over and shook Barlow's hand. Actually, they seemed to be trying to crush each other's hands. 'Gentlemen,' he said.

'Speak for yourself,' said Lummis. 'You know everyone here, right? Don't know if you've met . . . Golly, what's your name again?'

'Jake Landry,' I said, shaking with Rylance.

'Clive,' Rylance said. 'So are you a new member of the executive team?'

'Just filling in for Mike Zorn,' I said.

'Good,' he said. He looked around at the others and laughed. 'Phew. I was starting to feel real old there for a second. Say, anyone seen Hank around?' he said.

'Last I heard, he was hot on Cheryl's trail,' Barlow said. 'Had something he wanted to raise with her.'

'Raise all the way up her ass, I suspect,' said Lummis. 'So, Jake, you ready to be inspired and motivated by our fearless leader?' He fanned his hands in the air like a preacher rousing his flock. 'The symbol of our company is the lion,' he said in a falsetto, not a bad imitation of Cheryl Tobin. 'And I'm here to make that lion *roar*.'

I laughed politely, and both Rylance and Barlow guffawed loudly, then Barlow leaned in close to the guys and muttered out of the side of his mouth, 'It is a goddamned *gynaecocracy* around here these days.'

The bartender took my order—a Macallan single malt—and Rylance pulled up a stool on Lummis's other side. Then Kevin Bross passed by, wearing black workout shorts and a black sleeveless shirt that showed off his broad shoulders and sculpted physique. He was drenched with sweat. The wristband of his heart-rate monitor was beeping rapidly. Bross looked like he spent more hours in the gym than at the office.

'Good workout, Coach?' Clive Rylance said. 'Hey, did someone strap a time bomb on you or something?'

'Huh?' Bross said.

'Sounds like you're about to explode.'

'Oh, that,' Bross said, and he reached under his shirt and tugged at a chest strap. It came off with a Velcro crunch. 'Heart-rate monitor. What about you, big guy? Brits don't exercise?'

Rylance hoisted his tumbler of Scotch. 'Just my left hand,' he said.

They both laughed.

'We gonna do Zermatt again this year, Kev?' Barlow said. 'I want to see you wipe out doing the slalom again. That was a blast.'

'Cram it, Upton,' Bross said jovially, 'or I'll tell them what happened to you at the top of the Blauherd lift.'

Barlow tipped his glass and laughed. 'Touché. So, is the sauna co-ed this year?'

'Clothing optional, I hope,' Rylance said, and everyone cracked up.

Just then I saw Hank Bodine—or, to be accurate, I *heard* him. He was standing on the other side of the room, hands on hips, talking to someone.

No, actually, he was yelling at someone.

As soon as I realised that the person he was chewing out was Ali, I jumped up from my seat and, without thinking, bolted across the room.

ALI WAS SITTING in a chair while Bodine stood right in front of her, obviously trying to intimidate. She'd changed into a white skirt and a peach-coloured silk blouse, cut just low enough to emphasise the swell of her breasts. She had gold bangles on her wrists and a necklace of tiny gold beads interspersed with large teardrops of polished green turquoise. She looked stunning.

She also looked angry.

I could hear Bodine saying, 'You want me to take this up with Cheryl, that it?' He was clearly holding back a great deal of anger.

'Obviously I can't stop you from talking to Cheryl,' she said. 'You can do whatever you want. But not before the meeting starts. Sorry. She's busy.'

I stopped a ways off, not wanting to barge in.

'This sure as hell isn't the agenda I cleared,' Bodine said.

'You're not the CEO,' Ali said. 'You don't get to clear the agenda.'

'Well, sweetheart, I never heard a single *goddamned* mention of anyone giving a speech here called "Hammond and the Culture of Corruption".'

Ali shrugged. 'I'm sorry . . . Hank.' I could tell she had been about to counter that 'sweetheart' with something acerbic but thought better of it. 'That was a last-minute addition.'

'You don't make last-minute additions without running them by me first. That's how it's always worked.'

'I guess things have changed, Hank.' Ali folded her legs. I saw a ghost of a smile flit across her face, as if she were enjoying facing him down.

Bodine rocked back on his heels, took his hands off his hips and folded his arms across his chest. 'Let me tell you something, young lady,' he said. 'You are making a serious mistake. I'm going to do you a favour and pretend none of this ever happened. Because I am not going to have my team demoralised by unsubstantiated accusations about "corruption" in this company. And if the board of directors gets wind of the fact that your goddamned boss is trying to level charges that have no basis, heads are going to roll. And I don't just mean yours. You hear me?'

Ali gave him a long look. 'I hear your threats loud and clear, Hank. But the agenda stands.'

'That's *it*,' Bodine said, raising his voice almost to a shout. 'What room is she in?'

'Cheryl's preparing her remarks,' Ali said. 'She really doesn't want to be disturbed.'

I could no longer hang back and watch Bodine talk to her that way. I walked up to him, tapped him on the shoulder. 'Didn't your daddy ever teach you how to talk to a lady?' I said lightly.

Bodine looked at me with fury. Before he could reply I said, 'I got you the information you wanted. About the E-336.'

'You,' he said, jabbing his index finger into my chest. His cheeks were flushed. 'You might want to watch your ass.' Then he strode away.

As soon as he was gone, I leaned forward and extended my hand to Ali. 'I'm Jake Landry,' I said.

'I GUESS HE'S JUST not that into you,' I said.

'What'd you do that for?' I could tell she was secretly pleased.

'Because I don't like bullies.'

'I didn't need your help, you know.'

'Who says I was trying to help?'

'You butted in. You shouldn't have. I can handle Hank Bodine. I don't need a protector.'

'That's obvious.'

'What's that supposed to mean?'

'It's called a compliment. You handled him way better than I could have.'

She looked momentarily appeased. 'Anyway, the idea was for you to get on his good side. Not alienate him.'

'I don't think he has a good side. Plus, alienating him is more fun.'

'He could get you fired.'

'Your boss can overrule him.'

'Not if she gets fired herself.'

She had a point. 'I could always move back to upstate New York and get a job with the cable company again. Maybe the vent-pipe factory.'

'The factory's probably out of business by now. Just like every other company there.'

'True.'

She glanced at her watch. 'I think Cheryl needs me. The reception's about to begin.' She stood up. 'Nice to meet you, Jake. It was really great.'

THE PRE-DINNER RECEPTION was held in a small room off the great room.

They were serving blender drinks and mojitos and flutes of champagne, and voices got steadily louder, the laughter more raucous, as the guys got increasingly soused. The exception seemed to be Hank Bodine, who was talking to Hugo Lummis, looking really annoyed. Ali was in Cheryl's suite talking through the evening's schedule. I stood there holding a mojito and looking around when someone sidled up to me. One of the guys I'd seen earlier whispering in the hall upstairs—*caught* whispering, I thought. The blond one.

'You're Jake Landry, right? I'm John Danziger. The corporate controller at Hammond,' he said.

We shook hands, and I went through my standard pitch about how I was Mike Zorn's stand-in. But instead of giving me the expected response, about how big the shoes were that I had to fill, Danziger said, 'I'm sorry if I was rude to you upstairs.'

'Rude?'

'That was you in the hall upstairs, right? When Alan Grogan and I were talking?' He had a pleasant, smooth baritone voice, like a radio announcer.

'Oh, was that you? Looked like an intense conversation.' That meant he'd seen me coming out of Ali's room. If, that is, he knew it was Ali's room.

'Just work-related stuff,' he said. 'But sort of sensitive.'

'No worries.' I couldn't figure out why he was making such a big deal out of something so trivial. Maybe he was afraid I'd overheard something. Whatever it was, he had probably been too preoccupied to pay much attention to me or where I'd just come from. 'So can I ask you something?'

Danziger gave me a wary look. 'Sure.'

'What does the corporate controller actually do, anyway? Besides . . . controlling things?'

'I wish I could tell you.'

'You mean, if you told me, you'd have to kill me?'

'If I told you, I'd put us both to sleep,' Danziger said. 'It's too boring.'

Someone tapped Danziger on the shoulder. It was Ron Slattery, the chief financial officer Cheryl Tobin had brought over from Boeing. He was a small, compact man, bald on top, with prominent ears, and heavy black-framed glasses. He was wearing a blue blazer and a white shirt.

Apart from on the plane earlier, this was the first time I'd ever seen Slattery not wearing a grey suit. He was the sort of guy you could imagine going to bed in a grey suit. Danziger excused himself, and the two men turned away to talk.

'Hey, there, roomie.' Geoff Latimer grabbed me by the elbow. 'Having a good time?'

'Sure,' I said.

He faltered for a few seconds, looked as if he was searching for something to say. Then: 'Everyone already knows everyone else. It's kind of a tight circle. Would you like me to introduce you to some people?'

I was about to tell him thanks but no thanks, when there was a tink-tink-tink of silverware against glass, and the room quietened down. Cheryl Tobin stood by the entrance with a broad smile. She was wearing a navy-blue jacket over a long ivory silk skirt and big jewel-studded earrings. Ali stood close behind her, studying a binder.

'Ladies and gentlemen,' Cheryl said. 'Or maybe I should just say, gentlemen.' Polite laughter.

Clive Rylance said loudly, 'That rules out most of us,' and there was a burst of laughter. Kevin Bross, standing next to Rylance, leaned over and said something mildly obscene to him about Ali. He probably meant to whisper, but his voice carried. I wanted to slam the guy against the peeled-log wall. Bodine and Lummis and Barlow were all standing together. I could see Bodine whisper something to Lummis, who nodded in reply.

'Well, you know me by now,' Cheryl said smoothly. 'I always expect the best. I'd like to welcome everyone to a Hammond tradition I'm proud to join. The annual leadership retreat at the remarkable King Chinook Lodge. From the minute I arrived at Hammond Aerospace I've heard stories about this place.' She paused. 'Some of which I can't repeat.'

Some low chuckles.

'What's that you guys say—"What happens at King Chinook stays in King Chinook"? I guess I'm about to find out what that's all about, huh?'

'You know it,' someone said.

'It's not too late to escape,' someone else said.

'Not too late to escape, hmm?' she repeated. Her smile had grown thin. 'Easier said than done. It's a long swim to the nearest airport.'

She was making a good show of pretending to enjoy the testosterone-rich rowdiness, but at the same time you could sense the steel. As if she were willing to be a good sport, but there was a point beyond which she wouldn't go. She also looked as if she wanted to get the hell out of there. Back to corporate headquarters, back to her big office where she could be the CEO instead of one of two sorority girls at a frat party.

'And believe me, I've thought about it,' she said. 'Especially after hearing about the courses that Bo's about to take us through.'

She looked across the room towards a giant of a man with a shiny bald head and a big black moustache. That had to be Bo Lampack, the team-building coordinator. He stood in the back corner with his arms folded across a great broad chest.

Lampack gave a conspiratorial grin. 'We haven't lost anyone.' He paused for dramatic effect, then added, 'Yet.'

A burst of raucous laughter, laced with cheers.

Cheryl held up her hands. 'Well, we'll hear more from Bo at dinner. And tomorrow, you guys are all going to see that we women can keep up with men—not just in the office but on the ropes as well.' She looked around. 'I'm not just the first outsider to lead Hammond Aerospace, but I'm also the first woman. And I know that makes some of you guys a little uncomfortable. I understand that. Change is always difficult. But that's one of the . . . challenges . . . I hope we'll get a chance to work through this weekend.'

The room had gone quiet but for a few pockets of restless stirring. Both Bodine and Barlow stood watching her in identical poses: their right arms folded across their bellies, supporting their left elbows. Their left hands clutched tumblers of bourbon. Like babies holding bottles of formula.

'If not,' she said, 'I hope you're all strong swimmers.' She looked around for several seconds. No one laughed. So she continued, 'You know, they say a general without an army is nothing. I need each and every one of you in there pulling—not for me, but for this great company. Let me remind you that the symbol of the Hammond Aerospace Corporation is the lion. And with your help, together we're going to make that lion roar.'

Lummis elbowed Barlow so hard that Barlow dropped his glass of bourbon. It crashed against the plank floor and shattered into a hundred shards.

A FEW MINUTES LATER, as we all filed into the great room for dinner, Hank Bodine put a hand on my shoulder. Upton Barlow was at his side. 'So you have some information for me,' Bodine said. His tone was curt.

'I'm pretty sure I've figured out why the E-336 crashed,' I said.

'Well, let's hear it.' His hand came off my shoulder.

Barlow's raisin eyes regarded me curiously.

'Maybe we can talk in private, later on,' I said.

'Nonsense. We have no secrets. Let's hear it.' To Barlow, Bodine said, 'Jake here says he knows why the Eurospatiale plane wiped out.' There was something defiant in his tone, as if he didn't believe me.

I paused. Cheryl and Ali were approaching from behind Bodine. 'How about later?' I said.

'How about now?' said Cheryl. 'I'd like to hear all about it.' She extended her hand. 'I don't believe we've met, actually. I'm Cheryl Tobin. Will you sit next to me at dinner?'

Bodine gave me a look of pure, unadulterated loathing.

A LONG TABLE had been set up in a bay of the great room that overlooked the ocean. Night had fallen, and the windowpanes had become polished obsidian, reflecting the amber glow of the room. You couldn't see the ocean, but you could hear the waves of Rivers Inlet lapping gently against the shore.

Cheryl Tobin was seated at the head of the table. I was at her immediate left. On my other side was Upton Barlow, then Hugo Lummis, whose pot-belly was so big he had to sit way back from the table to make room for it.

Lummis was telling some long-winded anecdote to Barlow. Meanwhile, Cheryl was talking with her CFO, Ron Slattery. His bald head shone: oddly vulnerable, a baby's. He was saying, 'I thought your speech was absolutely masterful.'

The table was covered with a stiff white linen cloth and set with expensive-looking gold-rimmed china and gleaming silverware. An armada of wine and water glasses. Next to each place setting was a narrow printed menu listing six courses. A white linen napkin, folded into a fan, on each plate. A card with each person's name written in calligraphy.

There was nothing spontaneous about Cheryl's decision to seat me next to her. If she wanted me to spy for her, I really didn't get it.

I buttered a hot, crusty dinner roll and wolfed it down.

Hank Bodine was down near my end of the table, but in no-man's-land, if you believed in close readings of dinner-table placement. Ali was on the other side, between Kevin Bross and the Brit, Clive Rylance. Both alpha males seemed to be putting the moves on her.

A couple of Mexican waiters ladled lobster bisque into everyone's bowls. Another waiter poured white wine. Upton Barlow took a sip, grunted in satisfaction, and pursed his moist red lips. He said out of the side of his mouth, 'I don't have my reading glasses—this a Meursault or a Sancerre?'

I shrugged. 'White wine, I think.'

'Guess you're more the jug-wine-with-a-screwtop type.'

'Me? Not at all. I like the gallon boxes, actually.'

He laughed politely, turned away.

Ron Slattery was keeping up his line of sock-puppet patter to Cheryl Tobin. 'Well, you've got the entire division running scared, and that's a good thing.' His mouth was a thin slash, barely any lips. His heavy black-framed glasses might have looked funky, ironic, on someone like Zoë, but on him they were just nerdy.

'Not too scared, I hope,' she said. 'Too much fear is counterproductive.'

'Don't forget, a jet won't fly unless its fuel is under pressure and at high temperature,' he replied.

'Ah, but without a cooling system, you get parts failure, right?'

'Good point,' he chortled.

Then she turned to me, raised her voice. 'Speaking of which, why'd it crash?'

She clearly wanted me to tell her in public, in front of everyone else.

'An inboard flap ripped off the wing at cruise speed and hit the fuselage.'

'Explain, please.' She really didn't need to speak so loudly.

'A three-hundred-pound projectile flying at three hundred miles an hour is going to do some serious damage.'

'Obviously.' Exasperated. 'But why'd it rip off?'

'Chicken rivets.'

'*Chicken rivets*,' she repeated. 'I don't follow.' People around us were listening now.

Even though she'd been the EVP for Commercial Airplanes at Boeing before she came to Hammond, I had no idea how much she actually knew about building aeroplanes. Lots of executives rely on their experts to tell them what to think. I didn't want to talk over her head, but I also didn't want to condescend.

'Well, so Eurospatiale's new plane is mostly made out of plastic, right?'

She gave me a look. 'If you want to call carbon-fibre-reinforced polymer "plastic" instead of composite.'

You got me there, I thought. So she did know a thing or two. 'Most of the old-line metal guys, the senior guys, still don't trust the stuff.'

'The "senior guys" at Hammond?'

'Everywhere.'

She knew what I meant, I was pretty sure—the senior execs at all the aeroplane manufacturers were inevitably older, and what they knew was metal, not composites.

'So?'

'So all the flaps on the wings are made of composite, too,' I said. 'But the hinges are aluminium. On the wing side, they're bolted to the aluminium rib lattice, but on the flaps, they're cut in.'

'The hinges are glued on?'

'No, they're co-cured—basically glued and baked together. A sort of metal sandwich on composite bread, I guess you could say. And obviously Eurospatiale's designers didn't quite trust the adhesive bond, so they also put rivets into the hinges, right through the composite skin.'

'The "chicken rivets",' she repeated, unnecessarily loud, I thought. 'Called that why?'

I glanced up and saw that more and more people around the table were watching us. I tried not to smile. 'Because you only do it if you're "chicken"—scared the bond won't hold. Like wearing a belt and braces.'

'But why are "chicken rivets" a problem?'

'When you put rivets through composites, you introduce microcracks. Means you run the risk of introducing moisture. Which is clearly what happened in Paris.'

Upton Barlow signalled one of the waiters over and told him he wanted to try whatever red wine they were pouring.

'How can you be so sure?' she said.

'The photographs. You can see cracks at the stress concentration points. You can also see the brooming, the—'

'Where the composites absorbed water,' she said impatiently. 'But the plane was new.'

'It made maybe twenty test flights before the show. Flew out of warm, rainy London up to subzero temps at forty thousand feet. So the damage spread fast. Weakened the joints. Then the flap tore off its hinge and hit the fuselage.'

'You're sure?'

'I saw the pictures. Nothing else it can be.' Ali looked at me, a glint of amusement in her eyes.

The younger of the two Mexican waiters poured red wine into Barlow's glass. It was deep red, almost blood-red. I guessed that meant it was good.

Then the waiter's hand slipped. The neck of the bottle struck the glass and tipped it over. Wine splashed on the tablecloth, speckling the head of Hammond's Defence Division's starched white shirt.

'For Christ's sake, you clumsy ox!' Barlow cried, and the lines in his forehead deepened.

'I sorry,' the waiter said, taking Barlow's napkin and daubing at his shirt. 'I very sorry.'

'Will you get the hell out of here?' Barlow snapped at the kid. 'Get your goddamn hands off my stomach.'

The waiter looked like he wanted to flee. 'Upton,' I said, 'it's not his fault. I must have knocked into it with my elbow.'

The waiter glanced quickly at me, not understanding. He couldn't have been twenty, had an olive complexion and close-cropped black hair.

The manager came out of the kitchen with a small stack of cloth napkins. 'We're so sorry,' he said, handing a few to Barlow and laying the others neatly over the stained tablecloth. 'Pablo,' he said, 'please get Mr Barlow a towel and that spray bottle of water.'

As Pablo left, I said to the manager, 'It wasn't Pablo's fault. I hit his glass with my elbow.'

'I see,' the manager said, blotting at Barlow's shirt.

Cheryl watched with shrewd eyes. After a minute, she said, 'Well, at least

Hammond would never do something so stupid as to use chicken rivets.'

I glanced at her quickly, then caught the sharp edge of Hank Bodine's menacing stare. 'Well, actually, we did,' I said.

'We did . . . what?'

'Put chicken rivets on all the wing control surfaces. Other places, too.'

'Wait a second,' she said. She sat forward, intent. 'Are you telling me our SkyCruiser team didn't *know* this might cause a serious problem?'

The waiter returned with a stack of white towels and handed them to Barlow, who said, 'I don't *need* any damned towels. I need a new shirt.'

'Excuse me,' I said to Cheryl. Then I touched the waiter's arm. '*Mira, este tipo es un idiota*,' I said softly. '*Es sólo un pendejo engreído. No voy a dejar que te meta en problemas*.' The guy's a jerk, I told him. A pompous asshole. I'd make sure he didn't get blamed for it.

He had an open, trusting face, and he looked at me, relieved.

'*Gracias, señor. Muchas gracias*.'

'*No te preocupes*.'

'You speak fluently,' Cheryl said.

'Just high-school Spanish,' I said. She didn't need to know that my 'teachers' were Latino gangstas-in-training, at a juvenile detention facility.

'But you've got the idiom down well,' she said. 'I spent a few years in Latin America for Boeing.' She lowered her voice. 'That was sweet, what you just did.'

I shrugged. 'Never liked bullies,' I said quietly.

She raised her voice again. 'You're not seriously telling me that we made the same stupid mistake, are you?'

'It's not a matter of being stupid,' I said. 'It was a judgment call. Remember a couple of years back when Lockheed built the X-33 launch vehicle for NASA? They made the liquid fuel tanks out of composite instead of aluminium. To save some weight. And during the tests, the fuel tanks ripped apart at the seams. A very public disaster. So our people looked at that, and said, man, throw in some rivets just in case the adhesive fails like it did with Lockheed.'

'"Our people". Meaning who? Whose . . . "judgment call" was it? Some low-level stress analyst?'

'I'm sure the decision must have been made at a higher level than that.'

'How high a level? Was it Mike Zorn?'

'No,' I said quickly. 'I don't really recall.'

'But the name of the engineer who signed off on it is a matter of record, isn't it?' she said. 'I'll bet you've got the spreadsheet on your computer. With the CAD number, listing the employee number of the stress analyst who signed off on the chicken rivets.' She smiled thinly. 'Am I right?'

She knew a hell of a lot more than she was letting on. The guy who signed off on all the wing drawings was a stress analyst who'd been with Hammond for fifteen years, a very smart engineer named Joe Hartlaub. I remembered how he argued, long and hard, against putting rivets through the composite skin. Remembered the emails between him and Mike Zorn. Zorn took Joe's side—then Hank Bodine jumped in and overruled them.

Bodine, who'd been building metal aeroplanes for decades, considered composites 'voodoo'. And he had the power to overrule both Zorn and the stress analyst. Bodine was the boss. He always won.

'I'm sure one of our stress analysts stamped the drawings, but the decision would have had to be made at a higher level,' I said.

'By whom?'

'I don't know.'

'Meaning that you know and won't tell me?'

'No. Meaning I'm not sure.'

'Probably an old-line metal guy, as you put it. A senior executive?'

I shrugged again.

'Because now it's clear, based on what happened in Paris, that the wings are going to have to be scrapped and rebuilt from scratch. Which will delay the launch of the SkyCruiser by six months, even a year.'

'A delay like that, we could lose billions of dollars.'

'And if we sell planes that we know to be defective, we're criminally negligent. So we don't have a choice, do we? Which is why I want to know who made the idiotic decision that's going to cost us so dearly.'

My theory was right. She was determined to use the Eurospatiale crash to undermine Hank Bodine, then get rid of him.

I just nodded.

'Well, I intend to find out who it was,' she said. 'And when I do, I will cut him out like a cancer.'

Chapter 6

The waiters cleared away the bowls and the gold-rimmed serving plates and began setting out a battalion of fresh silverware and steak knives with curved black handles and sharp carbon-steel blades.

Then the food came. And came. And came.

Raw oysters served with a pungent ponzu sauce. Saffron-buckwheat crepes with a ragout of lobster and chanterelle mushrooms. Saddle of venison stuffed with quince. Tiny braised wild partridges seasoned with juniper berries on a bed of cabbage laced with tiny cubes of foie gras.

Of course, I didn't know what half the stuff was, so I studied the menu like a lost tourist clutching a street map. I was full before the main course, and I didn't even know what the main course *was*.

At the foot of the table, Bo Lampack, the team-building coordinator, stood up and cleared his throat. The hubbub didn't subside until he clinked on his water glass for a good fifteen seconds.

'I don't know, think there's enough food here tonight?' he boomed. 'Might have to go out to McDonald's for a QuarterPounder later on, huh?'

The laughter was boisterous.

'Oh, yeah, *right*. No restaurants around here for a hundred miles. So I guess you better eat up, folks.' He looked around the table. 'Looks like we got some ladies with us this year, huh? Two beautiful ladies. You ladies think you can keep up with all these tough guys?'

I stole a glance at Cheryl. An enigmatic smile was frozen on her face like a mannequin's. Ali smiled bashfully, nodded.

'Actually,' Lampack said, 'maybe the real question is, can you tough guys keep up with the ladies? See, in case you guys are thinking you're old hands and you got a head start on the ladies—sorry. Doesn't work that way. We're going to be doing some new things this year. Get you out of your comfort zone. Some fishing—only not the kind you're used to. Some kayaking. A great new GPS scavenger hunt. Even extreme tree climbing—and lemme tell you, it ain't like when you were a kid.'

Some nervous titters.

'This isn't all fun and games, kids,' said Lampack. 'The programme is called Power Play, but it's not going to be like any play you've ever done before. You're all going to have to sign liability waivers as usual. There are dangers. We don't want any of you executives falling off tightropes and bashing your heads and delaying the launch of your new plane or anything.'

There was a weird, hostile edge to Lampack, I was beginning to see. Like he secretly resented the corporate executives he worked with and took a kind of sadistic pleasure in taunting them.

'I won't lie to you,' he said. 'There's gonna be scary moments. But it's moments like that that tell you who you really are. When you're thirty feet off the ground you learn what you're really made of, OK? You learn to confront your fears. Because this is about personal growth and self-discovery. It's about breaking down inhibitions so we can *build team spirit*.'

He reached down and picked up a large reel of half-inch white rope. He pulled out a length. 'You know what this is? This is not just your lifeline. This is *trust*.' He nodded solemnly, looked around. 'When you're walking across a cable thirty feet off the ground and someone's belaying you, you've got to trust him—or her—not to drop you, huh?'

He set the spool down. 'You'll be challenged mentally and physically. And you're all going to *fail* at some point—our courses are designed to make you fail. Not our rope, though. Hopefully.' He chuckled. 'These tests are some of the most brutal trials you'll ever go through.' He paused. 'Except maybe one of Hank Bodine's PowerPoint presentations, huh?'

Bodine clicked a smile on and off. No one laughed.

'See, I'm going to get you all out of your comfort zone and into your *learning zone*.'

A sudden explosion came from somewhere outside: the loud pop of a gunshot.

But it made no sense. This wasn't a hunting area. Everyone turned.

Lampack looked both ways, shrugged. 'Guess a grizzly must've got into someone's garbage.'

'Really?' Ali said.

'Happens all the time. Tons of grizzlies and black bears in the woods. Not supposed to shoot 'em, though people do. Get up early in the morning, and you might even see one washing himself down by the shore. Just leave 'em alone, and they'll leave you alone.' He nodded sagely. 'Now, we'll be evaluating the progress of your team development at the end of each day using the Drexler-Sibbet Team Performance Model—'

Another loud pop, then a door banged: the front door of the lodge, it sounded like.

A large man in a hunting outfit, camouflage shirt and matching trousers, and a heavy green jacket, traipsed into the room. He was well over six foot tall, heavyset and gone somewhat to fat. He was around forty with short jet-black hair that looked dyed, dark eyebrows, a neatly trimmed black goatee. *Mephistopheles*, I thought.

He stopped in the middle of the room, looked around with beady dark eyes, then approached the dining table.

'Man, oh, man,' he said loudly. 'What do we got here?' His teeth were tobacco-stained.

Lampack folded his arms. 'Private party, friend. Sorry.'

'Party?' the hunter said. 'Jeez Louise, ain't you gonna invite me in?'

He spoke with a Deep South accent so broad and drawling he sounded like a hillbilly. But there was something cold in his gaze.

He took a few steps towards the sideboard, where some of the serving dishes had been placed. 'Christ, will you look at that spread.'

'I'm sorry, but you're going to have to leave,' Lampack said. 'Let's not have any trouble.'

'Chill, Bo,' warned Bross quietly. 'Guy's probably drunk.'

The hunter approached the table, arms wide as if awed by the opulence of the spread. 'Man, looky here. Christ on crutches, look at all this *food*.'

He shoved Ron Slattery aside and grabbed a partridge right off his plate with grimy hands. Slattery's eyeglasses went flying. Then the intruder stuffed the partridge whole into his mouth and chewed open-mouthed. 'Damn, that game bird's *good*,' he said, his words muffled by the food. Grabbing a wineglass, he gulped it down like Kool-Aid, his Adam's apple bobbing. 'Mmm-*mmm*! Even better than Thunderbird.'

Hank Bodine said, 'All right, fella. Why don't you just go back to your hunting party, OK? This is a private lodge.'

The giant leaned over the table, reached for Cheryl's plate. He dug his soiled stubby fingers into the mound of porcini-potato gratin.

'Oh God,' Cheryl said in disgust, closing her eyes.

'Mashed potatoes, huh?' He made a shovel out of his forefingers, scooped up a wad, and crammed it into his mouth. 'Dee-*lici*ous.'

'Where the hell is the manager?' Cheryl said.

From the far end of the table, Clive Rylance said, 'All right, mate, just get on your way, now there's a good fellow. This is a private dinner, and I'm afraid you're outnumbered.'

The hunter gave Clive a stony look. Then a slow grin.

'You a Brit, huh? Limey?' He leaned over between me and Upton Barlow, jostling us aside. He smelt of chewing tobacco and rancid sweat. Grabbing a crepe from Barlow's plate, he said, 'You folks eat flapjacks for supper, too? I love flapjacks for supper.'

Barlow's face coloured. He pursed his lips, exasperated.

'Will someone get the manager already?' Cheryl shouted. 'My God, are you men just going to *sit* here?'

'You folks celebrating something way out here, middle of nowhere?'

Another door slammed somewhere in the back of the lodge.

A second man now entered the great room from a side hallway. This one was maybe ten years younger, also tall and bulky. He, too, wore a camouflage outfit, only the sleeves of his shirt had been ripped off, exposing biceps like ham hocks, covered in tattoos. His undersized head was shaved on the sides, a blond crew cut on top. He had a big, blank face and a small, bristly blond moustache.

'Wayne,' the first hunter called out, 'you ain't gonna believe what kinda situation we just lucked into.'

The second one smiled, his teeth tiny and pointed.

'Get your butt over here, Wayne, and try one of these here game birds.'

'Bo, would you please get Paul Fecher right this instant?' Cheryl said. 'We've got the cast of *Deliverance* here, and the man's nowhere in sight.'

Obviously she didn't see what it meant that the manager still hadn't emerged. He had to have heard this commotion; the fact that he wasn't here meant that something was very wrong.

'We don't need to shoot no deer,' the goateed hunter said. 'Never liked venison anyway.'

Lampack, relieved to get out of there, ran towards the kitchen.

'Hey!' the goateed guy shouted after him. Then, with a shrug, he turned to his comrade. 'Wait'll he meets Verne.'

The blond guy sniggered.

Bodine rose slowly. 'That's enough,' he said.

I whispered, 'Hank, don't.'

The goateed giant looked up at Bodine, and said, 'Sit down.'

But Bodine didn't obey. He walked down the length of the table slowly, shaking his head: the big man in charge, asserting his authority.

'Back to your seat, there, boss man.'

'Hank,' I whispered as Bodine passed me, 'don't mess with this guy.'

Bodine kept going, a man on a mission.

Lummis muttered to Barlow, 'Gotta be a hunting party that got lost in the woods.'

'We're in a game preserve,' Barlow replied, just as quietly. 'Great Bear Preserve. Hunting's against the law.'

'I don't think these guys care about the law,' I said.

BODINE STOOD MAYBE six feet away from the black-haired guy, his feet planted wide apart, hands on his hips, obviously trying to intimidate him.

'All right, fella, fun's over,' Bodine said. 'Move on.'

The goateed guy looked up from the food and snarled, mouth full, 'Siddown.'

'If you and your buddy aren't out of here in the next sixty seconds, we're going to call the police.' Bodine glanced over at the rest of us. He was playing to the crowd.

But the black-haired hunter just furrowed his heavy brow and gave Bodine a satanic smile. 'The po-lice,' he said, and he cackled. 'That's a good one.' Then he looked over at his comrade, potato mush on either side of his mouth. 'You hear that, Wayne? He gonna call the po-lice.'

The second intruder spoke for the first time. 'Don't think so,' he said in a strangely high voice. His eyes flitted back and forth. His arms dangled at his side, too short for his bulky torso.

Everyone had gone quiet, staring with frightened fascination, as if watching a horror movie. I said, 'Hank, come on.'

He waggled his index finger dismissively in my direction, telling me without words, *Stay out of this. None of your business.*

From the kitchen came a cry. A man's voice.

I saw the realisation dawn on people's faces.

Bodine moved to within inches of the goateed man. He was doing what he must have done hundreds of times: invading an adversary's personal space, intimidating him with his height, his commanding presence.

'Let me tell you something, friend,' Bodine said. 'You are making a serious mistake. Now, I'm going to do you a favour and give you an opportunity to move on. I suggest you take it. It's a no-brainer.'

Suddenly the man pulled something shiny and metal from his jacket: a stainless-steel revolver. He took the weapon by the barrel, and slammed the grip against the side of Bodine's face. It made an audible crunch.

Bodine let out a terrible, agonised yelp, and collapsed to his knees.

Blood sluiced from his nose. It looked broken. One hand flew to his face; the other flailed in the air to ward off any further blows.

The reaction around the table was swift and panicked. Some seemed to want to come to Bodine's assistance but didn't dare. Some screamed.

Cheryl kept calling for the manager.

'For God's sake, somebody *do* something!' Lummis gasped.

I sat there, mind racing. The second hunter, the one with the blond crew cut, hadn't moved. He was speaking into a walkie-talkie.

The goateed man, muttering, 'Call me a goddamned no-brainer,' held the weapon high in the air. It was, I noticed, a hunter's handgun, a .44 Magnum Ruger Super Blackhawk six-shooter. I'd never used one: I didn't like to use handguns for hunting.

Then the goateed man slammed the gun against the other side of Bodine's face. Blood geysered in the air.

Bodine screamed again: a strange and awful sound of vulnerability.

He fluttered both of his hands in a futile attempt to shield his bloodied face. He cried hoarsely, 'Please. *Please*. Don't.' Blood fell in large drops from his nose, spattering his shirt.

I wanted to do something, but what? Go after the guy with a steak knife? Two armed men: it seemed like an easy way to get killed.

'Buck!'

A shout from the front door. The black-haired man paused, handgun in the air, and looked. A third man entered, dressed like the other two, in camouflage trousers and jacket. He was tall and lean, sharp-featured, a strong jaw, around forty. Scraggly dark blond hair that reached almost to his shoulders.

'That's enough, Buck,' the new man said. He had a deep, adenoidal voice with the grit of fine sandpaper, and he spoke calmly, patiently. 'No unnecessary violence. We talked about that.'

The goateed one—Buck?—released his grip on Bodine, who slumped forward, spitting blood, weeping in ragged gulps.

Then the long-haired guy pulled a weapon from a battered leather belt holster. A matt black pistol: Glock 9mm, I knew right away. He waved it back and forth at all of us, in a sweeping motion.

'All right, boys and girls,' he said. 'I want all of you to line up on that side of the table, facing me. Hands on the table, where I can see 'em.'

'Oh sweet Jesus,' Hugo Lummis said, his voice shaking.

Cheryl said imperiously—or maybe bravely—'What do you want?'

'Let's go, kids. We can do this the hard way or the easy way, it's up to you. Your choice.'

THE WORDS TOOK ME BACK momentarily and I was ten years old again.

'We gonna do this the hard way?'

Dad's shadow fell across the kitchen floor. He loomed in the doorway, gut bulging under a white sleeveless T-shirt, can of Genesee beer in his hand. 'Genny', he always called it, sounded like his mistress.

Mom standing at the kitchen counter, chopping onions for chilli con carne. His favourite supper. Her hand was shaking. The tears flowing down her cheeks, she'd said, were from the onions.

I didn't know how to answer that. Stared up at him with all the defiance I could muster. Mother's little protector.

'Don't you ever hit her,' I said.

She'd told me she'd slipped in the shower. The time before that, she'd tripped on a wet floor at the Food Fair supermarket, where she worked as a cashier. One flimsy excuse after another, and I'd had enough.

'She tell you that?'

Blood roared in my ears so loud I could barely hear him. I swallowed hard. I had to look away, stared at the peeling paint on the door frame.

'I told him it was an accident.' Mom's voice from behind me, high and strained and quavering, a frightened little girl. 'Stay out of this, Jakey.'

I kept examining the peeling grey-white paint. 'I know you hit her. Don't you ever do that again.'

A sudden movement, and I was knocked to the floor like a candlepin.

'Talk to me like that one more time, you're going to reform school.'

Tears flooding my eyes now: not the onions.

'Now, say you're sorry.'

'Never. I'm not.'

'We gonna do this the hard way?'

I knew what he was capable of.

Through eyes blurry from tears, I examined the ceiling, noticed the cracks, like the broken little concrete patio at the back of the house.

'I'm sorry,' I said at last.

A few minutes later, Dad was lying in his ratty old BarcaLounger in front of the TV. 'Jakey,' he said sweetly. 'Mind fetching me another Genny?'

SLOWLY WE ALL BEGAN to gather on one side of the table. Except for Kevin Bross and Clive Rylance, I noticed. They both seemed to be edging away, as if trying to make a sudden break.

'Where's Lampack?' Ron Slattery said, his bald head glistening with sweat.

'Let's go, kids,' the long-haired man said. He pointed the Glock at Bross and Rylance. 'Nowhere to run, *compadres*,' he said to them. 'We got all the exits covered. Get over there with the rest of your buddies.'

Bross and Rylance glanced at each other, then, as if by unspoken agreement, stopped moving. I looked for Ali, saw her at the far end of the table. She appeared to be as frightened as everyone else.

Was this guy bluffing about having the exits covered? How many of them were there?

The man took out a walkie-talkie from his jacket, pressed the transmit button. 'Verne, you got the staff secured?'

'Roger,' a voice came back.

'We got a couple of guys itching to make a run for it. You or Travis see 'em, shoot on sight, you read me?'

'Roger that.'

He slipped the walkie-talkie back into his jacket, then aimed the gun at Bross. 'Which one of you wants to die first?'

Hugo Lummis cried, 'Don't shoot!'; someone else said, 'Move, just *move*!'

'Don't be idiots!' Cheryl shouted at the two men. 'Do what he says.'

'Makes no big difference to me,' the long-haired man said. 'You obey me, or you die, but either way I get what I want. You always have a choice.' He shifted his pistol a few inches towards Rylance. 'Eeny, meeny, miney, mo.'

'All right,' Bross said. The Big Ten football jock raised his hands in the air; then he and his British colleague came over to the table.

'What do you want from us?' Cheryl said.

But the long-haired guy didn't reply. He wagged his pistol back and forth in the air, ticking from one of us to the next like the arm of a metronome. He chanted in a singsong voice, 'My—mother—told—me—to—pick—the—very—best—one—and—you—are—not—it.'

His pistol pointed directly at me. 'You win.'

I swallowed hard. Stared into the muzzle of the Glock.

'It's your lucky day, guy,' he said.

My reaction was strange: I wanted to close my eyes, like a child, to make it go away. Instead, I forced myself to notice little things about the gun, like the way the barrel jutted out of the front of the slide.

'Huh,' I said, trying to sound casual. 'Never seen one of those up close.'

'It's called a gun, my friend,' he said. His eyes were liquid pewter. 'And when I pull this little thing here, which is called a trigger—'

'No, I mean I've never seen a Glock 18C before,' I said. 'Pretty rare, those things. Works like an automatic, doesn't it?'

He smiled slowly. He was a handsome man, except for those eyes, which were cold and grey and didn't smile when his mouth did. 'Sounds like you know your weapons.' He kept his gun levelled at me.

'Of course, seventeen rounds on auto won't last you very long,' I said, then immediately regretted saying it.

'Well, why don't we find out?' he said in a voice that, in any other context, you might describe as gentle.

Everyone was quiet, watching in mesmerised terror. The air had gone out of the room.

'Do I get a choice?' I asked.

HE LOOKED AT ME for a few seconds.

Then he grinned and lowered the gun. I exhaled slowly.

'All right, boys and girls, here's the drill. I want all of you to empty your pockets, put everything on the table right in front of you. Wallets, money clips, jewellery. Watches, too. Got it? Let's go.'

So it was a holdup. Nothing more than that, thank God.

'Buck, some back-up over here,' he said.

'Gotcha, Russell,' said the goateed guy, taking out his .44. I noticed he was no longer speaking in that hillbilly accent. He'd been putting it on.

'When these folks here are finished emptying out their pockets, I want you and Wayne to search 'em. Pat 'em down.'

Buck began orbiting the table, watching everyone drop wallets and money clips onto the table. Ali took off her necklace and bangles, Cheryl removed her earrings. The men removed their watches.

Russell holstered his gun and began strolling nonchalantly round the room, picking up objects, examining them with idle curiosity, then putting them down. He walked with the loose-limbed stride of someone used to a lot of physical activity. An ex-soldier, I thought, but of an elite sort—a Navy SEAL, maybe, or a member of the Special Forces.

He stopped at a long table on which one of the hotel staff had stacked blue loose-leaf Hammond binders. He picked one up and leafed through it.

Buck was making a circuit round the table, his back to me, and Wayne was frisking my room-mate, Geoff Latimer. So for a moment, no one was watching me. I moved my hand slowly across the tablecloth, grabbed the handle of a steak knife, slid the knife along the table towards me.

Then I lowered it to my side, held it flat against my thigh.

I gripped its smooth handle and ran my thumb along the knife edge. It would slice through human skin as easily as it dissected saddle of venison. Against a handgun it wouldn't do much, but it was the only weapon I had.

Russell ripped out a sheet of paper from one of the binders, folded it neatly, and put it in his jacket pocket.

Hank Bodine was now struggling to get to his feet. His face was slick with blood; he was badly wounded.

'You can just stay put,' Russell told him. He grabbed a handful of linen napkins from the table and dropped them in front of Bodine. Bodine looked at them dully, then squinted up at Russell, not understanding.

'You got a choice,' Russell said. 'You can try to stop the bleeding or haemorrhage to death. All the same to me.'

Now Bodine understood. He took a napkin, held it to his nose, moaned.

I flexed my left knee and brought my leg up behind me. Moving very slowly, I slid the knife carefully into the side of my shoe.

The lights flickered for a second.

'What the hell's that?' Russell said.

'It's the generators,' Kevin Bross muttered.

'What's that?' Russell approached Bross.

'This place is powered by generators,' Bross said. 'One of them's probably failing. Or the system switched over from one generator to another.'

Russell looked at Bross for a few seconds. 'You almost sound like you know what you're talking about.' Then he turned to Upton Barlow. 'I like your wallet.'

Barlow just stared back, his expression fierce but his small dark eyes dancing with fear.

'Guy gives you a compliment, you say "thank you",' Russell said.

'Thank you,' Barlow said.

'You're quite welcome.' Russell picked up the wallet, flipped it open. 'What's this made out of, crocodile?' He pulled out a black credit card. 'Bucky, you ever seen one of these? A *black* American Express card? Heard about 'em, but I've never actually seen one up close and personal.'

Buck approached, looked closely. 'That can't be real,' he said. 'They don't make 'em in black.' Now that he'd dropped the phoney bumpkin accent, he spoke with the flat vowels of a Midwesterner.

'Sure they do,' Russell said. 'Friend of mine told me about it. It's one step higher than platinum, even. You can buy anything with it, I heard. Sky's the limit. Yachts, jet fighters, you name it. You only get one if you're a real big cheese.' He looked closely at the card. 'Upton? That your first name?'

Barlow just stared.

Suddenly Russell had his pistol out and was pointing it at Barlow's heart.

'No!' Barlow cried. 'Christ! Yes, *yes*, that's my first name.'

'Thank you,' Russell said. 'Upton Barlow. Hammond Aerospace Corporation. You work for Hammond Aerospace, Upton?'

'Yes,' Barlow said.

'Thank you kindly.' Russell reholstered the pistol. 'I've heard of Hammond Aerospace,' Russell said. 'You guys make aeroplanes, right?'

Barlow nodded.

'You make military transport planes, too, don't you?'

No one spoke.

'Been in one of those for sure,' Russell said. 'Never had one crash on me, though, so you must be doing your job. Good work, Upton.'

He chuckled, low and husky, and advanced along the table to Kevin Bross. He leaned over, picked up Bross's wallet. He shook it, scattering the credit cards across the tablecloth, and picked one up. 'This guy only gets a platinum,' he said. 'Kevin Bross,' he read. 'Hammond Aerospace Corporation. You all with Hammond Aerospace, right?'

Silence.

'I saw those binders on the table,' he went on. 'Said something about the "Executive Council" of the Hammond Aerospace Corporation. That's you guys—excuse me, you ladies and gentlemen—right?'

Silence.

'No need to be modest, kids,' he said. 'Bucky, we just hit the jackpot.'

The lights flickered again.

Chapter 7

The others had no idea what kind of trouble we were in.

I'm sure they figured, like I did at first, that this was just a rowdy bunch of hunters, hungry and larcenous, who had stumbled upon an opulent lodge full of rich businessmen, no cops around to stop them.

But I was sure this was something far more serious. At that point, of course, I was going on nothing more than vague suspicions and instinct.

Russell, the ringleader of the hunters, ordered the crew-cut one, Wayne, to go upstairs and search all the rooms. 'I have a feeling we're gonna find laptops and whatchamacallits, BlackBerrys and all that good stuff upstairs.'

Wayne clumped across the floor and thundered up the stairs.

'Bucky, will you please make sure none of our executives here . . . "forgot" . . . anything in their pockets? Now, I read something about opening remarks by the chief executive officer. That's the boss, right? Which one of you's the boss?'

He looked around the table. No one said anything. Buck started at the far end of the table, frisking Geoff Latimer.

'Come on now, gotta be one of you guys.'

Cheryl spoke up. 'I am. Cheryl Tobin.'

'*You're* the chief executive officer?' He looked sceptical. 'Chick like you? You're the boss?'

'Chick like me,' she said. Her mouth flattened into a straight line. 'Strange but true.' The slightest quaver.

'A lady CEO, huh?'

'It happens,' she said, a little starch returning to her voice. 'Nowhere near often enough, but it happens. How can I help you, Russell?'

'So all these guys here work for you? A woman orders them around?'

Her nostrils flared. 'I lead,' she said. 'That's not quite the same as ordering people around.'

Russell grinned. 'Well, that's a good point, Cheryl. A very good point. I have the same philosophy. So maybe you can tell me, Cheryl, what you're all doing in this godforsaken fishing lodge in the back of beyond.'

'We're on an offsite.'

'An *offsite*,' he said slowly. 'That's like—what? A meeting, sort of? Chance to get out of the office and talk, that it?'

'That's right. Now, may I say something?'

'Yes, Cheryl, you may.'

'Please, just take whatever you want and leave. None of us wants any trouble. OK?'

'That's very kind and generous of you, Cheryl,' Russell said. 'I think we'll do just that. Now may I ask you something?'

She nodded. Her bosom rose and fell: she was breathing hard.

'A lady CEO gets the same money as a man?' he said.

She smiled tightly. 'Of course.'

'Huh. And I thought I read somewhere how women CEOs only get sixty-eight cents for every dollar a man CEO gets. Well, live and learn. Bucky, what do you take home on your welding job?'

Buck looked up. 'Good year, maybe thirty-eight grand.'

'You make more than that, Cheryl?'

She exhaled slowly. 'If you want me to apologise for the inequities of the capitalist system, you—'

'No, Cheryl, not at all. I've got no beef with the capitalist system. I'm just saying you might want to spread some of that around.' Now he was standing directly in front of her, only the table between them.

She looked exasperated. 'I don't carry much cash, and you're taking my jewellery.'

'Oh, I'll bet you got plenty more.'

'Not unless you plan on leading me to a cash machine at gunpoint so you can empty out my checking account.'

Russell shook his head slowly. 'Cheryl, Cheryl, Cheryl. You must think you're talking to some rube, huh? Some ignorant Bubba. Well, don't misunderstand me. You run a very big company. Makes a lot of money.'

She pursed her lips. 'Actually, we haven't been doing all that well recently. That's one of the reasons for this meeting.'

'Really? Says in that book there you have revenue of ten billion dollars and a market capitalisation of more than twenty billion. Those numbers off base?' His thumb pointed at the long table stacked with loose-leaf binders.

She paused for a few seconds, caught by surprise. 'That's not my money, Russell. The corporation's assets aren't my own personal piggy bank.'

'You telling me you can't get your hands on some of that money? I'll bet you can make one phone call and send some of those . . . assets . . . my way.'

'I'm sorry. There are all sorts of controls and procedures. I sometimes wish I had that kind of power, but I don't.'

Russell slid his pistol out of its holster and pulled back the slide. It made a *snick-snick* sound. He raised it, leaned across the table, and pointed it at her left eye. His index finger was curled loosely round the trigger.

Her eyes filled with tears. 'I'm telling you the truth.'

'Then I guess you're of no use to me,' he said softly.

'Don't!' Ali shouted. 'Don't hurt her, please. *Please!*'

Tears trickled down Cheryl's cheeks. She stared right back at Russell.

'Wait.' A male voice. We all turned.

Upton Barlow. 'We can work something out,' he said.

Russell lowered the gun, and Cheryl gasped. He turned to Barlow with interest. 'My friend Upton, with the good taste in wallets.'

'Let's talk,' Barlow said.

'I'm listening.'

'We're both rational men, we can work something out.'

'So you're the go-to guy. You're the man.'

'Look,' Barlow said, 'I just hammered out an offset deal with South Korea on a fighter plane. Everyone said it couldn't be done.'

I remembered that offset arrangement. He arranged for Hammond to transfer billions of dollars in proprietary software to Seoul so they could build our fighter jet for us, giving the Koreans everything they'd need to build their own fighter jet in a few years. It was a lousy deal.

'You sure you got the juice to make it happen?' Russell said.

'There's always a way.'

'I'm liking the sound of this, Upton.'

'And in exchange, you and your friends will agree to move on?'

'Now we're talking.'

'So let's get specific,' Barlow said. 'I'm prepared to offer you fifty thousand dollars.'

Russell gave that low husky chuckle again. 'Oh, Upton,' he said, disappointed. 'We're not even talking the same language.'

Barlow nodded. 'Do you have a figure in mind?'

'You think you can get us an even million, Upton?'

Barlow examined the table. 'Well, I don't know about that.'

'See, now, that's too bad.' Russell strolled along the table, head down as if deep in thought. When he reached the end, he circled round behind me, then stopped. 'What if I kill one of your friends? Like this fellow right here? You think that might get us to "yes", Upton?'

I felt the hairs on the back of my neck go prickly, and then I realised he'd put the gun against the back of Hugo Lummis's head. The Washington lobbyist started breathing hard through his mouth.

'Put that gun down,' Cheryl said. 'Aren't you the one who was talking about "no unnecessary violence"?'

Russell went on, ignoring her, 'You think you can dig up a million bucks, Upton, if it means saving Fatso's life?'

Droplets of sweat broke out on Lummis's brow and his big round cheeks.

'Yes,' Barlow shouted. 'For God's sake, *yes*! Yes, I'm sure it can be arranged if need be.'

But from my other side came Ron Slattery's voice. 'No, it can't. You don't have signing authority for that kind of money, Upton.'

'Signing authority?' said Russell, keeping the barrel of the Glock against Lummis's head. 'Now, that's interesting. Who has signing authority?'

The CFO fell silent. You could tell he regretted saying anything.

'For God's sake, Ron,' Barlow said, 'the guy's going to kill Hugo! You want that on your conscience?'

'Give him the goddamned money,' Lummis pleaded. 'We've got K and R insurance—we're covered, situation like this. Good God!'

'All right,' Barlow said. 'We'll make it happen somehow. Please, just put down the gun and let's keep talking.'

'Now we're cooking with fire,' Russell said. He lowered the gun. Walked up to Barlow and stood behind him. 'Because if you can get me a million dollars, company like yours, you can do better.'

After a few seconds, Barlow said, 'What do you have in mind?'

'I'm thinking a nice round number.'

'Let's hear it.'

'I'm thinking a *hundred* million dollars, Upton. Twelve of you here, that's'—he paused for maybe two seconds—'eight million, three hundred thousand bucks and change per head, I figure. OK? Let's get to "yes".'

THE STUNNED SILENCE was broken by Ron Slattery.

'But that's—that's impossible!' said the CFO. 'Our K and R insurance coverage is only twenty-five million.'

'Come on, now, Ronny,' Russell said. 'Read the fine print, bro. Gotta be twenty-five million per insuring clause. Twenty-five million for ransom, twenty-five million for accident and loss coverage, twenty-five million for crisis-management expenses, another twenty-five million for medical expenses and psychiatric care. That's a hundred million easy.'

'This is ridiculous,' Cheryl said. 'You're dreaming if you think our insurance company's going to write you a cheque for a hundred million dollars.'

Russell shook his head slowly. 'Oh, no, that's not how it works, Cheryl. The insurance companies never pay. They always insist that you folks pay, then they pay you back. Legal reasons.'

'Well, we don't have access to that kind of money,' she said.

Russell sidled up to her, his head down. 'Cheryl,' he said softly, 'Hammond Aerospace has cash reserves of almost four billion dollars in cash and marketable securities. I just read it in your binders over there.'

'Look,' said Slattery, turning round to look at Russell, 'even if we *could* somehow access that kind of money, how the hell do you think you're going to get it? Cash, unmarked bills, all that?' His slash of a mouth twisted into a sneer. 'I don't even know where the nearest bank is.'

'Now, you see, Ron, you're talking down to me, and I don't like that,' Russell said. 'Obviously I'm not talking about stacks of bills. I'm talking about a couple of keystrokes on the computer. Electronic funds transfers and all that. Takes a few seconds. I do know a thing or two.'

'We have controls in place,' Slattery said. 'Security codes and PIN numbers and callback arrangements. And which account do you imagine this hundred million dollars would go into? Your checking account? Do you have any idea how fast you'll have the FBI up your ass?'

'What I hear, the government ain't so good with offshore banks, Ron.'

Slattery was quiet for a few seconds. 'You have an offshore account,' he said. A statement, not a question.

'Anything can be arranged,' Russell said. 'If you know the right people.'

Slattery shook his head. 'Well, be that as it may,' he said, 'it's all theoretical anyway. We don't have the authority to move money like that.'

'You don't?' Russell took a folded piece of paper from a pocket in his jacket and held it up. 'Says here you folks are the "Executive Management Team" of Hammond Aerospace. CEO, CFO, treasurer, controller, blah-blah-blah. All the top guys in the company. You telling me you guys—and gals, excuse me—don't have the "authority" to transfer corporate funds?'

Slattery shook his head. His bald pate had begun to flush.

'Russell.' It was Upton Barlow.

Russell turned. 'Yes, Upton?'

'What you're really asking for is ransom, isn't that right? If you call it ransom, all you've got to do is call our headquarters in Los Angeles and make a demand. We have kidnap-and-ransom insurance. The company will have no choice but to pay you the money, then you can be on your way, simple as that. Everybody wins. Except maybe Lloyd's of London.'

Ali and I exchanged glances. She seemed as astonished as me that one of our own would actually *suggest* a ransom.

'Well, Upton, I do appreciate the suggestion,' Russell said pensively, as if he were a fellow executive helping to hash out the details of some complicated marketing strategy. 'But kidnap-for-ransom, as I see it, is for amateurs. Or banditos in Mexico or Colombia. It never works here. You think I want me and my buddies trapped in here with SWAT teams all around, shouting at us through megaphones, using us for sniper practice, helicopters circling and all that? Uh-uh. No way, José. Not when we got all the players here who can make our little deal happen.'

'I told you, we can't do that!' Cheryl said.

'Now, see, Cheryl, I'm not talking to you. You and Ronny, you seem to be the naysayers around here.' He raised his voice, addressing all of us at once. 'OK, kiddies, here's the deal. I'm gonna make a call to an old buddy of mine—a guy who knows how all this stuff works. Meanwhile, you guys have a little powwow. Figure out how you're gonna get me that money. Hey, Buck, when you're done searching everybody, I want you to tie 'em all up at the wrists. Hands in front of 'em so they can use the john if they have to.' He took out his walkie-talkie. 'Verne, you and Travis bring the staff in here, please.'

'Roger,' a voice said.

'There's no need to tie anybody up,' Cheryl said. 'Honestly—where the hell do you think we're going to go?'

'Well, Cheryl,' said Russell, 'you folks might be here a little while, see, and I never like to take chances.' He had the pleasant, confident voice of an airline pilot announcing that we'd just encountered a little 'heavy weather'. 'All right, boys and girls, my buddies here will take good care of you. By the time I get back, I'm hoping we'll all be ready to rock 'n' roll.' He smiled. 'Gonna be a kinda carrot-and-stick approach. You cooperate, we do our deal, and me and my buddies pack up and move on.'

'What's the stick?' asked Ron Slattery.

'You,' said Russell. 'We'll start with you. Thanks for volunteering.' He was talking to all of us now, his eyes hooded, nonchalant. 'You folks give me any problems, I'm going to kill my little friend Ronny. Call it a penalty for nonperformance, isn't that what you guys say?'

Slattery went pale as Russell stowed his walkie-talkie. 'I want everyone on the floor where we can see 'em,' he ordered his men.

As Buck went to grab the big reel of climbing rope that Bo Lampack had held up at dinner, the manager, Paul, and his son, Ryan, were led into the great room. Paul's face was bruised, and he was limping. The reading glasses round his neck were bent, the lenses shattered. He must have put up a struggle. Behind them followed the rest of the hotel's staff—the waiters who'd served us dinner, a podgy guy with a moustache I recognised as the handyman, two Bulgarian girls who did the cleaning. Then Bo Lampack, a long red welt across his forehead and right cheek.

Behind them came two men with guns. One was a younger version of Russell, only not as tall and with a weightlifter's build. *Prison muscles*, I thought. His head was shaved. He was in his mid-twenties, with intense greenish eyes. His face was soft, but that delicacy was counteracted by a fierce scowl. The edges of what appeared to be an immense tattoo peeked out of the crew-neck collar of his shirt.

The other, probably fifteen years older, was scrawny and mangy-looking, with dirt-coloured hair. His face was pockmarked and crosshatched with scars that were particularly dense below his left eye, which was glass. Under his good eye three teardrops were tattooed. That was prison code, I knew, meaning that he'd killed three fellow inmates while he was inside. His glass eye told me he'd also lost a fight or two.

Russell briefed the two of them. The young guy he called Travis; the older jailbird, the one-eyed man, was Verne. They took turns with the hunters I now knew as Wayne and Buck cutting lengths of rope, frisking and tying people up, then moving them one by one over to the wall on either side of the immense stone fireplace.

'Palms together like you're praying,' Verne ordered Cheryl. He wrapped a six-foot piece of rope several times round her wrists.

She winced. 'That's way too tight.'

But Verne kept going. He moved with quick, jerky motions, blinked a lot. Even before he got to me, I could smell him. He gave off a nasty funk of alcohol and cigarettes and bad hygiene. He had an alligator smile. His teeth were greyish brown, with tiny black flecks. Meth mouth. The guy was a methamphetamine addict. 'Much rather be frisking that babe down the end,' he said to Buck as he set to work patting me down. They both leered at Ali.

The steak knife I'd concealed in my shoe had become uncomfortable, even a little painful. I wondered whether there was a visible lump in the shoe leather. As Verne's hands ran down my chest and back, I held my breath so I didn't heave from the smell. My eyes scanned the dining table. The closest steak knife was just a few feet away, but if I made a grab for it, Buck—standing behind me with his revolver at the ready—wouldn't hesitate to kill me. Verne felt each of my pockets and seemed satisfied that they were empty. I didn't have a choice but to let him tie me up.

Now his hands moved down my trousers legs, down to my feet. All he had to do was to slip his fingers into the tops of my shoes, and he'd discover the knife handle. Verne's hands grasped my ankles. I looked down. A few drops of sweat trickled down my neck under my shirt.

'See that guy over there?' I said.

'Huh?' He looked up at me. 'Don't try anything.'

'The silver-haired guy with the bloody face. He needs to be taken care of.'

He sliced a long piece of rope into smaller sections, using a serious-looking tactical knife. 'I look like a doctor to you?'

'You guys don't want to lose him. Then you'll be facing a manslaughter charge on top of everything else. I know first aid,' I said. 'Let me take a look at him before you tie me up.'

'Uh-uh.'

'Your friend Buck has a gun pointed at me and I don't have a weapon.'

'Let him,' Buck said. 'I'll keep watch.'

'Thank you,' I said.

Bodine was sitting with his legs folded. His face was battered and swollen. He looked up at me, humiliated and angry, like a whipped dog. I sat down on the floor next to him. 'How're you feeling?' I said.

He didn't look at me. 'You don't want to know.'

'Mind if I take a look?'

'Lost a couple of teeth,' he said.

I gingerly felt his face, under his eyes. He winced. 'You might have a broken cheekbone,' I said.

'Yeah? So what am I going to do about it now?' he said bitterly.

'Take some Tylenol. Or whatever pain meds we have.'

'Not going to happen with these assholes,' he said quietly.

'We can try. Your nose might be broken. If we can get some Kleenex or some toilet paper, you should stuff some up your nose. Just to stop the blood flow. We've got to get you medical attention.'

Bodine gave me a fierce look. 'Yeah? When?'

'Soon as we can. Soon as this is over.'

'When's that going to be?'

I was surprised he'd said it. It was a sign of how far he'd fallen, how demoralised he was. Hank Bodine was always in charge.

Buck yelled to me, 'Time's up. This ain't a church social.'

I said softly to Bodine, 'Depends on how we play it.'

Bodine nodded once.

I said, 'There's blood and stuff all over your trousers. Let me see if they'll get you another pair from your room. Least they can do.'

He watched me as I got up, then said, 'Hey.'

'Yeah?'

'Thanks.'

Chapter 8

The whole place smelt of cigarette smoke: Verne was chain-smoking at the other end of the room as he frisked Ali, paying a bit too much attention to areas on her body where she wasn't likely to hide a weapon.

We sat on the wideboard floor on either side of the fireplace, in two groups. On the other side—which might as well have been miles away—were the manager, the other lodge staff, and John Danziger and Alan Grogan. Hank Bodine, lying on our side, seemed to be unconscious. All the lights were on, giving the room a harsh, artificial cast.

Verne had wound the rope round my wrists a little too tightly, before tying the ends expertly with a couple of overhand knots. 'There we go,' he'd said. 'Try and get out of that. Harder you pull against it, tighter it gets. Give yourself gangrene, you're not careful.'

Geoff Latimer, next to me, tried to shift his hands to get them more comfortable. 'I wonder if I'm ever going to see my wife and daughter again,' he said softly. He looked ashen.

Cheryl said, 'This damned rope is too tight. I'm already losing circulation in my hands.' She looked weary, suddenly ten years older. Without her big earrings she looked somehow vulnerable, disarmed.

'I wish I could help you,' Ron Slattery said. 'But my hands are tied.'

If that was his attempt at black humour, no one laughed.

I said, 'You want me to call one of them over here to retie you?'

Cheryl shook her head. 'The less we have to do with them, the better. I'll get used to it. Hopefully this isn't going to be too long.' She paused, looked at me, spoke quietly. 'We have to get the word out. Somehow we have to tell the outside world what's going on.'

I didn't think our captors could hear us. Russell was outside somewhere, and the guy I was convinced was his brother, Travis, was patrolling the room, his gun at his side, a good distance away. The blond crew-cut lunk was back upstairs grabbing loot. The other two—Buck, the black-goateed one, and Verne, the junkie, were at the far end of the room.

'How?' Kevin Bross said. 'You have a sat phone you're not telling us about?'

Cheryl glared at him. 'No. But the manager has one. He keeps it locked in his office. I know, because I've used it.' She glanced at the stone wall that made up one side of the fireplace. 'Maybe one of us can sneak over there.'

Bross snorted.

Upton Barlow straightened his shoulders. 'Now, isn't that interesting,' he said with heavy sarcasm. 'And I thought we were all supposed to be "offline", as you put it.'

'One of us had to be reachable, Upton,' Cheryl said icily. 'I am the CEO, after all. And I wouldn't get too high and mighty if I were you,' she said. 'Wasn't it you who made Russell an offer—put the whole ransom idea in his head? Brilliant.'

'That idea was already in his head,' Bross said. 'He and his thugs broke in here to rip us off.'

'Forgive me for my clumsy attempt to save your life,' Barlow said, his syrupy baritone dripping with contempt. 'Or maybe you've forgotten that he was pointing a gun at your face at the time?'

'Cheryl,' said Lummis, 'he *was* about to kill you and me both.'

'And wasn't it you who told him about our K and R insurance?' Cheryl turned to face Lummis. 'In violation of our strict secrecy agreement with Lloyd's of London? Do you realise the policy becomes null and void if you reveal its existence to anyone outside the executive council?'

Lummis's plump cheeks were slick with sweat. 'Good God almighty, I'd say this qualifies as a situation of extreme duress.'

The fact that we had a kidnap-and-ransom insurance policy was news to me, too, but I didn't get what the big deal was about revealing its existence. Hammond Aerospace was a multi-billion-dollar company with very deep pockets anyway; would knowing about the policy encourage potential kidnappers to escalate their demands?

'Hey, folks, let's all just count to ten,' said Bo Lampack. 'I know tempers are short, but we need to work together as a team. Remember, if we all row together, we'll get there faster.'

'Oh Christ,' said Bross. 'Where'd this knucklehead come from?'

Lampack looked bruised. 'Hostility's not productive.'

'In any case,' Cheryl said, 'it would be grossly negligent of me as CEO to allow us to give in to this extortion.'

Lampack, ignored by everyone, now just watched in sullen defeat.

'You have a responsibility,' Barlow said, 'to protect our lives. The lives of the people who run this company.'

'Cheryl,' Slattery said, in a reasonable voice, 'you know, we lost a whole lot more than that last quarter on the telecom satellite we're building for Malaysia, right? If we have to take a hundred-million-dollar charge for an extortion demand, or ransom, or whatever we call it—'

'Which I'm sure is covered by our K and R insurance,' Lummis put in.

Cheryl was shaking her head. 'You know this is not how it works, Ron. In Latin America, when the *secuestradores* kidnap an American executive, they never get more than thirty per cent of their initial ransom demand. If you pay them any more, they'll think they didn't ask enough. This guy's demanding a hundred million dollars, but the moment we go along with him he's going to think, If a hundred million was that easy, why not a *billion*? Why not *four billion*? Why not demand every last goddamned dollar we have in our cash reserves?'

I nodded; she was right.

'We don't know that, Cheryl,' Slattery said. His glasses were smudged, the frames slightly askew. 'He won't necessarily escalate his demands.'

She shook her head. 'No, Ron, I'm sorry, but one of us has to say no, and that's got to be me. We're going to refuse to give in to his demands.'

A panicked expression flashed across Slattery's face, but he said nothing. You could see his loyalty warring with his survival instinct. Russell had promised that he'd be the first to be killed if we didn't cooperate. Yet he was Cheryl's man, the only one here who owed his job directly to her. Her only ally on the executive council. Except for maybe Geoff Latimer; but Latimer seemed to be the sort who was careful not to take sides.

'She's going to get us all killed,' Bross said, shaking his head.

'How easy it must be for you to issue orders, Cheryl,' said Barlow. 'After all, you're not the one he's going to shoot first if we don't cooperate.' His eyes shifted from Cheryl to Slattery. He'd seen daylight between the CEO and her toady, and he was determined to widen the crack.

'Oh, come on,' Cheryl said. 'These buffoons aren't actually going to kill anyone. They're thugs, but they're not murderers.'

'Oh Jesus Christ,' Bross snapped. 'These are a bunch of trigger-happy outlaws with guns. You are so out of your league here, Cheryl.'

I agreed with Bross, but I wasn't going to say so.

'They're hunters who got lost,' Cheryl said. 'They're tired and hungry and all of a sudden they see this lodge, and they get the big idea to try a holdup. They won't do anything so stupid as to kill one of us. They're hunters, not hired killers.'

I couldn't hold back any longer. 'I don't think they're hunters,' I said softly.

'Why don't we find out what your CFO has to say about this,' Barlow said with a malevolent smile. 'Ron's the one who gets his brains blown out first.'

Slattery looked at Barlow, the panicked look returning, but he didn't reply.

Bo Lampack was trying to get everyone's attention, so we stopped and looked at him.

'If I may say something?' Lampack said. There was silence, so he went on. 'Let's face it—a gun is really a phallus. Men who wave guns around are just waving their dicks around. To challenge them outright is to emasculate them, which could provoke a really hostile reaction—'

'Will someone tell Russell to get in here and shoot this guy?' said Bross.

Lampack looked round for support, and when no one came to his defence, he sat back, looking deflated.

'They're not hunters,' I tried again, a little louder.

Finally, Cheryl looked at me. 'What makes you so sure of that, Jake?'

'For one thing, they're not equipped like hunters.'

'And you know this how?'

'Because I hunt. I shoot.'

'You shoot?' Bross said. 'What, paintballs?'

'You want to hear me out?'

'Not especially.'

'Let the kid talk,' Barlow said wearily, then complained, 'I've got to get to the john before my bladder bursts.'

'Start with their outfits,' I said. 'The camouflage. It's not the kind of camouflage you get at a hunting store,' I said. 'It's old military-issue.' The pattern was the chocolate-chip camouflage, which the army had discontinued around the time of the first Gulf War. 'They're also wearing genuine military jackets, with gear clips and mag pouches.'

'So maybe they picked up their outfits at some Army-Navy surplus store somewhere,' Cheryl said.

'That's possible,' I said. 'Sure. But they're carrying banana clips on their jackets. I've never heard of a legit hunter carrying a banana clip. And that gun that Russell was waving around was a Glock 18C.'

'Yeah,' Bross said with heavy sarcasm. 'We were all impressed by your knowledge of firearms.'

'Excellent,' I said. 'That was my whole point—to impress you, Kevin.

Then again, maybe I was trying to figure out how much he knew about it. Maybe even where he might have got it. See, the Glock 18 is banned for sale to anyone who's not in law enforcement or the military.'

'What—what are you saying, they're ex-soldiers?' Slattery said.

'Were you in the army?' Barlow asked.

'The National Guard Reserve. But my dad was a Marine,' I said.

'Maybe they're one of those home-grown militias,' said Slattery. 'You know, those crazy survivalist gangs.'

'A couple of them look like they've done time in prison,' I said.

'I wonder if they're fugitives of some sort,' Latimer said. 'Remember that old Humphrey Bogart movie called *The Desperate Hours*? These escaped convicts are looking for a place to hide, and they break into this suburban house and they hold the family hostage—'

'What difference does it make who they are?' Cheryl said. 'Their threats are hollow.'

'You're partly right,' I said. 'It doesn't really make a difference who they are or where they're from. But their weapons tell me two things. One is that Russell knows what he's doing. He's no amateur.'

'More speculation,' Cheryl said.

'And what's the other thing?' Slattery asked.

'That these guys aren't here by accident,' I said.

'What do you mean?' Slattery said. 'You think they planned—'

But then we fell silent as Verne brought Ali over. He held a gun on her: a stubby little stainless-steel Smith & Wesson with a two-inch barrel.

'I enjoyed that, sugar tits,' Verne said with a manic leer. 'Let's do that again soon without our clothes, huh?'

Ali gave him a glacial stare. Under her breath, she said, 'I'm not really into short-barrelled weapons.'

He heard it and he hooted. 'Whoa, that chick's got a *mouth* on her!'

'Hey, Verne,' I said.

He turned, eyes wild.

'You touch a hair on her head, and I'll take out your good eye.'

'With what?' He smirked. 'You can't even take a piss unless I say so.'

'Hey,' Barlow called out. 'Speaking of which, I need to take a leak.'

'So?'

'What the hell am I supposed to do?'

'Wet yourself for all I care,' Verne said with a cackle.

I gave Ali a questioning look: *Are you OK?*

She smiled cryptically. She seemed more angry than frightened, which wasn't surprising. That was Ali: she was a fighter, not easily intimidated. I'm sure it was something Cheryl had recognised in her immediately, a trait the two women shared.

'Excuse me,' Latimer called out. He looked haggard. 'I need my . . . insulin.'

'Your what?' Verne said.

'There's a kit upstairs in my room. In my dresser. With syringes and a blood-test kit and some insulin. Please. Just let me go up and get it.'

'You're not bringing a bunch of needles in here. Sorry, guy. Deal with it.'

'But if I—please, if I don't get my insulin, I could go into a coma.'

'Hate to lose a hostage,' Verne said, swivelling away.

'I didn't know you were diabetic, Geoff,' Cheryl said. 'How serious is this?'

'It's serious, but I don't have any symptoms yet. Just really thirsty.'

'Did you mean it about going into a coma?'

'If too much time goes by, it can happen. Though I think I'll make it for a couple more hours. If I drink a lot of water.'

'*Damn* them,' Cheryl said. She turned round and yelled, 'Someone get this man a glass of water *now*! And his *insulin*!' Her voice echoed.

Travis came over, gun levelled. 'What's the problem?' he said, scowling.

'Get this man some water,' she said. 'He's a diabetic, and he needs water immediately. He also needs his insulin shot.'

'And I need to use the rest room,' Barlow added.

'That's up to Russell,' Travis said. 'I'll see.' Looking uncomfortable, he turned, crossed the room towards the dining area, and began speaking to the crew-cut guy, Wayne, who'd come back down from upstairs.

'Thank you,' Latimer said. 'Even if they won't get my insulin, the water should help.'

'I still haven't heard why Landry thinks this whole thing was planned,' Slattery said.

'They're wearing the wrong brand of hunting jacket,' Bross cracked sarcastically. 'A big fashion "don't" in your world, that it?'

I refused to let him get to me. 'They came in here knowing exactly where to go and what to do. They knew where everything was the second they arrived—the kitchen, the front door, the upstairs. They knew which exits to cover. As if they'd scoped the place out in advance. It just feels too well planned to be a coincidence but they were trying to make it look like a random, unplanned break-in.'

'Why?' said Cheryl.

'I don't know,' I admitted. 'But I'll figure it out.'

'I think Jake may be right,' Ali said. 'Look at who comes here—mostly rich people and corporate groups. Who else can afford it? All these rich folks out here in total isolation. Sitting ducks.'

'Russell knows too much about Hammond,' I said. 'All that stuff about our cash reserves—I doubt he figured that out tonight, on the spot, by looking at a balance sheet. He already knew it ahead of time.'

'It's all out there on the public record,' said Barlow.

'Sure. But that means he did research on Hammond before coming here.'

For a few seconds, everyone was silent.

Then Slattery said, 'But how'd he know in advance that we'd be here?'

'You guys come here every year around the same time,' I said. 'It's no secret.'

'Excuse me,' Bross said. 'I don't even know why anyone's listening to you. Did anyone ask you for your opinion? You're not even a member of the executive council, or have you forgotten that? You're a substitute.'

Amazing: here we were, held hostage at gunpoint, and all Bross wanted to do was one-up me. With Hank Bodine at least temporarily incapacitated, Bross probably considered himself the reigning alpha male.

'I got news for you, Kevin,' I said. 'There's no more executive council. Not any more. Not now. Your life is no more important than mine or anyone else's. Neither is your opinion. We're all just hostages now.'

I heard a groan, then a familiar rumbling voice. 'Well put, Landry,' Hank Bodine said.

BODINE'S SILVER HAIR was mussed, clumps of it standing on end. His eyes had all but disappeared into the swollen mass of his cheeks.

'There he is,' Bross said. 'How're you doing?'

'What do you think?' Bodine tried to sit up. 'What's this, they tied me up, too? The hell they think I'm gonna do?'

Bodine's mere conscious presence had reordered the group like a magnet waved over iron filings. You could tell it rankled Cheryl. She needed to take charge. 'The issue isn't who they are or how they got here,' she said. 'The issue is how we're going to deal with it.'

'Tell me something,' Lummis said. 'Do we even have the ability to do this—to make a funds transfer from here—if we wanted to?'

No one replied for a few seconds, then Ali said, 'I'm sure he knows about the Internet connection in the manager's office.'

'That's not what I mean. Can it be done from here? Can we really transfer a hundred million dollars out of the corporate treasury to some offshore account, just using the manager's laptop?'

More silence. Cheryl looked at her chief financial officer: she didn't seem to know the answer either.

Slattery took off his glasses and ran a hand over his forehead. 'I could transfer funds out of one of our accounts from a laptop at Starbucks.'

'You're kidding,' Lummis said.

'No, unfortunately, I'm not,' said Slattery.

'Hold on a second,' Bross said. 'Are you telling me that any lunatic could just put a gun to your head and empty the company's treasury? We don't have any security procedures in place? I don't believe it.'

There was something about Bross's tone—he sounded incredulous, but in an exaggerated way—that made me suspicious. Then there was the look of irritation that Slattery gave him in response. Bross, I realised, already knew the answer. He gave a quick, furtive glance at Bodine, seemed to be performing for him. Bodine's eyes were open, but the lids were drooping.

'It's more complicated than that,' Slattery said.

'Ron,' said Cheryl, 'you don't need to get into this. It's beside the point.'

'Well, I want to hear it,' said Bross. 'It's very much the point.'

'Don't even dignify that, Ron,' Cheryl said.

'The fact is,' Slattery said, 'the bank's computers don't know if they're talking to a computer inside Hammond headquarters in LA or some old Macintosh in a fishing lodge in British Columbia.'

'How is that possible?' said Bross.

'Well, it's—anytime you log on to our system from outside the headquarters building, you're creating a virtual tunnel into what's called the VPN, the Hammond virtual private network. All the bank computers see is a Hammond IP address. For all the bank knows, it's getting a message from my office on the thirty-third floor on Wilshire Boulevard.'

'Ron,' Cheryl said, '*enough*.'

But Slattery kept going. 'For large, sensitive transactions the bank requires two authorised users to make the request. Then on top of that, there's dual-factor authentication.'

'Which is?' Barlow's raisin eyes narrowed.

'Forget it,' said Cheryl. 'We're not making any transfer.'

'Sounds to me,' Bodine suddenly said, 'like you're trying to shut him up. I want to hear this.'

Cheryl just shook her head, furious. She did seem to want to keep Slattery from talking.

'You enter a user name and password as usual,' Slattery said, 'but you also have to use a secure ID token. Which generates random, one-time passwords—six-digit numbers—every sixty seconds. You take the number off the token and enter it on the website.'

'So, if we don't have one of those doohickeys, we can't do the transfer,' Barlow said. 'I'm sure you don't carry one around with you, right?'

'It's on my key ring, upstairs in my room,' Slattery said. 'But Russell's probably got it by now.'

'These fellas aren't going to know what it is,' Barlow said.

Slattery shrugged. 'If they know what they're doing, they will. The bank logo's printed right on it.'

'Anyone else have a token like that?' asked Barlow. '*I* don't.'

'Just the ones who have signing authority for financial transactions greater than, I think, fifty million dollars. Authorised users.'

Cheryl turned slowly to Slattery. 'I don't believe I have such a token,' she said.

'That's because you don't need to dirty your hands with all that financial . . . plumbing work. It's just for the guys like me who're involved directly with the finances.' Slattery was starting to sound evasive.

Cheryl was unrelenting. 'Who has the signing authority at that level? Besides me, I mean.'

Slattery gave a tiny shake of his head, as if cueing her to stop asking.

'What are you telling me?' she said.

'I mean—well, actually, you don't have signing authority,' Slattery said. 'Not for a one-off cash transaction of that magnitude, anyway.'

Cheryl's cheeks immediately flushed. 'I see. Then who does?'

'I do, of course,' Slattery said. 'And the treasurer. The general counsel, and the controller. Grogan, Latimer and Danziger.'

'And Hank, I assume.'

He nodded.

'I see,' Cheryl said.

'Did I just hear what I thought I heard?' Bross said. 'You actually don't even *have* the power to stop us from wiring out the funds, do you? Since you don't have the power to authorise it.'

Cheryl looked at him for several seconds, her nostrils flaring. 'Perhaps not. But I'm the CEO of this company, Bross. And if I hear any more of your insubordination, you're going to be cleaning out your office.'

'If any of us survive,' Barlow said.

'We're not wiring a hundred million dollars to these criminals,' Cheryl said. 'It's as simple as that. *I will not allow it*.'

'Cheryl, please,' said Slattery. 'We all know what he's going to do if we refuse. *Please*.'

'Once we give in to this extortion, it'll never stop,' she said. 'I'm sorry.'

'You know,' Barlow said, 'I don't think you have the power to stop us. Am I right, Ron?'

Slattery glanced anxiously from Cheryl to Barlow, then back again.

Cheryl examined the rope round her wrists. 'Ron,' she said in a warning tone, without looking up. 'I expect your complete support.'

Slattery turned to her. 'I'm—I'm sorry, Cheryl. But this is just—this happens to be the one case where we disagree. We really have no choice but to give the guy the money he wants. But—'

'That's enough, Ron,' Cheryl said, cutting him off. You could almost see the icicles hanging down from her words. 'You've made yourself clear.'

I saw the tears in Ali's eyes and felt the bad wolf start to stir.

Chapter 9

'Guys,' I said, 'how about we spare the office politics and concentrate on trying to get out of here alive? Cheryl's right: if we give in too easily to Russell's demands, there'll be no reason for him not to keep jacking the price up.'

What I didn't say, of course, was that I didn't really care how much money Hammond Aerospace paid out in ransom.

'Yet we can't just say no. Because whoever these guys are, you don't carry weapons like that if you're not prepared to use them.'

Cheryl arched a quizzical eyebrow. 'So what are you suggesting?'

I turned to Slattery. 'What's the account number?'

'Which account number?' Slattery said.

'If you want to access our cash management accounts at the bank, you've got to know the account numbers, right? You have them all memorised?'

Slattery looked at me as if I'd lost my mind. 'Of course not. I keep a list in my office . . .' His voice trailed off as it dawned on him. 'But not here.'

'You need to call in to the office to get those numbers. Right?'

'Excellent,' Cheryl said.

'You think he'll let me make a call?' Slattery asked.

'If he wants his money, he will.'

'What good does that do us?' Bross said. 'That buys us maybe five minutes. That's pathetic.'

'It gets him on the phone with one of his assistants, Kevin. And then maybe Ron can communicate that everything's not OK here.'

'Oh, sure,' Bross said. 'Right. Russell's going to just stand there while Ron asks his secretary for our bank account numbers, and says, "Oh, by the way, I've got a gun to my head, so you might want to notify the police."'

'There's something called a duress code,' I said to Bross. I kept my tone calm—but condescending, as if explaining to a particularly slow child. 'A distress signal. A word or phrase that sounds perfectly normal to Russell but actually alerts whoever he's speaking to that something's wrong.'

'You got a better idea, Bross?' Hank Bodine said.

'Yeah,' Bross said. 'Keep it simple. All we do is tell him we can't wire money from any computer outside of Hammond headquarters.'

'No,' I said. 'If he's done his homework, he'll know that's not true.'

'Most of *us* didn't know if we could or not,' Barlow said. 'Why should he know any better?'

'And what if he has a source inside the company?' I said. 'We sure as hell don't want to get caught lying to him. Do we, Ron?' Slattery didn't reply. He didn't have to. 'Let's not find out the hard way what he knows and what he doesn't,' I continued.

'Then we just pay it,' Bross said.

'And after we pay the ransom,' I said quietly, 'what makes you think these guys are going to just let us go?'

Bross started to reply, but stopped.

'They're not wearing masks or hoods,' I said. 'They're not concerned about being identified. Why do you think that might be?'

'Oh Jesus,' said Barlow, realising.

'There's only one possible reason,' I said. 'They don't plan to leave any witnesses.'

Lummis exhaled audibly, tremulously, and his large frame went slack.

'I don't have any duress code worked out with my office,' Slattery said.

'Just say something unexpected,' I said. 'Something *off*. Something that might alert someone who knows you well enough that you're in trouble.'

'But what about Grogan and Danziger?' Slattery turned to me. 'For all I know, one or both of those guys has our account numbers memorised. They might think they're being helpful and volunteer the information to Russell, then there's no phone call.'

I nodded. 'We have to get to them. Make sure they know the plan.'

Grogan and Danziger were sitting on the other side of the river-stone fireplace, twenty or thirty feet away. The fireplace jutted out a good six feet. They were so far away that we couldn't even see them.

The only way to speak to them was actually to get up and move round the fireplace to the other side. But the moment one of our kidnappers saw anyone attempting that . . .

The front door banged, and Russell entered.

'YOU LOST YOUR MIND?' Dad said.

'I don't know what you're talking about.'

'Trying to rip me off? You didn't really think you could get away with it, did you?'

Suddenly he had the crook of his arm round my neck and was squeezing hard. I could smell his Old Spice, his boozy breath.

'Hey!' I felt the blood rush to my head. 'Cut it out!'

'We can do this the hard way or the easy way. Up to you.'

I tried to prise his arm loose, but he was much stronger. I was thirteen, tall and scrawny. Everything was bleaching out.

On the bulging muscle of his upper arm, the Marine Corps tattoo: an eagle, a globe, an anchor, a circle of stars, 'USMC' in Old English lettering.

'You know how easy I could break your neck? Either you're gonna give me back the fifty bucks, or I'm gonna break your neck. Which it gonna be?'

I'd taken the money from the cigar box in his dresser to buy a bus ticket and get the hell out of the house. A cousin was at college in Bellingham, Washington. I figured the fifty dollars would get me at least halfway across the country, and I'd beg or borrow or steal the rest. Once I showed up at Rick's apartment, he wasn't going to turn me away. The worst thing was leaving Mom alone there with Dad, unprotected, but I'd pretty much given up on her. I'd begged her to leave, and she wouldn't.

Finally, I gasped, 'All right!'

Dad loosened his grip, and I sank to the floor.

He held out his hand, and I fished the crumpled bills from the back pocket of my jeans. Tossed the wad onto the wall-to-wall carpet.

He smiled in triumph. 'Didn't I teach you nothing? What kind of pussy are you, can't defend yourself?'

'I'll tell my guidance counsellor what you did.'

'You do that, and I'll tell the cops how you been stealing money from your parents, and you know what's gonna happen to you? They'll send you right to the boys' home. Reform school. That'll straighten you out.'

'Then I'll just take one of your guns and steal the money.'

'Hah. You gonna rob a bank, Jakey? Or the 7-Eleven?'

I sat there, head spinning, as he went downstairs to the kitchen. Heard the refrigerator door open. The hiss of a pop-top: a can of Genny.

Mom was standing at the top of the stairs in her Food Fair smock, tears in her eyes. She'd seen the whole thing.

'Mom,' I said.

She gave me a long, imploring look, and for a moment she looked like she was coming to give me a consoling hug.

Instead, she gave me another sad look and went down the hall to the master bedroom to change out of her work clothes.

'WHO'S BEEN SMOKING?' Russell said.

He sniffed the air, turned towards the dining table. 'Verne, that you?'

'What about it?' Verne said.

'I don't want to be breathing secondhand smoke. You take it outside next time.'

'Sorry, Russell. OK if I go out for a smoke right now?'

I had a feeling he was going to do more than smoke a cigarette.

'Make it fast,' Russell said. He clapped his hands. 'All right, let's get down to business. Where's my little buddy Ronny?'

He crossed the room to our side of the fireplace. 'How're you doing there, little guy?'

Slattery nodded sullenly. 'Fine.'

Barlow said, 'I need to use the bathroom.'

Russell ignored him. 'You have a family, Ronny?'

Slattery hesitated.

'Three daughters, right?'

Slattery looked up suddenly. 'What are you—?'

'Divorced, that right? You cheat on your wife, Ronny?'

'I don't have to answer that.'

Russell patted his holster. 'No, you don't,' he said. 'You have a choice.'

'*No*,' Slattery said. 'I'll—I'll answer. I didn't start seeing anyone until after our marriage pretty much—'

'Ronny,' he interrupted, shaking his head and making a *tsk-tsk* sound. 'If a man can't live up to his marital vows, why should anyone trust his word? You love your daughters, Ronny?'

'More than anything in the world,' Slattery said. His voice shook, tears flooding his eyes.

'How old are they, your daughters?'

'Sixteen, fourteen and twelve.'

'Aw, that's nice. But girls can be difficult at that age, am I right?'

'Please,' Slattery said. 'I love them with all my heart. Russell, *please*.'

'They don't live with you, do they?'

'They spend every weekend with me,' Slattery said, 'and every—'

'That the best you can do, Ron? Weekends? But I guess it's better than nothing, right? Better to have a weekend dad than no dad at all.'

'Please,' Slattery said, 'what do you want?'

'I'm counting on you, Ronny. To make sure everything goes smoothly.'

Slattery nodded frantically.

'I need to take a goddamned *piss*!' Barlow shouted abruptly. 'I'm about to *explode*. You want me to do it right here on the floor?'

Russell grinned. 'Upton, sounds to me like you've got an enlarged prostate gland. Guy your age ought to be taking saw palmetto extract. It's the only body you got. You really should take care of it.' He raised his arm, flipped his fingers. 'Buck, please escort poor Mr Barlow to the head.'

Buck sauntered over at a leisurely pace, and grabbed Barlow roughly by the arm.

Cheryl said, 'I need to use the rest room as well. I'm sure others do, too.'

'Thank you for the suggestion, Cheryl,' said Russell. 'Anyone else needs to use the facilities, my team will assist you, one at a time. Now, Ronny, have we figured out how we're going to make this transaction work?'

Slattery swallowed hard, nodded.

'Look,' Bross said, 'let me tell you something that everyone else is afraid to tell you. We don't have the ability to make a bank transfer from here.'

'No?' Russell said.

Bross nodded. 'No. Online bank transfer requests can only originate from computers inside Hammond headquarters.'

Russell looked at him curiously for a moment, tipped his head to one side. 'Tell me your name again.'

'Kevin Bross.'

'Bross,' repeated Russell. 'Bross Balls, huh? Well, Bross Balls, maybe you can explain that to me a little more.' He was speaking in that fake-innocent way I'd begun to recognise. 'Use small words, please.'

'See, every computer has what's called an IP address,' Bross said. 'And the bank's computers won't talk to another computer unless it has the right IP address.'

'Really?' Russell said. 'Gosh, that's bad news.'

Bross nodded. 'I'm sorry to break it to you, but that's just the way it is.'

'This is interesting,' Russell said. He reached into his pocket, pulled out a small grey plastic object a few inches long. At its round end was the bright green logo of our bank; at the narrow end was a digital LCD read-out.

'Because when I called your bank about setting up a corporate account, they said I could initiate a wire transfer from anywhere in the world, no problem. Just a wild guess, Bross Balls, but I'm thinking this here might be an RSA SecurID authenticator.'

Bross licked his lips. 'Right, but Hammond Aerospace has a whole system of security protocols in place, Russell—'

'I thought you were just telling me how the bank's computers won't recognise an unauthorised IP address, Bross,' Russell said softly. 'We weren't talking about your internal security procedures, were we?'

Bross faltered for a few seconds. 'I'm telling you everything I know, to the very best of my knowledge—'

'You know something, Bross? I'm disappointed in you, executive vice-president of Sales and all. So now we're gonna have a change in plans. I'm going to have a little talk with each one of you separately. You're each gonna tell me *privately* everything you know about how to transfer money out of Hammond. That way I'll know if anyone's trying to pull a fast one on me. See if there's any contradictions. Anyone lies to me, we're gonna have a little downsizing, you might say. Oh, and one more thing. The price just went up. Teach you kids a lesson. It's five hundred million now. Half a billion.'

I turned to look at Ali, but all at once the lights went out, and we were plunged into darkness.

'WHERE'S THE MANAGER?' Russell called out in the darkness.

'Over here.' A voice from the other side of the fireplace.

The clear night sky was filled with stars, and the moon was full. The room was bathed in pale grey-blue light. My eyes quickly adjusted. Russell went to the other side of the fireplace.

'What the hell's wrong with your power?'

'I don't—I don't know,' the manager said. 'Must be the generator.'

'Well, who does know? Who fixes stuff around here?'

'Peter Daut,' the manager said. 'He's my handyman.'

'All right, Peter Daut,' Russell said. 'Identify yourself.'

'Right here.' A muffled voice.

'What's the problem?'

More muffled voices. The handyman seemed to be talking to the manager. Then I heard the manager say, 'Yes, Peter, please.'

'You want to cooperate, Peter,' Russell said. 'No power means the satellite modem won't work, which means I don't get what I want. Which means I start eliminating hostages one by one until I do.'

'The generator blew.'

Peter the handyman, I assumed.

'Water in the fuel filter. The diesel's always absorbing water out here, and I can't drain the tanks, so I just keep changing out the filters. The fuel filter needs to be changed, out at the shed.'

'Wayne?' Russell said.

'Yo, Russell,' Wayne replied from the far side of the room.

'Please take this gentleman outside so he can fix the generator.'

While Wayne lumbered over, Russell returned to our group. 'Ronny, you're my first interview. Come with me, please.'

Slattery struggled to his feet. With his hands tied, it wasn't easy. 'Would you mind if I use the rest room first?' he asked.

'When Upton gets back. One at a time. OK, Travis, Ronny and I are going to have a talk in the screened porch down at that end.' He pointed in the direction of the dining table. 'Keep a watch on our guests, please.'

IN THE SHADOWS I could make out Travis striding along the periphery of the room, a compact stainless-steel pistol at his side. He'd removed his long-sleeved camouflage shirt and wore only a sleeveless white tee. But his arms were so densely tattooed that it looked like he was still wearing camouflage.

'Nice job, Kevin,' Ali whispered to Bross. 'That was a great bluff.'

'I didn't see anyone get killed, did you?' Bross said. 'I tried, and it didn't work—big deal. I'm still here.'

'You don't get it, do you? Not only did you get the ransom jacked up, but now we're totally screwed. He's going to question everyone separately, and we didn't even get a chance to talk to Danziger and Grogan.'

'Go ahead,' he said. 'Why don't you just go and tell them yourself?'

'You'd like that, wouldn't you?' Ali said. 'Have me get shot? Didn't you listen to a word Jake said? We all agreed to tell him we don't have the account numbers.'

'Hey, I didn't agree to anything,' Bross said. 'And we all know why you're defending this loser.'

'Because he obviously knows what he's doing. And you don't.'

'The only thing that's obvious is that you two used to sleep together.'

Ali was silent for a few seconds.

'I don't think you want to be too high and mighty about office *romances*, Kevin,' she said, biting off the words. 'Or should we ask—'

'Ali,' I said.

'Landry?'

'Never let an asshole rent space in your head. The guy's not worth your time. We've got to get to Grogan and Danziger now. Before Russell does.'

Bross made a *pffft* sound. 'Who's going to do that, you?' he said.

I didn't answer.

I WATCHED TRAVIS, trying to get a fix on his rhythm. I was beginning to think that he hadn't just done prison time; the way he walked, that soldierly cadence, convinced me that he'd also served in the military.

He was also taking his job seriously. Any of the others would probably have sat in a chair, watching us. But maybe that was a good thing: it meant his back would be turned towards me for at least sixty seconds at a stretch. And given how dark it was in here, he could hardly see us anyway.

For the moment he was the only guard in the room. Wayne was outside with the handyman. Verne had just gone outside for a smoke—and a toke, or a snort—and might be back in a minute or two. Buck would return from the bathroom with Barlow at any minute. I had no idea how long Russell would spend with Slattery.

So if I was going to get to Grogan and Danziger, it had to be done right away or my plan was doomed to fail.

Not that it wasn't doomed to fail already. Too many things could go wrong with it. Russell—too canny, too suspicious—might not fall for the phone-call thing. He might simply scare the information out of someone at gunpoint: your company's money or your life. I knew what I'd choose.

He might not pick Slattery to do the transfer if he knew that there were four other executives—Grogan, Danziger, Bodine and Latimer—who also had the power. Whoever he did pick could easily screw it up, not figure out a way to communicate duress without Russell picking up on it.

And what if he already knew the account numbers?

So here I was, risking my life for a gambit that was likely to fail anyway.

But to do nothing, I was certain, was to ensure that some of us, maybe even all of us, got killed.

Russell was wrong: you don't always have a choice.

THOUGH THE TWO MEN were only maybe thirty feet or so away, on the other side of the enormous fireplace, it might as well have been a mile.

I waited until Travis had completed a circuit, did his military-style about-face and passed us. And then I tried to get up.

But rising from the floor with my hands tied together, palms in, wasn't easy. I had to swing my knees over to one side, then lean my torso all the way forward. Extend my hands as if I were slaloming. Then I pressed the back of one of my hands against the floor and pushed myself up to my feet.

It took almost five seconds. Which was way too long.

By the time I was standing, Travis had almost reached the end of the room. There was no time for me to run round the fireplace to the next alcove before he turned round.

Now what? I asked myself. *Do I sit back down, wait until Travis's next circuit?*

Then a screen door slammed. Verne, back from his cigarette break.

I NO LONGER had a choice. I had to move.

I took long, loping strides, as fast as I could, as lightly as possible. A matter of a couple of seconds, but it felt like for ever.

All the while my eyes were riveted on Travis.

He came to the end of his circuit and turned just as I sank to the floor next to the manager's son, Ryan. He—and everyone else around him—looked in astonishment. I gave a quick headshake to tell them to be quiet.

Travis glanced over but maintained his steady pace. He hadn't noticed.

Verne entered from the back hallway, humming some tune, amped. When he was out of range, Ryan Fecher said, 'What the hell—'

I put a finger to my lips, slid across the floor.

Alan Grogan and John Danziger were seated next to each other.

'Are you out of your freakin' mind?' Danziger said. I noticed the large bald spot under his fine blond hair. His light blue shirt looked as if it had been ironed. He was one of those preppy guys whose clothes always fit perfectly, who had a certain natural, aristocratic ease.

'Yeah,' I said. 'I must be.'

I quickly explained the situation. As I did, Danziger and Grogan exchanged looks—of disbelief, then scepticism and apprehension.

'I don't have the account numbers with me, either,' Danziger said.

'Well, I do,' said Grogan. 'In my head.'

'Figures,' Danziger said with feigned disgust. He turned to me, and said, with obvious pride, 'Grogan's a USA Math Olympiad gold medallist.'

Grogan glared at Danziger. 'Thanks, pal.' The moonlight caught the network of fine lines round his hazel eyes.

'Hey,' Danziger said, 'if that's the only dirty little secret about you that comes out here, you're lucky.'

'Russell doesn't know you have those numbers memorised,' I said. 'So you don't say a word. We clear?'

Both men nodded.

'Having a gun pointed at you does funny things to people,' Grogan said. 'We don't know what the others might do if Russell threatens them.'

'That's a risk we're going to have to take,' I said.

We sat in silence for half a minute or so while Travis passed by. Then Danziger whispered, 'Listen, there may be something else.'

I looked at Hammond's corporate controller.

'When you mentioned a duress code—it jogged my memory. You know, I set something up with the bank a while ago, but we never had an opportunity to use it. It's sort of a silent alarm—an electronic duress code.'

'Electronic? How does that work?'

'If you enter a nine before and after the PIN, it trips a silent alarm. Tells the bank officer that the transaction is fraudulent, probably coerced.'

'Then what happens?'

'Well, first thing, they freeze the account. Then a whole emergency sequence gets triggered—calls are made to a list of people. My office, the CEO's office, the director of Corporate Security. Telling them someone's probably forcing a company officer to access the bank accounts.'

'But are they going to know where it's happening?'

'Sure. Our security people can dig up the IP address we logged in from—that'll tell them exactly where the duress code originated.'

I nodded. 'Would Russell know we tripped an alarm?'

'Not at all. He'll see a false positive response. He'll think the transaction was successful.'

'He'll know it wasn't as soon as he checks his account balance.'

'True. No way round that.'

'So when he sees that the transfer didn't go through,' I said, 'we'll just tell him it must have been intercepted along the way. Maybe at some higher level at the bank. By then, the word will be out that we're in trouble.'

'Exactly.'

'Could work,' I said. 'Right now, it's all we have.'

Chapter 10

The manager's son, Ryan Fecher, slid over towards me.

'I recognise a couple of those guys,' he said softly.

'From where?'

'From here. Last week, we didn't have any corporate groups, just separate parties. That guy—Russell? The leader? And the one who keeps bringing people in and out? I think they're brothers.'

'Travis. What'd they do here?'

'They kept to themselves, didn't want to do any of the normal stuff like fishing. They mostly hung out here, took a lot of pictures of the lodge, the grounds, the dock, all that. They said they were into architecture and they'd heard about this place. Wanted to know how many staffers we had. Whether we had land-line phones or satellite phones. The Internet. How we got supplies like food and stuff. I pretty much gave them what they wanted but then I got busy—we were short-staffed last week—so I just told them to look around themselves.'

'They didn't seem suspicious to you?'

'Well, there was the architecture thing—I mean, this *is* one of the oldest lodges in Canada—and they said they were thinking of opening their own fishing lodge in Wyoming.'

'You never told me this,' his father said.

'I never gave it any thought until now,' Ryan said. 'Why would I?'

If Russell and his brother had come to the lodge a week earlier to scope it out, they'd been tipped off by somebody.

I asked the manager, 'Who knew we were coming?'

He looked defensive. 'I'm not sure what you're getting at.'

'These guys knew the top officers of Hammond Aerospace were going to be staying here. This whole thing was planned. That means they had a source. An informer. Maybe even a member of your staff.'

'Oh, come on.' He was indignant. 'The only ones who get the booking schedule in advance are me and my son.'

'People have to order supplies.'

'I do the ordering. There's no one else.'

'How do you get supplies in here?'

'A contract air service does a supply run every three days.'

'When's the next one?'

'Saturday.'

I nodded, wondered whether Russell knew that, whether it figured into his timing. 'How'd they get here, do you think? Through the woods?'

He shook his head. 'The woods are way too dense. Had to be a boat.'

'There must be old hunting trails.'

'They're all grown over. No one has hunted around here for years.'

'Since it's been made a wildlife preserve?'

'Before that, even. There's really nothing to hunt. The deer are way too small. Used to be a grizzly hunt, once, a while back. But not in for ever.'

'How far's the nearest lodge?'

After a few seconds, he said, 'Kilbella Bay. It's across the inlet.'

'So these guys must have taken a boat or a seaplane.'

'Would have had to. But I always hear boats coming in, and I didn't hear any motors. And I sure would have heard a plane.'

'So maybe they rowed in.'

'Maybe. Or took a motorboat in partway, then cut the engines and rowed the rest of the way in.'

'Which means they probably left their boat down on the shore, right?'

He shrugged. After a moment, he said, 'I did hear a gunshot.'

'We all did.'

'Come to think of it, I haven't seen José. He's one of the Mexican kids. I told him to hose out a couple of the boats earlier tonight, but . . .'

'Around the time these guys showed up?'

'It would be, yeah.'

'He probably ran into the woods,' I said.

Paul Fecher glanced at me, looked away. 'Yeah,' he said. 'Probably.'

I began sidling away, when he stopped me. 'This lodge is my whole life, you know.'

I nodded, listened. He wanted to talk, and I let him.

'I mean, when it was built, a century ago, it was sort of a madman's folly. A rich guy came out here when there was nothing else around except a couple of salmon canneries and decided to build this huge, beautiful fishing lodge.' He smiled sadly. 'I'm not even the majority owner. He's in Australia. Only comes up here when we have movie stars visiting. I put in the sweat equity.' He closed his eyes. 'My wife left me. Couldn't stand the isolation. So now it's just me and my son, and he wants out, too.'

'That's not true, Dad,' Ryan said.

'This is a time for complete honesty,' Paul said to his son. To me, he continued, 'You know, my chief pleasure in life is when guests leave happy. It makes me feel like a host at a great dinner party. And now . . . this.'

'Some dinner party.'

'I don't know what I could have done differently.'

He seemed to consider that for a few seconds; he looked unconvinced. 'Once he gets the ransom . . . We're not getting out of here alive, are we?'

I didn't reply.

He closed his eyes. 'Dear God.'

'That doesn't mean we can't try to do something.'

I WAITED FOR TRAVIS to pass by again.

A thought had occurred to me, and I shifted round to Danziger.

'If we have kidnap-and-ransom insurance,' I said, 'doesn't that mean we have some firm on retainer that specialises in rescuing hostages?'

Danziger smiled, rueful. 'That's only in the movies. In the real world, very few risk-management firms actually do retrievals. They do hostage negotiation and make the payment arrangements. But this isn't a ransom situation. Russell's too smart for that.' He paused. 'Russell does seem to know an awful lot about how this all works.'

'So do you.'

'It's part of my job. At Hammond, the controller is also what they call the "risk manager". That means I work with Ron Slattery and Geoff Latimer to arrange for all the special risk insurance coverage. Told you I'd put you to sleep if I told you too much about what I do.' He seemed distracted, looked at Grogan. 'How does he know so much about K and R, do you think?'

'I've been wondering the same thing,' Grogan said. 'You remember when Latimer told us about this security firm in California he thought we might want to have on retainer? Some law-school classmate of his founded it?'

'Right!' Danziger said. 'They did recovery and retrieval, not just hostage negotiation. A lot of child abduction cases. One of their employees got arrested in South America on a child recovery case he was working, charged with kidnapping under the international treaty agreements. Did a couple of years in prison in the US. That pretty much cooled me on them.'

The two men exchanged glances.

I said, 'You think that's Russell? That guy?'

Danziger shrugged. 'How else could Russell know so much?'

'What do I know so much about?'

A voice with the grit of fine sandpaper. Russell.

I looked away, stared at the log walls. I didn't want to catch his eye. Didn't want him to notice that I'd moved.

My heart hammered.

'I know a lot of stuff,' he said. 'Like the fact that you were sitting over there before.'

I looked at Russell, shrugged nonchalantly.

'I think you and I need to have a talk, Jake,' he said. 'Right now.'

AFTER I'D BEEN at Glenview a few months, Mom was allowed to visit.

She looked like she'd aged twenty years. I told her she looked good. She said she couldn't believe how I'd changed in a few short months. I'd got so muscular. I'd become a man. It looked like I was even shaving, was that possible?

Most of her visit we sat in the moulded orange plastic chairs in the visitors' lounge and watched the TV. She cried a lot. I was quiet.

'Mom,' I said as she was leaving. 'I don't want you to come here again.'

She looked crestfallen. 'Why not?'

'I don't want you to see me in here. Like this. And I don't want to remember why I'm here. I'll be out in a year or so. Then I'll be home.'

She said she understood, though I'll never know if she really did. A month later, she was dead from a stroke.

THE SCREENED PORCH was cool and breezy. It had a distinctive, pleasant smell—of mildewed furnishings, of the tangy sea air, of the oil soap used to wash the floor. The moon cast a silvery light through the screens.

'Come into my office,' Russell said. He'd taken off his tactical jacket and had put on a soiled white pit cap that said DAYTONA 500 CHAMPION 2004 on the front and had a big number 8 on the side.

He pointed to a comfortable-looking upholstered chair and I sat down. He sat in the one next to it. We could have been two old friends passing the time drinking beers and reminiscing.

Except for his pewter-grey eyes, flat and cold: something terribly detached about them, something removed and unnerving. The eyes of a sociopath, maybe; someone who didn't feel what others felt. I'd seen eyes like his before, at Glenview. He was a man who was capable of doing anything because he was restrained by nothing.

'You want to tell me what you were doing out there?' he said.

'Trying to help.'

'Help who?'

'I was passing along word from the CEO. Telling the guys not to cause trouble. To just do whatever you say so we can all get out of here alive.'

'She told you to walk over there to tell them that?'

'She prefers email, but it doesn't seem to be working so well.'

He was silent. I could hear the waves lapping gently against the shore, the rhythmic chirping of crickets.

'Why'd she ask you?'

'No one else was crazy enough.'

'Well, you got balls, I'll give you that. I think you're the only one out of all of them who's got any balls.'

'More balls than brains, I guess.'

'So if I ask Danziger and Grogan what you were talking about, they're going to tell me the same thing.'

The hairs on my neck bristled. 'You're good with names, huh?'

'I just like to come prepared.'

I nodded. 'Impressive. How long have you been planning this?'

I registered a shift in his body language, a sudden drop in the temperature. I'd miscalculated.

'Am I going to have trouble with you?' he said.

'I just want to go home.'

'Then don't be a hero.'

'For these guys?' I said. 'I don't even like them.'

He laughed, stretched his legs out, yawned.

I pointed to his cap, and said, 'I saw that race.'

'Huh?' It took him a few seconds to remember he was wearing a Daytona cap.

'Dale Earnhardt Jr,' I said.

He nodded, turned away, looked straight ahead.

'Junior crossed the finish line a fraction of a second ahead of Tony Stewart,' I said. 'Yeah, I remember that one. Seven or eight cars wiped out.'

He gave me a quick sidelong glance. 'I was there, man,' he said.

'You're kidding me.'

'Also saw his daddy get killed there three years before.'

I shook my head. 'Crazy sport. I think a lot of people tune in just for the crashes. Like maybe they'll get lucky and see someone die.'

He gave me a long look, didn't seem to know what to make of me. One of the snotty rich executives who followed NASCAR? It didn't compute.

'Nothing like the old days,' he said. 'NASCAR used to be like bumper cars. A demolition derby. The old bump-and-run.'

'Reminds me of that line from a movie,' I said. 'Rubbin's racin'.'

'*Days of Thunder*, man!' He was suddenly enthusiastic, his smile like a child's. 'My favourite movie of all time. How's it go again? "He didn't slam you, he didn't bump you, he didn't nudge you—he *rubbed* you. And rubbin', son, is racin'." That's *it*, man.'

'That's it,' I said, nodding sagely. *Bond with the guy*. Connect. 'Sometimes a driver's just gotta shove another car out of position. Spin the other guy out. But that's all changed now.'

'Exactly. Now you race too hard, they sock you with a penalty.'

'NASCAR got sissified.'

He gave me another quizzical look. 'How come you're so much younger than the rest of the guys?'

'I just look younger. I eat right. Saw palmetto.'

A smile spread slowly across his face. 'You someone's assistant?'

'Nah, I'm just a ringer. A substitute.'

'That why you're not on the original guest list?'

So he does have a guest list. From Hammond? Or someone who works at the resort? No, it has to be a source inside Hammond: how else could he know so much about Ron Slattery's personal life?

'I was a last-minute replacement.'

'For Michael Zorn?'

Interesting, I thought. *He's keeping track*. 'Right.'

'What happened to Zorn?'

So his information was at least a day or two old. Also interesting: he knew a lot about money laundering and offshore banks, yet he didn't know everything about Hammond.

'Mike had to go to India for some client meetings,' I said.

'So how'd they choose you?'

'I have no idea.'

He nodded slowly. 'I think you're full of crap.'

'Funny, that's what my last quarterly performance review said.'

He smiled, turned his penetrating gaze away.

'But if I had to guess, it's because I know a lot about our newest aeroplane.'

'The H-880. You an engineer?'

'No. I'm the assistant to the guy in charge of building the SkyCruiser. I'm like a glorified traffic cop. Actually, forget the "glorified" part.'

'Any of that traffic include money stuff? What do you know about the payments system—how money's moved in and out of the company?'

'I know that my pay cheque gets deposited into my bank account every two weeks. That's about it. I'm the low man on the totem pole here.'

'That doesn't mean what you think. The lower part of a totem pole is actually the most important part, see, because it's what most people look at. So it's usually done by the chief carver. He has his apprentices do the top part.'

'Thanks,' I said. 'Now I feel better about it.'

'Of course, the other guys don't know about totem poles. So they treat you like dirt.'

'Not really. Though they do like to rub it in about how much money they have. Fancy restaurants and golf-club memberships and all that.'

'Well, it's pretty obvious you're nothing like them. They're all a bunch of pussies and sissies and cowards.'

He was playing me, too, but why?

'Not really. Some of them are serious jocks. Pretty competitive—alpha-male types. And they all make a lot more money than me.'

He hunched forward in his chair, pointing a stern finger. He spoke precisely, as if reciting something he'd memorised. 'Someone once said that the great tragedy of this century is that a man can live his entire life without ever knowing for sure if he's a coward or not.'

'Huh. Never thought about that.'

He glanced at me quickly, decided I wasn't being sarcastic. 'You ever see elks mate?'

'Never had the pleasure.'

'Every fall the bull elks fight each other over the females. Charge at each other, butting heads, locking antlers, making this unbelievable racket, this loud *bugling*, until one of them gives up, and the winner gets the girl.'

'I've seen bar fights like that.'

'That's how the females can tell which bulls are the fittest. They mate with the winners. Otherwise, the weak genes get passed on, and the elks are gonna die out. This is how it works in nature.'

'Or the corporate world.'

'No. That's where you're wrong.' The stern lecturer's finger again. 'My point. Doesn't work like that with humans any more. These days, everything's upside-down. Women don't mate with the fittest any more. They marry the rich guys.'

'Maybe the rich guys are the fittest now.'

He scowled, but I had a sense that he didn't mind the fencing. 'It's like Darwin's law got repealed. Call it the rule of the weak. I mean, look at these guys.' He waved at the wall, at the hostages on the other side. 'This country was made by guys like Kit Carson, fighting the Indians with knives and six-shooters. Brave men. But now, some pencil-neck geek sitting at a computer can launch a thousand missiles and kill a million people. The world's run by a bunch of fat-ass wimps who only know how to double-click their way to power. Think they should get a Purple Heart for a paper cut.'

'I like that.'

'Their idea of power is PowerPoint. They got headsets on their heads and their fingers on keyboards and they think they're macho men when they're nothing more than sports-drink-gulping, instant-message-sending, mouse-clicking, iPod-listening, web-surfing pussies, and God didn't mean for the likes of them to run this planet on the backs of real men.'

A knock at the door, and Verne came in.

'Now they're all bitching and moaning about how they can't sleep on the floor,' he said, shrugging and twitching.

'Tell 'em this ain't the Mandarin Oriental. All right, look. No reason to keep 'em there, with the hard floor. I *want* 'em going to sleep. Easier to keep watch. There's a room with a big rug, off the main room. The one with all the stuffed deer heads on the wall. Move 'em all in there.'

'Gotcha,' Verne said, and he left.

Russell leaned back in his chair. 'Aren't you the one who told Verne you were going to gouge out his good eye if he touched your girlfriend?'

'She's not my girlfriend.'

He surprised me with a half smile. 'You do have balls.'

'I just didn't like the way he was talking to her.'

'So how come you know about the Glock 18?'

'I did a year in the National Guard after high school.' When no college would accept me.

'You a gun nut?'

'No. But my dad sort of was. Some of it rubbed off.'

Dad kept trophy hand grenades around the house, a veritable arsenal of unregistered weapons: 'gun nut' didn't really begin to describe him.

'You a good shot?'

'Not bad.'

'I'm guessing you're probably a pretty decent shot. The good ones never brag about it. So you got a choice here. You're either gonna be my friend and my helper, or I'm going to have to kill you.'

'Let me think about that one.'

'Guy like you could go either way.' He shook his head. 'I still get a vibe off you like you might try to be a hero. Don't.'

'I won't.'

'What I got going here is too important to get screwed up by a kid with more testosterone than brains. So don't think you're fooling me. Someone's gonna have to be the first to get shot tonight, just to teach everyone a lesson. Make sure everyone gets it. And I think it might just be you.'

If he meant to scare me, it worked. I refused to let him see it, though. I paused for a second or two, then affected a light-hearted tone.

'Your call,' I said, 'but I'm not sure you want to do that.'

'Why not?'

'Maybe I'm the only one you can trust.'

He folded his arms, narrowed his eyes. 'How's that?'

'You said it yourself, Russell. Of all the guys here, I'm the peon. I don't get a bonus. I don't get stock options. I really don't *care* how much money you take from the company. A million, a billion, I don't care. I didn't even want to come here in the first place.'

'You telling me you don't really care one way or another if something happens to any of those guys? Sorry, I don't believe you.'

'Don't get me wrong, I don't want to see anyone get hurt. But it's not like any of them are friends of mine.'

'You'd care if something happened to your girlfriend.'

'She's a friend. Not a girlfriend.' I hesitated. 'Yeah, I'd care if anything happened to her. But I'm cooperating. I just want to go home.'

His pewter eyes had become dull, opaque, as if someone had switched off a light. 'Sounds to me like maybe we're on the same side here.'

He didn't mean it, and I knew better than to agree. 'I don't know about that,' I said. 'But I get it that you're not kidding around.'

'That's what I like to hear.'

'So what are you gonna do with half a billion dollars? That's a hell of a lot of money.'

His stare pierced through me as if he had X-ray vision. 'Don't worry. I'll figure something out.'

'Half a billion dollars,' I said. 'Man. Know what I'd do? If it was me?'

A long pause. 'Let's hear it.'

'I'd take off to some country that doesn't have an extradition treaty with the US.'

'What, Namibia? Northern Cyprus? Yemen? No thanks.'

So he had looked into it.

'There's other places,' I said.

'Such as?'

Was he still sizing me up, or did he really want to know? 'Costa Rica.'

'Forget it. That's like trying to disappear in Beverly Hills.'

'There's this place in Central America, between Panama and Colombia I think it is, where there's no government. Ten thousand square miles of real outlaw country. Like the Wild West in the old days. Kit Carson stuff.'

'You're talking about the Darién Gap.' He nodded. 'No roads. Mostly jungle. Full of Africanised honeybees. I hate bees.'

'There's gotta be decent countries in the world that haven't signed extradition treaties—'

'Signing an extradition treaty is one thing. Enforcing it's another. Sure there's plenty of decent places. You can get lost in Belize or Panama. Cartagena's not bad, either.'

'You've done your homework.'

A slow, lethal grin. He said nothing.

'I hope you've taken precautions to cover the money trail, too,' I said.

'You steal half a billion dollars from one of the world's biggest corporations, you're gonna have an awful lot of people trying to track it down.'

'Let 'em hunt all they want. Once it moves offshore, it disappears.'

'You know, our bank's not going to authorise a transfer of five hundred million dollars to the Cayman Islands or whatever. That'll just raise all kind of red flags.'

'Actually, I was thinking Kazakhstan.'

'*Kazakhstan?* That sounds even more suspicious.'

'Sure. Unless you know how often Hammond wires money to a company in Kazakhstan.'

'Huh?'

'It's all there on the Internet. On some—what is it?—Form 8-K on file with the Securities and Exchange Commission. Seems Boeing buy their titanium from Russia, so you guys buy it from Kazakhstan. One of the largest titanium producers in the world.'

'That right?' I wondered if he was making it up; I didn't think he was.

'Titanium prices keep skyrocketing, so you guys like to stockpile it. Hammond's got a ten-year contract with some company in Kazakhstan, name I can't remember, for over a billion dollars. So every year you wire hundreds of millions of dollars to the National Bank of Kazakhstan.'

'We wire money to Kazakhstan, huh?'

'Not directly. To their correspondent bank in New York. Deutsche Bank.'

'How do you know all this?'

'Like you said, Jake, I do my homework. So let's say I set up a shell company in Bermuda or the British Virgin Islands or the Seychelles and gave it the name of some made-up titanium export firm in Kazakhstan, right? Your bank wires it to this fake company that has an account at Deutsche Bank in New York—they're not going to know any better.'

'I thought the Germans cooperate with the US on money laundering.'

'Oh, sure. But Deutsche Bank isn't going to have it for more than a second or two before it goes to the Bank for International Settlements in Basel. And from there—well, just take it from me. I got this all figured out.'

He really did. 'I'm impressed.'

'Never underestimate me, buddy. Now, a couple of questions for you.'

I nodded.

'That lady CEO,' Russell said. 'Most of these guys don't like her, huh?'

'Most don't,' I admitted.

'How come? Because she's a bitch?'

I paused for a second. Some guys use 'bitch' interchangeably for 'woman'. 'Yeah, they're probably not comfortable having a woman in charge. But the fact is, like it or not, she's the boss.'

He shook his head. 'I think it's because they don't want her investigating them. They're scared she might find something. Like a bribe, maybe.'

'News to me.' Had Slattery told him about the internal investigation? 'Wouldn't surprise me, though. She's a real stickler for rules.'

'They'd love to get rid of her.'

'Maybe, some of them. But the board of directors hired her. Not them.'

'And she doesn't have the power to fire any of them, does she?'

'Never heard that before.'

'There's a lot about your company I know.'

'I can see that.' And I wondered how.

'She's holding out on me.'

'That's her job. She runs the company. But she'll come round.'

'Maybe I don't need her.'

'Maybe you do. That's the thing, Russell. You gotta keep your options open. Anyone who has signing authority is someone you might need around. The point is for you to get your money. Not prune the deadwood.'

'But she doesn't have signing authority, does she?'

'That's way above my pay grade, Russell. You get all this from Slattery?'

'I have my sources.' He winked. 'Gotta know who I need to keep alive.'

'You never know who you might need.'

'Only need one.'

I shook my head. 'Don't assume that. The amount you're talking, the bank's probably going to require the authorisation of two corporate officers. That means user IDs and passwords and who knows what else.'

'Once I get the user IDs and the passwords, I don't need 'em any more.'

'Russell,' I said, 'let's be honest. You don't know which names the bank has on their list. What if they insist on a phone call to verify the transaction?'

'Not going to happen that way. It's all going to be done over the Internet.'

'Right, but look at it this way. A request for half a *billion* dollars emailed from some computer outside the country—that's bound to raise all kinds of questions at the bank.'

'Not if we're using the right authorisation codes.'

'Maybe,' I said. 'Or maybe not. Let's say the wire request goes to some low-level bureaucrat at the bank. She calls back the number on file for the Hammond treasury operations office or whatever it's called, but nobody at Hammond headquarters has a record of any transfer request.'

'The top guys are all here,' he said. He sounded a little less sure of himself.

'So someone at headquarters says, gosh, I don't know anything about that, but here's the phone number of the lodge where all the honchos are. The bank lady, being so conscientious, calls the number here. Which happens to be the only telephone in the whole place—the manager's satellite phone. Maybe you answer the phone yourself. Whatever. But she asks to speak to someone whose name's on her list.'

'They'll talk to her, believe you me.'

'And maybe the protocol is, she's got to talk to two senior officers. So you want to have at least two of them around to say, yeah, it's cool.'

'She's not going to know who she's talking to. Shit, Buck could pretend he's Ron Slattery, comes to that.'

I shrugged. 'And if they have voiceprints? Half a billion dollars, you never know what sort of security precautions they might take. What if the bank has a list of two or three names you've got to call if a request comes in for a transfer over, I don't know, fifty million or a hundred million bucks. You're not going to know who's on that list.'

He was silent for five, ten seconds. Looked around the porch. Moths fluttered outside. Some big insect—a June bug, maybe—kept colliding with the screen. The crickets seemed to be chirping louder and faster. It was brighter outside than in here: I could see the glimmering of the moon on the waves, the silvery wooden dock, the boulders and rocks of the shore.

'You're pulling all this out of your ass, aren't you?' he said.

'You bet.'

He nodded, smiled. 'Doesn't mean you're wrong, though.'

'And another thing? One of the hostages needs his insulin.'

'That guy Latimer.'

'He could go into a coma. He could die. You don't want that. He's the general counsel. He might have signing authority, too.'

He nodded. 'Why're you being so helpful?'

'Maybe I want to save my ass.'

'If you're trying something, I'll know.'

'I told you. I just want to go home.'

We looked at each other for a few seconds. It felt like an hour.

'Stay on my good side,' he said, 'and you'll make it out of here alive. But if you try anything—'

'I know.'

'No,' Russell said. 'You don't know. You think you know what's happening here, dude, but you really have no idea.'

RUSSELL'S WORDS ECHOED in my head as Travis followed me out of the screened porch and through the great room. *You think you know what's happening here, dude, but you really have no idea.*

Travis took me to another room I hadn't seen before, some kind of parlour or reading room with antlers and moose heads mounted on the walls. The floor was covered with a large Oriental carpet, where some of the hostages were stretched out or curled up, and others sat in clusters, talking quietly.

A lantern on a trestle table near the door gave off a cone of greenish light. Nearby, two guards on duty, sitting near each other in railback chairs, murmuring to each other: Buck, the one with the black hair and goatee; and Verne, the ex-con junkie with the teardrop tattoos.

Only one door, I noticed. There were windows, but they were shut and, I assumed, locked.

Travis shoved me to the floor. Then he called Geoff Latimer's name. Latimer was lying on his side, pale and exhausted.

'You're in luck,' Travis said, helping Latimer to his feet with a gentleness I didn't expect.

'Thank God,' said Latimer.

Travis and Latimer left the room. Hank Bodine, Upton Barlow and Kevin Bross, the Three Musketeers, were whispering to one another off in one corner. I noticed that Ron Slattery had joined them.

Other hostages had fallen asleep already, worn out by the stress and the long day and the late hour. A few snored.

'Jesus, Landry.'

Ali was sitting ten or fifteen feet away with Cheryl and Paul Fecher, the manager, and his son, Ryan. I looked over at the two guards at the other end of the room. They were still talking quietly, their faces half washed out by the lantern's light, half in shadows. Slowly, I slid across the rug.

'We were worried about you,' Ali said. 'When he caught you on the other side of the fireplace—'

'It was a little tense,' I said.

'What'd he want to know?' Cheryl asked.

'Well, he figured out pretty quickly I didn't know anything useful. Mostly he seemed to be sizing me up. He asked about you and . . .' My voice trailed off, but no one else from Hammond was within earshot. 'He knew about the investigation.'

Her eyes widened for a fraction of a second, then narrowed. 'How in God's name? Why would anyone tell him?'

'I'm pretty sure he has a source inside Hammond.'

She nodded. 'He knows too much, that's for sure. Danziger thinks he may be a professional, in the K and R business.'

She glanced over her shoulder. John Danziger was lying on his side by the wall, asleep. 'He also briefed all of us on the duress code.'

'Much better than my original idea,' I said.

'At least you had a plan,' she said. 'I owe you an apology.'

'Why?'

'I misread them. You had them pegged. And the way you stood up for me—I won't forget it.' She seemed embarrassed. 'This isn't easy.'

'This isn't easy for any of us.'

The door opened. Travis entered with Latimer, then called out Danziger's name. Latimer sat down near us. He looked much better, now that his diabetic crisis had passed.

He smiled, mouthed *Thank you*.

I just nodded.

Suddenly the lights in the room went on, as abruptly as they'd gone off. Lamps and wall sconces blazed to life. A number of people woke up, looked around.

'Guess the generator's fixed,' Latimer said.

I nodded.

'You know, what you did before—getting over to the other side to talk to Grogan and Danziger? You could have got yourself killed.'

'I don't think so.'

'You're a brave guy, Jake,' he said.

'Just a survivor.'

There was a noise at the far side of the room. Wayne, the crew-cut one, entered with Peter, the handyman, who was sweating profusely.

Wayne whispered to the other guards for a few minutes, then led the handyman to the back right corner of the room.

A minute or so later, Russell and his brother entered, Danziger in front of them.

Danziger looked terrified.

Russell cleared his throat. 'Ladies and gentlemen,' he announced. 'We have a little business to transact.' He unholstered his Glock. 'Some of you guys apparently think you're gonna be clever,' he continued. 'Try to throw a little sand in the gears. Screw things up for everyone else. Like I'm not going to find out.' As he was talking, he popped out the Glock's magazine and held it up, scanned it as if to see if it was full. 'Didn't some guy say that we all gotta hang together or we'll hang separately? Like, George Washington or one of those guys?'

'I believe that was actually Benjamin Franklin,' Hugo Lummis said.

Russell looked at the rotund lobbyist. 'Why, thank you, Hugo.' He nodded. 'Not many of you got the balls to correct a man with a loaded gun.'

'I'm not correcting you,' Lummis said hastily. 'I'm just—'

'Quite all right, Hugo,' Russell said. 'I like learning stuff. Not everyone does, though. People get ideas stuck in their heads. That's why you're all gonna have a little lesson. A *seminar*. Shouldn't take too long, though.' He seated the magazine back in the butt of the pistol with a quiet click.

'John,' he said gently, 'could you please kneel right here? That's right. Not on the rug—on the wood. That's good.'

'Please, don't,' Danziger said. He knelt, his eyes darting around the room.

'Now, John,' Russell said, 'you and I are going to give all your colleagues here a lesson they're never going to forget.'

'Please,' said Danziger. He was kneeling on the wooden floor, facing us, his hands bound in front of his flat belly. He could have been in church. His light blue shirt had big dark sweat stains under the arms.

Russell strode up to Danziger at an angle, like a veteran teacher approaching a blackboard. His Glock was in his right hand.

On Danziger's other side stood Travis, also holding his gun.

Russell's voice was calm. 'So, John,' he said, 'what's a duress code?'

Chapter 11

We watched in terror.

'A "duress code"?' Danziger said. 'You mean, like a burglar alarm, when—'

'I don't think we're talking about a burglar alarm, are we, John?'

'I told you, I don't know what you're talking about,' Danziger said.

'You did, didn't you? So I guess you really can't help me.' Russell placed his pistol snugly behind Danziger's right ear. He snapped back the slide.

I shouted, 'Russell, don't do it!'

There was a sudden commotion: Alan Grogan struggling to his feet. 'Please!' he called. 'I'll talk to you. I'll tell you anything you want.'

'Is that Alan?' Russell said without even turning to look.

Grogan zigzagged across the carpet, round the other hostages. He tripped over something but got right back up, with a jock's agility.

'You don't need to do this,' he said.

Travis raised his gun and aimed it at Grogan.

'Alan,' Danziger said, 'sit down! You've got nothing to do with this.'

Russell turned to Grogan, a cryptic half grin on his face. 'You wanted to tell me something? Try and save your friend?'

'Anything you want to know,' Grogan said. 'Just put the gun down.'

'Alan, sit *down*,' Danziger said. 'You don't know anything about this.'

'I think he wants to help you, John,' said Russell. 'He doesn't want me to blow your brains out.'

'John, just *tell* him!' Grogan shouted. '*Please*. It's not worth it. Please.'

'It's not worth it, John,' Russell said. 'Do you know what's going to happen when I pull the trigger?'

'*Don't*,' Danziger whispered. 'Please. I'll tell you everything I know about the duress code. Anything you want to—'

'It's not pretty,' Russell went on. 'A nine-millimetre bullet has a muzzle velocity of, like, a thousand feet per second. First thing it does is punch out a round piece of skull, see. Drives the bone fragments right into your brain, OK? Then, at the same time it opens up a nice big cavity in your brain. Like a cave. Then your brain actually explodes, John.'

'Russell,' Grogan said, coming closer, 'you don't have to do this. No one's going to use any duress code, I promise you. That was just an idea, we talked about it, but it's *not going to happen*!'

Danziger was trying to talk over him. 'The duress code is nothing more than a couple of numbers,' he said. 'You type in a nine before the—'

'Little gobs of grey matter spurt out the exit wound,' Russell went on. 'The grey matter shoots out the entrance wound, too. It's not pleasant. Not for me, anyway. I might get some of your brain tissue on my clothes.'

Danziger was shaking, sobbing silently. Tears were streaming down his face. Sweat had soaked most of his light blue shirt.

'Stop!' he shouted. 'I'm *telling* you! *Please!*'

'Russell,' Cheryl called out, her voice trembling, 'you do not want to face murder charges. There's no reason to do this. No one's going to try to stop the wire transfer. You're going to get everything you want.'

'He's *telling* you!' cried Grogan. 'Listen to him. What else do you *want*?' He, too, was weeping now.

'Alan, I want you to stay right where you are,' Russell said. 'Don't come any closer.' He placed the Glock back behind Danziger's right ear. 'Do you want to tell me what happens after you type in that duress code?'

Danziger closed his eyes. 'It triggers a silent alarm,' he said, his voice trembling. 'It tells the bank that the transfer request is being made under compulsion.'

'OK, good,' said Russell. 'Now, John, tell me something. Is there any other *duress code*? Besides the nine, I mean.'

Danziger mouthed the word *No* but no sound came out.

'I can't hear you,' said Russell.

'No,' Danziger gasped.

'That's it? No other tricks that you know of? Nothing else your buddies might try to screw this up?' Russell twisted the Glock, swivelling the muzzle on that same spot behind Danziger's right ear.

Danziger's face was contorted and dark red. 'I—can't think of anything.'

'You'd be the guy who'd know, isn't that right?'

'Yes,' Danziger said. 'There's no one else who . . .' His voice was choked by sobs.

'Who what?'

'Who knows the—the systems—'

'Thank you, John,' Russell said. 'You've been very cooperative.'

Danziger gasped for air, nodded. He closed his eyes, looked drained.

'Thank you,' he whispered.

You could almost feel everyone breathe a collective sigh of relief. Russell was a sadist, but not a murderer. He had tortured the information he wanted out of Danziger, so there was no need to kill him.

'Oh, thank God,' breathed Grogan. Tears were streaming down his face.

'No,' Russell said softly, 'thank *you*. Goodbye, John.'

He squeezed the trigger and the gun jumped in his hand and filled the room with a deafening explosion.

Danziger slumped to one side.

The gunshot seemed to echo for an instant, as though it was merely an auditory illusion. I stared, unable to fully comprehend what I'd just seen.

Then the silence was broken as someone let out a gasp.

People began to scream, others to cry.

A large chunk of the right side of Danziger's head was missing.

Russell wiped his left hand over his face to smear off the red spatter. Verne let out a loud whoop and pumped his fist. 'Yeah!' he shouted.

A number of people dived to the floor. Some tried to cover their eyes with their forearms, ducked their heads. Ali buried her head between her legs.

I wanted to shout, but I couldn't. My throat seemed to have closed.

Russell stood up, lowered the Glock to his side, backed up a few steps. Travis stared furiously at his brother.

Hank Bodine bellowed, '*Goddamn you!*'

In all the chaos, my eyes were drawn to Grogan. He was on his feet, stumbling forward to Danziger's body. He was crying, his head shaking. He knelt next to his friend's body, reached with fettered hands to lift his ruined head, trying to cradle it. Grogan tried to speak, but no words came out, just deep gasps, like hiccups. Blood oozed between his fingers.

A slick of blood and something viscous had pooled on the floor next to Danziger.

Then Grogan leaned over and kissed the dead man's lips, and suddenly everybody understood.

Grogan lowered Danziger's head gently to the floor and knelt there for several seconds as if praying. Slowly he rose to his feet as a terrible anguished scream welled up from his throat, and he staggered towards Russell, his face contorted with rage and grief.

'You goddamned son of a *bitch*!' he shouted, spittle flying.

He lunged at Russell, jabbing his tethered hands at Russell's face as if to throttle him. '*God damn you to hell, you goddamned son of a bitch!*'

'Alan?' Russell said in a matter-of-fact voice as he stepped to one side.

'*Why?*' Grogan gasped. 'Why in God's name—?'

'You, too,' Russell said, and he fired one more time.

WAYNE CAME IN with a mop and a bucket full of suds. The two terrified cleaning girls—Bulgarians who'd come here for the summer to work—were untied and told to mop up the blood.

By now the hostages had settled down into a dazed, terror-stricken stupor, almost a trance state. No one spoke. No one even whispered. Ali was crying softly, and Cheryl stared grimly into space.

'What do you want us to do with the bodies?' Wayne asked in an unexpectedly soft voice, as he and Travis lifted Grogan.

'Take 'em into the woods,' Russell said. 'Maybe the grizzlies will eat 'em.'

Travis glanced furiously at his brother but still he said nothing. Verne followed them out.

Russell reached down and grabbed Danziger's ankles and dragged him across the floor. It left a long red smear.

At the threshold of the room he stopped. 'Was my lesson clear enough?' he asked.

No one answered.

ONLY ONE of the kidnappers remained in the room now: Buck, the one with the black hair and goatee. He sat slumped in his chair, looking pensive. His .44 Magnum lay on his right thigh, his right hand on top of it.

The manager was crying silently, lost in grief and shock.

Cheryl was the first to speak. 'Someone told him,' she whispered.

Silence.

'Was it you, Kevin?' she asked softly.

'How *dare* you—' Bross erupted, spittle flying.

'He could have got it out of Danziger himself,' I said. 'That's the point of all these "interviews"—playing us off against each other.'

Lummis was gasping for breath, wincing, his face deep red.

'Hugo, for God's sake, what is it?' said Barlow.

'I'll be fine,' Lummis gasped. 'Just need—to try—to calm down.'

Buck looked up, stared for a few seconds, then seemed to lose interest. Muffled, angry voices came from the next room: Russell and his brother, I guessed, arguing in the screened porch.

I cleared my throat and the manager looked up at me with wet, red-rimmed eyes.

'We need to get help,' I said. It was obvious that cooperating with Russell and his guys would only get us killed. We had to contact someone, anyone, in the outside world. Even if no one else would do anything, at least I would. 'Where do you keep your sat phone?'

Clumsily, he tried to wipe the tears from each eye with the backs of his bound hands. 'My office,' he whispered. 'But that crazy guy—Verne?—asked me about it and made me give him my office key.'

I thought for a moment. 'Your office—you keep it locked? Do you hide a spare key somewhere?'

He nodded. 'Under the base of the lamp on the legal bookcase outside my office door. But I told you, he took the sat phone.'

'That's all right. There's other ways.'

Ali, who'd been listening to us, said, 'The Internet.'

'Right. They obviously haven't cut the line if they're planning on using it to do the wire transfer.'

'Landry, there's five guys with guns. You've really lost it.'

I looked towards the window.

Two silhouetted figures in the silvery moonlight struggled with a body, moving in the direction of the forest.

'I have a feeling that Russell told his brother he was only going to put a scare into Danziger and Grogan. Not bullets in their heads. As long as we can hear them arguing, we can count on them being distracted.'

'What about this guy?' She glanced at Buck.

I explained.

'Are you out of your mind?' she said.

I LAY ON MY SIDE as if asleep and drew my left knee up to bring my foot closer to my roped hands.

I'd lost a little feeling in my fingers, because my palms had been clamped together in the same position for so long. They felt prickly and thick and useless. But soon I was able to extend my hands and grasp the blade of the steak knife. Fumbling, I got hold of the handle and pulled it slowly, carefully, from my shoe.

Meanwhile, Cheryl was talking to Ali in a low, soft murmur. 'It puts all these petty games into perspective, doesn't it? One minute I'm vowing I'm going to take this fight to the board of directors and the next minute I'm wishing I could call my children and tell them I love them.'

'How old are they?' Ali asked.

'Oh, Nicholas is a sophomore at Duke, and Maddy's living in the West Village. They're grown. They're in the world. They don't need me . . .'

Now that the thing was out of my shoe, I realised it was as if a sharp stone had been stuck in there. To get it out was a relief.

'I feel like we've just got through the hard part. We had such a difficult relationship for so long. Nicholas still resents me for sending him away to prep school so young. He's convinced I wanted him out of the house so I could concentrate on my career.'

I turned to make sure Buck couldn't see me. He seemed to be dozing.

Keeping my back to him—and to Cheryl and Ali as well—I positioned the knife blade up and began moving it back and forth against the rope.

The blade was razor-sharp, but it was the wrong tool. Great for cutting steak, maybe, but not so great with climbing rope woven from twisted strands of polyester round a nylon core.

But I kept sawing away.

'I couldn't be mom and corporate executive at the same time, and I knew it,' Cheryl was saying.

'You needed a wife,' Ali said.

'Or a stay-at-home dad. But they didn't even have a dad at all for most of their childhoods. After Bill ran off with some bimbo.' She sniffled. 'So this is what I screwed up my kids for. So I could spend half my time trying to keep Hank Bodine from stabbing me in the back.'

Once I'd pierced the outermost polyester sheath, the strands began to fray, then splay outwards.

'I bet Hank's kids are screwed up even worse,' Ali whispered. 'Only he probably doesn't even care.'

Upton Barlow noticed what I was doing, and he stared in astonishment.

'And then die in this godforsaken fishing lodge in the middle of . . .' Cheryl's voice got high and thin and constricted, then stopped.

I went back to sawing at the rope.

'Didn't think you'd ever see a CEO cry, right?' Cheryl said.

'Cheryl,' Ali said gently.

'You know what they say—when a man's tough, he's decisive. When a woman's tough, she's a controlling bitch.' She sniffed again.

Finally, I was down to the last strand, and the blade broke through.

My hands were free.

Chapter 12

I gave Ali a quick nod.

'Excuse me,' she called out.

Buck came over, scowling. His jet-black hair looked stringy and unwashed.

'The hell do *you* want?'

'I need to use the bathroom.'

'You can wait,' he said, turning away.

'No, I can't,' Ali said. 'It's—look, it's a woman problem, OK? You want me to explain?'

Buck stared, shook his head slowly. He didn't want to hear details.

'It's gonna have to be quick,' he said at last.

She held up her hands, and he yanked her to her feet. 'Move it,' he said.

She walked, and he followed. Before they left the room, he slowly looked around. 'Anyone moves an inch,' he said, and he unholstered his gun.

I waited for a few seconds, then slipped my hands free of the rope and stood up. I trod quickly along the carpet. Behind me, I could hear faint rustling, soft whispers.

A low voice: 'You're a goddamned idiot, Landry.'

I didn't even have to look to know it was Bross.

'Shut up, Bross,' Cheryl whispered.

'No way,' Bross said, not even bothering to keep his voice down. 'I'm not going to sit here and let this kid get us all killed.'

I was just about out of the door when I heard the squeak of floorboards.

'I thought I heard something,' boomed a voice from the corridor.

Buck levelled his giant Ruger .44 at me. With his other hand he clutched Ali's neck.

She watched me evenly, her face a mask of calm.

Buck shook his head, cocked the revolver. 'Russell warned me you might be trouble.'

I PUT MY HANDS UP in surrender.

'Don't move,' Buck said.

I ducked my head, said quietly, 'You telling me Russell didn't let you in on our deal?'

'I told you, don't move.'

I took a step forward. We were now maybe six or eight feet apart. 'Can we take this out in the hall?'

'Maybe Russell wanted to cut him *out*,' Ali said. She winced involuntarily as he squeezed her neck.

I was close enough now to smell his oniony foulness, the wood fire on his clothes. 'I really don't want to talk in front of the others.'

'The hell you talking about?' Buck said.

'Why the hell do you think they even brought me here?' I said.

Another step. I looked up. 'Because I'm the treasury guy. The operations guy. Hammond Aerospace is a company with billions of dollars in cash, and I'm the only guy who can tap into it. That's why Russell told his brother to cut me loose. He didn't fill you in? Unbelievable.'

'Russell—?' That giant steel cannon of a gun was still pointed at the middle of my chest but Buck was listening now.

I took another step closer.

'I don't know how much they're paying you, Buck, but it's chump change compared to what Russell and his brother are taking.'

His expression was guarded, but there was a glimmer of interest.

'What're they getting?' he asked.

One more step. We were so close that I could smell his chewing-tobacco breath. 'This has got to stay between you and me,' I said in a voice that was barely audible. 'I mean it.'

'What kinda money we talking?' Buck demanded. 'I want to know.'

I dipped my knees slightly, but not so much that he'd notice.

'Why don't you tell *me*,' I whispered.

I didn't care what he said, just so long as he parted his jaws.

'Tell you—?' he began, and then I uncoiled, exploded upwards, the top of my head slamming under his chin with a sudden violent force.

His teeth cracked together so loud it sounded like the snapping of bone. He made a weird *uhhh* sound as he tumbled backwards, sprawled onto the floor with a loud thud. His Ruger crashed to the floor alongside him.

The impact had sent a jolt of pain through my skull, but it was surely nothing compared to what Buck felt the instant his teeth smashed together.

Ali gasped as she pulled free of his grip. Someone behind me cried out, then a few more.

Buck was unconscious. That I hadn't expected: I'd thought I might knock him off-balance long enough to grab his gun.

'My *God*, Landry,' Ali said. 'Where the hell did that come from?' She was looking at me with a peculiar combination of gratitude and respect and, I think, fear.

'I don't know,' I said. But of course I did. You don't spend time in a place like Glenview without something rubbing off.

Swooping down to retrieve Buck's stainless-steel Ruger, I tucked it into the waistband of my trousers. Then I turned round to face the roomful of my fellow hostages. Everyone was awake now.

'You goddamned *idiot*,' Bross said, even before I could speak. 'As soon as Russell sees this, he's going to start picking us off—'

'That's why I need help moving this guy,' I said.

Some looked at me blankly; some looked away.

'Come on. *Anyone*. Upton, you're a strong guy. I'll cut you loose.'

'Those guys are going to be back any second, Jake,' Barlow said.

'Let's go, Landry,' Ali said. She stood at the edge of the room, held her hands out to me. 'Slice these ropes off me.'

'No. They'll notice you gone right away. Paul, you know the layout of this place better than anyone. You'll know where to stash this guy.'

'I'm in no shape,' the manager said.

'How about your son? Ryan?'

Ryan shot me a frightened look, but his father spoke up for him: 'It's a suicide mission.'

'This asshole's going to get us all killed,' Bross said.

'How about you, Clive?' I said.

Rylance shook his head. 'It's madness, Jake.'

'Come on,' I said to the rest of the room. 'Someone? Anyone? Do I have to do this myself? Any of you guys?'

Silence.

'*Damn* it,' I said, and turned to deal with Buck's body myself.

'You got yourself into this,' I heard Bross say. 'What the hell did you think you were going to do—sneak out of here? Save your ass?'

I turned slowly. 'Trying to save all of our asses, Kevin,' I said. 'Because if you think just sitting here and being good boys and girls is going to save us, you're wrong. We have to get help.'

'That's exactly what got Danziger and Grogan killed.'

'Wrong. Russell killed them because somehow he found out they could identify him. They'd figured out who he is. And I'll tell you something else: Grogan was the only one who knew our bank account numbers. Which means Russell's not going to get his money. And you want to guess what Russell's going to do when he doesn't get his money, Kevin?'

Bross's mouth hung open in disgust. 'Why is anyone even listening to this moron? He's got his head up his ass.'

'No,' said Cheryl quietly. 'He's got guts. Unlike some of us here.'

'Just cover for me,' I said. 'When they ask where Buck is, all you know is that he said something about how he didn't want to go to jail for the rest of his life. And if they notice I'm gone, too, tell them I said I had to take a piss, and I couldn't wait. That's all you say, OK? Nothing else.'

I looked around the room. 'It only takes one of you to say something different, and we're all going to pay the price.' I looked directly at Bross. 'So even if you think I have my head up my ass, don't screw it up.'

Bodine was nodding. So was just about everyone else, except Bross, who scowled furiously.

'No one's going to screw it up,' Bodine said. 'Not if I have anything to do with it.'

'Thank you. Now is no one going to help me move this body?'

Silence.

'Me,' came a voice from the far back corner. It was one of the Mexican waiters. The one I'd talked to at dinner.

Pablo, I remembered his name was.

'I help you,' he said.

PABLO WAS SMALL and skinny, with short dark hair and widely spaced brown eyes. And something else I'd glimpsed at dinner, as he apologised for the wine: behind the innocent's eyes loitered a hell-raiser. A kindred spirit.

It was surprising how much easier it was to cut someone else loose than it had been to free myself. A couple of quick slashing motions using the heel of the blade, and the fibres began to give way, the strands splaying.

'There's no closet in this room, right?' I sliced through the rope, cutting it into two pieces, and tugged them off. Stuffed the two pieces of rope in the pocket of my trousers.

'No closet.'

'Out there?' I jerked my head towards the door to the hallway as he clambered to his feet.

'For the table linens,' he said. 'But basement is closer.'

No movement in the windows, no silhouetted figures. Not yet.

'How do we get down there?'

'I show you.'

He knelt at one end of Buck's body, grabbing under the arms.

The eyes came open just a bit, exposing little white crescents, and for a second I thought he might be regaining consciousness.

Turning round, I squatted between Buck's legs, grabbed his knees, leading the way out of the room. Two hundred and fifty pounds or more of unconscious man was even heavier than I'd expected.

The great room was dark and still smelt of dinner. *How many hours ago was that? Five, maybe six?* We threaded carefully among the jumbles of haphazardly stacked furniture.

'Where kitchen is,' Pablo said, directing me with his eyes. We struggled to balance the body between us, keep it from sagging.

'If they come in,' I said, 'we drop him and run, understand?'

He nodded, strain contorting his face.

I steered Buck's knees towards the kitchen door. The small round inset pane of glass was black, opaque. No one was in the kitchen.

The floorboards creaked.

I pushed against the door, swinging it open into the dark corridor. The cellar door, on the left, was sturdy oak.

'There,' Pablo whispered. 'Switch is on the wall.'

I let go of Buck's right knee to grab the big black iron knob. His right leg dangled, then his boot thumped loudly against the floor.

Somewhere a screen door banged.

Pablo and I were moving as quickly as we dared with our ungainly burden. The cellar door groaned open, rusty hinges protesting. I found the light switch, flicked it on, and a bare bulb illuminated a narrow, steep stairway. The ceiling was low and sharply canted.

'Careful,' Pablo whispered. 'The steps—no backs.'

We descended into the dank, dark cellar. The concrete floor, fairly recent, had probably been poured over the original packed earth. A new cinder-block wall ran along one side, partitioning off the fitness centre from the rest of the basement. Against the wall a row of metal shelving displayed miscellaneous junk: old lamps, cardboard boxes of light bulbs, an antique blender. An open pantry on the other wall was stacked with burlap sacks of rice, canned beans and giant tins of cooking oil.

'We need to tie him up to something that won't move,' I said. 'Where's the boiler?'

'Maybe something else,' Pablo said. He jerked his chin to the left.

We carried Buck's body along a narrow aisle between tall steel shelves of laundry detergent and bleach. Now, I figured, we were directly under the great room. Oddly, the concrete walls sloped inwards to what looked, at first glance, like the floor-to-ceiling bars of a prison cell. The light from the stairwell was too distant; I couldn't make out what it was.

Pablo gently set down Buck's head; I dropped the legs. Then he flipped the light switch, lighting a line of bulbs on the ceiling.

Behind the steel bars, I could see, was a room whose walls and low, barrel-vaulted ceiling were built from weathered red brick. The floor was gravel. Plain wooden racks held hundreds of dusty wine bottles. The wine cellar.

'Yes,' I said, grasping a bar and tugging. 'Good.'

I pulled the two lengths of rope from my pockets, held them up. 'We're going to need some more rope.'

'I don't think down here . . .'

'Anything. Wire. Chain.'

'Ah, maybe . . .' He turned slowly and headed back the way we'd come.

The wine cellar's grate was made of stout iron bars. The Château Lafitte wasn't going anywhere, and neither was Buck.

A guttural moan.

I spun round, saw Buck starting to sit up.

I SIDESTEPPED ROUND behind his back, then lurched forward, hooking my right elbow under his chin. The bristles of his hairy neck felt like steel wool against the crook of my arm. When I had his throat in a vice grip, I grabbed my right hand with my left, clasped them together, and squeezed.

Adrenaline coursed through my bloodstream.

He struggled mightily to free himself from the jailer's hold, flung his hands upwards, twisting and torquing his legs around.

My arm muscles trembled from the exertion. In ten seconds or so he'd gone limp. The carotid arteries on either side of the neck supply blood to the brain. Compressed, they don't.

Dad had taught me the blood choke. He'd actually demonstrated it on me once until I passed out.

Pablo rushed towards me, ready to help, then watched me set Buck's head on the floor. He held up a tangled mess of brown lamp cord.

'Perfect.' I handed him the steak knife and asked him to cut off pieces a couple of feet long.

In Buck's tactical jacket I found a black nylon sheath, out of which I pulled a knife. This was no steak knife. It was a Microtech Halo, a single-action front-opener. I pressed the titanium firing button, and a lethal-looking blade shot forward. A four-inch serrated blade that could take off a fingertip.

I handed it carefully to Pablo.

'*¡Dios mío!*' he breathed.

'Be careful.'

While he sliced lamp cord, I took out Buck's Ruger, thumbed the cylinder release, saw it was loaded. Several of his jacket pockets were stuffed with .44 Magnum cartridges; I grabbed a handful. There was a torch in one of his jacket pockets, and I took that, too: an expensive tactical torch.

When Pablo was finished, he handed the knife back to me awkwardly, blade out. He didn't know how to retract the blade.

I looped some lamp cord around Buck's wrists, and we used it to pull him upright. Then we shoved him against the iron grate and secured him, spread-eagled, in a standing position. Pablo wrapped cord around his ankles while I searched the dusty floor and finally found an oil-stained rag in a corner and stuffed it into his mouth, in case he came to again soon.

'I need to go back upstairs,' I said. 'To the manager's office. Is there any other way upstairs besides the way we came in?'

'No.'

'A delivery entrance?'

Pablo looked blank.

'*La entrada de servicio*,' I said. '*Ya sabes, el área donde se carga y descarga, por donde se meten las cosas al hotel.*'

'Ah.' He nodded, thought for a moment. 'Yes, but not to upstairs.'

'So there is another way out?'

'To the water only.' He went over to the iron bars, pointed out a gate in the centre that I hadn't noticed. Mounted on the gate's frame just to the left of Buck's lolling head was an old push-button mechanical combination lock. He punched in three numbers, turned a knob. Then he slowly pulled the gate open.

'In here,' he said.

I followed him into the wine cellar. He pointed to an arched section of the brick wall that had no wine rack in front of it. 'The old delivery entrance.'

The arched entrance had obviously been bricked in a long time ago. 'That doesn't really help us,' I said.

'No, no, look. Is where Mr Paul hides the very expensive wines.'

He reached behind a wine rack and pulled out a long metal rod, then poked it into a crack in the mortar between two bricks.

A clunking sound, and the entire arched wall jutted forward.

Not a wall: a brick-and-mortar door.

'What the hell—?'

Behind the brick-paved door was a small room. A few wooden wine racks, randomly placed, held maybe a few dozen dusty bottles. And a second iron gate. This chamber was actually, I saw, the mouth of a long tunnel.

'This goes right down to the dock, doesn't it?' I said.

Pablo nodded. 'When they build the lodge a long time ago, all the deliveries come by sea. They bring all the things in through this tunnel. But not for a long time. The old owners, before Mr Paul, they close it off.'

And they'd taken advantage of the renovation to build a hidden wine cellar for the good stuff.

'Everyone who works here knows about this?'

'No, just . . .' He was suddenly uncomfortable. 'José and I—sometimes we smoke, you know, the *mota*.'

'Weed.'

He nodded. 'Mr Paul, he fire us if he know. So José find this place under the dock.'

'I'm going to try to get upstairs to the office,' I said. 'I want you to go down to the water and look for a boat. Take any one that has a key in the engine. Or a rowboat, if you have to. You know how to use a boat?'

'Yes, of course.'

'When you get out there, move slowly and quietly, and don't start up the motor until the last possible minute. Take the boat to the nearest lodge and get help. The police, anyone. Tell them what's going on. OK?'

'OK.' He seemed to hesitate.

'You're worried about the noise from the boat's engine, aren't you?'

'They have guns. They shoot.'

'But you'll be far from the lodge.'

A sudden static burst came from Buck's two-way radio: 'Buck, come in.'

The voice echoed in the low-ceilinged chamber. I couldn't identify it.

I returned to the outer gate, pulled the two-way radio from Buck's belt.

'Buck, it's Verne,' the voice said again. 'Where the hell are you?'

'Maybe they look for you now,' Pablo said. 'Is not safe for you up there.'

I switched off the radio. 'You go,' I said. 'Get help. Don't you worry about me.'

AT THE TOP of the stairs, I switched off the light, stood in absolute darkness.

Quiet.

I pushed the cellar door open. The hinges squeaked no matter how slowly I opened it.

A few steps into the dark hallway, I stopped again to listen.

Voices now.

From the great room. I sank to my knees, out of sight, and listened.

Two voices, hushed and urgent. One was Verne's, manic, rising and falling, speedy and loud. The other was Wayne's oddly high alto. The tattooed ex-con conferring with the crew-cut blond lunk.

'. . . heard him saying he was going to bolt.' That was Verne.

'To who?' Wayne, now.

'—said he changed his mind. Got spooked after Russell killed those guys. Didn't want to go to jail for the rest of his life.'

'He told you that?'

'. . . the chick said.'

Something I couldn't hear, and then Verne saying, 'I'll take his cut.'

Something else, then Wayne: 'Where the hell's he gonna go?'

'Out there somewhere. Russell wants you to go look for him.'

'The hell's he gonna go? Not the Zodiac—'

'They got other boats down there.'

'. . . cut the spark-plug wires, so what's he gonna do, swim to Vancouver?'

Wayne said something else I couldn't quite make out, and then Verne said, 'Christ's sake, then look in the woods.'

'Can't go more than twenty yards in that forest without getting stuck.'

'You saw the guy in the jungle in Panama—he's an animal.'

'And if I find him?'

'Waste him, Russell says. Can't trust him any more.'

'I'm not going to waste Bucky for taking off. That's whacked, man.'

'You don't do it, buddy, Russell's gonna grease you,' Verne said. 'You know he will. He's not taking any chances. Not when we're this close to the big score.'

The jungle in Panama. Special Forces, then. Military, anyway. At least these guys and Buck, probably Russell, too.

So the cover story about Buck had worked. They weren't looking for an unconscious comrade but a defector. Nor had they realised I was missing.

That meant they'd search outside, not inside. I could hide here until they were gone and get to the office without being spotted.

The voices stopped. Retreating footsteps, then a screen door opening and closing. One of them had gone outside to search for Buck.

I slid across the floor, paused to listen again.

No one out there now.

I pushed the kitchen service door from the bottom, just a few inches.

Then, rising slowly, I sidled through the doorway and eased it closed behind me.

LOOKING LEFT, then right, I surveyed the room.

Through the cavernous shadowed space I moved slowly, cautiously, afraid I might trip over something.

Past the staircase landing, then into the hallway that led to the side entrance, the bathroom, the manager's office. Three identical wooden doors; all with black iron knobs and locksets. First was the bathroom, the next two unmarked, the fourth had a brass plaque that said MANAGER.

Just as Paul Fecher had said, a bookcase stood outside his office door. On top of the bookcase, a ceramic lamp. I lifted it, spotted the key.

The manager's office door was locked, but the old key fitted snugly in the lock. It turned with a satisfying click.

I pulled the revolver from my waistband, held it in my right hand as I turned the knob and opened the door with my left.

The room was small, windowless, absolutely dark. It smelt of old wood and damp paper. I pocketed the key, then shut the door behind me.

I pulled out Buck's tactical torch, and pulsed the beam on for a second. In one freeze-frame I could make out a small, roll-top desk, stored its location in my memory. On top of it, an Apple computer.

I had an Apple computer at home. When you pressed the power switch, it chimed like the opening chord of a Beethoven symphony. Unless the volume was turned down. But you didn't know until it was too late.

Even turning it on was a risk, but wasn't everything just then? I found the power button by feel on the back side of the base and pressed it.

In a few seconds it chimed. Loud.

I sat in an old rolling office chair and watched the screen light up and come to life, listening for footfalls in the hall, waiting.

The hard drive crunched and crunched, and finally a swirly blue pattern came right up. A row of icons on the left: Internet Explorer and the Safari browser. I double-clicked Safari and waited for it to load.

And waited. *Jesus*, I thought, *this is slow. For God's sake, hurry*. I found myself talking to the computer, all the while listening for footsteps.

But all I got was a big white box, a blank screen.

Then a few lines of text, not what I wanted to see:

Safari can't open the page http://www.google.com/
because your computer isn't connected to the Internet.

I quit Safari and reloaded it, and got the same error message. Either the modem was down or the satellite Internet connection wasn't working.

Switching on the flashlight, I traced the modem cable to a closet. The modem was right inside, bracketed to the wall.

Its power light was on, but the receiver light was off; it wasn't getting any satellite signal. I shut the modem down, waited a few seconds, then powered it back up.

No change. Nothing different.

The problem wasn't with the modem or the computer. Someone had cut off Internet access. There was no way to email out.

Or wire money out, either.

Chapter 13

That was the puzzling thing.

Russell's men must have cut the line. After all, once they'd grabbed the sat phone, the only way for their hostages to transmit a distress message was via the Internet.

Yet without it, there'd be no half-billion-dollar ransom. So, barring some accident during the takeover, they must have dismantled it.

I had to find out where and try to restore the link.

The summer after I'd got out of Glenview and before I joined the National Guard, I'd got a job as a cable-TV installer. Before the summer was over I quit, but not before I'd acquired a few useless skills, like how to splice coaxial cable.

Maybe not so useless.

I waited at the door, didn't hear anyone walking by. Holding the Ruger in my right hand, the key in my left, I unlocked the door, pushed it open a few inches, looked out.

No one in the hall that I could see.

As I crept along the dark hall, I glanced out of a window. No one out there. Maybe Wayne was still trudging through the forest, looking for Buck.

I kept looking, trying to locate the satellite dish. I vaguely remembered seeing one somewhere behind the lodge, mounted on top of an outbuilding. Which made sense: the dish didn't fit in with the rustic decor.

Sure enough, it was where I remembered: on top of a shed about 200 feet from the lodge. The cable that ran from the lodge to the dish would be buried, of course. If it had been cut, there were only two places it could have been done: at the shed, or on the exterior of the lodge.

Gently nudging the screen door open, I stepped out onto the soft earth, then pushed the door closed behind me so it wouldn't slam. Pine needles crunched underfoot. The delicious cool air smelt of saltwater and pine.

For a moment, I allowed myself to enjoy the illusion of freedom.

But of course I wasn't free. Not as long as Ali and all the others were trapped inside.

I walked slowly along the log siding, looking for a cable stapled to the concrete foundation. The wall outside Paul Fecher's office was the most logical place to find it. I couldn't risk switching on the flashlight; fortunately, the moon was bright.

In a few minutes I found it: a loop of cable sprouting from the concrete, a few inches above the ground. One end of the cable dangling loose.

It had been unscrewed from its connector. That was how they'd cut off Internet access. Quick and easy. Above all, easy to screw back in when they were ready to use it.

Except for one little thing: the connector was missing.

A little piece of precision-machined, nickel-plated brass used to join two pieces of coaxial cable. I'd spent much of that summer fumbling with the damned things, losing them on people's lawns.

I quickly searched the ground, just to be sure, but I knew what Russell had done. Simple and clever. He'd removed that tiny but crucial piece, to make sure no one could send out an SOS on the Internet.

I was impressed by Russell's thoroughness.

It also gave me an idea.

I raced over to the generator shed, where the satellite dish was bolted to the roof. At the back of the small, shingled building, I found where the cable came out of the ground and ran up the outside wall to the dish.

Kneeling, I took out Buck's knife, and with one quick motion, I sliced through the cable.

If I couldn't use the Internet, then neither could Russell. I doubted he or his men knew the first thing about how to splice coaxial cable, which sure wasn't like electrical wire.

I did, though. Those few weeks of tedium suddenly seemed less pointless.

Now I had something he needed.

But as I turned to head down to the shore, I heard a voice.

IT HAD COME from the front of the lodge.

A shout, quick and sharp: 'Stop right there.'

Pablo had been spotted; it could be nothing else.

I turned towards the shore, taking long, silent strides along the side of the building.

Down the hill a few hundred feet a bulky silhouette descended the wooden steps of the dock. An arm extended: a weapon.

'I'm not going to tell you again.'

Pablo was standing on the beach, torquing from one side to the other, as if trying to decide which way to run. Behind him, floating in the water, the black hulk of an inflatable craft moored to the dock.

I watched with a feeling of desperate helplessness.

Wayne wasn't going to shoot the kid, I was certain—not without Russell's approval, anyway. They'd bring him in, interrogate him, force him to tell them how he'd managed to escape. And where I was.

Would Russell then decide to make a 'lesson' out of some lowly lodge staff member? There'd be no reason for him to do it, not after Grogan and Danziger. But with Russell, you never knew.

Wayne descended a few more steps, then stopped, raising his other hand to steady his grip. Pablo gave a high, strangled yelp, his words obliterated by the crash of the surf. Wayne was much closer to the shore now than to me. Torn by indecision, I raised my gun, lined up the sights. His body was a distant blur.

No. I couldn't bring myself to fire at Wayne. Besides, at this distance, I had little chance of hitting the target. If I fired, I'd surely miss. And once I pulled the trigger, whether I hit him or not, everything would change at once. They'd hear the gunshot, know I was out here.

I had to help Pablo escape. That was all I could really do now.

So I did the only thing I could think of to distract Wayne, divert his attention and give Pablo the chance to run.

I picked up a rock. No way would I hit him at this distance but at least the sound of the rock hitting the ground might break his concentration, cause him to turn.

Pablo raised his hands in surrender, walked slowly towards Wayne, who said something I couldn't hear. Then Pablo did something bizarre: he clapped his hands, then put his arms behind him and clapped again.

What the hell is he doing?

I hurled the rock as hard as I could, and at that moment, Wayne fired.

Three shots in quick succession.

He probably never even heard the hollow *pock* of the rock hitting the wooden step.

I saw the muzzle flash, but the shots were distant, muted pops, masked by the sound of the ocean.

Pablo twisted, jerked forward, crumpled to the ground, a small dark shape on the beach.

He lay still, obviously dead. He could have been just another rock, another boulder, a pile of debris.

MOM'S VOICE WOKE ME, high and keening, from the kitchen downstairs: 'Please! That's enough! That's enough!'

Something hard crashing. My digital clock said two in the morning.

Dad, thundering, 'You goddamned bitch!'

I lay in bed, not moving, heart racing.

Mom's voice, hysterical: 'Get out of the house! Just leave us!'

'I'm not leaving my house, you bitch!'

He'd lost another job. As scary and foul-tempered as he usually was, when he got fired, he drank even more; he hit Mom even more.

Another crash. Something thudded. The whole house seemed to shake.

Silence.

Terrified, I leapt out of bed, vaulted down the stairs to the kitchen. Mom was lying on the floor, unconscious. Eyes closed, twin streams of blood running from her nostrils.

Some protector I was.

'Get up, you bitch!' my dad screamed. 'Get the hell up!'

My blood ran cold. He'd gone berserk.

'What'd you do to her?' I shouted.

He saw me, snarled, 'Get the hell out of here.'

'What did you do to her?' I lunged, hands outspread, shoved him against the stove.

At fifteen, I was as tall as my dad and starting to get some muscles on me, though Dad was still far beefier and more powerful.

For a second, his face went slack in surprise.

Then his face went deep red. He turned, grabbed a cast-iron frying pan from the stovetop, whacked it against the side of my head. I'd backed up out of the way, but not in time. The pan clipped my ear, the pain unbelievable.

I yowled, doubled over, my ear ringing.

'We gonna do this the hard way?' he shouted, and he swung the frying pan again.

This time, instead of backing up, I shot forward, pushed him hard, everything a blur. His sour perspiration smell, his beer breath, the grey-white of his T-shirt spattered with Mom's blood.

A flash of black, the frying pan, as he pulled it back to swing again.

The anger inside me had finally boiled over, and the pumping adrenaline gave me the strength to overpower the monster, to smash him back against the upper kitchen cabinet, the one with the glass windows in it and the neatly stacked dishes. To keep him from hitting me again, to stop him from hitting Mom again.

To be a protector.

The back of his head cracked into the sharp corner, where the wood veneer had peeled off, and he'd never got round to repairing it.

He roared, 'You son of a bitch, I'm going to kill you!'

But the anger and the adrenaline and all those years of storing it inside made me stronger than him, at least for the moment. My hands clutched the sides of his head, the way you'd hold someone you were about to kiss, only I shoved his head against the corner of the cabinet again, and again, and again.

He bellowed low and deep, like a beast. His eyes bulged, looking shocked and disbelieving and—was it possible?—afraid.

I didn't stop. I was in that dark tunnel now, had to keep going. Kept smashing his head back against the sharp corner until I felt something in his skull go soft. The awful bellowing stopped, but his eyes bulged.

I finally heard my mom's voice shrilling, 'Jakey, Jakey, Jakey, stop it!'

I stopped. Let go. Dad toppled, then slumped to the floor.

I stared.

'Jakey, oh my God, what have you done?'

My legs buckled. An icy coldness in my stomach, icy fingers clutching my bowels, my chest. And at the same time, something else, too.

Relief.

I STOOD IN THE COOL BREEZE and the dusky moonlight for what felt like a whole minute. It might have been only a few seconds, though: time had slowed.

Pablo was unarmed, no threat; he'd obeyed orders, had done what he'd been told to do. He had put his hands up. He'd surrendered. There was no reason to kill him.

Grief hollowed me out, and into that hollow place rushed a far more familiar emotion. Loosing the bad wolf, giving in to the rage: there was something strangely comforting about it.

It fuelled me, propelled me, focused my mind, sharpened my senses.

I knew now what I had to do.

WAYNE LUMBERED DOWN the dock steps to the beach. Maybe he wanted to make sure Pablo was dead.

I peered round the corner of the building, saw Verne emerge from the side entrance. He took something out of his pocket that glinted. The flick of a butane lighter, a puff of smoke. I heard him suck in the smoke, hold it in his lungs until he coughed it out.

I dropped to my knees, crawled along the front of the lodge. The porch ran the length of the building, raised about five feet above ground level. I moved quietly, staying close to the wooden skirting, struggling to maintain my balance. It wasn't easy, given the sharp incline from the shore to the building. When I reached the wooden walkway that connected the porch to the steps that wound to the pier, I stopped.

Inside the lodge, the great room remained dark. The only light spilled from the windows of the enclosed porch at the northwest corner.

I resumed crawling, went under the walkway, which was elevated a few feet above the steep hillside, shimmied through the narrow gap between creosote-treated timber pilings, then back along the porch skirting until I was beneath the screened porch.

Once I reached the west side of the lodge, I figured I should be able to crawl the short span to the woods unseen. That was the only way to reach the shore, and the boat, but getting through that dense forest—

Voices.

I sank as low to the ground as I could.

Russell was saying something I couldn't make out. Then came a reply, and I recognised Travis: '. . . ain't what we were hired to do.'

Their voices got softer, more conversational, and as much as I strained to hear, I couldn't.

I wondered how long it would take for Wayne to return to the lodge and report that he'd just killed a young Mexican, a member of the lodge staff—and a hostage. The first question would be how one of the hostages had escaped. There'd be a head count. They'd quickly realise I was missing, too.

Which would surely trigger further reprisals. More 'lessons'.

The ground was earthen and soft, but here and there were rocks and twigs that bruised my kneecaps. The narrow strip of lawn lay just ahead, and beyond it, the forest. The only way down to the water, the boats.

And then Travis's voice, whining, almost pleading: '. . . hundred million. Not five hundred million, man, come on, what are we doing here? Jesus, Russell, man, that's like a whole new level of, of—'

Russell murmured something lulling.

Travis spoke, but just a fragment floated through the air: '. . . your cellie from Lompoc.'

Lompoc, I thought. That was a prison somewhere. Russell's cellmate from Lompoc Prison, it had to be.

John Danziger: *One of their employees got arrested in South America on a child recovery case he was working, charged with kidnapping under the international treaty agreements. Did a couple of years in prison in the US.*

Now Russell raised his voice. 'No, Travis, you listen to me very carefully. All he cares about is getting the goddamned ninety-seven-point-five million dollars in his goddamned account in Liechtenstein by the close of business today. He gets that, he's cool, he's off the hook.'

Who was 'he'—Russell's prison cellmate?

My scalp prickled.

Ninety-seven-point-five million. Off the hook. Liechtenstein. So this wasn't just a clever heist dreamed up by a gang of ex-soldiers. They'd been *hired*.

I sat up, keeping my head just below the porch floor. I waited, listened harder, finally gave up. Then, my heart knocking, I rose slowly and raced towards the edge of the forest.

FOR A MOMENT, hidden in a dense stand of pines, I looked back at the lodge.

A tall, lanky figure stared out of the porch window: Russell.

Maybe he was simply impatient, wondering what was taking Wayne so long. He had a schedule to keep, after all.

I began scrambling down the steep hill towards the shore, through hellish, thorny underbrush, thickets of ancient, moss-covered spruces and twisted, gnarled pines. Branches whipped against my face.

As I stepped over a drift of leaves and pine needles, my foot struck something. When I saw what it was, I had to stop myself from screaming.

A well-manicured hand.

Through the blanket of leaves that had been strewn over Danziger's body I could make out the light blue sleeve of his shirt.

Next to it was another drift of leaves: Alan Grogan.

And a third body concealed by leaves and twigs. With the toe of my shoe, I cleared away just enough to see a dark-skinned young man in jeans and sweatshirt. José, I knew at once. Pablo's friend. The first one they'd killed, when they arrived: the gunshot we'd all heard at dinner.

Undone by what I'd just seen, I lurched forward, and tripped on a root; tumbled headfirst, then cracked my forehead against a rock outcropping.

I bit my lip, tried to will the pain away, then, head throbbing, I scrambled to my feet. My face, scratched and scraped from the branches, stung.

The roar of the waves told me I was close now.

The terrain had become so steeply pitched that I couldn't keep myself from sliding downhill. Only by grabbing at the branch of a downed tree was I able to stop just before plummeting off a scrabbly ledge into the ocean.

There was no shore here; the ledge was far too narrow. But the water was shallow, and it was the only way to the dock. Slowly, I lowered my feet into the surf, braced for a cold shock, relieved to find it wasn't too bad.

I waded along the shoreline, careful not to let the water reach my waist. Buck's revolver was in my pocket, and I wanted to keep it operational.

The shoreline wound past the trees to the small beachfront. There, out in the open, I could be seen from the lodge. I looked up, saw no one.

Wayne was gone. I assumed he'd made his way back to the lodge while I was climbing through the woods.

The Zodiac floated in the water, hitched to the dock.

On the sand nearby lay Pablo's body.

THE ZODIAC was a classic military inflatable, a commando boat with a skin of leathery black synthetic rubber. Around twenty feet long; probably seated fifteen people. At the stern was a twenty-five-horsepower Yamaha outboard motor, powerful enough but not too loud. A pair of aluminium oars rested in brackets: much quieter.

As I approached, though, I realised that the boat wasn't just tied up. It was locked. A cable connected the Zodiac to a steel horn cleat bolted to the dock. It was a strong cable, too—thick twisted-steel wire, coated in clear plastic, its ends looping through a sturdy brass padlock.

I tried to fight back the surge of desperation.

Was there some way to get the cable off? Hoisting myself out of the water, I climbed onto the dock, then immediately lay flat on the splintery planks so I wouldn't be easily spotted from the lodge. I leaned over, tugged at the cleat to see if I could prise it loose.

But the steel cleat was too secure, and the cable was too sturdy. I'd have to clamber back up the hill through the forest and look for a cable cutter. Maybe in the maintenance shed up the hill.

That meant exposure, more time. Could I risk it? If I had to . . .

Discouraged, I rose.

And felt a hand on my shoulder.

EVEN BEFORE I turned round I knew whose hand it was. I hadn't heard Wayne's approach: the surf had masked the heavy tread.

Now I found myself looking into the little black hole at the end of the sound suppressor threaded onto his black SIG-Sauer.

You don't put a silencer on a gun unless you mean to fire it.

'Boy, you're full of surprises, aren't you?' he said. 'Nowhere to run, you know.'

Buck's revolver was in my pocket. But an unsilenced gunshot would draw notice from the lodge. The knife would be a better idea.

If I could pull it out without him killing me first.

I took a long, slow breath. 'Who says I want to run?'

'Just put your hands up, Jake,' he said, 'and come back inside. I don't want to hurt you. I really don't.'

He didn't know I'd seen him pull the trigger.

I reflexively glanced at Pablo's sprawled body, on the sand behind him.

His eyes remained locked on mine; he knew what I'd seen.

'Come on, now, let's go,' he said. 'Hands up, Jake, and you won't get hurt. I promise.'

I'd barely heard him talk before. The man who'd just killed Pablo had a surprisingly gentle manner. His piping voice was almost melodious.

And he knew my name, which was interesting.

I'd killed once before and thought I'd never have to do it again.

I didn't want to.

Don't make me do this.

'Jake. You see, you really don't have a choice.'

'No. I really don't.'

'All right,' he said. 'Now we're talking.'

I bowed my head as if considering my options, and my right hand felt unseen for my back pocket, very slowly pulling out the knife.

Nodding, I thumbed the trigger button and felt it jolt in my hand as the blade ejected.

And then I lunged at him.

The man who'd just killed Pablo. I saw him as if through fog.

My heart raced. A quick upward swipe against his throat, and his mouth gaped in surprise, exposing the tiny jagged feral teeth.

His knees buckled, and he toppled backwards. The dock shook. His pistol clattered, slid almost to the edge of the dock.

Now I had the knife against his throat, my knees on his chest. The blade caught the moonlight. Blood ran from a gash just below his neckline.

'You know what this knife can do,' I said. 'Answer a couple of questions, and I'll let you go.'

He blinked a few times, and I saw, out of the corner of my eye, his right hand start to move. I pressed the blade against the skin. 'Don't.'

'What do you want to know?'

'What happens after you get your money? What happens to us?'

He was blinking rapidly: nervous.

'Don't worry, Jake,' he said. 'We're not leaving anyone behind.'

I studied his face, saw the very beginning of a smile, no more.

'What's that supposed to mean?' I said, though I knew.

He didn't answer. I slid the blade lightly against his throat. A fresh line of blood appeared. 'Who hired you?'

'You did.'

I slid the blade again, a bit harder this time.

'You don't get it, do you? We're just employees like you. Just doing a job. Come on, Jake. Seriously, now. There's no need for violence.'

I gritted my teeth. 'Tell that to the kid on the beach over there.'

'I saw that. It's a shame.'

'I saw it, too,' I said. 'Watched you put three bullets into him. One more question, Wayne. What did you say to him at the very end?'

Now he was unable to stop his smile. 'I told him to dance the *cucaracha*.'

Tears blurred my vision.

Wayne took a deep breath. 'He looked like a puppet, didn't you think?'

Blood roared in my ears, and I was in the dark tunnel, speeding along.

This time I slashed at his neck without holding back. He made a choking, gagging sound as his right hand grasped the air, the fingers twitching.

With both hands, I gave his body a hard shove. It made a great splash.

THE ADRENALINE BEGAN to ebb from my bloodstream, leaving me rubber-limbed, feeling played out.

I stood, though my knees were barely able to support me. Wiped the blood off the knife, then retracted the blade and slipped it into my back pocket. I fought off a wave of nausea. Then I remembered Wayne's SIG-Sauer, picked it up from the edge of the dock, slipped it into my waistband. Tried to summon the strength to go to the toolshed and try to find a pair of bolt cutters.

And then, from somewhere up the hill, came a high-pitched cry.

A female cry, quickly stifled.

Coming out of the side of the lodge, the area where Verne took his smoking breaks, were the silhouettes of two people, one of them shoving the other.

It was Verne, and he had a woman with him.

I RACED UP the wooden steps, right out in the open, no longer caring whether Russell or anyone else was watching.

For a few seconds I couldn't comprehend what was happening, why Verne was kneeling on top of Ali, pinioning her, why something had been stuffed into her mouth and her skirt was pulled up, and her soft vulnerable flesh was exposed, but the moment, the very second I understood, anger shot through my veins like high-octane fuel. I was possessed by a single-minded purpose. The world had collapsed to just him and me.

Verne looked up, startled, as I rushed up to him, but it wasn't easy for him to move. Not with his trousers pulled down that way, his discoloured white jockey shorts down around his knees. Not while he was struggling to hold Ali down with both hands and feet.

She was writhing and bucking against him, trying to free herself with all her strength, but her hands were roped together. Her face was red from exertion. Her cries were muffled by the panties he'd stuffed in her mouth.

Then, scowling at me, still kneeling on Ali's thighs, he lifted his right arm, swung it behind him to grab for his holster, entangled in his trousers.

I had Buck's gun in my pocket and Wayne's pistol in my waistband, but in my adrenaline haze I'd forgotten about them. I reared back and drop-kicked him, hard, in the throat.

Verne made an *oooof* sound, then emitted an enraged, animal-like growl. He wobbled, knocked off-balance, but quickly righted himself, got back up on his knees and tried to stand as he grabbed his trousers to hitch them up.

Ali twisted away. Her face was scratched, her blouse ripped.

Verne seemed to have given up on his gun, for the moment. Instead, as he propelled himself up from a squatting position, he grabbed my foot, twisted it, and slammed his other fist into my solar plexus. I doubled over, staggered backwards, the wind knocked out of me.

Back on his knees, he had his revolver out now and was aiming at me. He shuddered and twitched, his gun hand shaking. His eyes danced. The meth had fried his nervous system; he couldn't hold the gun steady.

I grabbed his gun hand at the wrist with one hand, twisted the gun in my other, and jerked it backwards. As I wrenched the gun out of his grip, his trigger finger bent way out of joint, obviously broken.

Then, flinging his gun out of the way, I slammed my elbow into his face. He toppled backwards, groaning and gasping for air.

I flashed on that image of Ali trapped beneath him, her nakedness exposed, her vulnerability, and what little restraint I had was gone.

Grabbing his sleeves from behind, I slammed the entire weight of my body against the back of his head, lifting my feet off the ground, forcing his head down. His neck bent all the way forward until his chin nuzzled his chest, and I felt his head jolt forward, then he made a short, sharp gasp as his neck audibly snapped.

For a few seconds, I lay on top of him. Then I rolled off him, heart racing, panting and heaving.

I rose, went over to Ali, lying exhausted on the lawn, and knelt and pulled out the gag. I threw my arms round her, squeezed hard. Her face was hot and wet as she began to sob against my shirt.

I held her for almost a minute. When her sobs slowed, I let go, took out the knife, and slashed through the rope to free her hands.

'WE NEED to get him out of here,' I said, picking up the rope I'd just cut off her and jamming it in my pocket. 'And we've got to get *ourselves* out of here, too. Before someone comes looking for him.'

'Landry,' she said, rising slowly. Her voice shook. 'What you just did—'

'Later,' I said. 'Come on, help me.' Verne's little stainless-steel revolver lay on the grass. I slipped it under my belt, then I grabbed Verne's legs, while she took his arms. The edge of the forest was just a few feet behind the shed. We'd only gone a few feet through the dense underbrush when she dropped his arms. 'I can't,' she said, panting.

'This is far enough.' The body couldn't be seen from the lodge. I began rummaging through his jacket, grabbing all the spare ammo I could find.

We stood behind the shed. Her face was shadowed. Gently, I put a hand up and wiped away her tears, the smudged make-up. I wanted to feel the satin skin of her face. She closed her eyes, seemed to respond to the consolation in my touch.

'Are you OK?'

She nodded, began sobbing again.

'Ali.' I stroked her hair.

'Who the hell are you, Landry?' she whispered.

'There isn't any time for that now,' I said. 'Any second, Russell's going to realise we're both missing. Right now I need your help.'

SHE HAD ANSWERS to most of my questions, her mind firing on all cylinders.

'"Close of business today" has to refer to close of business in Europe,' she said. 'Liechtenstein. Which is, if I remember correctly, next to Switzerland. Nine hours ahead of us. That means Russell probably can't transfer funds after seven in the morning here.'

'Did you notice a clock in the game room?' I asked.

'No. But sunrise here is around five a.m. this time of year—I remember going over the schedule. So it's maybe four thirty. The other thing is that he has to wait for our bank in New York to open. Around nine, I'd guess—six o'clock here. So he has one hour to make everything happen.'

'And we have about an hour and a half.'

'You know what's strange about this whole thing?' she said at last. 'How well briefed Russell seems to be. How much he knows about the company.'

'He has a source inside the company,' I said. 'Has to be.'

'But do you think he's actually *working* for someone inside Hammond?'

I was silent for a moment. 'That's what that guy Wayne said. I asked him who hired them, and he said, "You did." Meaning Hammond, I'm guessing.'

'Someone here?'

'Possibly.'

'But for what?'

'Good old embezzlement, maybe.'

'But why do something like this—a kidnapping? Why hire Russell and his men to try to pull off something so big and messy and downright *risky*?'

I nodded. 'Only one reason, I figure. If you're trying to make people think it's something it's not. You ever hear of something called an *autosecuestro*?'

She shook her head.

'Happens in Latin America from time to time. It's a staged kidnapping. A *self*-kidnapping. People fake their own kidnapping, to raise money from insurance companies or employers. Even from their own family members.'

'But . . . what kind of massive greed would make someone do something so insane? All this *bloodshed*.'

'Maybe the murders weren't supposed to happen. Maybe Russell's just out of control. And maybe it's not greed. Maybe it's desperation.'

'Huh?'

'Look at all the guys on our management team—they're not reckless types, right? Greedy, sure, but they're not motivated by the big score.'

'So what would drive them to do something like this?'

'Fear.'

She thought about that. 'But *who*?' she said finally.

I shook my head.

'Maybe the question to ask is, who had the chance to meet with Russell privately?' she said.

'We all did, right? When he did his "interviews".'

'But when problems came up, when decisions had to be made—whoever hired Russell would have had to talk to him in private. So he'd need a way to do that without the rest of us noticing. An excuse.'

'Anyone who asked to use the bathroom could have talked secretly with Russell, and we'd never have known it.'

'And Upton Barlow asked a bunch of times,' I said. 'And Geoff Latimer, with his diabetes.'

'Did you know he was diabetic?' she said.

'I never met him before. Though I did see syringes in his suitcase.'

'The weird thing is, when I was working in HR, I never saw any medical claims from Latimer that had anything to do with diabetes.'

'Geoff Latimer? Get real. Of all the guys here, Latimer strikes me as the least likely to do something like this. And besides, who's more loyal to Cheryl? He's one of her most trusted advisers.'

'And she's loyal right back. Slattery was pushing to strengthen computer security but Latimer persuaded her not to implement the plan on grounds of cost. But even with what's happened here you haven't heard her say a word against her general counsel. That's Cheryl. "The buck stops here" and all that.'

'Geoff Latimer,' I said, and stopped.

THE NIGHT SKY was still blue-black and clear and crowded with stars, but a pale glow shimmered on the horizon.

We raced round to the back of the lodge, staying low to the ground. Ali took Verne's stubby little Smith & Wesson revolver because it was small and fitted her hand. I kept the Ruger.

I stashed the SIG-Sauer to use as a back-up, just in case we needed it.

Tucked away in the trees behind the lodge was the maintenance shed. It was a rustic old structure, weathered and shingled. The paint on its door was peeling. An ancient brass padlock on a rusted steel hasp secured the door. It was unlocked, though; it came right open. Inside was the overpowering odour of oil paint and gasoline.

The floor was old plywood. I closed the door behind Ali, clicked the torch on, and set it down on a bench. It illuminated a circle against the shelving on one wall, casting the cramped interior in a dim amber light.

I unclipped Buck's walkie-talkie from my belt and switched it on. It was still on Channel 5, the one Russell's men had been using.

But Channel 5 was silent, transmitting only a thin static hiss.

'They could have switched channels, right?' Ali said.

'Or they're not using it. I want you to monitor this, OK? Listen for anything that might tell us what they're doing. And keep that gun in your hand.'

'Where are you going?' She sounded alarmed.

'I want to see where Russell and his brother are. If they're in the screened porch, I might be able to take them by surprise.'

'Take them . . .?'

'Shoot them, Ali. Take them down. One or both.'

'Jesus, Landry!'

'Can you fire the revolver if you have to?'

'I know how to use a gun.'

'I know you do. I'm asking if you can bring yourself to do it.'

She inhaled deeply. 'If I have to,' she said. 'I think so.'

THE PORCH WAS DARK and empty. In the game room, the wooden blinds had been drawn. They'd been open all night, though the windows had been shut. That meant they knew we were out here. They'd taken precautions.

I dropped to the ground and waited about a minute, listening for any movement, watching to see if anyone was looking out. When I was fairly certain I wasn't being watched, I got to my feet and ran back to the shed.

Standing outside the closed door, I said in a low voice, 'It's me.'

The door came open slowly. Ali stood there, revolver in her hand, looking like a natural. Her eyes were questioning, but she said nothing.

I went in, shut the door behind me. 'They know that I'm out here. Maybe that you are, too, by now.'

'How can you be sure?'

I explained.

'So what does that mean?' Ali asked. 'What are we going to do?'

'We go to Plan B. I'm going to shut off the generator. They can't wire the money without power *and* unless I splice the cable back together. Which means they're going to have to cooperate if they want the funds. It'll also disorientate them. And in the confusion, I'm going to try to get back inside without being noticed.'

'*Inside?* For what?'

'To get the others out. Meanwhile, I want you to stay here and see if you can find a heavyweight bolt cutter.'

'For the Zodiac?' she said.

I nodded.

'If there was a bolt cutter here, you'd have grabbed it already, Landry. I know what you're doing. You want me to stay here.'

I hesitated for barely a second. 'Right,' I admitted. 'I don't want you out there if they start shooting.'

'Yeah, well, I'm not staying inside here. I want to do what I can.'

I thought for a moment.

'All right,' I finally said. 'But at least wait here until the power goes out. Keep a watch on the house.'

I edged the door open a bit and looked out. 'When you see the generator shut down, run over to the kitchen entrance.'

Then I thought of something. I swept the walls with the torch. Tools hung in perfect rows on pegboard or on hooks on the wall. Cans of paint and paint thinner and plastic bottles of garden chemicals and hose-end sprayers lined the narrow wooden shelves. Piles of stuff on the floor.

Neatly folded on a shelf next to the paint cans, I found something that would work: a canvas dust sheet. I shook it open, then took out Buck's knife and sliced a long rectangle.

'Could you lift up your skirt?' I said.

She looked at me curiously, then got what I was doing. She pulled up her skirt. I positioned the little Smith & Wesson revolver on her thigh, and wound the canvas strip around both the gun and her thigh, just tight enough to secure the weapon in place: a decent makeshift holster. Then I pulled the skirt back in place.

'Element of surprise,' I said. She nodded.

'Try it,' I said. 'Make sure you can do it fast if you need to.'

While she practised, I ran the torch up and down the walls, shined the beam on the piles on the floor.

Noticed the crates that didn't belong here.

A cache of spare ammo, it appeared. Russell's men had brought the crates in with them and stashed them out of sight. My eyes were caught by several red cylinders about the size and shape of Coke cans. Black markings on them: AN-M14 INCEN TH.

'What are they?' Ali asked.

'Thermite hand grenades.'

'Hand grenades? What for?'

'The army uses them to burn things down fast. Much faster than splashing gasoline around, and a whole lot hotter.'

'My *God*. You think that's what they're planning to do before they leave? Toss in one of those? Burn the lodge down with everyone inside?'

'That's my guess, yes. But not until the funds go out.'

'Which he can't do until the power goes back on. And you fix the satellite cable.'

'Exactly.'

'Landry,' she said. 'These grenades. Are they something—we could use?'

'Maybe.' I was quiet for a few seconds while I thought about it. And then I explained how.

'I'm going out,' I said. 'You sure you want to do this? If you're at all—'

'Of course I'm scared,' she interrupted. She attempted a brave smile. 'But don't worry about me. I'll deal.'

'You always do,' I said, and turned to leave. 'I'll meet you at the back of the lodge. As soon as you see the lights go out.'

'Landry,' she said. 'Make sure you come back.'

THE DOOR to the generator shed was unlocked, of course. Inside it was hot, smelt of machine oil. I flipped open the generator's control-panel door and studied the array of knobs. There was a power knob, a fuel valve, various gauges and digital indicators.

The two-way radio, clipped to my belt, chirped.

I froze, listened. Heard nothing.

Turned the volume up.

That was the sound of someone pressing the transmit button. But no voice followed. As if someone had hit the button by accident.

I turned back to the control panel. Just shutting the power off wouldn't do much good. It might throw Russell and his brother into momentary confusion, maybe even flush them out of their sheltered positions. But just as likely it would heighten their paranoia.

The fuel valve, though, gave me an idea. Turn off the power, let the engine die, then close the fuel valve and wait a minute or two. When the power switch was turned back on, everything would look normal. But the generator still wouldn't work. Russell would send Peter, the handyman, out to deal with it. Probably accompanied by Travis, to make sure he complied.

It would take the handyman a long while to figure out what I'd done—he'd check out the control panel and find everything in the right place. Meanwhile, Russell would be getting desperate.

The radio chirped again. I stopped.

'Jake.' Russell's voice, tinny and flat. 'Time to come back inside.'

I stood still. *Don't answer, don't let him know you can hear him.*

In the background, frenzied shouts.

But Russell's voice remained calm. 'I know you're out there, Jake. You really should come back. Your girlfriend's worried.'

I SWITCHED OFF the torch. Turned the walkie-talkie's volume down, not off. The generator remained on.

I pushed the shed door open slowly, looking to either side. Keeping in the shadows, I crept along the perimeter of the yard, round the back towards the maintenance shed, where I'd left Ali.

Even in the gloom, at a distance, I could see the shed door open, the light on inside.

I took a few more steps, scanning side to side, alert for any movement.

The shed was empty. Ali was gone.

The radio chirped. 'It's over, Jake. She's right here. Hey, remember that Glock 18 you know so much about? Well, she's about to learn even more about it. First-hand. The best way.'

A second or two of silence, then a female voice, loud and frantic.

'DON'T DO ANYTHING HE SAYS STAY OUT THERE STAY SAFE DON'T DO WHAT HE SAYS—'

I almost didn't recognise Ali's voice. I'd never heard that kind of fear in her voice before.

Russell's voice cut off her cries. 'You don't want to test me, Jake. You know what I'll do. All I want is for you to come back inside.'

He paused. I kept silent.

'Once we do the transfer, you and your girlfriend and all your colleagues here can go home,' he said. 'But if you don't get back in here—well, it's your choice. Like I say, you always got a choice.'

THE SCREEN DOOR HISSED as I pulled it shut. The hall was dark, but light poured out of the open door of the manager's office.

I approached silently. Even before I saw who was sitting at the desk, I caught the faint sweet trace of his Old Spice.

Geoff Latimer looked up, startled.

'Roomie,' I said.

'Jake!' he said. 'You—were you able to get word out?'

I came closer to the desk. Saw a list of numbers printed on a sheet of paper next to the keyboard: Hammond's bank accounts. 'Couldn't get the Internet to work,' I said. 'You having any luck?'

He shook his head, eyes guarded.

'Stand up, Geoff,' I said.

'You shouldn't be here. Russell told me to do the funds transfer, and he's going to be back—'

'Where do you inject the insulin. For your diabetes. Where?'

'Jake, you're not making sense.'

'Only three places a diabetic normally injects insulin,' I said. 'What's your place?'

'My—my stomach—but we don't have time for this, Jake.'

I grabbed his shirt, yanked out the tails.

His smooth, pale belly. Not a mark.

I dropped the shirt. 'You told Russell to kill Danziger, didn't you?'

He swallowed. 'What the hell are you talking about?'

'John *knew*. He'd figured out you contacted Russell through some old buddy of yours who ran a security firm Russell used to work for. So Danziger had to die, isn't that right, you son of a bitch? Grogan, too.'

He glanced at the door. Maybe he was expecting Russell or Russell's brother to save him. Turning back, he said, 'Jake, this is insane. I'm trying to *help* us. You're wasting time we don't have.'

'That's true,' I said, and I took out Buck's Ruger and placed it against his forehead.

'*Jesus!*' he gasped. 'What the hell is this? Put that thing down *now*!'

'All to get rich, huh?' I pressed the end of the gun barrel harder into the pasty skin of his forehead. His eyes welled with tears.

'But I'm thinking it was more complicated than that. You stole money from the company, put it in some "special purpose entity" offshore. But then the investment tanked, right? And you had to cover the loss, fast.'

'Will you please put that gun down?' he whispered. 'That thing could go *off* if you're not careful! Are you crazy? I'm trying to get us *help*, Jake.'

'You needed to come up with a hundred million dollars. Right?'

'Who is putting these insane ideas in your head? Is it Bodine? Slattery?'

'I don't think you meant for things to happen the way they did today,' I said. 'You didn't hire Russell to hold the company up for half a billion dollars, did you? That was his idea. You were totally clear in your instructions, I'm sure. A hundred million, right? You told him to make it look like he and his guys were just some backwoods hunters who got the bright idea to take a bunch of businessmen hostage, hold them up for ransom.'

He stared at me, frantic.

I jammed the end of the barrel harder against his temple, and he gasped.

'You knew Russell had a lot of experience in situations like this, but you didn't do your due diligence, did you?' Then I added more softly: 'You didn't want people to die, did you, Geoff? Tell me that wasn't part of the plan.'

Tears spilled down his scrubbed red cheeks.

'No,' he whispered. His face seemed to crumple. 'It wasn't supposed to happen like this. It wasn't for me! I never made a *dime*!'

'How was it supposed to happen?'

But Latimer didn't answer. He closed his eyes. His lower lip trembled.

'So how *was* it supposed to happen?' I whispered. 'Russell would hold the company up for a hundred million dollars, then let us all go free? They'd get their cut, and you'd cover your loss? And no one would find out about the money you embezzled from Hammond? Was that how it was supposed to go down?' I grabbed his shoulder, shoved him towards the door.

'Please, Jake, do you think I had any idea what was going to happen?'

'Thing is, Geoff, you still don't,' I said as I pushed him down the hall.

I SHOVED LATIMER into the great room, the revolver at his back.

Russell stood behind Ali, an arm round her neck, his Glock to her temple. He didn't need to say anything: he had a gun to Ali's head and wouldn't hesitate to kill her if it suited his purposes.

I had Latimer, the man who'd hired Russell, but he was only useful if Russell still needed him at this point. And that I didn't know.

Travis was standing about ten feet to the side of his brother, his gun aimed directly at me. I tried to calculate the geometry of the situation, but there were too many unknowns. This much I knew for sure: it was two of them against me, and the only thing between Ali and her death was the twitch of a trigger finger.

Something struck my lower back, a supernova of pain exploding and radiating and doubling me over. I sprawled to the floor and as I rolled over onto my side, I saw who had kicked me from behind.

That jet-black hair and goatee, that towering physique, the pinkish face badly bruised. But otherwise the man wasn't much worse for wear.

'Well, what do you know,' Buck said. 'I had a feeling I'd be seeing you again.'

'LET HER GO, RUSSELL,' I said as I struggled to my feet, still clutching the Ruger.

'That your big idea, swapping Latimer for your girlfriend?' Russell said contemptuously. 'Come on, buddy. I really don't care what happens to him.'

But Latimer had broken free anyway. He now stood between Travis and Buck, his bodyguards. His face was flushed, his eyes furious.

'You know, I really should have killed you first,' Russell continued.

'That's all right,' Buck said. 'I'll do it for you. Happy to oblige.'

Ali was staring at me. She seemed to be communicating silently; but what, if anything, was she trying to say? I saw the fierce resolve in her eyes.

I raised the pistol, moving it from man to man to man, aiming at each, one at a time. But Russell knew I'd never risk a shot at him. Not while he had his gun on Ali. It would take no more than a jerk of his finger on the trigger at the instant of his death, and she'd die, too.

'You have to take him out,' Latimer said, his voice echoing. 'He's the only one who knows anything now.'

'I don't work for you any more, Geoff,' Russell said.

'Actually, Russell, I don't think Geoff's really thought this through,' I said. 'See, you need me alive. If you want the Internet connection to work, anyway.'

'Ah.' Russell nodded. 'I see. Well, it's all hooked up now.'

'No, it's not. One of your guys must have screwed up—cut the line.'

Russell smiled.

Buck said, 'Guy's bluffing, Russell.'

'Don't take my word for it,' I said. 'Ask Geoff.'

'How's the satellite working, Geoff?' said Russell.

Latimer hesitated a few seconds. 'Something's wrong with it. I couldn't get connected. He must have done something.'

'Should have brought your A team on this job,' I said. 'You see, Russell, I worked as a cable installer once for a couple of months. Not one of my favourite jobs, but I guess you never know when a skill might come in handy.' I waited a beat, but Russell didn't reply. 'Call me crazy, but I've got a feeling you're not really an expert in splicing RG-6 coaxial cable.'

Silence.

'Didn't think so. The handyman sure isn't. Ask him. When the satellite goes down, I'll bet you the manager gets on the sat phone and calls the satellite company. You planning on calling the cable company, Russell? Ask for a service call, maybe?'

'We don't need him, Russell,' Latimer said. 'I'm sure the handyman can figure it out. The main thing is, there's only one person who *knows* about all this. You have to take him out right now.'

Russell glanced at Latimer. Smiled again. 'You know, Geoff,' he said, 'I think you're right.' In one swift, smooth movement, he removed the Glock from Ali's head and an explosion rang in my ears.

Latimer slumped to the floor. Ali screamed, jumped, but Russell's arm held her tight against his body.

I stared, at once relieved and horrified.

'Now, Jake,' Russell said calmly as he replaced the gun against Ali's temple, 'my brother's going to escort you outside and watch while you repair the line. I know you care whether your girlfriend lives or dies, so I'm sure you won't try anything stupid. Place the Ruger on the floor. Slowly.'

I paused. Breathed out carefully.

Russell jammed the Glock into Ali's temple, and she gave a cry.

'All right,' I said. 'But here's the deal: as soon as I fix the cable, you let her go. I'll signal you when I'm finished, and you can check. Confirm the Internet connection's working. If I keep my end of the bargain, you keep your end. OK?'

Russell nodded, smiled. 'You don't give up, do you?'

'Never,' I said.

Chapter 14

Travis kept his distance, his weapon trained on me.

I knelt at the side of the shed where I'd cut the cable, and held up one end for him to see. A glint of copper in the moonlight.

'Can I have a little light here?' I said.

With his left hand, he took out his torch and switched it on. He shone it on the loops of cable coming out of the earth against the shed's concrete foundation, then at the severed ends.

I said, 'One of you guys must have cut this. You do this, Travis?'

Travis sounded surprised to be asked, even irate. 'No.'

'I'm going to need some stuff. A crimping tool, a couple of F-type male connectors, and an F-81 connector. And a cable cutter and a pair of pliers.'

Travis shuffled a foot on the gravelly sand. 'I don't know what the hell you're talking about.'

'If they have it, it's going to be in the toolshed. I'll have to look.'

He shone the torch into my eyes. I shielded my eyes with a hand.

'I'm going to have to ask Russell.'

'You check with your brother every time you wipe your ass? If they have anything, it'll be right here, in the shed.' I touched the shingled wall. 'Let's take a look. You guys don't have time to screw around.'

He hesitated. 'All right.'

Instead of coming round to the front to the shed door, I rounded towards the back.

'Hey! Door's over here.'

'Yeah, and the key's hanging on a hook back here,' I said, and kept going. I muttered, 'Or do you want to call for Big Brother and ask him for permission to get it?'

He followed, still trying to keep a distance, his gun on me.

'Will you point that torch over here, please?' I said, not indicating anything. 'And not at my eyes?'

'Where?'

'Damn,' I said, stopping by a gnarled old pine whose branches raked the shed's low roof. 'It's not here. You see it anywhere?'

The cone of light swept up from the ground to the shed's low roof, then down again. I could see him hesitate, trying to figure out how to get out his two-way while keeping the gun on me. As he did so, I stepped closer to him, pretending to search for the missing key. He clicked off the torch and felt for his walkie-talkie.

'Wait,' I said. 'I think I found it. Sorry about that.'

Wayne's SIG-Sauer, nestled in a crook of the old pine's tree trunk. I grabbed it, swung it around, and put it against Travis's ear.

'One word,' I said, 'and I'll blow your brains out.'

He hesitated just long enough for me to grab his gun hand at the wrist and twist it, hard. He was amazingly strong: all that prison muscle. But finally I was able to wrench it out of his hand.

His left fist crashed into my cheek. He didn't have much room to manoeuvre, but still the blow was incredibly powerful. A jagged lightning bolt of pain exploded in my eyes, my brain. I tasted blood.

But that didn't stop me from thrusting my knee into his groin. He grunted, expelling a lungful of air. I shoved the gun into his ear, but before I could say anything, his fist smashed into my temple, and pinpoints of light danced before my eyes. I kneed his groin again, slammed his head into the tree trunk, then swung the pistol against the side of his head with all of my strength.

He slumped against the tree and slid to the ground. He was out.

I tied him up with some of the rope I'd cut off Ali, then popped out the magazine of his Colt Defender, checked to make sure it was loaded. It was. The SIG was down at least three shots, so I jammed it into my back pocket as a back-up. Then I headed to the other shed.

MY FATHER HAD what he called a 'toy box' of war trophies and deactivated training grenades he'd brought home from Vietnam. When I was maybe six he explained to me what an incendiary grenade was. A little later that afternoon, as I ran circles round him trying to get him to play hide-and-seek, he hurled one at me.

To teach me a lesson.

Only after I stopped crying did he explain, with a hearty guffaw, that you had to pull the pin first or it wouldn't detonate. I'd always assumed it was a dummy grenade, but with my father you never knew.

There were four thermite grenades in the shed. I only needed one.

Five minutes later, when I'd finished my prep work, I returned to the lodge.

RUSSELL'S EYES NARROWED. He knew something wasn't right.

'We got a problem,' I said.

'What problem?'

'You,' I said, and I held up the grenade for a second. I grasped the pull ring, tugged it out, and then I hurled it at him.

'*You crazy son of a bitch!*' he screamed, diving out of the way.

Ali shrieked and jumped free, and Buck leapt away, too.

The confusion gave me enough time to pull the Colt Defender out of the waistband of my trousers and squeeze off two shots. Russell was a blur. When the bullet struck his shoulder, he roared, then crashed into the overstuffed sofa, his gun dropping from his hand, sliding a good ten feet or more.

Buck canted to one side. A crimson starburst appeared on his jacket.

Muffled screams from somewhere close by: the game room?

Russell, back on his feet, hesitated for an instant, as if deciding whether to reach for his gun. The fury in his face told me he now understood that I'd removed the primer from the grenade; he didn't enjoy being duped.

I aimed the pistol and fired another round, but then something moved in my peripheral vision.

Buck, summoning a final burst of malevolent strength, had somehow managed to raise his gun. He fired. I glimpsed the tongue of flame at the end of the muzzle, felt a fireball of pain explode inside my right thigh.

The floor came up to hit me in the face.

My forehead and cheekbone felt broken, the pain ungodly. Everything was spinning. I struggled to get upright, finally managed to stagger to my feet, then Russell swooped at me, kneeing my solar plexus.

I sagged, fell backwards, retching, the gun dropping to the floor. I couldn't catch my breath. He grabbed my hair, jerked my head up, slammed it back down against the floor.

Blindly, I swung at what I thought was his face but connected with something softer: muscle. At the same moment he jammed his knee into my wounded thigh, and everything went white and sparkly.

The room and everyone in it danced and jiggered before my eyes, turned liquid. I could see Russell, purple-faced, reach back to slip something out of somewhere (was it his boot?)—and in his fist something glinted: a blade, a long-handled knife. With a guttural, bestial roar, he aimed the blade directly at my heart.

I was paralysed, watching Russell in his animal rage, the silvery gleam of the knife blade.

I thought, *This is the bad wolf.*

I tried to plead, but only a grunt came out, and I was slipping away, not strong enough to grab the gun out of my pocket, to do anything but—

The top of his head came off.

He toppled, blood everywhere.

Ali held the Smith & Wesson in a perfect two-handed grip, shoulders forward, an ideal stance.

Her hands were shaking, but her eyes were fierce.

Epilogue

The Canadian police kept us in Vancouver for almost four days.

The two surviving kidnappers were immediately arrested by the Major Crime Unit of the Royal Canadian Mounted Police. Buford 'Buck' Hogue was evacuated by helicopter to Royal Columbian Hospital in New Westminster, where he died in surgery. Travis Brumley was placed in a detachment cell at Port Hardy, then brought before a judge and charged with murder. As far as I knew, he hadn't killed anyone. But as the investigators pointed out, he was still the perpetrator of a violent crime.

The bodies of the victims and the hostage-takers were all airlifted to Vancouver for autopsy. The rest of us were subjected to some pretty lengthy questioning by the Major Crime Unit team, no one longer than I, after my wounds were bandaged up in the hospital.

Once the exuberant relief of our rescue had worn off, the exhaustion set in. We were all pretty traumatised. In between police interviews we slept a lot, talked, called our families and friends.

I couldn't help noticing that Clive Rylance and Upton Barlow and even Kevin Bross were a lot friendlier to me. I suspected it wasn't simple gratitude for what I'd done. These were men who could smell power shifts from miles away, and they all knew that Cheryl had big plans for me.

But Ali became quiet, withdrawn. On the second day, I finally got a chance to talk to her alone. We were sitting in a waiting room of the RCMP's E Division headquarters outside Vancouver.

'It's eating me up inside,' she said. 'I keep replaying what I did in my head.' She stared at the floor. 'I'm not like you, Jake. I don't think I'll ever shake it.'

I drew closer to her on the couch, took her hands. 'You never will,' I said quietly. 'I understand, believe me. More than I ever wanted to tell you.'

And then, taking a deep breath, I told her everything I'd never told anybody before.

ON OUR LAST MORNING in Vancouver, I was having breakfast by myself in the restaurant of the Four Seasons when Upton Barlow approached my table.

'Mind if I sit down?' he said.

'Not at all.'

'I underestimated you, my friend,' he said.

I didn't know how to respond, so I didn't.

'I still find it hard to comprehend that Geoff Latimer embezzled from the company. And on such a scale at that. You never really know people.'

I looked up from my coffee, saw the anxiety in his face. 'I think it was more complicated than that.'

'Well, no doubt,' he said, feigning an offhanded tone. 'What—what did he tell you at the end?'

Of course, that was what he really wanted to know: had Latimer revealed everything? As far as Barlow knew, Latimer had spilled his guts to me.

I leaned close to him. 'See, Upton, here's the thing. There's going to be a lot of changes at the top, as I'm sure you know.'

He nodded, cleared his throat. 'What do you know about these—changes?' He must have hated having to ask me that.

'I know Cheryl's going to look favourably on those who cooperate.'

'Cooperate?'

'Some people will get thrown to the wolves,' I said. 'You have to decide if you're going to be one of them.'

IN EXCHANGE FOR Cheryl's guarantee not to hand him over to the Justice Department, Barlow was only too happy to tell her everything.

About how her predecessor, James Rawlings, had asked his trusted general counsel, Geoff Latimer, to set up an offshore partnership in the British Virgin Islands.

It was Hank Bodine's idea, actually, but then Rawlings—a shrewd but aggressive investor—decided he wanted to triple the pot within a year and replace the funds in the company's coffers before they were discovered missing. Turn fifty million into a hundred and fifty. The ever-cautious Geoff Latimer had warned his boss that trading on margin like that was terribly risky.

But Jim Rawlings was willing to take the risk in order to amass enough untraceable cash for what he liked to call 'offsets'—facilitation payments, success fees, whatever: a slush fund for bribes.

To give Jim Rawlings his due, there was a reason why Hammond's foreign business was so strong during his tenure.

It wasn't just the lousy four hundred thousand bucks that Hank Bodine had told Geoff Latimer to wire to an offshore account he'd set up for the Pentagon's chief acquisitions officer. No, it was the millions that Bodine had dispensed to foreign ministers and Third World dictators the world over.

Jim Rawlings never expected the fund to go belly up, of course. He never expected to put Latimer in the desperate position of having to come up with a hundred million dollars to pay off a margin call when the investment collapsed. Had he lived, Rawlings would have taken care of things.

Then again, he never anticipated an outside investigation that made it impossible for Latimer to dig up the money in the Hammond treasury.

'If Rawlings hadn't dropped dead playing golf none of this would have happened,' Upton Barlow told Cheryl later. 'I never liked golf.'

I ALMOST DIDN'T MAKE the flight home.

I had the dubious honour of being interviewed personally by the head of the RCMP Major Crime Unit. Midway through his interrogation, he got a copy of my juvenile arrest record—yeah, sure, they promise you that your records are 'sealed', but they never really are—and from the way he started crunching his breath mints I could tell he was excited.

But finally he excused me, after everyone else had boarded the Hammond jet. They held the flight for me, though.

I limped up the metal steps and entered the main salon.

As I looked around for a seat someone clapped, and then a couple of people, and before long there was a smattering of applause. I smiled, shook my head modestly, plopped down in the nearest seat, which happened to be next to Hank Bodine.

He was talking on his cellphone, and as soon as he saw me, he rose and found another seat, off by himself. For the first half-hour of the flight, he made call after call, and I could see him getting more and more frustrated.

Then Cheryl summoned me to her private cabin.

ALI LET ME IN but immediately excused herself. She went to a fancy mahogany desk in the corner and tapped away at a laptop.

Cheryl was sitting in one of the overstuffed white brocade chairs and she, too, was talking on a cellphone. I took a seat on a couch facing her, picked up a copy of the *Wall Street Journal*, skimmed the movie review, and pretended not to listen in on Cheryl's conversation.

'Jerry,' she was saying, almost coquettishly, 'you know I've been chasing you for years.' She gave a lilting laugh. 'Oh, you'll love Los Angeles. I'm sure of it. Don't you get tired of all the *rain*? I did. All right, then. Good to reconnect, and I'm glad we could come to terms. I'm *thrilled*.'

She snapped her cellphone shut and looked up at me. She seemed to be in a giddy mood.

'Jake, as you can imagine, we have a lot of work to do when we get back to the office. Quite a few senior positions to fill. There'll be a number of vacant offices on the thirty-third floor, and I'd like you to take one of them. As one of my special assistants.'

'Thanks,' I said. 'I appreciate it. But I'm not really cut out for the thirty-third floor. I'll mix up the salad fork and the fish fork. You never know what I might blurt out. It's just not my scene.'

She looked at me for a few seconds, her eyes grey ice. Then her expression softened. 'Actually, I could use some more straight talk on the thirty-third floor.'

'Thing is, I can't let Mike Zorn down.' I smiled sheepishly. 'Gotta deal with the whole chicken-rivet thing.'

After a few seconds, she said, 'I understand, I guess. But I'm sorry—'

At that moment, the door to the cabin flew open, and Hank Bodine stormed in.

'What the hell is going on?' he yelled. 'Every time I call my office, I get some damned recording saying I've reached a "nonworking extension at Hammond Aerospace". I can't even reach my own admin.'

'Gloria Morales has been reassigned, Hank.'

'*What?* You have no right to do that without my sign-off!'

Ali approached Cheryl, handed her a burgundy leather pad with a single sheet of paper on top of it. 'Thank you, Alison,' Cheryl said. She picked up a large black fountain pen from the marble end table, took her time uncapping the pen, then dashed off a bold signature at the bottom of the page. She held the paper up and blew on it to dry the ink. Then she gave it back to Ali, who wordlessly took it over to Bodine.

'What's this?' he said warily. He snatched the paper from Ali's hand and stared at it, his eyes steadily widening. '"Violation of fiduciary duty of loyalty" . . . What the hell do you think you're doing?' He shook his head. 'Nice try, Cheryl, but you don't have the power to fire *anyone*.'

'Really?' Cheryl inspected her fingernails. 'You might want to ask Kevin Bross about that. I'm sure you've noticed he's not on board. Try him on his cell. I didn't think he merited a ride on the company plane.'

Bodine emitted a sharp bark of laughter. 'You'll never get this past the board of directors. They specifically took away your power to hire and fire.'

She sighed. 'The executive committee of the board of directors met this morning in special session, Hank,' she said patiently. 'Once they read the emails that Upton kindly provided, they realised they had no choice.'

'Upton!' Bodine said.

'They quickly realised how far-reaching the legal consequences will be. And, of course, none of them wants to be hit with a lawsuit *personally*. They simply wanted me to clean up the mess you made. Which I was happy to do. As soon as they restored my power to do so. Quid . . . pro . . . quo.'

Bodine's face had gone beetroot-red.

'From their standpoint, of course, it was . . .' Cheryl paused, pursed her lips as if savouring a delectable chocolate, then smiled. '. . . a no-brainer.'

AS THE METAL STEPS rolled up to the plane, I looked out of the window and saw a crowd of photographers and television cameramen and reporters.

When the plane door opened, a roar came up from the crowd, and the reporters closed in, shouting questions. Cheryl was the first to exit, then Ali, then the rest of us.

It was a bright, sunny, perfect California day. Suddenly something streaked out of the crowd, tracing frenzied circles on the tarmac.

'Gerty,' I yelled. 'Come!'

She ran towards me, her leash flying behind her, and vaulted into the air. Her tongue swiped my face. Then she bounded away and knocked a photographer's very-expensive-looking camera out of his hands. The poor dog was crazed with joy and relief.

Zoë shouted an apology to the photographer, tried to nab the dog, then gave up.

As I headed towards the parking lot, Gerty straining at the leash, Ali called out to me.

I stopped, looked round.

'Did I hear you turn Cheryl down?'

'It's nothing personal,' I said. 'I just like being good at what I do.'

She shook her head and smiled. 'Maybe someday I'll figure you out.' She bent down and caressed Gerty's head.

'When you do,' I said, 'fill me in.'

She ran her fingers through the dog's silky ruff, saying, 'What a good doggy.' Gerty's tail wagged like crazy and she swiped her big tongue all over Ali's face.

'So this is the dog-wife, huh?'

I nodded.

'She's beautiful.' Ali glanced back at the limousine. 'You still live in the same apartment, right?'

'Of course.'

'Mind giving me a ride to my place?'

'Sure,' I said. 'But I gotta warn you—there's dog hair all over the car.'

'That's all right,' she said. 'I can deal.'

JOSEPH FINDER

Likes: loyalty, honesty & generosity
Dislikes: arrogance, pomposity & pretension
Website: www.josephfinder.com

RD: What gave you the idea for using an executive bonding weekend as a setting?

JF: I've heard from friends in the corporate world about these ridiculous offsite retreats, where everyone does 'trust falls' and rope courses and other team-building exercises. Sometimes they take place in remote locations. So I began to think: what if something happened? What if the entire leadership of a huge corporation were gathered in the middle of nowhere—and suddenly they were all taken hostage?

RD: Is the lodge where the novel is set based on a real place?

JF: Yes. A friend told me about an incredibly luxurious, yet rustic, fishing lodge in British Columbia where his company had an offsite retreat. No phones or cellphone reception or Internet. Completely off the grid. That got me wondering . . .

RD: What made you set the novel in the aerospace industry?

JF: I wanted my fictional company to be a really macho, all-male kind of place—because I wanted their new CEO to be a woman. Also, I've always been fascinated by the airplane business, particularly the technology. And there's a long history of bribery and corruption which I knew would give me an intriguing, built-in story line.

RD: Why did you want the CEO to be a woman?

JF: There are a lot of female executives but very few female CEOs—not yet, anyway. Women make great leaders, but many boards of directors, traditionally mostly male, are reluctant to name a woman to run a major corporation. I think that's largely because of old prejudices. And plenty of male executives chafe at being led by a woman. Any kind of conflict like that makes a drama that could play out in interesting ways. I did talk to a few female CEOs, who shared some great anecdotes with me.

RD: There are some very unpleasant executives in the book, are they based on specific individuals?

JF: Absolutely. I meet a lot of people in the corporate world while I'm doing research, and most of them are terrific people. But every once in a while I meet a real jerk, and I think: 'Hey, great—thanks. I need a villain. You're going into my next book.'

RD: Was it fun putting the executives into such a challenging situation?

JF: Very much so. I loved the concept of having all these Alpha Males, who are accustomed to snapping their fingers and having their every order obeyed, suddenly facing hard men with guns who have nothing but contempt for these desk jockeys.

RD: When you did the research for the book did you find that people in big companies were happy to talk to you?

JF: At first the people I talked to were quite nervous, especially those in the kidnap-and-ransom industry, who are usually extremely secretive. In fact, most companies aren't permitted to disclose whether they even have kidnap-and-ransom insurance, let alone how much—they don't want to encourage potential kidnappers. But after a while I began to break through the wall of silence.

RD: You've said that you don't like your books to be described as corporate thrillers. What's your thinking on that?

JF: I don't, because to many readers it means spreadsheets and PowerPoint presentations and boring stuff like that. The fact is that the corporate thriller—at least as I see it—simply refers to a suspense novel that involves intrigue in the workplace, touching upon things that we all think about—friendship and colleagues and relationships, ambition, success and betrayal. Done right, the corporate thriller can be tremendously appealing and extremely real.

RD: What's the most difficult aspect of writing a novel for you?

JF: Getting started. No question about it. Once I've begun writing, it really moves. But each time I start a book, I feel like I'm standing on a really high diving board. Once I plunge into the water, I love it. But standing there, high in the air—it's kind of scary.

RD: You write about some very violent people. What keeps you awake at night?

JF: Nothing. I always sleep well. Though I have to say that when I'm writing full-blast, I don't seem to dream. It's as if I use up all the creative, dream-making stuff during the day.

RD: Do you have rituals when you are writing?

JF: All sorts of rituals. I start my writing day with a good espresso and a big mug of ice-cold water. I need to have a view of trees, nothing else, just trees. But the truth is, when the writing is going well, I can write just about anywhere, and the fussy stalling rituals go out the window.

RD: What's the best thing about being a successful writer?

JF: Being your own boss. I was never very good at office politics, so it's a relief not to have to be nice to jerks at work.

THE GHOST © 2007 by Robert Harris
Published by Hutchinson

SACRIFICE © S.J. Bolton 2008
Published by Bantam Press

THE MAN IN THE PICTURE © Susan Hill, 2007
Published by Profile Books

POWER PLAY © 2007 Joseph Finder
Published by Headline Publishing Group

Illustrations, Photos and Acknowledgments:
Page 4–5: Robert Harris © Jane Bown; Susan Hill © photograph by Penny Tweedie, Camera Press, London; Joseph Finder © Joel Benjamin.
The Ghost: 6–8: image: Stockbyte; design: Darren Walsh@velvet tamarind; page 162 © Jane Bown.
Sacrifice: 164–6: image: Altrendo Panoramic.
The Man in the Picture: 338–40: image: Lee Frost; design: Curtis Cozier; page 402 © photograph by Penny Tweedie, Camera Press, London.
Power Play: 404–6: image: Stephen Strathdee and Litwin Photography; design: Stephen Mulcahey; page 574: © Joel Benjamin.

Dustjacket spine: image: Stockbyte.

Printed and bound by GGP Media GmbH, Pössneck, Germany

020-252 DJ0000-1